The Rafters

The Somnambulist Saga

Book One

A.C. MONTGOMERY

D1301923

INTRASOMNIUM PUBLISHING

The Rafters

- World Maps-

-Lux Lumetía-

Caulder

Teal

Landel

Fannin

Ripolis

Belles

Seward

Mirrón

Archer

Tartel

Gamlin

Willow

Castle

Jardin

Vaulton

Satin

Rallis

Vessel

Polly

Sampton

Bleekar

★ Grand Theatre Casavella
● North Market
✡ The Hinge
◯ Café Roscalla
⬤ Rhyus arrival portal
★ CavonRué

⬢ The Tower
■ PrōmissĭoFountain
⬡ Randál Vanaché
▢ Crimson Glass
▲ Crystal Harbor
● Umbra Halls

...Adelaide   ...Arienette   ...Eve   ...Ravenna   ...Valencia

-Atrum Unda-

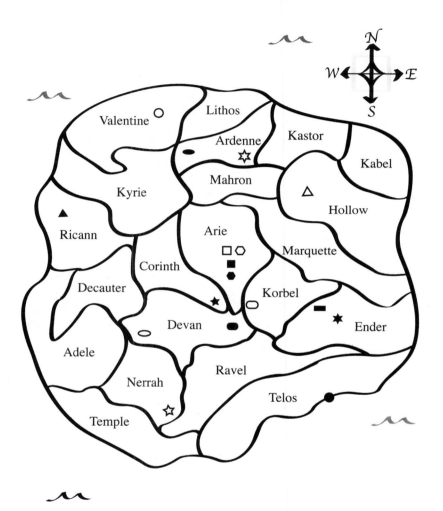

✹	Tavokk's Home	⬢	The Tower
⬭	Niall Trace's Shop	◼	SŭsurrusFountain
✪	Scribe's Den	◯	Cosmos
⬭	Helena's Home	▢	Wishing Well
●	Shadow Market	▲	Callis' Home
★	Tazo's Home	●	Stone Shelf
◯	Fisher's Home	△	The Dome
☆	Ĭnauro Manor	◯	Fado's Butchery
		▬	Crest Falls

-Insula Palam Vita-

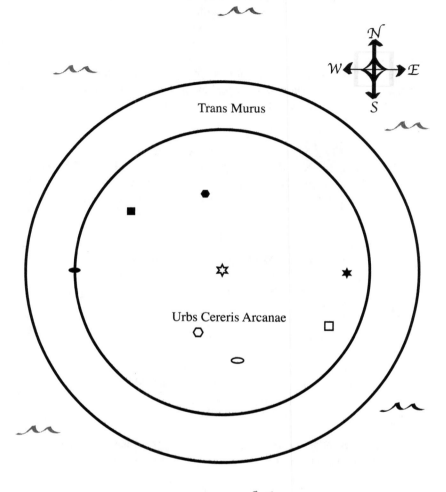

Trans Murus

Urbs Cereris Arcanae

★ Lenim's House   ⬣ FeNelle
⬬ City Entrance   ■ MadamCorvin's House
✡ The Grounds   ⬡ Cafe Kampnel
⬮ Pub Ralikoo   ☐ Sultan's House

This is a book published in the United States by
IntraSomnium Publishing, LLC
Omaha, NE
All rights reserved.

www.IntraSomniumPublishing.com

Library of Congress Control Number: 2010912317

The Somnambulist Saga ; bk 1
Second Edition
Summary: Rhyus Delmar, the Key Calling, begins the journey to fulfill his destination, which lies before him entirely unknown.

ISBN: 978-0-9829223-5-4 (hbk)
ISBN: 978-0-9829223-4-7 (pbk)
ISBN: 978-0-9829223-6-1 (epub)
ISBN: 978-0-9829223-7-8 (epdf)

The primary text type of this book is set in 12-point Times
Typeset and book design by Allison C. Sojka

Printed and bound in the United States of America
by BookMasters, Inc.
Ashland, Ohio, September 2011

This book is dedicated to Michaela and Amy
For their continuous eagerness
Toward
The Somnambulist Saga.

To Steven, Mandy, and Jeff
For
All of their support & the help they have given.

And to Gene, who without
None of this
Would have been possible.

- Table of Contents-

Character Maps- In Back:

The Rafters

O: Prologue

A young man awoke in an unfamiliar city. *An ominous* feeling pervaded his senses. Dazed, he lay still, unknowing. Atrum Unda, the Dark City, a place of never-ending rain. Thickly woven, black clouds dropped harsh, icy rain on his prostrate form. But not icy enough to burn the exposed flesh of his arms and face. Brisk air ate through rain-drenched clothing causing an uncontrollable shiver. He laid blinking wearily and half conscious. He looked desperately around, trying to assess his surroundings.

Where am I? he wondered.

As he blinked, trying to clear his vision, two winged men swam into focus through the pelting rain. The black marble figures were dressed in elegance, their faces concealed by masquerade masks, adorned with images of the sun and moon.

The dark sea crashed against the edges of the slick, stone shelf on which he lay. His perch pressed against the base of a high, stone cliff where a steep, narrow stairway angled up the vertical face to meet a lush, thriving forest at the summit.

Something moved. There it was again. He strained at the blurry periphery of his vision to determine if the rain-drenched haze was playing tricks on him, or if indeed, something was out there.

All went black.

With a start, after several unconscious minutes, his eyes opened to see a shadowy figure looming over him. He discerned a man's voice. *What is he saying?* Unsuccessfully, he strained to make out the words.

A sudden, sharp explosion of pain struck him, hard and square, snuffing the feeble flicker of his consciousness. Unaware, he curled into a writhing fetal position. He couldn't breathe…and once again, everything went black.

1: Lux Lumetia

An obscure figure leaned against the side of a black building. With a half-hearted kick, he scattered a clump of blue, sapphire granules with the tip of his square-toed shoe. They skittered away in a hazy blue cloud, beneath the dim glow of a sputtering streetlight. Tilting his head upward, he luxuriated in the coolness of the omnipresent rain that so much characterized the city of Atrum Unda. It spattered his shades and streamed down his angular, pale face.

The man, Vincent KyVeerah, concentrated his energies toward another somn, similarly wired to his mental wavelength. A somn in a distant city, Lux Lumetia, the City of Light.

"Venn." He drummed his long, manicured nails on the stone, waiting impatiently for a response. Nothing.

"Come on, Venn. Pay attention!"

"Vincent! What in Blue Ravenna are you up to so early in the morning? Mucking around this time of day is just plain, damn uncivilized! I certainly would not be out now, if Marion hadn't dragged my ass here." The rich, deep voice, tinged with sleep, was heavy in its disapproval. Venn, himself, tended to get up around nine or nine thirty. Going out to the city walkways any earlier was beyond his liking. Marion had insisted that they must go before dawn in order to get the best of the early market produce.

"You know I prefer KyVeerah, p-lease." Amusement thinned KyVeerah's already fine lips and carried through his thoughts. *"Hang on, Venn, I need you to concentrate."*

In an instant, KyVeerah sent a mental image to Venn of a young man landing in a Lux canal of the very city where Venn himself dwelt, and then he disconnected his mind.

୧ୠ

The bright first light of a beautiful morning shone down on Venn and Marion as they scouted North Market. As they walked, Marion babbled at his side, delighted with everything she saw. With each step, her soft brown, chestnut curls bobbed as she bounced along.

He envied her youth. At twenty-seven years old, Venn had long ceased being excited about the wonders of the North Market. He would much prefer to be back under the soft, warm covers of his luxurious bed. He longed for a few more hours of rest.

Tiring of the market's incessant noise in short time, he exited north toward an airy bridge spanning a distant canal. From there, he could watch over Marion but still enjoy his tranquility.

At the moment though, Venn had blocked the bright colors and pungent odors of the market from his thoughts. Staring down into the crystal clear water below, he concentrated on the message that Vincent KyVeerah had just planted in his mind.

An image formed. Suddenly, he found himself peering down into another canal, almost identical to that immediately below him. He could see a boy, or rather a young man, lying unconscious on a crystal slab, partially submersed in the clear, blue water. He appeared to have fallen down a short flight of three wide steps. One arm draped over the bottom step with his head partially supported by the same. Venn grimaced as he recognized the location of the canal portal where the young man lay. It would be quite a jaunt to get to the Ripolis District where KyVeerah expected Venn to retrieve him. Then he showed a wry smile. Since when had Vincent KyVeerah ever made anything easy?

"Lucky the little bastard landed face up," Venn muttered. "Maybe he won't drown before I can get there."

Venn narrowed his ice blue eyes in frustration. Precipitously, KyVeerah had cut the connection before he had any chance to register a response. Having closed his mind, he also managed to block any further attempt for Venn to express his disapproval at the folly of his plans.

Venn's emotions roiled. Though twenty-eight, just two years older than Venn, KyVeerah frequently used the slight age difference, among other factors, to justify his self-appointed superiority. Now, he thought it acceptable to just dump the young man of the vision in Venn's lap.

&)C&

Barely aware that Venn had departed the scene, Marion moved cheerfully among bright stalls and animated market vendors. Lusty voices called out, offering the finest meat, fruit, wine, and especially, sweetmeats, which she would need for the coming week.

"Hey lady! You can't pass this up!" A handsome vendor pressed a woven basket at her, ignoring all rules of spatial propriety.

Turning away in reflex, Marion came to a sudden stop. A whiff of exotic herbs brought her right back around.

"I haven't smelled a bouquet like this in ages!"

"And you won't in many more. I guarantee it!"

A warm glow filled her brown eyes, as she grinned at the vendor, examining his wares, and adding, "I love experimenting with new dishes."

She winked, with a conspiratorial whisper, "The man I cook for is a hopeless loss with a pot or pan, but he certainly knows how to get the most out of a well-contrived dish!"

Marion added his wares to her basket and continued searching until she found a goodly supply of Aci fruit. Acidic and sour to the extreme, it was nonetheless wonderful in many dishes, especially in the next she had planned.

Finished, she pranced to the nearest merchant to purchase her gatherings.

"Find everything all right?" the pleasant vendor asked.

"I certainly did. And more!"

"Have a good time?"

"Wonderful! But," she pouted, "I guess there always comes a time to head home."

Returning to Venn, Marion moved further north through the Archer District. She continued past the market strand to approach him, unsteadily balancing her bags of purchases. As he came into sight, she couldn't help a brief appraisal. At the apex of the sparkling, white bridge, he appeared a glowering, dark giant. At a towering six-foot-three, his powerful frame was accentuated by a mane of jet-black hair, falling to the middle of his back. Random strands lifted, dancing in the cool breeze, creating a halo effect in the early morning light of both suns. Marion slipped a wry smile. A halo was not what she would associate with Venn. His brute power, rectangular glasses, broad chiseled features, and exquisitely tailored clothing announced a refined aristocracy—not divinity.

Hearing Marion's footsteps, Venn turned, eying the load she carried. "Actually, you need to get some more. Much more. It would appear that we are going to be having a guest."

Marion, with only twenty years behind her, accepted change with the resilience of youth. After shooting a brief, questioning look at Venn, she shrugged her shoulders, dropped her bags at his feet, and headed back to the line of market stands. In truth, she thrilled at the prospect of bartering more with the hard-driving vendors.

Venn watched her from the bridge, as she flounced back toward the market strand. Her wavy, chestnut hair shone bronze in the intense sunlight as she made her way. She amused him, the way in which she carried herself so spirited and carefree, as she wandered from stall to stall, haggling with the vendors. A pale blue sundress complimented her flawless skin. It fit her petite form perfectly, as though it had been made specifically for her. Then again, it had in fact been tailored exactly to her specifications. A crooked grin appeared on Venn's face. As he continued watching her, the ice in his eyes melted into a limpid blue.

"Oh Marion."

&)CR

Venn and Marion left North Market, winding their way in silence through a shimmering labyrinth of white stone buildings and crystal-lined waterways. As Lux Lumetia consisted of a series of scattered islands, linked by canals, they had to cross numerous bridges, much like the one on which Venn had stood outside the market. The city walkways shimmered in the suns' light. They were constructed of the same white stone as the buildings; however, small amounts of the same, gleaming crystal that lined the waterways was crushed with the white stone, giving the finished surface of the walkways an attractive, silver sheen.

Moving quite some distance to the Ripolis District in the northeastern corner of the square city, the two of them reached the edge of a particular canal, the canal of Vincent KyVeerah's mental-sent image. Venn knew exactly where to find this Lux canal portal, through the clarity of his mental communication from KyVeerah.

Marion's hands reflexively tried to cover her mouth, but they failed to make it there, weighed down by all the heavy grocery bags that Venn made her carry. She gasped as she spotted the striking young man that Venn had been expecting all along. The young man laid waterlogged and unconscious, his head supported by the lowest step to an underwater boat dock. With his face just inches above the water, his head buffeted side to side by gentle rolling, blue waves.

Venn trudged halfheartedly down the short, wide steps to the submerged dock, grimacing as water soaked his fine, handcrafted boots. Crystal docks were generally meant for the city's inhabitants to use in boarding passenger boats. Some, such as this one, also offered a portal at the top of its steps. The portals, known to only a limited number of somns, offered a more secretive passage. The young man had traveled that route, only to roll down the steps onto the platform. Venn gave a ruthless smile, thinking it probably didn't help the kid much that he was unconscious before being stuffed through the portal at the other end.

Dragging the young man up the steps from the canal, Venn deposited him unceremoniously on the dry walkway. He lay quiet, unmoving.

"Do you think he's even alive?" Marion asked.

With a quizzical expression, she studied him for a long minute before planting a not-so-friendly kick in the ribs.

In response, he choked out a guttural sound, half gasp and half grunt.

Venn smothered a surprised laugh at her action. Instead, he raised a judgmental, black eyebrow.

"Hey now, is that really necessary, Mae?" He scowled. "The kid's obviously been through enough today. And it hasn't even reached midday."

Marion shrugged, indifferent, smiling sweetly up at Venn.

"Why do I always get stuck taking care of Vincent's messes?" Venn sighed, in exasperation.

"Did you say something?" Marion asked rhetorically. "If you ever hope to marry, you had better start speaking a little louder. Mumbling is a rather unattractive quality in a man."

"So is lecturing your elders," Venn muttered.

Unabashed, Marion pressed on with a grin," What was that again? Would you please repeat that?"

Not on your life, Venn thought.

Instead, he barked, "Let's just get him home and out of these wet clothes. How in Blue Ravenna would I ever afford a physician to care for him if he became ill? Not that it wouldn't serve his stupid ass right to catch his death." Venn stooped down. With a single, effortless movement, he swept the unconscious youth up to rest over a heavily muscled shoulder.

Marion rolled her eyes at the absurdity of Venn not being able to afford a physician. Hell, he could afford every island in the city. With a hidden smile, she kept her head down. She knew for a certainty that having a physician around, giving the orders for a change, was what would kill him.

Gleeful, Marion chattered on to Venn, as they made their way back over the lengthy distance west through the city. She ignored his ever-darkening mood, as he contemplated this new burden that KyVeerah had dumped on him. Bystanders gaped at the trio. The whispering and the stares didn't faze Marion. After having lived with Venn for two years, odd experiences had become commonplace and expected from time to time.

After the extensive return trip to the northwestern-most district of the city, the Caulder District, they turned down a long, narrow alleyway. From clotheslines, stretching high above, dangled old, tattered rags, abandoned some years back. Rustling leaves skittered across the ground, spiraling toward an unknown destination. At the far end of the alley, where precious little sunlight penetrated the darkness, Venn pushed open a metal gate and proceeded into an ancient, high-walled courtyard, tucked away from the city's light.

Scattered, anemic weeds poked through cracks in the worn, drab cobblestones of the vast courtyard. Nestled against the east and west walls, sat two stone benches, having long ago taken maximum advantage of the rising and setting suns. At the very center of The Courtyard, as it was simply entitled, stood an enormous, ancient tree. Its massive, gnarled branches had once created a natural arboreal ceiling, painting a pleasant patchwork of light and shade over everything below. But a home had been built around The Courtyard, long ago. Ever since, the tree had risen through a designated hole at its center. Its branches draped protectively over the roof, though the sunlight no longer shone brightly overhead. Around the tree stood a metal fence, replicating the pattern of the main entrance gateway.

At the north end of The Courtyard, an exquisite pair of statues bracketed a set of large, metal double doors, its heavy set of knockers framed by an array of skillfully crafted stars. Midway between the doors and tree stood a raised stone dais. A decorative, metal rod stood planted firmly in the ground just before it.

Ignoring the heavy load that Venn had toted clear across the city, Marion quipped, "Are we almost home yet? These groceries are getting heavy. I certainly wasn't expecting to carry them all by myself." She bit her lip, suppressing a mocking smile.

Venn stopped dead in his tracks, peering down at her diminutive form. He paused just long enough for Marion to notice the bulging veins in his neck and the rippling muscles of his clenched jaw.

"Marion, my dear," Venn said, through clenched teeth, "when we get into the house, please remind me to slowly kill you."

"Oh, don't be moronic," Marion said, "you love me far too much to do away with me. Besides, who would feed you if I weren't around?"

Venn, still carrying the young man, scowled and trudged on behind Marion, as she frolicked through The Courtyard to push her way through the heavy, metal doors. The doors led into the opulent home, built around The Courtyard many centuries ago, and still in pristine condition.

Once inside, they spiraled up a stone staircase to the second floor. They pushed through a second set of double doors and stepped into the large hallway that stood directly over The Courtyard, surrounding the ancient tree. Just to the right of the doors, Venn dropped the deadweight onto an antique, yet generally comfortable, chair.

As he stretched the kinks from his back and arms, Marion frowned back at him, scolding, "Now Venn, the poor boy isn't a sack of potatoes. You don't have to be so brutish!"

Venn scowled at her in confusion. Was this not the very same young lady who had proceeded to nonchalantly kick the kid in the ribs just hours ago? He muttered, "Sometimes I just want to—"

Cutting him off, Marion said, "What Venn? Sorry, can't hear you. You know what they say about mumbling! Besides," she added, "the one of us who can cook has to start dinner!" She shoved through a door and into the kitchen.

Holding his head, Venn growled something incoherent and escaped to the den—his favored getaway. He would never witness Marion's mischievous grin and twinkling eyes as they parted ways.

She hummed a merry tune, planning the makings of a sumptuous feast. "Venn is going to be ecstatic when he tastes this!"

ᔕᗉᘖᔕ

Opening the door to the den, Venn breathed in the heady aroma of leather, parchment, and wood smoke. He leisurely surveyed the room. Well-worn wood floors stretched across the large den, as they did through all of the rooms in the house. Ornate, golden designs skillfully augmented the warm, burgundy glow of an exquisite antique rug, which stretched across three-quarters of the room.

Overstuffed, wooden bookshelves lined the walls, breaking only for an enormous fireplace and an opulent wet bar with an oversized, ornately framed mirror placed above.

In grateful anticipation, Venn walked over to the bar and lifted a crystal decanter of clear amber liquor. Pouring a stiff drink, he threw himself down onto a soft leather armchair in front of the fireplace. After gulping down the smooth, yet fiery, liquid in a single draft, he tilted his head back, closed his eyes, and began to relax his mind. Concentrating his mental energies, he successfully connected with Vincent KyVeerah.

"Vincent, we need to have a chat." A brief pause.

"Now really, Venn, how many times must we go through this? I prefer to go by KyVeer—"

"Now is not the damn time! Stuff your pathetic ego for a moment! Can you handle that?"

"A little cranky, sunshine?"

"Marion has already had two years to drain my patience. You had no right to dump her on me then, and you have absolutely no right to drop this kid on me now!"

"Oh, come now. What did I do?" KyVeerah asked, in innocence.

"What did you do? Be serious! If you had to send him here, and you didn't need to, by the way...why couldn't you have at least used the portal here at Umbra Halls? You made me cross the entire city to fish out the half-drowned kid from a canal and carry him all the way back here! During which entire time, the whole city gawked, and Marion decided that I needed to be verbally tortured! What's up? Why should I be wasting my time on this godforsaken boy?"

"Would you like some cheese with that whine?" KyVeerah prodded, with a chuckle. *"My, my, you really have had quite a day, my lovely."*

With a deep breath, Venn tried to suppress the frustration welling up inside of him. *"How about it? Are you going to enlighten me about what hole you've dug for yourself this time?"*

"There will be plenty of time for that later. What I need for you to do now is sit tight. I will contact you in a couple days, give or take. Then, I will explain everything."

"Oh, shit, he's planning on coming here!" Venn thought, understanding the implication of KyVeerah's words.

"Uh, remember, I can hear you."

"Dammit!"

"That too, darling."

"Fine. But I had better get a damn good explanation for all my troubles."

"All in good time. Take great care of our little starshine. He is top priority! Trust me!"

"Yeah rig—" Venn began, but KyVeerah had already broken

their connection.

"I hate that prick!" Venn cursed, to the empty air around him.

Disgruntled by his fruitless communication with Ky Veerah, Venn ventured back out into the hallway. Glancing up, he spotted Marion dancing toward him. "I hope you are hungry. I have prepared all of your favorites!"

Perking up, Venn felt all the troubles of the day peel away. Nothing revived his spirits like great food. His mouth watered at the incredible aroma rolling down the hallway. Expectantly, he beamed at Marion.

"Oh, by the way," Marion said, with a wide smile, "he's awake!" Without awaiting a response, she ducked back through the kitchen door.

"Son of a bitch!" Venn slumped. Placing his head in his hands, he sighed. "I'm getting too old for this."

2: Atrum Unda

A rapid clanking filled an otherwise silent room, as a man stirred on a spacious, black sofa. His hand pressed into the suede fabric of the sofa arm, forcing him upright. Upon the low, glass table, rattled several bottles and empty glasses from the previous night. He had not drifted to sleep until late morning.

"What a night," the man muttered, blinking bleary eyes. "Damn. Nothing like a mid-afternoon hangover." Swinging his legs down and leaning forward, he rested his throbbing head in his hands.

The floor beneath his feet shook again, as did everything else in the loft. Stirred to action, he untangled himself from a black, fleece blanket, grabbed as many glasses and bottles as possible, and carried them to the kitchen sink where they clanked for a moment before coming to a halt, for the time being at least.

Stretching, he cracked long, slender fingers and ran them through his disheveled, raven hair. He cracked his back and dragged his feet to the refrigerator.

The idea of food had been appealing, but at the sight of it, his stomach rebelled. Dragging back to the living room, he sank back onto the sofa. Inhaling deep, he shut his eyes and burrowed his face into one of the couch pillows.

ℰↄⒸℛ

A persistent knocking on the door jolted Jereth Tavokk awake. Bolting upright, he prepared to defend himself from attack.

Another knock. Realizing his foolishness, he proceeded to the door, questioning, with sharp words, "Who is it?"

"It's me, Jimmy, Mr. Tavokk. I have a message for you," informed a young voice.

Though only half dressed, Tavokk opened the door for a red-haired child. "Jimmy, my boy! Why didn't you say so?"

"I've been trying, Mr. Tavokk! Many times! I always deliver my messages exactly when you request!" the boy replied, with enthusiasm.

"Of course," Tavokk replied dismissively, to the freckle-faced boy. "About that message. What've ya got for me?"

"A note from Mr. Morgandy!" the boy gushed, proudly handing over a silver envelope. "It's my twelfth birthday today!" he added, with a hopeful look.

"So? What do you want? A cookie?"

"Well…actually, Mr. Tavokk, mother says money is really tight right now. I thought maybe a little extra? To help out the family?"

"Well, aren't we a little knight in shining armor?" Tavokk snorted. "Listen kid. Money is tight for everyone. This is Atrum Unda after all."

"I understand that, Mr. Tavokk," Jimmy said, but he couldn't disguise his watering eyes, as he bit his lip to hide its quivering.

"Oh, by Valencia's light, don't give me that look! It's pitiful!" Tavokk cringed. He sighed in frustration. "Wait here."

Sounds could be heard as Tavokk disappeared through the door to rummage through his belongings. He returned to the door and looked down at Jimmy. A coy smile played on the boy's lips.

Tavokk shook his head. "Don't give me that face you little hoodlum," he said, handing over the usual. It was a pale blue envelope filled with a considerable sum, especially for a boy of Jimmy's age. "Here's the standard amount. And this is for your mother." He winked slyly, shoving a glass bottle of liquor into Jimmy's hands.

Jimmy looked at the bottle in question.

"Trust me. Your mother needs it with a cheeky kid like you."

Jimmy showed an innocent smile.

"And remember, Jimmy, if you ever tell anyone about our *delivery arrangement* I will have to dispose of you," Tavokk dissembled, in a dark whisper, sliding a well-manicured fingernail across his throat, as he made a slicing sound through clenched teeth.

Jimmy, gawking wide-eyed at the unkempt man, swallowed hard. "Honest, Mr. Tavokk, I ain't never tellin' nobody!"

"Oh, don't look so frightened, I'm only kidding," Tavokk relented, flourishing a dismissive hand.

With a cautious smile, Jimmy began to turn away. "Uh, thanks, Mr. Tavokk."

"Hold on," Tavokk said, placing a hand atop the boy's small head. He turned it to face him, adding darkly, "but really…" and gave one last wide grin at the startled boy before shoving him out and shutting the door behind him.

〜◯〜

Tavokk walked to a bookshelf by the sofa and poured a glass of opaque liquor. Settling onto the couch, he reflected on the silver envelope in his hands. Turning it over, he read the distinctive embossing:

Mr. Jereth Javokk

From the reflective tabletop, he picked up a slim, ornate dagger with a curved blade. He sliced open the envelope, retrieving a single, neatly folded sheet of silver paper that read:

Jereth,

Tonight. Usual place. Usual time.

C. M.

Tavokk smiled. *Callis certainly has a way with words.*

He reached for his newly poured glass, but considering his already aching head, quickly set it back down. Thinking aloud, he declared, "Perhaps this should wait."

〜◯〜

Many hours and several wardrobe changes later, Tavokk was ready. White, netted sleeves fell to the middle of his hands. He sported an open, black vest with many pockets. High, red boots and a black belt with a large, metal skull accessorized fashionably discolored, black denim pants.

From a bureau drawer, he slipped a pocket watch into an inner pocket of his vest. Studying the mirror, he pulled his shoulder-length, black hair into a loose ponytail and threw on his shades.

He grinned, admiring the roguish stud grinning back at him from the mirror.

Grabbing his keys, he exited the loft's side door to a rickety flight of stairs. While making his way down the black, grated-metal steps, a tram screeched by, shaking everything around and sending sparks flying every which way.

He scanned his surroundings in a quick glance, and satisfied, stepped from the base of the stairs and headed west. Walking slowly at first, he steadily gained speed. The red lining of his long, black leather coat caught the dim light with his swift movements. As he hurried along, though concealed by his jacket, tattoos over his scapulae began to glow. Behind dark tinted shades, his eyes began to illuminate with violet iridescence, and as he approached, a dark streetlight in the near distance began to flicker. Brighter and brighter it glowed, until Tavokk reached it. He vanished. The light went dark.

୫⑤෪

A moment later, in the Arie Sector at the center of Atrum Unda, a sharp wind whistled. Jereth Tavokk appeared through the darkness, his jacket whipping behind him. The unseen, white glow of his tattoos dimmed and faded away as he came to a standstill. The sudden blast of wind died.

Tavokk stood at the base of a large, sapphire hill. Before him, at the very center of the city, loomed The Tower of Atrum Unda. A watchful eye, it glowered high over the city, overshadowing the tallest buildings. Its metallic-flecked black marble gleamed in dark reflection off of the river below and obscured the remaining, black marble buildings surrounding it.

"Hmm." Tavokk steeled himself to move ahead.

He started up the hill. Rain, falling lightly when he left home, fell steady now. City lights shimmered off of the blue granules beneath his feet. Nearing the top, he veered to his right, away from The Tower and the metallic bridge spanning the moat surrounding it.

As he moved past, he studied a large, black marble structure known as the Sŭsurrus Fountain. Inlayed throughout with intricate designs in white and blue, it held significance that many did not realize. Although the blue was the same as the sapphire granules so ubiquitous throughout Atrum Unda, the white stone could be found nowhere else in the city. It had been smuggled from its rival sister city, Lux Lumetia, long ago.

Two winged figures, in captivating costume and masquerade masks, sat upon the uppermost platform of the black fountain. This was the only place in Atrum Unda where both sun and moon figures could be seen adjacent to each other, displayed as one.

Tavokk knelt, picking up a large blue granule. Throwing it into the Fountain, he wished, "Let this be a valuable encounter."

He proceeded past the Sŭsurrus Fountain to a small, empty

plaza. A minimalist landscape greeted him, with a path veering to either side. To his left, a long set of stairs spiraled down to a single, low building known as the Wishing Well. To the right, a similar set laced upward, around a small hill, to a second building, the Cosmos. Both were popular bars, but the Cosmos was Tavokk's destination tonight.

With quick, light steps, Tavokk ascended the marble stairs. He studied the bar's dark tinted windows and peered up at the flickering, neon sign. Forcing the heavy door open, he stepped inside.

Adjusting his shades over his eyes, Tavokk surveyed his surroundings. A girl sat at a high-top table to his left.

Too young to be here, he thought. But who gives a damn in this city?

There, straight ahead, beneath a suspended, blue neon sign, sat another young woman. This one was stunning and surely of age. He smirked, to no one in particular, and strolled in her direction.

The distance between them closed with each step.

Then it widened again as he passed on by, depriving her of another glance.

ℰᏣᎡᏣ

"Hello, gorgeous," Tavokk greeted, with a smile, as he approached the occupant of the next table.

"Hello yourself, Jereth!" the man at the table replied, flashing an equally bold smile.

Glancing at the man's dark, heady brew, Tavokk grinned. "Ah, that does look delicious. You're my kind of man, Callis."

Callis jumped up from the booth, waving down the nearest bartender, a burgundy-haired beauty. "Tazo, bring another of these for me and two for my dear friend here!" he hollered, over the blaring music.

With a wicked smile, he turned again toward Tavokk.

Similar to Tavokk, Callis sported multiple piercings, including several earrings, an eyebrow barbell, and a lip ring. Numerous tattoos adorned his body, though most were covered this evening.

Unzipped sleeves exposed his elaborate forearm tattoos while his black pants were neatly torn, showing white inner pockets, and were complimented by a white belt. An open, metallic blue jacket revealed white stars on a low-necked, black shirt, which glowed eerily in the overhead black lights of the bar.

Tazo brought three glasses of iced, dark liquid and handed them to the two men. "Why, thank you," Callis offered, with an honest nod.

Tavokk slid his shades down just the slightest and gave a charming wink.

Tazo couldn't help but smile. "My pleasure." Masking her smile, she returned to the bar, though slipping a lingering glance back at the charismatic gentlemen.

Tavokk looked Callis in the eye. "On a more serious note, what news do you have for me?"

Callis hesitated for a moment, cautiously scanning the room. "You might not believe this. It's a little crazy, what I've heard."

"Callis Morgandy, how long have we been in business together? Crazy or not, it must be of great interest, or you wouldn't have planned this lovely meeting. Am I wrong?"

Callis pondered a moment, nodding in agreement. "Most true."

"Well then, what is the juicy gossip?"

"Rumor has it, there is a special water portal hidden in the city. An old relic from the past."

Tavokk leaned closer, eager eyes glowing. "How old?"

"Older than The Tower of Atrum Unda, possibly dating back as far as The Ancients and Rafters."

"Rafters?" Tavokk reacted, with a bit too much volume, taken off guard. "You mean The Rafters? They are a myth!"

"Hush!" Callis quelled. "According to my informants, the so-called 'myth' is just as real as you and me."

"Intriguing." For a moment, Tavokk was lost in his own thoughts. If Callis had access to such informants, he might be even more useful than anticipated. He knew Callis well enough to realize that he would torture and kill for such knowledge as he, Jereth Tavokk, already possessed. Knowledge of The Rafters and what really lay beyond the Dark City, beyond The Darkness.

His answer to Callis was a wide-eyed smile.

"Curious, I see?"

"Oh. You have no idea," Tavokk murmured, with a mysterious spark in his eyes. With a hand propped under his chin, they danced beyond his shades.

Callis responded, with a look of bewilderment, "Are you keeping something...?"

"Oh look, our drinks are gone. This just will not do," Tavokk interjected. "How 'bout you summon your stunning lady friend to bring over another round?" He offered a directive tilt of his head toward Tazo.

Callis turned to the bar, signaling with two fingers and an empty glass for Tazo to bring more drinks. She held up a bottle, and Callis assented, an attractive smile lighting his handsome features.

With Callis distracted, Tavokk changed the subject. He skillfully hijacked the conversation toward weather, rain as always in the City of Dark Water, and other topics of interest, such as past underground dealings and encounters.

ℰᏳᏰ

Focusing his attention on Callis, Tavokk was unaware that their little meeting had attracted the attention of another in the room. Sitting alone, nursing a nonalcoholic beverage, she sat studiously avoiding them. While flirting innocuously with a blushing youth across the room, the young woman had every sense glued to their conversation.

Through her "professional associations" Helena Meretrix had dealt with both men. But she was now amazed, and in truth a bit shaken, to find that they evidently knew each other.

Coming in such a small package, Helena was a contradiction in terms. Her petite frame and soft feminine curves belied the fact that she was, in truth, a cross between a viper and an unstable explosive. Ample breasts, suggestively revealed, insured that she had plenty of time to sum up any man before she had to talk to him face to face. Even then, she could keep him mesmerized with her green eyes and full, pouting lips. Beneath a shining halo of short, strawberry-blonde hair was hidden a restless brain, malignant in its incessant drive toward ruthless power and control.

Helena had achieved much in her short career. But given her insatiable lust for power, it seemed next to nothing. Holding her current position was in itself a huge feat. Even with that, she rankled at being on the elite operation's bottommost rung.

Life had never been kind to her. Now, at twenty-three years of age, all she could remember of her previous life was an endless succession of dirty ragged dresses, and even dirtier old men who sweated and grunted as they labored over her tiny frame after crossing her mother's palm with a greasy wad of bills.

Even worse had been that occasional strapping young man. In another world she may have found some of them attractive. But every single one had been aloof, cocksure, and arrogant. Not one had seen her as anything more than a temporary plaything. And she had seen them as nothing more than an enemy.

With an angry grin of satisfaction she remembered that by now she had personally seen to it that not one of them would ever sweat or grunt again. The old ones she had simply dispatched of with no more thought than one would toss a bag of stale garbage. But the younger ones, the self-absorbed monsters, had given her ample fodder on which to perfect her craft.

Even now as she thought of it she tenderly caressed the stiletto blade cradled gently in a special sling. Just below the rim of her purse. Countless times, she had practiced snatching that blade to bear. By now it was pure reflex. When the need arose, she often found that she already had blade in hand. Before she consciously realized the need for it.

With a quiver of pleasure, her mind drifted away from the pair across the room. One by one she ran through the litany of young men she had dispatched. With each one, she had steadily learned to exact her revenge with ever more finesse. And no rule in her book said a fight had to be fair. Nothing in life was fair.

Taking her time, like a cat with a mouse, she found that she loved the process even more than the final result. On light dancing feet she would dart in with quick jabs of her razor sharp blade. With each lightning thrust, she could feel the blade drinking the bright red blood. And with each thrust she felt an electric surge of excitement, almost overwhelmingly sensual in intensity.

Time and again she would strike, laughing and bouncing lightly out of the way. With each strike she reveled in the thin crimson rivulet that drained away the life force of her prey. At last, when nothing remained but a quivering mass of flesh on the blood-drenched ground, she would turn silently and walk away. Strangely hollow and empty inside.

Still lost in her reflections, Helena continued to search back through the list. She had so longed for a man, just once, who might be kind. One who might attempt to actually know her and who might even give a little rather than just take. But that man had never come.

As she had grown older in this hard city of Atrum Unda, she had sadly come to understand that for a man to survive, let alone flourish here, a powerful sense of self—even to the point of arrogance—was a necessary trait for basic survival.

In order to advance, the women also had to affect an outward persona to interface with the needs of such men. More than once

Helena had heard herself referred to as "that big-breasted bimbo." She smiled to herself, knowing that in truth, she was a sleek and lethal bird of prey. She had taken great pains to perfect her "fleshy persona." Much to her benefit. Even the agony brought on by the ātrāmento—the chemical shower-mist used to alter one's skin pigmentation—was well worth her while.

Her fabricated persona made men stupid. And in women it engendered either a jealous anger and disgust or an uncomfortable sense of competition. Either way it achieved the goal of keeping them at bay. And that was exactly as it needed to be. It was the very means through which Helena had climbed to her current position as an assassin. And aside from assignments, it gave her full latitude to develop her plans for power all by herself.

Unbidden, from somewhere deep inside, crept the memory of a place she had heard about. A "City of Light." It was said to be a place where somns could casually go about their day without continuous need of preplanning or cover stories. For a moment she felt the demon that is despair. Frowning, Helena was afraid that she would never know any world other than that of assholes and whores. Speaking of which...

Once more she raised her eyes to study Callis and Tavokk across the room. As she strained to listen, her eyes hardened with every unheard syllable of their conversation. She mused, *What reason would Jereth Tavokk and Callis Morgandy have to speak with one another?*

ॐ

Two rounds later, Callis interjected, "You know, I heard something rather odd today." He looked somewhat dazed, as he watched the room tilt unnaturally side to side. "I heard that a Calling has been awakened."

With a conspiratorial whisper, he intoned, "They say this one is different from the others."

"Different how?" Tavokk pressed, now wary.

"They say he will determine the balance of realms."

"That's a hefty task to rest on a single Calling, wouldn't you say?" Tavokk queried, with a concerned expression snaking over his features.

Behind him, Tavokk did not notice that the expression on Helena Meretrix's face was no longer one of curiosity, but rather one of sheer frustration. She needed to know what these men had to discuss. It couldn't be anything light of importance.

"It's what I heard. What do I know? It could happen though. There hasn't been a recorded Calling in years. Other than Nyx Crucian's, but that must have been a waste of a prophecy," Callis declared, his eyes masking a hidden emotion that Tavokk couldn't decipher. "And there definitely hasn't been a Calling summoned to such a momentous task in centuries," he babbled on, only loosely aware of his conversation.

Seeing Callis' sudden, altered expression, Helena scowled.

"Nyx?" Tavokk questioned. "Who exactly is this Nyx Crucian?" he continued pressing, to discover all Callis knew of the particular somn.

While listening for a response, Tavokk frowned. He knew Nyx Crucian as a treacherous man who had masterminded his way into a position of underground authority in Atrum Unda. The two-faced son of a dagger was up to no good.

But what does Callis know of Nyx? Does he know him personally? he pondered. Only select somns truly knew Nyx. Those who did were ruthless crowds. Tavokk's mouth twitched as unpleasant images came to mind. He knew much more about Nyx Crucian than he would tell.

"Nyx is no one," Callis stammered. Something in the back of his reeling senses warned him to shut up.

"He must be someone," Tavokk said, with innocence. He attempted to make himself sound more as though he were asking a question, rather than interrogating a man with too many drinks on board.

Tavokk carried on pressing about Nyx, but after continued failure, he yielded with a glower.

Flustered, Tavokk pushed back from the table. "It's getting late. I must be going."

"The night is still young!" Callis exclaimed, drunkenly unaware of time.

"Perhaps," Tavokk replied, stepping up from the booth. "However," he continued, "I must get up early. There are some things that need to be settled."

"Well...all right, Jereth," Callis said, suddenly morose.

"No worries, Cal. We'll see each other again before long," Tavokk said, as jovial as he could muster. He gave Callis a solid pat on the back and headed for the door. Giving one last glance to the man with the vibrant red hair, he turned back toward the exit.

Heaving the door open, he stepped out of the bar.

"I will see you again soon, my friend." He scowled. "That is a promise."

Ⅎ∾ℳ

Tavokk made his way through the never-ending rain and down the stairs from the Cosmos. Nearing the plaza and its blue covering, he paused.

Who is following me?

3: Another Nuisance

Venn walked through the main hallway located overtop The Courtyard, passing the tree that grew up through the hole at its center. Branches overhung the balustrade, as the central tree continued upward, stretching high over the roof. He reached out and ripped a leaf from a nearby branch, as he aimed toward the kitchen.

Proceeding through the doorway, Venn anticipated the food that smelled so wonderful.

"What in the world is that?" Marion inquired, harshly.

Startled, Venn jerked his head up. "What is what?"

"That!" Marion snapped, pointing an accusing finger at Venn's hands.

"Oh," Venn said, baffled at the tone of her voice, "just a leaf."

"I don't care what it is! Why the hell are you shredding it all over my clean kitchen?" Marion scolded, hollering without need.

"It's just a leaf for crying out loud," Venn muttered. Looking up, he startled once again. He hadn't expected to see the boy from the canal sitting at the table. He cringed, noting that the boy had changed into a set of his favorite clothing.

Venn glared at the young man who sat, shifting awkwardly, unsure what to expect.

After turning his attention briefly back to Marion, Venn's eyes shifted about the room. "Marion, please explain how it is acceptable for you to freak out about a little leaf when you can't even close a damn cupboard!" Venn understood that the best defense was a good offense.

"It's my kitchen, and I can leave as many cupboards open as I like!"

"Uh, excuse me? Whose kitchen?" Venn responded, his hostile eyes like crystal blue ice behind his glasses.

"My kitchen! I'm the one who cleans it! I'm the one who cooks in it! Not to mention, I'm the one who buys and gets stuck carrying all the groceries home by myself! If it wasn't for me, you wouldn't even have food to stuff in that obnoxious, pessimistic, whiny-ass mouth of yours!" Marion shrieked, in a single breath.

Venn stared wide-eyed, his mouth agape. Speechless, he felt eyes on him. He glared at his unwelcome guest, and snarled, "What the hell are you looking at?"

Marion eyed the young man and then Venn. "Don't yell at him! If you can't control yourself, then you will go without dinner! Get out!" Turning away, she dismissed him with a wave.

Venn flushed scarlet, and taken aback, he searched for a response. All he managed was another venomous snarl. He spun abruptly and stormed out of the kitchen, slamming the door behind him.

Still seated in the kitchen, the young man whistled, labeling a close call.

Marion slammed a plateful of food on the table before him. "Shut up and eat."

ℰ⊃ℂℛ

Venn stomped to the den. Excluding his bedroom, it was his one place of quiet sanctity, sacred to him alone. He headed straight to the bar for something appealing and numbing. Uncorking a glass bottle, he poured a stiff libation. He dropped into his soft leather chair, taking a large swig and staring into the fire.

Oh Vincent, he reflected. *Two years ago, you dropped Marion into my care. What is your plan with this boy?*

Relaxed after a few drinks, Venn arose. Setting his empty glass on a small side table, he exited the den. Ignoring the delicious, lingering aroma, he approached the kitchen. *Too quiet,* he thought.

He cracked open the door, apprehensive about the greeting he might receive. Deep down, he regretted his first impression on his new houseguest.

The room was empty. The dishes had been rinsed but left unwashed. Curious, Venn wandered the upstairs rooms, searching their whereabouts. In the center hallway, he detected a distant, harsh cackle. *No way to mistake Marion's laugh.* A half-smile crossed his lips as he envisioned an old crone, instead of a lissome young girl.

The sound had come from The Courtyard below. Making his way downstairs, he pushed through the heavy doors, into the open. Marion and the young man were sitting on the stone bench off to Venn's left.

Marion offered a dazzling smile, apparently over the recent spat. Venn sauntered toward them, his boots making their way over the cobblestones.

"I believe we've met," Venn offered, in dry sarcasm, extending a bold hand to the young man.

"Uh...yeah," the young man replied, with discomfort. He reached a cautious hand in return.

Marion smiled wide as the two shook hands. She had become well accustomed to Venn's curious ways.

"What is your name?" Venn asked.

"Rhyus," Marion blurted. "His name is Rhyus Delmar, but don't call him Rye. He hates it!" Freezing, she pursed her lips. It was not her place to answer.

Venn turned a raised eyebrow to her. "Marion, thank you so much for the inestimable enlightenment." Though his words were clipped, a half-smile remained.

"Sorry," she whispered. She bit her lip, while maintaining her pleasant smile.

Rhyus flashed her a grin, amused by her quirky personality. He shifted his gaze back to Venn, nervous to break contact for long.

Venn returned his attention to the young man, "Rhyus, eh?"

"Yeah," Rhyus drawled, "that would be me."

"Hmm." Venn's brow furrowed at the snippy rejoinder. "Well *Rye*, how exactly did you end up here?"

"I...I thought you brought me here," the boy intoned, confused.

"No. No," Venn snapped. "Not here, as in my home. Here, as in Lux Lumetia," he growled. "Why here? And why show up in such an outlandish way?"

"Oh," Rhyus hesitated, as Venn tilted his head in expectation.

"Don't look at me like that! I don't have a freaking clue!" Rhyus retorted. He regretted his brash response, noting Venn's hostile glare of reproach.

"Not a clue," Venn repeated, peering over his rectangular glasses, clearly unconvinced.

"W-well," Rhyus stammered, "it was dark. And raining." He paused before continuing, his voice holding a note of reflection, "I saw two large statues. They looked like winged guardians or something. Actually, they looked just like those." He pointed to the sculptures at the head of The Courtyard. "But they were black not white."

Venn's expression relaxed, as he focused on Rhyus. He pressed, "Continue."

"A man shoved me onto a hard patch of ground. Stone perhaps? It was wet...strong pain...my memory's hazy...a flash of light. That's all. Then I woke up here."

Venn shuffled his feet. "And the man?" he inquired. "You are positive it was a man?"

"I…he said something. It was a man, yes, but I know nothing more of him."

"Concentrate! What exactly did he say?"

"I don't know. He spoke out loud, but no one else was there."

"What did he look like?"

"I couldn't focus. It wasn't night, but dark. Raining." Closing his eyes, Rhyus strained diligently to recall. "Not as big as you. And…strange…even though it was dark, he had shades on."

Vincent, Venn speculated to himself. *It has to be Vincent. In Atrum Unda? Is that where he has been? What business is holding him in such a horrid place?*

Yet, more to the point, Venn's thoughts carried on, *who is this boy? Where does he fit in? I don't like this. Not at all.*

"What's wrong?" Marion called, as Venn spun toward the exit gate. She jumped off the bench, catching up to him.

"It's nothing," he said, still moving.

"Wait Venn! If it's about the leaf…I don't care!"

"Don't be absurd," he said, just loud enough for her to hear. "That doesn't matter. I'm not mad at you." He reached out, squeezing her hand for encouragement. "Just watch over *Rye*. But, whatever you do, don't follow me." He stressed the cryptic warning, as he disappeared through the metal gate and into the alleyway.

ഇരൻ

Lux, the City of Light, had been dark for hours. Two of the five moons were currently present. Valencia, glowing silver, and Ravenna, blue-violet, cast their light from above like spotlights following Venn, as he made his way through the lifeless city streets.

Walking briskly across the silver, luminescent ground of Lux Lumetia, he enjoyed its eerie beauty at this silent time of night.

After negotiating many streets and bridges, Venn stepped into an Eastside tavern, the Crimson Glass. He had found the city's nightlife. Here, some came to gossip, some to find companionship, and some simply to drink away their problems. Venn's reason was the first.

With a brief survey, he spotted his target. Mona, daughter of the widowed tavern owner, had celebrated her seventeenth birthday just prior to their last encounter. Radiant, with pale gold hair and sparkling, golden makeup to match, she was a treasure trove of the latest talk of the town. Dreaming to be hired as a city journalist, she strove to stay on top of her sources.

"Hello, Mona. I so much enjoyed our last meeting."

"Welcome back, Venn." She eyed him through heavily darkened lashes. "It's been awhile, how have you been?"

"Oh, good. Suppose I can't complain too much." Making such small talk, he straddled the barstool beside her. "And you?"

"Oh, you know." Mona toyed with one of her tight, shoulder length curls, asking, "Where's Marion?" She glanced about the room, saying with a smile, "You can't have lost her? You two are practically inseparable."

"Don't get me started," Venn groaned, waving for a bartender.

Mona chuckled. "What trouble have you gotten yourself into this time?"

"That's what I'd like to know."

"Pardon?" she questioned. "You should speak up. You know mumbling—"

Abruptly, Venn cut her off, "Actually, I came here to ask you something."

He turned momentarily from the girl, as an attractive bartender approached. "What can I getcha, handsome?" she asked, eyeing him up and down.

Mona, behind the bartender, put her index finger to her mouth, gagging her silent disapproval.

"A double. Hard," he ordered, and then added casually, "despite coming here often, I do not believe we have had the pleasure of meeting." His face expressionless, he was unaware that this brunette came on strongly to even any imagined encouragement.

Handing the drink to Venn, her fingers brushed his. "My name is Lucille. But call me Lucy." Winking, she purred, "Just let me know if you need *anything*, dear."

Ignoring her connotation, Venn raised his glass. "Will do." At this point, he no longer noticed. His mind was elsewhere. Tightening her lips, she stalked off to her other customers.

With Venn to herself again, Mona smiled and leaned closer. With a conspiratorial whisper, she asked, "So, what do you want to ask me?"

Venn, absorbed in his own thoughts, startled to alertness. "What?" he asked, focusing again on Mona.

Mona's smile dropped to a petulant frown.

Studying her, Venn considered the best way to start. "I have heard rumors. Strange occurrences have taken place these last few days. Have you any knowledge of such?"

Mona pondered with a finger to her lips. "Do you mean other than a strapping, raven-haired man carrying an unconscious boy over his shoulder through Lux Lumetia?" She wrinkled her nose coyly at him.

Venn peered over his glasses with a stern gaze to stress his seriousness, informing, "This is no laughing matter. If you know of any useful tidbit I would greatly appreciate it."

Mona kept her voice to a whisper as she said, "Well, there is one thing."

"Yes?" Venn held his breath.

"Lord Abel and his White Guard are on alert. The Guard is actively patrolling the walkways. It is also said that Lord Abel and The Tower Scholars are disputing something behind closed doors."

Emptying his glass, Venn pondered this information. Then, slamming the glass on the bar, he rose. "Thank you, Mona. Your words are worth a fortune." He offered her a short smile and turned brusquely away.

"Hey! Venn!" Mona called after him, however the music drowned her out, as he rushed through the door.

ℰℂℛ

Venn picked a steady pace, agitated, but studying his surroundings this time around. From the corners of his eyes, he spotted armed men in the shadows, keeping an attentive watch on the city. Mona had been right. The White Guard was on patrol. Through careful observation, he had discerned their true purpose. They weren't watching all the walkways. They were concentrating their attention on all the main portals between Lux Lumetia and Atrum Unda.

No wonder Vincent used such a haphazard portal to smuggle Rhyus into Lux, Venn thought. Though it may have been wise to use that hidden portal, the boy had been lucky not to drown in the crystal canal. Realizing the gravity of the situation, he hurried back toward Umbra Halls.

Venn weaved back home through the moonlit city. Fitting the pieces together, he flogged himself at his stupidity. Picking up the boy, he had noticed the tattoo, but it had never registered. He now knew what Vincent KyVeerah had in mind. *Damn him! He could have at least warned me to be discreet, rather than let me flaunt the kid across the whole city. How could I have been so ignorant? And does Vincent really believe that little loose cannon could be his...*

His thoughts trailed off as he reached the gate to The Courtyard. Making his way over cobblestones, and around the tree, he pushed his way inside. Climbing the stairs, he opened one of the hallway doors.

"Oh, shit!" Venn yelped, ragged nerves on edge. He glared at Marion who had camped out in the chair beside the double doors. And by the look of the snacks she had piled up, she had settled in for the long haul.

"What are you doing up, missy? You scared the shit out of me!"

"Waiting for you, obviously," Marion sniffed, with disdain. "You had me worried."

"Look. I am very capable of taking care of myself," Venn huffed. "Think about it. If I thought you could take care of both yourself *and* Rhyus, don't you think I might be capable of caring for myself?"

Taking offense at her unappreciated concern, Marion barked, "Fine, next time I won't bother myself about you! You big jerk!" Brushing an unwanted tear, she turned and stomped away.

Venn hesitated before reaching out and grabbing her shoulder. "Wait. I'm sorry."

"Don't touch me!" she snapped, as he attempted to make her face him.

"I apologize," he quietly said. "That was rash of me." He waited a moment until both of their breathing calmed. "What do you wish to tell me?"

Marion looked him in the eye and gave into his honest remorse. Then, looking back at the floor, her feet shifted in apprehension. "Well, you see. It's about Rhyus."

"Oh, Ravenna..." Venn's breath caught. *Am I too late?*

4: A Robed Encounter

Rain poured from the dark night sky, but besides the eerie feeling cast by it, Jereth Tavokk felt an intrusive presence.

Descending the staircase from the Cosmos, he felt it close. Sliding behind the large statue a short distance from the stair's base, he waited. A stealthy, robed figure covered the remaining steps. Moving swiftly, Tavokk grasped the thin wrist of his pursuer, twisting its full form into a locked grip.

Holding tightly with his left arm, he reached up with his right. Removing the cerulean hood, Tavokk looked down into a pair of bewitching, green eyes. He offered a twisted grin, "Hello, darling."

From her supple form, a spicy, woodland fragrance filled Tavokk's senses. In her struggle, the young woman had turned toward him. Soft, full breasts pressed against his chest, as his arms wrapped around her feminine form. As one arm kept a tight hold across her lower back, he placed the other behind her head, grasping onto her strawberry blonde hair.

"Helena Meretrix, what a pleasant surprise," he said. Adjusting his grip, he moved his lips just inches from hers, surprised by the warm sweetness of her hot breath. "To what do I owe this chance encounter?"

"Well...I was coming up from the Wishing Well earlier and saw you heading to the Cosmos. I figured that, since it has been awhile, you must have missed me," she said, haughtily. She tried to readjust her stance, failing in the tight grip of her captor.

"No. I could have handled a few more weeks, or months, or hell, I could have handled never seeing your face again. Yes, I believe that would be the correct choice," Tavokk pondered aloud. "No offense." He flashed a wicked smile.

Helena glowered.

"Oh, don't be so put off. You are a little close to hold such aggressive feelings. Wait, I'm not used to this vantage point. Are those crow's feet I see?"

Helena's jaw dropped.

"So really, what do you want from me, kitten?"

Preferring to slap him, Helena maintained a necessary restraint and vented her curiosity instead. She demurred, "I wanted to ask you something."

Tavokk peered over his shades, remaining only inches from Helena's face. "Yes?"

"I'm looking for a boy. Or a young man perhaps."

"Looking for a good time, are we? And you've come to me. Why, you are right, darling, it has been awhile, hasn't it?" He gave her a look of intrigue. Readjusting his grip, he slid a sensual hand to her hip.

Shivering despite herself, she strove to look through his dark glasses, curious of his true intent. She snapped out of it. "No, not like that!" She blushed. "I have heard of a boy who has come from another place, beyond our own."

"And you want him." Tavokk raised his eyebrows.

"Yes. No! Not in the way you are implying!"

"Pray tell, how am I implying?"

Helena snarled.

"You know, that isn't so attractive from this angle. Do your nostrils always flare like that? Or only when you are angry?" Helena tried to pull free of Tavokk's hold, but he reined her in.

"What do you want with the boy? He can't be more beautiful than myself?" Tavokk cocked an eyebrow.

"Unbelievable! How conceited can one asshole be? The boy is rumored to be of great importance." Lowering her voice, she continued, "I have heard a Calling has risen. If I can get to him before some terrible somn does, I can lead him to great things."

"And how do I fall into this grand scheme?" Tavokk asked, suddenly serious.

"Who are you kidding, Jereth? We both know that you have connections."

He raised his eyebrows, intrigued once again. Not many somns referred to him by his first name. Generally it was left at Tavokk. "What would I get out of this?"

"What do you want?" she asked, with cold hostility.

"Well." He leaned in closer, pulling her slowly toward him with his left arm, feeling her heat as he drew her near. He was surprised to feel the hot blood begin to pound in his temples.

Just as surprising, Helena closed her eyes and tilted her head back. Quickening, she began to press her soft breasts into his hard chest, leaning her lips toward his.

"Whoa now!" Tavokk leaned back. "Are you coming on to me?"

he asked, with a crooked grin.

Helena growled, "Why you!"

In his distraction, she managed to push away. In the flash of an instant too late, Tavokk glimpsed a metallic glint, followed by a sudden sharp pain on the side of his face. Just as quickly, the knife had disappeared, and the petite young woman stood before him, balanced lightly on the balls of her feet.

"Jereth," she hissed, "you gotta watch out. I may be small, but my sting is sharp."

Then, without another word, she flashed a smile that was half invitation and half deadly warning. With a brief pucker of her full, sensual lips, she blew him a kiss and turned away, walking with a slow gait that accentuated the sensual undulation of her hips.

Rarely at a loss for word or action, Tavokk stood stock still, tasting the bright, coppery salt of warm blood on his tongue. *The little bitch stabbed me!*

Watching her walk away, he remained unmoving. Feeling the throbbing quickening of his pulse, he wondered at the fine line between bitter anger and ardent lust. Thin lips tight with rage, he watched her sultry form dim into the ever-pervasive mist.

"That wasn't very polite, puppet," he yelled out. His rage dissolved into a smug smile. "Oh, and by the way, I'm not interested!" He watched until she disappeared from view. With absolute certainty, he knew that they would meet again. *And*, he vowed, *that meeting will be most interesting.*

He turned and walked off into the night. Picking up speed, a light began to flicker at the bottom of the hill. He descended and vanished.

5: Visual Transformation

"What happened?" Venn asked, anxiously.

"Well. It's not good," Marion shied.

"Just tell me, Marion!" Venn shouted, anticipation devouring his insides.

"He found something. Something valuable."

"What? What in the world do you mean?" Venn was growing irritated now.

"The den. He found the den."

"Oh *hell* no!"

"Venn!" Marion shrieked, as he stormed off. She tried to restrain him, but he continued on, dragging her along like a little rag doll.

Venn threw open the door to the den.

Rhyus sat nonchalantly in Venn's chair with his bare feet on the footrest and his back to the door. Burning wood crackled in the fireplace, and the boy's wet shoes lay sprawled on the luxurious rug near it.

Wary, Marion recognized the characteristic traits of a furious Venn. Veins in his neck began to pop as muscles in his neck and jaw tightened. His fingers blanched as he clenched his fists.

Rhyus had scattered Venn's books in piles on the floor surrounding him. Some closed and some open, pages bent helter-skelter. A few more on the side table served as drink holders for Venn's favorite liquors.

Desperate, Marion tried one last time to pull Venn from the room.

"Oh, you're home," Rhyus said passively, turning his head toward the door. He turned back, but not before Venn noted the particular book in Rhyus's hands.

Venn's blood began to boil. That was the last straw. "What the hell are you doing?" he roared.

"Reading of course," Rhyus said. "What does it look like I'm do"Reading of course," Rhyus said. "What does it look like I'm doing?"

Marion squeezed between Venn and the door. Peeking around Venn's shoulder she cut in, "Umm, Rhyus..."

"Yeah?"

"You should…" Marion tried to warn, but Venn was already half way across the room. He reached over the chair, ripping the book from Rhyus's hands. "Get out," Venn whispered the threat.

"What's your problem? Are you always this psychotic? Or is today my lucky day?"

Marion's eyes widened with horror. She shook her head rapidly, "No, no, no. Not good. Not good at all," she thought aloud, from across the room.

Venn's face suffused with white rage. "I dragged your ass across this city once. I wouldn't be afraid to drag you back and toss you head first into that canal!"

"Oh, really? Is that what you're going to do?" Rhyus smirked.

Gripping its back legs, Venn viciously wrenched the leather chair from underneath Rhyus, crashing him flat on his back, his feet still up on the ottoman.

"Holy shit! You are insane!" Rhyus yelled, scrambling up to distance himself from Venn. He stumbled backward toward Marion whose hands covered her mouth in fear that Venn might actually kill him.

"Get…out…" Venn threatened, through clenched teeth.

Marion assisted Rhyus, pulling him from the den. Rhyus hesitated, searching for a rejoinder.

"NOW!" Venn's voice echoed off the walls.

Pulling the door shut behind her, Marion shoved Rhyus into the hallway.

"What the hell were you thinking?" Marion demanded, in a furious whisper.

Rhyus, ignoring her, snatched his arm back and moved toward the double doors.

As Marion watched, he pretended he couldn't care less about what had transpired. She sighed in exasperation.

୫ଠଓ

Dejected, Venn dropped into his chair. Rubbing his temples, he couldn't believe that the boy could be of any importance. *Then again, Vincent seems convinced. This is a serious matter for him. How the hell did Vincent ever manage to be tied to such a self-centered, obnoxious little prick?* Venn's primary refuge had been breached, and he felt strangely defiled. Without thinking, he picked up a half-empty glass and downed a large swallow.

"Good lord!" he spat. "Kid can't even make a decent drink!" He cringed, both repulsed and infuriated.

Deciding to retire, Venn surveyed his books lying in disarray about the room. He quelled a brief urge to sort them, knowing he would more than likely smash one through the mirror over the bar. Or worse.

Exiting, he nearly tripped over Marion, sitting against the wall, legs hugged against her breasts. Venn snarled, as he walked by, "Do *not* go in there. If I find that boy in there again, I'll kill him!"

"I—" Marion began. Venn did not allow her to get a word in.

"I don't want to hear it," he said lethally. He tramped downstairs to his bedroom, the one true place nobody would dare bother him.

With its understated black-and-white elegance, the room embraced him like an old friend. Below, a rich wood wainscot wrapped the room. Above, ran exquisite crown molding. Both had been stained lustrous black with ornamental, black-and-white paper covering the walls between. The only accents were the midnight blue sheen of a pair of lavish, floor-length drapes and the matching comforter on his bed.

Venn sighed and shut the door. Hurling his shirt onto a worn, black leather chair, he swept a pile of arranged pillows from the bed to the floor. He crawled in and buried his face in a remaining pillow, to block his racing thoughts. Soon, he grabbed another, covering his head to block all light and sound. Eventually, he drifted into a restless sleep.

ଛେଠ

Morning arrived, but the brilliant suns never shone through the windows of Umbra Halls. Waking late, Venn donned a pair of loose, pale blue denims and a sleeveless, gray undershirt. Hungry, he bathed quickly and charged upstairs. Marion offered a cursory greeting from the same hallway chair where she had awaited him the previous night. She immediately shifted her attention back to the puzzle book in her lap.

Giving brief acknowledgment, Venn padded bare feet over the worn, wooden floor to the kitchen. He pulled a large corrfruit from the fridge and took it to the table where he dispatched it with little ado. Done, he crossed the hallway to the den, closing the door behind him, as always. Marion had peeked up as he passed by.

Caressing his books, Venn gently sorted them back into their rightful places. Lifting the books from the side table, he carefully wiped them dry. Doing so, he spotted the glass that contained such a disgraceful excuse for a drink.

Rhyus, he reflected. *If this whole situation is as serious as I suspect, I must keep close watch over him. Great. Exactly how I would love to spend my time. But no doubt, the boy has questions of his own. I had better give him some answers before he falls into the wrong hands.*

Back in his room, Venn changed into a pair of dark blue denim pants and a long-sleeved, button-up shirt. Shoving feet into wide, black sandals, he grabbed a necklace with a prominent black star sapphire pendant from a hook by the door and hurried out.

Smiling from her usual perch, Marion assessed him, "Lookin' good stud."

"Where is Rhyus?" Venn half questioned, half demanded.

"Still asleep, the last I knew."

"You can't be serious?" Venn gave a disapproving look.

"Uh, yeah. Pretty sure."

Sighing with annoyance, Venn headed down to the guest bedroom. Though available for centuries, it rarely entertained guests. Nonetheless, it now held Rhyus.

Venn pounded relentlessly on the door.

A grumbling moan came from inside.

"Get up!" Venn ordered. "It's after noon, and there are things to take care of."

"What. You're not gonna throw a chair at me, are you?" Rhyus mocked, still half asleep.

Venn boiled. "Just get up!" Throwing his hands in the air, he stormed back upstairs.

"He is impossible!" Venn groused to Marion, mainly to get the thought out of his head and into the open.

ℰᴑℭℛ

Rhyus rolled over with a groan. He pulled a green-cased pillow over his face, and then threw it roughly across the room. He lay quiet, pondering who he was and where he had come from. *How the hell did I get here?* The unknown answer left him infuriated. He knew that his cocky attitude really pissed Venn off. But for Rhyus, it was just his way of whistling in the dark.

Eyes opening, he surveyed the room, which he had been introduced to the previous evening. Dark wood paneling accented cream-colored walls. A plush, emerald comforter covered snow-white sheets.

Standing, he donned a pair of loose denims and a white, short-sleeved shirt that Marion had left folded on the window seat. Being Venn's, they engulfed him. Rhyus cinched the belt to snug the pants around his slender waist.

After a shower to ready himself for the day, Rhyus headed upstairs. Unnoticed, he ventured upon Venn and Marion, who sat at the kitchen table, concentrating over a game of chess. The board and its playing pieces were exceptional, crafted from the very crystal that lined Lux's water canals. Venn, eagerly grasping one of his bishops, moved it brusquely.

"Checkmate!" Venn crowed, flashing a smug grin at Marion.

"Wow, Venn. You finally won a game."

"Ooh, too low," Venn pouted, at Marion's mocking.

Rhyus cleared his throat.

Venn spun on the backward chair that he straddled. He raised a brow toward Rhyus. "Oh really?"

Marion tightened her lips and frowned up at Rhyus, still standing in the doorway.

Rhyus studied the floor, avoiding Venn's gaze. He felt icy eyes burning into him from behind Venn's glasses.

"Let's make a deal," Venn proposed.

"What kind of deal?" Rhyus asked, looking Venn in the eye now.

"I was thinking along the lines of, 'If you avoid annoying me, I fill you in on some tidbits that you may find to your interest and benefit. And if you maintain your smartass attitude, I throw a chair at you in possibility of paralyzing you from the waist down'. How does that arrangement sound to you?"

Rhyus paused a moment. "All right," he answered, "you're on."

"One more thing," Venn said, "you will do something with that hair before I will be seen with you in public. I don't want to look as though I've found myself a wet animal to drag around."

Venn adjusted his glasses. "Marion, my dear, won't you please assist in grooming the poor lad?"

"Sure thing." She smiled at Rhyus's obvious discomfiture, and then commanded him to follow, "Come Rhyus."

Marion frowned as they walked. "Don't sulk. You look like you're on death row."

"If only. This is much worse than death row," Rhyus mumbled, but not quietly enough for Marion to miss. She stopped in her tracks, turned, and placed her hands on her hips.

Caught by her abrupt halt, Rhyus crashed into her.

"Good Ravenna. Are you trying to run me over?" Marion scolded. "Venn asked me to help with that pitiful rat-mop you call hair, so that's what I am going to do whether you like it or not!"

Rhyus cringed, but he recovered quickly. Shaking it off, he responded with his arrogant cover.

"Yes, ma'am," he saluted, locking his legs and clicking his heels. A cocky grin covered his face.

Marion started back down the corridor, muttering, "Smartass."

Rhyus laughed but stopped, realizing that they had come to a standstill before Marion's room.

She gave him a look. "I need to grab some things so we can begin your, uh...*transformation*." As she rummaged through her dresser, Rhyus, unsure what to do, stood awkwardly in the doorway.

Marion smirked. "You know, you can come in. If Venn finds out, I won't let him hurt you...or throw a chair at you."

"Ha, ha, very funny," Rhyus scoffed, before coolly adding, "Venn doesn't scare me." But he warily looked over his shoulder before entering.

He noted trim similar to the guest room, which had been painted clean, crisp white. Variegated, turquoise stripes adorned the walls, and an overstuffed, white sofa chair rested on a large, white rug. A canopied, four-poster-bed, lavishly adorned to match, rested in the center of the room.

Clean, classy, and fresh, Rhyus appraised, though darned if he would let her know he truly thought so.

He whistled as a man would over an attractive woman.

"What's that supposed to mean?"

"Nothing," Rhyus responded in innocence, "it's nice."

A frown creased Marion's face. "There's *nothing* wrong with my room," she declared angrily, directing him to the bathroom.

"I didn't say that there *is* anything wrong with it. In fact, if I recall correctly, I said that it is *nice*."

Marion glowered at him. "You didn't mean it that way."

"Don't be ridiculous. Of course I meant it that way," he crooned. "But mine is nicer." He made the last comment quietly, though intentionally loud enough for Marion to hear.

"Why you!"

"Are you going to do my hair or not? I assume Venn isn't one to be kept waiting."

Marion glared, but she didn't pursue the conversation. She arranged various hair products across the counter. Studying Rhyus's reflection in the mirror, she said, "You're too tall."

"I'm sorry?"

Marion sighed, "Just grab that stool and sit down."

"Aye, aye, captain." As Rhyus promptly sat, he peered at Marion in the mirror.

Marion misted Rhyus's hair, working product into it. "How old are you?"

"Twenty-two," Rhyus answered, in short.

"Ah, only just older than me," Marion chirped, enjoying the current activity.

After a few moments of silence, Rhyus spoke in a mocking tone, "Do you play personal hair stylist for Venn too?" He turned his head to assess the reaction to his comment.

Her smile turned to an immediate frown as she forced his head straight. "Hold still! And no. I don't. Venn, unlike you, knows how to coordinate his appearance with style. And wipe off that smirk. You are *not* that funny."

"Actually, a lot of somns find me *quite* funny." He flashed a rakish grin.

"Please. The only somns you know here are Venn and myself. I just told you how funny I find you. And Venn, need I say?"

"Ouch. You wound me so." Rhyus feigned a wounded expression.

Marion stepped back, saying, "Don't be ridiculous. Get up."

Confusion played over Rhyus's face. "Wait. I was only joking. Come on, I didn't mean it."

"No, Rhyus, I'm done. You can get up now." Marion gathered her tools in obvious dismissal.

"Well?"

"Well what?" Rhyus questioned, unsure what Marion was asking.

Rolling her eyes, she sighed, "What do you think? Of your hair?"

"Oh," he said, with a sheepish expression, before studying the mirror. "Hot damn, I look sexy. Oh, and the hair's nice too."

Marion scowled at him.

"No," he laughed. "I like it. Really. I do."

"Agh! You are *so* ungrateful." Marion directed him to the hallway.

"Thanks Marion," Rhyus tried, in a note of reconciliation, as she pushed him out.

"Whatever." Slamming the door, she disappeared from view.

Rhyus, still grinning, made his way back upstairs. The grin

disappeared as soon as he saw Venn leaning smugly against the elegant stone balustrade, arms crossed, waiting for him. Venn tossed a costly, red jacket forcefully at Rhyus, warning, "You damage it, I will destroy you."

Marion ducked through the doorway and underneath Rhyus's arm, which remained holding one of the doors open. She came to a halt just before his motionless figure.

Seeing the jacket in Rhyus's other arm, she eagerly butted in, asking, "Where are we going?"

"Whoa, you're not going anywhere, missy," Venn said. "Someone must stay home in case I receive more intruders. You see, it seems I am being mistaken for an orphanage. Someone must be here to turn these poor, unfortunate souls back to the streets. Two is already two too many — if you catch my drift."

Marion gaped. Venn stood haughty as she gave him an injured look.

After a long moment, Venn broke the tension by casting a wink at her. "Oh, don't worry, Mae. You belong here." Turning to Rhyus, he intoned, "Rhyus, if you ever make this lovely young lady cry, it will be the end of you." Venn turned to Rhyus, and then back to Marion, a grin on his face.

He looked at Marion, as though asking if she was satisfied.

"Uh, thanks?" she said, somewhat puzzled and beginning to blush.

"We're off," Venn declared, starting into the stairwell, pushing past the young man. "Come, Rye," he called. He shouted back to Marion, "We'll be back by nightfall, Marion. Dinner would be marvelous!"

Rhyus, with a confused scowl on his face, threw the red jacket on, as he followed Venn down the stairs. Marion watched them pass beneath, through The Courtyard.

℘℩℧

Rhyus followed Venn down the alley behind The Courtyard. Despite the alley's darkness, the suns shone brighter with each step toward the white walkways of the city. "Don't you worry, leaving her alone like that?" Rhyus asked.

"I could have done worse," Venn said dryly. He glanced up at the distant Tower of Lux Lumetia. It stood at the city's center, looking regally down over all it surveyed.

"Oh really, like what?"

"For instance, I could have made her put up with the two of us. Or worse, I could have left her with you." Rhyus was unaware of Venn's thin smile. "But I'm not that cruel."

Perplexed, Rhyus sighed, attempting to shake his bangs out of his face. They refused to move. His dark brown hair remained shaggy, but it was fashioned tastefully thanks to Marion.

The trip to the Eastside was long. Venn and Rhyus walked quietly. Unable to bear the silent tension any longer, Rhyus spoke. "As much fun as this is, it would be nice to know what we are doing."

"Impatient are we? Are you in such a rush to get back to our dearest, Mae?" Venn asked coyly.

"You know that's not what I'm talking about!"

"If you must know, we have errands to run, which is why I didn't want Marion tagging along." Venn turned south. By now, The Tower at the city's center was far behind them.

"What could we possibly be doing that you don't want Marion to know about?"

A frown creasing his otherwise flawless features, Venn said, "If you are too daft to have noticed, I tend to downplay my wealth. Having said that...here." Still walking, Venn transferred a wad of cash from a jacket pocket into Rhyus's hand. "You might need this. But don't you *dare* mention a word of this to Marion." Venn issued a warning glare over the rectangular frames of his glasses. "As a matter of fact," he continued, "nothing we do or discuss today is to be relayed to Marion."

Rhyus, taken aback, stammered, "I-I don't understand." He shuffled through the wad of pale-colored bills before stuffing it into his pocket. "Why don't you want Marion to know about this?" Rhyus pressed, using a tone that he should have learned by now did not fly with his temperamental host.

Venn stopped dead. Even at Rhyus's height, Venn glared down into his emerald eyes, the blue luminosity of Venn's consumed them. "I do this because I do *not* want you coming to me every time you need something."

"And Marion?"

Venn erupted. Throwing his hands into the air, he roared, "What I do with my money is none of her damn business! Or yours!" Realizing that somns were staring at them, Venn reined in his temper.

Speaking with clipped words, he carried on, "I have enough to deal with. I do not need Marion giving me grief for actually doing something nice for you." He turned hastily down the street, leaving Rhyus to catch up.

Now in the Rallis District, the heart of the Eastside, they had reached the wealthiest part of the city. Buildings here sparkled with a luminous intensity. Walkways glistened with a polished sheen. The same architecture as the rest of the city was found here, but significant modernization had created bold, magnificent new structural lines.

"We're here." Venn said abruptly.

Rhyus stared at the building before them. There was nothing to hint what Venn might be getting him into. Beautifully sculpted white marble doors revealed no knobs or handles.

Venn placed a powerful, yet finely manicured, hand upon a raised protuberance of the sculpted door. It hinged aside, revealing a small, metallic box attached by two cords. After pressing a sequence of buttons, it buzzed three times, loud enough to be heard over the city's noise but quiet enough that no one else would notice.

After the third buzz, Venn moved the box to his slender lips. "Cyrus," he said, "it's Venn."

With a new, long buzz, the door opened. Venn stepped through the narrow opening, directing Rhyus to follow.

"You're not planning to kill me, are you?" Rhyus joked, yet an unexplained shakiness slurred his voice.

Venn turned his head in a way that Rhyus could see his profile. A grin unfurled slowly over his lips. "Only one way to find out."

℘℃

Looking around, Rhyus gaped. "You gotta be kidding me! You dragged me along to shop for clothes?"

"For you," Venn replied.

A baffled expression settled over Rhyus.

"I can't have you living in my clothes, can I?" Horror covered Venn's face at the thought. "Besides," he added, "they look god awful on you. You couldn't pull off my look if your life depended on it."

Venn threaded a hallway lined bilaterally with display windows. Stunning mannequins, male and female, displayed one particular brand. Rhyus was disturbed at how lifelike they looked. Almost living beings. They even altered their posture to maximize viewing when they were passed. At the end of the lengthy hall, a set of glossy, black curtains hung, and in front of them was an elegant sign that read *Randál Vanaché*.

Once through the curtains, the hallway opened into a large room. A man greeted them, walking forward, as they entered.

"Ah, Venn! It has been too long my admirable friend!" he exclaimed, in a concise, clipped accent. With slim features and fair skin, his short, platinum hair sported a black patch over the left temple. Eager, he greeted Venn with two enthusiastic pats on the back. Venn returned one himself.

I'll be damned, Rhyus thought, *he can come off as almost pleasant*.

"How are you, Killian?" Venn asked, with a genuine smile. Rhyus still stood in disbelief.

"Marvelous. Wonderful!" The man flashed a set of dazzling, white teeth. "Cyrus will be down momentarily. He is finishing up a project. I left him upstairs in the studio. Tell me, how is our darling, Marion?"

"The same as always," Venn said, with another heartfelt smile. Rhyus's jaw nearly dropped off.

The room had a spiral staircase at the end and lounge chairs at the center. On each side, three tiered steps ran the length of the room where clothing and accessories began displaying themselves, and more black spiral staircases led up to a second level of display. The black-and-white floor glistened.

Soon, Cyrus bolted down the stairs. Rhyus winced at his violet and platinum hair, fashioned just longer than Killian's.

"Venn! By Arienette above! How are you?" he squealed, with Killian's exact accent.

"Good, good," Venn said. "Killian, Cyrus, this is Rhyus," he politely introduced Rhyus, who couldn't help but throw a minor glare at him. Who the hell did Venn think he was fooling with his good-guy facade?

"Feisty, isn't he?" Killian mocked playfully, noting the look Rhyus had thrown Venn's way.

Venn laughed in agreement. Cyrus followed suit with a heady cackle of his own.

Right. No wonder Venn gets along with these pretty boys, Rhyus sulked inwardly.

Still grinning ear-to-ear, Venn said, "The boy needs proper clothing and accessories. I leave him to your unmatched expertise."

"But of course!"

Rhyus cringed at Killian's exuberance. With his fingertips lightly on Rhyus's shoulder, Killian guided him toward the men's apparel.

Killian understood price was not an issue. He dragged Rhyus around like a play doll throughout the store. Pulling things from racks and shelves, he made Rhyus model, followed by personal critiquing. All the while, Venn relaxed on a violet couch across from Cyrus. Exotic drinks and conversation were abundant.

As Rhyus underwent Killian's ministrations, they conversed as well. He confirmed that Killian and Cyrus were indeed twins. A great uncle who raised them had started the clothing line with his wife. They hyphenated his first name, Randál, to her last to capitalize on the Vanaché family status. After his death, the family name reverted back to Vanaché, due to notoriety on so many levels.

The Vanaché brothers had traveled far before establishing this location. All items were limited and exclusive. They only admitted somns with exceptional taste and unlimited wealth. Despite their apparent youth, they had prospered. Venn and Marion were huge favorites. "Beautiful beings!" Killian stressed, in admiration.

After being dolled-up as long as Rhyus could tolerate, Venn calmly paid the exorbitant total.

"One last thing!" Cyrus exclaimed. Running upstairs, he returned toting a light brown messenger bag with bronze buckles and clasps. "Just finished," he beamed. "It's on the house."

"Thanks. I really appreciate this." Rhyus said graciously.

"Delighted." Cyrus nodded.

"Now don't be strangers!" Cyrus said, as they exited through the glossy, black curtains.

"Indeed. And tell our beloved Marion to stop by soon. We may or may not have a surprise in store for her!" Killian flashed that same, flawless smile and winked farewell, as Venn and Rhyus made their exit.

6: Conflict at the Piazza

After leaving Randál Vanaché, Venn and Rhyus continued walking in a northwest direction, The Tower remaining ahead of them all the while.

Nearing the western border of the Willow District, Venn stopped unexpectedly and was tripped into by Rhyus, taken unaware. "Watch it!" Venn scolded.

Rhyus frowned. *Back to Mr. Loveable, I see.* Evidently, the influence of his Vanaché pals had already worn off.

They had reached a beautiful piazza, and at its center, a large white fountain, known as the Prōmissĭo Fountain, glittered. The focal point of the fountain was a white statue of two winged women—one sitting, one standing.

Moving forward, Venn stopped a short distance away, studying it.

"What do you see here that is peculiar?" he asked, without a hint of a glance toward the boy.

"Well, the women have wings."

Venn turned his head, eying the boy critically.

"The sphere?" Rhyus tried again.

"Thank you!" Venn stressed. "I thought I might have to strangle you, and honestly, that would just prove to be a complete waste of my time."

The sitting figure displayed in her hands, a black, glinting orb. The one standing stared transfixed at it, suggesting she were being offered a gift of immense significance.

"The orb," Venn intoned, "is made of a mysterious stone. It comes from a city beyond our surrounding waters, from beyond The Darkness."

Rhyus raised a surprised brow at Venn. "Are there truly places beyond The Darkness?"

"Yes, places limited somns travel to. Precious few would ever have reason to travel there. In fact, common citizens of Lux Lumetia do not even remember that anything exists beyond The Darkness. They are raised in ignorance. They are told stories to keep them blind. To hide them from the truth."

"So," Rhyus asked, "how does one travel through The Darkness?"

"Some have ventured across the Dark Waters by boat, but that is often a treacherous stunt. The Darkness sinks in and has driven many who have tried to madness. So, predominantly, the means of travel is through specially designed portals. They act as a secure shortcut."

"But why go in the first place?"

Venn studied the young man before him, watching for any glimmer of response or recognition. *Does he really have no idea who he might, in fact, be? Or even where he is from?* Venn frowned. It would seem that Vincent KyVeerah had a special knack for finding souls with no memory of their past. First Marion. Now this boy. *But why always dump them on me?*

In spite of his frustration, Venn continued, "There are certain somns who are chosen, for one reason or another, to be educated. From birth, they are raised in a domain of knowledge and fact. Some of these somns are raised to positions of authority. Some others are raised for considerable other purposes."

"Why are you telling me this?" Rhyus asked with a blank expression. "I know there are things you would much rather be doing than giving me a tour and one-on-one story time."

Venn responded with a withering look. "You've got me all figured out, huh? Did it ever dawn on you that there might be some reason you landed on my doorstep?"

For a long while, Rhyus pondered over Venn's question. "Wait, are you trying to tell me that you took me in because I'm supposed to have some kind of significant purpose? It all sounds kind of cheesy and story-bookish if you ask me."

Venn studied Rhyus closely, asking, "Can't you recall anything?" He continued, with an evident repugnance, "Think about it. You don't really believe I would have taken in someone such as yourself solely out of the goodness of my heart?"

Rhyus paused again, rubbing his neck. "No, probably not."

"Obviously!"

Venn scanned the area around them. Turning away from the Prōmissĭo Fountain, he headed toward a more obscure structure of white covered archways. Lowering his voice, he whispered, "The Tower is very near. We must be discreet about drawing attention to ourselves."

"So, these portals," Rhyus asked, once they had achieved a more secure cover, "is there any way a common somn, who wasn't specifically educated, could figure out how to use them? Could they use them to travel to these outside worlds?"

"Well," Venn said, "I suppose it might be possible. But very unlikely. They would have to know what to do and then obtain the proper means to do it. It would be a ridiculous amount of work. And an untrained somn could never be certain of the final result."

Rhyus countered, "Has anyone ever just gone into The Darkness to try to reach something beyond?"

"Well, yes. There is actually a term for such somns. We refer to them as Rafters."

"Rafters?"

"Yes. The title traces back to The Ancients. In the time of The Ancients, they were known as *The* Rafters. However, now somns are taught to think that The Rafters were fiction. Mythical beings."

"Well, are they?"

Venn laughed. He gave Rhyus a look of contempt, "You have *got* to be kidding!"

"No need to be condescending," Rhyus mumbled, giving Venn a dirty look from the corner of his eye.

After a drawn-out look of disapproval, Venn relented. He stood and scratched his head. He spoke as though relating a story to a child. "Where should I begin? The Rafters were very real. There are even Rafters who operate today. Right now. However, modern-day Rafters operate almost in antithesis of their namesake. Rafters of current times are more like suicidal sailors. Their actions are impetuous and reckless. One must study for years before heading out through The Darkness to a world beyond our own. Even if a modern-day Rafter miraculously made it to another land, they would have no idea what they were up against. They would not know where to go or whom to trust. They would be clueless about tradition or etiquette. They would not understand the history, politics, or a myriad of other crucial insights about where they landed."

Rhyus sat quietly, considering Venn's words. At length, he spoke. "So, if we are able to go to places out there," he looked at Venn, "are there others who are capable of coming here from those other places?"

"Of course. Such is the balance of this world," Venn said. "There is a notorious group who thrive on traveling from place to place. There are two types of these specialists. Messengers and Callings."

"Come again?"

Impatient, Venn sighed. "Messengers and Callings," he repeated. "They are inextricably joined. These are somns who are destined for things much greater than this mundane life of ours, although without each other, both are lost. They must act together to meet their full potential, to find their true destination."

He elaborated, "A Messenger's express purpose is to act as a guide or guardian to his or her Calling. And it is *crucial* for a Calling to find and to stay on the right path. Otherwise, unbridled, the intrinsic power of a Calling may wreak untold havoc of unimaginable proportions!" With these last words, Venn's eyes bored distinct meaning into those of his listener.

"And you think I'm somehow lumped in with these *destined* beings?"

"I never said anything of the sort!" Venn spat back, far too quickly. Recomposing himself, he raised his chin in an arrogant pose.

Rhyus frowned his irritation. "Well then, where the hell do I fit into all of this? There must be a good reason you tromped me all the way out here to tell me this, or do you just get some sort of sick joy in leading me on, without actually telling me a damn thing?"

Venn displayed a twisted smile. "Now, what reason would I have to torment you? It's not like you have ever done anything to anger me since I've so generously taken you in."

With an awkward look of regret, Rhyus shifted his eyes toward the ground.

"We're done here. Let's go." Without even looking to see if Rhyus followed, Venn continued northwest, beginning the return trip to Umbra Halls.

"Wait! I still have more questions!"

Ignoring Rhyus's protests, Venn hurried over the twinkling pavement.

At length, they crossed The Courtyard of Umbra Halls. Venn ordered Rhyus to take the bags of clothing immediately to his room, though Rhyus wasn't quite sure why. He must have realized that Marion would see them sooner or later, most likely sooner.

$\wp\circlesseqgtr\wp$

Venn stood in The Courtyard for a few minutes, taking in the crisp air. Suddenly, the silence was shattered. Venn jumped as a shrill scream emitted from above. He looked upward.

Marion!

Bolting for the double doors, he crashed through, flying up the stairs. Rhyus had clearly heard the scream as well, for he was hot on Venn's heels.

"Marion!"

7: Down the Rabbit Hole

A shrill wind filled the air, whipping its way through littered walkways between shabby buildings. The rain separated as Jereth Tavokk appeared in the darkness. He looked up at his own building, moving toward it with his jacket flapping behind him. Its red liner caused fiery glints to dance under the dim city lights in contrast against the wet sapphires around him.

The metal was slick under Tavokk's red leather boots as he ascended the rickety grated stairs, ignoring the railing. He pulled his keys from a jacket pocket at his waist. A tram screamed by on its high track, shooting sparks in every direction. This made it difficult to place the silver key into the lock, due to the violent shaking of the stairs beneath him.

Stepping inside, Tavokk was welcomed by the sound of glass clinking, courtesy of the passing tram. Carrying on to the bedroom, he draped his coat over the chair in the corner, sat on the bed, and dropped his wet boots on the floor. Sinewy muscle rippled across his lean frame as he stretched wearily.

His mind racing, he pulled back the dark comforter and collapsed onto the exposed sheets. He reached for a corner of the comforter.

Lying on his back, half covered, Tavokk closed his eyes in an attempt to relax. Physical details and endless slices of conversations recycled through his mind.

"A special water portal hidden somewhere in the city...back as far as The Ancients..." Callis's words echoed, as he swirled his glass between drinks. *"A Calling has been awakened..."* The red-haired man viewed the room with a singular, smooth effort. *"Determining the balance of realms..."* The odd intensity in Callis's hard, brown eyes. *"There hasn't been a recorded Calling in years. Other than Nyx Crucian's..."*

The feel of a nearby, once familiar feminine figure. *"A Calling has risen..."* That spicy, woodland perfume. *"If I can get to him..."* The long, batting lashes and black outline of those enthralling, green eyes. *"We both know that you have connections..."*

He slipped off to sleep.

Tavokk awoke to the dark afternoon. He sat up, surrounded by a wall of bedding. Heavy, slanting rain beat at his windowed wall. "By the moons, I have got to quit these late nights." He rubbed his throbbing temples.

Escaping the covers, he pulled on a pair of sleek black pants that fell long, allowing only his toes to remain visible. He tied them at his slim waist. In the bathroom, he studied the mirror, admiring numerous black tattoos across his pale flesh. Pressing his hands mid-back, he cracked his spine. A deep scowl formed as he caught sight of the cut Helena had so recently left on his cheek. *Damn that bitch.*

Still glowering, Tavokk wandered to the kitchen where he prepared a light meal and pulled a large flagon of juice from the refrigerator. He sat at the small kitchen table, enjoying his breakfast, which would likely also constitute his lunch. The food helped in ridding his mind of current grudges.

"What shall I do today?" Tavokk asked the spoon held up before him. Noting his inverted reflection in the spoon's surface, he boasted, "Why, what a charming fellow you serve!"

Once finished, he added his dishes to the growing stack above the broken washer, vowing to catch up someday.

A mangled copy of the daily news, *The Atrum Chronicles*, had been forced beneath the door. Pulling it free, he flipped through its pale sienna pages. In large bold font, a particular heading caught his eye. Its black letters read *Tomfoolery of a Townsman.*

"Odd," he thought aloud. He pulled the paper nearer for a better look, as he headed toward the living room.

Skimming the article, his eyes grew with interest. "Curious."

The article discussed an Atrum Unda citizen, Fyfe Van Ingen, who had been declared accountable for spreading dangerous rumors.

"The Key Calling has come!" Van Ingen was quoted as shouting throughout the city's walkways in a wild frenzy. Tavokk knew the Key Calling to be a unique Calling who had been whispered of for decades. This Calling was to be wonderful yet potentially dangerous. None could say what momentous task he or she was destined to fulfill. Citizens only knew that his or her power was to be unbelievable, and that their impact would be unimaginable.

"I haven't heard mention of this in years." He pursed his lips, thinking.

The article continued. The Black Guard had taken Van Ingen into custody in The Tower of Atrum Unda for safety of the general public. This order, the article claimed, was carried out under direct command of Lord Cain himself.

Hmm. Tavokk stroked a long nail along his chin. Running this same hand through his tousled hair, he frowned in speculation. *What more does Fyfe Van Ingen know about the Key Calling? Does he know his identity? His purpose? Even more to the point, does he know who the Calling's Messenger might be?*

Throwing the paper aside, Tavokk growled his frustration. "Damn it!" he cursed. *If Fyfe knows this, then how long before Lord Cain manages to torture it out of him? And if Lord Cain learns of it? Then Valencia, help us all!*

Tavokk searched his memory. He had met Van Ingen on many occasions, usually at bars or other wild revelries. Only one year his senior, Van Ingen always seemed somehow wiser than his years.

Thinking, Tavokk paced about. *Though quite a party animal, Fyfe draws a line of control. So, what drove him over the edge? Did he ever actually go over? Did he indeed run amok, or was it a story to mask Lord Cain's true intentions?* He frowned. "I wonder exactly where he is being held captive."

Tavokk lay back, kicking his feet up onto one arm of the long black couch and sinking into the cushions. He crossed his arms beneath his head, drifting as he stared at the ceiling's metal beams, thoughts running through his head. Somehow, Tavokk had to get an inside track on just what the hell was coming down.

His eyes snapped open. "Of course!" he shouted. Jumping from the couch, he swiped the paper back up without looking at it. *Written records.* "The Tower Archives!" he exalted. The glow of his eyes suddenly wavered as his mind switched gears. "If I got in there, I could look for records about Callis's ancient water portal!"

"Perfect!" he exclaimed, eager to tackle the illicit challenge. Though he faced certain death if caught, he grinned like a schoolboy. "Those fools couldn't catch me if they tried."

ℰᏗᏟᎡ

Lips pursed in thought, Helena Meretrix sat on the couch staring into the fireplace. The flames had long flickered, igniting the thoughts that continued to race through her mind. For hours she had been trying to piece together why in the world Jereth Tavokk would be meeting up with Callis Morgandy at the Cosmos. The only possibility—webs of the Underworld—didn't even make sense. Their lines of underground work were so separate from one another. In theory, they would only come into contact on very unfortunate grounds.

Helena was angry that her attempt to press Tavokk for some tidbit of information ended without luck. The day before, she had heard some wild man in the streets carrying on about the rising of the Key Calling. For the briefest moment she had seen a spark of recognition on Tavokk's face when she mentioned it. But with the grace of an expert, he had immediately erased any trace of surprise.

She shook her head in concentration, thinking harder on the two men's overlap: the Underworld. Both Callis and Tavokk operated in circles of power at the highest order. This couldn't be just coincidence. Anything to do with the Key Calling would involve power of infinite possibility. And she was sure neither of them would be long out of the chase.

Reaching far back in her memory she recalled odd bits and pieces that never seemed to fit into her immediate everyday fight for survival. So naturally, they had gone long ignored. Scattered pieces about The Ancients, cities of other realms, and important somns known as Callings and Messengers. But now, a *Key Calling*? This had to be of significance.

If those two were on the trail of this thing, she would have to stay close somehow, for there were none better at ferreting out information. In addition, if she played her cards right, either would be a powerful ally. She shivered. If she were caught playing a crooked card, either would be a dangerous foe as well.

Again she reflected on her Tavokk encounter. Damn the man. Her whole life she had sailed freely, never once risking the slightest feeling for any man. But somehow, he had briefly managed to penetrate that iron shell. What had it been? Could he have actually cared? Could he have been the one that she had always imagined but never dared to touch? Or did he just see her as a challenge? An impossible nut he had to crack? For a moment, when he had held her close, she nearly gave in to her old passion. She had managed to block him out almost completely. But evidently, old desires die hard.

Whatever the case, there had been too much baggage on both sides and things had never come to pass. She thought she had completely forgotten the man. But now, here he was. Just as compelling. And just as arrogant. *That sniveling bastard.* What was it he had said at their parting? Oh, yes. *"By the way, I'm not interested!"*

This infuriated Helena on more levels than she could count. Just as he had intended. Tavokk was a master of mind games. Although she knew this, the thought failed to soothe her. However, one thought brought a smile to her face. He may not have given her anything, but at least she had left him with something to remember. Still smiling, she reached down to pat her beloved blade. It was the only thing she had ever truly been able to rely on. Even though "safe" here at home, she was wise enough to never let it leave her side.

She lifted it, tenderly admiring the heft and balance. She had lived with it for so long that it was a natural part of her. She admired the firelight that danced off its razor edge. At length she slid it back into place, still pissed that Tavokk had managed to move her so far off her guard. Again.

Callis Morgandy and Jereth Tavokk think they're so damn special! Her manicured nails cut into her palms as her fists tightened further. *Just wait. One day I will overpower both of you. Then you will come to me looking for favors!*

Her mind switched over to her boss at The Dome. Nyx Crucian. She was a member of his White Band, third in ranking behind the Crimson Band, and the highest Black Band. *Someday I will stand at his side.* The thought struck a new chord. "The hell with that! One day I will tower over him. And over every one of the sick egotistical bastards who think they are in charge here!"

₧)₨

Nearly prepared, Tavokk fastened the wide, silver buckles of a long black coat, with the exception of the ones along his upper chest and throat. His thin-soled boots had been chosen for stealth.

Groomed to kill, Tavokk donned a pair of indigo-tinted shades. He retrieved his pocket watch from the bureau before making a hasty exit through the side door. He glided down the rickety stairs, encouraged that the rain was lighter than usual. *Good weather for good hunting!*

Instead of hyperspacing, he took a land route, allowing extra time to enjoy the weather as well as to develop a plan of attack.

Tavokk passed several merchant booths. The vendors dozed on stools beneath transparent shelters to block the omnipresent rain. A few times, he encountered random civilians wandering the city.

Finally, he looked up at the colossal Tower standing rigid over

Atrum Unda. It looked to him like a giant sundial. *An appropriate analogy if the suns were ever to decide to relocate to the city of Atrum Unda.* Tavokk chuckled at the thought of the suns suddenly appearing. The entire city would enter hysterical meltdown. He ascended the hill with blue granules shifting at every step.

Stopping at the summit, Tavokk admired the exquisite Sŭsurrus Fountain, constructed of black marble with two sculpted figures on its highest platform. He was, however, taken aback by the sheer size and strange, dark beauty of The Tower behind it. Though the structure was visible from most any point in the city, he had only stopped to truly take in its remarkable form on one other occasion. In general, he chose to ignore both The Tower and the authorities slinking within its glinting structure.

From a distance, The Tower looked like a tall, glittering pillar that some paranormal being had planted to scar the city's surface — heaping the blue ground around it into a monstrous hill at the city's center.

But up close, it was a different beast. Its monumental structure, faultlessly constructed of the usual, silver-flecked stone, formed an upward spiral, escalating to the clouds. A somn may think he or she could climb to a world beyond Atrum's skies, beyond the rain.

Dense clouds generally masked the upper stories, but a dazzling light emitting from The Tower's topmost section bluntly reassured the population of its continuing dominion. Dark tinted windows lined the tall spiraling levels of The Tower. They were easily overlooked by the uninitiated, camouflaged against the glinting black stone.

Tavokk studied a metal bridge with equally impressive metal gates before it. It spanned a wide moat guarding the structure within. The deep, dark water ran off into two rivers, both running in a southwestern direction. He exhaled a single, short breath, scanning the foot of The Tower with water lapping its smooth black surface.

Turning away, he strolled toward the Sŭsurrus Fountain. He skirted three wide steps at its base. Then, with sinuous strength, he made two impossible leaps onto a high ring of stone at the second level. Water from the fountain now mingled with the light rain falling over him. Stepping along the watery surface, Tavokk looked up into the shadowed eyes of a handsome young man. The sculpting was remarkable, as though some enchanter had turned a warm, breathing being into hard, cold stone. Down on one knee, he leaned forward with his hand extended, offering assistance.

Accepting the winged man's offer, Tavokk gripped his slick, marble hand. He planted his foot in a camouflaged niche and hoisted himself upward. Gripping the statue's shoulder with his free hand, he pulled himself onto the highest ledge where he came face to face with the second figure. Also faultless, this figure stood upright. Behind his cosmic mask, callous eyes bored into Tavokk's own. A chill ran down his spine as he realized the haughty sculpture couldn't care less if an insignificant lowlife such as himself failed to heed its dire warning.

Despite the forbidding gaze, the figure's stone hand angled toward the kneeling man's cape, lying spread across the top level. On close inspection, Tavokk saw that it was indeed formed from several independent pieces of marble.

Placing his long, slender hands on a particular fold in the man's cape, Tavokk began to push a section of stone away from the center of the platform. As Tavokk grimaced in great effort, the tattoos on his shoulder blades began to glow beneath his shirt and jacket, and a violet radiance flared from behind his shades.

After a few moments, he removed his grip from the wet stone. Breathing heavier, he looked before him.

"Hah!" he laughed, amused by the fact that the hidden passageway did in fact exist. He had once heard rumor of it from a highly secretive being, but had never known whether it truly existed. The man was, in fact, a somewhat sketchy character after all.

A vertical tunnel was now revealed just before him, a ladder descending into the dark passage. *How far down must it go?*

Tavokk spun around, sending water flying in every direction, as more continued running down him in a way suggesting he had become a part of the fountain. Gripping the rail, he jumped down onto the first rungs.

8: Subliminal Stipulations

Venn yelled out for Marion, receiving only silence. "Marion!" he tried again. "Where are you?" Panicked, he looked about, deciding where to search. He scolded himself: *I should have never left her alone!*

"In here," came a voice from the kitchen.

Bolting through the kitchen door, prepared for a fight, Venn saw only Marion bent over a pile of ingredients on the kitchen table. He studied her quickly, making sure there were no traces of cuts or bleeding.

"What are—?" Marion began. Venn's face shifted from worry, to relief, to anger, seeing that she was all right.

"Venn? *Breathe* Venn!" she ordered.

"What the Hell!" Venn roared, breaking his silence. Rhyus cringed in the background. Venn's last outburst had been on his behalf. He was grateful that this one was not.

Marion glared back, taking offense at Venn's overblown reaction. She finally spoke, "Can you believe this?"

"Believe what? Answer me!" Venn barked.

Marion held up a rabmelon in her palm, as if it explained everything. Venn still looked confused.

"The fruit vendor gave me West Bay melons when I specifically asked for Plush! I even paid extra for them! I'm certainly not going to cook with these, that's for damn sure."

Venn snatched the bright red melon out of her hand. "Rabmelons? "You scream like bloody hell over melons?" He raised his arm.

Rhyus, afraid he was going to throw it at Marion, yelled, "No, she didn't mean it!" Too late.

Venn had already hurled it. "Do you have any idea how worried I was?"

Unfazed, Marion glanced at the far corner where he had thrown it. The blood red melon had bypassed her, hitting in an explosion of epic proportion. Blood-red gore dripped from the walls and ceiling.

Rhyus looked like he might faint. He could not believe her nonchalant attitude.

Marion calmly folded her hands, but her eyes were liquid fire.

"I am not the one cleaning that up," she said. Then she addressed Venn in the quiet manner one would use with a child. "I'm sorry I screamed. I was angry. I calmed down. But now, thanks to you, I'm pissed again." Marion crossed her arms.

She explained, "Do you even know the difference between a Plush and a West Bay melon?" She shook her head at his blank expression. "I thought not. Plush melons, a premium brand, are the only ones suitable for eating. West Bay melons, on the other hand, are repugnant, suitable only for the scum in the districts that grow them."

Not a speck of empathy showed on Venn's face. "I recall specifically telling you to keep an eye on the house and not to leave, especially to go melon shopping!"

"Excuse me for trying to prepare a nice surprise for you, while you two leave me here all alone so *you* can go have some quality child-to-brute bonding time!"

"I'm not a child," Rhyus sulked. Neither Venn nor Marion acknowledged him.

"Well *I* already ate since *some* people decided to abandon me forever. There are leftovers in the fridge. And don't forget," she eyed the corner, "to clean up your mess. I shall be in my room."

Rhyus quailed at being left alone with Venn. *Great, now he can turn it on me.*

However, completely ignoring Rhyus, Venn marched straight to the fridge for the leftovers. He slammed them onto the kitchen table, and then grabbed a plate for himself, apparently having forgotten his unwelcome guest.

He yanked out a chair, sat, and dug into his cold meal, not wasting the effort to reheat it. Cocking his head at Rhyus, he snapped, "Well, what are you waiting for? Eat, or get the hell out of my sight!"

Rhyus took a plate and sat down for an intense, awkward meal with the silent Venn.

Finished, Venn threw his unrinsed dishes into the sink. *No doubt expecting Marion to clean them*, Rhyus thought, watching Venn's movements cautiously from his seat at the table.

Without warning, Venn's eyes flashed toward Rhyus, noting his gaze. "What? You think it's acceptable to stare at whomever you want, whenever you damn well feel like it?" he snarled, eyes glowing a paranormal blue. "Well guess what," he continued, "that doesn't fly here!"

Rhyus tried to respond, but Venn cut him off, ordering, "Clean up those blasted dishes." He grumbled something under his breath and stormed out of the kitchen, slamming the door behind him.

℘ℭ℞

Rhyus sat alone. The hour was late. He looked at the kitchen sink, and then to his half-empty plate. With a deep sigh, he gathered the remaining dishes and rinsed them before placing them, one by one, into the dishwasher.

Running a hand through his hair, he sighed again before dragging his feet in heading toward his bedroom. And as he had walked to the double doors, he had noticed light spilling under the door of the den out into the dark hall. Upon reaching his room, he put on a pair of forest green sweats that Marion had carefully folded and set on the window seat.

Rhyus laughed that his sweats clashed with the emerald bedspread. Then he frowned that he even noticed such a fact.

He lay wondering, *How much of this can I stand? How has Marion tolerated Venn for two years? Or why? Did she get here the same way I did? Then again, how did I get here? More than that, where did I come from?*

Perhaps I was brought here to care for Marion? No, even if I were here for that reason, Venn would never allow it. What caused Venn to become such a brute? No normal somn could be so heartless, but then again, there is nothing normal about Venn. He's so capricious, so impossible to read.

Reflecting back on his conversation with Venn at the piazza, he did a mental countdown on his fingers.

Portals: Evidently these are a means designed to travel to other places without traveling the Dark Waters.

Rafters: From the time of The Ancients. They did indeed travel over the waters. But wait! Venn said there were Rafters operating even today. What did Venn call them? Oh yeah, "suicidal sailors."

Messengers and Callings: Somns who routinely use the portals. They are raised in knowledge and for special purposes. "Destined for things much greater."

How does Venn know such things, he wondered on. *Was he raised in the knowledge? Has he been beyond The Darkness? Does Venn personally know some Rafters? If he does, he certainly isn't fond of them or their ideals.*

I wonder if The Rafters came from the same place as the black orb of the fountain? Rhyus thought back to the piazza and the attractive Prōmissĭo Fountain. *I bet it's beautiful there. More so than here in Lux Lumetia. Best of all, there would be no Venn. Anywhere Venn is not has to be better!*

Rhyus sprang upright. *Oh, shit! What if Venn is a Messenger and I am his Calling?* he thought, in horror, nearly sickened at the thought. *No! It's not possible,* he decided. *A Messenger would be intelligent, charming, and amiable. Everything that Venn is not. Other than his fortunate appearance, Venn has nothing.*

Long into the night, he puzzled over his situation. Wary, he thought, *I don't really know anything about these Callings and Messengers. They could be anyone for all I know.*

Rhyus's head ached in intense concentration. *If only I knew how I got here. Why was I in that crystal canal?*

His thoughts faded as sleep drew him into her undefined arms, pulling him into the depths of subconsciousness.

ℬℭ

The late night found Venn sunken into his soft leather armchair in the den, his feet on the ottoman. One hand gripped a half-filled glass, while the other pressed three powerful, yet elegant, fingers to his brow. Eyes closed, he felt the blood pulsing through his veins, past his ears and beneath his temples.

What am I supposed to do with the boy? he asked himself. *How long will I be stuck with him? Forever, for all I know. Dear god!*

Recalling that Marion was originally to be a "temporary guest," Venn bristled at the fact that she still remained. *Vincent,* he thought, in resentment. Why could he not take the boy or even Marion at that? Not to say that he hadn't become rather fond of her. But the thought of being used rankled within him.

A voice jostled Venn out of his melancholy, moping state.

"Venn!" The voice snarled, having been unintentionally disregarded in its initial efforts.

"Vincent?" Venn said. Startled, but attentive now.

"Who were you expecting? Lord Abel?" KyVeerah jeered.

"No, no. It's just that I honestly wasn't expecting you. At least not for awhile."

"You speak as though you lack familial, brotherly love! Why forfeit all joie de vivre? Not all energy and love of life is dead, my dear Venn." Even through his thoughts, Venn could hear KyVeerah's mocking laugh.

"I have finished my business here. I am sure you have had plenty of time to bond with the boy by now."

"If by 'bonding' you mean that he is still alive," Venn muttered, angry at the very idea of bonding with Rhyus.

"Smashing! I will see you in two days. Technically sooner, I suppose," KyVeerah said, breaking connection.

Venn exhaled a heavy growl. Irritation filled him, as air returned to his lungs. *Less than two days?* he thought. *Which could be worse? Vincent's coming? Or him not coming?*

Sighing again, he threw his feet from the footrest and pushed up from the chair. Running his fingers through his hair, he tucked it behind his ear, though most still fell in front of his shoulder.

℘℃℞

Rhyus jolted upright. It was early morning. The suns would not touch his window at this hour, even if they were to decide to reclaim Umbra Halls. A cold sweat overtook him, as he moved panicked eyes to the windows, the door, then back to the windows.

True sleep had been impossible. Distracting dreams had held him between sleep and awareness. *It was all so real.* Rhyus shuddered beneath the sheets, grasping the slick comforter tight in his fists.

The dreaming had not varied. Instead, it had consisted of a single dream, circling repetitively through his subconscious. Each time, he was told to awaken. Each time, he wakened to the same place:

Cool, crisp air filled Rhyus's chest. He awoke suddenly in the shadowed Courtyard of Umbra Halls. He found himself lying on the ground. Face down. Trying to rise, the abnormal ground shifted with every movement.

Startled, he saw myriad tiny, blue granules entirely concealing The Courtyard's worn cobblestones like a sea of dazzling sapphires. Although beautiful, the small, sapphire grains sliced at his skin. His eyes strained upward, away from the ground on which he lay.

The two white statues bracketing The Courtyard's large double doors were different somehow, but Rhyus could not discern just why. "Look," the winged figure to his right exhorted, her white marble lips unmoving. She did not move her eyes from him; nevertheless, he followed her urging, lifting his eyes beyond the stretch of sparkling blue.

The metal doors stood tall, their forged stars slowly shifting position. The doors opened to the sound of a crashing sea. Glancing around, The Courtyard walls had disappeared and darkness swallowed the place where he lay.

Repositioning himself, he saw the ground had solidified into a gray, stone shelf. Looking back, the white marble statues had also transformed. He now saw two black, glinting figures. These figures, unlike the white, were male. Still winged and masked, they stood apart from one another. The base of a narrow stone stairway rested between them.

The stairway reached high to the top edge of a steep cliff, against which the low shelf was situated. At the top loomed a large, stone arch. Vines covered much of the ancient structure, now engulfed by a vast forest stretching far beyond it. A breathtaking view. With the exception of the cliff's side, a pounding sea surrounded the shelf.

Rhyus, with what strength remained, propped himself to sit. A harsh storm raged. Dark, hovering clouds dropped cold rain. He shivered, wondering where his jacket had disappeared to.

The sense of someone's presence intruded. A shadowy figure made its way swiftly, yet gracefully, down the narrow stairs. It descended about half way, and then, in the blink of an eye, stood looming over him.

"You've been trying my patience, you know. I have waited a very, very long time for your arrival." The voice projected a serious note; however, a moment after the statement, Rhyus caught the vague suggestion of a grin on the man's shadowed face.

Without cause, the wind was violently knocked out of him. Alarmed, his eyes clenched as he struggled for breath. Though the impossibility of breathing seemed to last a lifetime, it unexpectedly vanished, just as promptly as it had occurred.

ꕥ

When Rhyus's eyes snapped open, he stood gaping upward at an enormous, domed structure, constructed elaborately of metal and dark tinted glass. He spun to view his surroundings, but before he could successfully turn, he found himself standing on top of the dome, 160 stories above the city floor.

Utter blackness enveloped this dome structure and Rhyus in every direction. As his eyes adjusted, pale pinpricks of light began appearing all about. They looked like stars, but they must have belonged to the city below, for the space above him remained a solid, empty black. The rain, becoming colder, continued its downpour as a crackling boom of thunder reverberated through the air. The ground began to shake as, in each of the four cardinal directions, colossal towers began to protrude from the ground far below. One by one, they cut through the city's surface.

In the west, the familiar white Tower of Lux Lumetia projected beyond the immense height of the dome on which Rhyus stood, awestruck. As The Tower achieved full height, with its tallest tower at the center and its three smaller connecting towers around it, the brilliantly illuminated cell at its apex began to dim. The crystal-powered energy captured within diminished slowly at first, then ever more rapidly.

As the light cascaded into darkness, Rhyus turned involuntarily to the north where a new tower rose like a sculpted mountain of fine, white sand. Composed of numerous defined levels, the immaculate sand fell to its destruction before ever reaching consummation. As he observed its total decimation, the structure seemed all too familiar. Anger pumped through Rhyus's veins as he watched the structure crumble in ignominy to the ground.

A force pulled Rhyus to the east where he witnessed the birth of yet another tower, drilling up through the city floor. This one, sleek and glittering brilliantly, was comprised of glinting black stone spirals that stretched to the sky. Its crystal energy source, similar to that of the Lux Tower, glowed brighter and brighter as it matured to hover high above. Completely entranced, he strained to watch the great crystal light source as it increased its luminosity, reflecting off of, as well as penetrating inexplicably into, his eyes. Adrenaline rushed through him.

At last, he was heaved before a fourth and final tower in the south. The stunning brilliance of this structure eclipsed anything he had ever seen. Its construction consisted of astonishing blue-crystal ice. The main centerpiece of the structure stood tallest, continuing far beyond the highest point of the dome. Extensions, appearing as bridges of sorts, reached out from the center. They stretched horizontally in various directions and distances. Then, changing direction ninety degrees, they created a series of surrounding blue-crystal shafts that stretched down to the ground.

This fourth tower, at its final height, dwarfed the white and black towers into insignificance. It stood proud, sending a trembling wave cascading over the dark city floor, as it ground to a halt.

"Magnificent," Rhyus gaped. But he realized he had spoken too soon as, abruptly, one of the resplendent extensions broke away, splintering on the ground with a heart-wrenching shatter. It was followed as each piece in succession fell away. Adrenaline continued to surge through Rhyus, flooding his entire being.

"No!" he cried, taking a few helpless steps forward.

No good though. The extensions continued to fall and shatter until all that was left was the monumental centerpiece. Rhyus stared, unable to look away or even blink. And then it began. The sound of ice cracking away entered his ears, and large chunks began to fall before his eyes. As the outer shell broke away, the center began to melt, spilling out over the crumbling casing.

Fierce anguish erupted, tearing at Rhyus to his very core. "No! I can explain!" he cried out, as the last of the ice tower disintegrated into oblivion. He knew now, it was his fault these things had occurred. He brought this shame upon himself, and he realized that it would affect far more than him.

Someone stood behind Rhyus now. The bystander knew Rhyus's guilt and anger, yet he remained standing silent, just beyond view. Rhyus dropped to his knees. And once again, everything went dark.

ℰℭ

Through the darkness, a barred slot appeared just before Rhyus. A dim light lay just beyond it. He felt the confinement of the small, lightless room enclosed around him now.

An unfamiliar voice warned, "You must hurry!" The door with the barred slot disappeared and a man stood before him. He was clothed in a slate gray robe. A cowl draped over his head, obscuring his face from view.

"Leave this place at once. Before it's too late! The path of The Rafters will guide you." As if the man had never stood before him, the robe fell empty to the floor. Rhyus turned away in frustration, his fingers pressing his damp hair against his skull and away from his face.

∞Ↄ⚬

Suddenly, facing in the opposite direction, Rhyus realized that the cramped room had opened up. Stained glass windows reached high to a vaulted ceiling. He stood before an altar. The wooden church had clearly existed for centuries. Though timeworn, the archaic structure carried an aura of significance, imbued in its heavy air.

A floorboard creaked behind him. He remembered awaiting someone's arrival. Turning toward the sound, he now faced the pews and the entrance doors. Rhyus discerned the very somn whose presence he had been anticipating.

The young woman was garbed in undeniable extravagance. Adorned in luxury, Glasco brand articles encased her, head to toe. From her tall, slim black heels to her large-lens sunglasses encrusted with the intricate crystal word *Glasco* running toward her temple, she was stunning. The sleek, delicate lining of her black halter-neck dress whispered with a gentle sway as she strutted arrogantly between the weathered pews up the aisle toward him.

Her black satin clutch, embossed with the same meticulous logo as her glasses, was intricately crafted with alternating rows of blue crystal and silver. The platinum band of an ostentatious watch hugged her wrist, bragging of incalculable value through an exquisite inlay of rubies and diamonds.

I look an absolute mess, he admonished himself. *And she…she is astonishing. She looks like a goddess, bejeweled in black.*

Marion.

He stood transfixed as she made her way to the altar, grasping its edge with her free hand.

"I beg of you!" Rhyus shouted, in desperation. A hand raised in supplication unintentionally caught her glasses, tearing them from her face and throwing them far down the wooden boards of the isle.

She offered him no more than a stone-cold glare. Stunning makeup, rendered in black and violet, served only to enhance the void in her heartless eyes.

"How…? What…?" Rhyus inquired with a single, questioning movement of his hand toward her, as he fought to repress his spiraling emotions.

She cast Rhyus an icy glare. "Beware Armani," she said, as though that explained it all.

She then shifted her attention to the fallen Glasco glasses, commanding, "Get them."

"What?" Rhyus asked, but he quickly realized the meaning behind her demand. In her current state, he welcomed the opportunity to distance himself. As he retrieved the costly item, he felt low, untouchable. He leaned to rescue them from the floor, and then he made his way back to the altar.

As he proffered the glasses to her, he stammered in a last attempt, "I-I need you."

With a peculiar glint, her eyes hardened even further in rebuke of his appalling betrayal. Snatching the glasses, she secured them back into place. Then, silently, she thrust out her usually delicate hand with an imperious movement.

He looked at her in confusion.

"Take it."

Hesitating a moment, Rhyus reached to accept the bronze envelope. The initials A.C. were elegantly scripted upon the surface. He could feel the weight of an object concealed within it. As he studied it, her voice came to him again.

"You can wake up now."

"Rhyus, wake up."

"Wake up!"

෫෨෬

Rhyus's hands were clammy. "So real," he said, with unsteady breath, recalibrating to the room around him.

What was that? he wondered. *What did it all mean? And Marion...*

Rhyus threw off the comforter, and standing, he brushed the matted hair from his face. Stumbling, he grabbed a bedpost to stabilize himself, feeling the quaking of his lean muscles.

The grandfather clock indicated 4:40 a.m. Shaken by the vivid dreams, Rhyus crept down the hall to the bathroom. *Well, I'm sure as hell not going to get any more sleep this morning.*

Once he stood before the sink, he drenched his face with cool water. "What the hell," he said aloud, to the reflection in the mirror. Dark circles rimmed his bloodshot eyes.

Rhyus quickly looked away, ignoring the disturbing somn

standing in the mirror's glass. Putting a closed hand on his bare chest, he felt his heart pounding far too fast.

Photographic images flashed behind his bloodshot eyes...high-heeled shoes and slender feminine legs...a flowing dress as a once-fragile beauty glided toward him...dark makeup and cross lips... that enticing figure...

"Perhaps a shower will clear my head."

Hot steam rose over the frosted shower doors, fogging the large bathroom mirrors so he did not have to see the man in the mirror.

Once in the shower, the hot water pouring over his skin helped to purge the racing emotions within.

"You must leave. Now!" Rhyus whipped around, expecting the gray-robed man from his dream. The severe voice would have sent him into a sweat, but for the hot water already pouring over the hard musculature of his sleek body.

There was no one on the other side of the frosted glass. *Foolish*, he scolded himself. But the voice had been so clear. And so near to him.

Stepping from the shower, Rhyus listened apprehensively, as water dripped from him. Closing his eyes, the collapsing blue-crystal ice tower invaded his mind.

"No." His eyes snapped open, as venomous adrenaline surged again through his every cell. Grabbing a black-and-silver towel, he hastily dried and made his way back to the bedroom.

Marion had cleaned the clothing from his arrival two days ago. He hastily donned the intentionally faded and torn denims. A man's simple face, wallowing in sorrow, decked his blue-gray, short-sleeved shirt. The black hooded sweatshirt, left unzipped, had on its back a single abstract street lantern, lighting a path to a distant city.

To avoid waking anyone, and to fill the early hours, he decided to explore the city, stuffing Venn's wad of bills into his pocket in case of emergency. On the way out, he hit the kitchen, looking aimlessly for something to eat, but he had no appetite so early.

In the main hallway, Rhyus dropped into Marion's favorite lounge chair to slide on his worn, flat-soled shoes. He grabbed the new messenger bag that Cyrus and Killian Vanaché had given him and pushed through the double doors. At first sight of The Courtyard, his recent dream came crashing back into his mind. He threw a hand up to block the image of the sea of sapphires. Suddenly, the gray-robed man stood again before him. The harsh voice, issued from under the dark cowl, admonished again, "You must leave now! Before it's too late!"

Then, he laid again, on the sea-stormed ledge, the shadowed man standing over him. The horrible, sick feeling. He couldn't breathe.

୫୬

Gasping the cool morning air with the largest gulps he could manage, Rhyus threw his head back, shaking off the visions. He felt his heart again, thundering in his chest. *What does it all mean? These hallucinations...* He threw the question to the sky. *Or are they dreams? Can I not escape whether asleep or awake? Must I leave now? If I don't, why will it be too late? Should I go... or should I stay?*

Clenching and unclenching his hands, his vision swam back to The Courtyard. The one that had been there before him all along. Rhyus glanced at the white, shimmering statue to the left of the forged double doors. She stood graceful and still, eyes focused on the elevated stone dais before her.

Rhyus passed the tree and stepped through the metal gate and out into the alleyway. Tiny specks of light grew larger and more frequent as he approached the still-dark city. The suns still crouched, hidden far below the horizon.

Rhyus wandered aimlessly. Umbra Halls, he had learned from his trip with Venn, was located in the northwest corner of the city. The Westside, known as the West Bay, was sullied and inhospitable. The Eastside was typically more salubrious. The majority of the city's wealth collected there.

So Rhyus, true to his form, headed southeast.

9: Acquaintances at the Prisoner's Quarters

Tavokk made his way swiftly, yet cautiously, down the ladder running through the Sŭsurrus Fountain. Falling rain effortlessly worked its way through the opening in the man's marble cape, causing the rusted metal rungs to grow slick beneath his hands. He grimaced. Though used to unsavory places, the slimy feel of the rungs did not suit his usual, fastidious nature. His discomfort was magnified as the black stone of the passage served to magnify the darkness.

Intriguing, Tavokk considered the passage through the marble cape. *This approach must have been abandoned long ago. Considering the narrowness of the passage, yet the tremendous force required to slide the stone, access would certainly have been limited to only a unique few individuals.*

The ladder met perpendicular with a tunnel about eight stories down. Tavokk jumped the last several feet, leaving the bottom rungs undisturbed by the thin soles of his boots. Pleased, he found that the passageway widened to a body length, with a ceiling easily twice as high. The floor of individually crafted, black marble cobblestones differed from all the other surfaces, which displayed the same black stone.

His eyes adjusted to the dank darkness, broken at intervals by pairs of tarnished silver sconces. They emitted a dull light through once-brilliant, crystal lamps, now covered by the grimy coating of many centuries.

A telltale trail of likewise-coated blue granules denoted prior passage of some far, distant soul.

Adjacent to the ladder sat a small, ancient metal table and chairs. A deck of cards, abandoned mid-game had become tattered and worn by the grimy dampness. A wonder they had not simply dissolved into nothingness. *Hmm, an old guard post,* Tavokk noted. *I wonder what happened. The final watch must have ended abruptly.*

He made his way in silence, except for the faint pattering of rain below the Sŭsurrus Fountain's entryway. Quickly, he closed the distance to a point somewhere beneath The Tower.

He reached another wall and another ladder. Looking up into this new shaft, he displayed a crooked grin. He hoisted himself to the third rung, and then scurried upward in anticipation. He could hear water rushing nearby. The flowing water of the moat, undoubtedly.

Atop the second ladder, less rusted than the first, a hand-wide platform encircled the opening. Straddling the shaft, he examined the tight enclosed space in which he now stood. It seemed hopeless.

How in the world? Tavokk puzzled. After a moment's pause, he pushed against the marble walls surrounding him. He shuffled, wary of his footing, continuing to search for an exit. When a wall budged, Tavokk pulled away, startled, slamming into the curved wall behind him.

"Hah," he laughed a hushed retort, at his own jumpy reaction. Bracing his feet, he exerted extreme force against the wall that had just moved. Again, Tavokk's eyes and shoulder blade tattoos began to glow at the excess anomalous energy. The wall gave, opening outward toward an adjacent black wall.

He peered out from his enclosure. Silence. Realizing that he had come up through one of numerous marble pillars, he scraped muck from his boots on the handy narrow ledge within the pillar and stepped into the vacant level. He had heard that one seldom encountered anyone on the lowest level of The Tower.

The floor at this level was extraordinary. The usual glittering flints had been multiplied, compelling even the slightest traces of light to reflect powerfully upward. Tavokk followed the path of this light toward the ceiling. He stood mesmerized.

Tavokk could see upward many stories. Hallways of indestructible glass caused each level to resemble a round spider web. The negative spaces were filled with black marble. Threads ran like spokes from the center, as concentric rings divided each section into trapezoidal rooms — increasing in size toward the outer wall.

Tavokk hoped no one from above had noticed him exit the pillar; however, the glaring light from below should keep anyone from looking down. Besides, everyone he could see above him appeared rather distracted.

Without further ado, he walked toward the center where on every floor stood a statue encircled by four elevators. The exceptions were floors 80, 160, and 240, which sliced The Tower into four equal parts.

These floors had spiral staircases connecting to the subsequent levels, allowing efficient coverage of an immense height of 320 stories—each elevator covering 80 floors.

Reaching the elevators, Tavokk pressed a small, silver button on the wall. When the sound chimed, a white light illuminated the star-shaped crystal fixture above the door.

He entered the unoccupied elevator. Noting a row of silver buttons, corresponded to floor numbers carved into wall beside them, he pressed the button for floor 80. Glancing around, Tavokk grinned at the unexpected sight of himself in a mirror covering the entire ceiling. He rarely missed the chance to admire himself when the opportunity presented itself. He took a deep breath, becoming quickly infuriated as he spotted the tiny white scar on his cheek. Enraged, he swore at Helena. Despite the fact that he healed quickly, she had left a disfigurement that could very well last forever. His thoughts simmered. *How could I let her get a strike on me?* Strangely, he still couldn't shake the memory of her spicy, woodland fragrance, pouting lips, undulating hips...

"Dammit!" He shook all such thoughts aside, still glaring at the image reflecting back at him, as he felt the elevator begin its rapid ascent. *How does Helena even know that a Calling has risen? Besides, someone of her level shouldn't be getting ideas such as going after this rumored, powerful Calling,* he fumed. *I wonder what it might mean...No matter,* he vowed, *next time we meet, the outcome will be different.*

The same glass used for hallways also encased the elevator shaft, allowing Tavokk to view somns as he passed each floor. All seemed intent on reaching their own destinations. Few noticed each another, even when passing closely. He did not fear being spotted as the elevator rose.

He arrived abruptly. Although he could see through the 80 levels of glass flooring, clear to ground level, he was immediately blinded by light blazing upward from the glinting ground's surface. *I was right. I couldn't have been seen entering.* Blinking away tears, Tavokk strode to a silver spiral staircase. He followed it up to the next set of elevators where he caught a lift on the opposite side, taking it to floor 130.

Watching the rooms on each floor, he muttered to himself, *those rooms are so confined.* Each had but one small, horizontal window and sconces similar to those in the underground passageway. *It must become god awful dreary, seeing nothing but black walls for hours on end.*

Another chime, another lit crystal star, and the doors opened at Tavokk's destination. This time he avoided looking downward, but he realized something was different about the rooms here. *No. This isn't right.* These rooms contained no windows or light fixtures. Noting the unusual presence of narrow, eye-level slots with vertical bars across them, he realized his location.

This is the Prisoner's Quarters. It was floor 132 I wanted.

The newest addition to Nyx Crucian's White Band, Jett Milan, stood silently beside his boss's most infamous assassins, Armani Saint and Julian Gallows. Nyx had ordered Jett to accompany them on their excursion to The Tower. Likewise, Nyx instructed the duo to elucidate the workings and layout of The Tower to Jett.

Having no desire for conversation, Jett eyed his superiors silently. He had only encountered the notorious duo from a distance. Jett had been initially intrigued by their nefarious reputation. After observing them in closer inspection, they had proved to be disappointing. Until today, he had never spoken to them. Now, he wished things had remained that way.

"Nyx must have taken quite a liking to you to have *us* spend our time giving you a tour of The Tower," Julian said, becoming sick of the silence. He stared curiously at Jett with his aqua eyes. Jett remained silent.

"Cat caught your tongue?" Julian teased. Armani's lips held back a smile. Jett focused his attention on his reflection in the metal of the elevator doors.

"The dark and silent type, eh? Well, no matter. You won't need to speak for what we're doing today," Julian said. Jett's brow furrowed in curiosity.

"Today, we'll be interrogating a prisoner. He was in *The Atrum Chronicles* today. You may just observe," Armani informed.

"Fyfe Van Ingen?" Jett asked.

"Well, would you look at that? He does speak!" Julian snickered. Jett's face dropped into a scowl, and he exited the elevator as it reached floor 80. Armani and Julian followed after, keeping pace easily with Jett.

Jett sighed. *Why me.*

"To answer your inquiry, yes. Van Ingen is the man we will be *visiting* today," Armani said, as they proceeded up the staircase to floor 81. Reaching the top, Jett started down a corridor, pausing when he realized Armani and Julian were no longer following behind.

"What are you doing?" Jett asked. The duo looked back at Jett from near the elevators that would lead them to Van Ingen's confinement.

"We're going to the Prisoner's Quarters to interrogate Van Ingen. I thought we went over this?"

"We did," Armani affirmed in agreement with Julian.

"You need the authorization papers from the Mandate Magnate in order to interrogate a prisoner," Jett said.

Julian grinned. "How about *you* go get the papers, and we will go interrogate the prisoner? Sound good? Meet us after you've done so."

"But it's *protocol*," Jett insisted. Ignoring Jett, they headed toward the elevators. Armani and Julian rarely followed protocol. They got the job done. That's all that mattered to Nyx. Jett watched as they entered the elevators and disappeared from view. *Unbelievable.* Turning from the elevators, he began to make his way to the Dictum Division to obtain Van Ingen's authorization papers.

ℰℭℜ

Tomfoolery of a Townsman, indeed, Helena Meretrix mused, over the riveting heading that had caught her attention earlier this morning. *This Van Ingen character is exactly the break I've been waiting for! With him, I won't need Jereth Tavokk.* She smiled as she walked purposefully through The Tower, having just left The Archives.

To make things even better, the Black Guard was kind enough to arrest and imprison him within The Tower. Helena chuckled darkly as she stepped into an elevator. *I should thank them for saving me the time of hunting him down. He has nowhere to run. Soon I'll have all that I desire!* The elevator chimed, and the doors slid open.

Fyfe Van Ingen. You'll be wishing you kept your big mouth shut by the time I'm done with you.

As the elevator descended, Helena admired her reflection upon the metallic surface of the doors. So far, Helena's endeavors for the day had proved fruitful. After entering The Archives, she had sought out information pivotal to her plans with relative ease. *Well, mostly,* she thought. The first somn Helena had approached proved to be a waste of time. *The stuttering fool was so nervous, I couldn't understand anything he said.* A sultry smile crossed her stained lips. *Fortunately for me, I was saved from the bumbling idiot by the very scrumptious Albert.*

Helena had the luck of encountering the young Tower librarian, Albert Young, a handful of weeks ago at a nightclub. When Helena had first met Albert, she considered him just as she would any other man of intrigue: A handsome dope just begging to buy her a drink. After talking to him for a while, she discovered he could prove beneficial to her plans. *In more ways than one,* she thought now, as she smoothed the hem of her skirt.

By making sure to keep in close contact with him, Helena had managed to obtain not only the book she sought from The Archives, but also information that was worth more than all of the Atrum beryls combined. *Only way to get your hands on one of those babies is to pay a hefty price in the underground circuit,* Helena thought, recalling the rare gem, more commonly known as the Dark Water beryl. Few somns knew how to obtain the precious gem from the depths of The Darkness. The gem's properties were as mysterious as The Darkness from where it came. But that was beside the point. *Albert has proved quite useful, but I need to focus less on gems and more on valuable matters at hand. Like Van Ingen.*

Stepping off the elevator and onto floor 81, Helena navigated her way. Although she had never needed to meet with one of The Tower's prisoners, Helena knew the procedure for interrogation. Before being allowed access to Van Ingen, The Tower authorities would require her to obtain the necessary authorization papers from the Mandate Magnate. Without the Mandate Magnate's seal, nothing was held licit in view of Lord Cain and the other Tower authorities. There was only one place a somn could acquire such documentation.

As she approached her destination, a familiar somn emerged from the Dictum Division at the end of the hall. She clicked her tongue. *What the hell! What is Jett Milan doing here?*

"Jett!"

A dark-haired young man caught sight of the last White Band member he ever wanted to encounter. Not enthused to see her, he spun around. Seeing The Tower's outer wall shortly before him, and realizing he had nowhere to go, he slowly turned back around as Helena drew near.

Ugh, he cringed.

"Who gave you authorization to be here?" Helena demanded, quick to the point.

Jett stared blankly, before answering, "Black Band orders."

"What? You're the newest recruit! What could *you* possibly have to offer the Black Band?" she scoffed. He remained motionless, his dark eyes void of emotion.

"Well?" she pressed.

"Errands."

"What kind of..." she began, but he had already brushed past her in heading to the elevators. Helena glared after him, as she wondered, *What Black Band member is he getting authorization papers for? Not to mention, which prisoner?*

ഇരുന്നു

Tavokk twisted his mouth in thought. He had been to The Tower just once, years before. Although he recalled most key levels, he had evidently mixed up the floors of the Prisoner's Quarters and The Archives.

Hearing a sound, Tavokk turned, wincing at the rustling of his long jacket. Alert, he discerned a woman's voice nearby. A deep, scratchy voice answered the first.

Inmates. As Tavokk listened, they conversed across the way, only able to see one another's dark, beady eyes.

"Didn't you hear about him, Haley?" the deep, scratchy voice questioned.

"About who?" the woman, Haley, responded. She had an equally unpleasant voice.

"Fyfe Van Ingen, that blasted man we encountered at the Crumpets' big bash just last month. Do you remember him?"

"You don't mean that fellow that fought old man Reginald?" the woman inquired.

"Yes, yes. That is the very one."

"Fallon, you mean he is *here*?"

"Indeed. That is what I overheard them guards discussing last night." The rough voice added, "They said they are keeping him in 003H."

Tavokk tuned out the continuing conversation. *Fyfe.* Distracted by his plans to break into The Archives, he had forgotten about Van Ingen's imprisonment here. *003H,* he speculated. *This could be fortuitous.*

Moving soundlessly over the glass floor, Tavokk weaved his

way between cells in searching for cell 003H. Growing irritated and about to give up, Tavokk spotted it.

"Aha! There you are," he said. The particular cell was one of the smaller ones toward the center, not far from the ring of elevators.

Creeping to the marble door, Tavokk rested his hands on either side of the small, barred slot. He leaned as close as possible, placing an eye between two of the thick, metal bars.

Suddenly, two eyes appeared. By pure reflex, Tavokk issued a startled yelp, ducking to the side of the door.

"What the hell was that?" a nearby prisoner inquired. Tavokk cast his eyes in the direction of the voice. He crouched, perfectly still.

He slid back toward Van Ingen's cell. The eyes had disappeared from view. "Fyfe?" Tavokk intoned.

A pause. "What? Who?" Shifty eyes returned, peering from the darkness. Disheveled hair covered much of the dull, once livid, eyes.

"Jereth?" the skeptical voice questioned.

"Yes?" Tavokk moved up to the slot, eager at the calling of his name.

"I haven't seen you in months. By Eve, what the hell are you doing here?" A baffled expression radiated from Van Ingen's eyes. His eyes were lifeless. The usual, rich darks and the brilliant caramels that normally glowed from them had been drained, sucked out by the shadows of the cell and the general absence of all color.

"Speaking of hell, you sure look the part, my good man." Tavokk directed his statement toward the black and purple bruises puffing Van Ingen's right eye.

"That doesn't answer my question," Van Ingen pressed, retaining no trace of his usual charisma.

"Well, we certainly can't meet at any respectable parties from in here now, can we?"

Van Ingen's eyebrows drew together in his candid displeasure.

"My, Fyfe, a short time in this pit has done a job on your charming disposition." Tavokk raised an eyebrow.

Van Ingen glowered.

"Eeh. Well then, if you really must know, I am here to check out a book."

"Uh huh. A book. Sure. You want me to believe you dragged your ass to this hellhole to look for a book." It was a statement. Not a question. The vehemence coating Van Ingen's words pained

Tavokk. It was uncharacteristic, upsetting.

A brief chime filled the awkward silence as an elevator came to a stop. Tavokk, instantly alert, moved a short distance from the cell door, pressing against the wall as he heard the elevator doors open.

"But really, Julian, you could have at least dragged something more out of him before clocking him. You knocked him clean out!" A rich, beguiling voice spilled out through the doors as the elevator opened.

"I couldn't help myself, Armani. You know how I get. *He* should have known that would happen," a second voice replied. This resonant voice, though enchanting as well, lacked the musical timbre. The degree of allure in both men's voices, however, far exceeded expectation. They spelled poison to a dangerous, unnatural degree, which one would never appreciate, unless hearing firsthand.

"Unconscious, Julian! He was unconscious for nearly a day! I thought his eye was going to bleed right out of his skull!"

Julian sighed, bored with the appraisal, which he had heard too many times already. He rolled his eyes condescendingly.

Tavokk turned rigid, as though he were carved from the black marble that created Atrum Unda. The hair on his neck stood on end, and a shiver ran down his spine.

Shit!

Struggling for the ability to move, Tavokk mustered just enough to dodge hastily back, hugging Van Ingen's cell door. The fearful eyes, hidden in the heavy shadows of cell 003H, demonstrated that Van Ingen was just as aware of the danger these men presented as Tavokk himself.

Tavokk whispered, urgently, "I must go, but I will be back. I *will* get you out of here."

Eyes filled with desperation, Van Ingen moved his mouth to object, but then he closed it. He knew that these men could not find Jereth Tavokk here. He flashed a look, as though aware how closely Tavokk and these men, Armani Saint and Julian Gallows, were acquainted. *Could it be so obvious?* Tavokk wondered.

With a nod, Van Ingen shrank back into the utter darkness of his tiny cell.

With violent, wrenching guilt in the pit of his stomach, Tavokk moved away from Van Ingen's cell. The two men from the elevator were very near. Only a couple rings of cells and elevators separated them from him. This meant that either of two hallways would lead them directly to him.

As Armani's musical voice drew closer, Tavokk slowed his breathing to quiet the pounding of his heart. His abnormally keen hearing allowed him to hear their conversation from his current location.

"Julian, why must you behave so? You act as though I bore you to death." Silence. Tavokk's heart skipped a beat. Then, with a clear, melodious laugh, Armani collected himself and carried on. "I'm bluntly surprised you didn't kill him. I thought you were going to sell his soul to Goddess Eve and claim the beating heart from his chest. Who would have thought you merciful enough to leave him merely unconscious and bruised." Another laugh.

The men moved in Tavokk's direction. He heard them in the hallway to his left. He dodged to his right, moving further from the center, to another wider, circling row of cells.

Tavokk crept low along one of the many black cells. Peering out, he pulled back instantly as the two pallid men appeared in the nearest webbed hallway.

The figures moving elegantly before him, he had met. And he had hoped never to have the pleasure of meeting them again. The duo held a merciless reputation in the underworld of this city. They were inseparable, and it was practically impossible to survive them if a somn picked the wrong time and day to cross their path.

Although vastly alluring, theirs was a deadly trap. Their bewitching eyes could devour one's soul. A being could easily flounder in Julian's eyes of unfathomable turquoise, deeper than the seas themselves. Then there was Armani. His eyes had a fatal quality, blacker than coal, but allowing bands of lava red to seep venomously through, exposing the will of Eve, goddess of the life after death. Together, the duo would be easily capable of consuming the entire city.

Armani halted. "Do you smell something?" A large, gold hoop adorned his left ear beneath short styled, dark bronzed hair, which was naturally lighter on top.

"Yeah," Julian said, frowning. "Smells familiar." Closing his eyes, he inhaled the vague hint of some opulent cologne. "Hmm." Julian's shoulder length, dark hair appeared utterly black in the dim lighting of the Prisoner's Quarters.

Tavokk's eyes widened. *How could I have been so foolish!* Fortunately, he had worn so little that they soon forsook any pursuit.

Dropping the matter, Armani and Julian proceeded to Van Ingen's cell, each placing a hand upon the door within two separate, shallow boxes. As their energies connected, creating a circuit, the door slid back and receded into the wall.

I must help him! But after thinking again of the notorious duo, Tavokk's thoughts quickly altered. *Then again, maybe not. He can fend for himself. He's a tough one.*

Making his way past Armani, Julian peered cynically down at Van Ingen. "So? Are we enjoying our stay here at the magnificent Tower?"

"Accommodating enough, I hope," Armani cut in. "We went to great trouble to get you this remarkable cell. Not everyone receives such *security*." A grin embellished his flawless features.

Tavokk stood behind a distant cell, listening. He clenched his fists at the mocking. *Don't do anything stupid, Fyfe. Don't say anything stupid.* He couldn't imagine being in Van Ingen's position and having to put up with this.

"Go to hell," Van Ingen snarled.

Tavokk smacked a silent palm to his forehead.

Armani and Julian arched a collective brow. Julian turned an eye toward Armani, saying, "He doesn't seem at all enthusiastic about our efforts."

"Not at all," Armani agreed, in wicked delight. "Perhaps we should teach him some gratitude. Maybe he would be more appreciative afterward?"

"May I?" Julian's expression twisted eagerly in Armani's direction, asking permission. Sickening malice spilled from his glassy, aqua eyes.

Armani remained standing in the doorway, satisfaction lacing his features. "P-lease do."

Crouching, Van Ingen risked a glance up, as Julian closed in. A predator engaging its prey, Julian, eager for the coming pain, lashed a backhand to Van Ingen's unbruised eye, followed by a swift kick to the solar plexus. In agonizing pain, Van Ingen dropped, gasping on the slick, stone floor. Julian leaned forward, wrenching Van Ingen's head back by his hair.

"Have we decided to cooperate like a respectable little house guest?" Julian scoffed. Van Ingen just gaped painfully at him, unable to speak.

As Julian prepared to strike again, Armani gracefully snatched his arm, saying, "Now, now. We mustn't repeat our mistakes. We have questions that need answering."

Guided by Armani, Julian turned away, but not without one

last merciless kick to the ribcage. Armani shot a reproachful look, but Julian swaggered to an adjacent wall and leaned back with an arrogant grin.

Armani crouched over Van Ingen in his fetal position. "What do you know about the Key Calling?" he crooned.

Tavokk, in hearing this, leaned too far into the open hallway, his curiosity overwhelming caution.

Van Ingen quelled in sincere terror as Armani's demonic, scarlet eyes glowed, penetrating the darkness of the cell.

"I thought you didn't believe in the Key Calling," Van Ingen spat, a rough sarcasm slurring his words.

"Hah!" Julian blurted, at the little tête-à-tête before him, unable to keep out of Armani's private conversation.

Armani cast a stern, warning look back at Julian. He took pleasure in his glory moments, and he was not about to allow Julian to disrupt him of his own accord. Suddenly, he came to alertness, eyes searching the hallways around them. He tilted his head, eyes narrowed, as he listened.

In response, Tavokk jumped backward, falling. He scrambled up, attempting to regain cover. He had felt a strike of anxiety that Armani might have sensed his eavesdropping. Reaching cover, he closed his mind and slowed his breathing.

At length, Armani turned back to Van Ingen. "Don't be daft. Of course we believe in the Key Calling. It's the general public that has a fragile mind. We can't allow a panic over things beyond their comprehension."

"Why should I—" Van Ingen groused, but the elevator chimed, cutting him off. Armani, Julian, and Tavokk all perked up.

Tavokk hesitated, wishing to remain where he stood, but he realized this might be his only opportunity to escape up to The Tower's Archives without being noticed by the callous twosome.

When the doors opened, Jett Milan strolled out. He was several years younger than Armani and Julian, who were just into their thirties. His startling brown eyes rendered black and merciless, masked by a shock of draping black hair.

Must be one of their guys, Tavokk decided, stealing toward the elevator. As Jett turned, moving toward Armani and Julian, Tavokk dove through the closing doors.

*10:*Departure

What is south? Rhyus queried, walking on and on. Lux Lumetia was deserted at this hour, which appealed to him. He enjoyed having the world to himself. It gave him time to think. Besides, he wasn't in the mood to talk to anybody.

The Tower, nearby now, was much larger than it had appeared from the piazza. The dazzling white stone structure kept a vigilant eye over the entire city. From here, he could see that the colossal central tower connected to three mid-height towers that formed an equilateral triangle.

The multiple bridges connecting the center tower to each shorter one divided them into precise, vertical thirds. *It's even more remarkable than I perceived in my dream.*

He marveled as the beacon at the apex of the central tower shined over Lux Lumetia. *Extraordinary. I wonder how it works. Where does it derive its energy?*

"Hello, son."

Rhyus jumped, startled at the voice.

A middle-aged man sat upon a glimmering white stone bench. His fresh face had a kind smile as he chuckled at Rhyus's reaction. Rhyus flushed lightly.

"What brings a young man such as yourself out at this early hour? The city still sleeps."

"Nothing in particular," Rhyus said, rubbing the back of his neck. He looked at the ground, avoiding eye contact.

"You look troubled, son."

Images of encounters with his current host flashed through Rhyus mind. He stammered, "I-I believe that would be an understatement."

"Oh? Perhaps you would like to discuss your troubles? It helps to capture a listening ear." He grinned as if this were some sort of inside joke.

"I don't mean to be rude," Rhyus started, "but who *are* you?"

"You may call me Abel. And you are...?"

"The name's Rhyus." At that, he glanced briefly at Abel. His wavy, blond hair was so far beyond platinum that its silver sheen clashed against his lightly tanned flesh. Hypnotic, liquid amber eyes sat deep in his lean face.

"You know," the man said, shifting his weight, "I thought I would recognize anyone who might cross my path in this city. Our encounter has proven otherwise."

"Yeah, well, I don't get out much."

"Again, these troubles, what might they pertain to?" The somn's wish to help seemed most genuine.

Rhyus tried to hedge, but something drew him to open up. "I am caught in a predicament. I am having problems in the household where I am staying. I also have no idea what I am supposed to be doing or who I am. What is my life?" Rhyus frowned, feeling overwhelmed. He continued to see his night's dream.

Abel smiled at Rhyus's decision to speak out. He knew that no good resulted from keeping everything inside.

"This place where you are staying— sit isn't with close friends or family, I presume?"

"How'd ya guess?"

"A man who has been around like I have has his ways." Abel laughed, despite his cryptic tone. "Would you care to take a seat? There is plenty of room, and I am more than willing to share."

Hesitant, Rhyus sat on the bench, though as far to the end as possible without falling off.

"You know," Abel started again, once Rhyus had situated himself, his bag leaning up against his leg. "Sometimes things are better off left to take care of themselves. On the other hand, sometimes we are meant to assist them along."

"How do you mean?"

"For instance, where you are living—if you remain, perhaps things will work out in due time. Then again, maybe you are meant to pack up your bags and take some time to find your true self. By the time you return, everything between your hosts and yourself may have resolved, and all will be well."

"Right," a dubious Rhyus replied.

"We each have our own destiny. We are intended to discover that purpose. For some, it becomes apparent with no effort. Others must go out and search. We must travel. We must strive to find our destiny."

Abel's pleasant disposition caused Rhyus to put his dream further behind him. "But how do I know which of these categories I fit into?"

"My son, you must trust your instincts. Look for a sign. Perhaps there'll be many signs. Either way, in time, the answers will come."

Rhyus shuffled his feet upon the hard, stone ground. His eyebrows knitted together, deep in thought.

"You must go now," the voice of the robed man from his dream entered Rhyus's head, as real and as clear as ever. Rhyus lifted his head in a quick motion.

Concerned, Abel awaited some explanation.

"I know what I must do." Rhyus stood abruptly without explanation. He leaned forward to grab his messenger bag, slinging it over his shoulder and across his chest.

"Off then?"

"Yes, I must hurry. The suns shall reach the horizon soon."

The man offered a charming smile and said, "Then a new day and a new journey await."

Rhyus returned a respectable nod and turned on his heel.

Moving quickly in a northern direction, Rhyus soon found himself among a handful of vending stands with merchants standing or sitting nearby, preparing for whatever business the day may bring. More stands were in the process of having their day's displays set up.

This must be North Market. He continued north, admiring the colorful stands and their varying contents and merchants.

"Plush melons are delicious this time of year."

Rhyus stopped in his tracks, peering over his shoulder at a diminutive, young girl. Blonde, tight spiraling hair fell loosely past her shoulders.

Boldly moving to stand next to her, Rhyus picked up a red melon in one hand, turning it over a couple of times. "So, are these Plush melons really that good?"

After inspecting Rhyus shortly from the corner of her eye, the girl turned her head toward him. A laughing smile showed on her lips. "Yes. They're absolutely wonderful! But this," she wrinkled her nose at the rabmelon in Rhyus's hand, "is not Plush." She grabbed the West Bay melon from Rhyus's hand and set it back into its proper basket. "This, on the other hand," she picked up a brilliant melon from a basket just before her, "is Plush."

With a smug smile, she slipped the rabmelon into Rhyus's hand.

"How rude of me not to introduce myself." She batted her eyes. "My name is Mona. My mother owns the Crimson Glass, a tavern located in the Eastside. I apologize, but I don't recognize you. Are you from around these parts?" Her finger absently traced the outline of a white bird on her pale orange fabric bag.

"Pardon? Oh, no." Rhyus shook his head. "I am staying with… acquaintances."

"Where in the city? Somewhere nearby?"

"I'm staying in the Caulder District. In the northwest."

"Oh yes," Mona nodded. "I know the place. It was the luxurious part of the city, decades back. But isn't it rather run-down now? I've honestly never been there myself. Just what I've heard."

"I suppose. Where I am staying still exudes wealth. But yeah, you're right, the surrounding area is pretty decrepit."

"So are you going to get any?"

"What?" Rhyus asked again. "Oh, right." He looked down to his hand still holding the bright, plump melon.

She gave an amused grin. The blue of her eyes twinkled. "Well?"

"I think I will."

"They aren't for you, are they?" she asked, in response to Rhyus's expression.

"No…they are for one of my hosts."

"More like host-ess?" she pressed, curious.

Rhyus flushed. "Yes, a host-*ess*," he said, copying the way she had stressed the word.

Her grin widened. "Ah hah."

"Speaking of which, I need to be getting back." He looked at the rabmelons, baffled by which to choose.

"Let me help you." The girl rummaged through the basket searching for only the best. As Rhyus opened his bag, she placed them gently into it.

"That should be plenty." Rhyus flashed a genuine smile. "Thank you for all your help."

"Certainly. As you are new in town, if you ever need any information, stop by the Crimson Glass. I am a pool of information! Hope to see you around," she said truthfully, walking away with her own loaded bag. Her long, violet skirt swung in rhythm with her swaying hips.

Paying with his stash from Venn, Rhyus watched her disappear, and then he headed back to Umbra Halls.

The suns beat Rhyus home by a good hour. Irritated, he dashed through The Courtyard and up into the kitchen, hoping that Marion had not risen early. He couldn't be sure with her.

Gently, he replaced the rabmelons on the table with the Plush ones he pulled from his bag, smiling at what Marion's reaction would be. He opened the last one, taking a large bite out of it. *Wow. These really are good.*

Still munching on the melon, Rhyus grabbed his bag and headed downstairs. Marion's door was closed. Pressing his ear against the door, he heard no sound from the other side. *Good. She must still be asleep.*

He walked to his bedroom where he stuffed his bag with the new clothes from his wardrobe. Slinging the bag back over his shoulder, he took one last look at the room. *It could be a long while before I have another comfortable room to stay in.* With mixed emotions, he walked out, closing the door behind him.

Reaching the kitchen again, gripping the door handle, he paused. Looking back at the door of the den, he dropped his hand and made a stealthy trip back to it. Once inside, he strode quietly over the ornamental rug to Venn's large wooden desk. Pulling the dark leather chair back, he shuffled through the desk drawers. He came across a black pen with an intricate silver inlay that looked intriguing. Rhyus removed the cap and set it aside.

No paper was currently out on the desk's surface. There were only a few piles of books as well as a couple of open ones. Without thought or consideration, Rhyus grabbed an open book with a deep violet cover and silver-edged pages. He scribbled a quick design at the bottom corner to test the pen. The ink, a shocking luminous blue, raised an embossed imprint as he scrawled across the page.

Leaning over the book, he began writing on a book page with *Chapter 20* in an elegant, black font at its top.

"Finished," he said aloud, completing his letter. He ripped out the page and stood up. As a last thought, Rhyus folded it in half. He picked up the pen for a last time and wrote on the outer side, *Marion.* The blue script embossed itself once more, completely hiding the small text beneath. He dropped the uncapped pen onto the desk. Without closing the book or sliding the chair back into place, Rhyus exited the den hurriedly, moving toward the kitchen.

Rhyus tucked the book page where he was certain that Marion would discover it, among the gift of new Plush rabmelons. As he stood, looking at the arrangement, he leaned forward and removed the West Bay melons from the edge of the table and placed them into his messenger bag.

Exiting, he passed through The Courtyard, past the large tree, and through the metal gate. He turned his head with a final glance back. It was daytime now beyond Umbra Halls, but The Courtyard was still blanketed in shadows. As a shrill wind whistled through the open space, he walked quickly out into the alleyway.

ℰℭ

Marion yawned softly, as she stretched her arms and legs. Cuddled beneath a fluffy comforter, she pulled it up, tucking some under the side of her face to create another pillow. She blinked, though there was little light to adjust to. After a few quiet minutes, she stepped to the cool wooden floor. The simple mirrored face of her watch read 7:23.

Still in her blue satin nightgown, Marion yawned her way to the kitchen. With the refrigerator door ajar, she stood, popping fresh berries into her mouth, one by one. While placing a plump berry between her slender lips, Marion caught sight of something unexpected. With a cheery smile, she glided softly to the table and picked up one of the melons.

Plush, she observed, delighted. *Who would've had time?* Something new caught her eye. She picked up the folded piece of paper, written with nowhere near Venn's elegant script. Her smile widened, in realization, *Rhyus*. Embossed script read:

Marion,

I am leaving. It's nothing personal. I have my reasons. Thank you for your kindness and hospitality. I hope you understand and will forgive me. Don't follow me. This is something I must do on my own.

Rhyus

P.S. Hope you enjoy the Plush rabmelons.

Oh, and ditch the brute. He doesn't deserve you.

The cheerful smile lingered before falling to a frown. He couldn't be serious, after they had so graciously taken him in. She narrowed her eyes.

Placing the melon down, Marion sped back downstairs. She stripped, showered, and dried off in record time. Grabbing her toothbrush and paste, she shuffled through both dresser and wardrobe for something to wear. She decided on split-leg blue denims, with turquoise ribbons at the seams, and a tight, thin-strapped top that matched. She slipped Rhyus's note into her pocket.

Marion hastily made neat stacks of carefully selected clothing, which she placed into a beige bag with three wide diagonal black stripes. Its scarlet script read *Randál Vanaché*.

Marion slid into a pair of comfortable boots, zipping them to a point high on her calves. She hurriedly tidied her hair and makeup. *Oh, one more thing.* She grabbed a page of stationary from a pile beneath her bed, along with her puzzle book and pen, before rushing upstairs.

Marion set the bag gently on her favorite, antique chair and slipped into the den. Still, carrying the piece of stationary, she leaned over Venn's desk, taking a glass pen from the top drawer. As she wrote, scarlet words filled the bordered paper. Just as Rhyus had done, Marion folded the paper in half, creasing it with her fingernail.

As Marion carefully replaced the pen, she gasped at the philosophy book lying open on the desk. *The Ship Sinks, but It Is Our Grave.* Venn absolutely loved this tome on the veracity of significance.

Marion shook her head, yet she found it amusing that Rhyus had managed to choose this particular book from the vast collection filling the room. She carried the book with her, placing it into her bag. *Best Venn never witness this desecration.*

In the kitchen, Marion carefully moved the crystal chess set from its awkward location above the refrigerator to the table, habitually straightening a few pieces. With a wistful smile, she slid her note beneath an edge of the checkered board. The beautifully scripted scarlet *Venn* was displayed in its entirety.

She loaded the rabmelons from Rhyus into her bag, along with water bottles and some other necessities.

From the main hallway closet, Marion drew a black leather jacket. It fell to mid-thigh, with silver zippers and buckles over a good portion of its surface. There was a clean tear on the left arm, but it remained important to her. It was one of the few things she had to remind her of her previous life. The life she had before coming to live at Umbra Halls with Venn. Donning the jacket, Marion fastened a few buckles from diaphragm to hip level.

Slipping the costly bag over her head, she closed the closet and stepped to the double doors. After taking a final look around, she hastily walked down to her room to grab one thing she had forgotten. It was her first, and most significant, gift from Venn. The watch, kept hidden in a secure drawer of her nightstand. As she replaced her simple, mirrored watch with the new one, a dazzling circle of diamonds around the face threw a shower of rainbows coruscating about the room. She buckled the watch's silver bracelet band around her wrist.

8:49, it now read. She had taken more time than she had hoped. Venn would be rising soon. *I must find Rhyus before he can catch up to us.* Marion headed through the double doors and hurried beyond The Courtyard.

Now...to find Rhyus.

11: Escaping The Archives

Tavokk crouched in the corner of the elevator. Being that the upper walls were glass, he waited until Jett Milan was far enough away to avoid notice. Reaching his arm up, he pressed floor 132, where he would find The Archives. As the elevator rose, he straightened, pursing his lips to calm his breathing. He had not been prepared for the close encounter with Armani Saint and Julian Gallows. In reality, being prepared for such a moment would be nigh impossible.

During the short trip to floor 132, he regained his composure. *If that call had been any closer, I would be hanging by my coat buckles. Fyfe would not be the one receiving the worst treatment. But then, I had no reason to risk a return, until now.*

The chime sounded. Smoothing his raven hair and straightening his jacket, the doors parted and Tavokk strolled out. He had returned to his usual confident self. Once beyond the elevator's safe black marble flooring and lower walls, he realized, *This floor is glass... though I can't look down, Armani and Julian could easily spot me if they were to look up. Then again, I'm sure they are so used to the insignificant activity of others around them that they don't even notice it anymore.*

Lost in thought, Tavokk bumped into an abandoned cart of books that waited to be filed. Luckily, with a swift reaction, he caught the books before they fell. Though he may have appeared in control, his quivering hands revealed the lie. Hands still trembling, he straightened the wayward books.

Distracted, he had failed to notice a man approaching. Tavokk tried to think of an appropriate statement to justify his presence, but still vexed by Armani and Julian, he simply ended up sounding awkward. "Ah. Here are The Archives." He looked around, chin up, as though proudly observing. "The very place I have come to increase my knowledge...about books...and things...in the library...the great Archives...Go Lord Cain!" Tavokk made a pumping gesture with his fist, cheering in enthusiasm.

The man brushed right on by, toward the elevator. While rushing past, he shook his head at the moron in disgust, grumbling,

"D-Damn, ignorant r-rook."

"Yes…all right," Tavokk said, playing the part until the man disappeared.

Now, where do I begin? If what Callis said at the Cosmos is true, there must be a book or some articles about water portals. Why haven't I heard of this before?

The Archives was immense, comprising two floors of endless bookshelves. Decorative spiral staircases connected the floors in each of the cardinal directions, augmenting the quartet of elevators. Both levels had higher ceilings than the other levels of the Tower. The perimeter of both floors was lined with bookshelves. But the upper floor had a wide, glass-floored balcony around its entire perimeter, lined by silver railings, broken at four intervals, allowing access to lounges with glass tables surrounded by black leather chairs. The rooms on the floor below supported each lounge.

Looking around the second level, Tavokk made sure he was alone before skimming the shelves for anything he might use. All the while, he kept an eye out for intruders.

Occasionally, he pulled likely books out for examination. After rejection, he simply tossed them over his shoulder. After all, this was not his home and these were not his books. He grimaced as he accidentally tossed a book over the thin, silver railing, hearing it thump down on the first floor. He gulped, remembering Armani and Julian's presence, just two levels beneath The Archives.

Frustrated, he stood with his hands on the decorative railing. He scanned the deserted lounge areas. Silver flecks glinted light in every direction. *Wait…the rooms.*

But of course! Tavokk rushed back down a staircase to look at the smaller, central wall of one of the first-floor rooms.

As he studied, letters began forming in the marble, burning with a red glow, hot from being etched into the solid black stone. He watched, fascinated, as letters carved out their fiery warning:

No book to leave room. Severe fine for violation. Comply so all may benefit.

Tavokk's mouth twisted. Odd. As he finished reading the engraved warning, a new red-hot point etched a flawless square on the wall. The previous words vanished as new ones took their place:

Place hand below to accept terms.

Tavokk placed his hand within the glowing square outline. He jumped at the electric blaze that coursed down his arm to his spine. But nothing happened. The wall refused to budge. *I am not one to take rejection kindly,* he scowled. Rejection had been boiling just beneath the surface, and images of Helena coursed through his brain. Over and over, countless scenes of rejection flashed like a neon sign. "Dammit!" he cursed under his breath. He had tried so hard. At least he convinced himself he had. At first he had tried to get closer to her. Then to forget about her. Neither had worked.

The images of Helena Meretrix were enough, however, to give him the motivation he needed now. He strained against the wall, tattoos glowing with the effort. When still nothing happened he became infuriated. Calling on his most powerful emotions, he deliberately gave in to his mental circus of pain. The first images were pleasant, but in no time, they became twisted and hard. He allowed their times together to flip past—igniting a fire within. Every conversation was etched in flaming letters upon each page. Dancing, as their words around things, which had gone unspoken. He knew of her abominable past and the things she had done…with others. To others. To herself…

Tavokk's eyes burst into a violet luminosity behind his shades.

Thank you. You are now permitted to enter.

The wall proceeded to melt. Tavokk pulled away in consternation, as some flowed onto his hand. Forced from his thoughts, he examined it from every angle, perplexed that nothing remained on it.

The wall had only been an intricate holograph, overlying a dark tinted glass door. Black marble pooled at his feet before vanishing into nonexistence. Regrettably, he could not fully admire the impressive illusion, due to the blinding light reflecting upward.

Unexpectedly, the glass door slid into the wall above, revealing long rows of books that ran the perimeter of the room. A shimmering silver rug covered most of the floor. It reflected the dim luminescence of star-shaped clusters of crystal lights above, arranged into systems of constellations.

"All right." Tavokk walked to a bookshelf, resuming his previous activity. At one point, a faded title, *Tales of The Hidden*, grabbed his attention. "Ooh, stories! I do love a good story." Tavokk unbuckled his jacket, sliding the musty old book into an inner pocket.

Finding nothing more of interest, Tavokk headed toward another room, which boasted much tighter security. This wall was not a holograph, and these engravings were solid black as opposed to the burning, ember red.

Again, he placed his hand within the etched box. He jumped at the electric blaze that ran down his arm to his spine. But nothing happened. The wall refused to budge. *I'm not one to take rejection kindly*, he thought. The image of Helena flashed briefly through his mind, giving him just the motivation he needed.

He strained against the wall, tattoos glowing with the effort. When, still, nothing happened, he became infuriated. His eyes gleamed with radiant, violet luminosity behind his shades. Volatile energy caused more tattoos to glow, one by one, until the majority had ignited. The reaction between the marble and him became nearly unbearable, like an overheated supermagnet, powerful enough to disintegrate any normal being.

With a blast, he was thrown to the floor. The marble wall split in two, each half sliding back a step and then horizontally into the sidewalls. The walls, once again, resembled single sections of black marble devoid of any seam. Though lying on the floor, Tavokk couldn't help being impressed at the room's innovative engineering.

Regaining his composure, he cracked his neck, adding a sarcastic afterthought, *And wasn't that fun.*

He did a lithe kick to a standing position and walked nonchalantly through the room's large entrance.

This new room resembled the one he had just exited. Well, before he had carelessly turned it into a disaster zone. At the center of the room, there rested an elegant pedestal. He quickly disregarded it, distracted by tiny, red lights indicating that he had just passed through a security scanner.

Just as before, he plowed through the room, tossing books everywhere. The fact that the books were very old and valuable didn't hinder him a bit. Toward the outer edge of the room, he came across a faded, rust-colored book entitled, *The Beginning: Rise from the Water*. With high hopes, he removed it, flipping through the book's worn pages. Chapter titles included: *Creating a New World, Atrum Unda, Lux Lumetia, Travel Limitations*, and most importantly, *The Intrinsic Value of the Water Portal*.

Perfect, he grinned wide, elated at his finding. With the book at his side, he walked to the exit, disregarding the security sensors.

Deeee-brr-eep, a piercing noise blasted. On a previously invisible wall, glowing, red letters appeared:

Warning! Disable security system or General alarm will sound.

Tavokk cringed. *This can't be good.* He watched, unsure what to do as the message erased itself and appeared for a second time:

Warning! Disable security system or General alarm will sound.

Goddammit. Tavokk pressed his empty hand to his head with no clue of how to disband the alarm.

His casual stroll now became a backbreaking sprint, as he shot to the nearby elevators. He pounded at the silver button, demanding an elevator to receive him at once. The brief wait was interminable.

The instant a door opened, Tavokk leapt inside, groping for the ground floor's button. *Shit!* The elevator only went to floor 81. Tavokk dropped to the floor, concealing himself behind the black marble walls of its bottom half.

When the elevator reached its destination, he looked out, bothered by the fact that he hadn't yet heard an alarm sound. He ran toward the black spiral staircase. Due to the slick surface, he had the fortuitous luck to slide past the stairway entrance.

Making his way back, something Tavokk had *not* expected caught his eye. In the hallway between the sets of elevators across from him, he noted a head of fiery, crimson hair. The man was moving away from the elevators and down a webbed corridor. With an involuntary, high-pitched yelp, Tavokk registered the red-haired man's identity. It was his drinking buddy from the Wishing Well. *Oh, by Eve. Callis!*

Unable to move, unable to breathe, his brain processed the repercussions of crossing his dangerous friend.

After the accidental sound of his horror had escaped his lips, Tavokk swiveled with blinding speed onto the staircase, crouching below the banister to avoid Callis's field of view. *If Callis discovers me here, it definitely won't be pleasant.* His stomach wrenched at the thought. Crouching low, he spiraled down the stairs, his long black leather jacket trailing behind him.

೮ාය

Hearing an unusual noise, Callis Morgandy swiveled his head

toward the stairwell. His sharp gaze combed the entire structure. *I could swear I just heard something much like a shrieking bird.* After evaluation, he dismissed it with a shrug.

ಏಂೞ

Only a quarter of the way down, Tavokk threw himself over the railing. Still grasping the book in his left hand, he dropped like lead, through the wide central opening of the staircase. The impact of his landing pulsed through his body. He grimaced. *I'm going to be feeling that one.*

Recovering quickly, he leapt to his feet, racing for the final set of elevators. Again, he pounded the silver button, writhing in impatience. He leapt into the southwest elevator, stabbing at the first floor's button repeatedly.

Dropping to the elevator floor once again, he gratefully noted that in his white-knuckled hand, he still held the worn book. He loosened his grip just the slightest.

Just then, an ear-piercing alarm began to sound.

ಏಂೞ

Armani and Julian had just climbed into the elevator from the Prisoner's Quarters. They rode, proud of the results with their latest victim, Fyfe Van Ingen. They were certain he would soon divulge the valuable information they were awaiting. Very soon. Just before reaching the eighty-first floor, an alarm sounded. When the doors opened, the two of them flew out into the circular space between the two sets of elevator shafts, scouting The Tower about them.

ಏಂೞ

Exiting one of the offices of the Dictum Division, Helena fumed at the absurdity of what had just taken place. The first insult had been in making her sit for hours, quietly filling out a mountain of paperwork. After the hundredth redo, they immediately denied any authorization papers. She had demanded to know how it was that the newest member of Nyx Crucian's White Band, Jett Milan, received priority treatment, and all she received was the shaft?

The snooty woman behind the counter hadn't even felt the need for any response. Other than that they did not remember ever hearing of a Helena Meretrix in connection to any of Nyx's bands. White, Crimson, or Black. With an exaggerated sniff, the old bat had then headed toward the back to attend to more important matters.

The tall, pock-faced man had also remained silent. Merely eyeing her with that same hunger she had seen far too many times before. It was difficult, but Helena had learned that when one worked for Nyx Crucian, it was not worth the pleasure of losing one's patience toward the never-ending bureaucracy of The Tower.

Silently counting to ten, Helena turned away and stalked toward the room's exit. It was at that point that he had found the temerity— or more the stupidity—to say to her back, "That doesn't say much about you, does it?"

As Helena turned slowly back toward him, it had taken every fiber of her being to leave her blade safely tucked away. But she knew that with this emaciated puke she wouldn't need such weaponry to control the situation. Step by slow step, she advanced. As she continued his way he had began to stammer, uncertain what he should do. True to the potential of his bird-brain, he merely stood there. Dumbly doing nothing.

Staring down at the mere slip of a girl, he swallowed, seeing the fire burning in her eyes. However, she smiled. Confused, he attempted to smile back. But all he achieved was a crooked grimace that immediately disappeared as one hand shot out to squeeze his scrawny neck. The other hand caught his scrotum with an iron grip.

At this point, her smile had become genuine. She wrenched his head down to hiss in his ear. "Little big-man, from this point on you had better remember Helena Meretrix. Any time I come here, for any reason—even if it be to see Lord Cain himself—you will jump up with a 'Yes m'am.' You will sign the papers and get the hell out of my way." As a punctuation mark, she allowed each hand a final squeeze that left him gasping and retching on the floor.

With this, Helena had enough, and began her walk back to the elevator. She had just raised a finger to press the elevator button when she was interrupted by a deafening sound.

ℰↃ℃ℛ

Callis, rushing to the elevators at the screeching alarm, saw his fellow Black Band members, Armani Saint and Julian Gallows, exiting an elevator with pangs of eagerness igniting their eyes. Not expecting to see them here, he closed the space between them with quick, long strides.

Armani, seeing Callis's high-speed approach, greeted him. "Ah, Callis." Julian, who had been preoccupied in scanning the far side of The Tower, whipped around with surprise.

Armani crooned, condescendingly, "What brings you here? Did Nyx—"

Julian cut him off, "Not now, Armani." He turned his attention back to Callis. "What the hell is going on here, Morgandy?" he demanded, referring to the alarm.

As if in answer to Julian's question, red letters appeared, glowing across every dark tinted window, high on the walls of each black marble room. The letters also ran across the back wall of every elevator, both inside and out.

Drawn by the alarm, somns began congregating in the webbed corridors. They filtered into, and around, the elevator lobbies on every level. The red letters continued to run:

CODE: 7. 51. 72. B D...Intruder Alert...Repeat...Intruder Alert...

The warning continued, cycling over and over.

Armani and Julian exchanged a sudden look of amusement. "Aha!" They said, simultaneously.

Armani turned to Callis with a beguiling lift of his eyebrows. "Coming, Callis?"

With a distracted voice, gaze locked on the staircase, Callis brushed off the invitation. "Uh. You guys go on ahead. I'll catch up."

Armani patted Callis's shoulder, following Julian without a second glance. Julian shoved others out of his way, irritated that they were delaying his fun. He summoned an elevator.

The head librarian, who had just recently exited The Archives as Tavokk had entered, squeezed between others in a desperate attempt to reach the elevator now opening directly before Julian. As he tried to squeeze past Julian and move into the elevator, Julian threw out his arm.

"Out of my way, peasant," Julian demanded, sideswiping him into a sprawl on the floor.

Armani, disregarding them both, took an elegant step over the man on the floor and past Julian into the elevator. "You really should have gotten out of his way," he reproached.

"B-but...The Archives...I-I am the head l-librarian. I m-must check on the books."

Armani raised an eyebrow at the cowardly form, too nervous to get up off the floor. Julian, now in the elevator, advanced toward the man. Armani pulled him back. "Not now, Jules."

As the elevator closed, Julian remarked, with a vicious sneer, "Oh, don't worry. I'll be sure to check on your books." All the while, the piercing alarm continued to sound throughout The Tower.

As soon as Armani and Julian disappeared, Callis ran to the spiral staircase, weaving between those standing around. Grimacing, he hurled himself over the railing.

He fell rapidly, his long, vivid blue jacket trailing behind. "Ugh!" Callis grunted, as he painfully slammed, in a perfect crouch, onto the thick glass floor below. The landing would have shattered the bones of any average being. But Callis was way beyond average.

Powerful energy surging, he opened his brown eyes. Pushing upright, he dashed for the southwest elevator, noting its rapid descent. He pounded brutally at the silver button, ordering it to stop. The red numbers refused to rise; however, the familiar chime sounded and the crystal, star-shaped fixture ignited above the elevator to his left. *Thank Ravenna.* Callis descended rapidly through the shaft. Suddenly, it slowed to a complete stop, between floors 6 and 7. "NO!" He slammed his fist on the door.

A holographic screen appeared on the back wall of the elevator.

Tavokk crouched, ready to sprint when the elevator reached ground level. But much to his consternation, the doors remained closed. A static sound issued from behind him. Peering out, there was nobody in sight on this lowest level, yet he noted multitudes of people cramming the hallways on levels as far up as he could see.

The elevator's back wall revealed a middle-aged man, with silver streaking his combed-back hair. A seer, at the top of The Tower's authoritative chain, he appeared irritated and cross. The shrieking of alarms slowly ceased.

"Attention. This is not a drill," the man intoned. His voice projected a sharp growl. "As you all know, I am Vander Boniface of the Velvet Order. There has been a breach of Tower security. All personnel shall remain in, or return to, their rooms. Otherwise, proceed to the nearest station on your current floor.

"The main gates and entrance are in lockdown. For your safety,

Lord Cain has ordered all elevators shut down. After this message, occupied elevators will open briefly on the nearest floors to allow exit, then shall reenter immediate lockdown. Again, please refrain from boarding any open elevator. Report to the nearest stations and stand by for further instruction."

The holographic screens vanished, replaced again by the glowing red warning messages, running horizontal and cycling:

CODE: 7. 51. 72. B D...Intruder Alert...Repeat...Intruder Alert...

And the horrendous, shrieking alarm returned.

℘)Ⅽℛ

Armani and Julian, trapped midway between floors 131 and 132, were relieved once the holographic screen disappeared, and they exited on floor 132. They strode out into The Archives, thankful that they had not been sent uselessly down to floor 131.

Julian grinned. "Good Karma."

"What do you mean?"

Julian shrugged. "We have to put up with so much crap around here. We deserve to be let off on the right level." His grin widened, ready for a little fun. He dashed from one room to the other, Armani in hot pursuit. The culprit was gone, but the wreckage declared his recent rampage. As Julian continued his fruitless search, the grin turned to a mask of malice. He kicked a cart into a nearby wall where its books scattered, joining the rubble in every direction.

Realizing that The Archives' intruder had escaped, the duo rushed back to the elevators, which had already been put into lockdown, refusing to open, even for them.

Armani crossed graceful arms, suppressing his rage. "Here we are, my friend."

"Goddammit!" Julian screamed, pounding a useless fist on the impervious door.

As though in response, a faint, rupturing explosion sounded far below. Vibrant, green light reflected up into the room, continuing upward throughout the entire Tower. Armani and Julian turned to one another, consternation written on their faces.

Tavokk bounced breathlessly on the balls of his feet, as the elevator came back to life. It moved two final feet, coming to a proper standstill and opening its doors. As soon as the doors had parted enough for his agile form to chivy through, Tavokk broke out, sprinting for the access pillar. A few steps from the elevator, he felt the tremendous concussion of an explosion, just floors above.

His face paled, mind flickering back to Armani, Julian, and Callis, all within The Tower's walls.

Behind him sounded another nearer explosion. Green light flooded the room, illuminating the wall before him. *Shit! I am going to die.* His pace rose to an impossible speed.

After what seemed an eternity, Tavokk reached the pillar. Tattoos ablaze, his energies merged with the heavy marble, wrenching the hidden door open. He slid inside, standing on the narrow, circular ledge and using his energies to close the camouflaged pillar doorway. Stepping to the ladder, he charged down the vertical shaft.

ᏕᎧᏟᎡ

Callis growled as the holographic screen vanished. He flinched as the god-awful alarm and red code warnings started up again. Impatient, he stood inches before the doors, the tip of his nose grazing their slick surface.

As the elevator shifted to its final position, he shoved his way out, irritated by all of the somns who had not yet returned to their rooms. The only way down, other than an elevator, was the endless corridor spiraling the entire periphery of the Tower. *Preposterous. Six floors will take forever!*

He turned back to the elevator, whose doors were nearly closed. "Stop them!" Callis cried, shoving brutally through those standing in his way. He reached it too late.

He noted the *01* above the southwest elevator with a venomous expression. That very elevator had assisted the Intruder in his or her escape. Approaching it, Callis pounded the button, willing it to open. Already in lockdown, it refused. He pounded the door violently, leaving an obvious dent, knowing he would be later reprimanded.

Brushing fiery locks from his eyes, he pulled on a pair of black leather gloves, flexing his fingers in preparation. Callis's muscles began to bulge, tattoos glowing beneath his jacket.

An explosion of energy fired outward from Callis as he reached forward and violently wrenched the elevator door. It gave with a shattering roar, cracking the thick glass and blowing the emergency door. Sparks and energies flew in a crescendo of brilliant green light, up the elevator shaft and throughout The Tower.

A woman screamed from the lobby, joined by other frightened and accusatory shrieks. Somns fled the area, throwing looks of accusation from a safe distance, as the perpetrator planned his next move.

Throwing himself into the shaft, Callis scrambled down the maintenance ladder, more frustrated with each step.

Ripping his white leather belt from black-denim loops, he roped the elevator cables and jumped back, plummeting toward the ground-level elevator. Crashing in a perfect crouch onto the emergency exit, he yanked it aside and jumped down into the elevator, panting, as rivulets of sweat ran down his face.

A second, booming explosion erupted as Callis destroyed the "indestructible" metal doors.

As he jumped from the shattered elevator, he spotted movement. He raced to the far wall, looking frantically around. The perpetrator was nowhere to be found. "I know I saw him!" he roared, in anger.

"I know that was him!" Callis slammed his iron fist into the marble pillar beside him. Gasping for breath, he dropped to a single knee, leaning up against it.

℘◯℃

Tavokk, scurrying down the ladder in the dark vertical shaft, stiffened as he heard the roar emitted by who could be none other than his dear friend, Callis Morgandy. A harsh chill raced through him. He looked upward, wide-eyed, as a puff of dirt showered down on him. Tavokk shook his head roughly, shaking the grime from his hair, though careful not to send his shades flying.

Nearing the bottom, he jumped from the ladder, falling the short distance to the ground. He landed with a splash in the slick layer of moisture and muck. He could hear the rushing of the river just beyond the marble walls of the underground passageway.

Running through the high-ceilinged passageway, his thin-soled boots pattered rhythmically over the grime-coated cobblestones as he scurried toward the second ladder.

The dim light from the wall sconces, which had earlier felt warm and welcoming, now cast an eerie feeling, like a bad omen.

Colliding with the metal table, sending the soiled playing cards shamed to the filthy ground, he reached the ladder that would lead him to his official escape, out into the open air and familiar rain of the city.

Tavokk scurried up the slick ladder rungs, still disgusted by their texture beneath his flesh. Rainwater from above spilled down over him, heavier now than it was at his initial arrival. Looking upward, water falling over his shades, he could see the opening.

Finally, he reached the opening and heaved his body up out of the dark shaft and onto the uppermost platform of the black, glittering fountain. Heart still racing, he climbed down, making his way to the second level, and then leaping to the lowest, widest ring. Making his way down the steps, he threw one last half-glance toward the colossal Tower. He ran as fast as he could to the northeast, careful not to slip and fall on the blue granules covering the enormous hill.

At the bottom of the hill, a streetlamp had already begun to flicker. *Thank you, Eve!* Deep in gratitude, he drank of the cool night air. Descending the hill, he met the flickering light. The rain parted and he vanished.

12: Sailing Into The Darkness

Rhyus passed through the metal gate into the dark alleyway, now so familiar in the short time of his stay. Tattered clothing still fluttered from lines strung high above, as leaves skittered in the subtle breeze toward the city beyond.

Since his earlier sojourn, it had begun to drizzle. It was strange considering Lux Lumetia rarely saw anything other than a blue, sunlit sky. During his stay, Rhyus had never even spotted a cloud. *I haven't been here more than a few days, yet it feels like I've been here a lifetime,* he recounted.

While packing, Rhyus had absolutely no plan of attack. He just knew that the robed man in his dream was right. He had to leave. Walking toward the open city, he felt the call of the sea. *I need a boat.*

Rhyus, following a shimmering, white path along the northern shoreline, moved quickly, though careful to avoid attention. *There must be a port nearby. This city is a collection of islands after all.*

He hoped to find a dock nearby, before the usual morning activity started. Further east, a port would be too secure, and any vessel found there would be far more costly and complicated than what he needed. But ultimately, he must disappear before, god forbid, Venn could hunt him down.

Then, through the light rain, he spotted them. Ship masts jutting above the dark water. Gratified, he walked faster, though still careful to avoid suspicion.

Rhyus stopped dead in his tracks. *I need a watch to navigate. At sea with no chronometer, I couldn't figure my longitude. I would just float aimlessly, with no sense of time, to god knows where.* Noting the exact location of the port, Rhyus turned toward North Market. From sparse information he had gleaned, the docks ran a double shift, one group leaving before sunrise, the other, late morning. He had to find what he needed and return between those times.

Zipping his sweatshirt and throwing up his hood, Rhyus glared at the sky, *Damn, I hate rain!*

Nearing the strip, he saw women with bright baskets dragging children from stand to stand. A few clusters of men stood in desultory groups, gossiping.

After a fruitless search, Rhyus sought assistance from a copper-haired young woman standing behind several woven baskets of vegetables. A charismatic young man, a few years older, lazed on a chair behind her.

"Pardon me, miss."

Loose curls bouncing, her honey eyes glowed at him from beneath long, dark lashes. Her painted lips turned upward, delighted to see the wayward stranger.

Momentarily losing his line of thought, Rhyus grinned. He shook his head. "I'm sorry." Looking back into her golden eyes, he asked, "Do you know where I might possibly find a watch?"

With a surreptitious smile, she leaned close. "There," she whispered.

He followed her finger to a man with odd glasses and a navy blue coat, far too large for his body. Taking a few steps in that direction, Rhyus turned to thank her, but she had already been drawn away by a surly woman with a whiny, fit-throwing daughter yanking at her empty arm.

A shame, Rhyus's grin returned. He waited while the man crouched before some young boys, convincing them that their mothers should buy the knickknacks that he held before them. Failing the sale, he began to walk awkwardly away, bowlegged and waddling.

"Excuse me, sir!" Rhyus shouted, from behind. The man did not acknowledge. Rhyus quickened his pace.

"Pardon me, sir."

The man stopped in his tracks, shifting the entire left side of his body around to face Rhyus. "Why Hellooo, sonny!"

"Uh, hello, sir."

"What can ol' Archie do ya for today?" The man grinned, awkward and anything but genuine.

"Well, I hear that you may have something to sell that would be of use to me."

"Ah, but of course! What exactly is it that ya are lookin' for, boy?" Asked the caricature of a man.

"Well, a watch actually." Rhyus wondered whether this just might have been a practical joke. "But if I was misinformed I under—"

"But of course I have watches for ya! Ya've absolutely been correc-it-ively informed. I got as many as ya could possibly be interested in buyin'!"

Without another word, the man turned, beckoning Rhyus to follow. Passing by, Rhyus grinned as he caught the copper-haired girl's gaze. She blushed, looking down, embarrassed that he had caught her observing him.

Walking behind a stand, Archie adjusted his glasses.

"Wench, get me my special case!" he shouted, to an old crone sitting in a chair behind the stand.

Retrieving a tattered briefcase with golden clasps, she handed it to him. Rhyus wondered again whether the copper-haired girl had been toying with him by sending him to speak to this man, Archie. He looked along the market strand, though he knew she was too far away to see.

Without thanking the woman, the merchant turned his attention immediately back to Rhyus.

"Now sonny, I've many from which to choose. Ima sure ya'll find one to fitch your pleasing."

Agghk! Rhyus startled, at the horribly disturbing, snaggle-toothed grin. The image nearly made him shiver. However, Archie did not comment, so Rhyus assumed he must not have noticed.

"Wad'd'ya tink?" The garbled question took Rhyus a moment to comprehend. As Rhyus viewed the briefcase's contents, he did give the man some credit. He indeed had a multitude of watches to choose from.

Each watch was individually wrapped in a thin, durable case. As Rhyus rummaged, Archie kept a careful eye on him, thinking at any second he might grab one and run for it.

"Perfect." Rhyus chose a watch with a chronometer in its rectangular face. Just what he required for the upcoming journey.

"I'll take this one!" he gushed his enthusiasm, at the find.

As soon as the words left Rhyus's mouth, Archie slammed the briefcase shut, his face transformed with a fresh, keen brightness. "Brilliant! A beaut, ain't she?"

"Uh, yeah. Yeah, she is." Rhyus lowered a skeptical brow, at the chimerical salesman.

He shoved the briefcase back into the woman's arms and quoted an exorbitant price. Rhyus haggled, but in the interest of time, he grudgingly overpaid so he could get back before the next wave of fishermen arrived at port.

Passing the market's northern end, Rhyus felt a hand on his arm.

The copper-haired girl stood beside him with the same pleasant smile.

"Sorry about that." Her smile widened, as she removed her delicate grip, blushing at her own audacity.

Taken once more by her stunning, delicate features, he couldn't help grinning back. Despite the rainy overcast, her copper hair shone brilliantly, as did her beautiful, honey eyes.

"It's all right. I really did need a watch, after all."

"Would you, perhaps, be interested in grabbing a cup of mallow or dreg with me later this morning? I must tend to the stand until ten thirty, but after that I am free." A hopeful look in her clear eyes overshadowed the shyness in her voice.

"Well...I would love to, but..." Rhyus's eyes shifted, breaking contact between them.

"Oh no. I understand." She looked away. "You have someone." Rhyus could not tell what disquieted him more, the embarrassment on her face or the disappointment in her voice.

"No, no. It's not that. I have to leave for a handful of days, perhaps longer. I must leave port by ten. But maybe..."

"Once you return?" Hope radiated from her golden eyes.

"Yes. I'd love that. Maybe I may find you here upon my return. But I don't have the slightest idea how long I will be gone."

"Well, you certainly have something here to return for." Copper looked down, demurely.

"Well then." Rhyus swallowed, regretting that he had to go. "I already look forward to it."

After brief reflection, she looked up again. "By the way, my name is Cassandra. Cassandra Hollis."

"Rhyus." He wished he had a more eloquent way of introducing himself.

"Well, *Rhyus*. Safe travels and an early return." Cassandra's liquid eyes touched his one last time as, tossing her long curls behind her, she turned back to the vegetable stand.

Rhyus watched her elegant movements, denim cuffs darkened from the rain-soaked pavement. She turned with one last smile. Rhyus couldn't help a wide, crooked grin. He lowered his head and made toward the shore.

Fumbling to fasten the silver buckle of his watch, Rhyus gaped at the time. The correct time already set, it read 8:45. *Shit!* Rhyus took off sprinting.

Gasping for breath, he saw masts growing high against the blackening sky. Ships, large and small, came into view as he ran past white buildings to his right. Hearing distant voices, he ducked, panting, into a secluded cove.

The boats towered over him. They looked bare with sails neatly furled away, awaiting departure. As Rhyus followed a particularly large mast upward, he squinted against the rain, now dropping with relentless fervor.

Great! I chose the only day in a frikkin' million years that it decides to rain in Lux Lumetia! Well, I need a boat, but what kind? Rhyus walked the lengthy, crystal dock examining boats, each moored to its capstan by a transparent, blue hawser. *This won't do. This one is too large...too small.* Anxious, he knew that haste was in order.

As he searched for a ship, Rhyus couldn't help the ache in the pit of his stomach when he looked far out to the Dark Water. He remembered Venn's ominous words in the back of his mind, "Suicidal sailors, reckless..."

Perfect. Rhyus, at last, stood before an average-to-large, two-master with an elegant canopy protecting its stern. Two large lanterns at bow and stern promised ample light. Kneeling, Rhyus fumbled at the unfamiliar knot. *Now...how the hell am I going to sail this thing?*

₭)р

Marion tore through the dark alleyway toward the open city. Pausing to scan the area, she was gratified to note that the Caulder District was as abandoned as usual.

She thought quickly. *Rhyus will want to get as far away as possible...wait.* Remembering the times she herself had planned to leave, she realized with dismay...*He is headed for a port.*

He must go to the only port on this shoreline...Then again, who knows with that boy. He does some rather unintelligent things. She squinted in thought. *The kicker will fall, only if Rhyus has heard of another port. But that would require quite a trip, and he will be hurrying. It's the Crystal Harbor. If I am wrong, I may never find him.*

Marion prayed fervently, *Please be there. Don't be gone yet!*

She ran quickly, as the drizzling rain soaked her flawless hair and clothing in no time. Although hurried, she admired the shimmering quality of the silvery path, despite the shadows and rain.

She continued swiftly to the secluded Crystal Harbor. She had forgotten how much she loved to sit here, with her feet in the clear water, when she needed to get away. That was long ago, when she was first taken to Umbra Halls. *I wonder where Vincent is now,* Marion thought, about the somn who had first brought her to Umbra Halls, Vincent KyVeerah. Then, her thoughts turned to Venn. *Will he be all right without me?* A light twinge of worry met her as she recalled his living habits before she settled in.

Then she saw him, crouched before the crystal capstan of a charming boat. She recognized his black hood with the parchment-colored streetlamp and distant city on it. He had worn that sweatshirt when Venn and she first discovered him in Lux Lumetia. Rhyus didn't notice Marion's silent approach in the quickening rain.

"Rhyus?" Marion's words were overwhelmed by the clash of waves against the rocking boats.

"Rhyus!" she shouted. Startled, he dropped the hawser into the water.

"Whose boat is that, Rhyus?" Marion frowned, in accusation.

Rhyus looked up with a growl, resentment and frustration all too clear. He dropped onto his stomach, forcefully slinging his arm over the dock's edge to retrieve the blue rope from the rough sea. Grasping hold, he pushed into a kneeling stance as the sky opened up, beating down on him.

Refusing to let Rhyus get in a word first, she shouted forcefully, over the heavy rain, "I know what you are doing. I am coming with you!"

Rhyus tried to interrupt, but she continued. "I've made up my mind. You can't stop me!"

Marion stood still, a twinge of apprehension sparking within her.

Rhyus looked up, shouting back. "Do you know how to sail?"

"Nope. You?"

"Not a chance." Rhyus shook his head. Slowly, a rogue smile played across his face. "This might not be pretty, but it ought to be interesting."

"Wait. Have you thought this through? Somns go mad out there. The Darkness gets inside them. Most never return!" Marion wore a shocked expression, as she pulled her matted hair into a ponytail.

"Yes?" Rhyus answered quizzically.

"You are letting me come? Just like that?"

"Well," he shrugged, "you said it would be futile to argue." Though half-glad Marion had decided to come, Rhyus couldn't shake a vague feeling of ambivalence.

A sudden flash from his dream appeared through the rain... Marion's entrancing black dress swaying as she crossed her legs elegantly, one in front of the other, as she made her way down the wooden aisle toward him. That dark, enthralling makeup and those long, slowly batting lashes…

Rhyus jerked his head away from her, peering out at the blackened sea. The sea had always seemed so blue, so light and transparent. Not today. Today it was solely a vivid reminder of his dreams. He could remember that stone shelf on which he had lain with the cold rain beating down and angry waves crashing all around. Only now, here, the rain fell warmly. And the waves rocked more gently in this present world. This world of reality.

Ignoring Rhyus's sudden, strange brooding, Marion chirped, "I didn't think you would give in so easily. You really are different from Venn."

Offended, Rhyus snapped, "Do *not* compare me to him."

Seeing the hurt look on Marion's face, he abjured, "I'm sorry. Speaking of which, is Venn OK with this? Are *you* OK with leaving *him*?"

"Oh, he will be furious. But if he cares about me, as I know he does, he will understand and let me make my own decisions. Who knows fate? It may not be long until I see him again."

"*If* you do." Rhyus added, just softly enough to be muffled by the rain.

"What?"

"Oh, nothing." He shook his head.

Marion laughed.

"What is so funny?"

"He is going to blame you." She smiled.

"Yes. He will." Rhyus smirked, in return. "What are we waiting for?" He helped Marion onto the boat, and then hoisted himself aboard.

"Well, miss. How do we get this thing moving? We need to be away before the second shift starts arriving. *If* they are crazy enough to endure these conditions." He winked.

Laughing agreeably, she moved closer so they wouldn't have to shout. "Well, this boat, *Quinton Paris*, is from the Philosopher's Collection.

"I thought you said you didn't know how to sail."

"But I didn't say that I didn't know *about* boats now, did I?" She beamed.

Rhyus pondered a response.

"It doesn't require knowing how to sail to get this boat going."

Rhyus was perplexed.

"The Philosopher's Collection are automatic, I suppose you could say."

Rhyus still looked lost.

"I'm just saying, I think I can figure this thing out. A friend once took me out on a Philosopher. He taught me how to control it, but it has been a while." At that, Marion headed to the bow. He followed aimlessly behind.

Marion fiddled with some buttons, causing the sails to unfurl. Another button drew the large canopy over two rows of cushioned bench seats at the stern.

Rhyus gaped. Marion, with a single finger, pushed his jaw closed. Laughing quietly, she turned her attention back to the command station. In no time, she had the boat heading to open sea.

Marion grinned at Rhyus.

"I could never have managed without you." He touched the side of her face, looking down at her. "Thank you." Then he playfully pressed her face to the side.

Marion brightened. His playful manner assured her that he was glad to have her company. "Where to, mate?"

"Might I suggest east?"

"Aye, aye, captain. Off into the blackness we go."

"Into *The Darkness*, you mean," was Marion's ominous reply. "So. Tell me about this *friend*."

"It has been a long time." She shook her head. "We don't see or talk to each other anymore. It's complicated."

"Fair enough." Leaning on the rail, Rhyus traced a finger over one of the letters. "Quinton Paris? Must be an important guy."

"He *was*. Got himself killed in a brawl a year ago. He was interesting. I met him a couple of times with Venn. Venn knows a lot of somns."

Marion leaned against the rail next to Rhyus. They both stared down as a long line of wooden oars, just above the water, rowed untiringly.

"So, where exactly is this boat taking us?"

"To the stars." Marion tried to keep a straight face, but couldn't.

"Nice."

"Well, you better hope it's somewhere good or you're gonna pay."

"Oh really? Is that a threat?"

"Maybe. But look ahead. What do you see?"

"Umm, black."

"Exactly. A little unnerving?"

A shiver ran down Rhyus's spine, and not without Marion seeing.

"As I said. Exactly."

They both looked out into The Darkness. Rhyus exhaled. "Well, shit."

13: A Long-Awaited Visitor

"Venn!" a voice shouted frantically.

His eyes opened. It was just a dream. But as his eyes readjusted to the black and blue images of his bedroom, an unsettled feeling continued to overwhelm him. Thick, knotted ropes of muscle dancing along his arms betrayed his anxiety, as he propped himself up in bed.

Venn moved his eyes to the black, stained door. He watched it for a long while, eyes concentrating and his insides churning over a feeling he could not quite fathom.

Climbing from the bed, he slipped into a dark pair of denims, low on his hips from the lack of a belt. After stretching, to relieve the tension across his heavily muscled torso, he slipped a sleeveless, black shirt over his head and made his way to the door.

The house was exceptionally quiet. The clock in the main hallway read 9:47. Though he thought it wasteful for everyone to sleep in, he did enjoy the peace and quiet.

In the kitchen, he pulled a container of fresh assorted berries from the refrigerator and made his way to the den. Shutting the door quietly, he set the container by his chair and moved to the dark wooden bookshelf beside the fireplace. He skimmed the colored book spines for something intriguing to quiet his restless mind.

His eyes landed on a burnt orange spine, a book entitled *Curiosity Killed the Cat: Which of Nine Lives Matters?* Venn loved all things philosophical. He could contentedly read books on philosophy for all eternity. This book, by Silas Salazar, was one of Venn's personal favorites. He had also written another of Venn's favorites entitled *The Ship Sinks, but It Is Our Grave*.

Venn flipped through the book as its pages' golden edges caught the flickering firelight. He kicked back in his favorite chair, feet up, and began to read. A faint smile formed on his lips, and light shone behind his rectangular framed glasses, while he lost himself in the world of philosophical theory. Eventually, breaking his attention, he glanced at the ancient clock over the desk. The time read 12:56.

He had still not heard a sound from either Rhyus or Marion. *I do get wrapped up in my reading. So, who knows?* He scrunched his toes on the ornamental rug and stretched. Seeing the empty container on the side table, his stomach growled. Marion should have lunch ready by now.

Crossing the den to the large, open hallway, yet still hearing no sign of Rhyus or Marion, Venn frowned.

Marion's cooking is far better than anything I can scavenge. How could she still be sleeping?

Venn wandered by the laundry, biding his time. Rummaging through a basket of neatly folded clothes for a pair of pale blue denims and a dark red, short-sleeved shirt, he glanced at the clothes he had tossed about, and shrugged knowing Marion would fold them again.

Heading to the shower, he surveyed the bathroom's new theme of crimson, black, and gold. *Definitely a Marion touch*. He smiled. Tossing his glasses aside, he climbed into the hot shower, as steam rolled out over the shower walls.

How can those two just sleep in all the time, he thought reproachfully, while rinsing his hair. *Honestly, I don't see why Vincent is so worried about me keeping an eye on them. That boy in particular. Vincent must know I will be half-tempted to kill the kid by time he decides to pick him up. OK, more than half tempted.*

After drying and tastefully styling his long black hair, Venn dropped the towel on the floor and pulled the shirt carefully over his head. On the front was his favorite chess piece, a black knight. Leaving his other clothes sprawled about the bathroom, he made his way back up to the kitchen with lunch on his mind once again. *Still no Rhyus or Marion!*

Just then, Venn spotted the crystal chessboard resting on the table. *Ready for a rematch already, is she?* He grinned crookedly, eyes dazzling. *Wait*. Noting the pale bronze sheet of paper tucked under the edge of the game board, he recognized the bold red script that read *Venn*. His grin faded as quickly as it had appeared.

He walked to the table and grasped the bronzed paper. Sliding it from under the board, he unfolded it with a single hand. Using his other hand, he adjusted the rectangular frames of his glasses and pushed his hair back out of the way. The letter read:

Dear Venn,

Now don't panic. I have everything under control. Rhyus has decided to take a leave of absence. But don't worry. I'm going after him. We will be back before long.

She can't be serious. Venn put his fingertips to his brow.

There is plenty of food in the fridge to tide you over until I return. You should be set for at least a week. They are labeled, so you will know what to eat first. I also put reheating instructions on them. So don't be afraid to actually use the oven. Trust me, it isn't really that difficult.

Blue Ravenna. Venn shook his head.

I did laundry last night and folded it all. The basket is to the left of the dryer. All you have to do is put everything away in its proper place. IF you decide to do any laundry while I am away, just remember—

To wash-
  1. Separate the colors.
  2. Use only ONE scoop of sillsand.
  3. Wash on cold, normal wash.

To dry-
  1. Use normal dry.
  2. Clean out the lint vent after use.
  3. Take out the load as soon as it is done. You know how fussy you are when your clothes are wrinkled, don't you?

Oh, and please try not to drink TOO much. You know it isn't good for your health.

Love, Mae

P.S. That melon mess had better be cleaned up before I return!!

After reading Marion's note, Venn stared blankly at it, unsure how to feel or how to react.

Then the frustration kicked in. Crumpling the paper, he hurled it across the room. *Who the hell does she think she is? I can damn well take care of myself. I have been around plenty long, and I by no means need someone hovering over my every need! Besides, where the hell do they think they are going to go?*

Venn gave a half-glance toward the broad splatter of bright red pulp on the adjacent wall, dried now. With a look of disgust, he stormed out, in a customary Venn sort of way, moving from the kitchen to the den. Repudiating Marion's request, he headed straight for an ornamental, glass bottle. Filling a glass with an excessive amount of deep amber liquid, he dropped into his soft leather chair. The surface, cool against his angry burning flesh, sent a shiver down his spine.

As soon as he crossed his feet on the large ottoman, an appalling realization hit him. His brilliant eyes widened behind his glasses... *Vincent!*

Vincent will be arriving at any moment now. He did say tonight, did he not? How in the world do I tell him that both Rhyus and Marion have run away? True, I haven't seen Vincent in a while, but knowing him, this is not going to be good.

Venn kicked himself upright. Nursing his drink, he paced the edge of the luxurious carpet.

He clenched his free hand. *Vincent is going to massacre a mob when he discovers them gone.* He sighed, stuck between a rock and a hard place. *I must go and find them. No! I have to trust Marion. And I can't search for them until Vincent has come. If he arrives to an abandoned house, there will be hell to pay. Besides, who knows exactly when he will show? He claimed he will arrive this evening, but he is full of surprises.*

Venn's pacing ceased as he collapsed back down into his chair. *This is preposterous. I have to find them, but I can't leave. What the hell am I supposed to do until Vincent gets here?*

He picked up the empty container from earlier and stormed back to the kitchen. From the fridge, Venn grabbed one of the few items without handwritten labels. *Nothing like leftovers.* He trudged to the table and slammed the container and silverware down, and without caring enough to heat the contents, ate stubbornly from the new container.

Once finished, he sat motionless for several long minutes, elbows propped on the table, head in his hands. Then, from nowhere, he hurried to the sink where he guzzled three glasses of water without stopping for air. Catching his breath, he threw the dishes into the sink and escaped once more to his usual getaway for the hundredth time that morning.

In his study once again, Venn lumbered to the desk on the far wall, running an appreciative hand over the smooth, dark wood in admiration. It had been unused for far too long. From the lowest drawer, he removed a thick, leather-bound book. It was a gift from a family member years ago. He had filled it with philosophical theories and concepts of his own; however, it had rested untouched within that drawer since before Marion came to Umbra Halls. *Perhaps if I write out my quandary, an answer will come to mind.* He flexed his fingers, calculating.

Opening the journal, he flipped to the most recently written page. A smile of anticipation touched his features. Venn pulled the top drawer open and hefted a sleek, black pen with thin golden rings running down its entirety. This pen had been a gift along with the journal. As thoughts began to stir, he placed the tip to the top of the next empty page and began writing.

His exceptional script elegantly filled the page, golden ink matching the previously written pages. Though he had never abandoned his reading, he had forgotten his own fondness for the act of writing. *Foolish,* he declared, to himself.

Without intent, he lost himself in his writing, unaware of the rapid passage of time. After several pages of his deepest thoughts, he stretched. The clock's dark hands now read 6:14.

Where could they be now? Has Marion found him? And where the hell is Vincent?

Leaving the journal open, Venn wandered back to the kitchen. He devoured another unheated container, not tasting a single bite in his worry over Marion. Again, he guzzled several more glasses of water before returning to the den.

Dropping back into his chair, he grabbed his book and picked up where he had left off. When the clock reached nine thirty, Venn fumed at Vincent's absence. *Damn his hide! Is he coming tonight or not? If I had any clue he'd be this late, I could have had Rhyus and Marion back by now!*

He slammed the open book down and began pacing the rug once more. It was a surprise he had not worn the rug clean through to the old floorboards by now.

Eventually, pouring a strong drink, he lit a fire in the fireplace and settled into his chair. He propped his feet in their usual position. After a few more drinks, his blood warmed and he closed his eyes, trying to relax his racing mind.

℘↺

A loud thud pulled Venn instantly to consciousness. He blinked. *I must have fallen asleep.* And a deep, distracting sleep it had been.

The once soothing light of the fire now reflected wildly in his startled blue eyes, as brilliantly as the flames of a burning ship out on the sea's blue waters. He craned his neck toward the door.

Moments passed. Still peering around the side of the chair, body twisted, he listened intently for another sound. *I must have imagined it.* He faced back into the flickering flames that danced, glowing in their hypnotic hues of blue, red, orange, and yellow.

Without warning, a tremendous crash reverberated down the hallway. Alarmed, Venn's wide eyes tried to see through the door. Jumping up, he threw it open, looking frantically around. Then, barely catching his eye, a shadow interrupted the dim light spilling under the kitchen door. Adrenaline coursing through him, Venn crept toward the kitchen, grabbing the slender, crystal vase from beside Marion's antique chair.

He stood outside the door for a split second, and then he heaved it open, blue eyes blazing, vase raised, ready to strike.

"Eeek!" A startled voice shrieked.

Surveying the scene, Venn erupted in fury. "Vin-*cent!*" White and clear crystal pieces lay scattered all across the room. Lowering his arm, Venn knelt, carefully picking up a single, shabby piece with a crown at its uppermost point. Cradling the tattered piece in his gentle hand, he stood, glaring down at the apprehensive figure before him.

The crystal chessboard had been shattered beyond recognition.

"What have you *done?*" Venn roared. Raising his arm, he hurled the vase across the room where it shattered with an earsplitting crash, adding more crystal shards to those already present. Now, the entire room glittered with the shattered remains.

Crouching, KyVeerah raised a hand, warding off both the infuriated Venn and the crystal projectiles ricocheting in every possible direction. Once the last piece had settled, he rose, surveying the disaster that they had created.

"Huh. You would think crystal from the Lux canals would be sturdier." KyVeerah rested his chin in his hand, mimicking actual contemplation.

Animosity shot through Venn from head to toe. Flinging the partial king piece to the table, he closed the distance between KyVeerah and himself.

KyVeerah warily stepped back. Dodging around the table, he made a run for it. He shrieked as Venn caught his shirt collar, reining him in, gasping and choking. Readjusting his grip, Venn held him firmly by the neck from behind. KyVeerah tried a futile escape, which only resulted in his running hopelessly in place, hands scratching desperately at the air before him.

"Now Venn, don't be hasty," KyVeerah gasped. "Accidents happen."

"*You* are the problem. Accidents *always* happen whenever you are around!" Venn enjoyed a sadistic pleasure at KyVeerah's obvious discomfort.

"Come now. You don't want our darling Rhyus and Marion to walk in and see us acting like savages now, do you? They might. After all, there has been quite a ruckus!" KyVeerah shut up, wincing at the electric blue flare from Venn's eyes. He had hoped to get across to Venn before being beaten like a dirty rug.

Venn's color plummeted from its deep crimson to pale white. The mention of Rhyus and Marion had caught him off guard. He released his hand from KyVeerah's neck, causing him to somersault, while tripping and pulling a kitchen chair down with him.

Sprawling on the ground, he collected himself quickly, holding the chair as a shield.

Venn growled, "I need a drink." He abruptly departed, leaving KyVeerah on the floor with a puzzled look upon his face. KyVeerah's expression lifted immediately, as the mention of alcohol registered in his mind.

Discarding the chair, KyVeerah stumbled to his feet. Though unheard, he babbled, filled with anticipation, "Did you say drink? I love drinks!" Following Venn, KyVeerah saw him spitefully rip a handful of leaves from the overhanging tree, as he stomped toward the den. Disregarding Venn's current resentment toward him, he continued to follow Venn through the door.

As Venn lumbered to the bar, KyVeerah attempted to make his presence known. He waved his arm in the air. "Umm, Venn..." Venn ignored him.

KyVeerah tried again. "Actually, I am feeling quite parched. You wouldn't, by chance, happen to have any Antum Regal? Would you?"

Irritated, Venn righted the bottle, which he was going to pour for himself. He set the bottle down, glaring at KyVeerah. However, as the cogs in Venn's head began to turn, a wicked grin snaked across his slender lips.

"Antum Regal?" Venn asked, as KyVeerah still stood cautiously near the door—in case the need arose for a quick escape. "Yes," he said, smiling enigmatically. "I do believe that I have that."

He crouched, opening a wooden cupboard, well stocked with a wide assortment of alcoholic beverages. He dug through various colored bottles, in one of several concealed refrigerators, until his hand fell on the object of his search.

"Oh look," he said, scathingly. "There happens to be only one left."

KyVeerah perked up eagerly. But Venn removed the cap from the bottle and pressed it to his lips, chugging its contents in large gulps.

KyVeerah's jaw dropped. "Uh, V-Venn," he stammered, "could you possibly pour me a wee bit?" He pinched his left eye closed, gesturing with his thumb and index finger.

Ignoring him, Venn continued to drain its contents. KyVeerah pleaded, stepping toward the bar, forgetting his previous precautions.

Reaching the bar, KyVeerah stretched a hand out for the vanishing rum. Venn turned an inhospitable shoulder to him before extending his arm. His fingers pressed KyVeerah's face, scrunching his features while keeping him at bay.

Around Venn's hand, KyVeerah mumbled, "Please, Venn. This isn't fair, I promise not to break anything ever again."

Venn, unable to believe the words that had just come out of KyVeerah's mouth, paused in short, rolling his eyes. Then, he carried on drinking.

For quite some time they continued, KyVeerah becoming more agitated as Venn, who had neglected to consider the unintended consequences of torturing KyVeerah in this way, steadily succumbed to the effects of the strong liquor. At last, Venn slammed the bottle onto the bar. His head lolled on his shoulders, as he looked at KyVeerah with a mocking expression.

In a forlorn voice, KyVeerah asked, "Not even a drop left for me?"

Venn snatched the empty bottle off the bar, shoving it into KyVeerah's hands. Satisfied, he staggered to his lounge chair before the fireplace.

Shaking the empty bottle, KyVeerah moped, "Too cruel, Venn. Too cruel." He rummaged through the bar in search of another bottle. *There must be one somewhere.*

Out of the blue, amidst his perversely elaborate inspection, KyVeerah asked, "Where are Rhyus and Marion? A pretty quiet bunch, eh? They can't be sleeping already? No one's that slothful. Not even me, and that's saying something." KyVeerah nodded, agreeing with his own self-assessment.

Slurred words came from across the room. "I hath shou."

"What was that, my dear? Didn't quite catch that," KyVeerah derided. He wondered to himself, *I hath shou...I hathe shoe...I hate you!*

"Aha!" KyVeerah exclaimed, proud he had solved the puzzle. Then, realization sunk in. "Aww..." he sulked.

Though the hands of the grandfather clock were reflected in Venn's besotted eyes, he could not focus on them. As he struggled to discern the time, KyVeerah continued rummaging under the bar.

Ah hell, KyVeerah thought. *Venn was telling the truth. That really was the last bottle.*

Glancing toward where Venn slouched, KyVeerah threw both of his arms up in the air, exclaiming for a second time, "Aha!"

"Idi-esh," Venn slurred.

Choosing to ignore Venn's impolite comment, KyVeerah grinned. *I may still have a bottle stashed in my room from my last visit!*

Looking at Venn once more, KyVeerah shook his head.

Sensing eyes on him, Venn snapped his own open and glared

intently back at KyVeerah. Or to be more accurate, he glared in his general direction considering Venn was hazily looking at two Vincent KyVeerahs.

"Oh dear goth, not two of hem," he drunkenly murmured.

"You aren't looking too good, my lovely. Perhaps we should get you off to bed for a little nappy."

"I am purhfectly cap-abuhl of gohing to bed myshelf."

"All right. Stand up then," KyVeerah challenged.

"I am, moron," Venn growled, still slumped into his soft leather chair.

Sighing, KyVeerah heaved Venn's arm over his shoulders and wrapped an arm around his waist. "Come on."

They staggered from the den, down the stairs, and into the east hallway toward Venn's bedroom.

Dear lord. Talk about dead weight. I'm going to need someone to carry me by the time we get him to his room and laid down. Maybe I should have asked Rhyus to help me. Where is that boy anyway? Marion too?

KyVeerah finally got Venn into bed. "There you go, big guy, all nice and snug. I have some errands to run, but I'll check on you in a few hours." He patted a hand gently upon the lustrous blue comforter, as he tucked it more tightly around Venn.

"Hwait," Venn slurred. Trying to prop up on an elbow, and failing, he fell back into the confinement of his lush bed. Gathering his energies, he sat back up, with no trouble this time. "We need to talk, Vincent." His voice was strangely sober, as he grasped KyVeerah's arm before he could get away.

More in control now, KyVeerah looked down into Venn's eyes, now aglow with brilliant, blue ice. He stated, with a haughty air, "It's KyVeerah, please. And whatever it is, I am most certain it can wait until I return. When you have…uh…returned to your usual jolly self." Escaping Venn's tight grasp, he waved his hand with a dismissive flourish.

"No. *Now*, Vincent," Venn demanded, in severe authority, slowly enunciating KyVeerah's first name.

"All right." KyVeerah tapped his fingers together. "It's your call. Talking sounds like a *marvelous* idea." He hid his apprehension beneath a veil of sarcasm.

For some time, Venn refrained from speaking, staring into space. The muscles framing his face were tight, and his eyes were as hard and solid as the crystal lining the Lux canals.

"Umm, Venn?" KyVeerah nervously waved his left hand in front of Venn's face.

"The kid's gone."

Startled, KyVeerah jumped back. Venn waited in silence, waiting for the realization to sink in.

KyVeerah's face fell stark white, as his eyes widened with horrified disbelief.

"What did you say?"

"Rhyus. He has gone. Who knows where?" Venn controlled his breath, willing himself to sobriety. He was preparing for the inevitable reaction.

"You lost him?" KyVeerah shouted, in accusation.

"Marion too."

It took another moment to settle in. KyVeerah's eyes widened even more. "You lost *both* of them?" His voice raised an octave.

"Technically, they ran away."

"What!"

"Rhyus first. Marion followed after in search of him."

"You are kidding me! This isn't really happening!" KyVeerah paced, enraged, at the end of Venn's bed.

"How, Venn?" KyVeerah threw his hands up. "How in the world did a recently waterlogged boy and a mere girl escape your hold? He wasn't even here three whole days!"

"It's not my fault!" Venn roared, in defense.

"*One Thing*, Venn. I asked you to do one thing for me. Even I have never screwed up this bad!"

Venn growled, "*First*, two years ago, you dropped Marion on my doorstep saying that it was only for a 'short while,' and *now* you pulled the *same* stunt with that godforsaken boy! And without a single, damn explanation!"

"Aargh!" Exasperated, KyVeerah threw his hands back into the air. "This is getting us nowhere! Besides, you are in no condition to go out on a hunt. We will go in the morning!" He turned, venting his rage at the window. "Dammit!"

He turned his head back toward Venn who, fading away, nodded his reluctant agreement.

Venn fell asleep. Taking this as his official dismissal, KyVeerah walked to the door, closing it behind him.

Familiar with Umbra Halls from the vast amount of time he had spent within its walls, he headed to the large bathroom just beyond Venn's room. Making himself at home, he showered and exited to the bedroom at the end of the hall, where the stained black woods were richly adorned in crimson as opposed to the blues of Venn's room.

He dropped onto a cushioned bench seat with many extravagant pillows resting against the wall.

KyVeerah sat a while, fuming at the loss of Rhyus and Marion, pondering and planning what steps that they would need to take when morning came. After a long time concentrating and holding his hand to his aching head, he lay back. *Oh well*, he finally sighed. *Let morning bring what it will. No use throwing away the moment, worrying about something that can't be fixed until tomorrow.*

Dropping down along the edge of the seat, he slid a hand under the pillows, searching. "Aha!" A grin spread ear-to-ear as he grasped the object of his search. "Brilliant. A bottle of Atrum's finest, Antum Regal, and nearly full."

Letting the towel fall, KyVeerah strode to the wardrobe, proudly viewing the display of his own clothing before him, which he had long missed. Grabbing something sleek and minimal, he headed for the bed.

He slid beneath the lavish comforter, taking several large swigs from the bottle, enjoying the smooth fire running down his throat. He had quite an interesting time preparing for this official meeting with Rhyus. It had also been exhausting. Before he could lift the bottle for another drink, he had fallen fast asleep. But he knew that a good night's sleep was in order, for tomorrow the hunt would begin.

14: The Underworld Stands Sentinel

Moving briskly down one of the many corridors, winding through The Dome of Atrum Unda, Callis Morgandy shook the omnipresent rain from his radiant, red hair and his long jacket, sending a shower to fly off in every direction. The immense Dome was a formidable structure, daunting in every aspect. Dark tinted windows and colossal, silver beams ran from their massive expanses at the ground to narrow at the peak where the beams still spanned over thirteen feet across.

The Dome, being the center of operations for Nyx Crucian and his subordinates, was the Underworld's high kingdom. Nyx's third-highest assassin, below only Armani Saint and Julian Gallows, Callis was well versed with the ins and outs of The Dome.

Though half the height of The Tower's 312 stories, The Dome's circumference gave it an equal amount of living space. Even the sketchiest of lowlifes knew to avoid The Dome and those connected with it at all costs.

Nyx's close connections with The Tower granted him power and authority throughout the city. While Lord Cain's authority stretched throughout the general citizenry, Nyx reigned as a supreme authority of both the underground and commonplace markets.

Having entered The Dome through its black glass, metal-framed doors, he stormed across the dark stone floors, glimmering with the common silver flecks.

A central staircase ran clear to floor 154. From there, the top five floors required special elevator keys. Nyx controlled access to all keys, going to none other than his valued assassins.

The Black Band consisted of his top five assassins. A level down, the Crimson Band, held two. And his lowest White Band numbered five. Each assassin received a key from him, and each band had its own floor and its own commons room. A separate staircase led between 155 and 156, the White Band and Crimson Band's floors. A third ran from 157 to 160, which only Nyx and his Black Band members could access.

Four spherical elevators cut The Dome into equal quarters. Reaching one, Callis slammed the small, black button and watched the white number over the door count down to ground level. Fumbling for the intricate, silver key, he pressed 157. The spherical elevator stayed level as it traversed the sloping exterior wall of The Dome. The outer glass shaft allowed Callis to look out over the dark city during the ascent.

Reaching his destination, he proceeded to a room at the far end of the hallway, grasped the silver door handles, and threw wide a set of massive black, frosted doors. Leaving the doors open, he made his way across the vast space.

Scattered leather sofas and armchairs rested between bookcases, along frosted black windowed walls. To the left stood an ostentatious silver and black pool table with colored, yet transparent, balls. Even further to the left, at a large mahogany table, Armani Saint and Julian Gallows were engaged in a heated game of chess.

At Callis's not-so-subtle entrance, Armani stood, throwing his arms wide in an enigmatic gesture. "Ah, here he comes, the talk of the town!" His voice flowed musically, and the single, large hoop dangling from his left ear upstaged numerous other piercings lining his ears. In a single elegant motion, he flipped his bronze hair from before his captivating black and red eyes.

Julian refused to even look up. As the board demanded his undivided attention, he grumbled something incoherent. It was quite obvious by the tone of his voice that it was something rather discourteous.

"Now, Jules, no need to be jealous. We're all a team here."

Julian muttered, "*Someone* tried to keep all the *fun* for himself. Pretty selfish, if you ask me."

Ignoring Julian, Callis made his way to a sofa, throwing his burgundy trench coat onto a silver coat rack.

Heavy musculature stretched his black long sleeves and tailored red vest as he sat, arms crossed, with a deep frown disrupting his flawless features. He bit at his lip piercing in aggravation.

Armani, raising an eyebrow, glanced back and forth between the sulking Julian and the somber Callis. A booming roll of thunder broke the silence of the room, echoing into the distance. A stillness descended once more with exclusion of the torrential pounding rain against the tinted glass. Armani breathed a sigh of irritation.

As Julian reached for a chess piece, Armani intercepted, snatching the piece just as he touched it.

A violent flame of anger shot through Julian. Jumping to his feet, his chair flew backward. He slammed his fists on the table, rocking the chess pieces from their posts.

"What the hell, Armani!" Julian roared. He tried to steal the piece back, but Armani blithely kept it out of his reach. In a wild fury, Julian flung the board across the room, sending frosted red and white glass pieces to scatter in every direction. They all shielded their faces from the flying glass shards.

Julian threw his hands into the air. "Goddammit, Armani! Now look what you made me do!"

"If you can't behave like a civil being, you don't deserve to play," Armani calmly scolded.

Watching with amusement, Callis chortled.

"What?" Julian hissed, eyes wide. "You have something to say, Morgandy?" Julian cocked his head, the fumes practically visible.

Callis matched Julian's threatening gaze with a sinister look of his own. "Do you have *any* idea where I just came from? Let me have the pleasure of enlightening you." Callis stood, taking a few forceful steps toward Julian. His boots crunched glass shards until he halted, only a small space remaining between them.

"I've been a *guest* of the Black Guard. Them assholes took me in for questioning. Why? Word got out that the Intruder two days ago was a six-foot-one, crimson-haired man whose touch and temper brought destruction to everything in his path!" Callis's eyes darkened demonically as ferocity poured from him. His hair fell forward, framing them to create an even more daunting appearance.

Armani, maintaining his serene disposition said, "Really, Callis. You must admit that was to be expected. Perhaps you went just a *teensy* bit overboard?" He pinched his index finger and thumb together.

Before Callis could interrupt, he continued, "Seriously Cal, Jules and I could see the aura of your energy blast all the way up in The Archives."

Julian, forgetting his anger for the moment, threw his head back in a harsh cackle. "And despite all that fuss you made, the damn bastard still escaped your grasp."

Growling, Callis snatched his coat and crunched back across the room and through the doors that he had left wide open.

A dark-haired somn named Royce Elwood, who was just younger than Callis himself, called out, laughing as he approached, "Hey, Cal! I hear you let The Archives' Intruder get away! God, I can't imagine—"

Callis, eyes straight forward, threw out a powerful arm, making clean contact with his fellow Black Band member. The man's body hurled backward sprawling into the room, across the glass littered floor.

As Callis disappeared down the long hallway, Julian broke into a harsh peal of laughter.

Armani tilted his head toward the man sprawled on the floor, small pieces of glass protruding from his flesh, stating the obvious, "Probably best not to mention that, Royce. Our Callis, it would seem, is in a rather foul mood."

Royce nodded in agreement, pulling a particularly large shard from his forearm and applying pressure with a thumb to staunch the flow of blood streaming down toward his wrist.

15: A Key Possibility

Helena Meretrix closed the book in front of her. She caressed a finger over its smooth surface. *Within these pages lie the hidden mysteries of Atrum Unda. Soon, all will be revealed to me. The author of this book will be the key to unlock it. Very soon.* For a while Helena sat in silence, planning when she could make the trip to find the book's author. Hopefully he would be as informative and accommodating as his nephew, Albert, had been. Her momentary smile turned into a frown as the vision of Albert dissolved from her mind and the sight of Jett Milan—likewise engrossed in a book—reached her from across the White Band's commons room.

Soon after Jett's initiation into the White Band, Helena had concluded that she had no use for the reticent young man. From the start, he had shown no interest in her. Actually, she seemed to have just the opposite effect. May times she had tried to engage him in conversation or to ask his opinion—if for no reason than to feed his male ego and to make him feel important. But always to no avail.

His restraint didn't so much bother her, as much as it created a challenge for her. She had practiced the fine art of wrapping any man around her finger in a heartbeat. When a man was in such a position, he tended to think with only one part of his anatomy. And that was the part she certainly knew how to control.

In truth, she was worried. If she found herself in the field with a man who reacted in the same way as Jett, it could be quite dangerous for her. That, if for no other reason, was why she had to figure out Jett Milan.

Helena pursed her lips in thought. Perhaps she hadn't been approaching him the right way. Maybe she could coax him into a conversation. "What are you reading?" she asked softly, leaning forward over the table. Jett remained silent, focused on his book. She frowned, but decided it was worth a different approach. "Where are the others? I haven't seen Stella and Wylan around lately." She bit her lip, waiting for a reply. Ignoring her attempts, he continued reading. Jett's expression was unreadable.

"Jett?" she began again, refusing to give up. "I want to apologize for my behavior the other day. You know, at The Tower. My harsh words were uncalled for. I know you haven't been with us long, but it's already obvious that you could be a powerful ally. Even for me," Helena crooned, in her sweetest voice. "That was pretty intense at The Tower. With the break-in and all. You weren't far from The Archives, right? I hope you don't mind my curiosity, but whose authorization papers did you obtain? They appeared to be for the Prisoner's Quarters."

Jett set his book down and folded his arms across his chest. His brown eyes darkened as he stared Helena down, sending a shiver up her spine. *At least I have his attention.*

"Listen," Jett said. "Stop talking."

"What?"

"I don't care for you." Jett enunciated each syllable, and then returned to his book.

Helena's temper flared, but she kept her cool. "You know. In this line of business, there are times we must cover each other, regardless of our own personal feelings. *Your* survival could someday depend on mine." She was about to continue her lecture, but was interrupted when a willowy young woman with long flaxen hair bounced in to greet her.

"Helena, sorry I'm late!" said Angelina Pratt.

About damn time. Helena stood up to confront her comrade. "I've been waiting here forever, Angelina. Where have you been?"

Jett came out of his shell to mutter, "I bet I know. I bet she's been with Royce Elwood of the Black Band. Again."

Helena shot a sharp glare at Jett. But he ignored her.

"Whatever," Helena said. "Just forget him. There is something that I need to tell you. *In private.*" An anxious crease formed between Angelina's brows.

"It's all right," Angelina whispered. "We can go elsewhere to talk."

"Like hell! We aren't going anywhere," Helena said. She turned to Jett. "You can leave now. You have already indicated that you are not willing to share any of your business with the *team*. So it would not be proper for the *team* to share any of its business with you." Helena turned back to Angelina with a conspiratorial smile, as though Jett had already gone.

"Right." Jett stood up, snapping his book closed. He'd had enough of Helena Meretrix, and needed to get out of here anyway.

As he headed toward the doors, Angelina called out, "Oh, Jett!" He stopped. "I delivered Stella and Wylan's next assignments. Just exactly as you told me to."

"Good," he said, without looking back at her. "Thank you." With that, Jett exited the room.

"We're all alone now, Helena. What was it you wanted to tell me?"

"What was that?" Helena growled.

"What was what?"

"That! I would like to know where in the hell Jett Milan gets off giving orders to White Band members!"

"Oh. He wasn't giving orders. The orders came down from Nyx, as usual. Nyx just hands the assignments to Jett. And then Jett disperses them as he sees fit. That's all," Angelina explained.

"That's impossible. Why would Nyx entrust such a task to Jett?"

"Well," Angelina said. She shifted uncomfortably. "Jett is kind of the White Band's new leader."

Helena stared.

"Nyx must see something special in him. Even though he's our newest member, Nyx has already sent him out on a mission with Armani Saint and Julian Gallows of the Black Band!" Angelina was squirming with excitement, as though this would be welcome news to Helena.

"It's so impressive! At this rate, it won't be any time before Jett skips up to the Black Band himself!" Angelina persisted, the excitement growing in her blue eyes.

"That's impossible," Helena snapped again. "Jett Milan does not have one single trait that would qualify him for the Black Band." Her words were said hollowly. As though saying them would make them come true. Her brow furrowed in thought. She definitely needed to keep a closer eye on him.

"You're just jealous that he hasn't given you any assignments yet."

"I am not jealous! But now that you mention it, why *hasn't* he given me an assignment?"

"Let me think." With a slight smirk, Angelina pretended to put on her thinking cap. "Let's see. Well, you haven't been reporting in lately. You're always off making some big plans of your own. It's not like Jett can hand you an assignment when you're not here. Hey. Exactly where have you been?" Angelina couldn't hide her sudden curiosity.

"That's actually what I wanted to talk to you about. But if you would rather we just stand here singing Jett's praises...?"

"Oh. Come on. Tell me Helena. I'm sorry. OK?" Angelina pleaded.

Angelina Pratt was twenty-three, just as Helena. Although of the same age, seeing her actually bouncing on her heels reminded Helena of a little girl. She couldn't help but smile at her enthusiasm.

"Very well," Helena said. "I can't say why right now, but I need an access key to the upper levels of The Dome. That said, I need you to hit up your man, Royce. To borrow his key. Can you manage to acquire it?"

Helena maintained an open smile, but her thoughts took another course.

I know she can. Royce is always visiting her for their special "sparring" lessons. Why, by Ravenna, does Nyx even keep such a whore-monger as Royce Elwood in his Black Band? She had heard that he frequently jeopardized his missions, as well as put his partners at risk. This particular trait, Helena had earlier decided, must be how so. She had—more than once—imagined Royce going off on little side excursions. She didn't know what her comrade, Angelina Pratt, saw in him. *It doesn't matter*, Helena told herself now, *as long as I get my key*.

"I don't know, Helena. I *really* like Royce. I don't want to—"

"You'll take orders from a creep like Jett, but you won't help out a friend?"

Angelina chewed the inside of her cheek as she studied Helena's crestfallen features. She did not want to use Royce like that, but she didn't want to disappoint her friend either. They had been through so much together.

"Well?" Helena pressed, knowing that in a battle of wills, she could always win over Angelina.

"All right," Angelina said. Looking like a small cornered animal, she added, "I'll try, but I can't promise anything."

Immediately brightening, Helena reached out to give Angelina an uncharacteristic hug. "Wonderful!" she said. "But don't take too long. I'll be needing it very soon." With that, Helena spun on her heel and exited the commons room before Angelina had any chance to think about what she had just promised.

ഓരോ

Staring at the empty door, Angelina frowned. She really did not want to do what Helena had asked. But as long as band members completed their required tasks, everyone was *technically* allowed their own plots—though doing so was highly unsuggested if you didn't want someone eventually sent tailing after you, due to Nyx's growing suspicions. Nevertheless, these side-missions occurred, and more often than not, the others were not usually aware. It was one of Nyx's *ways* of keeping his assassins happy.

Band members also often asked for favors of their comrades without need for explanation. If a favor was promised and not fulfilled, all too often a plan would fail and an associate—and possible friend—would meet death.

At length, Angelina started to laugh. Doing this small thing for Helena was certainly the lesser of two evils. When Helena had asked her for a secret meeting, she feared she was being asked to participate in a hit.

It wasn't that she didn't enjoy missions with Helena. The woman was just a consummate planner, and she usually found some strange way to keep the mission interesting. But all too often she got caught up in the sick joy of the process and ended up with blood strewn from one end of the horizon to the other. That wasn't always a bad thing. But if the hit was supposed to be kept on the down-low, they sometimes ended up spending a significant amount of time working to clean up the carnage. Once in awhile, they even had to drag out leeches to help cover things up.

In a nutshell, missions with Helena were usually great fun. But generally a lot of extra work.

16: Fado's Butchery

Having left the Black Band's commons room, ignoring the laughter behind him, Callis hit the button for the elevator. Once at ground level, he stormed through the exit into the dark gloom, accompanied, as usual, by heavy pouring rain.

Tightly clasping the silver buckles of his coat, Callis moved across the city with the tails of his trench flapping behind him in the wind. After crossing through several sectors, he entered the Valentine Sector, a run-down part of Atrum Unda consisting of rough, black stone buildings that swallowed any light.

It was a prime location for underground dealings, yet even Nyx Crucian didn't have many contacts here, and the ones he had weren't reliable. These locals avoided association with Nyx and his people in every way possible.

Callis entered an isolated building with a large, metal sign reading *Fado's Butchery*. A bell above the door tinkled in contrast to its surroundings causing the solitary man behind the counter, chopping a large hunk of meat, to look up.

He was portly with a stout face covered in freckles all the way up to his balding head. His only hair was an unruly red beard and straggles of matching hair dotting his massive forearms. Beady, black eyes added the final touch to his brutish features.

"Hello, Fado." Callis threw a charming smile. "How's business?"

In a gruff voice, Fado replied, "Callis, it has been awhile. And by *business* do you mean the meat business or the *other* business?"

A crooked grin on his face, Callis answered, "Both, as always."

"You're a good man, Callis, especially for a man of your kind and vocation. A rare breed, you are." The man gave a wholehearted grin. "All's well as can be expected with the butchery, but as far as the other...you best speak to Mordion. He's downstairs in the back. You know where to find him." With a tilt of the head, Fado pointed to a doorway at the left of the room behind the counter.

Callis nodded generously. "Gotcha. Thanks, Fado."

"For you, Callis, anytime. Now scat." The red-bearded man waved a massive hand in a half joking, yet at the same time serious, manner. "And let me get back to my business." With that, Fado dismissed Callis with a wave of his razor-edged cleaver.

"Ah Fado, haven't changed a bit, have you." Callis smiled and shook his head, as he strolled back around the counter. Beyond the doorway were two sets of stairs. One led up and the other descended to the darkness below.

Without hesitation, Callis descended into the dark. Having made this trek on many occasions, he followed the path, directed only by a soft glow at the end of the narrow, concrete hallway.

He reached a large, crude door with a small, horizontal cutout at eye level. Pressing a worn button, Callis heard grumbling, followed by a loud cursing as something crashed to the floor. Sharp steps made their way to the door, followed by a pair of blue eyes peering through the slot. An irritated voice snapped, "Who the hell is it? I'm busy. If you're not worth my time, get the fuck lost."

"If you don't want my business, I shall be happy to take my leave, Mordy."

The crystal blue eyes squinted into the darkness of the hall. "Callis? That really you?" But before Callis had time to respond, the eyes disappeared and the air filled with the sound of bolts and bars sliding away. The door swung open, sending out a warm flood of light. Callis squinted, having become accustomed to the dimness.

"I'll be damned. It is you, Callis. Don't just stand there. Come in, come in!"

The wine cellar's racks had been removed except for one in the back and three on the left wall. One of these was pulled down, revealing a hidden chamber that was used as a safe.

One large table held an assortment of junk such as scattered papers, smokes, an ashtray, and a small electronic device. The man sauntered to the desk after relocking and securing the door.

He shuffled papers around, failing to create an illusion of organization. Of medium build, his dark, spiky hair was disheveled and matted. He ran a hand through it, adding to its disarray.

"Stressed, Mordion?"

"Man, you have no idea. As you know, my brother, Fallon, is indisposed, so this is all my responsibility now." He waved an open palm at the disgraceful mess overtaking the table. "This is a two-man job. Nor does it help that I must watch my niece, Brika. Man, she's a li'l nightmare," Mordion rambled on, more to himself than to Callis.

Callis laughed, "At least she has her grandfather. It can't be that bad, right?"

Mordion choked, "Fado? All's he does is spoil the li'l she-devil. If her mother, Mina, were still around, she wouldn't tolerate Brika's behavior. You know, Fado still blames my brother for his Mina's death? What a load a crock, I say! If my brother wasn't such a worthless piece of—"

Before Mordion could prattle on, Callis interjected, becoming serious. "Actually, that's why I'm here."

"Huh?" Puzzlement spread across Mordion's features.

"You recall the purchase I made about eight months ago? I know you remember our encounters well."

"Of course, but what does that—" Mordion began, but Callis cut him off again.

"Circumstances have changed. I now need the accessory to go with it."

Baffled, Mordion replied, "Oh, right...all right." He paused, appearing to be in thought, then added, "But I can only sell it to you as a set of two. They're hard to come by, and they must be programmed to link to each other."

"Oh come on, Mordion, I don't need two. I only *need* one."

"Sorry." Mordion shrugged. "You know the trade, Cal."

"I really can't use two of them...But I'll take both nonetheless."

"Perfect. Follow me on back," Mordion capitulated, leading Callis to the safe that camouflaged as a wine rack. It was a long narrow room, also with a metal table at its center. Metallic storage compartments covered the walls, each with a numeric keypad.

Callis respectfully remained by the table, as Mordion plugged the red cord from a small, rectangular device into a keypad, creating a high-pitched hum.

With a respondent sound, the compartment unlocked, allowing Mordion to withdraw a small object. He resecured the compartment and set the object before Callis on the table. It was small with a shiny wrapping around it.

"These aren't cheap, Cal. I hope you're offering up something good in exchange."

"More than enough," he assured, pulling a set of papers from his jacket pocket and sliding them across the table.

"What's this? Wait! Fallon's release forms? How in Ravenna's name did you get these?" Mordion looked up, bewildered. "He's not even up for parole for another sixteen years."

"Due to The Archives incident, of which I'm sure you are aware, I've been kept 'preoccupied' there. I do, in fact, have several contacts within The Tower. Oh, and one more thing." Callis had a new expression on his face.

"Yeah?"

"I want a vessel."

"Callis, I—"

"I know you have one, more than one. Don't even try to deny it. And the payment you hold in your hands is well worth the electronic chips and the vessel. Unless, of course, you wish me to recant the release forms. As you said, Mordion, I know the trade. And yes, I know it well."

Mordion rubbed his shoulder, contemplating.

"Well, how about it?"

"All right. But I don't like to give these sorts of things out, Callis. Not to anyone. It leads to entirely new levels of trade, very risky ones, at best."

Reluctantly, Mordion approached a new compartment much further back. He returned with three objects individually wrapped. Two were in silver paper, one in orange. Taking a seat, he unwrapped each.

The first was a locket with a black star sapphire where the picture would normally be. The second turned out to be a silver ring with a black star sapphire mounted in its face. And the third item, in the burnt orange paper, was a watch. Mordion demonstrated how, with a miniscule switch, the watch's face popped up, revealing a black star sapphire hidden inside.

Callis immediately rejected the locket. He liked the watch idea, but it wasn't a style he would be caught dead wearing. The ring, however, would be very obvious. Armani and Julian would notice it straight away.

"The ring," Callis declared. "I'll take the ring."

"Ah, Cal. I never doubted you would pick the costliest one. He began to wrap the other two back up.

"What can I say?" Callis said, "I have exceptional taste." He shrugged, smiling. "Now that is out of the way, take the forms to The Tower and your brother will be released, promptly, a week from tomorrow."

Callis snatched up both of his packages in the palm of his hand. "I'll be taking these now, if you don't mind."

"A week? Why not—"

"Just to make sure these beauties work." Callis held up the box containing the two electronic chips.

"Oh, and if for some reason they aren't up to par, I can cancel the release of your dear brother. Just in case, but I trust you. You've never let me down yet, Mordion. Just another thing to keep in mind."

"I'll be taking my leave now. It was good seeing you, Mordy, and try not to stress so much. You'll go bald like Fado." Callis smiled and winked at the speechless Mordion.

"W-Wait," Mordion stammered, "Callis...I...thank you."

Callis turned back with a crooked grin. "It's just business, and I'm a business kind of man, Mordion. Remember that and never forget it."

Reaching the crude door, Callis unhinged the locks and bars. Without another word, he headed out.

As he started for the upstairs exit, Fado caught his eye.

"Find what you were looking for?"

"As usual. Can always rely on ol' Mordy."

"Yeah. He's not a bad kid, especially compared to his brother."

Callis's grin widened. "Well, be seeing you, Fado."

"Take care, Cal."

As Callis opened the door, he nearly bumped into a girl in her early teens. With warm, copper-brown hair, her gray eyes widened the moment she caught the eyes of the beautiful, crimson-haired man.

Callis flashed his most charming smile. "After you." He stepped aside, motioning her to enter.

She didn't move. She simply continued to stare at Callis with captivated eyes.

Fado leaned over the counter, barking, "Brika, get on in here! You're in the man's way."

Her grandfather's rough voice woke Brika from her stupor. Blushing, she rushed past him, around the counter, and up the stairs.

Fado guffawed, "Oh, Callis. Thank Ravenna, my little Brika is *far* too young for you. You would certainly bring trouble to any woman's living quarters." He laughed again.

Callis shrugged a humble agreement. "Goodbye, Fado." He shook his head, descending again to the streets of Atrum Unda.

Callis pondered the events of the past few days, as he cut through the mist. It was late, and the Valentine Sector was not a place in which to venture once late night came.

Maneuvering the labyrinth of darkened streets, he eventually reached the Ricahn Sector, an exclusive sector that exuded wealth, and where he maintained his residence.

Nearing his place, he spotted a familiar face.

I'll be damned. It's Jimmy. What is he doing all the way on this side of town? Realization dawned. *Hmm. I suspect this has something to do with Jereth.*

Stealthily, Callis crossed the walkway, closing the distance toward Jimmy. He came alongside the boy, a half step behind him. Keeping his gaze focused straight ahead, Callis murmured, "Don't react. See that alley coming up on the right? Follow me there. Act casually." The streets seemed lifeless, but Callis hadn't survived in his profession this long by taking foolish chances.

Startled, Jimmy blurted, "Mr. Mor—"

"Shh!" Callis warned, picking up his pace and moving a few strides ahead of Jimmy. He slipped into the dark alley without anyone other than Jimmy noticing.

Shortly, Jimmy poked his head into the alley. Not casual in the least. He looked back and forth between the public streets and the shadows of the alley.

Good Lord. An arm shot from the shadows, pulling Jimmy into the alley by the collar. The boy yelped in surprise, but Callis quickly covered his mouth.

Jimmy's initial reaction faded instantly as Callis released his grip. "Mr. Morgandy, I was just on my way to see you!" the boy chirped, happily and much too loud.

Callis put a finger to his own lips, "Lower your voice, Jimmy. We don't want anyone to hear us. It would defeat the purpose of meeting here like this."

The red-haired, freckle-faced boy looked up at Callis. Warm brown eyes, very similar to Callis's own, grew wide. He hunched his shoulders, whispering, "Oh, right. Sorry Mr. Morgandy. Is this better?"

"Yes. Yes, Jimmy. Much. No need to apologize. Just tell me what you have."

Eagerly bobbing his head, Jimmy responded, "Of course! Mr. Tavokk sent me one of his silver messenger beetles. It told me to retrieve a letter from his house meant for you, Mr. Morgandy." Jimmy retrieved Jereth Tavokk's characteristic, pale blue envelope from inside his jacket and handed it to Callis. "I tried delivering it twice before, at the specified times, but you weren't home."

"Unusual circumstances detained me," Callis explained. *So I was right. Jereth has been trying to contact me.*

Proudly, Jimmy added, "And I made sure not to forget to slide Mr. Tavokk's little silver beetle back under the door this time." In the dim light, color rose to the boy's freckled cheeks as he remembered the last time, when he *had* forgotten to return the messenger beetle.

"Well done. I wasn't expecting to meet you here at all. So you'll have to excuse me for not sealing your payment in its usual form," Callis said, stuffing a thick wad of bills into Jimmy's hands.

Jimmy displayed his coy, little smile. "No problem, Mr. Morgandy! Thank you very much!"

"Now run along home. It's not safe for you to be on the streets this late at night. Take the express train. And don't speak to anyone. Stealth is the key!" Callis warned, shooing him away with the flick of a wrist.

Jimmy hurried away, enthusiastically waving. "Take care, Mr. Morgandy!" he shouted. Callis shook his head with a sigh, but he couldn't suppress a wry grin as he watched the boy bounce around the corner.

Once Jimmy disappeared, Callis reemerged with Tavokk's letter tucked safely away in his pocket. Nearby, Callis made out the massive structure that contained his home as well as many others.

The building was constructed, without surprise, of the same silver-flecked black marble found throughout the city. It housed several grandiose train tunnels at its lowest level as well as tracks for express trains that weaved in and out of the building. Housing began several levels above the trains, increasing in value toward the top, furthest from the noise and bustle of the busy station.

However, before the station came into clear view, Callis changed his mind. *I need a drink. Besides, I'm too restless to go home just yet.* He crossed the city back in an eastward direction. As the evening progressed, the streets became ever more deserted.

Nearing The Tower, he reached the two spiraling paths leading down to the Wishing Well and up to the Cosmos. He started to hike up the path leading to the Cosmos, but not before noticing soldiers of the Black Guard lurking in the shadows.

Damn fools. Do they really think the Intruder is going to pop up in the near vicinity of The Tower? As if he would be hiding in the bushes or some other such nonsense! Callis tried to silence the anger welling up inside of him. Taking a sharp breath of the cool, crisp air, Callis exhalation was slow, though a bit ragged. After several deep breaths, he entered the Cosmos and made his way back to his usual, secluded booth.

Tazo, with her appealing, burgundy hair loosely piled on top of her head, strolled to where Callis, one of her favorite customers, sat drumming his fingers on the table in thought. On anyone else, her hair would look sloppy, but it made her appear like a delectable, dark angel.

Watching her sultry approach, Callis smiled.

"What can I get for you, Callis?" Tazo purred kindly, in her velvet voice, meeting his gaze with her alluring, foggy blue eyes.

"Surprise me. No. Actually, make it my usual. And bring me two, if it's not too much to ask."

Smiling with moist, painted lips, Tazo sweetly answered, "Expecting company?"

"No. Just a rough day. A very rough couple of days, actually."

"Ah." She frowned in commiseration. I'll fetch your drinks immediately and leave you to relax." She parted with another smile, returning to the bar.

"Greatly appreciated," he said, as just moments later, she returned with a drink in each hand, setting them on the table before him.

"Anytime, Callis," she murmured again.

After watching Tazo walk back to the bar, Callis took a large swig from one of the glasses. He reached into the pocket of his trench, which he had laid out across the table against the wall to keep it out of his way. He surreptitiously drew out the letter from his good friend, Jereth Tavokk. Swiftly tearing open the pale blue envelope, he unfolded the letter and glanced over the fine script within, written on matching, pale blue paper:

Callis,

This letter is to inform you that I will be out of the area for business's sake. I'm sure you'll understand. I shall be away for at least a week, if not a bit longer. I'll send word once I have returned.

Till my return,

Jereth

Callis thought back to what Jimmy had said about how he had already tried for two days to deliver this letter. *This letter is easily three days old,* he realized. *Damn intruders and interrogators.*

Well, on the up side, this means that Jereth ought to be back in about four days, give or take. I wonder if he has heard about The Archives Intruder yet. He shook his head, laughing at his own foolishness. *Don't be an idiot, Callis. Of course he has. Nothing gets past Jereth Tavokk, no matter where he goes.*

At that moment, Tazo approached with a new set of drinks, having observed that he had finished both of the previous ones. She also bore a small note in her left hand.

"I brought you refills, all on the house tonight," she said, winking one of her dazzling, cloudy blue eyes, accentuated by long, dark lashes and glittering blue makeup.

"Oh, that isn't necessary," Callis said, "but the gesture is greatly appreciated, nonetheless."

A smile graced her perfectly painted lips. "I insist. Oh, and before I forget again…this is for you. It was sent here earlier this afternoon." She slipped him the note. "Someone must have known you would make an appearance here tonight." She smiled pleasantly, once again, and took her leave, as Callis flipped the note open. Its paper was black, and its script glistened with a silver glow.

Of course, he thought, *a note from Armani. Damn him to Eve. He knows my habits all too well.* Callis felt ill at ease as he finished reading the note, a sense of irritation growing rapidly inside of him.

By the goddesses! Does it never end? According to the note from Armani, Nyx had called a Black Band meeting for the following day. *Guess I knew this was bound to happen sooner rather than later, just as Armani predicted. No doubt this meeting is about The Archives and the wretched Intruder that I let escape.* He sighed in irritation, downing the first of the new drinks that Tazo had brought with one swift gulp.

As he sat, more slowly nursing his next drink, Callis stewed.

I just don't get it. I had him. He should never have escaped me! Lines of tension stretched Callis's shirt, obvious, even in the dimness at the back of the bar. *The Intruder may have escaped The Tower, but the chase isn't over yet. No matter what he might think, I will find him.*

Grimly, he stared into the vacant space before him. *This game has just begun.*

17: A Gift From Eve

"Blast it to Eve!" KyVeerah stretched his fingers and neck, followed straightaway by his arms, legs, and back. His body was in knots. He raised a hand to the side of his jaw and pressed, cracking his neck. He then moved the same hand to the other side of his jaw, repeating the same movement.

Wouldn't it be nice to have the day to sleep in? But I can't. Yes, yes, I know. KyVeerah frowned.

Sitting up, he threw the extravagant comforter off, which doubled over on itself. Next, as though it were routine, he shoved the layers of the slick sheets aside, burying them beneath the comforter.

Another day, another job, he sighed, lacing his fingers behind his head. *If ever I had a whole day to entirely relax, I don't think I would have the vaguest clue what to do with myself.* Shaking his head from side to side, as though it were necessary for him to exhibit his answer for someone other than himself, he came to the final verdict. *No, I don't suppose I would.*

He twisted and slid his feet onto the floor, one on the cold wooden floorboards, and the other on the soft edge of the red rug. Resting his hands on the edge of the bed, he looked straight ahead at the black curtains concealing whatever lay beyond.

Come to think of it, I can't remember a time when there weren't curtains drawn over these windows. How out of place it would seem now if one could see the other side. It's almost as if one of the great mysteries of the world would be forever ruined.

From the corner of his eye, KyVeerah caught sight of the bottle of rum resting upon the nightstand. Realizing that the cap had not been put back into place, he slid toward the nightstand and grabbed the cap from the tabletop, twisting it on securely. *Whew. Never safe to leave full bottles open. It could definitely lead to a mess. More importantly, to a shameful waste of good liquor.*

He willed himself out of bed, though he would have much rather fallen back into it. He ambled to the wardrobe in the corner. Opening it, he selected what he deemed as tasteful enough attire to accompany him throughout the day. Still wearing next to nothing, he stumbled out into the hallway.

Turning toward the bathroom, he glanced at the hall clock. 6:24. *Far too early. Especially considering what time I finally made it to bed. Then again, Venn won't be up for a few more hours.* With that he grinned, knowing that Venn's head would be pounding much worse than his own. *Well, if he sticks to his old routine, which I know by heart, I can take care of a few things and return before he blows a gasket.*

Climbing into the shower, KyVeerah began to ready himself for the day. Finished, he dried and wrapped the towel around his waist while he fashioned his hair. Shaking his long hair, he checked to make sure that it felt as close to usual as possible since he was using different products than he was used to. His numerous earrings flashed in the mirror behind the reflection of his dark hair as he hurried through his ministrations.

Moving on, he tossed the towel to the floor, throwing on a pair of light blue denims and a black belt with a large buckle. He wrestled a formfitting, short-sleeved shirt over his head. It sported a contoured skull on its left side, wrapping from front to back, with black splatters as a background.

Back in his room, he slid on a pair of showy, black shoes with small spikes around the toe and heel. He then settled a pair of shades on his head, assuming he may want them for later. Who knew how long he would be out and about? And honestly, who wouldn't need shades in the City of Light?

Returning to the counter, he slid the numerous silver and black rings onto their proper fingers and clasped the necklaces around his neck.

He made his way up the stairs swiftly and quietly. Not necessarily to keep from waking Venn, but more from his own innate nature. Searching the kitchen for something to eat, he was annoyed that Umbra Halls' kitchen storage had been reorganized. As a matter of fact, the entire kitchen had been rearranged.

Who in their right mind? This kitchen's basic storage layout has never been changed. Not in my time. Why would someone need to change it now? It better not have been that boy's idea, or he'll be getting a talking to. That's for sure!

KyVeerah paused, staring at a wall of cupboards and drawers. Resting on a single foot with his arms crossed, he tapped the other foot in frustration. *I just want a simple bowl of oats. Is that too much to ask?* He eventually found the hidden stash, as well as a spoon, and a bowl. Then, he slid over to the fridge in search of milk, the one thing he could depend on to be in the same place. Yes, he opened the door, and there it was. *Halle-frikkin'-lujah!*

KyVeerah smiled. *The little things it takes to make a somn happy.*

After finishing two bowls, KyVeerah placed the milk back into its appropriate spot. *Hurrumph,* he grumped, noticing the neatly placed and labeled containers Marion had left for Venn. *I wish someone would go through the trouble of preparing and labeling meals for me.*

It must've been the girl. Would someone tell me why, by the goddesses, I gave her to Venn as a living companion? That was the worst idea I ever had. Ever. Cross my heart and hope to die, if in fact I tell a lie. He crossed the index and middle fingers of his left hand down at his side in realizing that perhaps that wasn't the "worst" idea he'd ever had.

Throwing his dishes into the sink, he stepped into the hallway and grabbed his coat from the center railing where he had left it on his arrival. Odd that Venn hadn't noticed it before finding him in the kitchen. He must have been very distracted.

Eeh. What a terrifying encounter that was. Hopefully we won't be doing that again anytime soon. A shiver ran down his back as he revisualized Venn storming into the kitchen with that crystal vase raised high. No doubt existed that Venn aimed to annihilate him.

Venn would probably have carved large holes into the centers of his books to hide the diced-up pieces of my body. Another shiver crept down his spine; however in reality, Venn would never do something so disgraceful to a book. KyVeerah knew that, after all the countless years they had known one another.

Slinging his long coat over his shoulders, he headed out in the same quiet and swift manner as before. KyVeerah moved elegantly through the shadowed space beneath the great tree and over the cobblestones of The Courtyard. He could feel the presence of the winged statues behind him, watching him with cautious eyes as he reached the metal gate and proceeded out into the darkness of the alleyway.

As he moved toward the open city, more early-morning light came to greet his eyes. Automatically, he dropped his shades down to avoid the suns' intensity, even at this early hour. Especially at this early hour. Even through the dark tinting of his shades, KyVeerah squinted against the silver glittering of the ground as he stepped from the alley.

He peered around. *How long has it been since my last stay in*

Lux? he wondered. *About two years?*

To the southeast, the Tower of Lux Lumetia stood white and dazzling in unison with the rest of the city. It hovered menacingly, gazing down upon the civilian population from its vantage point, high in the cloudless sky. In its powerful stance, it appeared to be waiting for someone to make a wrong move.

Auck! The ideal city. So clean. So tidy. So perfect. Even its ghettos projected an impression of tidiness and tameness, compared to the run-down parts of other cities. Then again, the majority of Lux's inhabitants would know no better, most having never left this city of their birth. Most beings were totally clueless as to what truly lay beyond the seas, beyond The Darkness. Considering the ways and the things the citizens were taught, and misinformed, it was small wonder that none other than those chosen to know the select secrets ever wished to travel beyond The Darkness. It would require a fool to wish for such things.

Lifting his feet, KyVeerah moved toward North Market. *Despite two years since I last stayed at Umbra Halls, I could still draw this city like it were the back of my hand. And in much more precision and detail, at that.*

Though KyVeerah walked swiftly, due to his innately agile manner, none would ever imagine that he was up to something or in a hurry. Although, at this literal moment in time, it was true that he was in no particular hurry and that his motives were generally innocent, he was certainly looking for something. Well, someone.

Half an hour later, KyVeerah reached North Market. Stands had already been set up, prepared to face the day. Vendors of all ages and types sat or stood around their stalls with a wide range of commodities.

Peering here and there as he passed, he admired what the stands had to offer, as well as eyeing what others were shopping for at this early hour. Many mothers appeared to be out. Several others, of varying age and status, were out wandering the strip as well.

Walking a bit further, his eyes rested upon a pleasant sight. He tilted his head forward, peering over the top of his shades. A charming young lady was making change for a middle-aged woman with two nagging children at her side. With smiles, they concluded their transaction. The woman dragged both her purchases and her children away with her down the strip.

Indeed! KyVeerah grinned lightly, as with his own elegant stride he made his way to the stand. The young woman leaned over the baskets, arranging their contents to be more visually pleasing.

He leaned forward, just inches from her ear. "Cassandra," he whispered her name, in his smooth, cultured voice. She jumped back, dropping some contents, which scattered over the ground.

"Vincent!" she gasped, in a hushed shout of shock. She held her hand over her breast, forestalling a heart attack.

"But of course, beloved." His grin widened, displaying flawless teeth. "I must say, Cassandra, you are looking absolutely stunning! Not saying that comes as a surprise." He tilted his head forward and raised his brows, peering characteristically over his shades. His enthralling eyes caught her, once again, off guard.

Cassandra blushed under the flattery. She dropped her eyes, then brought them back up to meet his gaze. She was struck by the unusual quality of his eyes, thinking them far more beautiful than any she had ever seen.

"It has been quite some time," she said, resuming her serene voice. "You are the very last somn I expected to find standing before me this morning. Any morning." She flashed her pleasant smile while pushing loose, copper curls behind her ear, only to have them fall forward again, framing her lovely face. It was the face of an angel. One any man would dream of.

"Yet here I stand before you. And I assure you, I am quite real."

Cassandra couldn't help but smile. She shook her head, eyes locked on his. "You haven't changed a bit."

"You wouldn't want it any other way."

"No, I expect not." She paused. "I wondered whether you would return one day."

"Oh, darling. For you, I will always return." His wide, characteristic grin matched the teasing in his voice.

"Vincent." She rolled her eyes playfully and shook her head.

"Speaking of my return, where is that delightful brother of yours?" KyVeerah peered around from behind his shades. No matter how intently Cassandra tried to look through them, she was unable to see that his eyes had shifted temporarily off of her.

"Jude? He took a quick trip to the Willow District to pick us up a couple cups of hot dreg. He should be back very shortly," she assured. "You are more than welcome to stick around here until he returns." She added, in a conspiratorial whisper, "I promise, I won't reveal your location."

Cassandra awaited his decision, though doubting he would be willing to stand and wait around, even for only a short time. One could never be sure with Vincent KyVeerah. Once someone thought they had him figured out, he would instinctively do the opposite of what was expected.

"Oh, what the hell. Why not?"

Knowing that he would expect as much, Cassandra gestured to a chair behind the stand. "You may as well make yourself comfortable. No need to stand around while waiting for my brother. Besides, I have a feeling you will be spending quite a lot of time on your feet."

Accepting, KyVeerah stepped around to Cassandra's side of the stand. He sat tilting the chair onto its two back legs, rocking back and forth, pushing his toes into the ground. Settling back, oblivious to his surroundings, he did indeed make himself comfortable.

Cassandra watched as KyVeerah seated himself where her brother, Jude, often sat relaxing. Jude had always told her that she was much better at handling the everyday common folk. Whatever that meant.

"Oh my word!" Cassandra threw a hand up to her mouth. In her distraction, resulting from the return of the long vanished Vincent KyVeerah, she had totally forgotten the morning shoppers coming to and departing from her stall.

"I am so sorry, madam," Cassandra apologized, gesturing with her hands exactly how much, as a woman gave her a disgruntled look at how long it had taken Cassandra to pay her attention.

KyVeerah chuckled, watching the dissatisfied old woman with her hand on her hip, her lip jutted forward. *As if contorting yourself into something even more grotesque is going to help your situation, old hag.* He twisted his lips delightedly, continuing to rock back in his chair. *Some somns. I just do not understand what circulates through such numbskulls. Do they really think they are going to achieve anything through the obnoxious things they say and do?*

Finishing with the disgruntled woman, Cassandra collected the items she wished to purchase while answering a million irrelevant questions. She also made change, which the old woman grabbed, stuffing it into a fabric clutch.

Turning back to KyVeerah, now that no customers were rummaging through her baskets, Cassandra glared at him. "Could you possibly be a little more discreet?" Her fair skin flushed, as she skewered him with a look of exasperation.

"My sincere apologies." KyVeerah grinned crookedly. "How do you do it?"

"What? Do what?"

"Deal with such drab lowlifes, such as that woman, all of the time."

She sighed, shaking her head at his imperious tone. "Oh, Vincent."

"What?" He cocked a brow above his dark lenses.

"Don't you have even the slightest respect for the somn race?" She hoped for a genuine response.

"Cassandra, Cassandra," he said, shaking his head slowly with an honest smile. "I hold the lack of respect for the somn race, simply because it deserves no admiration."

"Surely there is something?"

"No," he said, crossing his arms, "not when you get down to the core of things."

"What exactly do you mean?"

"I am merely saying that the heart does not fundamentally exist for the preservation of love, or the admiration of others, as we are manipulated to believe through the teachings of ethics and morality."

"Oh, doesn't it?" Cassandra pressed her painted lips together in obvious dispute.

"No, not in the least. Our hearts beat for one undisputable reason: to keep the blood flowing, in order to keep us alive."

"Well, yes. That's the obvious reason, but—"

KyVeerah cut her off. "Many believe that our reason for living is to love and to be loved, but honestly, what good would that do the world? We live to live. And that is that. We are willing to do almost anything in order to live, to survive this despicable world into which we are born. For instance, if we must either steal our neighbors' food or starve to death, we will steal their food. If we are ordered to kill another being or be killed ourselves, our bodies will instinctively tell us to kill the other being whose life is at stake."

For a moment he sat, pondering the sagacity of his own words. "I do realize, however, that it is difficult to understand what matters most, our morals or our lives? Is a life supposed to be the ultimate gift? Why would one allow it to be taken away if there were any other option?

"Some may opt to sacrifice themselves to save another. Wrong. That is against our true heart and instinct. In that last second, when it's too late, they realize that they made the wrong choice."

KyVeerah held a hand up, forestalling Cassandra's obvious

consternation. "Don't look at me like that, Cassandra. I know that sounds covetous in the most disgusting of ways, but it is the true core of the somn race. You don't believe me? If you were ever forced into such a decision, you would see the truth of my words. I know many, from every walk of life, and I know this is what lies below the morality taught by society."

Cassandra stared at him in disbelief. Her expression conveyed both repulsion for his words, pity, and doubt that he would even believe them. "I know you better than that, Vincent KyVeerah! I know there are those for whom you would sacrifice your own life in an instant!"

"No, beloved. You misunderstood my meaning. Yes. There are those for whom I would sacrifice my life in an instant, if only one of us could live. But that doesn't make it the correct decision. It may be the right decision in my mind, but my body would want to live."

Cassandra frowned for a moment in thought, but her reply was not what she originally intended. "Jude!" Her head turned to follow her eyes, and she stepped to the opening between her stand and that of her neighbor.

"Brother," she said, with a renewed smile.

"My darling baby sister." He approached, handing her a drink. He kissed her casually on the forehead. "I'm sorry it took me so long. I ran into a couple of fellows along the way that simply refused to let me pass up a good conversation."

Suddenly, the young man's eyes shifted beyond his sister. They rested upon the man who sat in his usual spot.

"Vincent? Good lord, brother! I thought you were long gone from this city, having long since plundered the only things you desired from it!"

KyVeerah's smile was wide, most pleased to see his good friend, Jude. "Come now, I'm not that merciless. And do you really think me that destructive? I beg to differ." He stood as Jude gladly approached him.

He grasped Jude's extended hand, as they vigorously patted each other on the back. "God, it's good to see you!" Jude examined his friend, back from who knew where. "You look just as I left you… or as you left us, I presume?"

"Yes, you all have my apologies. The necessity to abandon this place came very suddenly. I hope that I might receive the forgiveness of both of the beloved Hollis siblings?"

"Without doubt!" Jude took priority in answering for both his sister and himself. "I just can't believe it! I ceased to expect that I would ever see your face again. Honestly, brother, it's as though Goddess Eve has returned you from the dead! And I am glad that she has!"

"You are looking well," KyVeerah commented, gesturing toward his friend's costly attire. It was quite a departure from his usual wardrobe of the past.

"Yes, we came to inherit a small fortune. Apparently, our parents left us much more than we had originally expected. And you are looking very well. I hope my darling sister has been keeping you entertained? I hope you haven't waited too long?"

"Of course she has, as always in your absence. And no, I haven't been here long, not at all."

"Cassandra," Jude started, turning his attention back to his sister, "would you ever forgive me if I were to—"

"Go on." Cassandra smiled, flourishing her hand to shoo both of them away.

"What will you tell the Kolbys?" Jude asked his sister of the family with whom they shared the stand. The Kolbys had long been in charge of covering the afternoon shift.

"I will simply tell them that you are home ill or at least that you were when I headed out this morning. Honestly, would my brother whom they admire so much ever leave them with a lie?"

"You are an angel." Jude offered a final nod, as he led KyVeerah through the opening between the stands. Following, KyVeerah lowered his shades with a wink to Cassandra at his leave.

"It was great to see you," she said, in farewell.

"You as well. It's always a pleasure. I know I will see you again in good time."

18: Café Conversation In Sampton

Together, KyVeerah and Jude made their way south down the strip, moving in the direction from which Jude had just come.

"So, how in the world are you?" Jude asked, as they reached the southern end of the strip.

"I am doing quite well. There's never really enough time to relax, but I suppose that's what you get when you go into my kind of business. It's to be expected, I imagine."

Jude was a charming young man, only three years KyVeerah's junior, as opposed to his sister, Cassandra, who was even four years younger, at twenty-one. His body was slender, and his warm brown hair had a copper tone that was reminiscent of his sister's, but only when captured as highlights in the bright light of the suns. Rather long and shaggy, it was nonetheless well styled. On the other hand, Jude shared the fair skin and honey-colored eyes of his sister.

As they moved down the open walkway, KyVeerah reevaluated his friend's attire. Over a white shirt of thin, rich fabric, he sported an expensive brown jacket with matching belt and shoes. Unbuckled sleeves revealed tattoos running down his forearms, some spilling onto his left hand. The rings on his fingers were also princely. Jude wore two barbells through his left brow, and similar to KyVeerah, he had numerous ear piercings.

"So, where have you been all this time, Vincent? You couldn't have sent a single word? As far as I am aware, you never told a single soul you were taking off in the first place. I thought somebody had stabbed you bleedin' dead, chained you up, and tossed you into the depths of the faukin' sea! Damn, Vincent!"

"Shh!" KyVeerah peered cautiously around. He raised a warning finger, threatening, "Jude, this is not an appropriate time or place. In due time, but for god's sake, keep your voice down."

Jude capitulated. "All right, all right. But you have to understand that, given the business we are involved in, it is imperative to inform each other about what's going on! As one of your closest friends, I had to assume the worst had happened, considering I never heard a blasted thing. It's been two godforsaken years, Vincent!" He bared his teeth, biting off the end of his statement.

"Are you quite finished?" Vincent gave another warning look. "And the name's *KyVeerah*."

Clenching his teeth, Jude exhaled in vexation, wishing to press the issue. KyVeerah should have found *some* way to report to him. It didn't matter where in the world he had been. This involved business and more. "Yes," he snarled.

"Good."

Jude bit his tongue, leading silently onward.

"Where are we headed?" KyVeerah questioned. Many minutes of silence had passed as the two moved through multiple districts, and they continued moving forward.

"Just to the south. Sampton District. There is a café where we can grab a drink. You never know, maybe they'll spike them with a little of our favorite liquor, regardless of the early hour. Some kindly older women work there who I doubt would deny us anything we order."

"Well, you certainly haven't lost your touch, you old rogue." They both smiled slyly at each other, oblivious to their recent spat.

They crossed more bridges and walkways, coming in and out of view of multiple crystal canals, filled with perfectly transparent water. Abruptly, they halted before a sign reading *Café Roscalla*.

"Our destination." Jude extended his arm, ushering KyVeerah through the glass door.

Seat yourself, read a metal sign. "Will do," Jude said, in response to the painted words. He led the way through the maze of tables and booths with which he was clearly familiar. He stopped at a booth in the very back. From there they had seclusion, yet they could still view the room's entirety. Just as they made themselves comfortable, a middle-aged woman approached.

"Hello Marjorie." Jude offered a delightful smile that reminded KyVeerah of Cassandra's.

"Hello, sweetie. Oh, brought a friend along today, I see?"

"Sure have, madam," Jude charmingly replied. "Marjorie, this is my friend V. And this is my lovely lass, Marjorie."

"Oh, no need to flatter a woman, dear. I'm nearly twice your age." The woman waved a hand, excusing the flattery, but clearly enjoying it all the same. "What will it be this morning, my dears?"

"Marjorie, I know it is rather early in the day. But do you think, perhaps, you might be able to spike a couple of hot dregs? It's been a long couple of days, with more to come, I'm afraid."

The woman smiled sweetly, peering around the café. "Oh,

sweetie, no need for explanation. You know ol' Marge will take care of you."

"Wonderful. Thank you, very much, Marjorie." Jude flashed his charming smile once again.

"Any time, dear. I will be right back. It'll take just a bit to get those dregs brewed up for you."

KyVeerah and Jude each nodded graciously, as she turned to weave her way back toward the bar.

Jude smiled with a shrug.

"Hah," KyVeerah laughed. "Marvelous. So what does she believe *your* name to be?"

"Jarvis."

"You have got to be kidding. That's horrible! Oh goddesses, forbid that I ever meet a man *actually* named Jarvis!"

"Yes, I know. It's terrible. I couldn't help myself!" The sheepish grin on Jude's face caused KyVeerah to laugh again.

Shortly, Marjorie returned with two rust red ceramic mugs, filled to the rim and topped with a large spiral of whipped cream. Each mug rested on a small saucer with a small, silver spoon and a dainty triangular paper napkin.

"Thank you, so much," KyVeerah said, as she set one of the mugs before him.

She placed the second before Jude, smiling sweetly. "There you are, Jarvis dear."

Jude covered his amusement, expressing his appreciation. "Thank you, Marjorie. You have no idea how amazing this looks right now."

"Anytime, sweetie. And if you boys need a refill or anything else, just let me know." She gave a conspiratorial wink.

"Oh, we surely will."

Marjorie gave another small wink before turning back to the kitchen. As she disappeared, they both silenced their mirth.

"Jude Hollis," KyVeerah whispered, stabbing a finger at his friend, "you are a horrible, horrible somn. That poor woman." With a crooked grin, he shook his head.

Jude wiped his eyes, which had begun to water. "But, anyway—" He interrupted himself with a sip from his mug.

"So," KyVeerah said quietly, once they had set down their mugs. "Have you spoken to Galton recently?"

"Galton!" Jude choked in surprise. "What do you want with Galton? You never go to Galton unless you have something good in mind." Jude skewered KyVeerah with a severe expression. "What are you planning, Vincent? You don't show your face in the city for two full years, and now you hunt me down just to ask about Galton?"

KyVeerah ran a hand through his black hair, revealing his numerous piercings while tapping his lengthy fingernails rhythmically. "You didn't answer my question. When was the last time that you spoke with him? And lower your voice."

"Well, it was about four months ago. I had to obtain some professionally forged papers to cover our house. Cassandra's and my place."

KyVeerah paused his tapping to lift his mug for a thoughtful sip of the steaming dreg. Something Jude had said earlier returned to mind: *We came to inherit a small fortune. Our parents left us much more than originally believed.* KyVeerah mulled over the thought, for he couldn't possibly mean...

"What?" Jude interrupted, with a concerned look. "I don't know what you are presuming, but I know that look of yours, and I have never been fond of it—particularly when you are directing it at me."

Silently, KyVeerah took another sip. "Well, I was just thinking."   -175-

Jude's eyes narrowed, brows knitted together, realizing the accusation about to be voiced. Knowing KyVeerah, it would likely be a correct assumption. And it was something he did not wish to admit.

"I was wondering about something you said. That your parents left you more than everyone originally believed. And you needed Galton to help you obtain professionally forged papers. What can I say? You have certainly caught my attention. Jude, what kind of scam are you pulling?"

"I'm not pulling any scam!"

"Hush!" KyVeerah said, with a wicked gesture, about to reach over the table and strangle him personally. "You must keep your voice down," he snarled.

Calmer now, KyVeerah rested his elbows on the table, fingers interlaced. "Continue."

Jude mulled over his surfacing thoughts before speaking, dropping his honey eyes and stirring his dreg with the small spoon. "Cassandra and I received notice. We would be evicted if we didn't pay up. No questions asked, no debate. We had three weeks to come up with the entire amount. An outrageous sum.

"Then, a miracle. As though brought down by the goddesses themselves. While clearing boxes stored in Mother and Father's old room, eleven years after the incident, I came across a letter written in Mother's immaculate script. It was an account of a secret stash in case anything ever happened to them. The sum was beyond anything I could have ever imagined. The letter informed that it was to be divided among Cassandra, our Aunt Claudia and Aunt Lynette, and myself. My mother's sisters blame us to this day for the incident. They haven't spoken to us for eleven years.

"That was four months ago, right after the notice of eviction. I decided right then and there that our aunts would never see any of the money. And Cassandra and I were not going to be cast to the streets.

"I was the only living somn aware of the letter. If my aunts suspected so much as an inkling of the money, they would have ripped the house to shreds immediately after our parents' deaths."

Jude rested his head in his hands and sighed.

"Take a drink," KyVeerah said, setting down his own mug, which he had been sipping throughout his friend's story.

For a long moment, Jude sat motionless. Finally, taking the recommendation, he lifted his mug and took a few large swallows. Those were soon followed by a few more.

"So, you took this letter to Galton and asked him if he knew anyone who would be willing to adjust it for you?"

Another heavy sigh. "Yes, pretty much."

"So what payment did Galton exact for such a dealing?"

With an agonized moan, Jude threw his elbows back on the table, dropping his head back into his hands.

"That bad, eh?" KyVeerah peered from behind his shades, sensing Marjorie checking on them. Realizing that they had both finished their drinks, he waved for her assistance.

Surprised that V had been aware of her behind the kitchen door, she quickly made her way to their table. She gave Jude a look of pity, wishing to help in any way possible.

KyVeerah asked smoothly, "May we have another round of drinks, madam?"

"Oh, but of course." She snatched up their empty mugs and spoons, whisking them away. "I'll be back shortly, dears." She gave a pitying glance at her dear Jarvis before turning back to the bar to prepare the next round.

KyVeerah pondered what Galton had requested as payment from

Jude. Without delay, Marjorie returned with the new drinks perched on sea foam green saucers, which she plopped onto the table.

"Here you are," she bubbled, setting KyVeerah's before him, then solicitously sliding the second in front of Jude.

"Thanks again, Marjorie." KyVeerah offered her a small smile and a respectable nod.

Jude, wrapped up in his woe, didn't respond at all. Understanding, Marjorie simply offered another glance of pity. "Just let me know if there's anything else I can get for ya," she said, KyVeerah's way, smiling again.

He gave another nod, "Will do."

KyVeerah turned his attention back to Jude. He hadn't budged an inch. "Jude, if you don't mind me asking," he began quietly, "what exactly did you give Galton as payment?"

A long moment passed until Jude raised his head, appearing to examine the texture of the ceiling.

Finally, he looked intently into KyVeerah's shades, as if he were able to look through them and into his eyes, despite the intense tinting that would make it impossible.

KyVeerah slowly sipped from his mug, waiting for Jude's answer. He knew that, with time, it would come.

"I didn't pay him." Jude closed his eyes briefly. It was obvious how shaken and ashamed he was.

"You what?" KyVeerah almost jumped to his feet. "How? What?" he stammered. Jude had to have paid him *something*. Galton was not a man to do any dealing for free. And if there were a third party involved as well, he or she would certainly be expecting their own payment. KyVeerah pondered this new twist with a baffled expression.

"Vincent, I couldn't pay him. Do you understand? I had nothing, nothing at all. We were about to be evicted for that very fact. It's not like we had anyone here to help." His voice shook, as he cast an accusing eye at KyVeerah.

KyVeerah slid his shades to the top of his head. With a forceful gaze, his eyes bored into those of Jude. Expression filled with guilt and shame, Jude was unable to look away. If he were a weaker man, tears would have been spilling from his eyes.

"Nothing," Jude repeated, morosely, closing his eyes for another moment.

"So, what exactly was the arrangement that you struck with him?" KyVeerah pressed. He could plainly see there was more to the deal than Jude had explained.

"He knew the short term of my eviction situation. He knew there was no time left before we were kicked out. He told me, that in my case, he would make a rare exception, but that I would owe him a favor." Jude pressed his fingers together as emotion drained the color from his face. His skin was clammy. "You know, as well as I do, that any favor Galton might ask will be fraught with danger. I may have to sacrifice my own life. But that would be acceptable, as long as I know that Cassandra is safe, with the money that she needs and a place to live."

"Jude, stop it." KyVeerah squinted with the ferocity of his concentration. "So, you and Cassandra received all of the money from the account?" he questioned, just to reaffirm the fact.

Jude released a long, unsteady breath, trying to calm his nerves. He nodded.

"Wait! Does Cassandra even know about this? She can't. She must not know anything involving Galton or this business, or it could mean the life of both of you." KyVeerah frowned. Either way, things were not good.

"Good Valencia, Jude. This is some mess you've gotten yourself into." He slammed his fist on the table, causing the dishes to clatter unnervingly.

Jude shook his head again, eyes still angled upward. "I do have to say, Cassandra was surprised that mother would leave her own sisters out of her will." Jude finally managed to look at KyVeerah.

"She doesn't have any idea how much money was involved. If she did, she would never believe that it was all meant solely for us. Some of the money, I used to eliminate the entire house payment. I don't have the nerve to tell her. Not yet. She's going to know that something isn't right. Mother loved Claudia and Lynette to death, and she would never have deliberately left them out of that kind of inheritance."

"So, what exactly does Cassandra know?"

"She didn't even know about the eviction notice. I didn't want her to know until I had a plan. So I waited and told her about the eviction notice and the letter explaining the will all at the same time. By that time, higher officials had verified the money, and it had been transferred into a new account under Cassandra's and my name.

"I didn't even tell her about the new account. I only told her that we were receiving a large enough stipend to take care of our home, CavonRué. I told her that, once they worked out the official numbers, they would get back to us with the remainders. I don't even know what that means. But Cassandra seemed to buy it.

"I don't have a clue what Galton is going to ask of me, or when. I know that after the deal I offered him, there is no way he would accept cash as payment. I am sure he will wait until he has something horrendous in mind. It will be something dangerous, risky enough that he doesn't want to put his own men on the line. There is no way I can even warn Cassandra that there may be something coming up. If I told her, and they found out, I am certain they would have her killed. And that is the *last* thing that I would ever allow to happen in this godforsaken world."

They both quietly sipped their drinks, preoccupied by their own thoughts. "Wait a minute," Jude's expression altered. "Why did you want to know if I had spoken with Galton recently anyway?" His eyes filled with a dubious curiosity. "What might it have to do with whatever plan you are scheming up?"

KyVeerah nursed his drink, as he framed his words. "Galton isn't fond of those involved in business with him randomly disappearing for long periods without informing him of their whereabouts. He likes to keep a tight rein on his business acquaintances. That's where you come in."

"For sake of The Darkness, what do you mean?"

"I mean, my friend, that you are my ticket back to Galton. You are coming with me to pay him a visit." KyVeerah flashed a wicked grin.

"Oh no!" Jude's eyes widened. "No, no, no, I can't show my face to him right now. And I won't, Vincent! I will not do it! What if he should decide to go ahead and do away with me right then and there?"

"Jude, you are, in fact, the best friend I have in this damn city. I am certain that, in a moment, you are going to change your mind and agree to help me out by coming along." KyVeerah gave him a piercing look, expecting that moment to come very shortly.

"Oh, Vincent, please. Have mercy. I have already bitten off more than I can chew, as it is." Jude put his hand up to shield his eyes from KyVeerah's adamant stare.

KyVeerah sat quietly, waiting for his friend to change his mind. The look on Jude's face reflected the conflict warring within. After several minutes, KyVeerah finished the last of his drink, replacing the empty mug back on its saucer. "Are you ready?"

"Fine." Jude gave KyVeerah a scathing look. With a warning finger, he leaned across the table. "But if anything happens to me, it's on your conscience."

KyVeerah beamed in satisfaction, as though oblivious of any danger to his friend. "I knew you would come around."

"I had forgotten, Vincent. I really do hate you and all of your goddamned ways." Though Jude shook his head, he gave a short laugh all the same. Standing up, he hollered back toward the kitchen, "Thanks again, Marjorie!"

Between them, they contributed a large pile of pale-colored bills to cover their refreshment. It was much more than necessary, but worth the price of discreet service.

Readjusting his shades and straightening his coat, KyVeerah made the first move to leave. "Let's go see what awaits us."

Weaving once more through the maze of tables and chairs, they made their way toward the entrance of Café Roscalla, Jude one step to the rear. They pushed through the glass doors and headed west. KyVeerah laid down a thick layer of sarcasm, "Well, this ought to be a good time."

Jude raised his eyes toward the sky. Today there would be no spirits to assist them. "Peace with you, Goddess Eve. Keep us from your world."

19: The Perfect Analogy

The night was windy. Rain whipped through the streets with a sting in every drop. The streetlight offered only a stingy glimmer, glowing blue off the ground in showing her the way. To Helena, it seemed the perfect night to vent her fury at a life that had led her to such cruel loneliness. She kicked at the blue sapphires and stomped through puddles, splashing up icy droplets that glittered like an aura of icy shards around her.

The analogy was fitting. Deep inside, she felt her heart to be no more than a block of cold hard ice. But she had long ago come to the realization that there would never be anyone to share it with. Her childhood—and most of her adolescence—had been filled with nothing more than a steady stream of dirty faces and sweaty bodies.

Her mother had never been any comfort. Even in those few times they had spoken to each other. She was only happy she now had a daughter to take her place on the hardboard cot. That meant Mommy always had enough cash to be in constant possession of a half-empty bottle.

Helena's thoughts drifted back to that freezing night when she had been dragged to the guard shack at The Tower. Throughout that long night, she had been nothing more than a ragged toy—temporarily allowing the guards to forget the biting cold—as she was passed back and forth. The night had lasted until she lost all track of time and place.

In the morning, she opened her eyes to see nothing around her but drunken guardsmen collapsed into a mass of snoring piles. Rolling to her knees, she had tried her best to sneak quietly out the door. She needed to be gone and away before they had a clue. However, as she reached the doorway, a streaming ray of sunshine broke through. It fell glittering on the handle of a knife. For an eternity she stared. It was beautiful. Graceful figures etched into the handle. Attempting to disguise its lethal intent.

Trying to swallow the dry lump in her throat, she could barely breathe. She crept closer. Looking back now, she still couldn't believe she had the courage—or even more, the stupidity, to try such a thing. She had always possessed an innate sense of survival.

And to be caught at such an attempt would be a sure and cruel death.

But Goddess Eve had smiled on her that morning. She did finally reach her target. And not daring to so much as breathe, slowly slipped it from its well-oiled sheath.

The next thing she could remember, she was scurrying down a dark alleyway clutching her newly won treasure to her chest.

That moment had changed her life.

At first, the blade felt heavy and awkward in her small hands. But endless hours of diligent practice, slowly and steadily brought her the sense of secure protection that she had always longed for. Initially, she had only used her knife for protection. However, living the life she did, she had found a multitude of circumstances where she had to put it to use.

In one particular instance, she had been minding her own business when someone suddenly—and roughly—grabbed her from behind. Turning her head, she gasped. The man who now had his dirty clutches on her was the same man who had first taken her. He had been rough. He had been thorough. And when he finished, he still leered at her as he fished deeply into his pocket for a grimy wad of bills that he thrust into her mother's hand. Helena closed her eyes, feeling a bit nauseated as she remembered the greedy gleam that had come into her mother's eyes. That had been the last night—until she took the knife—that she had ever spent a night alone.

On recognizing him, every fiber of her being turned to ice. Ice that flamed, burning away every last vestige of civilized thought. Without even thinking, she was suddenly holding the knife, now planted in his protruding gut. The only warmth in the entire world was that which ran down her fingers and over her hand to pool on the sodden ground. With delight, she had watched the life trickle out of him, until he lay motionless, staring with flat dull eyes into a gray sky that he could no longer see.

From that moment on, Helena had stalked her previous tormentors, honing her skills. For some time, she had given herself over to an orgy of bloodletting. But as her opportunities for revenge had lessened, she had become more selective. With time, she had become adept enough to hire her skills out to others. They had paid well, and eventually her prowess had even reached the eyes and ears of Nyx Crucian. Never again did she have to walk in fear of others.

Now she walked wherever she wanted, certain that her reputation, as well as that of her comrades, was a powerful shield about her. But her life was still not all knives and roses. It was more like the pennātus bloom—with petals said to be the feathers of Goddess Eve's wings, which can never be touched. A black flower whose glossy petals sprayed out a venomous mist if somn flesh were ever to come too near. Helena had found that the more lethal and selective she became the more lethal and selective the enemy became as well. She had to be careful what she touched. And to know the full capabilities of an opponent before getting too near.

Helena had learned to keep her eyes and ears always open. And even more, she had learned to always have a plan. In fact, her entire life revolved about a series of plans. She had a plan for each day. She had a plan for escape. And now she was working on a plan for the future.

She smiled darkly. What a glorious future it was going to be. Yet, a small obstacle still lay in her way. She needed information—information about this Key Calling. She needed his power.

And she was pretty sure she knew where to start in her search.

With Albert's grandfather. Serlio Young.

20: Riding on Seas of Annihilation

Marion hummed as she sauntered away from Rhyus, who was leaning over the rail near the bow. He swayed with the hypnotic rhythm as the oars, rowing in circles, dipped in and out of the Dark Water. A light drizzle fell from the ominous clouds above, but at least it had stopped pouring.

Still humming, Marion made her way to the stern where a row of wide, cushioned benches lined each side of the boat, beneath a luxurious waterproof canopy. The comfortable cushions were red, one of her favorite colors. Appropriate, since Quinton Paris's trademark had been to write with nothing but red ink. That fact, along with other notable qualities, had always intrigued Marion.

Water-repellant screens, thin and transparent, extended from the true canopy to keep passengers dry.

Marion wiped the few droplets from a small section of the bench, despite the fact that her clothes were already soaked. She pondered the odd weather. She had never cared for rain, but she did love its coolness, and Lux Lumetia so rarely saw rain that it was a treat when it did occur.

She lay back. Sinking into the cushions and closing her eyes, she pondered Rhyus's comment: *"So...tell me about this friend who taught you how to steer such a respectable boat as this?"* Marion smiled. *Does Rhyus object that I may have had relations with him?* She couldn't help a silent laugh that Rhyus might be jealous. She thought she had stifled it, but Rhyus turned his head in her direction, which only caused her to laugh for a second time before closing her eyes again.

Where is he now? Marion wondered, about her friend from the past. *I am sure he is doing wonderful things. Carrying out important business or taking adventurous trips perhaps? I wish I could have stayed with him. Then again, what would I have done without Venn? He has been so good to me. Well, for the most part. I have been more than happy with him the last two years. What will he do without me there in Umbra Halls to keep him company, or more so, to take care of him?* A small frown touched her lips.

The gentle rocking waves lulled Marion into a deep sleep.

"Rhyus!" Marion jolted upward.

Rhyus, lying on the opposite bench, rushed to kneel beside her.

"Marion," he said, putting a hand on her arm. "Marion!" As she continued to frantically cast about, he put a hand to the side of her face, trying to calm her. "Marion, you're all right. It was just a dream."

Finally, her anxious, warm brown eyes rested on his, heart still pounding and her breathing ragged.

"Quiet Marion," Rhyus said calmly, running his fingers through her matted hair, pushing it from her face. Concerned, he took her hands in his. "Are you all right?"

She began to tear up.

"Oh, Marion." Rhyus's heart dropped. Taking a seat next to her, he rested her head in his lap, her legs curled back on the seat. He placed one hand on her side, as he ran the other through her hair.

She eventually drifted back to sleep. He looked down, as she rested lightly on him. *What was that all about? She looks so peaceful now. But that look on her face. I realize I've only known her a few days, but that was way outside anything she's ever shown.*

Suddenly, Rhyus recalled waking startled from his own dreams. It seemed like ages ago, but in reality, it had been just that morning. Random images flashed through his mind again.

That stone shelf with the harsh waves crashing around it... The Courtyard of Umbra Halls covered in a sea of sapphires...the presence of the shadowy figure before being knocked unconscious... the beautiful towers falling to their destruction...the eerie bystander who knew the wrongdoings of which Rhyus stood responsible. A chill ran through Rhyus causing Marion to alter her position. He tried to ignore his own flashbacks so he could comfort her, but they continued to pound at his mind.

The robed man who had told him to leave, to follow the path of The Rafters...and Marion...so beautiful...and who was this Armani? Why had she mentioned him? Were those his initials on the letter she had demanded he take?

Rhyus looked out at the black sea, visible only where light from the boat reflected on it. He shivered, thinking about the madness The Darkness was said to bring. He recalled the dread that had overtaken him when Marion had mentioned Armani in his dream. Wiping his clammy hands on the red seat, he avoided looking at Marion's still form, so peaceful, so delicate, and so different from the Marion of his dream. He shook his head, confused. His dreams were so mixed with his reality that he was unsure where his reality began and where his dreams ended. Or was it where his dreams began and where reality ended?

What about the robed man who told me to leave? He was so real and so convincing. But am I a fool for listening to his orders? Letting a stolen boat lead me into this black abyss to steal my mind, leading me to madness? Where is it taking us? For all I know, we may drop off the edge of the world. Another shiver ran through his lean frame, as light rain continued to land on the overhead screen, rolling off to join the Mother Sea.

The gentle rocking of the waves surprised Rhyus. He had assumed the oscillation would be much more forceful out here.

Looking up, he was also baffled by the brilliant stars lacing the ink black sky. They dazzled brightly, despite the steady drizzling rain. Perhaps the clouds had thinned enough to allow such mystical lights to shine forth in the lowering sky.

He frowned. *Why are there no moons?* On previous nights, he could swear he had seen from two to three moons circling over the city. And they had been full moons. *They can't be gone. Especially considering the starlight. They can't be covered by clouds or out of phase since they are so random, sometimes at completely opposite horizons.*

Tired from his previous dream-broken sleep and the early morning, he closed his eyes and drifted off.

℘℃ℛ

Rhyus stretched and yawned. Small lights had come on across the entire length of the boat. At the stern, a large spiraled source sent out beacons of light, which crawled eerily across the black waves, as though attempting to escape danger that surrounded the boat. Rhyus watched the ghostly traces fade away, skipping off the crests of the waves, far into The Darkness.

"You're awake," Marion said, sitting next to him and holding a ripe rabmelon.

"You're not going to poison me now, are you? Poison me and steal the boat which I have rightfully claimed?" Joking, he cocked an eyebrow.

"No, it's not poisoned. I promise."

"But you wouldn't tell me if it were, would you?" he pressed, with the same crooked grin.

"No." She nodded thoughtfully. "I wouldn't. But what good is a captain with a stolen boat and no first mate to do the bitch work?"

Rhyus laughed, snatching the red melon from her hand.

"That's what I thought."

He took a large bite. "You know, Marion, you were actually right. These are amazing."

"What do you mean *actually*?"

Rhyus paused, debating an acceptable response. "I was foolish to think that they would be anything less than you had earlier informed me that they would be." His tentative smile showed hope that she found his convoluted answer acceptable. At least it sounded to him like a good enough response to schmooze a woman.

She hesitated, before smiling. "Well good. I am glad you realize that I tell none other than the truth."

Satisfied, Rhyus took another large bite. Once finished, he hurled the husk out through a thin gap in the screen. As it hit the black water, Marion shouted in a shrill voice, "Rhyus!"

"What?"

She crossed her arms and exhaled heavily in curt disapproval.

"You didn't want me to leave it aboard to rot did you? Besides, I am sure it will make some fish out there far happier than it would make us, lying on our polished deck."

"You're an idiot. Don't you realize what a danger it is to leave any hint of a spore trail around us?"

After stubbornly refusing to speak to one another, Marion finally glanced toward Rhyus. Though he felt her eyes, he refused to show the slightest acknowledgment.

Annoyed, Marion finally gave in. "How did you have time to get those melons anyway?"

"I didn't sleep well. I got up early."

Marion gave him a malcontent expression for stating the obvious.

"What?" he sighed, as she continued to stare at him.

"I had a lot on my mind, and it kept me from sleeping. Since I was up, I decided to wander the city. There was nothing better to do so frikkin' early." Marion continued to stare.

"I wandered around for awhile. The North Market vendors eventually set up their stands. I overheard someone say something about Plush melons, and recalling you had been so set on having some, I thought I would be so kind as to pick you up a batch.

"While returning, I had time to think. I decided I was nuisance enough at your home, and that I should leave. So I returned, packed my bags, and headed out. Oh, and I wrote the note for you, hoping it would suffice as an acceptable self-dismissal."

Marion appeared somewhat appeased.

"How did you find me before I got away?"

Marion dropped her eyes. "I got up early. It didn't take long to find your note. I decided to go with you. I figured that you would want to get as far away as possible, and I knew the only way to accomplish that was by water if you're impetuous enough. You are. Not that that's a good thing...I also figured that you would follow the shoreline for the nearest dock. That would mean Crystal Harbor. And there you were, just as I had hoped." With a short laugh, Marion added, "However, I didn't know I would find you stealing such a respectable boat."

He shrugged with a genuine smile. "What can I say?"

Marion couldn't help but smile back.

They sat silently, each preoccupied in their own thoughts.

Occasionally, they chatted over irrelevant topics such as the abundance of stars or discovering and naming nonexistent constellations. Their favorite colors, Rhyus's being green, which Marion explained was ridiculous and ironic considering his eyes and his temporary bedroom color. "Good karma," he shrugged, with a sardonic grin.

Marion stated that her own favorite was black. Rhyus tried to claim that black was not a real color. His efforts failed. As they continued their desultory conversation, time flew rather quickly. Eventually, Marion went to the bow. Rustling through a wooden compartment where she had stored their packs, she returned with her hands behind her back.

"Pick one."

"Left," he said, pointing at her arm.

"That's my right arm."

"Whatever."

Bringing her right hand from behind her back, she offered another Plush melon, which he willingly accepted. In her other hand was an identical melon. "We have to ration our food. We could be out here a while."

"Indeed." After taking the last acceptable bite, Rhyus hurled the rind overboard and put his right hand out in a gesture of asking for Marion's as well.

Rolling her eyes, Marion placed the husk onto his outstretched palm. "I guess you might as well. It's too late now. Still, that was stupid, and you are still an idiot." She watched as he hurled hers overboard too.

He shrugged, a proud grin on his face.

"All right, smart ass. I'm going to bed."

"Oh come on." He offered her a pair of pouting eyes. "How can you be mad at this face?"

Marion couldn't maintain her frown. Rhyus noticing, silently congratulated himself. "G'night Captain."

She shook her head playfully, bidding him a good night.

Dousing the smaller lights throughout the boat, Marion curled up across from Rhyus who had already drifted off to sleep.

A few hours later, Rhyus awoke to a strange rustling. Once realizing it was Marion shaking, he noticed himself shivering as well. The cold breeze cut like a knife through his wet clothes.

Going to the compartment where he had seen Marion retrieve the melons, he unfastened the bronze buckles of his messenger bag, finding everything within it dry. In fact, the bag itself was dry, being impermeable to rain.

Fool. Had I known, I would have changed my sopping clothes long ago. The feeling of dry clothing was the best thing he had felt all day. *Well, maybe.*

Checking Marion's bag, her clothing was soaked. Rummaging through his own bag again, he pulled out another pair of fresh denims and a green shirt with a white tree on it.

"Marion." He pushed the hair out of her face. "Marion," he called a little louder. She jumped, taking in the sudden sight of someone right before her.

Noting it was Rhyus, she quickly readjusted.

"I brought you these. They're completely dry. I hope you don't mind, but I checked yours too. They are all soaked." He pressed the clothing into her hands.

Marion could just make out his kind expression, as he moved his hand to the back of his neck. "Ah. There is one dilemma with the dry clothes being mine. I forgot to pack ladies undergarments." Marion laughed as she caught him blushing, even in the faint light.

"Why thank you, kind sir." Marion shivered at the chillflesh running down her entire body.

"I will be over there." Rhyus pointed toward his side of the boat. "You know…in case you need me for any reason." He moved and sat facing in the opposite direction.

"Umm, Rhyus?" A meek voice called for his attention.

Rhyus swiveled around, noting the darling little Marion swimming in his clothes. "You look absolutely stunning."

"Yeah, yeah." Though dressed in dry clothes, chillbumps still covered her chilled body. She rubbed her arms in a failed attempt to warm herself.

"Watch out." He seated himself behind her, pulling her back toward him as he wrapped his arms around her. He held her close, rubbing her arms and legs in an effort to make her warm. The warmth of their nearness was a reprieve for them both.

"Stand up a second." Rhyus shifted, lying on his side. "All right." He patted the cushion in front of him.

Marion sat, and then lying down, curled up, tucked snugly against him. He wrapped his arm around her thin waist. "Now don't get used to this," Rhyus joked, though somewhat serious as he meant to make it apparent that this sleeping arrangement wasn't going to become habit.

"Oh, don't worry," she replied, however the closeness of his embrace was the greatest comfort that she could remember since coming to Lux Lumetia.

In no time, they drifted back to sleep.

෨ℭ

Morning arrived with no announcement. There were no suns, no chirping birds, nor any other greeting. Twinkling stars punctuated the same blackness and wait—two moons were now in sight, both glowing as full bright discs. *Odd*, Rhyus thought.

As Marion nestled against him, still sleeping, he shifted his arm from around her waist, up to her side. The unfamiliar movement caught her subconscious attention. She blinked her eyes, rubbing them and stretching each limb, one by one.

"Good morning, sunshine." He smiled, resting his head in his hand.

"Yeah," she replied, half roused, "you too."

Waking fully, she sat up. With a playful look of accusation from beneath her dark lashes, her eyes traveled to the hand that had moved from her waist to her side.

"What?" He looked innocent. "Nothing happened."

Marion laughed, shaking her head. "You are ridiculous." Rising, she walked to the bow.

Rhyus grinned widely, watching as she clutched the denims to keep them from sliding right off her thin frame. *Good thing she doesn't move much in her sleep.*

After digging through her bag, she leaned over the rail, toothbrush in hand.

"Good idea." Rhyus followed suit. Standing beside Marion, he noted the water bottle held captive between her feet.

"Wait a minute, is that my belt lying on the deck?" Rhyus accused, though he really cared less.

"Mway fahn shtay."

Rhyus burst out laughing. "Are those words, Marion? Do you really think you are allowed to rummage through my things for whatever you want?"

Marion leaned over the rail, up on her toes, and spat.

"Charming." Rhyus cocked an eyebrow.

Giving him a cheeky look, and taking a long swig from her bottle, Marion spit a stream far out over the water.

"*Most* charming." He smiled, and she smiled back in return. "And wait a minute," he added shortly. "Aren't we supposed to be rationing our water?" Marion twisted her mouth in brief before shrugging and handing her toothpaste out to Rhyus.

Accepting it, Rhyus followed suit once more.

As had become custom, Marion retrieved a pair of melons, tossing one to Rhyus.

They ate silently, Rhyus screwing up his face at the tart acid immediately following the sweet toothpaste. He laughed.

"What?"

"I was just thinking that a steady diet of melons isn't exactly the ultimate nutrition for crossing this black abyss."

"Yeah." Marion looked thoughtful. "I suppose you are right." She slurped back into her melon.

Finished, Rhyus disposed of the husks in the new customary way while Marion ignored him. They sat in silence again. Rhyus pondered where they could be heading. He thought about his trip to get the watch with the chronometer. It was obvious that had been a useless venture, traveling wherever the boat wished to take them.

Remembering the copper-haired Cassandra, Rhyus corrected himself. *Well, maybe not completely useless.* Having no clue of their destination, he wondered, *Will the civilians be friendly toward our arrival?* He hated to admit it, but Venn had been right. Wherever they landed, they would know nothing of the somns, their history, beliefs, alliances, geography, or customs. They would be like blind children, relying on luck and opportunity. *Perhaps they will instantly lock us up. Or worse.* He gulped.

Marion looked at him, asking in concern, "Are you OK?"

"Oh, yeah. It's nothing." Attempting to change the subject, he asked, "Are there two or three moons?"

"Well, actually there are five."

"You're kidding."

"Adelaide, Arienette, Eve, Ravenna, and Valencia," she said, naming them off. "They are like goddesses watching over us."

"Are they always so full? How is it possible for none of them to show, like last night?" he inquired.

"They never decay into crescents or darkness. They are always full, perfect circles of light. And their paths have no particular order. They do orbit, but their distance and location always vary, one night to the next. When at a distance, sometimes they disappear for days. I believe their orbital speeds are inconsistent as well. I don't know how it works. I'm just passing on what I've been told.

"In case you haven't noticed, their colors differ from one another also. It's the best way to tell them apart for anyone who can see the differences. I guess you could try to discern their markings too, but they don't have many, and they aren't too distinct. Nonetheless, these are the only two ways to distinguish them since their orbits make it impossible to know them by path or size.

"It is easiest if you go by color. They are named alphabetically in alignment with the color of the light spectrum. Adelaide has a red tint to her. Arienette is almost golden. Eve has an orange tint. Ravenna is blue-violet. And last, Valencia has a silver glow."

"Insightful." Was all Rhyus managed, wishing he could remember what she just said.

"I promise, it isn't that difficult after a while," she assured him. "Ravenna has always been my favorite. She comes off different. The others appear so warm and inviting. Ravenna, on the other hand, always seems mysterious to me, a little darker, as if she is hiding the secrets to our world." She smiled.

Rhyus gave her a quizzical look.

"I am beginning to sound like Venn. He loves philosophy, you know. He truly is a brilliant man." A pleasant smile remained upon her lips as she thought about him.

I dread the next time I cross his path, Rhyus thought, with a grimace just opposite of Marion's reaction. *He will likely grind my bones and feed me to the very seas on which I now ride. If he doesn't lock me up and torture me for the rest of eternity.*

Oblivious to Rhyus's discomfort, Marion quipped, "Do you like puzzles? Word and number puzzles, I mean?"

"Umm, I don't know. Maybe?"

"Hold on." She scurried to the wooden compartment, returning with a thick book. "Some of these can get pretty tricky, but others aren't too bad. It's a good way to pass the time."

"Thanks," he said, as she handed him the book and a blue pen.

"No problem." She smiled. "Do whatever puzzles you like. Doesn't matter to me one way or another." She turned around again, heading back to the bow.

"Wait." Rhyus looked at the vibrant blue pen.

"Yes?"

He shifted his eyes thoughtfully up to her. "Black isn't your favorite color." It was both a question as well as a declarative statement.

She grinned.

"It's blue." He was sure of the fact, thinking back to her bedroom, her combs and hair supplies, the dress that she had worn the day of his arrival, and this current pen. He looked at the pen again and then back into her soft brown eyes.

"Brilliant deduction!" She smiled wide before turning away again to the storage compartment.

While Rhyus began working the puzzles in Marion's book, she hunted for some loose rope. Finding some, she fashioned a makeshift clothesline for the clothes from her bag. The drizzle had ended at some point during the night, making the day a bit more tolerable, but the incessant Darkness still intruded into their very core. And the confinement, with nothing to do, was much more apparent. Who knew how long they would be out at sea?

Rhyus spent the long afternoon calculating and figuring out solutions to various puzzles. After Marion had strung her damp clothing, she had curled up close by. She became engrossed in a thick book from her bag. If Rhyus had been attentive, he would have recognized it as the very book he had desecrated earlier to write Marion's note.

Now and then, Rhyus or Marion stood to stretch their limbs, looking out into the oppressive blackness. The only proof that time had moved was the silent circling hands on their watches and the hypnotic circling of the boat's many wooden oars.

Many hours later, Rhyus stood where the rail attached to the high wall of the bow. He shook his head, feeling odd as though something unwarranted was creeping inside him. As though The Darkness was no longer only around him but becoming an integral part of him. Looking down at the painted words *Quinton Paris*, he released a deep breath. His watch read 6:42 p.m.

Good lord. I don't know how much more I can take. Rhyus ran a hand through his tousled hair. *What I would give for a shower. I'm sure Marion feels the same.*

Later, as they ate their last melons of the day, Rhyus dropped his head onto the wide wooden rail behind him. *I am going to starve to death if I don't die of boredom first. And it would be nice to have a barrel filled to the rim with water.* Rhyus sipped at the precious water that he had been rationing since morning.

At his nudge, Marion lifted her head from the leg she had been using as a pillow. Trudging to the bow, Rhyus brushed his teeth and spat over the edge of the boat. He looked guilty as it hit the water. "I should have swallowed it," he grumbled, before taking the last sip and tossing the bottle overboard. Shortly, Marion followed suit.

As the hours dragged, a breeze began to whisper over the cold, endless sea. Marion read while Rhyus simply stood at the stern, staring into The Darkness. They moved with the current now, but the light from their lamp still scampered away, fleeing the very site of the boat. Rhyus sighed. *This trip had better prove its worth.*

"Bedtime?" he asked Marion, sounding a bit too hopeful.

"Yeah." She stretched. "Sounds good to me."

"Would you care for some company? It's a tad bit frigid out here."

"That would be fabulous." Marion smiled flatly, but Rhyus could see that the endless Darkness had extinguished every spark of the usual vibrant enthusiasm from her eyes.

Marion, watching him change his clothes, flushed when he turned to face her. He grinned, as she damped the small lights. As Marion's clothes had not yet dried, she still wore what Rhyus had lent her. She removed the belt, buckling it around the canopy's support post to prevent losing it again.

As she curled into the nook formed by Rhyus's body, he slipped his arm around her waist again. "Like I said," he mumbled, "don't get to used to this."

"Oh, go to sleep." She smiled as she scolded him for his egotistical comment.

"Aye, aye, Captain."

Marion rolled her eyes, though he could not see it.

Rhyus's thoughts diverged toward sleep. *This trip has to end sooner or later. Yeah, I suppose I am enjoying my time with Marion, but honestly, I don't know how much longer I can last out here on the water. I will be amazed if boredom, starvation, or thirst doesn't kill us before we reach land.*

Closing his eyes, Rhyus was unaware of the constant Darkness creeping ever deeper; invading every cell, to the very core of his being. He gave another sigh, worried about what they would find when they did reach land. Marion snuggled more tightly against him. He pictured the endless repetition of the illuminated waves rolling beyond the stern, lulling him into the realm of sleep.

21: An Underground of Another City

Buildings and walkways shimmered in silver and white as the skies glowed above in a cloudless blanket of blue. Despite that, the heavy air began to feel less clean, and the overall atmosphere began to crawl over every citizen.

"Welcome to the Westside," Jude said, with a lack of enthusiasm. He maintained a steady pace, just a step behind and to the side of KyVeerah.

"Though it has been several years, I recognized the feel of this place a mile away."

"Just sayin'."

KyVeerah grimaced. "Just be thankful you don't live around these parts."

"No doubt about that, brother."

Up to this point in their travels, passersby had generally kept to themselves, avoiding eye contact with either KyVeerah or Jude, as they wove their way through the network of buildings towering overhead.

Now, however, with each step further west, the somns they passed began to show an interest in them. Curious eyes looked up from crouched bodies covered in clothing much too large, or on the other hand, far too revealing. A haggard misery exuded from both beggars and whores.

They must be freezing, KyVeerah thought. Though heartlessly, he did not pity the poor souls. He assumed the majority of them had brought such a vulgar lifestyle upon themselves.

It did not help KyVeerah or Jude that, over their good hygiene, they sported such flashy attire. Heads turned in suspicion as they neared their destination.

Clearly, no one trusts anyone in these parts, KyVeerah thought, eyeing the woebegone bystanders. *Absolutely revolting*, he cringed again, but he maintained an air of nonchalant disinterest.

The filth and pollution seemed to extract oxygen from the air, and they had to force themselves simply to breathe.

KyVeerah was aware of the uneasiness that exuded from his friend. He could sense his angst from the twisting of the rings on his fingers, to an apprehensive shifting of his eyes. Though his steps seemed steady and confident, he maintained a much smaller distance than he had in the decency of the city's center. KyVeerah hoped that Jude would be able to conceal his discomfort from others.

Galton will surely be able to pick it up from him. His vibe is far too strong. Hell, then again, he will probably be able to tell just by looking at Jude if he doesn't stop fidgeting like a nervous little schoolgirl.

At length, they reached a place neither of them truly wished to be.

A multitude of undesirable somns gathered here, where three districts converged forming the center point of West Bay. These somns sat or stood in clusters, rather than staying to themselves like most of those they had passed along the way. *Appalling.* KyVeerah kept the repulsion he felt from showing across his features.

As they reached an overcrowded crossroad, KyVeerah stopped abruptly. He motioned for Jude to step forward with a subtle gesture of the ringed fingers of his left hand.

Though the gesture had been most subtle, Jude noticed and moved forward to stand shoulder to shoulder with his friend.

"Collect yourself," KyVeerah warned. "You know this crowd as well as I do. If you don't pull yourself together, they might just rip us apart on the spot. If they detect any sign of weakness, you know they will certainly do so. He gave Jude a cautionary side-glance from behind his shades. From most angles, it was impossible to see KyVeerah's masked eyes, but from where he stood, Jude was able to discern an intense gleam emitting from them.

The circling lowlifes began to whisper among themselves, scrutinizing the two from their positions tucked away against the building walls. It seemed impossible that the dazzling white walls hadn't forced themselves to crumble to their own demise through sheer shame of association.

KyVeerah turned directly back toward Jude, whose golden eyes reflected fluidly back at him. "Ready?" KyVeerah needed to be sure that his friend was prepared before leading him to the wolves.

Jude nodded.

Satisfied, KyVeerah led north into the Castle District where they approached a tall, corner building. Its appearance was deceiving as it glistened in the intense sunlight of late morning, for the dealings and events that occurred within its stone walls were anything but charming.

They ascended four short steps. At the top, stood a set of wooden doors.

Vertical windows in each door had been boarded up from the inside, so that no outsider could look into the building's interior without first opening one of the two large doors.

KyVeerah quieted himself with long, steady breaths. He could hear Jude doing the same, but his doing so was unintentional.

"All right." KyVeerah yanked the left door open, stepping inside and holding the door propped open until Jude took hold of it. Making sure that Jude had enough space to enter, he sidestepped to the left of the doorway. In doing so, he nearly knocked over a tall, wooden display stand with a hefty book sitting open for show. A metal fastener securely anchored it to the stand.

Grabbing the tall stand with one hand, he grasped the book with his other hand. *Agh!* As soon as he was assured that neither would topple over, he yanked his hands back. Shaking them forcefully, he did his best to rid them of the thick, grimy layers of accumulated dust.

It was clear how little these somns cared for the upkeep of this particular place. Thick layers of dust covered bookshelves, books, tables, chairs, and every other item in the room.

A library. At least it had once been. It must have been centuries ago, judging by the disgraceful condition of the place. The only thing in the room not entirely covered in dust was a vague path across the floor. From this, the dust blanket had been carelessly brushed aside, revealing an intricate pattern of rich parquet inlaid flooring, from an age long passed.

Jude stepped forward to stand next to KyVeerah who peered over his shades, scanning the room. "I remember this place being out of shape, but I didn't recall it being quite this decrepit." He adjusted his head back to its usual, proud posture.

The Hinge. That was how the Underworld referred to this place, and it was the one place where Jude would truly love *not* to be right now, or ever.

"Why hasn't anyone come to greet us?" Jude inquired, in the quietest of whispers.

Having previously been used to at least some protocol of decorum, KyVeerah frowned, though his tone was more curious than concerned. "I don't know, to be quite honest."

Without another word, KyVeerah moved forward, following the narrow path that had been created by shuffling feet, both coming and going. The dense air had a thick, abhorrent feel that draped over them as they cut their way through it. They weaved past tables, chairs, and many rows of books, long untouched.

"Maybe they've moved their location?" Jude questioned quietly, half meaning the statement and half out of high hopes.

"No, I think not," KyVeerah said, continuing to follow the path.

"How can you be so sure?"

"The latest layer of dust has just recently been scattered. And here, it wouldn't take long for a new layer of dust to collect. So, someone has walked this path rather recently. And if my senses don't fail me, I would say that there are at least a handful of Hinge members here, right now."

The two of them reached the end of the path, where it intersected with a bookshelf. KyVeerah searched to see whether there was a way to trigger the bookshelf to move out of the way, so that they could continue on their journey. Every book seemed undisturbed, coated with thick layers of dust.

Peculiar. There had to be a way. It had been over two years, but every time he had come to this place before, there had always been someone to greet him, although not always in a friendly manner, by any means.

KyVeerah spun around, hearing a sudden yelp from Jude. He had sensed someone's sudden approach.

A man easily half a foot shorter had snuck up behind Jude. Holding a serrated blade to his throat, he yanked Jude down to his level. The blade was spotted with rust, and oddly, KyVeerah had a brief thought of what an unsanitary choice of weapon it was. *Then again*, he disposed of the thought, *it seems this man could care less about sanitation.*

The ugly little man, with a shaved head and beady little eyes, pulled Jude into a more secure hold. He pressed his serrated blade harder, until a thin line of blood trickled down.

Jude made a face at KyVeerah, demanding that he get him out of this tight spot.

"What is your business here?" The short man directed the question toward KyVeerah, assessing him to be the greater threat, especially now with a five-inch blade pressed firmly against Jude's throat. The stream of blood dripped down his neck and onto the delicate, white fabric of his collared shirt.

KyVeerah spoke confidently, without the slightest trace of concern, "I am here to speak with Galton."

"What business have you with him?" the bald man asked, as his squinted, beady eyes fixed on Jude. He flashed a yellow-toothed grin, then snapped his eyes back to KyVeerah after a short second. He feared to take his eyes off of him for long, and KyVeerah could feel that fact with all too much ease.

"Contacts, technologies, and documentation," KyVeerah said straightforwardly.

It was clear to the bald man that this stranger with the casually crossed arms, looking down from behind those dark tinted shades, was not a rookie at this trade.

"What about him?" The man shook Jude, still tight in his grasp. The motion caused the blade to shift, drawing a rugged stripe over Jude's jugular.

Pressing his lips together, Jude directed his eyes toward the high ceiling beams, attempting to maintain a convincing state of composure. In his current predicament, there was really nothing else he could do. He could only wait for KyVeerah to extricate him. Unless, of course, the hounds were set on him, rending and devouring his body until there was nothing left to be recognized.

Feeling the sting of the knife and the warm blood on his neck, Jude wondered how bad the wound actually was. He felt the knife shift briefly away before immediately exerting even more pressure over the freshly opened wound. He clenched his teeth to fight off the pain.

"He is my associate, and I will be needing him, so it would do me well if you would abstain from slitting his charming neck. You have made your point well enough, my good man." KyVeerah uncrossed his arms, extending a finger at the horizontal gash across Jude's neck. The vivid red blood was a lurid contrast against his fair skin and white shirt.

The man finally looked down, for the first time, noticing the open wound he had drawn across the flesh of his captive.

"Apologies." Embarrassed, the man lowered his eyes to the floor, expressing a nonverbal request for forgiveness, and he released Jude from his hold.

Jude straightened, moving swiftly to KyVeerah's side, though maintaining his best effort at composure. He had a strong urge to staunch the trickle of blood still moving down his neck, but he refrained from doing so. He threw an icy glare at the little man, feeling the bright red stain spreading past his collarbone and over his new shirt.

A creaking sound echoed throughout the large room as the bookshelf began to move forward. Jude and KyVeerah stepped aside, as it continued turning outward, revealing its hidden passage.

KyVeerah watched the appearance of a staircase. *I wonder how it works?* Constructed of a dark stone, the steps appeared even darker in the shadows. They formed a rectangular spiral, leading upward many stories.

While Jude looked to the newly revealed stairwell, which both his friend and he had taken on previous occasions, KyVeerah turned a quizzical eye toward the short, bald man.

"Go right ahead," he responded. "The fifth door you come to, that'll be the one you're after."

"Thank you." KyVeerah nodded respectfully.

"Just tell them that Hewitt gave you admittance." Once again, he shrugged a nonverbal apology for the inadvertent injury to Jude.

Jude focused his attention back toward Hewitt, scowling. He bit back both the stinging of his neck and his urge to strangle the man. It would be foolish to act on such an urge in this place.

KyVeerah gestured for Jude to precede him into the shaft. But Jude staunchly refused, his legs planted shoulder width apart and his arms crossed. He waited for KyVeerah to make his way first before he would will himself to follow.

Without a word, KyVeerah conceded to his friend's wishes and stepped into the shaft, ascending the dark stone steps.

"Oh, bleedin' hell." KyVeerah heard Jude utter the words under his breath. It was clear, as they passed the first door that the words were in response to hearing the bookshelf down below shifting back into its original place against the wall, sealing the stairwell. Jude now pressed his hand firmly against his neck, to staunch the blood still oozing down inside his collar.

They passed door two, then door three. "Breathe!" KyVeerah slowed his step to issue his command in a low whisper, when he ceased to hear Jude's hushed breathing from behind.

Realizing that he had, in fact, been holding his breath, Jude exhaled. He concentrated on slow, deep breaths, as they continued to ascend past door four.

Door five. Jude's steps had been quiet, and KyVeerah's even quieter, as they approached the fifth door. Nonetheless, they could discern that muffled voices on the other side came to a halt. A pair of stealthy footsteps approached the door from the other side.

22: Meeting The Hinge

Having reached the fifth story of The Hinge, KyVeerah raised a hand to knock. But thinking better of it, he lowered his arm back to his side. He felt it best to let those on the other side open the door without being sure of what they would discover in the stairwell.

Giving one last side-glance back to Jude, KyVeerah could feel the angst devouring his friend. At least Jude was doing far better at concealing the fact now, overriding it with an air of collected confidence. Jude shifted his footing, straightened his posture, and waited for whoever might open the door.

KyVeerah extended his fingers, stretching them in a last second of preparation. When the door flew open, he whipped a curved blade from the sheath on his belt, hidden by the thick layers of his coat. He held it up with his arm fully extended toward the now open doorway.

The man who opened the door stood a mere few feet from the tip of KyVeerah's blade. Scraggly, light brown hair falling to his shoulders was beginning to give way to silver. A matching beard clung to his almost nonexistent chin.

KyVeerah stared, deep with interest, into the pale blue eyes of the man. His eyes were so pale that they appeared to have almost no color at all. Black pupils dominated with the illusion that they were the only things filling the whites of his eyes. *How peculiar*, KyVeerah thought. *If I had crossed this man anywhere else, I would have unquestionably assumed him to be blind.*

The man held a knife in his hand, though it didn't appear that he intended it to be a physical threat. Not until good reason showed, anyway. His features were calm and expressionless.

"How have you come to reach us?" The man's voice matched his appearance, dull and expressionless.

"Hewitt gave us admittance," KyVeerah stated, calmly and maintaining his strong posture. He continued to hold the knife out defensively, clearly prepared should anyone in the room make a sudden move.

"What is your business with us?" came the same flat, listless tone. He appeared indifferent to the fact that Hewitt had admitted them.

"Contacts, technologies, and documentation," KyVeerah repeated the phrase he had told Hewitt, in an uncomplicated manner.

"Who is it, Flint?" A sinister voice demanded. A new man approached the doorway with a large katana in hand. He shoved Flint aside and pointed the katana toward KyVeerah's chest, his blade significantly longer than KyVeerah's own.

Shifting his weight, KyVeerah fought the strong urge to take up the spine-chilling man's threat by cutting him deep from his lips to his liver.

"Give me one good reason why I shouldn't drive this point straight through your heart." This man, with his long, wild black hair, and equally black eyes, advanced the tip of his weapon to contact with KyVeerah's ribs.

KyVeerah could sense Jude shifting in his own shoes behind him. He hoped, and expected, that his friend would refrain from doing anything rash.

"Because your boss will be glad to speak with me." KyVeerah left no room for doubt. The position of the door at the corner of the room, and the fact that the door swung backward, away from the corner, made it difficult to see the rest of the room.

The dark-tempered man scowled, his black eyes widening in obvious displeasure. His hair shifted as he shook his head in negation. His look demanded further explanation without the need of spoken words.

"I have never failed to bring your boss information which was overwhelmingly satisfying to him." Taking a subtle shift forward, KyVeerah felt the sharp blade bite into his flesh. Refusing to give the bastard before him any satisfaction, he maintained a strict, serious face without acknowledging so much as a single iota of pain.

The untamed man watched, somewhat bewildered, as he felt the pressure on his own end of the katana. He refused to yield his weapon, watching as the vibrant hue of blood began to stain through the gray fabric of KyVeerah's shirt.

Behind him, KyVeerah felt Jude alter his stance again, clearly unsure of what was going on. But Jude could see by the expression of the wild-eyed man that something was definitely happening.

Leaving Jude, both theoretically and literally in the dark, KyVeerah continued his verbal warning. "I assure you, your boss will be most displeased if you damage such a valuable client." He twisted his mouth with disdain and cocked an eyebrow, waiting for the man's response.

"Jory!" A strict voice shouted from somewhere in the room. The man standing before KyVeerah turned at the harsh calling of his name.

"Flint!" The man, Jory, ordered viciously, jerking his head toward KyVeerah.

The scraggly man, Flint, took Jory's place. But before giving up his position, Jory, with an evil grimace, edged his powerful body forward, pushing the weapon just deeper into KyVeerah's flesh.

With a low growl, he wrenched the weapon away, after first forcing it downward with a quick twist of his wrist, slicing down over two of KyVeerah's ribs, ripping flesh and fabric before the blade cleared his body. He cast yet another glower from his bedeviled eyes. Then, sheathing the katana, he stormed off to answer the voice that had sternly called out his name.

KyVeerah clenched his teeth when he felt the sharp sting of oxygen entering his open wound. He could feel warm blood spreading over his chest and abdomen. It was absorbed by his clothing, filling the black, contoured skull, bringing it to an unintended semblance of life.

Flint stood nervously, watching KyVeerah and occasionally throwing his attention to Jude, still hidden by KyVeerah in the shadows of the shaft. Even in the dim light, Flint could see the fresh gash on Jude's neck, left by Hewitt, and the vibrant stain it left on his crisp, white shirt. Although the expression on Flint's face remained empty, KyVeerah could read curiosity behind his ghostly, pale blue eyes.

Even Jude could sense the man's interest as he was carefully examined. Shifting his footing on the dark stone platform, he wished that he had shades similar to his friend, so that his golden brown eyes would remain hidden once they were forced from the shadows of the stairwell.

From the obscured recesses of the room, KyVeerah heard muffled voices, one of them the all-so-pleasant Jory, but there were at least two other voices involved in the conversation. One of the other voices caught KyVeerah by surprise. It was a female's voice. Although he could hear the tones of their voices, he could not make out their hushed words, even with his heightened senses.

Long minutes passed. Eventually, Jory came back into view,

although barely visible over Flint's shoulder.

After another moment, he took a few steps to the stairwell, but then turned back in the direction of those with whom he had been conversing. "Well, I sure as hell hope you are right!" he growled, displeased over words that had been passed amongst the group. He turned, taking a few more strides toward the stairwell, but paused again. He turned his back a second time. "Hale!" he hollered.

With that, Jory returned, and this time he was determined. Nothing was going to stop him. Behind him, the woman appeared in KyVeerah's line of sight.

Hale caught up to Jory with quick, soundless steps. He turned, placing a hand upon her upper arm. Leaning close, he whispered into her ear. Hale's eyes remained most serious though KyVeerah could swear he noticed a half-grin in response to what Jory had told her.

With a sensual hand, she brushed her hair back, stepping in front of Jory to approach the door. Her movements were almost imperceptible, but she soon stood directly before them. Neither KyVeerah nor Jude had heard the whisper of her footsteps, even at such a slight distance, as she glided over the creaky old floorboards.

Her hair glistened brilliant gold, interspersed with thin streaks of platinum blonde. It fell in luxurious, shining waves to the small of her back.

Stunning, KyVeerah couldn't help the thought swimming over the surface of his mind. She was beautiful indeed, but he could tell, with each nearing step, that such beauty did not denote so much as a hint of kindness.

Her eye makeup consisted of both dark and brilliant blue-violets, outlined with black to match her long lashes. Matching lipstick was also an intense shade of blue-violet. It was all in stark contrast against her fair skin but complemented her dark, form-fitting clothing and boots to perfection.

"I'm up here," Hale purred, with a sultry, dark voice, as KyVeerah's eyes moved instinctively from her knee-high boots, to the strategically revealed cleft of her breasts, and up over her well-defined collarbones. Her painted lower lip pressed forward in a pout. But it did little to alleviate her harsh expression.

Wait a minute! How did she...? KyVeerah questioned, knowing that the intensity of his dark shades would hide his eyes from anyone. He quickly wiped the baffled expression from his face. *She can't be a mind reader.* At least he certainly hoped not, as that would put both Jude and himself at quite a disadvantage. *Perhaps she was just making an assumption.* He couldn't help the tiny grin that twisted his lips. *If so, it was certainly an accurate one.*

Flint stepped aside as Hale dominated his space before the open door. Although Flint exceeded Hale's twenty-nine years by over a decade, she was not a woman to let anyone stand in her way.

As Hale neared, KyVeerah noted that Jory had also begun to creep closer. A wicked grin played over his features, showing plainly over both his harsh, curved lips and his nefarious eyes.

Hale's rich, lavender scent overwhelmed KyVeerah's senses. He could tell that Jude was expecting something unpleasant by the uneasy shifting reoccurring behind him.

"So, who have we here?" Hale's smooth, dark voice graced the heavy air. "Hmmm...I believe we've met," she said frankly, in a voice below a whisper, audible only to KyVeerah's exquisite senses. Her eyes narrowed, and as her dark lip pouted forward again, she fixed him with a witch-like stare.

He tried to read the thoughts in her striking, cerulean eyes, which stood out in such contrast against her pale skin and dark makeup and attire.

"Do you recall?" she queried, in the same hushed, testing manner. She seemed to be looking straight through the heavy mask of his shades. Refusing to say another word before he had a chance to think about it, she stood silent, boring through him with the harsh stare of her brilliant eyes.

"Ruby?" KyVeerah whispered, so low that only she could hear. His eyebrows knitted in scrutiny as he carefully studied her features. He gasped, "By Valencia above...Ruby Hale!" KyVeerah was hammered into a state of shock.

How can it possibly be? The Ruby Hale of KyVeerah's past had always been so friendly and delightful. Her every thought had been of pure joy. At that time, her straight golden hair often sported brightly colored ribbons, and she delighted in light shades of pink, copper, and red. She would never consider wearing dark colors. Whites, pastels, and bright colors matched her carefree personality. At that, she had repeatedly criticized KyVeerah for the frequency with which he wore such dark colors. "They mask the soul," she used to say, with a blissful smile. She never did manage to convince him of this.

What in Valencia's name happened to her? he wondered, in astonishment. It shook him to the core when remembering her previous, carefree nature. She changed so much that he hadn't even recognized her. And that, he would *never* have believed possible.

Five years ago, he had left Lux Lumetia, not for the first time nor would it be the last. That much was clear. When he returned just under a year later, his dearest friend, Ruby Hale, whom he had not informed that he was leaving, was gone. He had nearly pined away, searching desperately for her. But with time, he had eventually managed to block her from his thoughts. He had to.

Until now. It had been five years since he had seen her appealing face. It was apparent that she had still not forgiven him for leaving without explanation.

"Aha! So you do recall." The words slithered quiet and dark over her luscious lips.

Jory and Flint, from a respectable distance away, left Hale to do her own thing. Jory watched with anxiety in his wild eyes, and Flint with his usual, bored curiosity.

Hale stepped close to KyVeerah now. He had lowered his blade to his side, but despite this distracting encounter, he remained aware of his surroundings, particularly with regard to Jory and Flint.

Although he tried to keep calm, his pulse quickened. "Ruby…" KyVeerah said, quietly, as she continued to move closer. Behind her façade, he could not read the true meaning of the expression in her brilliant, blue eyes.

Hale halted mere inches from him. She refrained from any contact, but she slowly moved her hand up across his chest, and then toward his shoulder. Her eyes remained locked on his, which continued to invoke the impression that she could see right through his dark lenses.

She moved her lips just inches from his ear. "You broke my fucking heart!"

"Vincent!" Jude yelled loudly, breaking his long silence as Hale flashed him a lethal, withering look. Jude wrapped his arms around KyVeerah's shoulders, pulling him back out of harm's way. However, he was not quick enough.

Hale, striking abruptly, had lashed down at KyVeerah with the hand raised toward his shoulder. All along, she had held a palm razor, concealed in her hand, prepared for the moment to come.

Jude had managed to pull his friend back into the stairwell, but Hale had still inflicted a deep gash, from his right collarbone to his lowest, right rib.

KyVeerah's roar sent harsh chills through all in the room.

Hale stumbled back, extricating herself from being close enough for KyVeerah to reach her, once he was able to collect himself. She turned, scampering back behind Jory. It was evident that Jory hadn't expected her action, however, as Ruby's unexpected attack sent KyVeerah's weapon sprawling across the floor, he pounced to capture it.

Jude, who had fallen against the back wall of the stairs, needed all of his might to hold KyVeerah back. KyVeerah frothed with rage, eyes ablaze with living fire behind his shades.

Jude held him down, one arm locked firmly around his neck, until KyVeerah could regain his composure. Jude did not know exactly what his friend was up to, but he did know that he was here for a reason, and that it must be of significance. Given these particular circumstances, it had better be something mighty damn significant!

If it weren't one of his closest friends holding him back, KyVeerah would readily have broken his bones to escape the unyielding embrace. But wanting anything other than to hurt Jude, KyVeerah found himself in a desperate bind. His breathing began to slow as Jude squeezed him, slowing the air from reaching the depths of his lungs.

Finally, he ceased fighting and slid to the ground, though Jude kept him partially upright. Loosening his hold, Jude looked him over. From under his coat, Jude could see the spreading stain of blood, but the folds of his shirt kept him from assessing the true damage.

"For the sake of Eve!" Jude shouted, pushing himself to stand, while still supporting his friend. He had reached the end of his endurance for their stupid fucking games. "Are you imbeciles ever going to allow my good man to talk? Or are you cowards just going to continue whittling us down, piece by piece, instead of fighting us like men!"

Any anxiety that Jude may have entertained had vanished entirely by this point. He was furious.

Hale grabbed Jory's arm, requesting that he remain where he stood. She moved back in front of both Jory and Flint, still staying a safe distance from the stairwell. "Come out," she demanded. There was panic behind her eyes now, but she hid it expertly.

Jude looked down as KyVeerah began to regain his breath.

"Leave him," Hale ordered. "Move, now."

Jude gave one last glance at his friend before stepping out into the light of the room. He shook the long, loose curls of hair, which had fallen before his eyes, and squinted at the bright light in contrast to the darkness of the stairway.

Hale put up a hand. "Stop there." Jude stopped, halfway between her and the stairwell.

"Jory," Hale snapped.

Jory stepped to her side, looking to learn her new request.

"Take care of this—"

"Wait a second," he interrupted, holding up his hand. He moved a few short steps toward the man with the gash on his neck and the bloodstained shirt. "Don't I...?" he paused a moment, in thought.

A devious grin slowly unfurled over Jory's lips as he looked at Jude. "You. You are the one who couldn't pay up to save his sorry little ass and his pitiful little plot. Ha!" His wicked eyes lit with the realization.

"Jory—" Hale said again, but he interrupted her a second time.

"I'm taking this one to Galton," he told Hale, flashing his odious smile.

"You!" Jory pointed at Jude. "Down on your knees!"

Jude remembered Jory from his last trip to the Hinge. He hadn't recognized Hewitt downstairs. He didn't remember Hale either, and certainly would have had he ever met her before. There were, however, a couple of different men here during his last visit. Tyson and Tristan.

Jude glowered, biting his tongue yet again, to keep Jory from unsheathing his katana and slitting his throat. Forcing himself down on one knee, he then lowered the second to the floor.

"Hands on your head," Jory growled, rotating his index finger in a circular motion.

Jude, grumbling inaudibly, moved his hands up. He placed them on the back of his head, interlacing his fingers.

Jory glanced over to KyVeerah, who had also pushed himself into a kneeling position, but without any orders to do so. He had pulled his coat as tightly as possible over his upper body, covering the large, open wound. Blood stained his jeans, dripping down onto the dark, stone platform of the stairwell.

KyVeerah had placed his hands over his chest and abdomen, exerting as much pressure as he could to slow the bleeding. He bared his teeth as the shock wore off and the real pain kicked in. He fought to ignore the pain, realizing that he needed to be stitched up as quickly as possible, before he passed out from blood loss.

Jude avoided the temptation of turning to look at KyVeerah when he saw Jory look past him toward his friend. *Vincent can take care of himself through the worst of situations*, Jude assured himself. Up to this point, that had always proven to hold true.

Moving his attention back to the man kneeling before him, not finding KyVeerah a threat any longer, Jory circled Jude, leaving a wide boundary for precaution. "Try anything, anything at all, and your friend dies," Jory threatened. It actually brought comfort to Jude, when he realized that Jory saw him as a greater threat than KyVeerah.

Approaching Jude from behind, Jory kicked the sole of one of his shoes. He placed a hand on the back of Jude's neck, planting his long nailed fingers just above and below the open gash across his throat. Grabbing a switchblade from his pocket, he pressed it to the middle of Jude's back, ordering, "Stand."

Moving one leg in front of his body, Jude hoisted himself to stand, hands still behind his head.

"Now move. You know where the boss is," Jory hissed, into his ear.

"Hale!" Jory called, as Jude took his first step. "Take care of that one. Only bring him on back if you think he deserves a word with the boss."

"Get on, move it!" Jory shouted, as Jude paused for a last look toward his friend. His attempt failed as he was forced to turn back toward Galton, who was blocked from view by multiple rows of bookshelves, identical to those on the entry level.

Galton...Jude briefly looked up at the ceiling. *Ah, hell.*

He moved reluctantly forward, Jory pressing nails deeply into his neck and the switchblade held with just enough force for Jude to feel its unmistakable presence. He stepped forward, guided by the pressure on his neck. Even though, as Jory had just said moments before, Jude already knew the way.

23: A Quick-time Conversation

A burning fury simmered in KyVeerah's veins as he watched Jory lead his friend away in agony. He pressed his hands harder over his searing wound, denying the writhing pain building up within him. The gash Jory had left was merely a scratch compared to the one Hale had just given him.

With a cry of despair, too unbearable for even Flint or Hale to endure, KyVeerah shattered the silence. Each grimaced at the soul-wrenching agony of this man who had not deserved the reprehensible treatment that he had endured.

Flint turned away knowing that, out of his concern for Jude's safety, KyVeerah would not try anything that might jeopardize his friend. Flint walked to the far corner of the room, where the door blocked him from KyVeerah's view.

Flint had decided to leave the matter in Hale's hands since Jory and she had been the ones to make such an unnecessary mess of things. He covered his ears as another searing cry broke the still, heavy air. At this moment, Hale was the only person in the room within sight of KyVeerah. But she didn't notice, for at the moment, she was turned away, ripped apart by her feeling of guilt. She had long wished to get back at KyVeerah for abandoning her without any goodbye or explanation all those years ago. Now, she leaned her face against the empty wooden wall, shielding it with her hands on either side. She hid her eyes and her expression, while blocking his cries with thumbs pressed firmly over her ears.

She struggled to create a mindset of denial, pretending and wishing that nothing had happened. She wished with every fiber of her being that KyVeerah had never shown his face here while she was present. Her heart pounded. She fought the facts at hand. *What am I supposed to do? I can't just let him lie there and bleed to death.* Hale clinched her eyes even tighter.

Hale issued a heart-rending cry of her own but managed to muffle it with her hand, choking it into utter silence before anyone else could hear, or so she assumed. Suddenly, her eyes widened in abject horror as she was grabbed from behind. She was half dragged and half carried back to the stairwell. Hale looked around frantically for help, for while she was not paying attention, KyVeerah had taken advantage of the absence of Flint and Jory. Despite his intolerable pain, KyVeerah managed the situation well enough to subdue her while escaping back out of view, into the stairway.

Face suffused with rage, KyVeerah fought back the pain as he pressed Hale hard against the back wall of the shadowed stairwell. His breathing was heavy. He pressed nearer to her, tilting her face upward and staring down at her with a deadly gaze from his gleaming eyes.

"You will take me to Galton. And then you are going to sew up this detestable mess that you have made." KyVeerah glared at her, and without removing his eyes from hers, he grabbed her thin wrist. Forcing her hand open, he pressed it firmly over the open gash where his blood still oozed, fresh and warm. "Is it a pleasure to have my blood on your hands?" His mouth was hard. "It tears me apart and makes me sick to know that you are the only woman I ever...*truly*...loved."

The joy, which had arisen at his first realization that this was his Ruby, was now a thing of the distant past. He could see regret and the panicked confusion in her eyes now, but it meant nothing to him. Releasing her, he knew that she would not lead him to any more afflictions.

"Take me to him." KyVeerah pointed in the direction that Jude had been led at knifepoint. No longer holding her, he leaned against the wall for his own support. He cinched the coat tighter, grimacing at the pressure. His eyes were shut, but he could still feel the gaze of her radiant, blue eyes.

"All right." Her voice shook as her false composure, which had originally astonished him, began to crumble. "Can you walk?"

"Yeah," he said, with an ironic laugh, causing a new surge of pain to shoot through him. "But no thanks to you, my love."

He straightened his posture, his left arm still supporting him against the wall. Cocking an eyebrow, he watched as she stared at the blood staining his pale denims, running down onto the stone floor.

She bit down on her dark lower lip, turning to take the first cautious step from the stairwell, moving as soundlessly as before. Looking back at KyVeerah, she waited for him to follow her out into the room. If he tried to pull anything else, this time she would be ready for it.

"Come on. What are you waiting for?" The silky darkness had

returned to her smooth voice as she collected herself, using the sinister façade that she had worked so hard to perfect over the years, to re-create a false composure. With an unconscious gesture, she brushed the long golden bangs away from her cerulean eyes.

KyVeerah took a deep breath, and pushing himself erect, he followed. Every movement, every step, tugged at his wound, sending waves of searing pain to course throughout his body.

Hale gave him a demanding gesture to walk before her. As he moved past, she followed just a few short steps behind. She was impressed at the fluid elegance of his movements, despite the obvious agony of every step. *Admirable*, she thought, considering how very few could pull it off.

Together, they weaved back and forth through the rows of bookshelves. Hale noticed that, as they walked, a thin trail of blood dripped off of KyVeerah's coat, leaving a vibrant spotting on the worn, wooden flooring.

Faint voices became discernable with each passing row, as they approached their destination. At last, at the far end of the room, they stepped into an open space with an old table at the center and enough matching chairs placed comfortably around it to seat ten.

"Ah, Vincent. Goddess Eve must have brought you here considering that no one in his right mind would come crawling to me after two years of unexplained absence." The harsh greeting came in the form of a man's deep, rough, scolding voice. Galton.

"Yeah. Hello, Galton." KyVeerah managed to speak the words evenly, between deep breaths. Jude looked up at his friend from a chair at the far end of the table where he had been ordered to sit.

Galton stood, moving closer to KyVeerah. Jory was standing across the table from Galton, while another man stood just to the side of Jude. "Tyson," Jory hissed. The man, who KyVeerah had not recognized, held a large knife with one hand, as he tapped the fingers of his other hand on the back of Jude's chair.

KyVeerah detested Tyson immediately. In his mid-thirties, he had dirty blonde hair with a matching goatee and oddly dark eyebrows. His blue eyes cast an unnecessary, arrogant look at KyVeerah, which KyVeerah matched from his position far down the table.

Glancing at the floor, Galton became aware of the blood dripping from KyVeerah's coat. "I hope they didn't damage you too badly?" Galton questioned, in that same deep, rough voice. "You are aware of my policy on strangers, Vin. And it has been awhile, you know."

KyVeerah knew that Galton had always been fond of their business relationship, but he couldn't help other than to nod in acknowledgment of the facts, as Galton had laid them out on the table. "Of that, I am aware."

"However, I'm surprised they managed to make you bleed like that considering your usual, persuasive disposition?" He chuckled. "That must have taken incredible restraint on your part. He glanced down the table toward Jude. "But you evidently had a good reason for such discretion. I suppose it's fortunate for you that you brought this scalawag along with you." Galton pointed at Jude. "Your friend's lucky to be alive, ya know?"

"Indeed, I am aware of this as well." KyVeerah lowered his head, paying respect. "I realize that it has been too long, Galton, but I anticipated that you would not turn me away." KyVeerah now coolly met Galton's gaze.

Galton, a man in his mid-forties with broad, handsome features and a head of black hair, now running toward silver, managed a very tight ship. A well-trimmed beard dressed his chin. *The man does keep himself tidy. It is admirable, taking into account that most involved in this trade use it as an excuse to let themselves go.* That was another reason KyVeerah valued his relationship with Galton.

"I was hoping we might have a chat in private?" KyVeerah knew that Galton would never turn him down for such a request. "Also, I would appreciate it if you could assure me that my accomplice shall remain further unharmed in my absence."

For the sake of reputation, Galton appeared to be in thought for a short minute, then nodded. He turned toward the end of the table where his band had collected, including Hale who now stood beside Jory. She kept her eyes from meeting KyVeerah's, while Jory refused to move his off of him.

"You all," Galton said, pointing a moving index finger at each of them in a fluid motion. "Leave him be. Just keep an eye on him."

KyVeerah could tell that Jude was not pleased about being left alone with this unpleasant band of cutthroats. *It must be done.* He looked toward the sidewall as another bookshelf slid forward, swinging open like the entry-level bookshelf had done. Another stairwell showed behind this wall.

"Come on, Vin." Galton waved for him to follow into the stairwell, which sealed off behind them. Galton, initially upset at KyVeerah's lengthy absence, now seemed to have moved past it.

He had returned to his usual self, full of equanimity, with whom KyVeerah enjoyed working very much.

Following Galton down a single flight of stairs, they entered a new room. It was a lounge that KyVeerah recognized from previous visits.

"Have a seat." Galton gestured to a shabby, pale green lounge chair. After KyVeerah had taken a seat, Galton moved to the bar to pour a couple of drinks. He returned to an adjacent chair that matched the one KyVeerah sat in.

"Are you certain you want me to sit here?" KyVeerah indicated the blood that he was getting on the chair.

"Of course. Good mercy, what did you do to provoke them, Vin?" Galton handed him the drink. "And yes, most certainly. Keep your seat. We will have to get that stitched up here shortly. I'll have Hale do it. You do look rather more pale than usual. You gonna be all right till then?"

"Oh, yeah." KyVeerah waved a hand in dismissal. "I've definitely had worse."

Galton sat back in his refined manner, sipping from his glass, asking, "So, what can I do to help you?"

"Galton. Are you familiar with Insula Palam Vita?"

"Yes, I know the island. The Island in the Presence of Life. That is what they call it, for that's precisely what it is." Galton nodded. But, as always, he remained curious about KyVeerah's intentions. He knew he would be intrigued over the task currently at hand.

"I was wondering whether you would hunt down some information. I mean *thorough* information."

Galton stroked his well-manicured beard. "Just what exactly is it you are looking for?"

"I am seeking information on something called Medius Animus, the Middle Spirit." KyVeerah took two large swallows from his glass, readjusting his left hand to keep pressure over his wound."

"Medius Animus? I tell you, Vin, that sounds familiar. But honestly, I cannot currently recall what it is."

"Not to worry. What do you say? Can you get the information for me?"

"I give you my word as a gentleman of the best kind that I will put forth my best efforts."

"Thank you. If you can do it for me, rest assured that I shall repay you in full, and far better than those worthless souls you normally claim as clientele could ever dream of." KyVeerah raised a brow, clearly indicating that Galton would know exactly what he was saying.

Inadvertently, KyVeerah clenched his teeth, holding his breath as a sharp pain surged through him. Recovering, he tipped his glass for a couple large gulps.

"Ah." KyVeerah, recovering, held a finger into the air. "There is one more thing. I would like to claim Jude's debt from you."

This took Galton by surprise. "Vincent," he said, fixed with a serious expression now. "You know that is between Hollis and myself." Galton meant exactly what he said. But at the same time, KyVeerah could tell that he was holding a spot of consideration, sitting just behind his dark brown eyes.

"If, by chance, you might reconsider..." KyVeerah took another drink, readjusting his coat. "I seem to have come into possession of a mythological family ring. The Chrem Larose. I believe you may have heard of it?"

"No. I mean yes. But you couldn't have!" Galton's eyes widened in disbelief. Although, in reality, he knew the things of which KyVeerah was capable of accomplishing. A look of pure interest filled Galton's eyes now.

"Yes." KyVeerah placed a hand in his left pocket, withdrawing a small object as he held it between his thumb and index finger. It was a small platinum ring, with several diamonds lining its band. A large calligraphic letter C, at its top, was embellished with numerous minuscule rubies.

Galton gave a whistle of respect. "Vincent, you've got yourself a deal." He shook his head in dazed admiration. "I must say. You sure as hell know how to influence the outcome of the things you want most."

"And my information on Medius Animus?"

"Vin, your information is covered!" Galton gave a rough, hearty laugh. "I can't even believe it! I have no idea how in the name of our creators, you manage to collect such extraordinary things! It's impossible! But, somehow, you always manage it!"

"Gotta do, what I gotta do." KyVeerah grinned through his pain. Continuing, he added, "And time is of the essence. I know it's short notice. But I must acquire the information within two days. I know I can count on you, Galton."

"Very well, it will be done...you sly bastard." Galton chuckled again, admiring the ring in frank disbelief. "Now, let's get you upstairs and cleaned up." Galton stood, finishing the last swallows from his glass. KyVeerah did likewise. Then, he winced, noting that the green fabric had now become well stained with blood.

"Oh, don't worry about it," Galton said, as the covered stairwell was revealed once again. "After you." He gestured for KyVeerah to lead the way back up the stairs and to the next floor where they had left the others.

As the bookshelf moved, KyVeerah stepped once more into the open end of the room, by the large table.

He threw his hands in the air. "Jude!" Altering the direction of his accusation, he shouted, "For the sake of Valencia! What the hell have you done?"

24: Bad Omen

Sporting a new pair of orange reflective shades, Callis stared absentmindedly out at the dark surrounding city, as the elevator curved along the shell of The Dome. As it ascended, his view became only the dark clouds roiling across the sky. Hovering over the city, they threw flashes of lightning that zigzagged violently through the air, striking wherever they pleased.

Callis muttered to himself as he noticed something odd. "It's not raining. That can't be a good sign." A dark sensation left him feeling ill at ease, as the elevator chimed, announcing its arrival on floor 157.

In one smooth motion he pivoted to face the metallic elevator doors and removed the intricate access key from its slot.

Not hesitating, he took the path to his right. Well acquainted with the layout of The Dome, he made his way with ease, weaving through hallways. The black marble walls matched his dark and somber mood.

The only sound was the rhythmic click of Callis's boots, slicing through the eerie stillness. At a pair of frosted glass doors, the same seen throughout the entire structure, he raised his hand and knocked twice.

A smooth, deep voice responded from the other side of the thick door, "Come in."

Callis pulled the heavy doors open, this time closing them shut behind him with a self-imposed politeness, quite unlike his visit to The Dome the previous day.

The room Callis had just entered was similar to the commons room of the day before. The walls were lined with silver-flecked marble, and the outer wall was of the same thick, black-tinted glass that comprised the entire shell of the Dome.

This room, however, was much sparser than the commons room of the Black Band. A bar lined the wall to the right with a large, gilded mirror hanging on the opposite wall. At the center of the room, an onyx table was situated. Six silver, high-backed chairs with black cushions lined its sides. One lone chair occupied the head of the table with its back to the outer wall. In this chair sat a man with a uniquely severe appearance. This man now stared straight at Callis, eyes drilling harshly to his core.

"You're late."

"Yes, I know," Callis said, paying no attention to any of the room's other occupants.

"Nearly fifteen minutes late!"

Callis shifted his gaze toward the man sitting at the opposite end of the table. "Really. Is that so?" he answered, with false bravado, casually removing his shades and tucking them neatly within an inner pocket.

A deep frown creased the cold man's features as Callis maintained his arrogant, nonchalant demeanor.

The two men gazed intently at one another with ruthless stares. Callis acted as though the man in front of him was not the most feared man in all of Atrum Unda.

Although a muscular man with a build similar to that of Callis, his height was striking and his body more slender. A suitable, thin nose perfected his aquiline features. His eyes were ice, and the muscles in his strong jaw danced as the silence grew between Callis and himself. This man was Nyx Crucian.

Nyx, elbows propped on the table with fingers interlaced, wondered what his impudent, crimson-haired assassin would say next. Callis truly tested his patience.

A well-tailored, navy blue jacket complimented the cold blue of his eyes. Light glistened from silver buttons on his cuffs, sending sparkling reflections into the eyes of those around him.

Suddenly, a raven-haired woman, sitting to Nyx's left, broke the silence. "Perhaps we should commence with the meeting?" The question left no room for sidetracking suggestions or remarks.

Armani, at Nyx's right, added, "Ezra is right. Callis, would you be so gracious as to join us at the table?" He directed a hand to the empty chair between Ezra Stark, the Black Band's sole female member, and Royce Elwood, the man Callis had sent sprawling across the glass-covered room just the day before.

All eyes in the room waited to see what Callis's next move would be. Julian, off to Armani's right, grinned wickedly, arms crossed, as he enjoyed the intense standoff between Callis and Nyx.

Breaking his gaze from the silent Nyx, Callis did as Armani suggested. As he sat, the intensity in the air was tamed into submission by the uncompromising sound of Nyx's voice. "Very well. Let us begin."

The dark beauty, Ezra, began the meeting by feeding Nyx information that was of no importance to Callis. He tried to tune them out, but it became quickly apparent that he would not be given that chance as Royce, now to his left, quietly whispered, "Cutting it a bit close, eh, Cal? Good thing Armani and Ezra were here to save your ass!" He tried to suppress a smile, but it quickly disintegrated when Armani threw him a foreboding look, warning Royce to shut the hell up.

Armani, with his keen senses, could surmise Royce's words by his arrogant demeanor as well as noting that Callis was fuming inwardly like a demonic being ready to snuff out Royce's light. As Armani watched, Callis remained tense with clenched fists and jaw as he fought the urge to beat Royce into nonexistence.

Royce, one day I'll get the opportunity to snap that pretty little neck of yours. The thought comforted Callis, as he glanced sideways at his band member.

As Royce caught the wicked gleam and the subtle smile that slid slowly and maliciously across Callis's features, his throat tightened and he gulped. He quickly decided it would be best to ignore the terrifying man to his right.

Royce Ellwood was the youngest member of the Black Band at the age of twenty-six, a year younger than Callis. Although of a more lean stature than most of the group, he was more than qualified to be one of Nyx's top assassins. He had a finely shaped jaw with a chiseled cleft accentuating his boyish good looks. Attractive brown eyes matched his silky, auburn hair, creating a deceiving air of innocence.

To Callis's right, was an extraordinarily attractive woman of a long, lissome Two years older than Callis, Ezra Stark held a position below him in the Black Band. Her skin had a sun-kissed quality to it, and jet-black hair complimented her vivid green eyes. A characteristic beauty mark rested high on her right cheek, just below the eye. Her hair was trimmed in a clean, simple style, framing her relentless beauty to perfection.

Sensing that the topic of conversation had changed, Callis tuned into what Nyx was saying.

"Now that has been settled, let's move on to what I really summoned you all here for. And I know you are all aware of what that is." Scanning over his five top assassins, he continued, "Let me make one thing clear. I do not care who let this *Intruder* escape. The fact of the matter is that someone did the thing that everyone thought was impossible. They broke into The Tower and escaped alive. Nobody, in the history of Atrum Unda, has ever managed to pull such a stunt."

Callis felt the heat at the back of his neck, as anger welled up in the pit of his stomach.

Nyx continued his little tirade. "Not to mention the fact that this Intruder cracked the security of The Archives. There are very few beings in Atrum who have anywhere near the strength and energy required to accomplish such a feat, and most of them are in this room as we speak. Three of you were there, and he or she still escaped. This fact makes the situation even more inexcusable… and insulting." Nyx raised an aggrieved eye toward the ceiling. His even, white teeth showed in a grimace, as he lowered his gaze to collectively glower at everyone in the room.

Ezra piped up with a sharp edge in her voice. "Wait! Are you implying that one of us had something to do with The Archives break-in?" A tone of offense stitched her words.

"Don't be ridiculous, my dear," Nyx replied, giving her a brief, direct look before looking away to stare at the glass doors across the room.

"The feedback that I have received is this. Lord Cain and those damn fools of the Black Guard are completely worthless. They do not have a chance in hell of finding, let alone capturing, the man or woman who has already slipped right under their noses. This is precisely the reason I am assigning Armani and Julian the task of hunting down and bringing the Intruder in, to *me*." Nyx emphasized this last word to make it unquestionably clear that Lord Cain was to know nothing of the plan.

"I want him alive; otherwise he is of no practical use to me. Is that clear?" His eyes became even more venomous as he scanned the occupants around the table with a harsh solemnity.

Armani spoke for both Julian and himself, his obsequious words thick with pleasure. "Absolutely. We shall find the answers to the situation at hand…and the Intruder." His proud smile trapped a thousand cruelties behind those flawless lips.

Rage shot through Callis, and he slammed his fists on the glass table. He rose to stand, chair flying back. "What! You can't just give this to them!" He irately tossed his head in fury toward Armani and Julian, as they preened across the table, flaunting their superiority at him.

A satisfied smile slowly spread over Julian's face in response to

Callis's lack of self-control. Armani smugly maintained his state of composure, though it was easy to read the conceited victory in his eyes.

Nyx arched an eyebrow at the nonverbal battle before him. He slowly focused his gaze back on Callis, eyes devoid of any possible speck of benevolence. "Actually, Callis, I believe I can."

Callis's temper boiled rapidly, until nothing could contain it. His words burst out, of their own will, as he roared, "He is mine!" He leaned over the table toward Nyx. "This assignment should be given to me. Not them! If only—"

His calm, icy voice slicing the air, Nyx interjected, "No." He raised a severe finger at Callis, all mercy departed. Quietly, he intoned, "You had your opportunity. The mission of locating and recovering The Archives Intruder belongs to Armani and Julian. They have far more experience in these types of matters, or any matters at that, but especially when it comes to tracking. This is not about your pride and redemption, boy. It's about efficiency." Nyx's gaze was liquid fire, and he refused to break connection, cutting into Callis, despite his ineffectual efforts to ward it off.

Callis opened his mouth to object, but Nyx cut back in. "Besides, you have plenty on your plate as it is. You are my top negotiator when it comes to making deals and collecting payments from uncooperative clients."

In a low rumble, Callis growled, "Collecting and securing deals? That's grunt work! Make one of your goon babies from the Crimson or White Band handle your thug work. Better yet, Elwood here could do it!" He threw a glance at Royce.

Taking offense, Royce looked as if he was about to say something. But once again, a single glare from Armani silenced him. He resorted to sulking and giving Callis a dirty look. Callis paid no heed as his heated gaze remained targeted on Nyx. All the while, Julian had become nearly giddy in his seat, about to burst into a series of cackles at any second.

Nyx, eyes radiant with anger, quietly pressed one finger onto the table's surface. "Take your seat, Callis." Nyx's quiet voice held no room for remonstrations as his eyes drilled a hole right through his insubordinate assassin.

Nyx came to a stand, both hands resting on the cool surface of the table. "My decision is final and irrevocable. I shall not discuss this matter any further."

Eyes ablaze and jaw clinched, Callis glowered at his superior, struggling within himself as to his next course of action. He knew he was treading dangerous ground and that he couldn't push Nyx to any further action. Callis was a formidable opponent, but Nyx could, and would, obliterate the crimson-haired assassin with no effort if he felt such should become a necessity.

Recalcitrant, Callis relented and took his seat. His jaw was still locked with the rigid anger at both himself and Nyx. Nyx froze Callis in his gaze a moment longer before taking his own seat and smoothly returning to his previous position with his elbows on the table, fingers interlaced.

The gleam in Julian's eyes faded, and his smile receded in disappointment. Armani, realizing that fact, knew that Julian would have deeply enjoyed watching Nyx cut Callis down. Now, Julian appeared forlorn that things had cooled down so dramatically.

Everyone turned their attention solely back to Nyx, excluding Callis who stared down at the table, livid in his anger and humiliation.

Nyx's icy voice rang crisp in the still air. "Now that we are straight, let us bring this to a close. Royce." Nyx turned his head.

"Sir?" Royce replied promptly.

"I am putting you in charge of the Crimson and White Bands. See to it that they execute their tasks accurately and efficiently. Some of them seem to have forgotten their place. Use whatever means necessary, and do as you see fit in enlightening them."

Royce seemed confused at the sudden change in topic, but he recovered with a cocky grin. "As is your desire, sir."

Next, Nyx tilted his head in Ezra's direction. "And Ezra, my dear, you will continue working closely with the squad leader of the Black Guard over at The Tower. Inform me as soon as you have obtained the information that I requested." The word "requested" was stated in clipped syllables, showing he meant it as a requirement, not a suggestion.

In her own crisp voice, she answered, "Of course sir, it will be done without fail."

"Excellent." He nodded his head, pleased. "If there are no further questions," he scanned the group, especially noting Callis's reaction, but Callis kept his hard gaze directed far off into the distance. "You all have your orders. Dismissed."

25: The Seed of Obsession

After Nyx dismissed the Black Band, Royce was the first to stand and take his leave, followed by Ezra, right on his heels. Like a gentleman, he held the door open for her.

"After you Ez." He gestured her through with a polite wave. "Hey!" He followed after her. "Would you like to head out for a drink with yours truly?"

Without so much as a backward glance, she responded, "Don't be an idiot. Were you even paying attention to what…" Their conversation faded as they disappeared down the marble corridor.

By now, Callis had stood to make his exit, but he noticed that Armani remained seated, making small talk with Nyx. As for Julian, Callis had assumed that he would have already made his exit. He was always eager to be off and away from Nyx's watchful gaze. To Callis's surprise, however, Julian hadn't moved a muscle in the direction of the door. Instead, he stretched, leaning nonchalantly against the wall.

Nyx, with his usual, controlled grace, stepped away from the table while still speaking with Armani. He noticed Callis hesitating by the door. "Is there something you need, Callis?"

Armani and Julian, like a pair of twin bobble-heads, swiveled in his direction. A smug grin was plastered over Julian's features. They watched as Callis silently returned Nyx's cold stare. After a long minute, he stalked away, slamming the doors shut behind him.

A gut instinct warned Callis that something wasn't right. He made his way down the hallway to the first bend in the corridor. There, he came to an immediate halt, sliding around the corner. The conference room was no longer in view.

Closing his eyes, he focused inward with intense concentration. The energy from his core sparked to life, spreading through every cell of his body. The tattoos along his shoulder blades began to glow, though hidden beneath his clothing. His eyes snapped open, now glowing with a radiance that transformed their usual warm brown to a shining bronze.

Feeling the warmth along his shoulder blades, followed by further igniting tattoos, he stretched his senses outward to better hear the distant sounds filtering into his mind. The faint sounds continued to grow, creating a musical collage inside the walls of his mind. Eventually, the music transformed into words, clipped in a perfect cadence. It was Armani's voice.

"Actually, sir," Armani's voice sounded, "Julian and I have already taken it upon ourselves to look into The Archives matter."

A false curiosity seeped through Nyx's voice. "Really? I suppose I shouldn't be surprised. Especially from you two." His last words snapped like the crack of the whip, his voice hardening in a display of his obvious displeasure at Armani and Julian acting without direct orders from him.

A skewed grin crept onto Callis's face.

Nyx's voice continued. "What details do you have to offer?" He phrased it as a question, but it was clear that he was giving an order, demanding information about everything that they had discovered thus far.

Armani's voice echoed again. "During our investigation, we discovered a few things." He paused. "Including the identity of the Intruder."

Callis's eyes widened. *How could they know such a thing?* he fumed. *I was the one chasing him, and I never even managed to see his face!* Regrouping, he took a deep breath, calming his nerves so that he could concentrate on his eavesdropping.

"And?" Nyx pressed, after a long moment of silence.

"With all due respect, sir, we would prefer to keep that information to ourselves. At least until we can produce solid evidence. Right now, all we have gathered is mere speculation." Further silence.

Humor met Callis's eyes. *I can only imagine Nyx's face right now. I bet he is white with fury! Serves the bastard right.*

"Very well." Enmity thickly painted Nyx's words. "I shall allow both of you free reign while investigating this matter; however, I do expect a full report when you have acquired something of substance. And it had better be in the very near future."

"Of course," Armani replied, in a tight voice.

"I shall warn you, although I will grant you freedom to explore this on your own, if you should encounter any complications, you will not have my assistance, as you have chosen to leave me in the dark." His words were merciless.

Julian's dark voice cut in. "No worries, Nyx. We are well aware of what we are doing."

A rougher tone edged Nyx's voice. "Good. Is that all?"

"Yes. That's all."

"Remember what we've discussed," Nyx warned. "Dismissed."

Callis heard the shuffling of chairs and new steps clicking across the floor somewhere outside the room. He snapped out of his trance, remembering his surroundings.

With an unnatural swiftness, Callis zipped down the corridor. He took a left turn, followed by a quick right into a main hallway. He then headed back eastward with quick, muted steps that no one would detect.

Those two mustn't find out that I have been eavesdropping on them. Everyone would know that I'm up to something for sure, and I'll never get my chance at him.

"All will be ruined," he muttered the words, barely loud enough for even himself to hear. With a low growl, he picked up his pace.

Having yet to break his connection, having only weakened it in his need to protect his position, Callis heard the return of Armani's voice.

He could sense Armani and Julian growing nearer to the main hallway, down which he was currently making his way. At a considerable distance, he would still be in plain view of anyone who might enter the corridor. His bright crimson hair wouldn't exactly help him blend in with his surroundings. He picked up his pace to an even more unnatural speed as he felt them drawing nearer. He saw them step into the main corridor, but in that very last second, he dodged into a side hall to conceal himself from observation. He slowed his pace trying to regain his composure now that he was out of harm's way, at least for the moment.

"Wait," Armani's voice resonated. Their echoing footsteps halted.

Shit, Callis cursed.

Julian, with his very distinctive voice, queried, "Is there any particular reason you so desire to loiter out here like a bunch of schoolgirls?"

Callis gave a sigh of relief. Julian's statement was obviously directed at a group somewhere near them, along the main corridor he had exited. As the group dispersed, Armani and Julian began moving again, their footsteps echoing once more.

"Answer me this, Jules. What do you believe will happen if our assumptions are correct? Not to mention, when Nyx finds out?"

The realization dawned on Callis that he still had his senses tuned into the area surrounding Armani. He scolded himself. *No wonder*

I can hear his voice so clearly from this distance! He released a deep breath that he hadn't even realized he was holding. Aware that his presence still remained hidden from Armani and Julian's keen senses, Callis tuned back into their conversation. Julian was speaking.

"Who knows? Anyway, by the time Nyx finds out, I will have had my fun with the Intruder whether or not it turns out to be our old comrade."

Comrade? A baffled feeling flooded Callis. *One of us? Why haven't I ever heard of this other comrade? Once anyone joins Nyx, they never leave. Not alive.*

"Well, I wouldn't exactly call him our comrade, Jules. After all, he did refuse to join us, which, when you get down to it, is refusing Nyx."

Callis's jaw tightened. He didn't like the direction this conversation was taking.

Julian released a poisonous cackle. "If I remember correctly, Nyx fumed for days. His face was priceless. It still amazes me that Nyx allowed the little retch to leave unharmed."

"You do have a point there. I suppose it is fortunate that our dear Callis dropped into our laps so shortly afterward to fill the empty position left open by our smooth-talking friend."

What? It can't be true. The man who broke into The Archives and evaded me was their first choice for my position! Who the hell is this guy? Anger welled up within Callis. The very thought of being a secondhand pick for his position sent a sensation of needles violently piercing his skin.

Julian tilted his head, scrunching his eyes in thought. "Remind me, Armani, what was that name he always insisted that we call him?"

"KyVeerah. He preferred the name KyVeerah."

"Ah, yes. Vincent KyVeerah. I always thought that KyVeerah was an odd last name. But I suppose it suits him. I always thought he was a bit…off." Julian frowned, remembering the awkward man.

"Really? Personally, I had become rather fond of him in the short time he was among us."

"And people think I have unusual taste."

With the look of a predator, Callis engraved the name of his target into his mind. Vincent KyVeerah. Callis forced himself to ignore his own racing thoughts and to pay attention to Armani and Julian's continued conversing. He must find out everything possible about the Intruder, his prey.

In a stiff tone, Armani spoke. "Never mind my taste. We have faltered off course. If, in fact, it was Vincent who broke into The Tower, it would greatly explain why the Fountain entrance was left open. If not, then we have an immense problem. Not many are aware of that particular entrance."

Julian bobbed his head in agreement, and Armani continued, "Scant few have the capability of even opening such a passage. Vincent would certainly be strong enough to do it. But if, perchance, it wasn't him, there is no telling how skilled and formidable—"

Deadly serious, Julian interrupted. "Either way, it was a damn careless and moronic thing to overlook. And for that exact reason, it makes me think it was Vincent who broke in. The scatterbrained fool."

Callis bit at his lip ring, focusing on the information that had just been divulged. *Fountain? Secret entrance? He literally escaped from underneath me? The bastard. I'll kill him! What else don't I know? I wonder if Ezra knows? Or Royce? Impossible!*

Armani's sudden, clipped voice pulled Callis from his thoughts. "Someone is near. This conversation is over."

Callis's heart plummeted. *They know I'm here.*

26: Eavesdropping

"*There you are.*"

Callis flinched at the sound of the voice. He feared the worst, expecting someone to appear around the corner. Crouching, he prepared himself for the inevitable.

Still, from a fair distance away, he could hear the disdainful voice of Julian. "Do I know you?" His tone rang with insult.

Relief washed over Callis when he realized that the initial voice he had heard did not belong to either Armani or Julian. His presence still remained hidden from both of them.

However, the following voice did belong to Armani. "Jules, this is Jett Milan. You remember him, right? He joined us at the Prisoner's Quarters the last time we paid a visit to our dear friend, Fyfe Van Ingen."

At twenty-four years of age, Jett Milan was the unspoken leader of the White Band—the lowest band in Nyx's squad of personal assassins. His deep-set, merciless brown eyes looked unkindly from beneath a shock of thick black hair.

"Aha." A slow smile unfolded over Julian's face, his aqua eyes brightening. Any other somn would be uncomfortable in Armani and Julian's overwhelming presence, but Jett was indifferent, even quite at ease.

"So, you do remember him then."

"Nope. Not in the least." Julian accentuated the P in the word *nope*, as he turned his nose up.

Armani rolled his eyes. Turning to Jett with his most entrancing voice, he apologized, "You must excuse Julian. He tends to be rather rude, but he is actually a nice guy."

Julian coughed a short, gruff laugh in response to Armani's obtuse complement.

Both Jett and Callis cocked an eyebrow at this. *Julian? Nice? No one could be dense enough to believe that. Not even Royce.* Callis paused in consideration. *OK. Maybe Royce.*

Concentrating, Callis returned his attention to the others. Jett was speaking.

"Right. Well, I was hoping the two of you could help me."

Now it was Armani's turn to raise an eyebrow.

"Oh, really. Is that so?" Julian hissed, with an unusually light tone in his voice.

In his matter-of-fact manner, Jett said, "Yes. It would be moronic to disturb Nyx. Ezra is a cold, stuck up bitch. I should know with Angelina and Stella in my band. And Callis is a moody rage-aholic." He shrugged. "So, that leaves you two. You guys are known for being scary, right?"

Callis was perplexed at the manner in which the boy had approached Armani and Julian. His lips suddenly tightened. *Rage-aholic? Honestly, is he trying to make enemies with each and every member of the Black Band?*

Armani and Julian stared, mystified at the stony-faced Jett, as if he were a foreign being from reaches unknown. Julian spoke first, a terrifying smile upon his lips, but his voice was light. "I think I might actually like this kid, Armani." Turning, he remarked. "I may even remember you after this day, Milan."

Armani chose to ignore Julian, addressing Jett, "And Royce? Why not go to him?" It was obvious that Armani was testing him. Jett looked with serene composure back at him. "That's just it. Royce is nowhere to be found. He called a meeting for the White and Crimson Bands. It was supposed to take place right after your meeting with Nyx. He said to meet him in the Crimson Band's commons room in ten minutes. That was nearly forty-five minutes ago. Oh, and some of the others are missing too."

"Who else?" Armani inquired.

Julian butted in. "How did you know we had a meeting with Nyx? That was private."

"Helena Meretrix is missing, as well as Angelina Pratt. No surprise there. I am sure if we find Royce, we'll find Angelina. Her skirts get shorter by the day, especially with Royce around." Jett paused for a moment. And then, more to himself than to Armani or Julian, he corrected himself in a quiet undertone, "Maybe that was going too far, even for me." Then he spoke up again, "And who the hell knows where Helena might be? I just can't escape the impression that she is committed to her own personal agenda.

"And as for your meeting, everybody knew about that. It was expected to happen sometime soon with The Archives and all."

Julian nodded, acknowledging that fact.

Jett continued, "The others are getting impatient. We all have individual duties to carry out for Nyx. And as much as I would like to flake off on Royce, he is unfortunately my superior, therefore forcing me to wait for him to arrive to a meeting he called himself."

Armani, with a sibilant hiss, responded, "So, you thought we could help?"

"Yes," Jett answered bluntly.

Julian threw his arms up dramatically, in exclamation. "Then help we shall! Lead the way, Milan!" Julian raised an eyebrow, winking at Armani. Jett was unsure of what to make of Julian's peculiar behavior.

Armani just shrugged in defeat, "Very well. Let's head to the Crimson Band's commons room and see if Royce has turned up yet. The three men headed down the corridor, away from Callis.

As he broke the connection, Callis's hidden tattoos faded back to normal. He slid his orange-tinted glasses back into place.

"The last part of that was pointless and time consuming," he declared. *I guess I should be glad that Armani and Julian decided not to continue this way and grace me with their presence.* He strolled casually around the corner where he had been hiding and headed east down the same passage that, just moments before, had been occupied by Armani and Julian. *I've wasted enough time as it is. I should hurry.*

27: A Snag In Plans

"Helena!"

Turning, Helena saw the approach of her comrade, Angelina Pratt. She had been waiting for her at an agreed location, away from The Dome and prying eyes. The time for their arranged meeting had long since come and gone. But that didn't surprise Helena. Anytime Angelina saw that idiot Royce Elwood she lost all concept of time. Helena crossed her arms and fixed Angelina with a steely frown. "You're late."

Angelina flipped her straight fair hair over her shoulder. "Yeah, I know. I'm sorry. I told Royce I had to leave. But you know how men are." She sheepishly smiled.

Helena glanced wearily at the sky—the rain falling over her face. "Sure. I know they can be pretty overbearing. They never imagine that women may have agendas of their own. What's good for the guy at the moment is obviously what's good for everybody." *Especially—I'm sure—when it comes to that bonehead Royce.*

Too bored by now to engage in any more small talk, Helena leaned close. "Were you able to get it?"

Angelina shifted uneasily. "Actually, Helena—"

"Wait a minute. Are you telling me that you weren't able to come up with even a copy of Royce's access key?"

"It's not like I didn't try. I tried everything I could think of. He didn't even want to talk about it. And the more I pressed, the angrier he got." Angelina shuffled her feet. "You'll just have to get someone else's key."

Yeah. Like everyone in the city just happens to have one. Helena shook her head. "Angelina, you're not saying that you really *asked* Royce? Of course he would never *let* you borrow it! You were supposed to distract him, and then get the key! We could have had a duplicate made and gotten it back to him before he ever realized it was gone."

Helena rubbed her temples knowing that Royce would have convinced Angelina to fess up why she wanted the key. And given Royce's big mouth, the whole world probably knew by now. *Great.* Now even if she did manage to pilfer someone's key, she would automatically be the prime suspect.

"Helena. I'm sure you will manage to come up with a key," Angelina said, to cheer her up. "You are able to do anything you set your mind to."

Angelina started to turn away, but hesitated. "Oh, by the way, Royce has called a meeting of both the White and Crimson Bands. The meeting is running behind schedule, and we're going to have to hurry since we're already late."

Once again she turned, starting to hurry away. But she stopped when she realized that Helena had remained rooted to the spot. "Aren't you coming?"

With a wave, Helena brushed her off. "No. No. Go on ahead. I have a few more things that I really have to do," Helena said, seeming far away. Lost in thought. But as Angelina turned to go, she called out, "Angelina, remember. You didn't see me here!"

"Of course. See you later!" Angelina said. And with a wave of her hand, she disappeared around the nearest building.

Watching her go, Helena pursed her lips in disgust. *What a ninny. Looks like I'm going to have to do everything by myself, as usual.*

The more she pondered the situation, the bleaker it appeared. After Angelina's dimwitted move, certainly, every member of the Black Band would hang onto their access keys more tightly than ever. Helena was going to have to get one by stealth. *But how?*

She had to do some trailing. To learn their habits. She knew the movements of the White and Crimson Band members by heart... with the exception of Jett. But the Black Band was another story. Every one of its members was top notch. They were always aware of their surroundings. And anyone caught trailing one of them would be in a world of hurt.

Head aching, she pressed against her temples.

From everything she had gathered so far, she knew that her plans must involve a Calling. She knew she was close. But where could he be? Or better yet, *who* could he be? Or might it be a she? From everything she had learned, she was sure that Van Ingen had it right. But he had been shouting that the Key Calling has risen. *What is so special about this Key Calling? Is he out there right now?* She didn't know why she was so certain, but she was sure the Calling was a he. She could feel it in her bones.

Helena had spent endless hours poring over the book that Albert had given her from The Tower Archives, entitled *Theological Energy Disturbances and their Potential*. It was enlightening, but contained a lot of esoteric stuff that she really didn't understand. And it still left so many loose ends.

Just the same, she had spent countless hours planning exactly what to do if she should happen to come across a Calling. But now, as usual, she set her sights even higher. If there was really a Key Calling somewhere out there, why not set her sights on him?

Though unable to explain how, she had learned through experience that if you worked hard enough at something, some unlikely coincidence would bring it to pass.

In her reading she had picked up that there had been several Callings and Messengers. Also, that it was possible for multiple Calling-Messenger pairs to exist at the same time—if the confluence of energies was too strong to be contained in just one pair. It was up to the Messenger to lead his or her Calling to their true destiny. *Somehow*, Helena thought. The book had just barely touched on that. It was more about *Universal Energies* and *Theological Energies* and something about The Ancients that she couldn't sort out.

Something she did know was that Albert Young had a grandfather. In fact, he was the one who had written the book. What she needed to do was meet up with him for a firsthand explanation. Sure the book's content was interesting, but it never really explained the primary point that would be most useful to her plans. She needed to know just how much energy these Callings could handle. And even more to the point, how she could hunt a Calling down. Or recognize if she found one?

There had been brief mention of some sort of strange somns who just sat around in confined rooms of The Tower—meditating— waiting to recognize The Awakening of a Calling or Messenger. Evidently, if one of these special somns recognized an Awakening, they would have the individual rounded up and brought to The Tower to receive a marking. A Messenger was always recognized before the paired Calling. And once both were found, their markings received would be identical. Helena was uncertain, but thought that these tattoos must somehow help a pair find one another.

Although she still didn't understand the reasoning behind the whole process, it did give her an idea. Since she had no clue who the Key Calling might be—or any Calling—she had another aim.

Helena knew that she now had to meet the author of the book, Serlio Young. Perhaps through him she might be able to figure out a way to narrow down this Calling's Messenger. And since the

Messenger would have a tattoo identical to his or her Calling, she would then have something to look for.

And Ravenna only knew, thanks to her mother, she had probably seen more damn tattoos in her life, than any other girl in Atrum Unda.

28: Return to The Archives

Callis continued east until he reached the elevator. He pressed the button to take him down to the first floor.

Even through his shades, Callis could clearly see the sky, as the elevator curved downward along the exterior shell of The Dome. *Still no rain. This day just keeps getting worse and worse.* As if in agreement with him, a deep roll of thunder echoed in the distance. Ding.

Leaving The Dome, Callis headed out into the rainless city, pointed south. At the Marquette Sector, he altered his route toward The Tower, which hovered eerily over the center of Atrum Unda.

He couldn't brush aside thoughts of what Armani and Julian had been discussing. *So, Vincent KyVeerah was the one who invaded The Tower to break into The Archives. And he managed to escape one of Nyx Crucian's top assassins. Me. And the worst part is that this man, Vincent, rejected the very position, which was then offered to me.* The thoughts ate through him like a slow burn, burrowing their way deep into his brain.

Revenge. Something had been stolen from Callis the day of The Archives break-in, and he wanted it back. The only possible way to regain what he had lost was to find and capture Vincent KyVeerah, despite Nyx's orders. *I will find more on this Vincent KyVeerah. I will start at The Archives and then the fountain. If there is a secret passage there, I will find it.*

Moving along the walkways of Atrum Unda, Callis's thoughts lingered on the Intruder. *He was offered my position, but he turned it down. Why?* He clenched his jaw in thought. It bemused him, and more to the point, it infuriated him that this man was desired first for his position. It was insulting.

The Tower came closer as Callis passed into the Arie Sector. He approached The Tower's entrance with a single mindedness in his step. Two members of the Black Guard stood attentive at the gates leading to the bridge and ultimately the doors of The Tower. The one to his left made a motion to stop him from entering, but the other Guardsman interceded, nudging the first and whispering something into his ear. His eyes altered in recognition of the man that he had attempted to stop from crossing through the gate.

The two Black Guardsmen stepped out of his way, the second nodding and addressing Callis as "sir." He passed by without the slightest acknowledgment of their pitiful existence. Everyone in Atrum Unda knew better than to block the path of one of Nyx's men, and Callis Morgandy was no exception, especially considering the day that he had already endured.

Moving through the large gates, he crossed the bridge that spanned the water surrounding The Tower. He entered, walking with a decisive step through the open space containing not much more than a series of pillars, radiating out from the center. As he moved directly to the center-most point, Callis couldn't help but glance at one particular elevator. The shaft that he had so uncaringly massacred during his pursuit of the Intruder had been roped off with large signs reading *Currently Out of Service*.

A deep frown creased his features. Under normal circumstances, Callis would have actually been pleased with the havoc he had wreaked, but this elevator only served as a cruel reminder of his failure. And failure was never an option for Callis, nor was it something that he was accustomed to.

Passing the crippled elevator, he slammed a fist down on one of the small, silver buttons, waiting impatiently for an alternative elevator to come for him. The chime sounded, as a star-shaped crystal fixture came to life above the door.

Callis entered, pressing the button for floor 80, the highest he could reach from the ground-level elevators. He leaned against the back of the elevator as it rapidly ascended. Catching sight of his crimson hair and orange reflective shades, but he looked away as his thoughts fell on how reports had indicated that The Archives Intruder was a raging, crimson-haired man.

His stomach churned as the elevator came to a sudden halt. The chime sounded again, and another star crystal illuminated, though this one was located within the elevator itself. When the metal doors opened, Callis pushed himself away from the wall, making his way to the center of the floor.

There, he quickly ascended the spiral staircase to floor 81 where he impatiently pounded his fist on yet another silver button. He expressed his frustration at the slowness of the new elevator by slamming the next button before he was even fully inside. He exhaled, with a snort of disgust, as it ascended to level 132, The Archives.

Once there, Callis took in his surroundings. Enormous bookshelves lined the perimeter of both levels. On the lower level, the floor was similar to the spider-web appearance found throughout The Tower; however, his attention was focused on the four narrow rooms extending outward in each cardinal direction.

The entire place seemed pretty desolate at the moment, and Callis believed himself to be the only living soul in the expansive chamber. He found it strange that no one was present. As he looked about, a loud clatter and a muffled squeak emitted from somewhere above on the second level. His gaze snapped upward, as he fired up his senses to determine from which direction the sound had come.

Following it, he headed up the nearest of the level's four staircases. Callis came upon a large pile of books, ranging in size and color. A man had just emerged from the cascade of books and was brushing the dust and debris off of himself, all the while carrying on an animated conversation with the lifeless articles.

Turning around, and catching sight of the unexpected and quite terrifying visitor, he yelped in surprise. Callis raised a brow of inquiry. "Is that really necessary?" He lowered his brow. "No, I think not."

The man stumbled over his words, trying to address Callis. His gray eyes were filled with uncertainty and a touch of fear. "W-who are y-you? Uh, I m-mean…how c-can I help you?"

Without answering, Callis countered, "And who might you be?"

"I-I'm Moore Pamby, Head Caretaker of The Archives."

"You mean like a librarian?" Callis questioned, a belittling tone in his severe voice.

"Uh…y-yes. That's right." His pale face was an unpleasant, ashen white, giving the appearance that he was about to pass out from sheer anxiety.

"I see. Well, I am Callis Morgandy. I am the man who readjusted some *aspects* of The Tower's interior a couple of days ago."

A loud, throaty gulp issued from Moore as his trembling hands dropped the book that he had been holding. Moore looked as though he couldn't speak, even if he wanted to. Callis, noting as much, discerned that it would be up to him to move this conversation forward, or they would both be there for a long while. Callis rolled his eyes. *Good Lord, he's going to give himself an aneurysm at this rate.*

"Enough of the formalities. I need your assistance. I need information regarding the Intruder. I want to know what books he stole and everything else you might know pertaining to him. Considering that you are the Head Caretaker, I'm sure you can assist me with this task." He offered a wide smile.

The smile had been meant for reassurance, but it had the exact opposite effect on poor Moore, causing him to fret even more. He remained mute, unable to make himself speak.

Growing impatient, Callis snapped, "Well? Answer me, dammit!" He took a step forward, causing Moore to stumble backward in retreat, tripping over the books again and falling flat on his back. Moore issued a panicked squeal.

"Oh, by Ravenna's wrath! I'm not going to hurt you! Just tell me what I want to know. I don't have all day!"

Moore didn't have much faith in Callis's words. "S-S-sorry," he stuttered.

Hollering in frustration, Callis clenched his hands out before him. "Don't be sorry!" This resulted in even more squealing, as Moore held a protective arm up. He scurried away to burrow himself behind the pile of books, fearing Callis was about to hit or strangle him.

Callis sighed again, trying to contain his displeasure. "I mean... um, Moore — that is your name, right?" After another pause of silence, Moore gave a weak nod. With the most reassuring voice that he could muster, Callis continued, "Please. Your assistance would be most valuable to me."

Moore, seeming to process some of this, and tried to speak. Yet nothing but an awkward squawk escaped from the man. He did manage to pull himself up off of the floor, and he ran a hand through his dirty brown locks. Clearing his throat, he tried again, "Y-yes. Of course. W-well, you see, the information you seek is not available."

Callis exploded. "*What?*"

Trembling once more, Moore still managed to explain. "You see, the Intruder made quite a mess, and there is no specific book checkout system. There has never been a need for one —"

Callis interrupted, "So. What are you getting at?"

Nervously, Moore continued, "Well, there are lots of books missing, and not all of them due to theft. According to the information that I have put together, it appeared as though he had interest in the high-security vaults."

"And?" Callis's voice deepened in irritation.

"That being said, it will take a bit of time to discover what exactly he stole."

"How long?"

"We should have the information in a few days or so. But—"

"But what?"

"Uh. Well. Only Lord Cain and The Elders are permitted access to the information regarding what the Intruder may have taken from the high security rooms. Those are strict orders from Lord Cain himself. No other personnel are authorized to know—except for myself, of course. It's entirely confidential. That is why it is necessary for the rooms to have such high security in the first place."

Callis closed the short distance toward Moore with incredible speed. Before the poor man had a chance to react or even realize what was coming, Callis had him pinned roughly to the nearest bookcase. A shower of books fell, raining down to the floor, joining the already large pile of books.

"Confidential?"

"I-I'm s-sorry. I can't—"

Fury consuming Callis, he grabbed Moore by his collar and dragged him to the railing. Snatching him up by the folds of his shirt, he lifted him high over it. Moore squeaked out a terrified whimper.

Snarling, Callis spat, "You can't what? Listen very carefully. I will have that information, and you will provide it to me, one way or another."

"I-I c-can't—"

Callis loosened his hold on Moore, letting him slide downward with his strength being the only thing to keep the man from certain death, as the levels of The Archives were in fact the tallest of all of The Towers floors. Moore emitted a loud yelp of fear, his eyes snapping closed.

"Do you even know who I am? I am one of Nyx Crucian's top assassins. And you dare to deny me? You will give me the information I require, or I will end your life. Right here. Right now. Is that clear?"

"Y-yes. It w-will be d-d-done."

With a demonic glare, Callis heaved the man over the railing to the safety of solid ground. He released his grip, allowing him to tumble hard to the thick, glass floor. His eyes burned with intense ferocity, as he commanded Moore, "I will check back in two days to see if you have found any information. And for your sake, I hope you have. Don't even think of doing anything foolish before our next encounter. Don't forget with whom you are dealing. Good day, Mr. Pamby." Without another word, Callis turned on his heels, exiting back to the staircase.

Back in the elevator, Callis slammed the button with even more heat than he had on his ascent. Despite its rapid descent, the elevator couldn't have seemed to move any slower. Reaching the eighty-first floor, he retraced his steps back down the helical staircase.

Just before Callis could hit the next elevator button, the familiar chime sounded and the star crystal lit up. The metal doors opened of their own accord. As they did so, he found himself standing eye to eye with one of the last somns he would possibly want to run into. Ezra Stark.

Green eyes widening, her severe features gave way, but she quickly recovered. In a cool voice, she addressed the unwelcome surprise, "Callis. I didn't expect to see you here." She strolled out of the elevator, as Callis backed further into the lobby.

The light reflecting throughout The Tower gave Ezra's lightly tanned skin a radiant glow. She may have even appeared as attractive if Callis wouldn't have loved anything more than to push her from The Tower's highest ledge. Still in a foul mood from his recent exchange in The Archives, Callis glowered, "Nor did I."

"Really. What brings you here? Doesn't your current assignment require your attention elsewhere?" Her question was authentic, though her words flew at him as a crisp accusation.

"I don't believe that is any of your concern, Ezra."

Not unaccustomed to Callis's gruff demeanor, she answered, "I beg to differ. It is quite my business."

"How so?"

"Your actions here reflect on the Black Guard, which reflects on me. Now, answer the question, Callis." Her eyes were stern, lips pressed together.

"No, I don't believe I will." He brushed past Ezra, ruthlessly jamming her shoulder with his own and stepping onto the elevator that she had just exited. Ezra's eyes shot fire, as she warned, "Callis. Remember your place."

Callis slapped a hand against the elevator door, preventing it from closing. His sharp eyes cut into her, as she returned his gaze. "There will be consequences if you don't follow Nyx's orders. For all of us. Just forget the Intruder, Callis. Let Armani and Julian take care of it."

"Thank you kindly, but I know my place. Mind your own." Before Ezra could reply, he let the elevator doors close and disappeared from sight.

Once again, Callis slammed the button for the main floor. *Pestering, harpy woman. I have more important things to deal with than her. His mind suddenly shifted gears…The fountain.*

As Callis exited The Tower, the air was thick with haze and a slight drizzle. His gaze touched on the two Tower Guards he had passed by earlier. *Hmm. It's time I rid them from my sight.*

Callis hollered at the two Black Guardsmen. "Hey, you two. Come here." They glanced at him, at one another, and then back to Callis, unsure how to best respond. "Now!" As the two men hurriedly snapped to attention in front of him, he retrieved a silver key, with an intricate design on its face, from one of his coat pockets.

"I need you two to do something for me." Callis made his statement bluntly, leaving no room for question; however, both men opened their mouths to object.

He raised a hand of intercession. "Refusal is not an option. This is an order directly from Nyx Crucian. And as Nyx holds such close ties with your Lord Cain, I highly recommend you do as I say."

One of the Guardsmen, recognizing his authority, answered, "Yes, sir. Can we assist you?"

"Take this key to Ezra Stark. She's within The Tower."-243-

The Guardsman replied, with a puzzled expression, "That's all?"

"You dare question the task that I have entrusted to you? It is a key, you fools." His intense, brown eyes declared them complete numbskulls not to comprehend the immense importance of the task he had given them.

"Of course not, sir. Consider it done." The two men saluted and began to walk toward The Tower. Callis interrupted, a single finger pointing in the air. "Oh, and one more thing." Both Guardsmen stopped in their tracks, turning back to face him.

"Relay this message for me to Ms. Stark. Tell her that she should be more careful, or there could be consequences."

"Yes, sir." They saluted once more and took their leave, pushing through The Tower doors. Watching as they disappeared, a satisfied grin slowly spread over Callis. *It's unfortunate that I won't have the pleasure of seeing the look on Ezra's face when she realizes that I swiped her access key to the crown of The Dome.*

With the Guardsmen now preoccupied, he was certain no one would be looking. No one inside The Tower ever had any interest in anything beyond its outer walls. He made his way to the Sŭsurrus Fountain, half the distance to the Cosmos and the Wishing Well.

The fountain was veiled with the same thick layers of mist that currently enshrouded the entire city. He mounted the three steps at its base, swinging his legs up onto the lowest stone ring. Squatting there for a moment, he peered around, attempting to see. He could barely make out the silhouettes of the sculpted figures on the highest platform. Taking a deep breath, he jumped into the fountain. The frigid water bit through his denims, but that was of no matter at the moment. *Thank Ravenna this is shallow*, he thought, as water covered him to his waist.

Callis ran his hands over the lower portion of the pristine structure, searching for any sign of an opening. He then hoisted himself up onto the next, higher ring. Water from the top now cascaded down over him, making up for the lack of true rain.

After several more long minutes of examining the second level, Callis began to doubt himself. *Was I misinformed? Perhaps I misunderstood their conversation.? No.* He shook his head, disagreeing with his own thoughts. *I can't be mistaken. Armani and Julian had no inkling of my eavesdropping. I'm sure of it.*

Eyes readjusting to the heavy mist, Callis studied one of the skillfully sculpted figures up on the highest platform. One figure was of a young man knelt down on a single knee. He was leaning forward, reaching out with one hand while the other gripped the edge of the uppermost stone rim. *Hmm, I wonder.* It seemed almost as though the young man was inviting him. He lifted himself up onto the highest platform, water coursing over him in waves now.

Once there, he studied the second figure, hoping for another clue, any hint at all. Both figures were masked. The second figure stood, faced partly away from him, but it appeared to be looking back in Callis's direction.

This figure's eyes, just like those of the kneeling figure, consisted of shining white inlays, giving them an eerie appearance in the gloomy atmosphere. Although only a figure of stone, the standing, black marble figure harbored great animosity toward Callis in its unpleasant stare. It held one hand out toward the platform where the kneeling man was located. Callis turned his eyes back to the kneeling man, squinting and scrutinizing the surface for anything out of place.

Irritated, he was about to give up. *Wait!* Suddenly, he noticed a thin line that seemed out of place in the otherwise flawless piece of work. There, along the cloak of the kneeling statue. Turning back to study the standing figure, his eyes retraced the path along the man's extended arm to where it was pointing. A small grin unfurled. *The cape!* Grasping the cloak of the kneeling man, Callis began to push at the heavy marble mass. Nothing happened.

Not allowing himself to give up hope so easily, Callis concentrated with fierce determination. Tattoos glowed intensely beneath his clothing. Sure enough, the heavy stone cape began to slide back, revealing the hidden entrance that Callis had so desperately been searching for. He continued to push, displacing the marble cape even further to uncover the entire circular opening at the top of the Sŭsurrus Fountain, which he had overlooked so many times before.

Tattoos fading, he peered down into the opening, not in the least breathless from the physical feat that he had just performed. A hole with a rickety ladder led down the dark shaft into a dark abyss. Callis's eyes grew wide with feral excitement.

"So, it begins, Vincent KyVeerah."

29: Darkened Moods on Dark Waves

Rhyus awoke, shuddering violently at a cold gust of air coming off the water. Eyes adjusting to the light from the spiral lamp, he noted that Marion was already up. He wished he could just sleep until they landed at their uncertain destination. His stomach growled angrily with nothing but the few melons to pacify it over the last couple of days.

Rhyus felt an uncomfortable darkness emanating from deep within. Every cell of his body was filled with angst. It sucked to wake up in such a sour mood. And he had a feeling that this one was not about to leave anytime too soon.

He sat up and tried stretching while breathing slowly to calm himself from his irritable state. After several silent minutes, he ran a hand through his hair and wiped the oily film onto his pants leg. He shook his head harshly back and forth like an animal shaking off water from a storm. The congealed strands of his hair moved soddenly.

Reluctantly, he trudged toward the bow where Marion leaned with her arms on the wooden rails. She was running her hand through her hair.

Sensing his presence, she turned.

"Hey," he said flatly.

"Yeah, morning," she returned, in similar fashion, lacking any of her usual emotion.

"I'm starving," Rhyus said, directing his voice nowhere specific, but he looked directly at the wooden storage compartment. Understanding, Marion made her way to it, pulling out a couple of the all-too-familiar red rabmelons.

Today, neither of them moved to sit on the benches. Marion approached Rhyus where he stood amidships.

"Here," Marion said, plopping a melon in his hand. Without another word, she walked back to her prior position, just above the painted name *Quinton Paris*. Leaning against the polished wood, it was now her turn to sigh.

Rhyus leaned back, watching Marion through the semidarkness. She had not yet turned on the small lights, but his eyes had adapted to straining through the universal dimness out on the Dark Water.

To Rhyus's own surprise, he didn't as much as crack the slightest grin as he watched Marion, with a desultory toss, throw her melon husk overboard. He merely took the last couple of bites from his own melon, which despite his hunger, he had momentarily forgotten.

Rhyus threw the remainder over his shoulder to sink down into the watery depths. He glanced up from the black endless waves to the equally black sky. *Three moons today*, he thought. He couldn't imagine how much darker it would be if somehow the moons and stars failed to perforate the inexorable dark.

After a short eternity, Marion pulled two water bottles from the storage compartment, along with the philosophy book and the large puzzle book Rhyus had been using. The blue pen was still clasped tightly onto a page inside the book.

"Catch," Marion muttered, tossing the book at Rhyus, followed by a water bottle. By reflex, he snagged both items from the air.

"Thanks," he said, with even less enthusiasm than he had intended. Regretting how sharp and unappreciative he had sounded, he pressed his lips together and looked down at the book with a mixed feeling of guilt and regret, only adding to his ever-growing ennui.

He seated himself near Marion, who was curled up at the stern, and began to read.

"So, what is the book you've been reading?" Rhyus asked, not expecting the slow smile that unfurled across Marion's twisted lips.

"You don't recognize it?"

"Umm, should I?" He pondered the question for a moment, but could come up with no possible solution why he might recognize it. He couldn't even remember the last time he'd read a book. Well, other than a few nights ago, when Venn had wrenched the leather chair out from under him, nearly shattering his spine. Rhyus thought harder, trying to recall the book he had been reading then. But he was sure this wasn't it.

"Really?" she pressed, in a manner that indicated she was half surprised and half intending to scold him for his lack of remembrance.

"No, I don't recognize it." He furrowed his brow in concentration.

"It's Venn's."

Rhyus shifted his thoughts back to the collection of books that he had sorted through that night in Venn's den. No luck. He looked up at Marion with a combination of vacancy and bafflement. She shook her head, smiling once again.

"It's the book from Venn's desk that you tore a page from. For your farewell note," she revealed. "A most horrible idea, I might add. It is Venn's all-time favorite book." Though she tried to throw him a look of accusation, she could not help but burst out laughing.

"Oh, right. About that."

Marion cackled. "When he catches us, he is going to kill you."

Rhyus nodded in agreement. "Even despite the book, Venn will kill me the instant he finds me. Goddesses forbid that happen anytime soon, or ever. There's no doubt that I would be a dead man."

Returning to their books, they soon drifted off into their own silent stupors—like every other day on the boat. From time to time, they stretched or ate a couple melons with rare occasion for conversation.

Throughout the day, the oppressive Darkness pressed ever more relentlessly upon them. They decided to retire early, as on the previous evening. Rhyus took the last sip from his water bottle. *If I could have just one more bottle…*Marion came up beside him, finishing her bottle as well.

Quickly changing his clothes, Rhyus laid on his cushions, facing the outer wall of the boat. He closed his eyes, begging for sleep to come swiftly.

As Marion's garments had finally dried, she pulled them from the makeshift clothesline and changed behind the large wooden compartment. It felt almost strange to be back in clothes that fit.

Halfheartedly, she doused the lights. Approaching the benches, she was aware of Rhyus's motionless slumber. Even in sleep, he exuded a very discomforting aura.

For a moment, Marion wished he would roll over to offer her a place next to him. She could feel the coolness of the night breeze returning. Settling onto her own bench, she curled up facing the boat wall, with no hope of blocking the cold breeze and missing the body warmth of the nights before.

Crossing her arms tightly, she tried to ignore the cold and the thoughts racing through her mind. At last, she faded into a deep, troubled sleep.

With the new morning, Rhyus felt chained to the floor by the blackest of foul moods. The inexplicable Darkness wrapped itself around every fiber of his being. Looking about, nothing had changed. Glancing at Marion, he wondered what thoughts, or dreams, might be running through her head. Lying back again, eyes closed, he tried his hardest to deny the day that was coming.

Hearing an unexpected thud, he noted that Marion had swung her feet to the deck. He glanced at her a moment before shifting his gaze back up to the sky.

Marion was unaware that Rhyus had looked her way. Believing him to still be asleep, she moved quietly toward the bow, sliding her feet over the deck. There, she stared straight ahead, as the black waves continued their determined task to outrun the boat while it sliced through them effortlessly.

Marion absently traced a small figure eight upon the wall's polished edge. She felt a gradual irritation as she stared impatiently out at The Darkness. She clenched her teeth, then realizing that she was holding her breath, exhaled heavily. She threw her head back and closed her eyes.

I hope everything is all right back at Umbra Halls and with Venn. I hope he is treating himself well. He had better be eating decent meals and not drinking any more than usual. She let out a long, shuddering sigh.

How do somns do it? she wondered. *Riding at sea like this? Then again, I suppose no one really ever has a reason to be at sea for days at a time. Everyone who goes out returns by the end of the day. I'm sure anyone planning to be at sea for any longer than a day would have a proper crew consisting of more than two novice shipmates.*

Gazing up at the sky, Marion acknowledged the golden moon, Arienette, far off in the distance. Most would have probably overlooked it, mistaking it for a large star. Not Marion though. She'd always loved the mysterious moons as they broke the darkness of the night. *I could never mistake any of the five moons for stars.* Her uncanny eyes easily differentiated their hues as well as any other distinguishing characteristics.

"I'm starving." Rhyus's voice had a strange, disconnected quality. His smug, yet playful, manner was entirely gone. He sat slouched, staring abjectly at the deck floor between his feet.

Marion gave him a quizzical look. *He seems so odd.* Normally, even when relaxed, his posture was always proud and confident. He was completely different.

Looking up, Rhyus noted Marion's gaze upon him. He glowered. "Who are you to judge me?" he snapped.

Marion merely looked at him, any form of response failing her. She closed her mouth, leaving only a disquieting silence to fill the air.

His unusual harshness nearly caused her eyes to pool. Breaking eye contact, she dodged toward the storage compartment and began digging through its contents, hands shaking.

Removing a single melon, she continued shuffling through the bag. Finding nothing left in her bag, she shoved it aside and quietly unclasped the bronze buckles of Rhyus's messenger bag. Rummaging through it, she quickly found what she was looking for and stood, backing away and shutting the door with her left foot.

"Here." Marion flipped a melon to Rhyus. She tried to keep her voice steady, but it was slurred by a tinge of anxiety.

As expected, Rhyus caught the well-aimed melon with the utmost of ease. Without giving it so much as a glance, he continued to stare straight at Marion. He cocked his head side to side with the dark, terrifying glare still plastered over his features.

Though Marion's hands were shaking, she hoped he would not notice. Drawn by the look emanating from his eyes, she knew that she would be unable to ignore him.

"Do you fear me?" The scathing question was genuine in that he did indeed wish for a response. His crooked grin, which was usually an attractive trait, had transformed into a sadistic sneer.

Marion still did not respond. She simply continued to stare into his emerald eyes. They held a queer, dark luminosity.

"What are you keeping from me?"

"Nothing, I'm not keeping anything from you."

"Oh really?" He raised his eyebrows in disbelief. Without removing his eyes from her, he broke the melon and took a large bite. Forcing a swallow, he demanded, "Put out your hand."

As Marion continued to stand motionless, Rhyus got up and advanced a step in her direction.

She held her hand out to him.

Glancing at the bright red, Plush melon in her hand, any small spark of amusement in this situation drained instantly from behind his eyes. He mocked, "I bet you think you are clever."

He made a swift and threatening move toward Marion. She shut her eyes tight and tried to shy away toward the closed compartment, yet her feet remained planted, refusing to move.

Reaching her, Rhyus grasped her arm. Careful not to cause her any actual physical harm, he pulled it toward him. Though her pale fingers tried to conceal its surface, he could see a great deal of the familiar skin of the brilliant red Plush melon within her grasp.

"How interesting." Rhyus raised a mocking eyebrow. In his other hand he held out the dull colored, West Bay melon.

Marion remained silent, unsure what to say or what his reaction was going to be.

"Marion, Marion." Rhyus shook his head. He pulled her closer. "I thought we were all about equality around here, *Captain*." He unkindly said the title. He forced her hand upward, closer to him.

Rhyus glanced back and forth, between the dull melon and the bright one in her hand. "It's easy to see that what is best for the Captain is not so for the crew."

Marion winced. Although she had not planned to be deceitful, she had assumed that he would not notice the difference between the melons.

"I think, perhaps, you should make it up to me."

Unsure of his intention, her eyes snapped to him in warning. Disregarding her look, he leaned slowly toward her as she pulled her face away. Pulling her wrist even higher, he spread her fingers and sank his teeth deeply through the husk of the bright red melon, as a stream of blood red juice filled her hand and streamed down her wrist.

He reached out and transferred his West Bay melon to her other hand while taking a firmer grip on the hand that held the Plush.

"Rhyus...please," she plead.

Suddenly, as an unintentional and unexpected explosion of energy and force emitted from Marion, Rhyus flew backward through the air. The recoil threw Marion in the opposite direction. Not expecting it, she fell awkwardly to the deck, while Rhyus managed to land steadily on his feet, though in a defensive stance.

Regaining his composure, he grinned and held up the Plush melon, now in his hand, with a large bite missing.

"You don't deserve it."

"Well," he glared down at her, "after what you tried to pull, I am damn well not giving it to you."

"Fair enough."

"What do you propose I do with it?" Looking down at the melon, he took one more bite, then impulsively hurled the remainder far out into the black abyss.

"Shit!" Rhyus sped to the rail in record time. "No!" He threw his hands into the air and slung his head back toward Marion. "Now look what you made me do!"

"I didn't make you do a damn thing, you fool. You just threw our last real excuse for food overboard!"

Rhyus clenched his hands before himself.

"You are pathetic." Marion pushed up off the deck. "Catch," she said angrily hurling the dull melon, with the bite out of it, at Rhyus.

He caught it mindlessly.

"I'm getting another one that you haven't disgraced."

"Hey, those are from *my* bag!" Rhyus said.

"And they are *my* melons. I am not going to starve on account of your bad mood."

Rhyus glowered at Marion, and turning hurled his dull melon to follow the Plush one.

Refusing to say another word to one another, they each grabbed a bottle of water and moved to opposite ends of the boat. Marion sat cross-legged with the book she had pulled from her bag, while Rhyus ignored her and sat down with the puzzle book.

Marion considered demanding her puzzle book back, but that would have involved speaking to him. She was aware that whatever they said to each other would invariably lead to some other ridiculous argument just as inane as "who got the best melon."

Many hours passed as they bent their heads, absorbed in their own, individual pursuit. As usual, there were the occasional trips, walking the boat to stretch their limbs and to visit the restroom below deck. There was a difference now. As The Darkness ate away inside them, they reacted to each other with aggravation and hostility.

Rhyus silently looked down at the chronometer that he had made the extra trip to obtain. A fat lot of good it was doing considering the boat was charting its own course to who the hell knew where? As he thought of the trip, he did smile at its one bright point.

"You know," Rhyus tossed out, in an arrogant tone, from a point far to the stern.

Marion finished the paragraph she was reading, deliberately making him wait before tilting her eyes up toward him.

Not to waste a single moment of her attention, Rhyus arrogantly tilted his head. "The most beautiful young woman invited me for drinks the day that we left port from the Crystal Harbor. I mean, absolutely stunning!" He made a gesture, emphasizing the statement. They looked warily at one another until Rhyus broke his gaze to look back out at the black waves.

Marion felt her face flushing in the dim light. Much to her chagrin, she could feel her hands becoming clammy, as she held the thick spine of her book. *Why the hell should I care what beautiful women he talked to in the few days that he spent in Lux Lumetia?* She scolded herself for succumbing to her body's automatic reactions. *It's not like beautiful women are uncommon in Lux. Besides, I'm sure far more unattractive women would have tried to hit on him during his short stay.* She told herself this, in an attempt to make an attractive woman hitting on Rhyus just part and parcel of the usual course of events.

With a surreptitious glance back at Marion, Rhyus hoped to catch a touch of jealousy. A satisfied half-grin played over him in response to his own boorish self-amusement.

Enjoying himself a little too much, he continued his game. "Oh, not to mention that appealing blonde earlier the same morning." He twisted his lips, putting a bent finger up to them.

Rhyus managed to catch Marion's eye for a moment before he looked away again. "But the one who invited me for drinks, who I unfortunately had to turn down for my little *voyage*, well, she asked if we could hook up once I have returned. She doesn't know a single thing about me, or about how long I shall be away. How quaint, don't you think? For all she knows, I could be on some charming boat right now with a divine, exquisite goddess of a young woman. But we, as the crew of this here ship, know that isn't the case now, don't we Marion?"

Marion looked away without comment, refusing to cry over his hurtful statements. *That is exactly what he wants. The puzzles aren't enough anymore on this boat with absolutely nothing to do and with all of this rationing of food and water. It is just going to his head.* Marion tried to convince herself that he didn't mean it. She told herself again and again, *That isn't Rhyus. He has never treated me like this. He would never...It has to be The Darkness moving in. I can feel it myself. It's just The Darkness.*

Regardless of her attempts, a single tear managed to spill over its barrier. By now, she had to set the book down in her lap, and she wiped the tear away quickly with the back of her hand. She knew that Rhyus could not possibly have seen it from where he stood, but it seemed as if he could feel it.

Rhyus watched with darkened eyes, maintaining his stance, as he watched Marion shy away from him, turning away to the bow. He had hurt her deeply, and he knew. He could feel her emotions permeate the air, filtering through it and into the depths of his mind.

Sighing with exasperation, he turned away to look out over the blackened waves. The reflections from the spiral light fled across the crests of the waves, fleeing that bad omen, which he could now feel deep down. There seemed to be a silent, mysterious laughter from the wind, the waves, and the sky, who had known all along that The Darkness would overwhelm them.

If the sea could speak, what would it say? What warning would it bestow? If Quinton Paris were here could he warn me of what is to come? What if there is simply nothing to come? Perhaps The Darkness will simply encompass and suffocate us, drilling us downward into a broken mental state of self-destruction?

Rhyus considered apologizing. He could not understand or believe his actions. But he could not do it. His behavior had been brutish, and he couldn't expect forgiveness for the horrible things he had said. For the intentional attack he had aimed upon her emotions.

Lowering his head, he watched the endless waves across the stern. The Darkness was inside him. It made him sick. He would give anything to reach land right now. Wherever they were headed, it would be better than out here with this asphyxiating presence.

The hours passed with no light, no sound, nothing but The Darkness. Rhyus's body ached. Something was wrong. He felt it. Anxiety built within, crawling down his spine, overtaking every inch of his body. His heart beat faster. Blood pulsed in his temples. All around, the world swam in a circle, faster and faster. Everything became black. Pitch black. Then he collapsed.

−−−

Blinking, Rhyus looked at the silver moon, Valencia, standing guard high above. A significant amount of time must have passed. He hadn't seen it since his conversation with Marion about the moons' names and colors.

Suddenly, he realized he was lying on the deck. Pressing a hand over his eyes, he lay for several minutes, trying to recall what had happened.

"Agh!" Rhyus cried out as something smashed into his ribs. With effort, he immediately sat up, swinging his legs around in case he needed to defend himself from a second attack. The movement sent stronger pain shooting across his ribs, and his head spun with the quick effort to sit.

It had been a boot. Marion's boot.

"What the hell!" he choked, his ribs still pulsing with surges of pain.

"Oh good, you're alive."

By her tone, he couldn't tell if she meant what she had said. "Damn woman!" he snarled. "Do not expect to ever get away with that again!"

Marion offered no more than a smug look, indicating that the occurrence would more than likely happen again. She stood hovering over him without a single movement. The expression engraved on her face clearly indicated that hurt had morphed into anger. Yet Rhyus could see something even more ominous. It was obvious that The Darkness had overtaken her as well.

"What the hell happened? How much time has passed?"

"You fainted. It's barely past four in the morning, though you would never know the difference out here." She exhaled heavily, showing her own exasperation with the sea and The Darkness.

"It's only been a day?"

"Not even," she scoffed. "It was mid-afternoon when you dropped."

"And you couldn't have as much as moved me from the deck?"

"Like hell! You really think that you deserve to have me haul your ass up onto those nice, cushioned bench seats?" By the look in her eyes, The Darkness was deep inside her. Perhaps her pain, at his earlier jab this morning, had unwittingly caused her to let her guard down.

"You are nauseating. You are lucky I came to see if you were even breathing!" Marion's expression twisted. "However, if you hadn't been, I don't reckon I would have tried to revive you."

Rhyus gaped, but before he could respond, Marion stormed toward the bow. Halfway there, she turned to hurl a melon at him.

"And you call Venn a brute! You could never be as great a man as Venn!" she spat, turning her back on him.

Rhyus was taken aback. Never did he wish to be compared to Venn, especially to hear that he was any less of a man than that fiend. He released a sound between a holler and a growl, and watched Marion pick up her pace. She gave only a half-glance back in his direction, but he could sense the panic in her eyes. He was not himself. Not the Rhyus she had befriended in their short time together in Lux Lumetia.

Rhyus swallowed a bite of the melon quickly, having no desire to savor its flavor. Auck! Horrible! He glanced at the melon. *I wonder if they're going bad?* Finishing it nonetheless, Rhyus chucked the husk overboard, far into the distance. Despite being unconscious for nearly half a day, he did not feel like he had received a single ounce of sleep. He crawled to his bench, where he threw himself down, facing the wall. In no time, he fell into an exhausted sleep.

ନ୍ଦ

Rhyus opened his eyes, as the yammering of a displeased Marion entered his mind, somewhere between sleep and awareness. Rolling his body away from the wall, he tilted his head upward. Realizing that he could hear Marion from the opposite end of the boat, he grumbled and dropped his head back on the cushions.

As Marion continued to complain, Rhyus threw his hands over his ears, clinching his eyes shut. *Good lord. There isn't even another being on this godforsaken boat! What in the world can possibly be upsetting enough to cause her to argue with absolutely no one at all!*

-256-

He lay listening for a moment longer, however as the minutes dragged and the noise ceased to end, he threw himself into a sitting posture, hurling his legs to the deck. "What the hell are you yelling about?" he hollered, furiously.

"What?" Marion yelled in return, glaring at him, as though he had just interrupted an important conversation.

Rhyus stared blankly back at her. That was anything other than the response he had expected.

He sighed. Mustering the will to push his body up off of the bench, he trudged to the bow where Marion stood.

For a moment, she was quiet, waiting for him to come nearer before she resumed her dispute.

"So, what is the problem?" Although Rhyus meant it to be a question, his utter lack of enthusiasm negated any attempt for it to sound as such. In fact, his monotone response only magnified the fact that he was just pretending to give a damn.

Rhyus knew that she was in dire straits when the normally sharp Marion totally overlooked the tone of his answer.

"The melons…"

"Yeah. They're repulsive, I agree," Rhyus cut in.

"No." She glared at him, annoyed with the interruption. "It isn't that. They have all gone bad. They don't have maggots or anything yet, but they're clearly rotten. Just look at them!"

"Oh, shit," Rhyus said, rolling a melon over in his hand. "I knew the one I ate this morning tasted bad. By the look of these, it must've been the best in the batch."

Looked up, he found Marion staring him straight in the eye with a look of accusation.

"What?" he demanded.

"You never believe anything I say!" she said, loud enough that Rhyus could hear it echoing off of The Darkness and the waves.

"Wait a minute!" Rhyus went silent. Alert, he held up a single finger, indicating that the conversation had ended. He was suddenly very attentive to their surroundings.

"What?" Marion's voice held quiet concern in response to the expression on his face. "What in Ravenna..." she added, noting something far off in the distance. Tiny pinpoints of light.

Rhyus could sense the same panic rising in Marion that had overtaken him the previous night.

"What is it?" Her voice was no more than a whisper. "Something doesn't feel right."

Neither of them removed their eyes from the strand of red, glowing lights beginning to grow larger as the boat moved slowly, yet steadily, in their direction. Rhyus whispered, "I'm not sure, Marion. But I do know one thing...not all sharks hide beneath waves."

30: A Stitch In Relations

Lying on the floor where he had fallen, Jude turned his head toward KyVeerah. His eyes were wide and helpless, and his skin stark white as he slid into shock. His lips moved, as if about to speak, but no words came. With blood oozing between his fingers, his hand wrapped around his upper arm, knuckles white with the force of his grip.

KyVeerah had stepped into the room just in time to see his friend sent backward onto the hardwood floor from a roundhouse kick by Jory. He was the one who had recognized Jude and hauled him away to Galton in the first place. Pleasure radiated from Jory's black eyes, and a wicked grin expressed his sick delight at Jude's pain. He removed the long-nailed fingers that he had held over an open wound on his own arm. Blood still oozed from it, but Jude had not hit anything crucial in his attempted defense.

By far on the worst side of the confrontation, Jude was bleeding profusely from his upper arm.

"Goddammit!" KyVeerah dropped to his knees, cringing at his own pain, but not giving a damn. He ripped the arm of Jude's coat off where it had been damaged and tore the upper portion to the shoulder.

Shit! Jory hit an artery. He shoved his shades up, kneeling over his friend, as the pool of blood around Jude continued to grow. It soaked the knees of KyVeerah's pants, mingling with his own blood.

"Jude." He grabbed Jude's clutched hand, forcing it further up his arm. "Press your thumb here as hard as you can!"

He followed the order, both of his arms shaking violently. His eyelids began to flutter.

"Jude! Come on, stay with me!"

Jude had already hemorrhaged a significant amount, as everyone in the room silently watched KyVeerah tear open his own coat, throwing it aside. He tore a large strip from the bottom of his bloodstained shirt, trying to avoid tearing away any cloth that had stuck to the blood congealing over his wounds. But a portion pulled away, creating a rivulet of blood that ran down his abdomen.

"I told you to keep your hands off of him!" Galton roared, entering the room just behind KyVeerah.

Flint stood with an innocent look, indicating that he had nothing to do with the mess, which Galton found quite believable. Ruby Hale bit down on her dark, painted lip, shifting her vivid blue eyes toward the floor. Wicked pleasure remained in Jory's eyes, but he managed to wipe the nefarious grin from his lips. He realized that Galton understood it was Hale and he who had created this whole mess. Tyson was nowhere in sight, but Galton didn't find this fact suspicious, having earlier put him on an assignment.

Meanwhile, KyVeerah forced Jude to move his hand again. Leaning down sent a surge of pain raging through his upper body as he made a tourniquet. He wrapped the large strip from his gray, skull shirt tightly around Jude's arm, cringing at the nasty wound.

Jory hadn't used his katana to cause this damage. Judging by the horrible, ragged edges of Jude's wound, KyVeerah could tell that the weapon he had used had a deeply serrated edge. It was far worse than the cut on Jude's neck from Hewitt's blade.

Galton continued to stand nearby.

KyVeerah looked up at him, eyes gleaming. Without his shades to block them, the light blazing from them was daunting. "Bring me antibiotics, ointment, and water. I also need bandages, Galton."

"Absolutely, Vin." Galton nodded in affirmation. He turned to his band. "If any one of you leave so much as another pinprick or scratch on either of them, I solemnly swear to Eve herself that I will remove your heads from your godforsaken bodies!"

Galton's eyes were harsh and uncompromising. He ducked back through the passageway to gather what supplies he could find for KyVeerah. Although he was not losing blood as quickly now, he had already lost far too much.

"Jude!" KyVeerah shouted again, as his friend began to succumb once more to unconsciousness. Jude's forehead had already broken out in a sweat, showing signs of fever.

Hale and Flint remained in their fixed positions. Jory, on the other hand, had pulled out a chair. Propping his feet up onto the table, he made himself comfortable. "Now, who'd have thought it would be such an amusing day?" he quipped, in a voice that was more like a hiss.

KyVeerah looked up, ferocity flashing from his eyes. It took every last drop of his willpower to keep from bounding up and removing both Jory's knife and his head in a single fluid motion.

He snarled, in a voice that denoted the veracity of his words, "You will get what's coming to you."

"Oh, yeah?" Jory yawned, raising a brow in further amusement. "And exactly how — " he began his snappy response, but he brought his words to a sudden halt as he saw Galton coming back into the room.

Having heard Jory's tone, Galton directed a warning glare.

"Vincent." Galton expressed the word with a stern voice.

KyVeerah looked up.

"Let me take care of him. You need care yourself. You're far too pale." Galton knelt beside Jude, lifting and carrying him past KyVeerah, to the table.

"Jory," Galton snapped, looking at the smug figure kicked back in the tilted chair with his feet up. "Never mind," he grumbled, keeping his cursing to himself.

KyVeerah remained kneeling on the floor, watching Galton move his friend. Galton had set the supplies he had gathered on a couple of pulled out chairs.

"Hale!" Galton commanded, with the same harsh voice that he had used with Jory. "Take Vincent downstairs and stitch him up. And don't you even think about pulling any funny business." He gave her a withering look.

Her voice trembled. "Yes, Galton."

Galton gave KyVeerah an assuring nod as he pushed up from the ground. Hale looked at KyVeerah, but could not look into his eyes.

Without a single word, KyVeerah grabbed his coat and followed her down into the stairwell. With one last glance toward Jude, he disappeared behind her, into the shadows of the shaft.

Hale stepped out of the stairwell, into the room, but KyVeerah hesitated in the doorway. An intangible, spine-chilling sensation emanated from every inch of the space before them. The appearance of the room did little to help alleviate the eerie foulness.

White. Everything had been painted white. The walls, the wooden floorboards, the cabinets lining every wall, and the ceiling beams were white. Even the one, solitary table in the middle of the room, and not to forget the bookcase they had just come through, was white.

Hale moved toward the opposite end of the room, her dark attire causing her to appear like a silent plague, disrupting the room's intended state. With his shades still placed on top of his head, the lurid reflections glared with foreboding light. KyVeerah continued to hesitate in the doorway.

"Come on," Hale snapped.

KyVeerah stepped fully into the room, feeling like a harsh disturbance himself. He strode smoothly across the room toward her.

"Lie down," Hale ordered, pointing to the white table.

KyVeerah raised an eyebrow.

"Oh come on," she said, rolling her eyes, "just do it." She turned away, moving toward various cabinets along the far end of the room. Crouching down, she rummaged through some, then stood up on her toes, high heels coming off the floor, to reach contents in the higher cabinets.

In the meantime, KyVeerah tossed his coat aside and eased himself back onto the table. He cringed. Every motion was difficult. The table was of cold metal with many layers of paint thrown over it. *That is certainly not a comforting sight*, he thought, noticing the dark stains peeking through the numerous layers of cover.

Lying back on the boxy surface, he turned his head back toward the entrance through which they had come. In doing so, his eyes ran along the length of the floorboards, following the blood trail, which he hadn't realized was trailing him.

Yes, I have officially disgraced the attempted façade of purity within this room, he thought, as Hale continued collecting her assortment of items. Still looking down at the floor, KyVeerah noted that many coats of paint had been thrown down over them through the years as well. Just as on the table, faint dark stains bled through, trying to expose themselves in spite of the deceiving cover. *Good Valencia, I wonder how many people have died in here?* he wondered, a bit less optimistic now.

"All right," Hale said, moving back toward him.

She pointed at KyVeerah's shirt, or what was left of it. "As much as I hate to tell you, you're going to have to lose that."

KyVeerah managed to grin, pulling the shirt up over his head. He gnashed his teeth as he ripped it away from the two gashes, separating them and tearing some sections back open where blood had bonded flesh to fabric. Hale grimaced as well. She tried to keep him from taking notice, but failed.

"Oh, no worries, love. Only a flesh wound." He peered up at her with enthralling eyes, as she examined the larger gash running across his torso. It disrupted the black tattoos that spilled onto his chest and sides from his back. "And yeah, you had best line those back up. *Exactly*." He gave her a look indicating that he was dead serious.

KyVeerah attempted to raise his arms to place his hands behind his head but instantly moved them back down to his sides, for the stretching was impossible to bear. He should have expected it. He tapped his nails against the painted metal, in a short rhythmic pattern, not looking forward to the moments to come. KyVeerah took a slow breath and exhaled, repeating the act twice more in his best effort to prepare himself.

"Ready?" Hale asked, and he could tell that she was actually expecting a genuine response.

"Dearest, the anticipation is the worst part of pain. You know?" He cocked an eyebrow assertively at her. "Try not to damage me any more than you already have, though. My body is a temple, after all." He grinned at her again.

With a look of derision, she narrowed her eyes. "You are absurd." Although on some level she agreed, or at least she used to.

"You are just being too narrow-minded. You have to open your eyes to the bigger, more important things in life. Like me, for instance. You can't really want to cause permanent damage to such an impressive figure?"

She shook her head with near disbelief at his audacity. With a choked laugh, she answered, "If I should ever meet a man who is more conceited than you, I don't know what I will do."

"Oh, not to worry, love. You never will." His grin widened.

"Stop it, now. Seriously. I'm going to take care of this, and you had better not make me cause you any further damage. You know—because we don't want to ruin the sacred temple." Hale rolled her eyes again, mocking him, and he could sense the humor behind them now.

"All right, have at it." A loud, writhing cry from Jude suddenly echoed down from three floors up, reverberating through the stone stairwell and throughout the white room. *Ah shit*, KyVeerah thought. *That is exactly how I am going to feel in a second*. At that same moment, Hale bit down on her lip and poured a bottle of absolute alcohol over the entire length of the wound.

KyVeerah dug his fingers into the edges of the metal table, chipping away sections of paint with his nails. Through hard, bared teeth, he released a heart-wrenching wail at the liquid fire in his wounds.

He threw his head back against the table, straining every muscle in his body, causing only more pain. His cry seemed to multiply Jude's by a thousand, probably audible throughout the entire district.

"Breathe!" Hale ordered. He barely noticed the blue eyes staring down, commanding him.

KyVeerah forced himself to take in a heavy, ragged breath. His body remained rigid, but he finally managed to reopen his eyes, which now focused on a spot where the ceiling met the wall.

"You devil woman," he strained, through clenched teeth, once he could finally manage to form the words. He still looked away from her at the ceiling. "You will pay."

Although he didn't see it, her look of compassion changed to one of resentment. "Well, this isn't going to feel much better." She picked up a needle.

"No. Nothing could feel worse than that." His hard, luminous eyes left absolutely no room for debate. "Give me a drink," he demanded, turning his blazing eyes on her now.

"No, Vincent. It'll thin out your—"

"Now!"

"O-OK...I'll be right back. Give me a second." She debated leaving him before he had been stitched back up, but ascended the stairway to the lounge.

Attempting to avoid another outburst, KyVeerah slammed his head back down onto the tabletop. He wrenched his hands from its rough edges and flexed his shaking fingers.

Hale returned with a glass that was filled to the brim with a dark liquid. She tried not to spill it as she hurried to the table.

As KyVeerah struggled to sit up, she winced, turning her head so that she did not have to witness the searing pain tearing his body. He snatched the drink from her hand and drained its content without a pause. "Coward."

She flipped her head back toward him, shimmering waves of golden hair flying. The rage in her eyes flew at him in disagreement.

He shrugged, looking back up at the ceiling. "Just saying." As another wave of pain passed through him, he suppressed it with a low growl and threw the glass across the room to shatter against the wall.

"You need to lie back down."

"So you think you can slice me open and then tell me what to do, thinking all the while that I will be happy to listen and act accordingly? Hell woman." He dropped himself back onto the table.

"All right," she said, overlooking his comment. Moving the point of the black threaded needle up against his separated flesh, all she could offer was an uninspiring, "Brace yourself."

Hale stitched carefully, sewing him up from his lowest rib to his clavicle. He lay silent, once again gripping the sides of the table and curling his toes within his boots. *It is nothing*, he told himself. *No worse than getting all of these blasted tattoos.*

Despite his best effort, another low cry escaped.

31: Bandages

"Done," Hale finally said, wiping the sweat from her brow.

"About time!" KyVeerah snapped. "Fuckin' Valencia! And you claim you've done that before? I've never seen anyone take so long to stitch someone together. I could have done it in half the time."

"Well, perhaps we should open it back up, and you can do it yourself!"

"You know, I am half tempted," KyVeerah muttered, sliding to the edge of the table and dropping his feet to the floor. He looked down to examine the job, which Hale had carried out.

Looking up from the seams holding his body together, he said, "Thanks, Ruby...you know...for nothing. If you wanted so much to spend time alone with me, all you had to do was say so."

Hale gaped, about to respond, but KyVeerah held a finger to her pouting lips. "No, no, beloved. It is far too late for that now." Quietly, but loud enough to make sure that she heard it, he added, "Especially after that horrendous, painful, and not to mention drawn-out, stitching job."

"Well, I *was* going to bandage you up, but now—"

"You had better watch yourself, woman." He pointed a finger at her, as he reached for his coat, which he had earlier cast to the floor.

He disregarded the look Hale threw at him. "I'm going to check on Jude."

Hale shouted up the shaft behind him, "Vincent KyVeerah! You are going to get a nasty infection if you don't come back down here right this moment!" Too late. He had already made his way back up to the sixth floor.

∾ଔ

"Galton!" KyVeerah shouted, as he exited through the bookcase. "How is my man, Jude?" He quickly approached the table.

"Well," came Galton's deep, rough voice, "I got the bleeding to stop and managed to clean him up. That is a nasty wound, but I fixed it the best I could."

KyVeerah rested the back of his hand on Jude's face, leaning forward as guilt flooded him. "Hear that, Jude? You're gonna be right as rain. And then we're going to go out on the town. Someplace where no unstable psychopath could ever think of trying to put a knife through you. I promise."

KyVeerah could sense the severe look that Galton was giving Jory. The latter simply remained in the same chair as before, but his feet now rested on the floor. He appeared to be examining a knife that he was turning over, and over, in his hands.

Jude's face was extremely pale, and his eyes remained closed. KyVeerah looked tenderly down at his friend.

"It could take some time for him to come out of it," Galton said, in a quiet voice.

"Galton. I know it is a lot to ask, but would you be able to keep him here and watch over him for awhile? You know this is the last place I would want to leave him, but I am sure you will keep a close eye on him. And there is something I really must tend to."

"Yes, of course, Vincent." Galton then fixed a commanding eye on KyVeerah. "And why haven't you been properly bandaged? You're going to get all sorts of infections, flaunting an injury openly in such a trap as this. What was that woman thinking?"

"Precisely. My question exactly."

"Go tell her to bandage you up properly. I can't allow someone such as yourself to leave The Hinge in such a state, without appropriate care."

KyVeerah sighed, looking down once more at his friend. "Yes, I suppose you're right."

Moving back down the stone stairs, KyVeerah reentered the white room. Hale, who was putting items back into their proper cabinets, turned, surprised to see that he had returned. "Yes?"

"I need your assistance. Won't you bandage me up?"

She frowned at him.

"Ruby. Please?" The smallest trace of a grin played over her lips.

"Well, what the hell are you standing clear over there for?"

KyVeerah grinned back, stepping toward the table.

"You're going to have to keep your arm out of the way," she informed, re-collecting bandages and tape. "No, just stay standing," she added, as she saw him about to hop back onto the table.

Carefully, Hale began to bandage the newly stitched wound.

"Ruby," KyVeerah said, once she had successfully applied bandaging to the topmost section of his chest.

She glanced briefly up at him, waiting for what he wished to say.

"I was wondering if I could ask you to do one *huge* favor for me?"

"And why in the world would I ever consider doing you a favor?"

"Because you owe it to me."

Hale couldn't help but burst out laughing at his reasoning. "Oh, really? And what kind of favor is it that you're asking of me?"

"Will you bring Jude to the Rundown tomorrow morning, just before dawn? I know that he shouldn't be subjected to much or anything really, in his condition. But I am asking you. He needs to be my responsibility, but there is no way that I can take him right now. He must rest a while. Six o'clock tomorrow morning, at the Rundown. Won't you, please, Ruby?" KyVeerah looked down at her as she paused in the middle of her bandaging, studying the black stitches and the realigned tattoos.

She released a quiet sigh, but KyVeerah could hear her response quite clearly, "Yes. Yes, I will take him there," she agreed, but she refused to look up into his eyes.

He gave her a genuine smile, "Thank you. Thank you, very much, Ruby."

Hale finished bandaging up the larger wound, as well as the wound from Jory. "You're done." She collected the items that she had set on the edge of the table, to put them away. Meanwhile, KyVeerah brought his arm back down, stretching it, twisting and bending it different ways.

"Vincent."

"Yes?"

"Why would you ask me to do something like that for you?"

"Honestly, Ruby, I know you would not be so shallow as to hurt my friend to get back at me. That would be too low, even for you. You know I am right, yes?"

She glanced back at him just long enough to catch the faint luminosity in his eyes. Standing still and silent, she finally gave a single nod.

"You should go. Don't you have business to tend to? I will have him there for you tomorrow morning."

"Will you wait for me? He shouldn't be left alone. Not for a moment."

"Yes, I will wait. But not forever, Vincent. *This time*, I will expect you to show as planned." She gave him her most serious look.

"That won't be a problem." He made his way back to the stairwell. "Tomorrow then. And thank you again, Ruby." He raised his arm, admiring the fresh swath of bandages. Then he disappeared, ascending the dark stairway before she could respond.

ℰℭ

"Galton, a word," KyVeerah said, coming back through the opening behind the bookcase for the last time. He walked to the far end of the table, opposite Jory, nearest to the simple maze of tall, wooden bookcases. KyVeerah kept a cold eye on Jory, as Galton came to stand by his side.

Maintaining his watch over Jude, KyVeerah stated, "I have spoken to Hale. She is going to bring Jude to me at a discussed time and location. But he must be watched over until then. And the antibiotics must be continued. I will need some for later."

Galton displayed a puzzled expression.

"It's a long and unnecessary story," KyVeerah replied, addressing Galton's obvious confusion as to why he would trust Hale after what she had so recently done to him. He gave a flourish of his hand, signaling his dismissal.

Galton nodded, "Of course, Vin. Give me a moment, and I'll throw some things together for you."

KyVeerah stepped back to Jude's side, as Galton collected an array of objects for him. Jude remained still with the exception of his chest rising and falling with every breath. His lips and skin were still far too pale.

"All right, Vin." Galton stepped back to KyVeerah's side, holding out a single-strapped black bag. "There are enough supplies in here for you to bring him back to full health, assuming that everything runs effectively and heals over well."

"Yes, thank you, Galton." KyVeerah nodded in respect, displaying his appreciation for Galton's considerations.

"Oh, and Vin—there's one more thing." Galton moved back, digging through a bag he had brought out earlier. Returning to KyVeerah, he held out a pair of dark denims and a dark, short-sleeved shirt. "I know that these aren't tailored to your elegant taste, but I think they will be a close fit for you. They belonged to Guy Letters. You may remember him and his unfortunate fall?" KyVeerah nodded.

Guy Letters had been ganged up on in one of the Vessel District's small bars. A man named Beck Scofflin, and a group of his followers, had dragged him outside and beat him to a bloody pulp, leaving him to die in a most dishonorable fashion.

Galton nodded. "I thought you might. The event was overexploited. A bit grisly, if I do say so myself."

"Thank you again, and for watching over him for the time being."

"Anytime, Vin. And don't stay a stranger now, you hear me?" Galton narrowed his eyes, giving KyVeerah a look, half warning and half portraying his own hopes and interests.

"You can change amongst these rows of bookcases. No one will be coming through to disrupt you." He cast a warning eye back at Jory. "Oh, and one last thing. I believe this belongs to you." Galton held KyVeerah's curved knife out, giving him one final nod. KyVeerah took the blade and nodded in return.

At that, he moved amongst the wooden bookcases.

32: Ever Nearer

Helena knew that this whole Calling thing had pulled her way off course. It had been much too long since she had been to one of the meetings of the White Band. She grimaced. The fact that Royce—and even Jett—generally ran the meetings didn't help. Of all assassins in Nyx's Bands, those were the two she just could not stand. When trapped in a room with either of them, it nauseated her to imagine they shared the same air.

Since she'd been taken in by Nyx, her life had been good. She still remained a loner, but what the hell, that had been the story of her life. She realized that despite the "freedom" Nyx granted his assassins to carry out their own personal plans, they must each carry their share of the load. And she had not been carrying her share. Not even close. She promised herself that once having found a few more answers, she would get right back on track again. However, after the hundredth time, even this promise began to sound unlikely.

Helena had almost finished the book from The Archives. It frustrated her that the main thrust of the book involved the historical evolution of the Energies. That still didn't get her any closer to her main goal. The text may have been interesting, but just the same, in many ways she actually found the text annoying. She had never been a strong reader to begin with, and this thing was loaded with all kinds of arcane references that made her head ache to think about. Despite that, she never gave up. If one single significant word in there brought her closer to her plan, it was worth the effort. If nothing else, once she committed to a plan, even the raw Energies themselves could not steer her from her path.

At least, since there was brief reference about the tattooing—or marking—of Callings and their Messengers, she did have something concrete that she could work with. It pissed her off, however, that there were only written references, and not one damn illustration.

But yet, somewhere deep in her mind's eye, connections had occurred. She could almost see and feel them, much like those hazy tendrils of dreamland that hung about for the first part of the day. And much as in those dreams, the more she tried to concentrate on them, the further they seemed to flee.

She knew with certainty that she was drawing ever nearer. As much as he would *dislike* it, Nyx was just going to have to wait a little bit longer.

33: Time to Take Leave

KyVeerah exited The Hinge wearing Guy Letters' clothing, which was just a bit large, but not too bad considering the way in which he had acquired them. He placed his own bloodied clothes into the black bag Galton had given him. Sliding his shades back into their proper position, he moved away from The Hinge, heading back to the southeast. He had to walk for a good while before returning to Umbra Halls. As he moved along, the tight tension in every muscle finally relaxed, and he released a long, shuddering sigh.

Looking around, he stopped in his tracks. He had the sudden realization that he had been moving unconsciously toward The Tower.

"Quite extraordinary, isn't she?" A faint voice reached KyVeerah from somewhere in the distance, but he knew the voice was speaking to him. He spun back around.

A man in his mid-forties sat on a glimmering, white stone bench. He had known KyVeerah would hear his words.

"You," was the only thing KyVeerah could manage. He stood still for a long minute before stepping toward the man with caution.

Despite wearing a long dark jacket with a hood pulled over his head, KyVeerah recognized him in an instant. Small wisps of light, wavy hair were visible, so light beyond a platinum blonde that it glinted with a constant silver sheen. His skin was slightly tanned, and eyes of liquid amber rested among his kind features. KyVeerah came to a halt some distance away.

"It has been quite some time, Vincent KyVeerah."

KyVeerah continued looking at him from behind his shades. He studied the area to be certain whether any soldiers of the White Guard might be around.

"They won't come near you," the man assured. "They do not see you as a threat. And I hope for things to remain that way. But there is a disturbed quality about you, Vincent." The man's face altered with a look of deep thought. "Yes, quite. You look troubled, son." His face now showed great concern, hoping that he might be able to offer a helping hand.

"It is nothing of your concern, Abel."

The man, Abel, only showed a warm smile at this remark. "You know," he began, "I spoke with a young man just yesterday about his troubles. He seemed to also have significant concerns, this one. You know what I told him?"

KyVeerah shifted his weight, offering a questioning tilt of his head.

"I told him that one must trust their instincts and look for a sign. I can see that you are also very troubled. And it is about much more than the difficulties currently resting foremost on your mind. You will discover what you are supposed to do and the right path for you to take." Sharing another warm smile, he regarded KyVeerah with his amber eyes, waiting for some response. "You will find a way to put the pieces together. You may not like all of the final outcomes, but generally you are not supposed to. Things have a way of working out in ways that are necessary for all involved."

KyVeerah sighed, and turning his head, looked away. *One of the few somns with senses as strong as my own. I am not fond of that fact in the least.*

Abel gave him a look that acknowledged his thoughts. "You need to loosen up, Vincent. You'll dig yourself into the ground." He allowed a moment for reflection. "Well, it has been good to see you again." He hesitated, "And Vincent," this time offering a look of serious concern, "please, I adjure you to take care of yourself."

At that, KyVeerah nodded his due respects, "Goodbye, my Lord." Then he moved past Lord Abel, who remained seated on the stone bench. Without looking back, he knew that the man leaned his hooded head down, once again hiding his face from the common folk passing by. If someone he desired to speak with passed near, he would sense his or her presence without the need of his sight. KyVeerah drew a deep breath for motivation and headed back northwest to the Caulder District.

Another sigh escaped KyVeerah's slender lips. He had moved at a steady pace until he stood just before the alleyway leading back to Umbra Halls. Beyond it was nothing but uninhabited forest, beach, and the sea.

Cracking his fingers, he prepared himself for the lecture that he was certain to receive from Venn. He swung, with his elegant stride, into the alleyway, which grew darker and darker until the light of the city vanished altogether. He pushed through the metal gateway and glided across the old cobblestones.

"Vincent! Is that you?" a stern voice shouted, from somewhere above the center of The Courtyard, through where the great tree protruded.

Agh. Good Valencia! KyVeerah rolled his eyes, but he had known this was coming. Then, as he pushed through the double doors at the head of The Courtyard, he could hear Venn push through the set just above. Hurrying, KyVeerah quickly ducked to the right, heading straight for his bedroom.

"Stop!"

KyVeerah stopped dead in his tracks, just two steps from his destination. Slowly, he turned his head, followed by the rest of his body until he faced Venn.

Venn glared at him with hard, brilliant blue eyes.

"Please, Venn! Not another word until I have had at least a moment to change." KyVeerah tried to tame the wild irritation in his voice.

"Wait!" Venn ordered, as realization sunk in. "Whose clothes are those, Vincent? Where the hell have you been? I swear, you haven't even been here an entire day, and you are already getting into trouble! And take off those shades!" He furled his eyebrows in certainty. "You're in the damn house. You'll be running into walls for sure."

KyVeerah shook his head. Turning away, he took the last steps to the door. He threw it open and ducked inside, but not without an agitated Venn stalking after him.

Venn stormed into the room through the open door. "What the hell, Vincent!" His furious expression evaporated when KyVeerah pulled the loose, short-sleeved shirt off, throwing it to the floor where he had already tossed his coat. "What *the* hell? Vincent?"

White bandages had been taped over the majority of KyVeerah's right side, as well as a separate piece just over his heart. Judging by their crisp cleanness, Venn knew they were fresh, most likely from today.

"Yeah." Shirtless, but still wearing his dark shades, KyVeerah flashed his annoyance. "It hurts. All right," he snapped. "Now you can stop staring, you aren't my damn mother."

"Too bad. By the looks of it, you need one to keep a close watch over you," Venn scolded, recovering his usual manner. The shock of surprise had already worn off.

"What is your problem?" KyVeerah snapped, mirroring Venn's approach. He threw his clawed hands into the air in a gesture of ferocity, like some wild animal. "Agh!" he cried, as the sharp motion shot pain across his torso. "Dammit!" The heavy ridge of muscle across his chest clinched in spasm, and the protective flexion of his abdominal muscles only served to elicit even more pain.

Venn rolled his eyes and raised a hand in a quick wave of dismissal. "I don't even want to know." He shook his head. "It's already running into evening, I had to wait for you before I could speak to someone about the possible whereabouts of Rhyus and Marion. Are you interested?"

KyVeerah's expression of irritation vanished. "Wait, are you actually inviting me to go along with you?"

"Oh, come off it, Vincent. You don't have to make such a big deal of it."

"Well, in that case, I really must shower, and then we can go."

"All right. But make it quick. I know how you can be."

"Fabulous." KyVeerah lifted his hands in an obsequious manner. "I'll be up when I'm ready then."

At that, Venn took his dismissal, shutting the door behind him.

80CR

KyVeerah stepped into the kitchen. Scooting crystal shards on the floor out of his path, he made his way to the fridge. Pulling out a small container of leftovers, he muttered, still annoyed at the kitchen's rearrangement. Grabbing a fork from the drawer, and without heating the container's contents, he began to wolf down the food.

Venn opened the door. "Hungry?" He took note of KyVeerah inhaling the container's contents. "Don't choke. That would be a pity now, wouldn't it?" Arms crossed, he leaned against the open doorway.

KyVeerah paused with his mouth open and the last bite halfway to his mouth. He shifted his eyes toward Venn, snatching the last bite from the fork held in midair. "Just a wee bit," he said, after throwing the empty container and fork into the sink, amongst the other dishes piling up there.

"And, what in the world happened there?" KyVeerah pointed to the far wall behind him.

"Oh, yeah. Never mind that." Venn shook his head, dismissing the drying crust of the filthy, splattered melon mess that had yet to be cleaned.

"Hmm." KyVeerah pursed his lips with curiosity, but simply

shrugged it off and moved past Venn and out into the hallway. As he walked, he pulled a leaf from the tree branch hanging nearby.

"Hey!"

"What?" KyVeerah looked up, still holding the leaf between his thumb and middle finger.

"Never mind. Let's go."

Stepping over to the large closet, Venn grabbed a long, black coat for himself, and then threw a deep aqua-blue coat KyVeerah's way. "Catch."

They put their coats on, making their way down to The Courtyard, KyVeerah following just behind Venn. Heading through the gate and into the dark alleyway, they found themselves together, out on the walkways of Lux Lumetia. The suns no longer shown at this hour, but frequent streetlamps kept the shimmering city illuminated.

Side by side, Venn and KyVeerah headed southeast in the direction of The Tower. They moved through the Caulder District, followed by the Mirrón and Gamlin Districts.

"Why do you wear those? It's night out." Subconsciously, Venn adjusted his own glasses.

KyVeerah shrugged. "Habit." He knew Venn was referring to his dark tinted shades.

Venn didn't respond to KyVeerah's comment. He simply continued walking alongside him.

"So, exactly where are we headed?" KyVeerah asked. By now, they were moving east of The Tower.

"We're going to a tavern on the Eastside, the Crimson Glass. It's not too much farther, just at the eastern border of the next district."

"Ah, indeed. I suppose I wouldn't mind grabbing myself a drink right about now."

When they reached their destination, the lounge was merely a small portion of a much larger building. A sign in red and white neon lights read *Crimson Glass*, and a matching image of a cocktail complemented the scripted title in the same glowing neon lights.

Venn paused, "We're here."

34: Seeking Gossip Where Gossip is Due

Venn pushed through the doors of the Crimson Glass and walked inside with KyVeerah a single step behind. KyVeerah looked around the tavern. The inside definitely represented its name with an abundance of crimson and white lights scattered throughout.

The tabletops and bar all had mirrored surfaces, reflecting light in every direction. The wooden floor was stained deep crimson and the white seats and bar cushions were bathed in the flood of red light.

As KyVeerah followed Venn toward the back of the bar, he spotted an attractive young woman sitting by herself on one of the silver and white barstools. She smiled as she caught sight of them coming near. She spun the straw in her glass with brightly painted fingernails, the same shade as her full, sensual lips.

Aw, Venn, you sly devil, KyVeerah thought.

Suddenly, he smacked into Venn, who had come to an abrupt halt. "By Valencia, Venn!" KyVeerah's voice was overshadowed by music piped throughout the bar. They still stood some distance from the young woman, but she continued to study them from the corner of her eye. She brushed long, dark hair back behind her shoulders, exposing lightly tanned flesh. KyVeerah was puzzled as Venn paid her no attention at all. And then he spotted her. A girl with pale gold, tight spiraling curls sat just next to where Venn had come to a standstill. The girl turned to face him. She was wearing bright green eye shadow and far too much eyeliner for her young face, at least in KyVeerah's judgment. She smiled at Venn, pleased to see him.

Incredulous, KyVeerah gaped. "This is your source?" he spat, with disgust and disbelief.

Mona, at first curious about the charming man Venn had brought along, was now insulted by his offensive reaction to her.

"She's a child!" Lowering his gaze to study Mona further, he sneered, "Isn't it past your bedtime?" He smirked, impressed with his own insulting humor, as Venn issued a warning look.

"That is no way to make friends. Besides, she is a font of very valuable information. She may very well be able to help us out. And perhaps *significantly*." Venn stressed the last word, hoping to draw forth KyVeerah's innermost interest.

Ignoring Venn's remarks, KyVeerah hissed, "And who said I wanted to make friends...with a *child*?" He pulled away from her, repulsed at the thought of being friends with a girl her age. "She can't possibly be more than seventeen!" he groused to Venn.

"Stop whining, Vincent. C'mon." Venn turned his attention back to Mona, who had a frown creasing her fresh, youthful face.

"Hello, Mona. How have you been?" Venn asked casually, taking a seat on the barstool to her left. "Pay no heed to the idiot at my side. Lord knows I don't." Venn lowered his brow and gave her a wink.

KyVeerah dropped his jaw, but he quickly recovered with a sulky scowl.

"Hello, Venn," Mona warmly stressed his name, ignoring KyVeerah and making it clear that she was going to talk to Venn whether his tag-along liked it or not. "I'm doing just fine."

Behind the cover of his shades, KyVeerah studied the attractive, black-haired woman he had originally thought they were meeting. Dissatisfied, he sat on the open stool beside Venn. He spun it away from Venn to face her, but he still listened for anything important that he or the young girl could possibly have to say. *If* either of them had anything important to say.

Simultaneously, Venn and KyVeerah motioned to catch the attention of one of the female bartenders. She had straight, warm brown hair and matching eyes. Acknowledging them, she finished placing some newly washed glasses into a freezer to chill. She flashed a beckoning smile, but then a frown tinged her features, registering that it was Venn. She immediately shifted her attention to KyVeerah, stepping nearer to him and leaned forward.

Having noticed her altered expression at the very sight of Venn, KyVeerah gave her a wry grin filled to the brim with curiosity.

"Hey there." The brunette's voice was warm and inviting, as the red light danced from two sets of large, dangling hoop earrings. "The name is Lucille," she said, with a smug smile. "What can I getcha, handsome?"

"Rum, straight up, would do me just fine." KyVeerah considered asking Venn whether he would like one as well, but quickly changed his mind. Reconsidering, he beckoned Lucille closer. With a whisper, he asked, "You don't, by chance, happen to keep any of Atrum's Finest here? Antum Regal?" At first, her eyes narrowed at the request for the illicit brew, but then she winked, giving him a conspiratorial nod.

"Brilliant! Make it two of them." He nodded to include Venn, soliciting a look of disgust from her. He lowered his head to return a wink over his shades. Lucille couldn't help but flush. He masked his eyes once more, and she headed off to get the drinks for him.

"Here you are." She offered a solicitous look behind her lashes. "And you can call me Lucy." She set the two glasses onto the bar's mirrored surface. "Just holler if I can get you *anything* else." She offered a new, seductive wink, revealing eyelids coated in bright yellows and oranges to match her top, though subdued by the red lights overhead.

KyVeerah tossed a handful of bills onto the bar's surface. "Will do." He nodded, raising his drink in a salute. As she turned away, he used the back of his hand to slide the second drink to Venn.

Venn grabbed the glass and lifted it for a couple of immediate swallows. He almost choked in a brief moment of surprise, lifting a brow as to the unexpected contents of the glass, but kept his intentions locked on Mona.

"Yeah, yeah. No need for thanks or anything," KyVeerah muttered, with thick sarcasm. Still receiving no thanks, he raised a glass to his own health and savored a few sips.

℘℘

"So, Mona," Venn thumped his glass down, "what's the new talk of the town?"

Mona's edginess faded as Venn conversed with her, facing away from the boorish man who had accompanied him. "Do you mean since our last encounter?" She gave him a light, mocking smile.

Now realizing that it had only been days since he last searched her out, he felt foolish for having not recalled the fact sooner. The last few days had felt like a hundred. He lifted his elbows to the bar, folding his hands together. "Well, yes. I suppose so." He had a twinkle in his eye.

Pleased with the opportunity to converse with Venn in general, and particularly at the chance to call him out on his absentmindedness, she gave him a genuine smile. "You've sure been curious about the goings on recently." She thought a moment, tucking some of her tight, gold curls behind her ear. "Lucky for you, things are always happening in Lux. And even luckier yet, you happen to know someone who is on top of everything that goes around." Mona flushed in response to her own self-aggrandizement.

Although neither Mona nor Venn could see him do so, KyVeerah rolled his eyes in disgust. He took another sip from his glass, muttering something incoherent under his breath as he set the glass back upon the bar's surface.

"Ah," Venn raised his glass, nodding his head in agreement. "Lucky indeed." He tilted his head back, finishing the last of the glass's contents. "Let's have it."

"Hmm…let me see." Mona placed a hand up to her chin, looking out of the corner of her eye, deciding which tidbits of hearsay to begin with. "Mary Joslin and Philip Quake were wed yesterday at the Naveen Cathedral. A large majority of the Eastside's wealthiest attended the mid-afternoon ceremony and the evening reception at Jonathan Quake's place. I'm certain you have heard of the Quake Estate? They are the largest landowners for several districts.

"And Mary Joslin was the sole daughter of the highest-ranked florists on the Eastside. Between Joslin and Quake, I'm sure there will be plenty of wealth to push around." As Mona swirled the contents of her cocktail glass, Venn could read the envy crawling over her features.

"Yes. I know them," Venn stated matter-of-factly, after a moment's silence. KyVeerah slid a second drink Venn's way, paying an unfamiliar, male bartender. Moving only his eyes, Venn noticed that Lucille was nowhere in sight.

Mona tossed a questioning look at Venn, seeing that his attention was clearly somewhere outside of their conversation. Catching himself, he jerked his attention back to her. "So…" He adjusted his rectangular frames. "Anything else of interest gone on?"

Venn sipped his new drink, fending off the girl's expression of accusation. For a second time, he failed to return even the slightest thanks for the drink he had just received. He said nothing, enjoying KyVeerah's clear irritation at the lack of displayed gratitude.

Mona continued to examine Venn, searching for an ulterior motive for his visit. Unable to land on anything definite, she picked up the discussion once again. "A serious bar fight took place a couple of nights ago."

That statement caught Venn's attention. He turned his entire body toward her with a concerned look. "What, here?"

"Oh. No. It wasn't here." She lowered her eyes, leaving only the bright green eye makeup to meet his gaze.

"Thank the goddesses above that everyone here is all right!" The rare look of concern remained on Venn's face, but it relaxed as he was assured that all was well here. With his composure regained, Venn rested his left elbow back upon the bar. "So then, at which bar did this 'serious' fight take place?"

Mona scowled at Venn's unkind mocking.

Venn returned to his drink. Glancing at the mirror over the bar, he could see KyVeerah looking at him. No, wait. KyVeerah was looking fixedly past him. Venn turned his head to see what could be holding KyVeerah's attention so strongly.

KyVeerah's eyes were fixated on the lightly tanned, black-haired girl with the dark, glittering makeup. He watched her get down from her bar stool, stumbling a bit, gripping the cushioned seat for stability. Attempting to steady herself again, the stunning young woman moved on past the bar, with a man just older than KyVeerah himself, and toward the exit.

Scowling, KyVeerah watched them pass right on by him without an ounce of notice. Wishing that he were the gent leading the well-figured beauty out, he looked back to the bar, studying the variety of colors and shapes of the bottles lining the many rows of glass shelving.

Venn slid a surreptitious hand beneath the bar, tapping the side of KyVeerah's leg. KyVeerah collected himself, as Venn discretely passed over some folded bills placed between his middle and forefinger. Perking up, KyVeerah summoned Lucille, who had reappeared behind the bar.

Lucille approached him. "How can I help you?" she questioned, in a way that opened room for the possibility of more than a simple drink.

"Just another round will suffice." He gave her a crooked grin, which she returned in her own, less crooked, fashion. Then she leaned too far forward, picking up the emptied glasses.

With a look from behind her lashes, her long hair fell forward. She tucked a strand behind her ear and stood straight again with a smirk on her lips.

"Venn?" Mona questioned, a bit snippy.

"What? Oh, right." He readjusted his expression, attempting to focus back in on their topic of conversation. Her look of displeasure thickened. "The bar," he added. "Where was the bar that this took place?" Mona continued to give him a voiceless glare.

Venn ceased to apologize for the disruption, sipping the new glass that KyVeerah slid his way. Mona gave in. "Well..." Venn turned his head back to her, encouraging her to continue. "Beck Scofflin left another man dead. At least it has been said that Scofflin was the one who did it, but you can never be sure. Especially when it comes to stories from West Bay." Mona pursed her lips, shaking her head in disapproval.

"Where in West Bay?"

"At the very heart. Scally Bar, in the Polly District. After a rough beating, a bottle was smashed right through the back of his skull. Quite a mess. There was some other damage, of course, both to the tavern and the other men involved. But everyone else made it out alive."

I wonder who was killed, or why? Again, Venn's mind wandered.

Mona carried on, "Oh, and Reigner Pace's boat went missing. Stolen, he says. The boat was one from the Philosopher's Collection, and a rather new addition to the series." Mona took another swig from her glass.

"Now, who would steal a boat?" she questioned, more to herself than to Venn. "Whoever it was will be caught. It's not like they could travel around all these islands unseen. Stealing a thing does not make it invisible. Whoever took it must be an idiot."

Maybe not, Venn thought. *A bit too judgmental, Mona?* He glanced to see if KyVeerah had caught this piece of information. But he was flirting away with the overly revealed Lucille, who was leaning much further over the bar than necessary. *Brazen hussy.*

Speaking of judgmental! Venn stifled the grin at his own hypocrisy. He turned his attention back to Mona when he realized that KyVeerah had sensed his eavesdropping.

"Oh!" Venn jumped at Mona's little yelp. "I haven't even told you the worst news of all!" she exclaimed. "A young man was hired as the new gossip columnist for the city paper. Although, of course, they don't call him the gossip columnist. His column has been titled "Evan on the Update," she huffed. She stared at a point out in space, pondering some deep question.

"I've got it! Evan Blakely. That's his name. The jerk starts officially tomorrow, and his first column will be published in the *Lux Lately* the day following." It was quite clear that Mona was bitter over the young man's newly created position. She repetitively tinked her fingernails against the bottom of her martini glass, which contained only an odd mixture of crushed genberries and a clear, carbonated liquid.

"I...we must be going," Venn declared, realizing that he had heard the last of any useful information from the distracted and razzled girl. "Vincent," Venn said, leaving no room for dispute. KyVeerah got up off of the barstool after leaving one last flirtatious wink for the bartender. Mona, on the other hand, hadn't even heard Venn's statement in her sour, self-absorbed state.

Before they had a chance to move more than a single step from the bar, a frantic man burst through the entrance. Acting like a loony, he climbed up on the nearest table, shouting and flailing his arms wildly.

"What the hell?" Venn asked, loud enough for only KyVeerah's keen hearing, as he focused on the man, attempting to make out the words he was shouting over the blaring music.

KyVeerah's eyes grew wide.

"Venn, we have to go." He turned and looked Venn in the eye, his face dead serious.

Vincent, what—?"

"*Now!*" This time, KyVeerah was the one leaving no room for dispute.

Grabbing Venn's jacket, he forced his way through the crowd surrounding the frantic man on the table. He made sure not to show the anxiety boiling beneath his skin.

KyVeerah threw the doors open, Venn following close behind. Together, they moved briskly away from the bar.

Shit! KyVeerah looked around with unease. "Shit!"

35: Down the Rabbit Hole...Again

With great restraint, Callis made his way carefully down the slick, rusted rungs of the ladder, moist from the mist filtering into the shaft from the world above. The opening was very narrow, and he felt a twinge of trepidation as he squeezed into it. Looking down from the top of the Sŭsurrus Fountain, he hadn't been sure he would fit, but sure enough, he made his way skillfully down through the tight space. His emotions were on edge, the lethal excitement of a predator on the trail of its prey.

Callis had never been comfortable in close or crowded places, which was unfortunate considering his line of work. He made his way down with caution, making it midway before pausing to analyze the situation.

Better test this ladder before I go any further. As a precaution, Callis shook the ladder with force, deeming it to be sturdy and dependable, despite its rusted surfaces and decrepit appearance.

With one hand clasping the slick ladder, Callis managed to reach into an inner pocket of his jacket to retrieve a pair of leather gloves. With his left arm wrapped around a single rung of the ladder, he stretched one over his right hand, using his teeth to pull the glove into place. He repeated this with the counterpart. Then, taking one last look at the never-ending gray sky above him, Callis shifted his grip and stepped backward into midair. His body dropped into the darkness, only his loosened grasp on the sides of the ladder to keep him from free-falling altogether.

He reached the bottom with a silent thud and peered around into the dankness. It was still narrow, but at least it was wider than the shaft, and the ceiling reached high. As he scanned the space, his eyes adjusted from the thick darkness of the shaft to his new, dimly lit surroundings. Filthy crystal sconces, embedded into the walls, cast muted light over the carved, marble cobblestones lining the floor.

A thick condensation lay heavy in the air with a moist layer of muck caking everything in sight. The bluish-gray sludge gathered into large puddles, fed by a thin stream of rainwater that trailed off to disappear down the corridor.

Still standing at the base of the shaft, Callis studied the floor. Glimmering sapphires had been tracked down over time to create revolting pools of slime that coated the cobblestones. He realized, however, that some of these granules had been carried down more recently.

With a scowl, he noticed several patterned indentations disturbing the muck as far down the corridor as he could see. *Footprints. And plenty of them.* Callis knelt to take a better look. *Still pretty defined. Especially these two sets.* He pondered a moment, determining the justification for their condition in quick time. *Armani and Julian, no doubt...which means that the third set of tracks belongs to him— the Intruder.* He studied the prints, burning their exact size and shape to his memory.

Callis stepped into the corridor with a locked determination in his step. He paused, nearly tripping over a metal card table lying on its side, a spray of moldering playing cards on the floor around it. In his distraction, he hadn't even given it notice. Judging by the marks in the muck, the table had slid from its original place near the base of the shaft, thrown sideways, scattering the cards throughout the small space.

Callis could tell without difficulty that the card table had been thrown over very recently. His gaze swept up and down the passageway. *I'm getting closer.* He increased the length of his strides, flying down the tunnel in a new revival of feral excitement.

In no time, he reached the far end of the corridor, which had a ladder almost identical to the one beneath the fountain. Not looking forward to entering a second narrow shaft, Callis stepped onto the lowest rung and began his ascent.

At the top, the space widened a bit. He pulled himself up onto a platform running around the shaft opening, finding himself within a new marble enclosure. *What the hell?* He felt around with his hands. Maintaining a precarious balance on the narrow platform, he searched the surface, spotting a thin, subtle strip of light running vertically along the outer curve of the structure.

He ran a gloved finger along the sliver of light. With the same hand, he tried to push it open. Nothing. With an irritated grunt, he shoved with determination against the wall of his marble surroundings, exerting a great amount of force. The curved wall bent under the pressure, finally caving outward with a loud thud. The wall opened, revealing the new exit.

Callis emerged from the cylindrical structure, stepping away for a better look at where he had broken through. His eyes widened in disbelief as he found himself standing in front of one of the many pillars that lined the main floor of The Tower.

Barely audible, even to himself, Callis whispered, "No!" White-hot anger flashed through him, as he balled up his fists, slamming the left one into a portion of the pillar that still remained in place. "*No!*"

He could feel the reverberation of the blow all the way up his arm. Every muscle in Callis's body was tense. Thick locks of his crimson hair fell forward, and his head hung low. He kept his eyes closed, as staring at the marble floor of The Tower usually resulted in a flash of temporary blindness. Leaning against the pillar, he lifted his head, eyes wide with rage.

Flashes of the past few days entered his mind. *I had him in sight! And then he just disappeared.* His anger escalated as he realized this was the very same pillar he had stopped at the day the Intruder had escaped. His furious eyes narrowed into slits. "I had him! I had the son of a bitch!"

Callis gnashed his teeth in blind fury. *I can't believe that creep crawled right out from under my very nose! I'd stake my life that only these few inches of marble separated me from him!* He looked toward the center of the room at the elevator that was still currently out of service. He turned back, moving with aggressive steps to where the opening in the side of the pillar led down into the long forgotten passageway.

With vengeful anger rising to the surface, Callis shoved his way into the pillar, releasing a wrathful scream, contained far too long, down into the blackness of the shaft. It thundered all the way down and through the tunnel that he had just exited. He could feel the throbbing pulse of his ferocity, as he took heavy gulping breaths, in and out. He raged, *I am going to find you, Vincent KyVeerah, and when I do, I am going to make you suffer. You are going to wish by the five lunar goddesses that you'd never escaped me that day.*

ᔓᑦᘉ

Staring down at the intricate silver key in the palm of her hand, Ezra Stark cursed under her breath. How could she have been so careless as to allow Callis Morgandy the opportunity to make her look like such a fool. And in front of two trainee Tower Guards, no less. It was a miracle that no one could see steam coming off of her.

She tightly clutched the key, digging sculpted nails into her palm. The dark, pitiless assassin noticed no pain in her vexation. Even if Callis and she were the only two who realized that his goal was to make her look and feel like a fool...well, that was beside the point.

"Of all the egotistical, chauvinistic—!" Ezra's scream echoed through the misty air, as she stomped her way back to The Dome. Even with all the other buildings towering over her, Ezra could still make out The Dome.

The only sounds as she crossed into The Dome's Hollow Sector were the crunching of her high-heeled boots and the quiet tapping of the rain. The product in her hair was wearing thin, and damp strands of raven hair stuck to the curve of her rosy cheeks. The black hair against her tanned skin made the green of her eyes all the more severe.

She tried to block the crimson-haired assassin from her thoughts as she entered The Dome's main entrance. Her earlier encounter with Callis and his smug attitude really pissed her off, which was not conducive to the need to appear calm and collected before her superior, Nyx Crucian.

A frown creased her striking features. *Wouldn't it have been just lovely if Callis hadn't returned to me the only key allowing me access to our upper levels? Nyx would not have been pleased.*

In her irritation, she twisted the pendant dangling from her necklace around her finger. It was a marvelous piece of work. The top portion, a flower sculpted from clear crystal, Lux crystal to be exact. It was the same crystal lining all of Lux Lumetia's canals, though Ezra was personally unaware of the fact.

Two silver, intertwined serpents formed the stem. The coolness of the simple silver chain had a calming effect on her. She had always thought the beauty of the flower and the deadliness of the serpents represented her personality quite accurately. An heirloom passed down through her family, it was the one and only thing in her life that she had any affection for.

Ding.

The chime caused her revitalized state of calm to evaporate. Taking a deep breath, she retrieved the access key from its slot and emerged from the elevator. Forcing herself to pause for a moment of recollection, she closed her eyes, taking another long, silent breath.

In her mind, she chanted her own personal mantra, "I am Ezra Stark, one of Nyx's top assassins. The first and only female ever to reach Black Band status." She paused a short moment before continuing, "I will never allow anyone to hinder, or limit, my thoughts or actions, especially in the presence of Nyx." Breaking her mental exercise, she muttered aloud, "Even if it is that callous and impudent golden boy of The Dome."

Having regained her composure, with all thoughts of Callis shoved into a far corner of her mind, Ezra strolled, self-assured, along the black, silver-specked halls radiating confidence and power. She gave two sharp knocks on the frosted glass doors before her.

A cool voice resonated from the room beyond, "Enter."

Ezra pushed the double doors open, letting them swing closed on their own behind her, as she crossed to the table where her employer, Nyx Crucian, sat.

Nyx's features revealed no possible emotion beneath his stony façade. Eyes alert, mouth stern, he greeted her, "I assume you are here to report your findings at The Tower, Ezra?" As was typical with Nyx, this wasn't a true question.

"Of course, sir," Ezra hedged. "Unfortunately, sir, I was unable to attain any new information from my informant." Noting Nyx's displeasure at her words, she continued in an attempt to explain her failure.

"It seems my informant, squad leader Clayton Benson, has taken an unexpected leave of duty for the next week or two. A family crisis, I'm told…which in my opinion, sir, is unacceptable and rather unbecoming of a squad leader." She looked for Nyx's reaction, but none was forthcoming. Finishing, Ezra looked as if she had eaten something sour. She had never been able to understand why people were so fondly attached to their blood relations.

Nyx raised an eyebrow. If one didn't know Nyx, they would have thought him "amused" at Ezra's distaste for family affections. In truth, it was one reason Nyx had brought her under his chain of command in the first place. She was known for her cold and cruel demeanor. She always executed her orders without question or hesitation, even the more lethal jobs.

"Yes…" Ezra's voice brought Nyx back from his inner musings. "However, even with Clayton's absence, I am positive I can track Lord Cain. Just give me a few days, and I will have your information, sir."

Nyx's glacial voice interrupted her, "That won't be necessary, my dear. This squad leader Benson's temporary departure may have come at an excellent time. Our dealing with Cain will have to be put on hold for a bit. Although he is an overwhelming nuisance, he is not an immediate threat to my plans."

This wasn't the reaction that Ezra had expected. It didn't represent the norm by any means, but before she could process her thoughts, they were disrupted.

"I have something more important for you to tend to, Ezra." She looked at him with curiosity. "It has come to my attention that Helena Meretrix of my White Band has been increasingly wandering off the path that I laid in front of her. She needs to be reminded of her place.

"Jett Milan, also of the White Band, reported the disappearance of some of his fellow band members earlier this morning, as well as one of your own. Helena Meretrix, Angela Pratt, and Royce. With the assistance of Armani and Julian, the latter two were tracked down." It was obvious that Nyx was not pleased. Ezra scowled at the knowledge that one of her fellow band members was involved.

"Unfortunately, the two were found together, and not in the most *proper* of ways."

Ezra's scowl deepened. *The idiot. His lustful behavior will be the death of him.*

Nyx's voice drew her attention back to him. "Anyway, to get to my main point, Helena was never located."

Ezra nodded her understanding. "You wish me to find and deal with her insolent behavior?"

Nyx's icy eyes brightened with approval. "Yes, but not quite yet. I believe that our little Helena is focusing her fealties on something that may be to our benefit. I don't know what she is scheming behind our backs, and that is why I want your assistance. Follow her. Find out what she is pursuing."

Excitement began to build within Ezra. "Yes, as you order, sir. I will attain your information and report back to you." Nyx nodded, in satisfaction. Ezra never argued with him over an assignment.

"Excellent, but Ezra, make sure that she has no knowledge of your pursuit. Do not, under any circumstances, approach her, unless you have discovered exactly what she is scheming. There is no need for you to confront her anyway, unless you truly believe something is extreme enough to require your immediate intervention. Otherwise, just bring the matter to me. I trust that you will use your judgment wisely."

"I am honored to serve." She gave a respectable nod, fighting an arrogant smile from slipping over her lips. "It will be done."

"Good. And one last thing, Ezra."

"Yes?"

"She must be getting close to her objective because she is becoming careless in her actions. Find her. Make it silent and quick." Nyx then ended their meeting, with his usual final statement, "You have your orders. You are dismissed."

઼ઝ

As the mist and drizzle of the day escalated into a steady downpour, Callis headed west, away from The Tower and into the Corinth Sector. With evening drawing on, the reviving, cool rainwater helped to soothe his ill mood. The four glasses of liquor he had just finished at the Cosmos may have had something to do with it as well.

He had been far too pissed off to go straight home after climbing up that wet, rusted latter through the Sŭsurrus Fountain's secret entrance. Therefore, he had been most grateful that the Cosmos, one of his favorite places in the city, was so close to The Tower. This held especially true as of recent days, since he had been practically living in The Tower.

Typically, he preferred a slow, steady rain, but this harsh and heavy rain was welcome. It helped remove the layer of debris that had collected on his jacket during his time underground, investigating the long forgotten passageway. The rain falling down over him helped him focus, though it was unable to damage his stylized hair, which contained thick amounts of the water-repellent product used by most in this city. At least those who would rather seem charming than like filthy life-likes.

Continuing further west through the Corinth Sector, Callis couldn't quiet the streaming chatter flowing incessantly in and out of his mind. He reflected:

> After Callis's furious outburst on the main level of The Tower, while standing beside the pillar that the Intruder had used to escape, he had choked down the remainder of his anger long enough to crawl back down the pillar's concealed ladder, backtracking through the dim passageway, the very way by which he had come.
>
> When he had reached the ladder at Sŭsurrus Fountain's entrance, he had tried to concentrate on his breathing. He thought he had subdued his temper, but when his eyes landed

upon the corroded table and chairs, so recently disturbed, his anger had flared again, causing even his tattoos to glow. Callis slammed his boot into the metal table, causing the cards and chairs to skitter away, smashing into one of the marble walls, and then collapsing on the grimy cobblestones at the entrance shaft.

His anger still not quenched, Callis grabbed the chair closest to him and smashed it into the nearest light fixture, fastened high onto one of the moist, black marble walls.

ഇൽ

Now, back in present time, Callis replayed this scene in his mind's eye. He remembered the way that crystal sconce had shattered, sparking viciously in retaliation for its destruction.

In mere seconds, Callis had left a path of destruction including the demolished sconce, a sprawled disarray of chairs, scattered playing cards, and a metal table that once had the ability to fold. *Then again*, he justified, *the table had been sitting useless for many years. My foot just made sure that it wouldn't ever be put to use again. Except, maybe for scrap metal.*

Callis now moved toward the Ricahn sector. From where he stood, at its edge, he could see the outline of his home in the distance. The massive station was visible, despite the heavy falling of rain.

Maybe I overreacted with the light fixture. Though he refused to acknowledge it, somewhere down in his subconscious echoed Jett's words, rage-*aholic*. Callis dismissed this thought as soon as it had formed. He didn't need to bring distress upon himself over such an insignificant thing, especially considering the steady downward spiral of his week's events. Now making his way through the Ricahn Sector, Callis tried to recall what he did after his outburst, but it all seemed hazy. Somehow, he had managed to crawl back up out of the fountain without ripping the ladder off of the shaft wall. The last thing he could remember was the moment he stormed into the Cosmos. He thought back to his trip into the bar, trying to remember:

Entering the Cosmos, in the worst of moods, Callis promptly removed the drunken moron who had dared to sit in his usual spot. He had grabbed the man by the collar, flinging him backward with quite unnecessary force, into a table yards away. In that moment, a hushed quiet settled over the bar.

The drunkard groaned in pain, but he somehow managed to stand, attempting to confront Callis. Having staggered to his feet, he began to argue with a threatening bottle in hand, swinging it around. After a single petrifying glare from the crimson-haired man, however, the interloper retreated. With that, Callis took possession of his seat, and the room returned to its normal boisterous evening atmosphere.

Tazo, seeing the state that Callis was in, changed her course, delivering him a drink that she had initially made for a waiting customer. Callis accepted the drink from her before she could even set it down, gulping it in two swallows.

"Another."

In record time, Tazo returned to Callis's table with not only another glass, but also the bottle itself. She poured him another libation, which he downed without delay. Tazo filled the glass yet again, to the rim this time. She repeated the process with yet another. After the bottle had fully expired, he dismissed her with a weak flourish of his hand.

Before returning to her other duties, she had told him with sincerity, "If you need me, just holler." And as an immediate afterthought, she added, "This is all on the house tonight."

Callis simply nodded, still without looking at her.

Concerned, she stood there for a moment longer, but realizing that he would want anything other than her sympathy, she turned and walked away.

She had moved on, bounding back to her other customers, while Callis sat at his table with closed eyes and clenched fists, trying to control his breathing. He had placed his elbows upon the tabletop and leaned his head forward, resting on his fists.

ഇരുഈ

Recalling all of this, Callis wondered if he had fallen asleep at the bar from exhaustion, or whether his brain had just shut down, boycotting its work as a result of the exhaustion from the events of the week. Feeling rather much like a brute, Callis ordered himself: *I must give Tazo a hefty tip next time I stop in. She is way overdue, especially with irritating assholes like me for customers. And in a city like Atrum Unda, I would stake my life that there are many others even worse.*

Callis trudged over the blue granules, moving nearer to the

station, which contained his home. As always, even through the darkness and the rain, the street lanterns managed to make the silver flecks throughout the structure reflect in a visually appealing way.

Multiple tracks ran through each tunnel opening. Callis watched a few of the express trains rush in and out of the station. It might seem strange that such expensive apartments were built above a train station, but it proved to be quite a desirable place to have one's home situated.

The trains themselves proved to be no problem as the high-tech cars operated smoothly, moving almost soundlessly over their white metal, talloy, tracks now being used for the new tracks in the wealthier parts of the city. No actual passenger stops were located within this station. Only train personnel boarded within. For the convenience of those who lived above the station, the nearest stop was less than a block away.

Callis made his way up a short set of stairs to a platform where an elevator would convey him to his luxury apartment. A set of elevators such as this one were placed at each corner of the building. Sensing Callis's motion, a small, blue light illuminated on the silver wall between the two sets of doors. He retrieved his apartment key, waving its mirrored face in front of the light.

An automated, feminine voice greeted him as the doors on the right opened:

Welcome.

Keys still in hand, he stepped aboard the elevator, waving the face of a second, smaller key before another light. The voice came again:

Thank you.

Four buttons listed possible destinations to choose from: Ground level, operations, workers lodging, or the residence platform. Callis selected the last option.

As the elevator ascended, he stared at his reflection in the polished metal of the door. *How long did I sit at the Cosmos?* Nothing had occurred to mark the passing of time since he had left the bar, and he didn't carry a watch. The rain and darkness were of no help. *Hopeless.* He gave up trying to figure the amount of time that had lapsed.

A short chime, in a minor scale, sounded and he turned to exit through a set of doors that opened on the back wall. Only somns who owned here could enter on this platform, with elevators leading to each resident floor, which was equally divided into four apartments, with spacious balconies wrapping their two exterior edges.

On this level, Callis lifted the mirrored face of the larger key once again.

The familiar automated voice sounded again:

One moment, please.

This elevator rose through the residents' balconies to drop passengers off at their front doors. Privacy was important in developing these luxury apartments—exactly why Callis was so fond of living here.

A holographic screen informed him to insert his key into the slot next to the floor he desired. A blinking arrow pointed at the row of slots. Callis inserted the larger key into the right slot beside number 23, the topmost floor. He had refused to have anyone living above him, and from this level, he had quite an exceptional view. The elevator ascended, and as it came to a steady stop, the voice came once more while an accompanying screen displayed its final message:

Thank you, Mr. Morgandy. Welcome home.

Callis retrieved his key. The elevator doors opened, and reaching forward with both hands, he pulled a second set of sliding doors apart, just long enough to step into his flat. He turned back around, closing the sliding doors behind him.

In the darkness, he reached for one of the many light switches to his right. He flipped the master switch, followed by a second that together bathed the room in warm light.

Kicking off his boots, he stood in a large entryway with a high ceiling. To his left, one set of doors contained a large coat closet, and another boasted the latest model washer and dryer, though Callis would never be caught dead doing his own laundry. That was what delivery laundry services were for.

Tossing his jacket onto a bench seat to his right, he proceeded forward over a deep violet rug. With a heavy sigh, he paused, reaching the middle of the living room. He tapped a foot on the gleaming, hardwood floor that was typical throughout the flat, the exception being the sumptuous carpeting in the master and guest bedrooms. To his left, the kitchen and dining room had no real barrier separating them.

The extravagant kitchen was equipped with every luxury one would expect to find in the home of someone as wealthy as Callis Morgandy. The dining room was furnished with another violet rug and a luxurious table with seating for ten. Three exquisite, geshem display cases were placed to the left and right of the table. None would dare ask the worth of the possessions in the cases, for if the truth be known, their jaw would likely dislocate as it dropped to the floor.

Callis searched out the small package that he had previously set on the enormous table, and began unwrapping the shiny, foil packaging. He had been most eager to purchase the item from Mordion the day before, but he had not yet had a breathing moment to sit down and open it, or stand and open it, as the case may be.

Within lay two circular memory chips. Callis slid one of these chips aside and neatly folded the other back up in its foil wrapping. Picking up the first chip, he turned and opened the doors of one of the display cases. Crouching down, he retrieved his small, silver messenger beetle from a secret compartment.

With steady fingers, Callis pushed the metallic beetle's mouth open, offering the fragment, inserting it half way. The beetle willingly accepted, swallowing to integrate it with its own circuitry. The instant the chip activated, the insect's eyes began to glow, acting as a holographic projector. Indigo words materialized, just inches from its face:

> You may record your message now. Your voice will trigger the beetle, automatically beginning your recording session. To end your recording session, simply press the beetle's mouth closed.

Callis arched a brow. Still crouching before the display case, he organized his thoughts, deciding what to say before he triggered the recording session to begin.

With the beetle facing him in the palm of his open hand, he spoke, "Jereth. Please excuse the unexpected arrival of this messenger beetle. You know I wouldn't contact you like this unless it was of great importance. Whatever business you are on, I'm sure you have knowledge of The Archives break-in. I'm sure you have also heard rumors that I let the Intruder escape." A bile taste filled Callis's mouth as his anger rose. He took a much-needed breath, quieting himself enough to execute the message to his friend, and business partner, Jereth Tavokk.

He picked up where he left off. "Anyway, it is because of this that I require your assistance, old friend. I need you to look into something very important for me. It has come to my attention that the man who broke into The Archives is a man who goes by the name of Vincent KyVeerah. See if you can find out anything about him. If anyone can collect information on Vincent KyVeerah, it's you, Jereth. I appreciate anything you can do for me, and I hope to be in more personal contact with you soon. Safe travels. Callis."

With that, he pressed the beetle's mouth closed. Its eyes began to glow a second time, projecting a new message:

Message recording successful. Ready for release.

Standing, he closed the doors to the display case with silver beetle still in hand. He opened the patio door to his left and stepped out onto the balcony.

Fierce bolts of lightning flashed in the distance as a wild storm awakened. With the beetle programmed to fly on course to Jereth Tavokk, regardless of his coordinates, Callis pulled his arm back, muscles flexing, and launched it far into the open air.

As it fell, the beetle, by design, beat its wings. It took flight of its own accord, vanishing from view, into the clouded sky. Callis followed the metallic glimmer until he could no longer distinguish its silvery form from the countless falling drops of rain.

Leaning forward, he grasped the balcony rail. Eyes dark in the shadow of Atrum's night, he stared out into the pouring rain.

Jereth will come through for me. He always does. A wicked smile settled over his strong features. *You're time and luck are running out, Vincent KyVeerah.*

36: "Ifs" of the Equation

A morose Helena sat swirling the cocktail in her hand. It had been a long hopeless day. She had planned on spending the day talking to Serlio Young about the book he had written, and other such things. But since Angelina failed to obtain Royce's access key, she had to spend the day devising some other plan instead. Every new idea had too many flaws. The fact remained that her only choice was to stick to her original plan. That meant she had to obtain a key from a Black Band member. It would be dangerous, but necessary.

Sitting up at the bar in the Wishing Well, sipping at her drink, her thoughts spun. *I should have had that Calling in my hands by now, but I don't. Why?* Her eyes were consumed by frustration. She put her drink back to her lips.

First, there was Jereth Tavokk. He will regret turning down my proposal. What a conceited asshole! Helena was used to Tavokk's games of cat and mouse, but something was different that night. Although he had teased her, Helena had the suspicion that he was hiding something. *He seemed uncharacteristically reserved. What does he know?*

Suppressing a bit of longing, Helena muttered, "Doesn't matter. He's all talk, anyway." Playing with the stem of her cocktail, she stared into the swirling, pink liquor. She forced her thoughts away from Tavokk. *Second, there was that whole fiasco at the Dictum Division. How dare those repugnant drones issue Jett Milan authorization papers but not me?* She could picture him. An imperious man, just a year older than her. With dark hair framing his unreadable expression…picturing him was enough to make her skin crawl. She quickly shook the image away. *Let him lead the White Band. He'll be dead before he is able to elevate his status. That, I will make sure of.*

Helena's surging thoughts were interrupted by the sound of incessant giggling behind her. The irritating noise reminded Helena of her comrade, Angelina Pratt. *Angelina proved more useless than Jereth and Jett combined! I may have to dispose of her someday. It would serve her right.*

She tapped a manicured nail rhythmically upon the bar's surface.

Her mind shifted gears. *My entire plan depends vitally on a lot of "ifs." If I can find a high-energy source. If I can obtain an access key. If I can find a Calling. If that Calling is strong enough to control the energy needed to fulfill my plan and secure my destiny!*

A wave of determination engulfed Helena. She swallowed the last bit of her drink, stood, and exited the Wishing Well.

It doesn't matter. None of it matters. I don't care what it takes! I will succeed, and may a swift death be cast upon any who dares to stand in my way! Her eyes burned with resolution, as her form was enshrouded by the heavy, penetrating rain.

37: Flee From the Eastside

Before Venn had a chance to ask KyVeerah what the hell was going on, or what in Blue Ravenna that crazy man on the high-top bar table was carrying on about, KyVeerah caught his forearm in a tight grip, pulling him, at a fast pace, to the north.

KyVeerah dodged into the nearest alley. Venn allowing himself to be forced along while still trying to analyze the situation, as they hurried away from the Crimson Glass.

KyVeerah released his grip once they made it out of the Rallis District. They crossed north into the Tartel District, weaving between buildings and darting over bridges and crystal canals, fleeing from some apparent threat that, by now, was far from sight. Venn tried to connect his mind to KyVeerah, but it was immediately clear that he was being blocked.

Peering around, Venn continued to follow near behind KyVeerah. He eventually decided that it must be safe enough to speak, but a severe look from his accomplice quelled his questioning a bit longer. When they entered the Seward District, Venn gasped, "Vincent! Where in this forsaken city are you leading us?" He kept his voice hushed, while using great effort to match KyVeerah's speed over the shimmering, lamp-lit ground.

"Umbra Halls, obviously," KyVeerah said, without turning his head. "I would have thought that even you, as closed minded as you are, could have figured that out."

Displeased with KyVeerah's words, Venn scowled. The possibility of heading home had crossed his mind, but he couldn't be sure. After all, he hadn't a clue what they were running from. Judging from the large bandages on KyVeerah's torso, whomever they were running from... there was probably a damned good reason for it.

KyVeerah continued on until they finally reached the Caulder District.

Umbra Halls was one of the most secretive places in Lux Lumetia, and therefore, one of the safest places to be. So they continued to run across the Caulder District, rushing past the abandoned alley, through the metal gateway, and into The Courtyard.

At long last, KyVeerah came to a halt, moving out of the way so that Venn would not collide with him. Venn stopped beside him.

Breathing heavily, though not as winded as any common somns would be after such an extensive run, they looked at one another. A serious edge remained sketched into KyVeerah's features.

They stood silently regained their breath. KyVeerah straightened, turning toward Venn in anticipation of the questions he knew would be forthcoming.

"So...are you going to...tell me what's going on?" Venn asked, between breaths. He spoke in a stern manner, though less harsh than a typical conversation between them. Considering KyVeerah's atypical behavior, Venn felt the need to stand down.

Quite in character, KyVeerah shoved his shades up with the back of his hand. Gritting his teeth, he leaned forward, trying to fight the waves of pain surging throughout his body. For some time, he remained like that. Venn waited with as much patience as he was capable. Finally, KyVeerah could stand upright again, refusing to acknowledge the pain any longer.

His unmasked eyes were illuminated, as he looked with intensity into Venn's. "Beck Scofflin," he said, in a serious tone. "He was headed to the Crimson Glass with a group of his men. They must have had a specific intention, but that man on the table said that Beck and the others would bring harm to anyone who got in their way. Especially, if they even slightly resembled anyone from a rival underground business."

A clear look of understanding entered Venn's eyes. Beck Scofflin. The very somn who Mona had discussed just before the crazed man had showed up and they fled from the bar. Beck and his followers had started the bar fight at the Scally Bar in the West Bay just the night before. It had resulted in a man declared dead. What reason would they have to ransack the Crimson Glass? Venn frowned, circulating the question through his mind.

"Good Lord." Venn's eyes widened. "We have to go back."

"What?" KyVeerah looked at Venn in disbelief. "You must be out of your mind!" His eyes deepened. "Have you heard nothing I've said?" he scolded, shaking his head and muttering something incoherent.

"Vincent, we can't just leave everyone exposed like that! We have to go back!"

"No."

"What?"

"There is no point!"

"Of course there is a point!"

"No, Venn. From the sound of it, Beck Scofflin would be there by now. In fact, he probably reached there some time ago." KyVeerah's words were severe and his eyes just as harsh. "It sounded like they were already very near. For all we know, he and his men have turned the place inside out and left by now!"

Venn couldn't believe KyVeerah's recalcitrance. It was entirely uncharacteristic of him.

"Look," KyVeerah said, putting his hands up in negotiation. "Not many would start a fight like that in West Bay one night and then do the same in the Eastside the very next. Yes, I've been gone awhile, but I think I know whom he is working for. And if I am right, it is a damn good thing that we left the Crimson Glass before Beck and the others arrived.

Arching a brow, Venn paused in silence, before speaking, "Sometimes, I swear, I don't even know what to make of you."

KyVeerah could only stare back in return.

Why do you deny it? The voice broke through the walls of Venn's mind, hissing in accusation.

"There is no need for that!" Venn roared. "What about the somns who remained at the bar? Do you think—?"

"Yes," KyVeerah snapped, before Venn could finish his question. "They probably caused damage. I could be wrong, but I suppose there could be a small chance that some of them were smart enough to get the hell out of there."

"Sometimes you make me wonder if you might view the somn race even more lowly than I do."

KyVeerah refused to take the bait.

"If you don't give a damn about those somns left there as the sacrifice, while we fled like cowards, what do you suppose we do?"

"We go catch up on our sleep."

"You can't be serious."

"Venn, this has got to be the safest place in all of Lux Lumetia. If anyone there recognized me and ratted me out, particularly if they connected you to me, they would do anything to track us down. He abruptly pushed the dispute aside, adding, "But really, Venn. You should be thanking me."

"Thanking you?" he interjected, as KyVeerah turned away. "Where the hell do you think you are going?"

"To bed." KyVeerah turned his back again, heading toward the forged double doors.

Venn caved in on the idea of returning to the tavern. *It will have to wait until tomorrow. If anything happened, it's surely over and done with by now. I'm sure it'll be in the paper and spreading through every gossip channel of the city by then.*

Shaking his head, Venn put everything aside and followed KyVeerah indoors for the night. He tried to push away questions of where KyVeerah had been and what he had really been up to. Then, he tried to bury returning thoughts of Rhyus and Marion. *If that boy puts a single finger on her, I swear...*

Eventually, Venn managed to clear the thoughts from his mind, overtaken by sleep.

38: The Rundown

KyVeerah's eyes snapped open, and he sat up with haste...
"Ruby!"

Ruby Hale had appeared, telling him to awaken with her cerulean eyes calling him. As his eyes adjusted to the darkness, he looked around. They landed upon one of the room's windows. After all these years, he had yet to see it open. For all he knew, there may be no window at all. Just a wall.

Throwing the sleek, yet airy, crimson comforter aside, he stretched and reached for a pair of white lounge pants. He pulled them on, stretching further, but being careful not to strain the wound along his right side any more than necessary.

Pulling the door open, he moved with quiet steps to the bathroom where he showered, being careful so as not to have to change the bandaging yet. *What an inconvenience!* This was the second time he had gone through this hassle since being stitched and bandaged.

So much had already happened, and he had been in Lux hardly more than one day. It seemed like forever since his arrival, when Venn had chased him around the kitchen for breaking his crystal chess set. He cringed at the memory.

Stepping back into the hallway, he looked at the clock, which read 4:54 a.m. *Ugh. Not a fan of these early mornings. Were I still awake from a wild evening, that would be one thing, but to deliberately get up at this time of morning. Ugh,* he groaned.

Once back in his room, he headed for the wardrobe. Then, returning to the bathroom, he dried his hair, hoping that his racket would not awaken Venn.

Pulling his hair back into a low ponytail, he pushed the long bangs from his face while grabbing socks and a pair of black boots from beside the bed. After fastening the large buckles of his footwear, he grabbed his wallet from the denims of the day before, now bloodied and ruined. Donning the jacket that he had removed just hours ago, he left, making sure to close the door.

Entering the bathroom one last time, he grabbed the pile of rings lying on the counter, placing them onto their correct fingers. He tied a black cord necklace around his neck, amongst others, and finally made his exit to The Courtyard.

The soft boot soles were silent on the cobblestones, as he passed the great tree. He moved through the metal gateway and stepped out into the alley.

The Caulder District may have been generally abandoned, but the white stone buildings and silver walkways continued to glimmer just the same.

Keeping a casual pace, KyVeerah had allowed more than enough time to make it to the Rundown by six o'clock, the appointed meeting time. Looking around as he moved through the Caulder District, he examined his surroundings.

Not much had changed. He assessed the various buildings, homes, stores, and cafés. They had long since been abandoned. All but the hidden Umbra Halls.

He continued southeast where, nestled into the wooded areas beyond the common districts, sat the Rundown. Casavella.

The Grand Theatre Casavella had been most popular in its day. Its beauty was astounding, and the entertainment drew everyone to enjoy its offerings.

An enormous stone wall created a border around its entirety. The circular wall was punctuated by three archways at its front. Handsome, carved pillars of matching white stone were placed evenly about the wall's full circumference.

Another exquisite touch finalized the entrance. Large pseudo-screens filled each of the three large arches, acting as brilliant mirrors. From outside the Grand Theater, one could only see the magnificent reflection of the city in them.

But these pseudo-screens were just that. False mirrors. They were only intricately designed delusions. One could walk right through them without feeling a thing.

KyVeerah stood a good distance away in admiration. *As stunning as ever*, he thought, with a smile, taking in the sight for the first time since his long absence.

Out of habit, KyVeerah put an unnecessary, protective hand before him as he stepped through the illusionary mirror. The wall was astonishing indeed, but what lay within its borders equaled its splendor.

Green. Even in the dimness of early morning, the ground was covered with grasses of various shades from yellow-green to blue-green and everything in between. The color variations interfaced perfectly, as if some artistic being had painted the blades one by one. They also remained at an ideal height, varying minutely to avoid monotony. Remarkable, considering that no one assisted in maintaining the grounds' well-kept appearance.

Glowing geshem cubes had been arranged into an appealing layout across the plaza. In the dark and early morning, the large geometric beacons blazed and then faded, alternating between blue, violet, and a charming shade of magenta.

KyVeerah crossed the grounds, noting that tables constructed of the same shimmering stone were still neatly scattered about. Stools around them sported water-repellant—for the rare-occasion rains—cushions in an impressive state of preservation, just waiting to be used.

Filling the western half of the circle, the grand stage compared in size to any large opera house or theatre. A very thin layer of geshem overlaying its surface gave it a brilliant sheen. Unlike pure crystal, geshem was extremely durable. It would take a tremendous blow to damage this topmost layer of the stage floor.

Many stage lights were still set on a curved path at ground level. They remained angled upward in hope that someday the shows would begin again.

Two cylindrical towers stood left and right of the stage front where those in charge of lights, backdrops, and other important effects had worked throughout each show. Vines for mere decoration on the towers had grown out of hand, blanketing the towers' surfaces.

A massive overhang, built to assist with lighting effects to illuminate the actions of the performers below, likewise had vines crawling over its surface.

Making his way between scattered stone tables and chairs, KyVeerah neared the stage with swift steps. Continuing past the left tower, he approached a wide stairway leading up to the stage itself. His boots moved without sound up the steps until he stood on the lustrous stage of Casavella.

Ruby Hale and he had started coming here after it had been officially declared shut down. Other than the overgrown vines, the theater appeared just as magnificent as in its operating days. The Rundown, Hale and he had begun to call it back in those days. Although some would have liked to see it reopen, the reputation of the West Bay had continued to decline, and the Caulder District cleared out as everyone migrated to the Eastside, the new upcoming center of wealth.

That was only a handful of years back. Now there wasn't anyone around to even consider passing through the imitation mirrors or even to admire them.

Hale and he used to lay together on this stage for hours, bathed in light from the constant fading and glowing crystal structures around them. The light had reflected in the rare white talloy of the overhang and off of the geshem of the stage. But that was before he had to leave the city of Lux Lumetia. Now those days were gone, and it was quite evident that the parting between Hale and himself had not gone well.

He approached a door to the side of the backdrop wall. Opening the door, he reminisced as he made his way back to the preparation room.

Closing the door behind him, his keen ears picked up a subtle sound. He moved toward a set of doors, from which the sound had emanated, and slowly pushed them open. Standing in the threshold, a tender smile crossed his lips. There, in the center of the room, amongst hundreds of costumes, lay his dear friend, Jude Hollis, with Ruby Hale kneeling beside him.

KyVeerah remained there for a moment. Having been silent, and leaving the hallway unlit, Hale hadn't even noticed his presence. With a hushed clearing of the throat, KyVeerah received immediate attention. Hale's eyes snapped toward him. Their cerulean shade pierced the surface of his shades, even in the dim light of the room. She had only turned on a single set of lights, causing dramatic shadows to fall over her features. She blinked a couple of times, looking up through her long, painted lashes. Sharp waves of golden hair with platinum highlights fell forward, framing the quiet expression on her face.

"You showed," she finally said. She dropped her eyes back to Jude. Lifting her hand to his face, she brushed the loose curls of his coppery brown hair from his eyes.

KyVeerah's grin mellowed as he watched Hale's tender movements. She brushed Jude's long bangs aside again as some of the loose curls shifted back before his eyes. She didn't look back up at KyVeerah, as he stood in the doorway. After a long silence, she said, in a quiet tone, "I wasn't sure you would come." Though subtle, her words held a bitter edge.

"Don't worry, it wasn't for you."

She flinched at this rejoinder but still refrained from looking back up at him, instead focusing on Jude's pale face and the dark shadows falling over it.

After further silence, KyVeerah released his grip on the door frame, moving forward.

Hale lifted her eyes mere millimeters, watching his shadow crawl toward her. Although, in some deep crevice inside she still loved him, she could not assuage the intense bitterness and injured pride at his total and unexpected abandonment. She remained angry. In fact, mere anger didn't even begin to cover the emotions she felt toward the situation...or the man.

KyVeerah's shadow crept over Jude and Hale, throwing both into further darkness. Slowly bending to kneel on one knee, he examined his friend whose chest slowly rose and fell as he slept soundly. Then he lifted his eyes to Hale, who refused to return his gaze.

"Ruby," he started, with an exasperated sigh. "Look at me. Just for one...blasted...moment." He paused between each word, trying to contain his brewing frustration. *Yes, she may have a right to be furious with me, but for Valencia's sake!* He absently shoved his shades up with the back of his hand. His violet eyes revealed the roiling state of his emotions.

Without thinking, Hale shifted her gaze upward. He could feel the range of intense emotions radiating from her, though he did not notice the strain in her facial features, as she did her best to suppress them. Even someone tough enough for a position with Galton had emotions if you dug down deep enough.

"Ruby," he whispered, now that he had her undivided attention.

Hale remained on the ground with her legs bent, propped up on one arm while the other rested on her side, occasionally moving to brush Jude's loose, copper curls from his face. She did not verbally respond to the restatement of her name, but KyVeerah could read the hard rejoinder in her eyes.

"I need to ask you another favor." He sighed again, but this sigh expressed a clear understanding that he was requesting favors where none were due.

The only reason he could request a favor of Hale would be in trade for her brutal slice from rib to clavicle the previous day. But the fact that she had brought Jude to him this morning was enough to make that up to him. If anything happened to Jude, especially as a result of his affairs, KyVeerah wouldn't know what to do. It would be one of those rare things for which he would never be able to forgive himself.

A question showed in Hale's eyes as she awaited the new request. KyVeerah could read the exhaustion behind them.

"You look like hell, love." His eyebrows knit together in a look of true concern.

At this remark, Hale managed to pull her gaze away, but only for a split second before returning to meet his. She searched for words, requiring a moment before finding them.

"G-Galton..." she stammered, before continuing in her smooth, dark voice. "He told me to stay with Jude after you left. He had business to take care of. He realized that you trust me, for some unfathomable reason. That was enough to convince him that I was up for the chore."

Hale tried to look away again, but couldn't detach herself from KyVeerah's intense stare, which searched desperately for the answers he longed for. The thought was disquieting, but she couldn't look away. She couldn't even close her eyes to block the gateway to the things he wished to know.

Many thoughts raced in disarray through KyVeerah's mind, but he refused to break the connection between them. *So? Galton is obviously already busy searching for information on Palam Vita? Good. I need that information. And he must have guessed something about the connection between Ruby and me.*

Finally, Hale forced her gaze downward, brushing Jude's bangs aside once again. "What did you want to ask of me?" Her speech was more straightforward now that she had managed to break the connection. When she looked up, her curiosity still showed. Her lower lip pouted forward in that distinctive manner of hers.

Her dark voice stripped the daze from his eyes. He blinked a couple of quick times, coming back from his own, unspoken thoughts as her rich, lavender perfume permeated his senses.

Her makeup contrasted from the dark blue-violets of the previous day, as black now only made a subtle appearance. It was overshadowed by a white shimmer that reflected up from the stone floor below them, catching every trace of light that danced off of it. Her lips were now pink in color. She almost looked as if she had reverted back to the Ruby Hale that had captured KyVeerah's heart.

"Vincent?" The questioning look remained in Hale's eyes, demanding to know what he wished of her.

"Oh, right." His brow furrowed as he gathered his thoughts. He continued to look into her eyes. "Jude."

Hale expressed her puzzlement.

"His sister," KyVeerah added. "I must go to his sister."

"What?" An alarmed look flashed through Hale. "You aren't going to tell her—?"

"Of course not! Who the hell do you think I am?" he scolded. "By the lunar goddesses, I'm not trying to get anyone killed!" He threw his hands into the air. "I'll be damned before I bring such harm upon her!"

Hale's expression altered from puzzlement to contemplation, and even a hint of jealousy. "What exactly are you going to tell her?"

KyVeerah stared at her, trying to uncover the true question.

"You know she is going to blame you for what has happened to him, no matter what you say."

"Are you worried for my well-being?" His tone was mocking.

She pretended not to give a damn about him or what he did, however he could tell that was not the case. Her pouty lips parted as she absorbed his disdainful comeback. "He deserves much better friends than your kind." She looked down at the sleeping man lying between the two of them. A hint of warmth had returned to his pale flesh.

"Please. I really must go to her. She will be worried sick at the fact that he has failed to return home by now."

She nodded a single time, causing golden waves of hair to shift. "Yes, all right. I will remain here and watch over him. But, Vincent...if you are not back by nightfall I will leave, and I will take him with me. And if that should be the case, I wouldn't expect to have him back anytime soon if I were you. And I definitely wouldn't expect any more favors from me. Ever again." Her severe eyes were glassy as she looked up.

He matched the hardness of her stare. "Well, I'm off." Without another word, he made his departure.

With a low growl, he kicked the final door open before him, flinching as the light of day met his eyes. Sliding his shades back into proper position, he grumbled and stepped back down the stairs.

Walking at his swift pace over the palette of green, he subconsciously noted a transformation to an entirely new range of color in the bright light of day. Weaving back through the tables, he groused his irritation. *She may be doing me a favor, but does she have to be such a...aargh!*

He continued to fret, raising his eyes toward the sky, wishing for an answer to his predicament. Leaning forward, he stepped through the master illusion.

What the hell am I going to tell Cassandra?

39: Insula Palam Vita

Marion and Rhyus stood in silence, staring up at the red lights in the distance.

"What should we do?" Marion asked. She had not forgotten her anger, but now her safety, and perhaps survival, was as stake.

For a moment, they both stood in silence, trying to decide on the best course of action.

"Maybe it would be best to steer away from it, at least for the time being. We don't know who they are or what they will lead us to." Rhyus remained uncertain about what would be best, as he continued to focus on the red points of illumination. "We could always backtrack to it."

"Look!" Marion threw her arm forward, forefinger extended.

Rhyus dropped his gaze from the lights high in the air. True enough, land could now be seen just ahead. "Well, I'll be damned." It had seemed this moment would never come.

Agreeing with Rhyus's opinion about steering the boat away from the eerie sources of light, Marion steered to their right, following the coast, as gentle waves rocked the boat.

"Keep an eye out for anywhere we can pull the boat in," Marion said, continuing to move the boat along the path of the shoreline and shaking off the all-encompassing Darkness that enveloped her, causing such a violent rift between Rhyus and her.

The near shoreline was a muddy strip of silt. Just beyond, a forest of dense vegetation pushed forward, protruding to the water's edge.

For some time, Rhyus and Marion had no luck finding a place where they might pull the boat in for landing. "Aha." Marion finally caught sight of a break where the coast moved inland. Approaching it, she turned the boat to follow the water's course.

"What, are you crazy?"

"We sure as hell weren't passing anything promising out there."

Moving further into the cove, Rhyus sighted large, still shadows beneath the water's surface. He moved his eyes from one dark spot to another, soon tracking one to a crystal formation jutting up out of the water. "Holy shit! Do you see those? Don't hit them! We'll be stuck here forever. And we don't even know where we are!" he rambled, in his rising panic.

"I know what I'm doing. I am not an idiot. Like you." She mumbled the latter under her breath.

"What did you say?"

"Nothing," she snapped back, steering the boat deeper inland.

"Look over there!" Rhyus pointed to the left. "Do you see it?"

"Yeah," she said, with a curious expression. A wooden dock was situated at the edge of the cove. Marion peered through the corners of her eyes, trying to discern whether anyone was around, as she pulled the boat forward.

She edged the boat right against the dock, as if she had done it a thousand times. Rhyus, with a last-second thought, retrieved his messenger bag from the storage compartment. Rushing back to the boat's side, he climbed up and leaped over.

"Good Ravenna, Rhyus!"

"Oh, stop worrying so much!" he shot back, hypocritically. "It's pretty worn and looks old, but it's stable enough." He had already tied the transparent, blue hawser to one of the wooden posts. Marion told the boat's motor to halt.

Just as impatient about getting off of the boat and as far away as possible from the pervasive grasp of The Darkness, Marion retrieved her own Randál Vanaché bag, throwing its single, beige strap over her head. She moved to the boat's rail, peering down at the dock with uncertainty.

"Oh, by the goddesses, it's fine!" Without as much as a helping hand, Rhyus turned away to a trail entering the unfamiliar, forested terrain.

Muttering something incoherent, Marion slid over the side of the boat. She double-checked the knot that Rhyus had tied, and satisfied, followed him into the forest.

It didn't take long to catch up to Rhyus. He hadn't traveled far. "Where are we?" she asked.

"How would I know? Stop harping at me!"

"Whatever."

"Don't you *whatever* me!"

"Or what?"

In their bickering, they hadn't noticed a slight change in the dark forest, closing around them. A subtle movement and a change of light went unheeded, due to the nervous energy circulating through each of them.

Without warning, a loud crack sounded nearby causing Rhyus

and Marion to jump. A man, who they hadn't noticed, stood camouflaged amongst the shadows and the trees. He stepped forward, tapping Rhyus on the shoulder. "Hello."

Surprised, both Rhyus and Marion screamed in a release of nervous energy. Marion, not forgetting her quarrel with Rhyus, hid behind him.

"Stop screaming!" the man said, recoiling from the horrid racket. He shielded his ears with long fingers.

At this unexpected reaction, both Rhyus and Marion fell silent. They stared at the man, eyes fearful and hearts pounding.

Slowly, the stranger turned back toward them, relieved that the horrendous noise had come to an end. He unwound his tall, slender form, head cocked well to the side. His rich, deep rust-colored bangs hung sideways, due to the position of his head.

"Who are you?" He gave the two of them a curious look. "Where have you come from?" Deep, midnight-blue eyes stared upon them with unblinking intensity. The man, of about thirty years, was very pale skinned. Despite dark blue-violet shadows beneath his eyes giving him a ghoul-like appearance, he was quite an attractive man.

Rhyus and Marion remained silent, timid, as they examined the unknown man.

Seemingly out of nowhere, Rhyus exerted a burst of courage, saying, "We are Rafters."

Marion could not believe what he had just said, but she did nothing to refute him. After a moment to process the comment, the strange man's expression altered with a new look of curiosity and fascination. He slowly straightened his head, and then he cocked it the opposite way.

"Rafters?" he repeated Rhyus words. "Did you say...*Rafters*?"

Marion remained behind Rhyus, both of them voiceless again, as he nodded in affirmation.

"I haven't met a Rafter in ages." Readjusting the angle of his head, his unworldly eyes drilled into Rhyus with a heavy sense of inquisition, and a mischievous smile touched the thin lips of his overly wide mouth. "And what are you *Rafters* names?" He finally blinked his eyes a single time.

Marion would have shut Rhyus up if she had the nerve, but as she did not, he replied, "I'm Rhyus. And this is Marion." He turned to direct toward her, not realizing that she had repositioned herself behind him. "Might I ask who you are?"

"I am a very important person." The man leaned toward them,

his smile widening to complement his declaration.

"Might I ask what your *name* is?" Rhyus asked, a bit baffled by the man's awkward introduction.

"Most certainly!" The man straightened proudly. "I," he placed a hand on his chest, "am Lenim Velent. You may call me Lenim." A change of expression suddenly flickered in the depths of his opaque eyes. "Rhyus..." he lowered his eyebrows, examining the young man.

"Yeah?" The way in which Lenim was studying him made Rhyus quite uncomfortable.

"I remem-eally need to get back to town," he adjusted his words midsentence. "Would you like to come?"

"Town?" Hope flooded over Rhyus as well as Marion who remained behind him.

"Yes. You know, buildings, somns, joined together as a community. The usual. Unless you'd like to stay here, of course?"

"No!" Rhyus and Marion simultaneously shouted.

Lenim pulled into himself, as he had previously, hands thrown back over his ears while he cringed. Finally, straightening up again, he rubbed his fingertips over his temples. "Must you *always* be screaming? You two were yelling before I was even finished..." he adjusted his statement again, "before I even approached you. Anyway, did you two want to come along?"

Rhyus and Marion nodded fervently.

"Then let us go!"

"Wait!" Marion spoke on her own for the first time since Lenim's approach. "What about the boat?"

In minor surprise, Lenim turned her way. "No one will steal it," he assured her. He seemed rather astonished that she would even consider that someone might.

"How can you be so sure?" she asked, not feeling so certain about the stranger's reassurance.

Lenim looked upward in thought. "Hmm. Let's just put it on the *trust tab*. Besides, I'm sure you two have such a lovely boat as this insured?"

Neither replied for a moment, as they looked everywhere but at him. They sheepishly shuffled their feet.

"Well, no," Rhyus finally admitted. "We kinda...stole it."

"Aha!" Lenim raised a finger, with his new declaration, "So, we resort back to the trust tab. Wonderful!"

"Yes. I suppose so," Rhyus agreed, with reluctance, though

Marion was still uncertain about abandoning their only getaway along the shore of the creepy little cove.

Lenim, deciding it was time to leave, turned and began moving away from the coast. "Come along."

Feeling they really had no choice, other than going back out to sea, which was not an option, and still feeling a bit of hope at the idea of heading toward a town, Rhyus and Marion followed behind Lenim. Together, they made their way through the dense vegetation.

As The Darkness over the black water had not yet begun to release its grip, Rhyus and Marion, still irritated and upset with one another, avoided any conversation. Nonetheless, the new environment surrounding them cast an eerie mood, keeping the two of them near one another and on their toes. They studied the surrounding forest while still making a point to avoid eye contact with each other.

Marion came to an abrupt standstill, giving a sharp yelp as she spotted a four-legged creature with an antagonistic face and multijointed, clawed appendages. The large creature stood bristling, no more than a dozen feet from them. Rhyus came to an immediate halt also, looking toward the creature that now bared its unpleasant teeth in defense. His eyes widened as neither Marion nor he moved in the slightest. He couldn't tell whether Marion was even breathing.

Without turning toward them, Lenim cringed again at the noise. Eventually relaxing, after a moment of silence, he queried once again, "Honestly, do somns always make such loud, painful noises where you come from? I think my ears must be bleeding." He brushed a finger across his ear, examining it for traces of blood.

"What the hell is that?" Marion demanded, in a hushed voice, somehow rediscovering the capability of speech.

"What? Oh, that little animal?" Lenim glanced at the creature, which continued to bare its teeth at them.

"What *is* it?"

"Actually, I'm not really sure what it is called. Hmm, how about that? But you know, they do taste quite good." He nodded, satisfied that he had provided an adequate explanation.

"Will it attack?" Marion asked, eyes wide and fearful.

Lenim gave a short, cackling laugh. "Oh no, definitely not. You are the ones more likely to scare the poor thing into sudden death."

"Are you sure?" This time it was Rhyus posing the question,

eyeing the crouched animal with its teeth exposed. It appeared as though it might pounce at any given second.

"Aren't there animals where you come from? Really. I mean, not all animals wish to harm a somn, you know? The little thing just wishes to keep us from getting any closer. He doesn't want us to harm him." Lenim peered back over at Rhyus, and then Marion, before continuing, "In fact, I think it much more likely to attack if we continue to stand here staring at it." It was a white lie, but without much thought required. Lenim decided it was the best way to trick them into continuing inland toward town. He choked back a chuckle, for sure enough, it worked.

40: Urbs Cereris Arcanae

"How long do you two plan on staying here?" Lenim asked, as he continued leading Rhyus and Marion inland.

Rhyus took it upon himself to respond, "We have not yet decided. As of this precise moment, we have no immediate reason to travel beyond these parts. Then again, that may come to change at any time. When we determine our next move, we will act upon it," Rhyus finished, as if he had previously determined these accounts.

"Of course." Lenim nodded, reverting back to his own mind's wanderings.

After a long while, distant sounds whispered through the trees. As they moved further, the sound of music from a sitar-like instrument sang to them. Its tuning was off as it carried on the breeze, playing in a minor scale.

Eventually, the thickness of the forest vegetation began to taper until it came to an abrupt end. Lenim stepped out from the tree line, and Rhyus and Marion looked about before following suit and stepping out from their wooded covering.

A man sat not far from them. He held in his hands the stringed instrument that had found them. The man did not look up at them as they passed by. He showed no recognition at all. He simply continued to play his melancholy tune on the instrument, which rested upon his skeletal, crossed legs.

Marion couldn't help but peer down at the emaciated, middle-aged man in his tattered clothing. As they passed by, a deep feeling of sympathy welled up inside of her. His eyes were detached from his surroundings, and dirt coated his hair, his skin, and his frayed apparel. His sorrowful song followed them, playing in the background, as they moved further from the vegetation line and on through the outskirts of the city.

"Trans Murus," Lenim said. "That is how we refer to these city-bordering parts."

Makeshift huts were strewn all about, and domesticated animals roamed here and there. Much to Rhyus and Marion's surprise, none of the Trans Murus somns paid them notice. Nevertheless, a trace of anxiety filled them both.

"Pay no attention to these dirty life-likes," Lenim said, in disgust. He waved his hand, dismissing the presence of the detached dwellers of The Outskirts.

Marion moved a little nearer to Rhyus, though still upset with him. She registered an uneasy vibe from these lowlifes, feeling that they would all turn their direction at any moment and come after them for trespassing onto their land. But they did no such thing.

Rhyus felt as though Marion, Lenim, and he had turned invisible. Why else would these somns remain so extraordinarily disconnected?

Forcing his mind in a new direction, Rhyus looked ahead toward their destination. The circular wall surrounding the entire inner city was remarkable, standing many stories high and several feet thick. It had been constructed of glimmering white stone and seemed to grow taller as they neared its base.

"Look familiar?" Rhyus asked rhetorically, looking Marion's way. She did not answer, but silently agreed that it did resemble the structures of Lux Lumetia. In fact, it looked identical to white Lux stone. Marion considered asking Lenim about it, but opted otherwise.

For a moment, the display nearly caused Rhyus to miss Lux Lumetia. But at the thought of Venn, a spine-chilling shiver ran through him.

Hovering above the wall's highest points, glowing orbs were placed in a systematic pattern around the entire structure. Energy sources that had to serve some purpose other than providing light, especially considering that it was midday and they still emitted a vibrant, artificial luminosity.

A security mechanism? Rhyus wondered.

Approaching the tall, narrow set of doors that served as the sole entrance to the inner city, they noted two figures, standing on either side of them. These guards wore masks with a more decorative appearance than anything they had witnessed thus far.

Strange, Rhyus thought, observing that their clothing was in much better condition than the somns of The Outskirts. In fact, they appeared quite costly. It was odd that they were contrived to match the peculiar masks.

"Hello again, my good men." Lenim bowed, his cape spreading along a single arm in the movement. The masked figures nodded their heads in response. Without a word, they moved toward one another and pulled the heavy doors open by their curved, bronze handles, permitting Lenim to enter the city along with his two companions.

They must hold him in high regard if they are allowing him to bring strangers into the city, Rhyus deduced. *And into a city with such a barrier as this. Do they receive many visitors? Maybe more visitors come here than I assumed?*

As they passed through, the two masked guards closed the doors behind them.

"Wow," Marion said, voicing the same thought echoing through Rhyus's mind. The city was a complete transformation from what lay outside its walls. Trans Murus might as well be an old, dirt graveyard compared to the city before them.

Lenim gripped the edge of his cape, extending his arm with a bow before his guests. "Welcome to Urbs Cereris Arcanae." He straightened back up into a dignified pose of self-composure. With interest, he watched the fluctuating expressions passing over Rhyus and Marion's faces, curiosity and fascination alike.

Urbs Cereris Arcanae, Rhyus repeated to himself. This new city was unlike anything Marion or he could recall having ever seen.

"This place is amazing." Marion gaped in awe, as she bypassed Lenim, excitedly looking every which way. "It's absolutely beautiful!" Her eyes glowed, reflecting the colors of the city. She noted the fact that there was another set of guards near them, here within the city's walls. They stood, keeping an eye on the city's entrance. However, they didn't seem to view this trio as any sort of threat.

The walkway beneath their feet was of a pale gold, textured stone that shimmered with warmth in the light of the midday suns. The golden walkways stretched out over the entire circular city, as far as they could see.

Straight ahead, yet some distance away, a large rectangular space stood out from its surroundings at the very center of the city. Three neat rows of brilliant pink, red, and white trees formed an organized perimeter all around the congregational area.

A sweet, floral scent wafted over Rhyus and Marion as it circulated throughout the welcoming city, trapped within its borders by the high, glimmering wall. Fruit and floral trees were planted in neat arrangements throughout the city, as were trimmed shrubberies and frequent rows of neatly planted flowers, varying in every color imaginable. Not a single plant looked out of place. Occasional somns could be seen strolling over the walkways.

Marion closed her eyes, exulting in the sweet aroma. Yes, she could smell it so clearly now, the scent of ripening fruits interlaced with that of fragrant blossoms and flowers. She spun around, opening her eyes and looking, with a cheerful smile, up at Lenim, awaiting his declaration as to where they should go now. Already, she could feel The Darkness releasing its grasp on her.

Marion hadn't felt this good in days. The same couldn't be said for Rhyus. He still stood further back, beyond Lenim, closer to the entrance doors. Rhyus peered around with cautious eyes, suspicious of their new surroundings.

Something about the enclosing wall left Rhyus ill at ease. *What are they really keeping out...or in? Surely, it cannot be those somns of Trans Murus. They didn't pay us as much as an ounce of notice. I can't begin to believe they could be a possible threat. They hardly looked able to hold themselves together, let alone tear apart a city.*

Feeling Marion's stare on him, he offered her no more than an unkind scowl before turning his eyes back toward Lenim, who seemed currently lost in his own thoughts. Marion also redirected her attention Lenim's way.

Sensing the scrutiny, Lenim snapped out of his daze. "Uh...well then." He pursed his lips. "Shall we carry on?"

Rhyus and Marion nodded in agreement, Marion smiling with excitement while Rhyus remained expressionless. As Lenim began moving, Marion stepped forward, moving along just beside him and leaving Rhyus to tag along behind.

They made their way through the city, past houses that only added to the flawlessness of the city. Their smooth, stone façades ranged from off-white to medium beige, but some had an orange tinge to them. Tile roofs were constructed of pale sandstone shingles. Each had wood paneled windows with flower boxes, all bountiful with a variety of flowers in bold, bright colors. Colored ribbons streamed from balconies, and paper lanterns skillfully embellishing them with complementary colors.

"Lenim?" Marion questioned, as they continued to walk.

He tilted his head down at her. "Yes?"

"Why must there be such excessive protection around the city? Have these walls always been here?" Still following behind, Rhyus perked up, listening in after hearing Marion's question.

A thoughtful look showed on Lenim's face as he mulled over a response to the question. "At one time, Urbs Cereris Arcanae was a much more free-spirited place. The stone wall wasn't like it is today. It used to be a decorative wall, constructed of sleek, colorful fabrics. Each cloth piece stood separate from the rest, on individual wooden supports.

"Back then, the somns who now dwell in Trans Murus also lived inside those colorful pseudo-walls, along with the rest. However, they began a huge controversy causing an interminable dispute. Eventually, they became dangerous and were kicked beyond the city's borders. They began destroying the wall, ripping the fabrics and burning them where they stood. Those who remained drew a line just beyond the colorful wall.

"It was ordained that, if anyone crossed the line, they would be eliminated on the spot. And if an inner-city somn left to gather resources, and the outskirts somns took him or her captive, they would pay for this too. Then, the inner-city somns began the clearing of trees from what is now Trans Murus. Once they completed a wooden barrier, the stone wall went up inside it. The troubles ceased, and in time the outskirts dwellers came to generally ignore the inner city altogether. However, the guards still take some precautions, as I'm sure you've probably noticed?"

Marion nodded, absorbing Lenim's words. "And those orbs?" She pointed to the top of the wall. "What purpose do they serve?" She turned back to face Lenim, as they continued walking.

"They are a further safety precaution," he informed. "They contain a source of energy that streams from one to the next. It protects us from anyone breaking in over the walls. The consequences of such an attempt would not be pleasant, to put it lightly."

Marion mulled over Lenim's words, as did Rhyus, still walking behind them. His assumptions about the illuminated orbs had been accurate.

They continued to pass the quaint little homes and occasional shops that blended in with a similar look. Intermittently, they passed other gardens and city dwellers. Some nodded pleasant greeting while others ignored them, though they covertly took in the unfamiliar faces. The well-kept vegetation remained consistent with fruit and floral trees, trimmed shrubberies, and orderly arrangements of colorful plants and flowers.

After some distance of moving over the pale gold walkways, a woman shouted out from a little house just ahead of them.

"Lenim! Oh, Lenim dear, how are you?" she called, eagerly approaching Lenim with the two unfamiliar faces tagging along beside and behind him. The round-featured woman, well into her forties, scurried toward them, as Lenim awaited her approach.

He crossed his arms over his chest. "Ah, Ellen. I am just splendid, as usual." As the woman drew near, he bowed courteously, hair falling forward. He stood back up, hair shifting naturally back into place, and peered down at the woman who had come near enough to touch. With an inquisitive look, she seemed very excited to see Lenim and the two outsiders.

"Ellen, this marvelous young lass is Marion, and her charming companion, Rhyus." Lenim motioned from one of his tag-alongs to the other. "They will be staying with us for an undetermined length of time." After a brief pause, he redirected his hand. "Marion, Rhyus, this is Madam Corvin."

"It is just so wonderful to make your acquaintance!" Madam Corvin took Marion's hands into her own as one would a child. "Are you hungry, dear?" she asked. "You dears look exhausted! You must have traveled far!" She nodded in affirmation of her own assessment.

Neither Rhyus nor Marion could help but perk up at the mention of their hunger, looking with hope toward an offering. Rhyus looked to the ground, expecting that Marion would answer well for them both.

"Yes, actually. We are famished! We have been living on very small rations since our leave several days ago," Marion explained. And then she looked away, feeling a tinge of shame for jumping on the woman's selfless offer as she had.

"By every moon above! The wonderful goddesses must have brought you to this place!" Madam Corvin expressed her thorough joy at the prospect of hungry mouths to feed. The wide, closed-mouth smile on her round face appropriately fit the rest of her features.

"You must come in!" The woman gestured to the house from which she had come. "I shall whip you all up something scrumptious!" Her kind words were lathered with hope and anticipation.

Still cradling Marion's hand, she shifted her gaze to Rhyus and then to Lenim. It would have been impossible for either Rhyus or Marion to refuse her offer. It had taken all of their willpower thus far not to simply devour fruit from the trees they had passed. The woman awaited their answer with hopeful expectation. Rhyus and Marion stood speechless, unsure how to respond without sounding blunt or discourteous.

"Yes, certainly," Lenim answered for them. "Lead the way, Ellen." He raised an extended arm in a *foreword ho* motion. Rhyus and Marion felt nearly giddy at Lenim's acceptance of her offer. Rhyus pressed his lips together, still looking at the ground, feeling guilty about the strong greed welling up inside of him. Marion, on the other hand, expressed an open appreciation of Lenim's response.

Madam Corvin's own smile widened in satisfaction. She released Marion's hand and scurried toward the house. Lenim followed after, in his own long stride, waving a hand for the two to come inside.

41: Unexpected Invites

Rhyus slid through the open door of Madam Corvin's house and closed it. Spotting Marion's bag on the floor by the wall, he pulled the strap of his own bag off over his head and put it down beside hers. He moved through the small entryway, following the sound of Lenim and Madam Corvin's voices to find himself in a room with the living space to his left and the kitchen to his right. Only the flooring, which switched from smooth stone to tile, delineated the kitchen space from the living room.

Either this house is brand new, or it has been very recently renovated, Rhyus decided, admiring the bright luster of the polished flooring.

"In here, dear," Madam Corvin called to Rhyus where he stood in the short hallway leading from the door.

As he joined everyone in the kitchen, Madam Corvin set two glasses on the counter, filling them with water for her guests.

"You must be so dehydrated," she said, presenting them with the refreshments. They accepted, finishing the contents in no time. Leaning against the opposite counter, Lenim watched in amusement as they guzzled their drinks. Indoors, the deep shadows beneath his eyes became even more apparent, magnifying their contrast with his unusually pale skin. Rhyus found his appearance quite disconcerting.

"Good gracious. Just as I thought." Madam Corvin put out her hands, asking for the glasses back to fill them a second time.

Without a moment of hesitation, Rhyus and Marion emptied their second glasses, then their third.

"Thank you," Marion finally said, as Madam Corvin handed them each a fourth glass. Marion's face flushed, a bit embarrassed over their ill-mannered thirst and their neglect to voice their appreciation up until now.

"Yes," Rhyus added, "thank you. Very much."

"You didn't think a woman such as myself would leave you out there walking about dehydrated and hungry now, do you?" She smiled kindly at them. Both Rhyus and Marion smiled back.

"Lenim, dear, would you care for a glass of iced mallow? Or

hot, if you're more in the mood for it? I know how you like it." Her manner insisted that he take her up on her offer.

"Why yes, Ellen. That would be splendid. Oh, and iced would be just fabulous."

Happy with his response, she turned back to the high row of wooden cupboards. "You dears just go take a seat in the living room. I will get a tasty meal going. And Lenim, dear, I will get that iced mallow to you shortly." Smiling, which seemed to be her usual demeanor, Madam Corvin turned back to the cupboard, humming a soft tune as she went to prepare the feast and the iced mallow.

Rhyus and Marion stood motionless, waiting for Lenim to make the first move to the living room. He eventually pushed his tall, slender form up straight and made his way from the kitchen, his boots clicking faintly with each smooth stride.

Following, Rhyus and Marion passed a wooden table, set for four. They sat on the couch, facing away from the kitchen, as Lenim made himself comfortable in a large recliner, crossing a leg with his ankle resting just above his knee.

Both the recliner and its paired couch had soft cushions of rosy-peach fabric that matched the wall in the kitchen. The living room walls were off-white, corresponding with the small oval rug on the floor as well as the kitchen's countertops.

All sat in silence, Rhyus and Marion sneaking looks at Lenim who appeared to have drifted into his own thoughts once again.

I wonder what is on his mind? Rhyus thought. *Either this man thinks so deeply out of habit, or something important is really bothering him.*

Madam Corvin shook Lenim from his daze as she handed him a glass.

"Why thank you, Ellen." He offered her a grateful smile.

"Just you let me know if you need another." She put a gentle hand upon his shoulder before resuming her cheery tune on her way back to the kitchen to prepare a meal for the four of them.

"So, where exactly are you two from?" Lenim asked, taking a swallow from his glass.

"It doesn't matter," Rhyus blurted, before Marion might reply with any ounce of truth. He would rather that information be kept to themselves for the time being. "It's not like we will ever go back."

Marion gave Rhyus a displeased look, as she squeezed her glass, taking a drink to hide her expression from Lenim, who was seated to Rhyus's other side. She wondered whether his words would prove true. As she lowered her drink, the thought of Venn alone in Umbra Halls seeped into her mind. For the most part, she had managed to keep such thoughts at bay, knowing that they would only trouble her, leading to no helpful answers, only raw emotions.

He must be lonely. She couldn't help but let the thought slip in. Then again, she knew that he would rather be alone than have anyone other than herself staying there with him in the large house. It had taken him quite some time to adjust to her staying there with him, as it was.

Lenim's voice disrupted her thoughts as he brought up a new question. "How did you find this place? Insula Palam Vita, I mean." He was genuinely interested in her response. He looked, unblinking, at Marion, having noticed her deep state of reverie. Elbows resting on the chair's arms and fingers pressed one against the other, his dark eyes looked into her own.

Rhyus scratched the back of his neck and jumped in before Marion could respond, "We knew we would run into it eventually." He tried to give a timbre of truth to the false words he was voicing. Nevertheless, he studiously looked away at a large painting of an elaborate flower garden.

With that, Lenim switched the target of his gaze, and Rhyus felt that if he looked Lenim in the eye, his words would easily be seen right through. This way, perhaps there was a chance his words might stand. *We just met Lenim this morning, for god's sake. How can we know his true intentions? We don't know who he is, what he does, or what he is capable of. Come to think of it, we don't know a single damn thing about him.*

Marion tried to pay attention to the conversation between Rhyus and Lenim, but the smell of the food Madam Corvin was preparing was an unceasing distraction. Her thirst may have finally been quenched, but the smell of a real meal was more than she could stand. Rhyus could still feel the intensity of Lenim's unblinking gaze, as he considered the young man's answer. The force of his piercing, opaque eyes seemed to penetrate into Rhyus, probing to discover the deceit in his words. Then again, maybe this feeling was just a result of Rhyus's awareness of his own voiced lies.

Lenim remained silent, chewing over Rhyus's answer. "So," he picked up, adjusting his position and crossing his arms over his chest, "you knew your desired destination?" The words were succinct. "You knew you were heading for Palam Vita when your journey at sea began?"

He adjusted his position again, giving Rhyus a skeptical look and waiting for any retraction.

This tactful interrogation made Rhyus very uneasy. Nonetheless, he took another swallow from his glass, trying to maintain a straight face in sticking to his story.

"Well, yeah. We certainly couldn't just set out without any idea where in the world we were heading. That would be a most outlandish thing for anyone to do." After the words had slipped past his lips, Rhyus realized that they were indeed, fact. At least that might make his story more convincing…hopefully. *When push comes to shove, where the hell are we?* he wondered. *What is this place we have come to? Why such intense security? And what did he call it? Urbs Cereris Arcanae?*

"True," Lenim said, after a moment of pause. He began bouncing the foot that was crossed over his other leg, and his eyes darkened further. As he fell into his own musings once again, his eyes stared forward at nothing at all.

Rhyus was unable to tell whether the man believed him. But did it even matter?

"What does it mean?" Rhyus forced the thought into a spoken question.

"What?" Lenim asked.

"Urbs Cereris Arcanae. That is how you introduced this place. What does it mean." Rhyus, forgetting his manners, neglected to put the thought into question form.

Lenim's eyebrows lowered, and his eyes narrowed into a warning gaze, signaling that Rhyus had better realize whose territory he had entered.

"Meal is ready!" Madam Corvin exclaimed to her guests, breaking the impasse. She had already set the circular, wooden table with food and utensils for each of them. "I hope you find it gratifying!" she chirped, as her guests approached the table.

"It's no ordinary salad. And I assure you, it is most delicious." She appeared very satisfied with the quick meal she had prepared for them.

In response to Madam Corvin's gesture, Lenim seated himself, followed by Rhyus and Marion. Rhyus intentionally situated himself across from Lenim, reluctant to be right beside him. Although, he soon realized that having to look directly across at him would be just as unfavorable.

After their early, yet long overdue, dinner, everyone returned to the living room at Madam Corvin's insistence. She, on the other hand, took care of the table and the dirty dishes. Neither Rhyus nor Marion had ever appreciated a meal so very much. The salad was just as delicious as Madam Corvin had guaranteed, and the side dishes of fresh mixed vegetables and pudding-topped fruit salad were just as pleasing.

"You two must come to the celebration this evening," Lenim declared, out of the blue.

"Oh, yes!" Madam Corvin exclaimed, turning away from the dishes and the sink filled with soapy water. "You two must attend!" she stressed, just as excitedly. "It would be a wonderful way to meet the city folk and to have a great time on your first night's stay!" She smiled, most cheerfully, at the thought, and then turned back to the dishes.

Rhyus and Marion looked at Lenim, a question on each of their faces.

"Tonight is the Eve of Festus Murus. The Festival of the Barrier," Lenim explained.

Neither Rhyus nor Marion changed expression.

"The anniversary of the night the great wall was finally completed and the threat of outsiders was declared forever gone."

At his words, Rhyus and Marion nodded in the slightest.

"Yes. You two certainly picked quite a day to arrive." Lenim gave them a mischievous smile.

"Yes. I suppose so," Rhyus said.

Does Lenim think we deliberately planned to arrive here on the night of this festival, Festus Murus? Rhyus wondered. He did, after all, tell Lenim that Marion and he had known where they were headed when they began their journey. Perhaps Lenim had just extrapolated his words to assume that they had planned their timing as well.

"So," Lenim tipped his head just a smidge, "will you attend?"

"Yes," Marion chirped up, before Rhyus had a chance to respond for the two of them again. She'd had enough of his act. "We wouldn't miss it." She smiled at Lenim whose overly wide grin grew even wider, his eyes beaming in reaction to her sudden response. Marion assumed that Madam Corvin would have expressed her delight as well, were she not caught up in a sink full of dishes.

Rhyus gave a sideways glance at Marion after her response

to the invitation. *Oh lord, Marion.* He pressed his lips together. *I don't know whether this is such a good idea.* Looking at Lenim, he watched the delight unfurl over his ghoul-like features. Rhyus could feel his stomach tightening in hesitation.

"Perfect!" Lenim exclaimed, settling into the comfortable chair with long fingers still pressed together before him.

Rhyus stood. "Excuse us a moment. I need to have a word with my shipmate." Rhyus was blunt, still reeling from Marion's response. She gave him a disbelieving look.

"Be my guest." Lenim's expression was inscrutable, as he gestured with a smooth motion toward the entryway.

Rhyus headed there. "Marion," he curtly said, turning his head only half back to her.

Although following him with her eyes, she sat motionless and offended, as he vanished down the hallway. Bitter and upset, realizing that he knew she would follow, Marion stood and tailed after him.

"I can't believe you!" Marion hissed, in hushed undertones once she met up with Rhyus just inside the front door.

Rhyus gave her a demeaning look. "You are a foolish girl."

"What!"

"You heard me. You should just let me do the talking from now on. I thought you'd have gotten that by now, but apparently not."

Marion's eyes began to water, but she held her eyes open wide, refusing to satisfy Rhyus by breaking down before him. "I have done nothing wrong," she spat, trying to steady her quavering voice. "Besides, it's you who should learn not to lie while you still have your head up your ass! You couldn't lie your way out of a paper bag! Rafters? What can of worms might you have managed to open?"

"We don't even know these somns!" Rhyus scolded, throwing a furious arm in the direction of Lenim and Madam Corvin.

"And you think it would have been better to deny their invitation?"

"I would think that obvious."

"What do you think they are going to do? Sacrifice us?"

Rhyus continued his look of accusation, his face still, along with the rest of his form.

"Who do you think you are?" A single tear managed to escape one of her glazed, brown eyes. "You don't even know *me*, Rhyus! How can you be so judgmental! Lenim and Madam Corvin have been nothing but kind to us since our arrival! If anything, they are the ones with the right to be skeptical. I mean, it is quite a coincidence that we have 'just happened' to arrive here on this very night of their important festival!"

"Just keep your mouth shut." He turned to walk back to the combined living and kitchen space.

Still sitting in the recliner, Lenim eyed Rhyus as he reentered the room. Rhyus approached the backside of the couch but did not walk around it to retake his seat. As he stood, neither Lenim nor Rhyus said a word. Once again, each had fallen into their own silent reverie.

At length, Marion returned. Rhyus maintained his stern look, turning away to gaze back at the elaborate garden painting.

Marion had stayed in the entryway a few minutes to collect herself, but now, just seeing Rhyus caused her eyes to well up again. She tried to convince herself that Rhyus's behavior was a consequence of being at sea in The Darkness for days.

"Oh, you poor dear!" In Marion's distraction, she failed to notice that Madam Corvin had finished the dishes. "You *poor* dear," Madam Corvin repeated. Approaching Marion, she took her hand as she had when they first met outdoors.

Marion, a bit ashamed of her pooling eyes and the corresponding flush of her fair skin, tried to force a smile.

"Your journey must have been terribly exhausting, " Madam Corvin crooned, in sympathy, still holding Marion's hand in her own. "I'll tell you what, dear. How about you spend the rest of your stay here with me?" In a motherly way, the woman extended her rounded, closed-mouth smile in hope. "I assure you, my home would be most accommodating. There is plenty of space and a guest bedroom you could use. However," Madam Corvin lowered her eyes in short, "I am not so sure I could accommodate both you and your...friend." Admitting this worried the woman, shaking her hopes that Marion would be able to take her up on her offer. She looked at Rhyus who kept his back to both women, and then she returned her gaze to Marion.

"Absolutely," Marion said, in relief.

The quick answer was not what Madam Corvin expected.

Marion vigorously nodded her head to express the solidity of her decision. Her long, chestnut waves rippled with the movement. "I would love to accept your offer." She forced another smile, but the woman didn't seem to pick up its false nature over her own delight.

"Will your friend be alright staying apart from you?" Marion could tell that this issue gave Madam Corvin great concern that she would change her mind. Nevertheless, the woman felt an ethical need to ask the question.

Marion cast another short glance at Rhyus, causing her eyes to gloss over again. But she pretended to have something in her eye, refusing to cry before her hostess. As she took the time to rub her eyes, she could feel her distress changing to bitterness. Somewhere, in a deep, far-away recess of her mind, she could hear a small voice chanting, "Good riddance to bad rubbish." She tried to push the feeling away.

"Yes," she assured the woman. "I'm certain that he can take care of himself. He will be just fine."

With a strong burst of intuition that something had gone amiss, Rhyus pulled his concentration from the garden scene and turned around. He gave Marion another skeptical, warning look.

Realizing that his attention was back upon her, Marion now lifted her proud eyes to meet his own, displaying a very satisfied expression.

He scowled, as he bit his tongue. *Dammit, Marion!*

42: *From Casavella to CavonRué*

KyVeerah walked at a more casual pace than was his norm, as he exited through the illusionary mirrors filling the arches at the entrance of the Grand Theatre Casavella. His thoughts circulated as he searched for possibilities and answers to the situation at hand. He moved over the silvery ground with such a strong sense of familiarity that one would believe he had never left.

His feet carried him east through the entire length of the Caulder District. He cut through several more districts, traversing over walkways and many bridges crossing crystal canals.

Pausing briefly, as he reached the Archer District, he found himself at a halt at the highest point on one of Lux's many bridges. He leaned against the bridge railing, looking down at the water just below. Its crystal lining was most beautiful with the suns' light reflecting off of it.

As his masked eyes followed the flowing channel, he allowed his mind to wander. So much was going on that it was becoming difficult, even for someone with his mental prowess, to keep everything straight.

He sighed, gazing at the city around him in attempt to remind himself why he had come back. Stepping from the bridge, he moved just a bit farther into Archer where he soon came to North Market.

Picking up his pace once again, he passed colorful stands with varying contents and animated merchants hawking their wares.

Moving down the strip, KyVeerah took in all the activities going on around him. The children running about, even at this early hour, those shopping, and the merchants themselves, either assisting customers or conversing in small groups near their stalls. However, none of them were the current target of his interest.

A little farther south, he spotted the particular booth he was looking for. He would much rather speak to her anywhere else, but she wouldn't be able to leave the stand and its produce unattended. He tried to think of any other possible solution. But he couldn't wait until the Kolbys took over for the later shift. And he couldn't leave Hale responsible for Jude much longer.

Weaving through customers and vendors alike, KyVeerah made

his way to the vegetable stand. When he reached it, near enough to touch the baskets and their contents, the copper-haired young woman was nowhere in sight.

Tightening his lips, he noticed a pleasant looking man and woman behind the stand where Cassandra ought to be. Of course, the Kolbys.

The man was sorting through some items behind the stand while the woman was finishing up business with a young lady who had purchased a variety of brightly colored fruits and vegetables.

"Can I help you, my child?" The woman behind the stand inquired. Her hair, pulled up into a loose bun, was the lightest shade of brown with strands of silver running through it. She had a plump face and a spirited smile to match eyes that sparkled in a merry way.

"Oh, yes," KyVeerah said, taking another look at her husband. With hair much more silver, he appeared every bit as kindly, and just as well fed as his wife.

They were two of the jolliest beings that KyVeerah had ever encountered. One might have even believed them to be Jude and Cassandra's mother and father if they didn't know better. But in fact, KyVeerah did know better.

"Pardon my asking, but are you Mr. and Mrs. Kolby?"

"Oh, yes dear. And don't mind the question." She looked at the charming young man before her. "What can I do for you?"

"Well." KyVeerah paused. "I was searching for the whereabouts of Ms. Cassandra Hollis. Might you know where I could find her? I thought I might run across her here."

Mrs. Kolby, a wide smile on her face, felt a new twinge of curiosity with hopefulness woven into it as the charming man asked about Cassandra, of whom she was very fond. "You are correct in your belief that she should be here, my child. But it would seem that her dear brother has fallen ill, apparently very ill." She shook her head. "Hopefully he will pull through all right. He is such a good man. A rare breed these days, you know? Is he a friend of yours? Any man or woman would be lucky to have Jude Hollis as a companion, or a lover even at that."

KyVeerah grinned, knowing that the woman's words held most true. But guilt seeped back through him as he considered Jude's true condition.

"Well," KyVeerah gave a final nod, "I thank you for your kindness."

"Anytime dear. And if you stop by to see her, won't you give

Cassandra our best wishes?"

"I will certainly do so." He turned, quick on his heel, and headed back north through the market strip.

Having reached the point where Archer bordered the Landel District, he changed course and began moving east.

As with traveling anywhere within the group of islands that constituted Lux, he passed over many more silver walkways, bridges, and crystal canals. The buildings surrounding him were of the usual stone, and the city began to grow crowded, as the suns reached higher into the sky. It was that time of morning when most were just heading out to face the day.

It had been some time since he had visited the Hollis's place. Reaching the Fannin District, where it was located, he rebuilt a clearer map in his memory, absorbing his surroundings.

Aha, he thought, as he spotted it, *CavonRué*.

KyVeerah congratulated himself on his impressive memory and good sense of direction, but then the thought circulating in the back of his mind crept forward, his sense of accomplishment evaporated. *What in Valencia's name am I ever going to tell Cassandra?*

He should have rehearsed his words during the walk from North Market, or better yet, ever since he left the Grand Theatre Casavella. He paused, debating his possibilities. He cringed. *This is probably not going to be good.* Taking a deep breath, he stepped from an alley, nearing the Hollis's place.

CavonRué was nowhere near the size of Umbra Halls, nor of many of the larger homes in the Caulder District or the Eastside. But it was still quite charming and of a decent size, nonetheless. A typical row house, it was narrow, tucked between buildings on either side. It sported three levels above ground and a small basement.

As children, Jude and Cassandra had grown up there with their mother and father. But since the incident eleven years ago, it had only been the two of them. Neither their Aunt Claudia nor their Aunt Lynette had been willing to take the children in, blaming them for what had happened. Jude had been just a lad of fourteen at the time and left responsible for both his ten-year-old sister and himself.

Ascending the stone stairway, KyVeerah reached the door. Once again, he paused before pressing the doorbell placed just to the right of the door, near a new crystal handle.

He stood with trepidation, listening for any sound from inside.

But nothing came. Not a single trace. But wait.

Tilting his head just an inch or so, he became still again. Yes. For a second time he heard the same sound. Listening, as the footsteps grew nearer, he stretched his ringed fingers, cracking them in apprehension.

The footsteps began to hurry. When they reached the door, he awaited the clicking of bolts being unlocked. KyVeerah took a single step back. When the last latch had been unhinged, the silver painted door began to open inward. A delicate hand with painted nails appeared at the edge of the door. A second hand appeared on the frame, and a woman's face came into view.

Cassandra. Her exhausted eyes were anxious as she recognized who had rung the bell. They were bloodshot and tired, for she had been up all night. Seeing KyVeerah sparked a glitter of hope.

She had been expecting someone with news of her brother, but she hadn't expected this.

"Vincent," she gasped. The look in her eyes fluctuated between hope, fear, and confusion.

"Cassandra." KyVeerah moved a hand toward the worried young woman. This sent her the wrong message. Well, maybe not *so* wrong.

She pulled her hand back from the door frame as his hand neared it. The reaction was more a result of her anxious state than her refusal to let KyVeerah reach out to her. Looking around, worry flooded her honey eyes. Her brother had been with KyVeerah. Why was he not here now? She knew Jude would never have stayed behind while his good friend, back from the dead, came to give his darling sister a message. Not any kind of message.

"Cassandra," he repeated, this time a bit more presumptively, reaching forth to rest his hand on her delicate arm, just below the shoulder. "He is fine," KyVeerah assured her, looking down at her with his masked eyes.

She attempted to meet his gaze through the dark shades, but doubt remained. She did not believe his words. She believed he would say anything to comfort her. But then again, it was very difficult not to be swept away by his beguiling tongue.

He brushed loose, coppery curls from her eyes and ran his ringed fingers through her long hair.

"Where—" she attempted to form a question, but he interrupted before she could do so.

"May I come in?" He used his most alluring voice, though he

already expected an invitation.

Cassandra tried a verbal response, but words failed her. She paused before nodding.

He waited, hand still on her shoulder. After another moment, she turned away, and his hand lost its grip as she took the first steps back into the house. Once KyVeerah was inside, he closed the heavy door, latching every one of the silver locks before turning back to observe the lovely interior of CavonRué.

A steep, wooden staircase opened on the right. To the left, he hung his jacket on a coat tree that had remained planted forever in one place.

The austere, yet comfortable, room held a rectangular kitchen table to seat six. A wooden bench lined each side of the table with two individual chairs placed head and foot.

Jude had told KyVeerah that his parents used this table since long before either Cassandra or he had been born. It was no wonder the Hollis siblings never considered replacing it with an upgrade.

His thoughts were cut short as Cassandra took a seat at the far end of the table. She cradled her head in her hands, her copper hair forming a veil over her features.

The floorboards creaked as KyVeerah pulled the end of the bench seat out, swinging a leg under the table, also taking a seat.

"Cassandra, are you feeling all right?" He put the question gently, acting as though there may not even be anything worth worrying about.

She didn't reply. Long moments passed before she raised her head, hair parting from her face. She studied her own reflection in his shades. "I couldn't sleep."

"I can see that. You look horrible, darling."

"I stayed up waiting for him. He always returns home. Or tells me if he won't be coming." She stared into space, pain and worry etched into her features.

"It grew rather late, even for him. I began to worry a bit. As time passed, I worried even more. I thought I was overreacting. However, I had a bad premonition that refused to leave. I knew something was wrong." Cassandra shook her head. "I couldn't fall asleep, so I came downstairs to brew a pot of dreg and tried to read, but I couldn't focus. My mind kept wandering from the pages."

KyVeerah could see the book still lying on the table. Its pages were open, facing downward as if it had just been set aside.

His eyes flashed with severity, startled, as with a quick fluid motion, Cassandra snatched the shades from his face. She had planned to demand that he have the decency to look at her with exposed eyes, but when she caught sight of the blazing fire in his unnatural, violet eyes, she opted otherwise.

"If you wanted me to remove them, all you had to do was ask," he hissed, his eyes brightly illuminated. Shocked, Cassandra drew back in her chair.

KyVeerah struck out his hand, snatching the shades back from her grasp. Resting the glasses on his leg, his radiant gaze fixed her in its sights, as though he were mentally trying to dissect her.

For some time she sat frozen, unable to move. Wrenching her eyes from his, she attempted to stand up and get away, but KyVeerah grabbed the arm of her chair. He pulled it nearer, causing her to sit once again, now just a few feet from where he straddled the bench facing her.

She stared at him, eyes wide, as his illuminated irises stared hypnotically into hers. Her nerves began to calm, and her heartbeat slowed as they sat in silence for several minutes. His gaze lost its violence, though retaining its serious tenure.

"W-what happened?" she stammered.

"Your brother was jumped, Cassandra." His voice was too smooth, too appealing to mean what the words implied.

Cassandra sat in silence, her mind circling in multiple rounds of denial. Shaking her head slowly, and then more quickly, she tried to block the pictures from her mind. "No."

"No? By Valencia, whatever do you mean, gorgeous? This is a fact, not a question of opinion." He lowered his brow, analyzing her lack of words and her hard expression.

She stared down at the floorboards, refusing to believe that her brother had been jumped.

"Beck Scofflin," KyVeerah began.

Cassandra's eyes jumped up at the mention of the name, filled with a new sense of worry. Her eyes pressed into him, wanting to know more, wishing that his next words would be anything other than what she anticipated.

"His men and he were out causing havoc last night, ransacking homes. They even started trouble at a local bar, the Crimson Glass. I'm sure you will hear news of it soon if you have not already. If you had but spoken to the Kolbys, you would know all of this already."

Her eyes continued to press into him, hard enough that he felt certain they would leave an imprint.

"Your dear brother was unlucky enough to get caught up in a moment of misfortune, however the moment I speak of was enough to cause some real damage."

Cassandra's eyes widened with fear, but she tried to fight it. She told herself it couldn't be true, yet KyVeerah's voice remained as smooth as glass and appealing as ever. The words just didn't make sense as they stitched themselves in amongst the enthralling tones of his voice.

"Jude and I fled when we heard from a frantic man what was coming, but Scofflin and his men were already too near. Jude was following just behind me as we were running to a safer location. A man leapt out of a shadowed doorway as we ran through an alley. I had run past him before he caught Jude by surprise. The instant I realized what had happened, I turned back. He took off running as soon as he saw me turn around. Unfortunately, he had already severed an artery in Jude's upper arm and left a long, ragged wound across his neck."

Cassandra threw a hand over her mouth, and a lone tear trickled down her cheek.

KyVeerah sat watching as Cassandra absorbed the news he had thrown her way.

"Is he all right?" she asked, fearful of the answer.

Nodding, KyVeerah assured her, "Yes, he will be fine." His words were even more convincing than his true opinion, though he did feel certain that Jude would pull through.

"Where is he?"

To this, KyVeerah only shook his head. "I assure you," he said, with a promise in his gaze, "that your brother is in good hands."

Cassandra closed her eyes, hand still raised to her face. Her eyelids quivered as she fought back the tears welling up behind them.

Suddenly, she stood up, placing both hands over her eyes. She began to shake, tears flowing down her face. KyVeerah quickly drew his leg from under the table, standing as well. He remained where he was, watching, but keeping the small distance between them. The sight of a sobbing woman generally caused him to recoil, but in this case he had expected her reaction, knowing that he had prompted it.

As tears continued streaming down, Cassandra dropped her hands. Closing the space between KyVeerah and herself, she began to weakly throw her hands at him, hitting him in her anger.

"How could you!" she sobbed. "How could you let this happen?" Her sobbing became more uncontrollable, and her blows weaker as she continued to pound her fists against him.

Protecting the wounds on his own body, KyVeerah grabbed her wrists. "That is quite enough," he said. She tried to pull away from him, but he pulled her in toward himself. She gave in, and he pulled her close. He placed one arm around her lower back and his other hand patted her head as she pressed herself, sobbing, into his shoulder, thankfully on the less-injured side of his torso.

She continued to tremble, as he braced her, leaning his head down upon hers. She still held her hands up to her face, trapped between his body and hers. Her sweet, honeysuckle scent enveloped the two of them. He swayed in his efforts to comfort the young woman, for whom he was candidly responsible for bringing this pain. But he could never confess the truth to her, not in a hundred lifetimes.

KyVeerah held Cassandra in his arms for some time. He ran a hand through her copper hair, soothing her while attempting to maintain his own composure, repressing his guilt enough to eventually look back into the wells of her eyes.

"Cassandra," he said, his head still leaning against her own, tucked up against his chest and shoulder.

"Yes?" she responded, in a faint voice, her sobbing beginning to calm, though tears continued to stain her cheeks.

"You must tell the Kolbys," he told her, in his smooth voice. "You must let them know what happened, that he was jumped during the Scofflin incident last night." He paused after this to run back over his thoughts. *I can't leave any holes unexplained or unaccounted for.*

Cassandra remained silent.

"Yesterday..." he started, in question. "Yesterday morning, when Jude and I left, did you tell the Kolbys that Jude was home ill?" He assumed such, as it was what Mrs. Kolby had said, but he had to be 100 percent certain.

She nodded. *Hmm,* he pondered, that does pose a bit of a problem.

"Just so they do not feel the need to question you any further, tell the Kolbys that Jude thought he was feeling a little better by last evening. Tell them that he told you he absolutely had to get out of the house, and that you tried to tell him no, but he was most persistent. Then Jude went for a walk and told you that he would stop by the store and pick up a few things on the way back, to at least give some purpose to his trip. Can you do that, Cassandra? Will you tell this to the Kolbys? It will be for the best." He said all of this to her in a crooning, hushed voice, as he continued to rock gently on his heels.

Cassandra thought it through for herself, and at last nodded. Pulling back, she slid her hands from her eyes, placing them upon KyVeerah's chest, just over his collarbones.

Trying hard not to wince at the pressure over his wound, he looked down as she peered up at him, eyes glazed over and tears still lingering over her fair skin. Her makeup was smeared, but she still looked beautiful.

"Thank you," she said, continuing to gaze at him through her glassy eyes.

This caught him off guard, and he couldn't help a puzzled look. "For what?"

"For watching over him. For always being such a good friend to him. And to me. You've always been so good to us both. I can't tell you how glad I am that you are back, no matter where you have been away to." She shook her head, emphasizing that it didn't even matter that he had left without telling them.

KyVeerah's expression changed from puzzlement into a hard, impassive stare. His guilty conscience flooded his entire being, and he fought to make sure that not a single ounce made its way to the surface.

Even in Cassandra's condition, she found a way to look at him now with that sweet, pleasant smile of hers. Her eyes were gentle as she looked out through their thin, glossy covering. They stood still, only a breath apart. Both of KyVeerah's hands now rested on her hips, and her hands remained on his upper chest.

A heavy wave of conflicting emotions overwhelmed KyVeerah as he looked down at Cassandra, the sister of one of his closest friends. As he peered deep into her captivating eyes, he envisioned the scene as he had exited the hidden stairwell of The Hinge to see Jude falling to the ground, becoming stark white in a matter of moments. He could see the pool of blood spreading over the wooden floorboards and feel the pain as he had dropped down at his friend's side, absorbing the blood into his clothing.

The combination of Cassandra's close proximity and his own relentless guilt and remorse made him almost nauseous as he peered down into her eyes. It felt as though they could reach out to discover the lies he held hidden within.

Without warning, KyVeerah pushed Cassandra away. The sudden action caused her hands to fall from his chest. He dropped his hands from her hips and turned away, readjusting his hair, securing it back into its low ponytail.

Bafflement flashed over Cassandra.

"I must go." His voice had become detached, though it retained its charming lilt.

"Vincent," her voice was stronger now, "I'm sorry."

KyVeerah, with a swift motion, turned back and pulled her close again, just inches away. He interrupted her apology with a single finger against her lips. She looked into his eyes, barely a lash away.

His lips, also no more than a whisper from hers, parted as he spoke, "I will have him back to you as soon as he is well. I promise you."

Once again, he pulled away with an abrupt movement. He turned toward the door, grabbing his jacket from the rack. Facing away from Cassandra, he threw it on, cringing as the action caused a strong surge of pain.

He stepped to the door and began to unlatch the multiple locks lining its edge.

"Vincent." Cassandra came up behind him while he unhinged the last lock. He opened the heavy door before turning around to face her. "Be careful." She placed one hand on his neck and the other on the side of his face, as he looked back into her eyes.

43: Trails and Trials

Helena knew that hunting down and locating the Key Calling, or any Calling for that matter, wasn't going to be easy, but she hadn't thought it would be *this* difficult. After the rumor involving the awakening of a Calling, and the ramblings of that partygoer, Fyfe Van Ingen, Helena figured someone would talk. Anyone. But no.

One minute the city was abuzz with talk of lost prophecies and Callings, and the next minute, nothing. *It's all because of that damn Archives break-in*, Helena thought, feeling rather annoyed. *Only thing anyone wants to talk about anymore is "Intruder this" and "Intruder that." So, the guy stole some books. Big frikkin' deal.*

Helena's visit to The Tower on the day of The Archives break-in had been anything but pleasant. *That blubbering fool of a librarian was no help at all, Helena fumed. Lucky for me, I found someone there who was much more accommodating. But after that, the Dictum Division refused me access to the prisoner, Fyfe Van Ingen.* She could just picture Jett's dark, expressionless features, as she had run into him. His nonchalant attitude had always pissed her off. *Why the hell are they allowing him to assist with Black Band matters anyway?*

For some time, Helena had devoted every bit of energy to elevating her status with Nyx's entourage of assassins. But she was certain that with morons and creeps like Royce and Jett calling the shots for the two lower bands, she would be forever getting nowhere. She tapped her fingers, contemplating her current plan to success. If it should come to fruition, Armani Saint and Julian Gallows would be so far down the power chain as to be almost insignificant. Even the great Nyx Crucian would have to ask permission to bow down and kiss her feet. She shivered with pleasure at the thought.

Helena pondered over all of these events, as she made her way into the Mahron Sector located in northern Atrum Unda. The Mahron Sector consisted of small boutiques and specialty shops.

As she caught a glimpse of her reflection in the window of a gourmet bakery, or so the fancy script on the store's sign read, Helena came to a halt. Up until this point, Helena found herself passing the shops without a single interest, but that was before she spotted a minor flaw in the mirrored image of herself. Retrieving a small compact mirror from her clutch, she examined the damage.

Minus a minor flush to her lightly tanned skin and the smudge of color in the corner of her supple mouth, everything seemed to be in place. Nonetheless, this was more of a flaw than Helena was willing to accept. With a manicured nail, she erased the easily disposable blemish.

With that taken care of, she snapped the compact case closed and exchanged it for a tube of lipstick. She reapplied a coat of color to her full lips. *Plum Desire. My favorite.* The warm, burgundy color complimented her emerald eyes and tawny skin. Now satisfied, she continued along her path.

Reaching the Mahron Sector's highest-priced businesses and boutiques, Helena paused again. Once more, she spotted a familiar face reflecting back at her, however this one was a face other than her own. It would be nigh impossible to mistake Callis Morgandy for anyone else with his prominent, crimson hair. A sultry smile unfurled over Helena's alluring features.

Hmm. Maybe I won't need Royce after all. The thought was pleasing as it crossed her mind. Helena's good friend and comrade, Angelina Pratt, had said that she could help in acquiring Royce Elwood's access key, one of the access keys granted only to Black Band members. The very key she needed for her ambitions to prove fruitful.

Helena had, at one point, considered approaching Armani or Julian, but she quickly relinquished the idea. It would be suicidal to attempt to seduce either of those demonic beings. Angelina had failed her. *Apparently, even Royce has his limits*, she thought, as her mind wandered back to the upsetting discovery.

Helena studied Callis up and down with a meticulous eye. *Not as easy of a target as Royce, but what the hell. Even Callis Morgandy must have needs. I'm sure. And judging by his volatile attitude and rigid stance, I'm guessing it's been awhile since ol' Cal's gone for a ride.*

⁊

"Hey, Callis!"

Facing the other way, Callis cringed. He was unsure whether it was a natural reaction to the general calling of his name, or if it was just the particular somn who was doing the calling.

With a forced effort, Callis turned to see where the voice had come from. He saw that a thin, voluptuous woman was closing the distance between him and herself. Callis took in the short, strawberry blonde hair, styled to frame her face, as well as the tawny skin and green eyes. Even with the remaining distance, he knew it could only be one person.

Ugh. Helena. His cringe deepened as she grew nearer, confirming his previous assumption. His reaction was definitely due to her. Callis was grateful for the dark, orange-reflective shades he had chosen for the day. Mentally prepared now, he turned fully to meet Helena, who came to stand before him. He tried to hold back his revulsion, as he addressed her, "Helena."

"So eloquent with words, Callis. As usual." Helena delivered a fake laugh, slapping playfully at his muscular arm. Callis swiveled his gaze to where Helena's manicured hand rested on his forearm. He closed his eyes for a minute behind his shades, feeling a headache coming on. Remaining unnaturally still, he asked, "What do you want? I'm busy."

"Now, is that any way to behave, Cal? I just came over to say hi. Besides, we never hang out anymore," Helena pouted.

Since when have we ever hung out? She is absolutely insane. Especially if she believes I'm falling for this, Callis told himself.

As Helena continued to pout her pleas of innocence, Callis noted something suspicious out of the corner of his eye. A woman, standing not too far in the distance, appeared to be weighing her choice in front of a floral stall with an intricate covering. She stood with a casual manner, but Callis could see that her eyes were shifted back to where Helena and he stood.

Callis focused his gaze on the distant woman while retaining his stance facing Helena. Looking closer, Callis saw the woman's raven hair framing her light, feminine features. No matter the distance, he made out a characteristic beauty mark set beneath her right eye.

Callis raised a pierced brow in curiosity. His inner voice held a tone of surprise. *Ezra? What the hell is she doing here?* Callis looked back down at Helena who appeared to be quite cross by his lack of attention. He looked back at Ezra. *She's not looking at us. She's looking at Helena.* Realization hit him. *She's following Helena. What reason would Ezra Stark have for tailing a White Band member?*

"I have to go now," Callis informed, causing Helena to flush in irritation.

"What? You haven't even answered my question, Callis Morgandy!"

Callis, ignoring her protests, easily released himself from her grip, simply saying, "I'm leaving." He could feel her heated anger as he walked away from her, as well as Ezra. He couldn't care less about offending Helena as he proceeded down the block, turning at the nearest corner.

His original plan had been to spend his day collecting "payments" from uncooperative clients of Nyx, and maybe completing some overdue paperwork back at The Dome. *But that can be put off*, he decided. *This is much more interesting. Besides, there's not much I can do until Jereth returns. These alternative tasks are only to pass the time until I receive any new information on Vincent KyVeerah.* Callis backtracked his way around the block until Ezra and Helena were quite visible, once again. But this time he was watching them.

He could see Helena making her way further north into the Ardenne Sector with Ezra not too far off. He paused before pursuing them. Stretching his senses, he concentrated on Helena, feeling the warmth of the tattoos along his arms and shoulder blades ignite into a fiery glow beneath his clothing and jacket. Making sure to keep distance between Ezra and himself, he picked up his pace.

Helena was too engrossed with her destination to notice someone following her, but Ezra wasn't so careless. *She would be livid if she caught me following her, and that wouldn't do either of us any good.* He could hear Helena mutter to herself.

"How dare he just turn and stalk away from me. Me of all people! I bet Callis Morgandy wouldn't even know how to properly handle a real woman."

Callis raised a brow. *Oh really? Is that what you think.*

Helena continued muttering, "Maybe I should ask Angelina to prod Royce again. Surely she can get him to relinquish his key for a short while..." But Callis could tell that even Helena doubted her words.

Wait a minute! Key? Our access keys? Callis pondered. *So that is what our little encounter was all about. I knew she wanted something, but I didn't think...*Callis puzzled over this new information.

A slow grin spread across his face. *If she thinks she'll attain an access key from Royce, she is mistaken. Despite his flaws, there's a reason why Royce has earned a position in the Black Band. He won't risk his own neck to impress a woman. Especially one such as Angelina Pratt.*

His grin turned to a frown. *What could Helena want with an access key? This news is quite unsettling. I don't like it. Even more of a reason for me to follow her. Ezra's good, but not as good as me.* His grin reappeared once more.

Callis continued to keep his distance while maintaining a clear view of both Ezra and Helena. Puzzled, he slowed his pace, mimicking Ezra. He soon realized why she had done so. Helena had entered a nearby building, and he watched as Ezra moved down an alley across the way. *Ezra will have a clear view when Helena emerges, but that won't be necessary for me.*

Stopping mid-step, he cut down an alley himself, though his was on the same block as the building Helena had entered. This allowed him no view of Ezra or Helena, however that would be no problem for him. Crossing his arms and leaning up against the cold lining of the alley, Callis made himself comfortable. With eyes closed, he focused his complete concentration on Helena. He continued to feel the ignited warmth of his tattoos. *All right, Helena. Let's see what you're up to.*

ɛɔ cʁ

Unknowingly, Helena led her two pursuers to the southeast portion of the Ardenne Sector. Atrum somns commonly referred to the Ardenne Sector as the historical sector. The buildings here flourished from the black brick of older times to the modern, speckled marble of current times. Even with the older, more worn-down buildings, this district remained as safe as any place in Atrum Unda.

The atmosphere here was that of classic antiquity, which somns took advantage of to charge higher prices, much like the gourmet bakery that Helena had passed earlier on. Helena had now come to an older, two-story building constructed of the old black brick with two large bay windows set on either side of a dark, wooden door. A sign in one of the windows read *Scribe's Den.* Below, in finer print, read *Books of Antiquity and Memorabilia.*

Standing before the shop, Helena reached for a small piece of paper that had been lodged between her large bosoms. *Oh, Albert. He turned out to be quite useful in leading me here…and fun, as always.* Unfolding the paper, she checked to make sure she had the correct address. *All right. This seems to be the place.*

Helena reached for the handle, opening the door and stepping inside. A little bronze piece tinkled above her head as she entered.

The air was thick with the scent of books, dust, and age—much what you would expect in an antique bookshop. Unattractively, Helena wrinkled her nose in distasteat the shop's musty smell.

A carpet runner lay over the aged wooden floor, which creaked as Helena progressed further into the shop. The shop looked like it was an old home, transformed to suit the needs of a business. She turned into the room on her left.

Bookshelves lined the walls while several antiquarian tables were placed throughout the room with more items laid upon them. Off to her left was one of the bay windows she had seen from outside. A steady pitter-patter of rain streamed down it. Before the window sat an old fashioned, wooden rocking horse with faded paint cracked over its form. Barely above a whisper, she muttered, "What an odd looking creature…is anyone even here?" Dismissing the creature, she moved further into the room. Off to her right sat another room, which Helena wandered into.

This room was very similar. Something on a small table with an intricate patterned doily caught her eye. A comb, set amongst various antiques, including a hairbrush, a perfume bottle, and a handheld mirror, was what had sparked her interest. It was one of those old-fashioned metal combs that women used to place in their hair. This one, however, had a beautiful black star sapphire inlaid in it. Helena noticed a crack in the stunning piece of work. She reached out a hand.

"Hey," echoed a rough voice. Helena jumped, turning to face the somn who had startled her.

Before her stood a man in his seventies with a combed back, thick head of hair in varying shades of silver. His frame was thin, but it wasn't fragile looking in the least. It was quite the opposite. Hard eyes and a strong jaw were clenched in cold judgment as he stared at Helena with little patience. "Don't touch anything unless you plan on paying for it. Besides, it doesn't work," he barked.

Helena, a little taken aback, replied, "Yes, I saw the crack…but what do you mean 'it doesn't work?' It's just a hair comb. Right?"

Frowning, the man said, "If you don't even know what it is, then don't bother. And like I said, it's broken."

"But—" Helena said.

"If you're not going to purchase anything, leave now. I'm much too busy."

Helena scowled. *Busy, my ass*. She flipped her scowl into a false smile. "Actually, I came here hoping that you could be of assistance to me. That is, of course, if you're name is Serlio Young?"

The man's gaze sharpened as he took in Helena's full appearance. Helena was decked out in a burgundy leather jacket with a shortened torso, which lay over a black corset, revealing her well-endowed chest. A black leather skirt—stopping just above her knees—and a pair of burgundy stilettos covered her lower half. Oversized, hoop earrings followed all of this as a final touch. Helena had carefully chosen this assemble, finding herself looking quite professional. The man's face displayed his opposing view.

He replied, distrusting, "You are correct in your assumptions. I am Serlio Young. But who are you and what do you want?"

With her fake smile, Helena said, "My name is Helena Meretrix. I am told you hold great knowledge on the original powers that connect our world to that of another." Her smile widened. "I was referred to you by an Archives librarian. Albert Young."

The crease of Serlio's frown deepened. "You know my grandson." It was a rhetorical statement, but Helena answered, nonetheless.

"Yes. He told me where I could find Serlio Young, the author of this very *interesting* book." Helena waved a small, paperback book she had retrieved from her clutch. It was entitled, *Theological Energy Disturbances and Their Potential*. Before Serlio could respond, she continued, "Albert also mentioned something about an energy pocket located somewhere beneath The Dome. Such a helpful young man, your grandson."

With tightened lips, Serlio said, "I see. How disappointing. Albert is normally good about holding his tongue. Especially when it comes to *privileged* information."

"Oh, he is capable of much more than just *holding* his tongue. Albert is a very *skilled* young man." Serlio looked as if he just swallowed something vile. His revulsion for Helena and her words was quite evident. Her sculpted eyebrows furrowed downward as she processed Serlio's blatant look of disgust toward her.

"Don't look at me like that, you old codger! You're grandson was a more than willing participant," Helena hissed. Serlio gave a curious look in reaction to her mini outburst. He considered snapping something back but shook his head, dismissing such thoughts.

After a moment, he said, "Albert was mistaken in referring you to me. I refuse to be of assistance to you. I think it is time you leave, Miss Meretrix."

"Oh, I think you will, Mr. Young. Did I forget to mention that I am one of Nyx Crucian's elite assassins?"

Serlio heaved a deep sigh of submission. "Yes, I do believe you forgot to mention that. Very well. Follow me."

Helena's face brightened. She hadn't expected him to cooperate so easily.

She followed Serlio to the door at the end of the main hallway. He retrieved a key from his pocket and proceeded to unlock it.

Nothing but a large window—revealing the never-ending dreary weather of Atrum Unda—lay before them once through the door. Serlio, however, led Helena to the right, which opened into a cozy little sitting room.

Moving past an L-shaped bookshelf, he took a seat on the couch. He motioned Helena to take a seat opposite him on a second. Once Helena had situated herself comfortably, he reached out to a huge old metallic kettle and poured them both a cup. He had been about to drink it when she had barged into his shop, and he was darned if he was going to let it get cold. A true gentleman, however, he could not ever refuse a guest, regardless the circumstances of her visit.

Clearing his throat, he started sternly, "Before I begin, tell me exactly what you know."

As Helena started to talk, Serlio listened with a deep scowl. He had been around way too long to be pushed around, and this bitch had certainly started off on the wrong foot. If she happened to be as stupid as she appeared, this would not take long.

At first Helena couldn't find any of the right words. This exercise was way outside of her normal realm.

After the first few sentences, Serlio knew he had been right. The girl not only had horrid manners, but she was stupid to boot. He was about to terminate the brief meeting, when she finally loosened up a bit.

Helena, so brash just moments before, did something she could not ever remember doing before. She apologized. She almost fainted when she heard the words escape her lips, but there they were. It wasn't until later that evening, when she had time to reflect, that she even partially understood the reason for her actions.

Her entire life had been lived in a world of macho power. Greed, boasting, power games, and threats she could deal with. Fighting back and intimidation were her bread and butter. But this was a world she had never seen. Sitting here, in a quiet room with a proper old man—surrounded by old books that held a power of their own—she was helpless. She could defend herself against weapons, but not against manners.

"I'm sorry that I can't explain much. I have read your book—a hundred times. Parts of it are beginning to make sense. But there are so many difficult sections. I just can't absorb them." When she had first walked in, all she wanted was some quick answers to basic questions. But sitting here now, strangely that all seemed, well, pretty childish. To tell the truth, for the first time she could remember, she was embarrassed.

Given her initial attitude, this took Serlio by surprise. He had been darn well ready to throw her out on her darling little ass. But something in her sincere humility gave him pause.

Sitting quietly, he took a few sips. Then he began on a different note. "You don't have to impress me, and there won't be a test." He surprised himself by smiling. "I ask because it will help me to know how to address the subject. I don't wish to bore you. But then again, I'm wasting both of our time, if I start way over your head."

This made sense to Helena, and the sincerity in his voice helped her regain a measure of her usual confidence. Before she began, she couldn't help but wonder how their interaction had gone so quickly from distrustful antagonism, to polite respect. Could it be that the

books surrounding them made doing anything else unnatural?

She hesitantly started again. But as he listened without any traces of judgment, she finally got beyond saying all the things she thought he wanted to hear. At that point she reached inside to put together the pieces of what she knew.

From his standpoint, Serlio was simultaneously amused by her shortcomings and amazed that a girl with absolutely no formal education had actually taken the time to think through what he had written.

When she finished, he offered a slight nod. Having never known him, Helena had no idea what a compliment it was. He sat pondering all that she had said.

"I am going to begin," he said, "by just telling the basic story. Now don't take that wrong." He raised a finger. "It's just that when trying to smooth out our ideas, often the beginning is the best place to start."

Serlio gently cleared his throat and took a sip of his drink. Then he settled back. Looking thoughtfully at the overstuffed shelf of books over the mantle, he began.

"As far back as time, there was darkness. Then from the darkness there pulsed a pinpoint of light. Many an age passed, until there was movement on the land. These minute creatures—living things— were filled with a force. The Energy of life. Through countless ages the creatures became larger and multiplied. As they lived and died, their Energies came together, and the light became brighter. With time, light and darkness became equal and formed the first true dichotomy of our universe. With time, there developed an ever more complex system. However, the duality of nature persisted, just as it does today. There were small and large, up and down, in and out, hot and cold, with and without, positive and negative, good and evil. I could continue the list all day long. But it is enough to make the point.

"Eventually, there developed two primary realms. One of coldness and ice. The other of heat and desert. At about the same time, there came to exist two peoples. One we refer to as The Ancients, the other as the somns.

"Who came first?" He shrugged. "Who knows?

"Exactly how did they come to be?" Again he shrugged, "Who knows?

"All around and between these two realms, were Energies. Both that of the somns, and different—but just as powerful—was that of The Ancients.

"Without any means of harnessing or controlling these Energies, there was constant turmoil. They flowed, clashing and bashing into each other willy-nilly. Eventually, a way was discovered to direct these Energy flows. For simplification we will call it a dipole. A positive and a negative pairing.

"Of course, a dipole large enough to control all the Energies required massive constructions. At that time, the two towers were built. One in the realm of ice, one in the realm of desert. And it worked.

"For countless millennia everything was as it should be. The two Energies carved out parallel paths, allowing them to coexist and travel side by side between the towers in peace. The dipole tower of the somns controlled one, and the Ancients' tower controlled the other. All was well.

"But then, and no one has any idea why, The Ancients had to leave."

At this point Serlio's throat was becoming dry. He stopped to sip his drink and briefly evaluate whether his audience was paying attention. She was sitting quietly and seemed to be watching with rapt attention. Reflecting, he had to admit, it had been ages since he had an audience. Especially one so breathtaking. In fact, he was taken enough to forget that she was one of Nyx Crucian's trained assassins.

Clearing his throat again, he continued, "As I said, The Ancients left. But there are many who speculate that they had actually planned on returning soon. They think this because instead of taking their Energies with them, The Ancients chose a particular somn. He was known for being very powerful—and very just. His name was…"

Serlio tried to come up with the name, but it just wouldn't come forward. He became flustered. It was a reminder to him that this was happening all too often. "Damn!" he said under his breath. He was afraid that soon he wouldn't remember his own name.

Helena surprised herself again. Leaning forward, she gently took the old man's hand and smiled. "It's OK. I really don't need to know his name. Everything you are saying is helpful. Even without it. I bet as soon as you stop trying, it will pop right into your head. Happens to me all the time." Still smiling, she waved a gentle finger in the air. An indication that she was eager for him to continue.

Serlio, also surprised by her touch and smile, stammered for a brief moment. He then settled back, took a deep breath, and carried on.

"Anyway. The Ancients chose this man. After meeting at length with him, they felt he would be strong enough to hold and maintain their Energies for the brief time they anticipated being gone. The problem, however, is that they never did return.

"This man…" Again Serlio struggled to come up with the name. This time, Helena sat quietly. As though she wasn't even there. She hoped doing so might lessen his frustration and embarrassment. Before long, he did settle down, and continued with the rest of his story.

"Anyway, this man…he did just what The Ancients expected of him. For many years, he maintained the smooth flow of the forces. Occasionally he slipped a bit and a small disruption caused some minor snowfall or dust storm. But never anything catastrophic.

"After many years passed, the natural powers of his youth diminished. He found that the weight of the Energies began to chip away his reserves. Getting ever older, he realized that they were literally causing him to deteriorate inside. He was falling apart."

"Being an intelligent man, and having no wish to disintegrate, he came up with a solution. He tried feeding minute bits of the Energies of The Ancients into the Energy stream of the somns. And lo and behold, it was accepted! The energy was picked up, and the disruptions that occurred were so small as to be unnoticeable. Perhaps a small cloud in the sky or dust devil. But that was as big as it ever got."

"The constant slow feeding took years. And those years took their toll on him. He knew that he was going to die before his task was completed. To insure that all the Energies were accounted for, he collected together all the remaining power—" Serlio hesitated here. He hoped he had managed to catch himself before revealing too much to one who should not be privy to such information. He felt it would be true, but not too revealing, when he continued. "And he placed it in a secure location."

Serlio stopped again. Helena wasn't sure if it was for dramatic effect, or if he just needed to wet his throat. When he started talking again, Helena was aware that he was beginning to slow down. And that his word choices were a mite more difficult. In that moment she realized, despite his strapping frame, Serlio was indeed an old man.

If she hadn't needed this information so badly, she might have encouraged him to stop for the time being. But this was important. Even though this background information was taking forever, she realized he needed to get through it. To set the stage for what she really needed. How the power of the Callings worked. And how she could get her hands on it.

Serlio coughed. He was gentleman enough to cover his mouth with a handkerchief. But when he pulled it away, Helena frowned at a small spot of red staining its corner.

With a breather and a few more sips, Serlio recovered. The brief respite did help, and he continued on.

"And it worked. For many years everything went smoothly. However, the Energies were no longer in their natural balance. And the added burden of handling multiple loads finally began to take its toll. The towers themselves began to crack and crumble under the heavy task. As they did so, there were more and more disruptions in the flow of Energies. And they became ever larger. In time, a constant barrage of windstorms, earthquakes, floods, hail, and every other possible catastrophe, plagued the realms. The somns were miserable—and in fear. If they did not find a solution, the realms of ice and desert, would soon exist no more.

"At length, a solution was found. The somn's son..." Serlio shook his head, frustrated that he still couldn't come up with the somn's name. "His son called together a small select committee. To help him decide how to manage the excess Energies and save the towers. Their plan was to place two cities in a dipole, creating an Energy loop perpendicular to their own. To fit the natural dichotomy of the universe, they chose a City of Light and a City of Darkness.

"By using some of the Energy that the somn had stashed away, his son mastered the task of pulling matter out of the surrounding universe. He and his committee were able to pull in enough to create two cities.

"At first their efforts were piecemeal, as they had not yet figured out how to transport huge masses of matter at one time. In this piecemeal manner, they cobbled together the first city. It was constructed using many individual islands of matter. These were connected together by a series of bridges. This was the City of Light. Lux Lumetia."

"As they worked, and their technology improved, they transported one gigantic mass to form the second city. The City of Darkness. Or as we so kindly know it, our own sweet city of Atrum Unda.

"Once the dual cities were completed, the somns immediately set to work building two great towers. When those were ready, Energies were slowly and steadily moved to them to create the second loop. At length, the two loops of Energy were both flowing smoothly. The ice and desert towers were repaired. And to this day, all four Towers have continued to operate smoothly, with no single Tower burdened by more than it can safely manage."

By this time Serlio had definitely slowed down. Some of his words were even beginning to slur together.

Helena swore inwardly. There had been no time to address the issues she really needed. But she realized that if she pushed now, she would soon be hearing nothing but gobbledygook. Hell, she might even push the old man over the far edge. If he stroked out or died she would never get the information she so desperately needed.

Pragmatic—if nothing else—Helena knew it was time to take her leave. It would be best to let Serlio rest, and continue the next day.

With a sultry stretch, she yawned. Keeping one eye on the old man to make sure he had noticed. He had. He wasn't that old yet.

With a warm smile she stood up and reached out to help him up as well. Once standing she stepped forward and gave him a long soft hug. She considered offering a light kiss as well, but given his sense of propriety, he might be offended. She had to be careful not to overstep her bounds.

"I'm kind of beat. I imagine your voice could stand a bit of a rest as well. To tell the truth, the thing I would like to learn most about is how Callings and their Messengers function. If you wouldn't mind, may I come back tomorrow?"

She smiled. "Perhaps we could pick up where we left off." She dared a subtle half-wink, just enough to make him wonder if he had really seen it, and to keep her meaning obscure.

As he walked her to the door he was actually stammering. "I-I'm sorry I couldn't remember the somn's name. The one who had to manage all the Energies."

Her smile was simple and sweet. "I'm still sure it will come to you."

With that she stepped back onto the street, turning only once, when she was halfway down the block. He was still watching. She blew him a tiny kiss, and turned away again. She headed back down the walkway, bubbling with anticipation at the information tomorrow might bring.

44:Quaint Accommodations

"I'm staying with Madam Corvin," Marion said, finding a way to steady her voice. She looked into Rhyus's shining, emerald eyes.

He stared back at her, voiceless. Motionless.

"What!" he finally said, thinking he better have misheard her.

"I am going to spend our stay in Palam Vita here…with Madam Corvin." Marion started to lose her evenness midsentence, but she pulled herself together enough to complete it.

Rhyus's eyes gleamed. For a moment he resembled Lenim as his eyes dried from a lack of blinking, but they continued to shine with a green vibrancy, nonetheless. A dark anger began to engulf him.

His ferocity spread, clawing through every inch of his insides. *Why does she have to be so goddamn difficult!*

He is so different from the Rhyus I met back in Lux Lumetia, Marion thought, in fear. She felt an overwhelming wave of regret. *I never should have left Umbra Halls. I wish Venn were here.* She couldn't stop the thought from forming; for right now, the wish held stronger and truer than ever.

Just as clearly as Marion could see his rage, Rhyus could see the circling emotions that had come over her. Hurt. Regret. And strongest was hatred toward him. *I deserve it…So what?* Rhyus knew his thoughts and expression were insolent. At that particular moment in time, he couldn't care less. The worst part was, he didn't know why. That was the most troubling of all to him.

"There isn't room for us both," Marion said, grateful at the words that passed over her lips. She was unsure how he would react or where he might stay. Then again, she didn't care, so long as she didn't have to be anywhere near him —not like this.

Silence filled the room. Lenim, still seated in the recliner, raised his eyebrows. A familiar sense of amusement showing in his deep blue eyes, his ghoul-like appearance grew by multiples.

"All right then." Rhyus's words were vulgar. "If you don't want to stay with me, I am sure I can find much better company and use of my time."

Marion ignored his attempt to hurt her further, but the task proved difficult to carry out.

Rhyus turned his attention from Marion to Lenim, breaking the strong connection Lenim currently held over her. He flicked his eyes back to Rhyus, demanding an explanation. Anger flooded Rhyus at the severe expression from Lenim.

Rhyus declared, "I think it's time we head elsewhere."

Lenim laughed at this newcomer who thought he could order those he had just met around. In his continued amusement, he cocked his head to the side. "Then I suppose we shall." His words were affable, but his overall demeanor consisting of his wide grin, unreadable eyes, and his incomprehensible motive in general, caused Rhyus to become angrier and unnerved.

With as much patience as he could manage, Rhyus waited for a sign to head for the entryway. To his dismay, Lenim remained still. Everyone in the room remained silent.

Finally, Lenim placed his pale hands upon the chair's arms, pushing himself up from its cushioned seat. He stretched his arms and back. "Ellen," he said to Madam Corvin, a finger beckoning toward the far corner of the kitchen, "a quick word."

As they shared a short conversation, Rhyus and Marion refused to look anywhere near one another.

Lenim swiveled around. "Rhyus, let us take our leave."

The two walked toward the hallway, Rhyus following Lenim's long stride. Marion stepped aside, refusing to give Rhyus a final look or valediction as he made his way past her. He offered her no more of a farewell.

Lenim, on the other hand, swiveled around upon reaching the entryway. "A delight meeting you, Miss Marion. I look very forward to seeing you again this evening at the grand Festus Murus." And as he had done in introducing the city, he gripped the edge of his cape, extending his arm and bowing before her.

Marion nodded cordially. "Yes, until tonight," she bid him farewell.

"Fabulous time, Ellen, as always." Lenim offered Madam Corvin the same act of departure before stepping out. Without a word, Rhyus swiped his bag up off of the floor, swinging the single strap over his head and across his chest. He made his way out the door just after Lenim.

At the last moment, Rhyus turned back with a sort of distracted appreciation. "Thank you again, Madam Corvin."

"Oh, anytime dear," the woman said, presenting that round,

closed-mouth smile. "I will see you tonight then," she added, before turning back into the house and closing the door, leaving Rhyus without a last word.

Madam Corvin moved toward her new guest, giddy with delight that Marion had accepted her offer to spend her stay at her home.

"My dear," a warm smile beamed from her rounded face, "I have a feeling that you would just love a shower about now?"

Marion lit up at the very mentioning. "Oh, I would!" The ear-to-ear smile on Marion's face was genuine to its fullest, and it brought Madam Corvin immense pleasure. The two of them headed upstairs.

Marion looked about as they reached the second floor. Windows lined the left side of the hallway, and a door led out to a balcony about halfway down. Every window had wooden panels on its exterior side with a box filled with flowers in full bloom. Madam Corvin had decorated the balcony with various colored paper lanterns and additional pots of flowers, meticulously spaced along the rail.

Everything in this entire city must be tidy and perfectly in place, Marion speculated, looking about the balcony as Madam Corvin had happily opened the door for her to explore. She enjoyed Marion's cheerful admiration.

Marion stepped back inside and followed Madam Corvin across the hall to the bathroom. She watched her open the linen closet to retrieve a towel, which she set on the far corner of the counter.

"Thank you," Marion said, with a kind smile, as Madam Corvin stepped out of the bathroom.

"Oh, of course, dear," The woman replied, smiling back. "You and your friend, such pleasant visitors," she added. "It's a shame we don't get more visitors around here."

Brushing her last comment aside, she peered back into the bathroom to make sure it was satisfactorily tidy, and then she returned her gaze to her new guest. "I will find something fresh for you to change into. I'll set it out here on a stool for when you are ready. Lucky for us, I just went shopping for a new outfit for the festival, and I happened to pick up a few additional parcels while I was at it." Madam Corvin attempted a guilty, yet cheerful, wink. "Some things for myself and a couple of gifts for Lilly Haddin who helps me with tasks from time to time. Such a pleasant young woman. She's about your size, so you will have some clean clothes until we find something to better suit you."

"Thanks again. I appreciate everything you have done for Rhyus and myself."

"Oh, pish posh. You youngins talk like I'm some sort of saint. I'm only a forty-seven-year-old woman who wants to help others in need. I'll be downstairs. And by the lunar goddesses, do take your time, dear. No hurry. We have plenty of time until the festival." At that, the woman turned to make her way downstairs.

Marion could only think how wonderful Madam Corvin had been to her thus far...and to Rhyus. Quite happy to do so, she stepped into the tidy little bathroom. She sighed with delight. *It has been far too long since I have taken a shower.*

ॐ)ल्ड

"Treat you well, did it?" a smiling Madam Corvin questioned, over the book she was reading from her place at the kitchen table.

"Oh, yes," Marion said. "The best shower I can remember."

"Good," the woman said, pleased, her cheerful demeanor never slipping for a second. "Those clothes are a little big on you, dear, but considering the unexpected need for them, they do fit you close enough. I do have a surprise if you are up for a little walk?"

Marion would normally feel uncomfortable going out into public in these oversized clothes. But considering the scurvy manner in which she had already been walking about the city, she couldn't care less.

"A walk sounds great," Marion said, feeling happier than she had since the last time she had been out about the city of Lux Lumetia with Venn.

"Wonderful then," the woman disrupted Marion's wandering thoughts. Placing a marker in her book, she walked over to the kitchen counter where her large baglike purse sat waiting.

Marion couldn't help but slip another smile. It looked like Madam Corvin was taking her out whether she agreed willingly or not.

"We are blessed that it is such a beautiful day! You really couldn't have picked a better day to arrive." Madam Corvin scurried past Marion who was standing at the edge of the room. "Come along, dear."

Madam Corvin handed Marion her boots. "You won't need that," she assured, as Marion looked over at her Randál Vanaché bag. It had been set in the corner of the entryway, upon the cushion of a wooden chair, which held no purpose other than decoration.

Easily accepting this, Marion allowed Madam Corvin to hold

the door open for her. Pulling keys from her purse, she locked the door and they headed northeast into a part of the city that Marion had not yet seen.

After a ways, Madam Corvin picked up in joyful conversation. "You know, I always wanted a daughter of my own."

Marion smiled at this, but she was unsure quite how to respond.

"Your mother must be a most charming woman, judging by your wonderful character and great beauty."

Marion dropped her eyes to the pale gold walkway. "I don't remember her," she admitted, after a short silence.

"Oh, my dear, I am so sorry." Madame Corvin paused in her tracks, turning to face Marion, worried that she may have said something she should not have.

"No," Marion said, shaking her head and raising her eyes, "it's fine. It has been so long. I mean, yes, I wish I could remember her...but after so many years...I don't remember my father either. But, again, the same holds for him." She offered her hostess a kind look, assuring her that it was OK to bring the topic up.

"Have you no children then?" Marion questioned, steering the conversation back to Madam Corvin's original remark. She started

walking, and the woman automatically picked up her own feet, leading the way once more.

"No, no. You see, dear, I am twice a widow. Unfortunately, neither marriage lasted long enough to bless me with a sweet child of my own."

Now it was Marion's turn to take on the guilt of having dug into a sensitive subject. Nevertheless, she continued walking. She could feel the tug of grief pulling at Madam Corvin's merry demeanor, proving the pain of the subject.

"That is why I am so very glad you decided to stay with me," the woman said, perking up and returning to her strong optimism. "Even if it ends up being only a short couple of days, I will be thankful for whatever time we have to spend together."

Marion found the woman's words touching. For a moment she wondered what her own mother had been like. She had never dwelt much on her clouded past. For the past two years, Venn and Umbra Halls had been her whole world. Her only family of sorts. But instead of bothering her, the thought was comforting. Shaking her head, Marion pushed thoughts of her home in Lux back down. They wouldn't do her any good right now.

The two continued conversing as they moved along, passing

more of the trimmed shrubberies, planted flowers, and fruit and floral trees. The bold colors and the wonderful scents of the city were relaxing, and they created such a different feel from Lux Lumetia. Marion took note of tall lantern posts here and there, though none were lit at this earliest time of evening. The two suns still provided too much light at this hour.

"Here we are," Madam Corvin's voice rang.

Marion came to a standstill beside her, looking at the building to their right. It closely resembled all of the houses they had passed, but wait. "What is this place?" Marion asked.

"FeNelle," Madam Corvin answered. "It's a specialty store. Young women's high-end fashion," she explained, with a guilty, cheerful look on her face. "They sell some of the most remarkable pieces of attire here."

Marion lowered her gaze and shook her head.

"Is something wrong, dear?" A look of concern appeared over Madam Corvin's face.

"It's just that...I don't have any money." Marion felt a bit ashamed. She had always had Venn these last two years to give her money to purchase her expensive clothing. "Rhyus...he is taking care of our expenses," Marion bluffed. She didn't even know whether or not Rhyus had a single bill on him.

"Pish posh. It's on me. I insist!"

Marion could tell how very excited the woman was about this shopping trip, so she simply nodded with a renewed smile.

"Wonderful!" Madam Corvin exclaimed, with a cheery shoulder shrug. "Well, come on then!" She waved her hand for Marion to follow as she moved to the door.

୫୦ଓଃ

Marion and Madam Corvin made their way back to the house after an enjoyable time at FeNelle. They left the store with not one, but two bags filled with so many items that Marion could not thank her hostess enough. They had not only purchased clothes, but also makeup and decorative pieces to wear in her hair at the festival later that night. The bags were simple, black with a script in pale blue reading *FeNelle*. The bags reminded Marion of Randál Vanaché, Lux Lumetia, Umbra Halls, and ultimately Venn. She mentally scolded herself for letting her mind slip to Venn, once again.

Madam Corvin had kindly offered to carry one of Marion's bags, and as they reached the door of the house, Marion took it so that she could fish her keys out of her oversized purse. "Thank you, dear," she said, as she unlocked the door.

"You look so very beautiful!" Madam Corvin said, as they moved inside. She had already told Marion this more than a dozen times. Her hostess had insisted not only to buy her the two bags of items, but she had also made her pick out an entirely new outfit that she could start to enjoy by wearing it home.

"I just can't wait to see you all dressed up for the festival tonight!" Madam Corvin exclaimed. "You will have all of the boys and men drooling!" Marion wasn't sure whether her hostess or she was more excited about the new purchases and the thought of her wearing them at the evening's event.

"All right. You go up to the bedroom, the second door down the hall, and rest. I will get you up after a while, and we will have plenty of time to do your hair and makeup and get you all fancied up before we go."

"Thank you again, so much, for everything." Marion accepted her orders, and taking her old bag as well as the new FeNelle shopping bags, headed up to the bedroom to lie down before the night's festivities really began.

45: Lure of the Sultan

Rhyus stood baffled as Madam Corvin closed the door to leave him facing none other than just that, the door. He spun around to catch up to Lenim who had gained distance already, considering the quickness of his long stride.

Closing the distance, Rhyus adjusted to the speed of Lenim's pace, though choosing to remain a step or so behind.

"Trailing along is a *splendid* way to express a lack of confidence, you know." Lenim said, in a sarcastic tone, not bothering to turn his head in the least.

Rhyus scowled. *Why does everyone think they can just order me around?* Displeased, Rhyus continued to follow behind.

In Lenim's opinion, he had done his share to help. "Suit yourself."

Rhyus wondered where this ghoul of a man might be leading. *He sure seems to have a lot running through his mind all the time. What could he possibly have going on in his life that he feels obligated to think so hard at every passing moment? I'm surprised that he is capable of noticing anything out in the real world around him.*

The two men walked farther from the city's entrance, moving northeast for a while before turning and walking sharply to the east. Rhyus, still content to tag along behind Lenim, spent the majority of the walk through the city staring downward, examining the texture of the walkways. Occasionally, he looked up to take in his unfamiliar surroundings; however, he had decided early on that once you had seen a single block of this city, you have seen it all.

Both Rhyus and Lenim were more than happy to maintain the silence between them as they walked, only the rhythmic pattering of Rhyus's shoes accompanying them. *Probably the most non-awkward silence I could imagine*, Rhyus thought, with curiosity. He continued to watch the path pass beneath him.

Time passed quickly, as Rhyus remained focused on his own thoughts. Glancing down at the watch he had purchased from the odd merchant, Archie, back at the North Market in Lux Lumetia, Rhyus noted that they had been walking for more than half an hour. Not too long, but it seemed they had left Madam Corvin's just minutes ago.

Amongst Rhyus's spiraling thoughts, he saw a clear image of Marion at Madam Corvin's, when he had realized she was up to something. Watching this reenactment, and that look upon her face, his blood began to boil.

His escalating thoughts eventually became too much to contain. He blurted, "I can't stand it!" Even from behind, Rhyus recognized an abrupt adjustment as Lenim was brought back to the here and now. It was like a switch had been flipped.

Continuing to face forward, Lenim asked, in an unreadable tone, "Can't stand what?"

"Marion," Rhyus said. "Why does she have to be so unreasonable?" He shouted the words too loud for Lenim's taste. He cringed, baring his teeth in revulsion.

"She should be somewhere I can keep an eye on her! To look out for her, I mean," Rhyus adjusted his statement. He realized, even in his fuming condition, that the statement made Marion sound suspicious and may therefore lead to questions in Lenim's eyes about both of them.

Lenim tensed a moment longer, making sure that the horrendous shouting had come to an end. Once certain, he swiveled around to face Rhyus.

"The shouting will cease to occur!"

A genuine surge of fear ripped through Rhyus at Lenim's unexpected reaction. Neither of Lenim's two typical faces that Rhyus had become accustomed to showed at this unpleasant moment. Neither the one of sarcasm nor the one that was blank and unreadable.

"For good."

"Y-y—" Rhyus tried for words, but realized they were going to fail him. He forced his eyes away and nodded. Something about Lenim felt all wrong. His sudden hostility, the ominous threat emitting from his dark, unusual eyes, and most important, Rhyus had come across no indication as to who this man really was or what in the world he may be capable of. But no matter the answers to these questions, Rhyus would rather not discover them in this particular way.

Lenim maintained his threatening stance, so unfamiliar to Rhyus. As usual, his eyes remained unblinking, without the slightest sign of strain. This was a sinister Lenim whose eyes pierced the young man before him.

Anxiety flooded Rhyus while the man stood menacing and

motionless, perhaps deciding how to slowly pick him apart into a thousand pieces. Where to begin, where to end? Rhyus dared not move, struggling to take slow breaths so as to not make a sound. He was unsure whether the air he was taking in even reached his lungs at all.

Satisfied with his effect on the young man, Lenim drew back. He shook the long bangs from his face. And as Rhyus dared to look back, the opaque eyes seemed to readjust and focus themselves once again.

It's like he is operated by some outside source, Rhyus thought.

Turning away, Lenim picked up his quick stride where he had left off. "Come on," he said, reverting back to that inscrutable nature of his. "We aren't far."

With still no idea where they were headed, Rhyus picked up his feet. This time, he damn well chose to tag along behind him, directly in his wake. Rhyus didn't want to feel as though Lenim could be watching him out of some abnormal peripheral vision. Not another word was said as they continued on their way.

"We are here," Lenim declared, coming to an abrupt halt. Rhyus, thankful of their arrival, had become accustomed to others stopping like this and managed to avoid colliding with him.

They were one stride from the walkway of another house. It didn't seem particularly different from any other they had passed, with one exception. Every other home and specialty store had been crowded close to one another. This house was set apart, surrounded by a spacious landscape.

It wasn't far from the wall, directly opposite from the point where the city's entrance was set into the enormous barrier. The familiar outdoor scenery was in place—the many fruit and floral trees in neat square patches, lengths of well-trimmed shrubberies, and an abundance of flowers. Walkways wove through the outdoor area, and bright lanterns hung on posts here and there.

Rhyus wondered what made this particular home so special that it sat apart from the rest. Other than its surroundings, it didn't seem out of the ordinary. Charming indeed. But extraordinary? Not in the least. *Wait a minute...Who is he dumping me on?* Rhyus grew irritated as he realized what was happening.

As if on cue, to amplify Rhyus's irritation, a man stepped through the front door and out onto the path leading down to where Rhyus and Lenim stood. He had not yet discovered the two waiting for him. Closing the door, he made it a few steps before spotting the waiting men.

"Ah, Lenim!" the man shouted. He picked up his feet, and with a quick, bouncing stride, hurried to the path's end.

"Yuri," Lenim said, flashing his distinctive grin.

The man moved a pair of pink-lensed sunglasses to the top of his head, returning a hearty smile. The lively quality of his eyes startled Rhyus. A vivacious, orange-amber, it seemed possible that they could lure anyone to him.

His hair, thick with unruly, crimped waves, was pulled back in an attempted low ponytail. His hair, if down, would reach barely past his shoulders, and it refused to stay back. Since the wavy lengths of his hair were layered, some simply sprang loose in a wild, free style. His bangs were momentarily pinned back by his glasses. Brown eyebrows, much too dark for his dirty blond hair, caused his orange-amber eyes to stand out even more.

When he reached Lenim, they gave each other a wholehearted pat on the back. Rhyus noticed that the man was well shorter than either Lenim or himself. As the two men took a single step back, Lenim set his hand on one of the man's shoulders. In unison, they turned toward Rhyus.

Lenim extended his other arm with his open hand toward Rhyus. "Yuri, my friend, this lad here is Rhyus. He will be staying here in The Urbs with us for an undetermined amount of time." Flicking his unblinking eyes to Rhyus, Lenim continued his introduction, "Rhyus, this good man here is Sultan. Pay him the greatest respects, and you will do just fine here."

Sultan? Rhyus thought, at the title.

"I wondered when you would be returning home," the Sultan said, to Lenim. Rhyus couldn't help but watch the man's hypnotic eyes, even from his three-quarter view.

Wait, Rhyus finally processed the words that had just been passed between the two men. *Returning home? Home to the city… or home to this house here in front of us?*

The following conversation did not answer his question, but instead veered completely off the topic and on to others that meant nothing to Rhyus. Giving up hope of gleaning any useful information, Rhyus tuned out, paying attention to nothing, not even his own thoughts for a change.

In his incomprehensive state, Rhyus failed to notice that Lenim and the Sultan had moved to the front door.

"Coming, Rhyus?" the Sultan asked.

"Uh, yeah," he said, scurrying toward the door as they pulled it open.

"Where did you say you were from?" the Sultan asked Rhyus, though neither of them had passed as much as a single word to the other.

"It doesn't matter," Rhyus snapped.

"Ooh, touchy subject?" the Sultan asked, with amused eyes, turning his vivid gaze from Rhyus, who had looked away, to Lenim.

Lenim looked toward the sky and shook his head, emphasizing that Rhyus's attitude was overdramatic and unnecessary. This was just expected conversation between an Urbs dweller and a newcomer.

As they entered the house, *Wow*, was the only word that came to Rhyus. Madam Corvin's house had been nice, welcoming, and recently renovated, but this house was extravagant and beyond.

"So, you are the city's Sultan," Rhyus blurted, in his amazement. He had only heard of cities with a Sultan in stories. Never had he heard of a true Sultan.

Both Lenim and the man entitled Sultan swiveled around with odd, inquiring expressions. Then, turning to one another, they began to laugh hysterically—Lenim with a harsh cackle and the Sultan in a giddy chuckling. Rhyus could only stare. He had no clue what to make of it.

As the Sultan's laughter calmed, Lenim's cackling also slowed as he tried to catch his breath. He slid a single fingertip beneath one watering eye. "Oh my," he laughed, once more.

"His name...His *name* is Yuri Sultan." That very amused grin reappeared as Lenim declared this. "He is not the Sultan. He is just..." he cocked his head in thought, "Well...Sultan." Looking at Rhyus, his laughing grin widened further.

"Uh, right." Rhyus lowered his eyes to the floor.

"I think I would enjoy taking him to find something appropriate to wear to the festival," Sultan said, to Lenim. "Once he has had a wash." Sultan cringed, as he cast a look at Rhyus.

"Be my guest," Lenim said. He waved a dismissive hand, and Sultan understood that he could lead Rhyus off. However, just as Sultan led the young man away, Lenim couldn't help but release another short burst of cackling.

46: *Festus Murus*

Late night had finally arrived, and with it a blackened blue sky accompanied by dancing flashes of lights and the sound of upbeat, celebratory music. Most importantly, it had brought with it the beginning of Festus Murus.

Rhyus walked with Lenim and Sultan as they left the house. He had learned that it was Lenim's house, but his friend, Yuri Sultan, was staying with him while his new home was being built. His had mysteriously gone up in flames, along with all of his worldly possessions.

The Grounds, their destination, was located at the very center of the city. The Urbs, as Lenim often referred to the city—short for Urbs Cereris Arcanae. Then again, it was everyone's destination. Somns moved over the golden walkways near and far, all making their way to where the festival was to be held.

Rhyus jumped as a small cannon fired, sending a bright flash of light high into the air. It whistled and whirred, separating into hundreds of individual, shimmering lights that spiraled madly about. The cannons had been going off for half an hour now, but this one was very nearby and caught Rhyus quite off guard.

"Anxious?" Lenim asked. He was clearly looking forward to the night's upcoming festivities. Sultan had also turned Rhyus's way with his own dashing smile in response to Rhyus's jumpiness. He gave a short, jovial laugh.

They wore masquerade masks. Lenim's covered over his eyes and nose while Sultan's covered most of his face but left his mouth and lower left side uncovered. Though he tried, Rhyus was unable to extricate himself from wearing a mask. His hosts were most persistent.

All three were dressed in extravagance from head to toe, costumes of true fashion. Sultan and Lenim had taken Rhyus to an exclusive male boutique where they had happily paid for everything. They had a ball making him try things on, finding just the right outfit for him to wear to the festival.

Rhyus had decided that it must be a rare opportunity for them to get out and do something of the sort. Most surprising was that, starting at the boutique, Rhyus found himself having a good time with these men. He enjoyed sharing in their hearty banter, even if they were a bit off. And more unexpected was that Rhyus looked forward to the night's events as much as Lenim and Sultan.

Conveniently, The Grounds was a straight shot from Lenim's house. They moved along walkways that shimmered in the warm glow of a multitude of colored lanterns. With every step, they could hear the celebration picking up steam.

Walking by rows of aligned floral and dripfruit-blossom trees, in white, pink, and red, they eagerly passed a waist-high sandstone wall that surrounded the grassy area bordering The Grounds, moving through one of four entrances at the cardinal directions.

Sultan nudged Rhyus as they approached the congregational area where Festus Murus was to be celebrated to its fullest. "Watch this."

Lenim broke free from the outer perimeter and out onto the short path to the center ground. Rhyus began to follow, but Sultan pulled him back with a firm hand on his shoulder. Confused, he faced Sultan with a questioning expression, though his mask mostly concealed it.

"Watch." Sultan waved his forefinger in a single circular motion before pointing back to Lenim who had proceeded onto a triangular dance floor, defined by its warm, sandstone flooring. Three golden paths led to its points. Along one of the floor's flat edges were three stepped, elliptical platforms of varying heights, two in the front with the tallest centered behind. They were all made of pale gold sandstone. Delicate waterfalls trickled down the geshem walls lining The Ground's rectangular perimeter, and fountains were placed in the two corners nearest to Sultan and Rhyus.

"Here it comes." Sultan's smile returned, set perfectly into the lower curve of his mask. Watching, Rhyus saw Lenim working his way up to the highest platform.

Standing face to face with a man who, up to this point, had been the sole occupant of the platforms, Lenim extended his elaborate, decorated cape, bowing in his typical way. The short, stout man returned a similar gesture but was nowhere near as flashy or compelling.

Everyone was instantly drawn to Lenim's presence on the high platform. A wave of silence fell over The Grounds, leaving only the boom of the cannons with all of the whistling and whirring sounds of their soaring lights.

Although unnecessary, considering that he already held the attention of everyone present, Lenim accepted the small microphone from the short man who offered it up with enthusiasm. He slid the ring base of the microphone onto his forefinger as he had a hundred times before.

"Good evening ladies and gents! Are we ready for a celllllebration?" Lenim's voice projected charismatically as he stretched the last word for effect. He raised his eyebrows, his grin making itself known. The crowd issued wild shouts and cheers. Some somns jumped about, whistling loudly.

Sultan smiled at Rhyus. "The crowd sure loves him, wouldn't you say?" He flaunted his eyebrows a single time, though they were hidden behind his mask. Like earlier in the day, his wavy, dirty blonde hair was pulled back into a low ponytail.

"Sure seem to. Maybe they're just excited for the celebration?"

"Oh no." Sultan shook his head. "They are certainly excited for the festival, without doubt, but these somns love Lenim to death." He smiled again. "Got charisma, doesn't he?" He gave a good-humored laugh.

"I guess I couldn't say otherwise." Rhyus let a smile of his own slip and turned back to watch Lenim up on the platform.

"Where is York?" Lenim asked, extending a hand upward in question. A section of the crowd began to holler again, and turning his head, Rhyus saw an average-built man in black and green walk out onto the dance floor.

"Ah, York! Where are your men, good sir?"

"Heading to where they belong." The man directed his sight to a section of grass to the right of the dance floor.

"Splendid," Lenim said. York's men were situating themselves amongst their instruments. They paused, nodding their heads and waving. Lenim, as expected, bowed to them. "York," Lenim said, returning his attention to the man on the dance floor.

"Yes, Lenim?" The man's mask was similar to Sultan's, but his hooked down around both sides of his mouth.

Lenim brought the microphone back to his lips. Turning his head just scarcely to the side, he grinned again, "Play us something *festive*, won't you?"

"Absolutely!" York bowed, moving over to his men.

"Let the evening begin!" Lenim threw both arms into the air. At this exact moment, a strip of water geysers shot up along the back edge of The Grounds, just behind the platform. Lights illuminated the geysers, changing color in unison with the music from green, to violet, and then to a bright orange, as they shot several yards into the air.

Lenim kept his arms raised and head thrown back as the geysers continued to dance. Everyone shouted and cheered even more, jumping up and rushing to the dance floor, some beginning to dance right where they stood. As Lenim dramatically thrust his head forward, arms back down to his sides, the geysers vanished. "Ladies and gents, Festus Murus!" With this, the musicians began to play. And just as was requested of them, their tune was loud, upbeat, and all in all festive.

Lenim removed the small microphone from his forefinger, tossing it into a floating orb placed near the narrow set of stairs. The orb caught it, holding it until another wished to put it to use.

As somns began to dance and socialize amongst one another, Lenim made his way back down to ground level. Numerous pairs of eyes followed as he moved through the crowd, but they left him his space unless he deliberately engaged them in conversation.

"Come on!" Without warning, Sultan grabbed Rhyus's arm, pulling him to the nearest large, geshem bin. The bins, Rhyus discovered, were filled with ice and various alcoholic beverages. Sultan informed that the smaller, silver bins were filled with beverages for the youngins. He accepted a bottle as Sultan handed it out to him.

"Will the whole town show?"

"Oh, yes. No one would miss it for the world."

Rhyus and Sultan conversed, mingling with others as they enjoyed the evening. Every so often, they returned to the geshem bins for another round of drinks for either themselves or others.

Sultan nudged Rhyus, whispering, "You're lucky you are wearing a mask. If everyone knew you were from elsewhere, you would be positively swarmed!" Rhyus realized this was probably true. Sure enough, later into the night, the somns who conversed with Sultan became increasingly curious of his new friend.

Several hours into the celebration, the music came to a temporary halt. Turning around, everyone noticed that Lenim had returned to the high platform. He raised his arms for silence, and everyone obeyed. "I have a request," he said, eyes moving over the crowd. "Where is the lovely Miss Marion, my new friend from afar?" Lenim's mask and clothing were dazzling in the artfully placed lights as he turned side to side.

Once again, a section of The Grounds erupted with enthusiasm. A spotlight fell over a young woman as those around her insisted that she step forward. Although shy, she moved forward, the light following her every move.

"Ah, Miss Marion," Lenim greeted her. He turned briefly, signaling to York and his men. He then looked back toward Marion at the opposite end of The Grounds. Grabbing the edge of his cape, he bowed low. Standing back up, tall and slender, he extended an inviting hand. "I would love to request this dance."

This drew a wide range of reactions. Cheering, shouting, and ohs and ahs mixed in with the buzz of the crowd. Returning the microphone to the orb a second time, Lenim descended to the dance floor. With long strides, he approached Marion who stood still as he drew near. Her striking outfit was accompanied by an equally attractive mask, attached to a long stem that she held in her hand. She lowered the mask, revealing her face.

"She is stunning, that one," Sultan crooned, not processing the fact that Rhyus and she had come to Urbs Cereris Arcanae together, nor how he might feel about this comment. Then again, he was right. She looked incredible, to say the least.

Lenim bowed again before looking her in the eye and extending a hand. "May I?"

She nodded and smiled, flushing, and then accepted his hand, answering, "Yes." He spun her a single time with her arms high in the air. With another grin and a nod, he led her out onto the floor.

A path cleared before them, and in reaching the floor, Lenim raised his arms. With a double clap of his hands, York turned back to his men, and they began to play another upbeat tune. Lenim in the lead, Marion and he looked like naturals as they danced over the cleared circle on the triangular floor.

Somns around continued to cheer, dance, and clap their hands to the music while Marion and Lenim enjoyed their moment together as the center of attention. Lenim was quite used to such a thing, but Marion, on the other hand, was not. Nonetheless, she took great pleasure in the occasion. Her dress twirled with her movements, and Lenim's cape swayed with every skilled step.

Sultan nudged Rhyus again with his elbow. "I think you need another drink." He smiled at the way Rhyus had been gawking at Lenim and Marion's flawless choreography, perfect to the point that one might think the two had rehearsed diligently prior to this night.

Rhyus pulled his eyes from the dance floor, turning to face

Sultan who let out a chuckle. "Bet you'd like to have a dance with that one," Sultan said, with a smile. "But good luck showing up my man, Lenim," he laughed again. Over the music, which had just raised a few levels in volume, he shouted, "Come on!" He angled his head, directing Rhyus to follow, and they weaved their way to the nearest geshem bin.

After uncapping a couple more drinks, Sultan dragged Rhyus out to the dance floor where somns outside the ring of those surrounding Lenim and Marion were dancing energetically and jumping about. They joined other ladies and gents in dancing and throwing their arms into the air at appropriate times with the music. They hollered and cheered with the rest of the crowd.

Having enjoyed many, many drinks up to this point, Rhyus's head was swimming by the time Marion and Lenim's dance came to an end. Along with everyone else, they turned toward the circle where Lenim and Marion now stood. Everyone threw his or her hands back into the air, cheering and whistling.

Lenim offered Marion another low bow. "And to my lovely partner on the floor!" he shouted, aiming another pleased grin toward Marion who curtsied to the circling crowd. A wide smile showed on her face, and her fair skin remained flushed beneath her mask from both the unfamiliar attention, as well as the heat from all the dancing.

Lenim reached out a hand, and Marion accepted it, placing her own into it. He pulled her hand toward him as he leaned forward, landing a gentle kiss. "Well done, my gorgeous lady. A true honor." His pleased grin encompassed his thin, yet very defined lips and his midnight eyes. He released the light grip on her hand and nodded, motioning with a single hand that she could take her leave to pursue her own path for the remainder of the night.

Marion left the circle, still being cheered, as she broke through its border. She rejoined the group of young women she had been enjoying the evening with prior to the unexpected invitation. They all welcomed her back, handing off a bottle and her mask. They giggled and snuck glances back toward Lenim before he too took his leave from the floor. The now empty circle soon filled with others who proceeded in their lively dancing.

Lenim wandered to where he had spotted Sultan and Rhyus, moving from the floor toward one of the geshem bins. "Hello, chaps," he said, placing a hand on each of their shoulders, making himself a place between them. "Having a splendid time, are we?"

"Oh, don't you know," Sultan smiled charmingly, his orange-amber eyes shining through the eyeholes of his mask.

"Excellent," Rhyus replied, as Lenim turned his way, expecting a further response. The alcohol was apparent in his speech, and Lenim grinned with amusement.

"Fabulous!" He pulled his arms down, reaching between them to the bin. Retrieving three more bottles, he uncapped them simultaneously on the side of the bin. "Cheers!" he shouted, raising his bottle. Rhyus and Sultan met him in the air, bottles clinking merrily.

Sultan took a large swallow before repeating, "Cheers!"

"Cheers!" Rhyus echoed.

"The night is still young," Lenim implied, in a hushed voice, then added, "Bottom's up!" with more volume, flaring his roguish eyebrows. He raised his bottle a second time, and they tilted back their bottles, draining every last drop.

47: Naughty, Naughty

A smile met Helena's lips as she heard knocking on her door. Not just any knock. She would recognize this pattern any day. Or night. For that was when it typically called out to her.

Tossing Serlio Young's book aside, she leapt up from the couch. After her meeting with Serlio at Scribe's Den, Helena had walked the long trip home. There were trams for faster travel, but knowledgeable somns in her sort of underground work never used them. They were too high-risk.

The somns hired by The Tower authorities to run the trams were given the job for a very specific reason. They were generally mentally unstable, but at least capable of their simple job: run the tram and watch the somns who get on and off through the single set of doors.

Their greatest skill was their memory. The Tower's trick didn't always work according to plan—less so, now that those high in the Underworld had learned of it. However, if any incident occurred of concern to The Tower, the Black Guard would speak to the tram runners, asking about who had boarded during the time of the incident. The Tram runners would always remember a somn. Every goddamn detail. Appearance. Location. Time of sighting. Creepier yet, they would recall any other time and place they had seen that very somn. "Goyrots" the Underworld called them. Like the nasty, oily muck called goyrot that was slapped onto the tram wheels to make them move faster, as they rattled on their tracks throughout the city.

But the walk had been rejuvenating. A positive energy filled Helena from head to toe as she made her way. She nearly broke into a skip halfway home.

Once inside, she had taken care of some quick chores. Then she had heated up a mug of hot mallow and plopped down on her couch with Serlio's book on her lap. She never once opened it. Her mind was far too busy running through what had happened. The things she had read, the story he had told, and the expectations of the following day.

With the warmth from the fire and the glow of excitement within, she had sat for hours in undisturbed silence. She couldn't believe that she had finally found the key to the knowledge she needed to find the loose Calling. And who would have thought—it was Albert Young's grandfather.

The rhythmic knocking came again, and Helena's smile widened as she scurried to answer the door. She smoothed down the little charcoal dress she had earlier changed into. And then she proceeded to unfasten the many locks standing between her and her caller. Pausing, she bent one knee slightly and placed a hand on her hip. Biting her cheek, she slowly opened the door.

"Helena," said a man a handful of years older than she. Golden highlights of his brown hair shone in the dim light of the lantern near her door. He held a bouquet of many long-stemmed blue-violet flowers. They were in full bloom, and Helena savored their powerful scent.

"Cupio?" she asked, with a grin.

"Their color. A reflection of Goddess Ravenna. The only woman as beautiful as yourself." He displayed a closed-lip smile, revealing deep-set dimples framing a triangular chin, as he offered the flowers.

Helena accepted, shaking her head playfully at the aphrodisiac she had been gifted. "Oh, Albert—you are a very naughty, naughty man."

Taking her reaction as an invitation, Albert stepped forward—closing what little space stood between them. As he reached around, placing a hand on her neck, Helena tilted her head back. She happily met his kiss, laughing when it unexpectedly ended, as he swept her off her feet.

Helena laughed again as Albert carried her, shifting through the doorway as they went. Stepping into her home, he easily kicked the door shut, without losing his grip on her.

"Lock it!" Helena said, in full laughter now, as he started kissing her neck—still standing in the entryway. With his lips still pressed against her skin, she heard—and felt—the laugh, which served as his response. "Albert!"

He pulled back, chuckling as his cool gray eyes met hers. "OK, OK," he said, "but you're not going anywhere." With Helena still secure in his hold, he turned to lock the door. Once done, he moved to the sitting room where a fire had already been lit.

"You know…" he said softly, pulling a bag off over his shoulder and setting it on the ground.

"Hmm?" Helena said, kissing at his ear.

"You must have bewitching powers. My grandfather doesn't like anyone…and I mean anyone…but you've got him all wrapped around your finger. He was grinning ear to ear when he told me about your visit today. And more unbelievable, he gave me a package for you."

"A package?" Helena pulled back, looking Albert in the eye. Her face was serious. Quickly however, her smile returned. She traced a finger over one of his tented eyebrows, as the wonderful feelings she had felt upon leaving Scribe's Den returned. "Oh Albert!" she said, wrapping her arms around him.

He looked at the couch, then at Helena. "This celebration calls for something special." His closed-lip smile showed again.

Moving to the kitchen, he propped his foot on a chair. Helena cast him a curious look as he pulled her to sit on his bended knee. He winked, and with a single hand, pulled off three flower blooms. Reaching around her he ripped them apart, showering the blue-violet petals over the table.

He gave Helena a smile as she shook her head. She waved her finger. "Naughty, naughty." Discarded, the bouquet fell to the floor.

Albert unzipped his jacket, and Helena pushed it from his shoulders to the floor. Ripping open his shirt, she sent it there as well.

Quickening, she unfastened his belt and denims. Snaking her arms around him, she pulled him close. Albert slid her onto the table and leaned in, gripped her thighs. Slowly, he slid his hands up under her dress, cupping her full breasts. Pressing against him, she could feel the burning heat of his desire.

Matching his desire, Helena lay back on the petal-covered table, pulling Albert with her. Instantly, they became as one.

৪০৫৪

"Well, Helena," Albert picked up his bag, crossing the strap over his chest.

She walked over and took a seat on the couch. Looking up at him, she smiled. What they had between them was far from true love. Nevertheless, she truly enjoyed their little get-togethers.

"Oh, I almost forgot." Unzipping his bag, he retrieved the package he had come to deliver. He leaned forward, placing it in Helena's hands. Placing a gentle hand on her cheek, he planted one last kiss.

Then he turned and made his way to the door. Unfastening the locks he opened the door. Pausing, he looked back at Helena with package in hand. "I tell you, pretty lady. That package had damn well be worth my trip out here." With a wink, he stepped out the door.

48: Return to the Grand Theatre

KyVeerah looked deep into Cassandra's eyes as she reached up, placing her hands on his neck and the side of his face. He could tell she was genuinely worried about him. When she told him to be careful, she didn't mean only for her brother's sake, but for himself as well. Her concern for her brother was a given.

Unmoving, KyVeerah stood as the warmth of her hands seeped into his cool skin. "Yes, I shall," he assured, as he turned quickly, causing her hands to fall from him a second time. He pulled the door open, descended the stone steps, and moved far down the walkway before he heard the sound of the closing door. Until that point, he could feel her eyes watching his every step, as he made his way from CavonRué.

Exiting the Fannin District, he began the lengthy trip back west. It took time, but he eventually stepped across the invisible divider into the Caulder District. *If I weren't in shape...*the brief thought skipped across his mind, as he ended his day's second rapid journey across the city.

Finally, he found himself standing again before the Grande Theatre Casavella. He paused, staring into the imitation mirrors, waiting for his heartbeat to return to normal. The city's reflection appeared just as impressive in the daylight. Again, placing his hand up before him, he stepped through the pseudo-mirror.

With quick strides, he passed over the palette of greens and between the stone tables and chairs. It was mid-afternoon, not bad considering the immense distance he had covered. Most somns would take far longer to accomplish the tasks that he had already undertaken and fulfilled.

Moving back around the high tower, stage right, KyVeerah ascended the wide stairs. His boots met the geshem surface of the stage, which reflected the suns' light much more vividly than its sister element, crystal, could even conceive.

He did not pause this time. The wheels of his mind rotated in a different direction than on his previous stop here in the early morning darkness. His lengthy walk had given him time to decide how to best care for Jude.

Pushing through the single door, KyVeerah traversed the dim hallway behind the stage without need for light. Throwing open the doors to the preparation room, his blood roiled at the sight before him. He hollered, "Ruby!"

She had fallen sound asleep, her unconscious frame lying a mere foot from Jude's own still body.

Ruby Hale jumped at KyVeerah's sudden outburst. Blinking rapidly, she turned to face in the direction of his voice.

"For the love of Valencia, what do you think you are doing? How the hell can you monitor him when you're dead to the world!" His shouted words seethed acid as he hurled them her way.

"Oh, by the moons above, chill out, I was only resting my eyes." Her lethargic words still reeked of deep sleep.

He rolled his eyes, along with his head in outrage. "Yeah, right." Trying to avoid a violent confrontation, he turned away, pacing with a ringed hand before his face, as he muttered to himself.

Finally turning back around, he glowered Hale's way once more, saying something incoherent before kneeling down to place a cold hand on Jude's face. His breathing was slow and steady, and his eyes flinched at KyVeerah's touch.

With both hands, KyVeerah pushed Jude's hair back. Still looking down, he snapped his eyes back to Hale who had finally struggled up onto a single arm, just as she had been when he entered this same room this morning.

"Shit, woman! I didn't leave you alone with my man so that you could take a damn doze beside him!"

Hale gaped with pouted lips.

"There would be no need to take offense if you had done nothing wrong. Wouldn't you say, love?"

She met him with a glare now. "Fine," she spat, "then *you* can take care of him on your own."

"I have already made arrangements."

"Well, good for you," she spat again. Shoving herself up from the stone floor, she stomped toward the doors, her heels clicking against the floor with attitude. "I wish you luck, Vincent. I have a very strong feeling that you are going to need it." She turned her head back to the doors, long strands of sharp, golden waves flying over her shoulder as she made her overdramatic exit.

KyVeerah could hear as Hale moved through the single door, down the stone steps, and over the considerable stretch of grass toward the theatre's entrance.

"Damn!" He hadn't planned on being so brutish in telling her that he had figured things out, but the sight of her sleeping on the job, when responsible for his dear friend, had infuriated him. *He could have died!* KyVeerah let out a heavy breath, hating the feeling of emptiness filling him now that she was gone. He turned back around to face Jude.

He couldn't have told Hale his plan, and she sure as hell couldn't have helped him carry it out. KyVeerah realized that there was no way he could take proper care of Jude and keep a careful enough watch over him. Too much was going on right now, and it was imperative that he keep the hounds at bay until Jude was whole again.

Taking Jude back to CavonRué was the only option. Cassandra should be the one to care for him. *But I can't get him all the way there by myself*, KyVeerah pondered. *I couldn't possibly have let Hale assist. It would be foolish to lead her to their home. Especially as she spends her time these days, working for Galton. It would have been most careless.* He nodded in self-agreement.

Twisting his lips in thought, he looked back at Jude. *How in the world...?*

Then he caught sight of an option. Releasing another heavy breath, KyVeerah moved a weary hand through his hair.

There is only one way.

49: The Demand for a Decision

"Venn!" KyVeerah hollered, proceeding through The Courtyard of Umbra Halls.

"Venn!" he shouted again, his eyes following up along the great tree, through the second-story opening where it rose.

Finally, he heard the sound of Venn's boots coming from the den where KyVeerah had assumed he would be. The door to the den opened and Venn shouted down, though not appearing over the rail. "You can't keep leaving like that, Vincent," he scolded, louder than necessary considering his knowledge of KyVeerah's keen hearing. He walked through the main hallway above, his voice becoming more distressed. "One of these days, someone is going to inform me that you got yourself killed, and I won't be aware that you had even left!"

There was no reply. Assuming KyVeerah was choosing to ignore him, Venn gave up his distant reprimand.

Venn burst through the double doors at the head of The Courtyard and walked briskly toward KyVeerah. "Now, what is it that you are holl—" Venn stopped mid-sentence. His attention had been fully focused on KyVeerah, but now it was torn away.

"What in Blue Ravenna?" Venn continued toward KyVeerah. "What *the* hell?"

"I need your help." KyVeerah shoved his shades up with the back of his hand. With eyes exposed, he met Venn's gaze as he came to a halt just feet away.

Venn could see the genuine need in KyVeerah's eyes. "Please, Venn."

Unsure how to react, Venn moved closer to the man KyVeerah was more than half carrying. "What, in the name of Ravenna have you done, Vincent?" His gaze shifted back to KyVeerah, and he could sense the guilt locked behind those violet eyes.

"Are these two his only wounds?" Venn questioned. He couldn't truly see them because of thick, fresh bandages, however he assumed they were serious taking into account the man's lethargy and the manner in which KyVeerah was approaching the situation.

"Yes."

"Here." Venn put an arm forward. "Let me take him." Venn's tone was cutting, but his actions proved his desire to help. Jude flinched with a small groan as Venn accepted his weight.

KyVeerah nodded once more, displaying his appreciation. Venn wasn't very fond of helping KyVeerah out with the frequent messes he got himself into, but for some reason, this hit him differently.

"Let's get him inside."

Leading the way back through the forged double doors and up the stairs, Venn reached the second floor and hung a right, into the kitchen. Crunching across the crystal shards left from the chessboard tragedy the night of KyVeerah's arrival, Venn pushed through another door.

They entered a large dining room with an extended table and numerous elegant chairs. For some reason, Marion had always maintained this room, ridding it of dust and filth. Perhaps she hoped they would use it someday. But the likeliness of that was not high at all.

"Vincent, get a rag to wipe down this table."

KyVeerah ducked into the kitchen, and then reappeared to do as he had been instructed.

Venn laid Jude on the table, pushing some of the surrounding chairs against a set of beautiful, antique display cases filled with dishware and impressive trinkets dating further back than the cases themselves. Everything within this room was worth a fortune. The window on the opposite wall stretched the full length of the room. It looked out over the uninhabited outskirts of Lux Lumetia where only forested areas and beaches were found.

As Venn studied Jude's bandages, a curious look fell over his face. "Vincent?"

KyVeerah looked up. He had also been looking down at Jude.

He was puzzled, as Venn seemed to tap his index finger on an invisible wall. KyVeerah looked downward, following the intangible path created by Venn's pointing finger.

"Your bandages, you numbskull."

KyVeerah still didn't quite understand what he was getting at.

"Did the same somn who bandaged this man put those bandages on you?"

Ah, realization hit him. Venn's peculiar face now made sense. "Uh…" KyVeerah extended and curled in his fingers down at his sides. He then raised a hand and scratched briefly at a point just behind his temple.

"I will take that as a yes." Venn returned his attention to the man on the table. "What is his name?"

"Jude." KyVeerah looked at the floor, as he supplied the answer. He didn't give answers so easily to anyone. But things were different when it came to his relationship with Venn.

"What happened to him?"

"It doesn't matter."

Venn threw him a look.

KyVeerah exhaled, exasperated. "He was jumped. Kind of...but yeah. And that's as much as his sister knows. And that is exactly where we have to take him. To his sister."

"Uh, huh."

KyVeerah paced the room, as Venn peeled back the bandages over Jude's neck.

"Goddamn!" An utter look of disgust fell over Venn's face. "What the hell did this guy get sliced with? A fucking steak knife?" He abhorred the thought of someone using such a deeply serrated weapon. Plainly not a proper weapon for slitting throats—not that Venn approved of throat slitting in most matters.

Slowing his pace, KyVeerah cringed as Venn removed the bandages from Jude's arm. "Oh, shit." Venn's look of repulsion continued. This was also the work of a serrated blade, but not the same one. This one was long and sharp. Venn's eyes narrowed. The knife had perforated the brachial artery.

"When did this happen?"

"Yesterday. Mid-afternoon. It wasn't too terribly long before I returned here."

Venn thought for a moment. "Well, at least it's clear that he has been well taken care of to this point." Another pause. "Where does his sister live?"

"He lives with her. They live over in Fannin."

Venn's eyes snapped back to KyVeerah. "Fannin? As in the Fannin *District* located at the entirely opposite corner of Lux Lumetia?"

KyVeerah twisted his mouth in thought. "Yeah, kinda...but at least they don't live in Ripolis." KyVeerah offered a hopeful look.

"They might as well! It's the only damn place east of Fannin!"

"Way to be optimistic."

"What?"

"Nothing, nothing."

"Just get out of here." Venn turned back to Jude. "I'll clean and bandage these back up. We will take him home in the morning."

Accepting this decision, KyVeerah exited the room as quietly as he could, though it was difficult with the scattered crystal shards he had to traverse in the kitchen. He headed downstairs, away from Jude. Away from Venn.

෯)෴

"Where are you?"

The voice entered KyVeerah's mind after Venn and he had taken a few hours to themselves.

"In The Courtyard," he replied, in thought.

His eyes were closed with his head leaned back against the wall, shades on top of his head. So many things were spiraling through his mind. He just needed time to relax.

Footsteps echoed from the ground-level hallway to the west of The Courtyard, the hall where Marion's room and the guest bedroom were. He focused on the steady footfalls as Venn approached more casually than normal. KyVeerah had seated himself, legs crossed, upon one of the benches on the east side of The Courtyard.

His eyes opened as Venn approached, taking a seat on the bench next to him.

Venn also leaned back against the wall, ankles crossed. They sat in silence.

Venn eventually broke the silence. "You know, I read an article in the *Lux Lately* about Beck Scofflin's little frenzy last night. It sounds like he did some damage, but Mona and her mother who owns the bar are both fine."

"Who?"

"From the Crimson Glass last night. From the bar."

"Uh huh." KyVeerah was not interested. In a mocking manner, he asked, "What about that attractive bartender, the one with the dark hair?" Eyes still closed, he flared his eyebrows, showing a tremendous lack of respect or sensitivity toward the evening's occurrence. In all honesty, he held no concern for the woman.

Venn rolled his eyes in irritation. "Yes. She is fine as well." He disapproved of KyVeerah's disdainful attitude.

KyVeerah broke the returned silence.

"Umm, I have a snippet of information," KyVeerah confessed. Venn only turned his eyes before he continued, "I'm pretty sure that Rhyus and Marion have left Lux Lumetia. Its entire borders." KyVeerah ducked in apprehension at Venn's coming response.

Venn had been unusually caring and was bound to come out of it sooner or later.

"What?" Venn asked, part in irritation and part in disbelief at the absurd idea. The mention of either Rhyus or Marion had become a rather sensitive subject.

"Remember what your *child source* said about that man's boat?"

Venn offered a mere look, pressing him to go on.

"Well, I think Rhyus and Marion may have taken it. Quite certain, as a matter of fact."

"Why in the world would you say that?"

"Well, think about it." KyVeerah counted the points on his fingers. "It seems obvious that Rhyus wanted to get away, most likely as far away as possible. And the boat was stolen on the very morning that they ran away." KyVeerah gave a side-glance, displaying his displeasure over Venn's letting them slip out from under his watch. "To a thinking person, it would be a simple conclusion."

"Son of a bitch."

"What?" KyVeerah's eyes snapped back to Venn, both curious and concerned. "What did you do?"

Venn had a self-irritated look on his face. "I mentioned The Rafters to Rhyus the day before he left."

KyVeerah's eyes widened. "You did *what*?"

"He needed to start learning *something*. Oh, and I also mentioned them damn ruffians nowadays who *call* themselves Rafters as they attempt to cross The Darkness. Damn rookies."

"Oh, good lord!" KyVeerah jumped up from his seat, throwing his hands up.

"Wait." Venn leaned forward, resting his forearms on his legs. "Why would they take that man's boat? It's not like either of them knows jack shit about sailing."

KyVeerah winced.

"What now?"

"It wasn't just any boat. It was from the Philosopher's Collection."

"So?" Venn didn't see any significance.

"You see…it just so happens that I took Marion out on a Philosopher's boat at a point in time before bringing her here."

"But it's not like she can sail the thing, Vincent."

"Actually," KyVeerah raised a finger, "I showed her how to control it. And they are automatic, Venn. Quite simple to learn. Once learned, it would be easy to figure out again."

"You have got to be kidding! Why would—" Venn began.

KyVeerah jerked his gaze to the small, metal gate.

"What is it?" Venn asked, not seeing anything suspicious.

"I'll be right back."

Venn was curious, but he nodded. If KyVeerah wanted him to go, he would have mentioned the fact, even if he expected to get turned down.

KyVeerah moved toward the entrance and out into the abandoned alleyway. With soundless steps, he crept to the alley's far end. Careful, sensing the right moment, he leaned from the protective covering of the building he was right up against.

Sure enough. No more than a dozen yards away stood a man. Perhaps not so peculiar, if this weren't the abandoned Caulder District. Nobody had come through in years.

Further, KyVeerah knew this man. His hair was short and dirty blonde with a matching goatee and dark eyebrows. His features wore a look of conceit. Without seeing them, KyVeerah could sense his cold blue eyes.

Tyson. Galton's man. KyVeerah had seen him just once before, during his recent trip to The Hinge with Jude. Jory had set Tyson to stand guard over Jude, and Tyson had set his hands on the back of the chair, a large knife in one of them. KyVeerah had hated him immediately.

There was only one reason he could be here that wouldn't mean KyVeerah was in a very dangerous position.

KyVeerah slowly pulled his knife. With a quiet swiftness, he closed the distance between them.

By the time Tyson had an inkling what was happening, it was too late. KyVeerah lunged, knocking Tyson down to his knees, forcing his arm behind his back with the curved blade at his throat.

"Tyson," KyVeerah hissed, in greeting. Tyson gave a sharp cry as his knees landed on the compressed ground. Good thing for KyVeerah's sake that no one else was around to hear his cry.

KyVeerah pressed the blade harder against his neck, though not hard enough to cause any real damage. As long as he didn't move.

"I know who you are. What is your business here?" KyVeerah demanded, wrenching Tyson's arm further back.

Tyson cried out again. "I was looking for *you!*"

"Well, here I am. What do you want?"

"Galton." The man's heart raced now.

"What about him?" KyVeerah hissed, his ominous words

needing to travel only inches.

"H-he wanted me to give you something."

"Then where is it?" KyVeerah whispered the words, with malevolence, into the man's ear.

"It's in my pocket. In m-my jacket pocket," the man stammered, sweat beading at the edges of his dirty blonde hair.

Not so intimidating now, huh? Again, KyVeerah pictured as this very man stood behind his dear friend, Jude, the knife in hand. Who could say this man had nothing to do with what happened to Jude? He had been in the room when KyVeerah had been downstairs with Galton in the interest of private business and a drink.

"Fetch it," KyVeerah ordered. "And if you pull anything, I swear to god, I will slit your pretty little throat."

Hand shaking, Tyson reached into an inner jacket pocket. Sweat rolled down the side of his face, some into his goatee.

Attentive, KyVeerah watched the man's hand emerge from beneath his jacket. In his hand were some ash-colored pieces of folded paper. His hand continued to tremble as he raised them into the air.

"Put them in my front jacket pocket. The one you can reach on the right."

Tyson looked dubious but kept his mouth shut. Swallowing hard, his throat shifted against the razor-sharp blade. Blood trickled down his neck.

Once Tyson had placed the folded papers into KyVeerah's pocket, he recoiled, pulling his arm back to his side.

"Is that all?"

"Y-yes."

"Good. Then get the hell out of here." KyVeerah shoved the man from his grasp, but in doing so, he made sure to leave a reciprocation slice in Tyson's neck, deep enough to scar for remembrance, though not deep enough to cause any vital damage. It resembled that which Tyson's comrade, Hewitt, left on Jude's neck. But KyVeerah's mark was sharp and clean, civil by the standards of such an area of business, unlike the tattered rip to scar his own man.

Tyson threw a hand up to his neck when he was released, resentment flashing in his eyes. He remained kneeling. His knees would be severely bruised, if not worse. He knew that he was in no position to fight, particularly against someone as proficient as this man who even his superior held in extremely high regard.

"What are you waiting for?" KyVeerah threw his head back,

offering to take on any challenge. A fair distance lay between the two of them.

Cringing, Tyson forced himself from the ground. Pain emanated from his knees.

KyVeerah maintained a vital distance but made sure to keep near enough to remain a threat. Tyson turned his head back to send one last look of animosity. Then, with difficulty, he started south.

"Be sure to pass my regards along to your superior," KyVeerah yelled after Tyson, who fighting the pain in his knees and throat, made distance as quickly as he could.

Tyson responded with an obscene gesture, and KyVeerah showed a small grin. He was certain his message would find its way back to Galton. And for the mark on his neck, they had that coming. As KyVeerah retrieved the ashen papers and unfolded them, the characteristic grin grew over his lips.

ℰℭ

Venn stood from the stone bench where KyVeerah had left him. "What happened?" he asked, taking a few steps closer. KyVeerah shoved the shades to the top of his head.

"Oh, nothing." KyVeerah shook his head, looking at the ground. His thoughts were preoccupied, as he moved through the gateway into The Courtyard.

Venn was unconvinced.

"I thought I sensed something. Apparently I was wrong."

"You were gone too long for it to have been nothing. Not to mention, you look a bit more worn than when you stepped out."

"Well, I thought I might come across something. But I was wrong." He met Venn's gaze with his familiar illumination. A light flickered in Venn's eyes as he sensed the deceit wrapped around KyVeerah's words. Venn was good at telling when KyVeerah was lying, and KyVeerah knew this.

"I'm exhausted," KyVeerah said, breaking the conversation. Turning to the doors, his eyes wandered over the metal stars, avoiding Venn. "I will check on Jude before I turn in."

He disappeared through the doorway while Venn, remaining motionless, did not respond. Nevertheless, KyVeerah knew that if Venn had reason or a wish to object, he would do so. That was Venn's way, after all.

50: Bidding Friends Farewell

KyVeerah knocked on the silver door of CavonRué. Venn and he had arisen at Venn's typical time of nine-thirty. After readying themselves, as well as Jude, they headed out for the lengthy trip across the city.

Jude had been given the comfort of Marion's bed for his night's stay. Marion always kept her room tidy and her bedding clean. So, Venn and KyVeerah thought it the best option. They took turns throughout the night, checking in on him.

On their eastward journey to CavonRué, KyVeerah led the way over the same path he had traveled twice the previous day. Venn followed just behind with Jude's arm around his neck for support. Jude attempted to walk on his own, but nevertheless, Venn carried most of his weight.

Just as the day before, KyVeerah heard nothing for a few moments after knocking on the door. Then he heard light footsteps approaching. The locks began to come unlatched.

"Vincent?" The sweet voice of Cassandra was heard as the door opened a crack. A curious expression showed on her face through the small opening between the door and its frame. She hadn't expected him to return so soon.

"Hello, beautiful."

"What are you—?" Cassandra started to question. She seemed less worried than the day before, though just as exhausted. She dropped her line of thought, stopping mid-sentence, as she yanked the door open, eyes wide. "Jude!"

Cassandra shoved the door to the wall and rushed out onto the landing to her brother, still supported by Venn.

She placed her hand on the side of Jude's face, some of his hair falling forward. Raising her other hand to his chin, he looked at her through straining eyes.

"Cassandra." His voice was barely audible.

"Yes. It's all right, Jude. You're home now. Everything's going to be OK." Her eyes welled up. Jude looked horrible.

She remained still, looking into her brother's weary eyes. "Follow me," Cassandra said, removing her hand from Jude's face and waving KyVeerah and Venn into the house. She led them up the stairs to the right of the entrance.

KyVeerah motioned Venn to go ahead as he turned back to the door, securing its locks. Once he had fastened the last bolt, KyVeerah darted up the stairs.

At the top of the staircase, KyVeerah found himself in a small living space, which took up a third of CavonRué's second level. Straight ahead was a lengthy couch with a low table in front of it.

A wall extending from the doorway at the top of the stairs divided the second level. KyVeerah moved through another open door and into Jude's bedroom. The others stood beside the bed where Jude now lay. Stopping at the foot of the bed, he looked down at Jude and then up to the others.

He gestured toward Venn. "I apologize, Cassandra. Have you been introduced?"

"Yes, thank you." Her voice was appreciative, though strained in concern for her brother who lay with his eyes closed again. Her eyes drifted back to him.

"Cassandra, may I speak with you for a moment?"

She paused, giving Venn a subtle side-glance before nodding. "Yes." She followed KyVeerah out into the sitting area where they halted a short distance from one another. "Cassandra," he began, unsure what to tell her. "Venn and I are going to be leaving the area for a while. That's why I wanted to bring your brother back here. You are the only other somn who should care for him while he comes back to full health.

"You won't be able to get a hold of me, but I am going to request that a couple of my close friends stop by from time to time to check in on you. Their names are Cyrus and Killian Vanaché. You will be most fond of them. I certainly am."

"Wait. You know the brothers who run Randál Vanaché?"

KyVeerah nodded, pleased at the fact that she was familiar with them. "Yes, we go way back. They are the greatest of beings, most kind and most entertaining." KyVeerah flared his eyebrows at the word *entertaining*, trying to lighten the mood.

Cassandra managed a small smile.

"That's what I like to see."

"Thank you, Vincent." She moved closer, wrapping her arms around his neck in appreciation. "Thank you," she repeated, as he placed his own arms around her in a brief embrace.

Releasing his hold, KyVeerah stepped back. "Venn and I really must be getting to Randál Vanaché to speak with Cyrus and Killian."

"Yes, of course," she said, understanding. "I'll walk you down."

Going back into the bedroom, KyVeerah leaned down. "Jude," he said, in a calm voice.

Jude's eyes flickered partially open at the calling of his name, looking into KyVeerah's revealed eyes. "Hang in there. I've gotta have my main man." KyVeerah grinned, though Jude's suffering rested heavy on his shoulders. "You'll be runnin' around in no time." He placed his hand on Jude's head with a nod, repeating, more quietly, "Hang in there."

KyVeerah pulled his hand back, standing straight. He shifted his eyes to Venn who was giving him a readable look. KyVeerah nodded in response. It was indeed time to go. Venn tossed one last glance at Jude, and then they exited the room. Cassandra, standing in the doorway, took the lead as they returned downstairs.

Once again, Cassandra unlatched the locks and gripped the crystal handle, pulling the door open. Venn gave her an assuring look before stepping out and descending the glimmering steps. Cassandra placed her right hand on the side of KyVeerah's face, just as she had the day before.

"Don't stay gone for so long again, Vincent," she pleaded. "You will come back soon, won't you?" Hopeful, she peered up into his entrancing eyes. "We need you here, Vincent. Both of us." She leaned forward on her tiptoes and, light and short, pressed a kiss just to the side of KyVeerah's lips. As she lowered from her toes, she reluctantly brought down her hand.

"Cassandra," he said, surprised by the longing look on her face. "I will be back sooner than later." He raised her chin, pushing her copper hair back from her face, his cool skin brushing over her temple.

"I will be back," he assured. "And you can tell your charming brother just the same. But I really must go." He put his cool hand to her cheek for a short second. Then, turning, he followed Venn out the door.

"Ouch!" KyVeerah threw his hand up to his neck. Venn turned with a curious look. "Nothing," KyVeerah said, shaking his head and dropping his hand back to his side.

Descending the steps, they made their way south. The moment they entered the heart of the Eastside, the wealthiest part of Lux Lumetia, was obvious. Moving into the Rallis District, they stood before one of the buildings that had very recently been polished to a sheen.

Approaching the stone wall, which separated them from Randál Vanaché, Venn looked to KyVeerah who answered with a flourish of his hand.

Venn stepped up, retrieving the hidden metallic box. After pressing a series of buttons, he paused until a buzz sounded three times, just loud enough for them to hear.

After the third buzz, Venn held down the larger button, pulling the box toward his lips, speaking in a quiet voice, "Cyrus, it's Venn. And I must say, I have *quite* a surprise for you."

Replacing the box, another buzz sounded, and the disguised door to their right opened. Venn stepped inside with KyVeerah just behind.

Traversing the entryway and narrow passage of display windows, KyVeerah thought about how phenomenal, yet creepy, the mannequins were.

Venn and KyVeerah passed beneath the high-suspended *Randál Vanaché* sign and entered through the set of black, glossy curtains.

"Ah!" KyVeerah yelped. In his distraction, he tripped right through the left curtain, ripping it from its support bar while trying to catch his balance. He flailed around on the ground until he finally managed to stand, throwing the curtain back to the floor behind him.

Venn rolled his eyes behind his glasses. Turning back around, both KyVeerah and he spotted Killian with his short, platinum blonde hair, black patch present, making his way from the far corner of the room.

"Venn, how are you on this fabulous day?" Killian asked, with enthusiasm, hands in the air as he hurried toward the entrance. "I didn't expect to see you back so soon! Shopping for yourself today, are you—" Killian's voice came to an abrupt stop. "Vincent KyVeerah?" Killian blinked several times, looking past Venn. "By the golds of Arienette, it *is* you!"

In response, KyVeerah twisted his mouth, peering back at the curtain now in a pile on the floor.

"Oh, no bother!" Killian said. "It happens all the time."

Accepting this, true or not, KyVeerah strode forward to meet Killian halfway, by a set of violet couches and lounge chairs. They threw their arms exuberantly around one another in a short embrace.

"I wondered when you would return," Killian said, with a handsome smile, as both men moved back a single step. His voice revealed no doubt that KyVeerah would, in fact, return at some point in time.

KyVeerah grinned, sliding his shades to the top of his head. "You know how it is. Business is business." He shrugged in jest.

"Absolutely." Killian returned a wink and a grin of his own. "So what brings you in? I know the opportunity to see a couple of old friends, no doubt...but," he hesitated, "I sense an additional motive, yes?"

"No pulling the coat over your eyes," KyVeerah answered. "I do have a favor to ask of Cyrus and yourself. I need to ask whether—"

"Vincent KyVeerah!" The shout filled the room, as a man with unnatural, violet hair, slightly longer than Killian's and with various platinum strands, stood at the top of the far, spiral stairs.

Looking up, KyVeerah threw an arm in his direction. "Cyrus, my good friend!"

Cyrus bounded down the steps, hurrying to where KyVeerah and Killian stood. He nearly tackled KyVeerah as he threw his arms around him. After a vigorous pat on the back, Cyrus stepped back and strongly clapped his hand to KyVeerah's shoulder. "Ho-ly Arienette, I can't believe it! It's wonderful to see you, Vincent!" he gushed, with the same, clear accent as his brother. "Good, lord. It's *so* marvelous seeing you!"

"You as well," KyVeerah rejoined, in high spirits.

"How long has it been, a couple of years?" Cyrus revealed a smile just as dazzling and faultless as Killian's.

"Ah, yes. Give or take."

"I have missed you and those wicked eyes of yours." Cyrus wagged a finger at his long-lost compatriot.

KyVeerah raised an eyebrow. "I would expect so."

Cyrus grinned, mirroring the expression on KyVeerah's own lips. "What might we have the honor of doing you for?"

"I was just about to explain to Killian. I need to ask an important favor of you both." KyVeerah shifted his gaze between the brothers. Each of them showed the inclination and interest to carry out any favor he could ask.

"A very good friend of mine has recently hit a lick of misfortune. His name is Jude Hollis. He was jumped. He has knife wounds to his neck and upper arm. The slice on his neck wasn't enough to cause any serious damage, but the knife through his arm did hit an artery. He lost enough blood that, in all honesty, he shouldn't be with us anymore. The bastards used deeply serrated blades. There's definitely a lot of extraneous tissue damage."

"Where is he now?" Killian asked, voicing what his brother and he were both wondering.

"Venn and I have just taken him back to his place, in the southeast corner of the Fannin District, so not all *too* far from here. He lives there with his sister, Cassandra. She will care for him. I was only hoping that you might check in on them every now and then to make certain all is well?"

Killian's expression stated that he need not even put it to question. "Of course, Vincent."

"We would be more than happy to help these friends of yours," Cyrus added. "After all, Vincent, any friend of yours is a dear friend of ours."

"Thank you, ever so much," KyVeerah said, before giving the Vanaché brothers clear directions to CavonRué.

"Venn!" Cyrus leaned past KyVeerah and Killian, waving for him to join them. Venn followed the request. "Good to see you back so soon," Cyrus said, flashing another flawless smile.

The four stood conversing for some time. They had known one another since childhood, and now it was infrequent that the four of them were together all at once.

"Ah, Vincent," Cyrus said, tapping a fingertip, with its finely shaped nail, lightly on KyVeerah's shoulder. "Before we forget, we have something for you. Give me just one moment, won't you?" His eyes darted between KyVeerah and Venn.

"Absolutely," KyVeerah answered, for them both.

In no time, Cyrus reappeared through the door at the top of the spiral staircase. Resuming his former position amongst the other three, he held a sizeable box toward KyVeerah. The slick, black lid contained the bold crimson script *Randál Vanaché* across its scaly textured surface. "The latest in fashion," he explained, with another charismatic smile.

"Well, open it already!" Killian exclaimed, eager for him to reveal the gift within. "Unless of course, you'd rather stare at a box all day?"

KyVeerah flicked his eyes back up to Killian with a grin. Reaching toward the box, still in Cyrus's hands, he pulled off the black-scaled lid and a few layers of tissue paper. His jaw dropped. "Good god." Just from what was revealed thus far, the color and fabric alone were impressive to behold.

KyVeerah gripped the edges of the smooth fabric, lifting the neatly folded contents. "Men of Valencia, you shouldn't have!"

Cyrus pulled the box away, leaving KyVeerah holding a long, deep blue-violet jacket of quintessential fabric and quality.

"Crafted true to your personal fit and style. For you and you alone." Cyrus offered a crafty, yet genuine, smile.

"By the lunar goddesses," Venn couldn't help but comment. "You guys have really outdone yourselves." Killian and Cyrus beamed.

"We thought this color would correspond best with those wicked eyes. We've been holding onto it for a while. We knew you'd come back eventually and deemed that an arrival gift would be appropriate when the time came around," Killian said, matter-of-factly, though still self-gratified with the exquisite masterpiece that his brother and he had created for one of their closest lifelong friends.

"Tested," Cyrus added. "The fabric is sun and heat resistant, water repellant, and won't stain or damage due to grasses or sands. It is like velvet steel. You should be well set," he assured, equally proud of the impressive piece of attire.

"I don't even know what to say," KyVeerah openly reveled in the jacket.

"Just promise you'll take care of it." Although he had looked it over a hundred plus times prior to this moment, Cyrus admired it for himself. "The best for the best, we figure."

"Well then, that would obviously be me." KyVeerah even wrinkled his fine, aquiline nose at the jest.

"I surmise that you two have a lot ahead of you. You ought to get home, it'll begin to get late before long, and you have far to travel," Cyrus affirmed.

"Yes." KyVeerah folded the coat lengthwise, draping it over his arm. "I suppose you're right."

"But it has been fabulous seeing you again, Vincent. And Venn." Cyrus nodded in a friendly and respectable gesture, and then tacked on, "as always."

They walked their visitors the short distance to the hallway entrance where the single curtain remained hanging near the Randál Vanaché sign. Killian merely brushed the fallen curtain aside with his foot, clearing the path.

"Well then," Cyrus said, feeling the familiar sorrow that their longtime, childhood friends had to be off.

"Come back. Anytime at all," Killian said.

"Yes now, don't be strangers," Cyrus added, before leaning to KyVeerah for one last wholehearted pat on the back. "So long, Vince. Come back in one piece again, ya hear?"

"Will do," KyVeerah replied, leaning in, giving and receiving another hearty pat on the back, from Killian this time.

"See ya around, Vincent."

Venn said goodbye in the same manner as KyVeerah. Then they moved through the opening where the second glossy curtain should have been hanging and down along the hall of mannequins until they reached the tinted entryway and the light of the afternoon's end.

KyVeerah exited, but glancing at Venn, he could swear that he saw a lingering smile.

"What?" Venn retorted, eyes flashing crisply. The smile vanished instantly from his face.

KyVeerah's only response was a deepening of his dimples, as he turned forward again and the two of them started the long walk back to the Caulder District, to Umbra Halls.

51:*Shadows of Prospect*

Slowly, and without a sound, KyVeerah opened the door to the den where Venn sat in his soft leather chair, his feet kicked up on the ottoman. He had an open book held up before his eyes and a fire danced in the fireplace. It had become late evening by now.

"What do you want?" Venn asked, sensing KyVeerah's presence, despite the absence of sound.

KyVeerah opened the door wider, sliding on into the room. He approached Venn in his chair, but stopped just behind it.

Venn lowered the book to his lap, peering through his glasses into the flickering fire, waiting for whatever KyVeerah had to say.

"I've come to a realization," KyVeerah said, placing a thoughtful finger to his bottom lip.

"Well, this ought to be interesting."

KyVeerah scowled before starting to pace behind Venn's chair. "I'm absolutely certain that Rhyus and Marion stole that boat."

"Lord, Vincent. We have been over this."

"I know, I know." KyVeerah gestured his frustration, having known that Venn would react in such a narrow-minded way. "But I know how we can find their location, no matter *where* that might be. Their *exact* location."

"Oh, really. And how exactly do you plan to do that?" Venn asked, expecting some absurd response.

KyVeerah continued to pace the invisible line on the ornamental rug. "I have learned that a man by the name of Fyfe Van Ingen is being held prisoner in The Tower—"

"How the hell is that supposed to help us?" Venn's tone was disgruntled at this beginning statement, which KyVeerah had not been allowed to finish. Venn dropped his legs off either side of the footrest. He closed the book with a single hand, relegating it to the side table where it bumped an empty glass. Leaning forward, he placed his elbows on the armrests, hands down on his legs.

"You see," KyVeerah picked up where he left off, "Fyfe used to work for a man named Galton who I have, umm, done business with." Though unable to see Venn's face, KyVeerah could feel his incredulity. "Fyfe worked for Galton, but he had *issues*. He apparently has unusually strong senses, which give him extraordinary power. However, in the past his senses were deemed uncontrollable, and he became a hazard, getting into all sorts of trouble, and not simple things."

"So?" It was obvious that Venn saw no significance in this information.

"So, he fled to Atrum Unda. And evidently the Black Guard, or someone else in high authority, has taken him captive. He's being held in a cell of the Prisoner's Quarters."

Venn remained unimpressed.

"For the sake of Valencia, Venn!" Aggravated, KyVeerah ripped the shades from his face. He threw his arms to the sides, violet eyes illuminated in ferocity. "We have to go to Atrum!"

"Oh, *hell* no!" Venn roared, pointing a finger to the door.

"Venn! What good is doing nothing but sitting on your ass reading your damn books?" KyVeerah knew he was crossing hot waters, but he realized it had to be done.

"What do you want to do? Break him out?" Venn mocked.

"Precisely."

"What?" He couldn't believe it. Not even coming from KyVeerah's mouth. "That is absurd! You're talking about *Atrum Unda* here!"

"Fyfe *cannot* be in the hands of The Tower. They may not know what he is capable of yet, but if they find out, it sure as hell won't be good!" KyVeerah strained, hissing the words.

Silent anger emitted from Venn as KyVeerah spoke.

"Venn, we *need* him! He is the only way we are ever going to find Rhyus or Marion—especially if we want to find them alive!" KyVeerah stood straight, taking a deep breath. "I used to associate with a shady bunch in Atrum Unda who have substantial ties to The Tower. They wanted me to become a part of their organization. But I declined."

"What in Blue Ravenna does that matter?" Furious, Venn blocked out the first part of KyVeerah's statement.

"During my brief association with this organization, I learned of a secret passage leading into The Tower. To the best of my knowledge, the passage hasn't been used in decades. The passageway used to be an old guard post and was rarely accessed, but now only a few rare limited somns know of it, including myself."

"Vincent, listen to yourself. This is preposterous! This is crazy, even for you! Who the hell would break into The Tower?" Venn shouted, before remembering that someone had done so just days ago. He dismissed the thought.

"Think about Marion! Fyfe is the only one who can tell you where to find her."

Venn was taken aback by the comment. The mention of Marion was the only thing that could have possibly broken through to him, and KyVeerah was well aware of this. Venn stood silent as his thoughts turned inward.

KyVeerah remained motionless, holding his breath, not wanting to disrupt Venn's unvoiced concentration. Doubtless, he was imagining the many horrible places she could be at that precise moment. Rubbing his fingers subconsciously at his sides, he was hopeful for a positive response.

"Go to hell," Venn finally demanded. Shoving his way past KyVeerah, he made his way to the door.

"And what is that supposed to mean?" KyVeerah shouted, infuriated that Venn had not given him a true answer, even if it would have been an unsatisfying one.

"We leave first thing in the morning."

"Wait…what?"

"First light. Be ready."

KyVeerah's jaw dropped. *I can't believe he actually agreed to go.* He continued to watch the door as Venn stalked through it.

"And shut off the fire!"

KyVeerah, still puzzled, rotated the switch beside the fireplace to deaden the flames. He turned and stared back at the door.

Well, this will be interesting. Tomorrow, we go to Atrum Unda.

52: The Package

Toying with the crystal pendant of her necklace, Ezra Stark's patience dwindled as she waited for Helena Meretrix to emerge from Serlio Young's shop. She stared at the sign in one of the bay windows that read Scribe's Den, and below it in finer print, Books of Antiquity and Memorabilia.

Ezra paced in irritation, surfacing from the shadows of the alley. *What could be taking her so damn long?* A flicker of something captured her attention, something that could not be mistaken. It was vibrant and unnaturally crimson. *Callis? What in the name of all creations is he doing here?* Ezra continued to stare as Callis's form dimmed, enveloped as he moved further into the mist and rain, until he faded entirely into the distance.

She curled her fingers—with sharp, manicured nails—clutching her hands into fists. A cataclysmic anger bubbled up in her throat. She could feel the verge of a shrill scream rising toward the surface, about to break through, but she held it at bay and pinned the thoughts to the walls of her mind.

৪০০৪

Settled comfortably in front of the fireplace, Helena studied the package in her hands. Its waterproof covering had the rich mellow patina of many years. And without even opening it, she could feel the aura of Ancient wisdom that she knew must be sealed inside. A chill ran through her as she tried to imagine what secrets it might hold.

With a soft smile, she thought of the gruff old man who had sent it to her. And with a wider smile, she recalled how she had thanked his grandson who delivered it to her. Closing her eyes, she let the moment slowly seep in. She imagined the chaos that she was going to unleash on Nyx and his crew once she had ultimate power. Half the city was in Nyx Crucian's pocket. And every one of them was going to fall when he went down. She would watch from her perch, enjoying every minute of the carnage.

With a frown, she hoped Serlio Young and his grandson, Albert, wouldn't be victims. *But there stands a chance*, she told herself sadly. *That's just how fate works sometimes.*

Breaking out of her daydream, she picked up her knife and made a clean slit around the end. Tipping the package, the ancient manuscript slid out into her hand. Reverently, she peeled back its cover. Her eyes went wide in horror.

Calling Anomalies of Atmospheric Perturbations, it read.

Her jaw dropped. *What the hell? How in the name of Ravenna is this going to be of help?* For the life of her, she hadn't a clue what one word on the cover meant. She furiously threw the manuscript into the fireplace. "I take it back! If this is that old bastard's idea of a joke, when I am in power, he and his little grandson can burn down with the rest of them! And they can be at the front of the line!" Her voice echoed darkly off the walls.

Bending over to throw the covering into the fire, she noticed an envelope lying on the floor. It must have been slipped between the pages of the manuscript. It was very old paper, with her name written in a rich cursive script. Slitting the end, she pulled out a sheet of sun-faded stationary.

Helena,

-- This old manuscript has been used for centuries, by those who watch the skies, for signs of Callings & Messengers.

-- Please disregard the title, for those academic somns love to sound smarter than they are. Some of this, you might not understand. But with study, I'm sure you will pick up a lot. I will try to fill in the gaps for you tomorrow.

Greatest regards,

Serlio Young

--p.s. I remembered the old somn's name. It was Deegan.

Helena stood speechless. Then, scrambling to her feet, she ran to the fireplace. Reaching in, disregarding the flames, she pulled the manuscript from the fire. Fortunately, the coating to protect it from the elements had acted as a flame retardant as well. It had resisted the fire for some time before igniting along its bottom edge. She anxiously batted the flames away and scanned it to assess the damage. The entire cover had scorched. She couldn't even see the obnoxious title. Holding her breath, she flipped the front cover. The writing on the pages was still intact.

With a sigh, she tossed the transcript onto the couch. She dropped down in relief beside it. After staring for a long while, she picked it up. She sighed again. *This is going to be a long night.*

53: Feeding Speculations

The room around Rhyus was unsteady. It swayed uncomfortably. In his hands, he clasped a slick, cool fabric. Green. Emerald green, he noted. The room around him was familiar; its off white walls with dark wooden paneling…the bay window…and of course, the slick, emerald bedding.

It finally clicked: *Umbra Halls.*

Rhyus jumped, as a man spoke from a corner of the shadowy room. However, Rhyus did not catch the words that the unfamiliar man had spoken.

Raising a hand to his head, Rhyus realized that it was throbbing. *What happened?* he wondered, in a thick cloud of confusion. *Umbra Halls…but how?* He closed his eyes tight with a hand pressing against his skull as the aching intensified.

∞)(∞

After a long, silent moment, Rhyus reopened his eyes. Unexpectedly, the throbbing ceased. Looking straight ahead, a curious expression came over his face. Just before him sat an oversized hourglass. Its intricate design was impressive as tiny, glittering grains of white sand shifted and fell through its center without a sound, falling in a constant stream toward the structure's encased floor. A few lights illuminated the hourglass while many other lights, placed in a circle around it, were directed away to light the room.

What will happen when all the grains have fallen?

"Time is running out," came a male voice from nearby. It was someone he had been speaking with, but whom?

Rhyus swiveled around on the high stool as casually as he could, not wanting the one he was conversing with to notice his failing memory. He caught sight of the man's vibrant hair but nothing more before his surroundings altered.

"Follow it," the man's demand reached Rhyus, just before Rhyus blinked his eyes to find that his conversational partner had vanished.

ℰℛ

Now, no one sat before him. The room was empty other than his own form sitting on the cold, hard ground. Even the colors of the room reflected the fact that he was alone, in variations of translucent and opaque blues and whites.

Frustrated, Rhyus released a sigh that he had been holding for far too long. He leaned back against the wall, quickly realizing that it was as equally cold and hard as the floor.

Focusing on his feet, he tried to direct his mind elsewhere. A failed attempt. The icy walls drained any motivation, along with blocking any capability to reach beyond them.

Then, his last willful attempt was disrupted as he heard the sound of two large objects sliding against one another, stone against stone or ice against ice. Rhyus jerked his head up, peering toward the room's sole door on the far wall.

"You have been vouched for," a man's deep voice said, from just outside the room once the door had been opened. Rhyus could not see the man as he said this. *What does he mean?* Rhyus felt a vortex of emotions whirling through him. The next moment was a blur.

ℰℛ

Without forewarning, Rhyus was on his feet where he had sat. Then he stood a quarter of the way across the room, and then two-thirds of the way to the door. Time ran slowly, though it also jumped, skipping miniscule fractions of time, as he moved toward the far wall. He shielded his eyes as he approached the door and stepped out through it.

ℰℛ

Lowering his hand from his eyes, he did not meet the light he was expecting. Instead, as he looked around, he realized that he was in the old church, and Marion was standing impatiently, waiting for him to turn back and look her in the eye.

He closed his eyes, shaking his head. *By the goddesses!* Had everything that transpired on the ship with her been a dream? Or was this the dream? *Where and when am I?*

Looking down again, he noted that, in his right hand, he still held the bronze envelope Marion had demanded he take. As he felt the weight of the object within it, his heated emotions became apparent, as his blood simmered. He couldn't stand it, and his sour feelings of regret roiled into a state of anger.

"Armani," he spat, when he finally whipped back around to look into Marion's eyes through the tinted glasses. They couldn't hide her eyes from him, and she knew it was so. She looked absolutely stunning, but his care and concern had numbed.

"What about him?" she snapped. She fought to deny it, but he caused tendrils of fear to stream through her.

"Is he what this is about?" Rhyus shouted. He hoisted the bronze envelope up before her eyes. "Maybe you should just grow the pair your pretending to have and tell me what the hell this is really about!" Rhyus's eyes were fierce with acidic highlights overtaking the strips of his irises.

"It has nothing to do with him!"

"Is that so?" he said, not believing her statement held an ounce of truth.

"Yes." She paused, taken aback by the desperation enveloping her reply. She turned curtly from Rhyus and began to walk away, descending the short set of steps leading straight down the center aisle.

He stared after her graceful form and her black, swaying garment, caught at a loss for any sort of response. At the bottom of the steps, she stopped, turning quickly on her high heels. She pulled the shades from before her eyes, framed with dark violets and blacks. "You *will* appreciate what we have done," she said, staring at him with intensity. She turned and walked away as quickly as she could while maintaining her look of composure from where Rhyus stood before the altar.

He watched her fleeing form move along the long wooden boards of the aisle, toward the church doors, until she faded from sight. He wondered when they would cross paths again. And as he closed his eyes, he faintly envisioned a memory. Four immaculate towers rose and fell to their demise, falling to the dark city floor, as he stood witness from his elevated position.

৪৩৫

Rain. Rhyus felt a chill rain pouring over him. And as he blinked his eyes, he realized that his sense of gravity was gone. He wasn't standing at all, but rather lying face down on a stone shelf. The harsh rain was pounding over him and everything else around. Ruthless waves crashed against the shelf's outer edges.

This place, why did he know it so well? It seemed so unfamiliar, but at the same time, it felt more comfortable than anything he had ever known. For a moment, he wished he could lie here forever. No more wondering or caring, just the pounding waves and the consistent downpour of the rain. Nobody even knew he was there.

Wrong. Rhyus looked through the corner of his eye to see the shadowed man looming over him. The man spoke to him. His words mingled with the rain, as they fell down upon Rhyus. A grin appeared over the man's barely visible lips. What intentions did he hold?

"Who are—?" Rhyus tried to question, but the words escaping him were no more than a whisper. They would never be heard over the rain and the waves.

As Rhyus forfeited his attempt, he turned his head with the side of his face striking the cold, wet stone. His eyes widened as he saw the man pull back his leg with its solid toed boot.

"See you on another side."

Rhyus barely heard the words before the man released his leg. It swung forward, slamming square into his abdomen, driving every molecule of air from his body.

Everything went black.

℘℘

Rhyus's eyes snapped open, and his arms at his sides ran rigid, as his fingers attempted to dig into the layers of fabric, and further, into the mattress itself. His eyes flicked about the room, and he threw a hand up to his chest. His pulse was hammering, but at least he was able to take in air.

I don't know if I can handle many more of these dreams, Rhyus thought, pulling himself into a sitting position.

Marion. Rhyus pictured the image of Marion from his dream, watching her legs, as she walked in those high heels, and the dress that swayed with her every move.

Marion, he thought again, however this was a startling here-and-now sort of thought. All of a sudden he was able to recall speaking with her the night before at the festival, Festus Murus. It had been sometime after Lenim and she had shared their much-enjoyed dance, a dance enjoyed by seemingly everyone else as well.

What did we even talk about? Rhyus wondered. *I can't even remember whether we were happy to talk to one another or if it was a forced encounter.* He could picture her dancing with Lenim though. *Brilliant. She was beautiful.*

Then a knock came at the door and Rhyus responded, "Yes?"

"Fabulous, you're awake!" Lenim exclaimed, throwing the door open. "How are we feeling this fine day?" Rhyus looked dully at him, not sure how to respond.

"Fine. Well, mostly," he altered his response. "My head hurts."

"No surprise considering the night's events, but it's good to hear if that's the worst of it all. Fortunate indeed." Lenim cocked his head and flared his eyebrows.

"What time is it?" Rhyus asked, realizing he had not a clue. All he could tell was that sunlight was shining in through the window.

"Just coming upon three o'clock."

"Wait, three? Like three in the afternoon?" This was not the answer Rhyus expected.

"Precisely," Lenim answered, with a grin. "But we did not get in until well after five this morning. And considering that you hadn't slept since your arrival on Insula Palam Vita, and also how much you had to drink…let's just say you probably needed it." Lenim's grin grew wider with this comment.

"Marion," Rhyus said aloud, without connecting the name with a true thought or phrase.

Lenim's eyebrows rose higher over his unblinking eyes in further amusement. "Yes?" he asked. Rhyus could tell that there was something Lenim wasn't saying. He was also making sure that Rhyus could easily pick that fact up.

"Nothing." Rhyus tried to brush the thought aside, but unable to keep it contained, he added, "I talked to her last night."

Lenim cocked his head with a curious expression now. "Yes?"

"I just…I don't really remember. But I kind of have a bad feeling about it." He looked down at his hands as he tried to jog his memory.

"Oh, yes," Lenim said. Rhyus switched his attention back to the man who was tossing his rich, reddish brown hair back from his face. Rhyus's expression lit up in a way that suggested Lenim ought to say whatever it was he was withholding.

"You two seemed to enjoy one another's company."

"But?" Rhyus pressed.

"Until you informed her that she was acting and dressed indecently, to put it mildly." Lenim grimaced. "That must not have been quite what she wanted to hear, seeing that she stormed away and ignored you for the rest of the evening. Probably not the best idea on your part. Just saying." Lenim gave a loose shrug, still leaning against the door, not caring or worried how Rhyus took his opinion.

Rhyus dropped his head into his hand. "Ah, shit." After a moment, he raised it, worrying his chin between a thumb and finger.

"What's done is done," Lenim said. "Go freshen up, and then come on upstairs."

Leaving no time for Rhyus to even consider responding, Lenim pulled the door shut behind him. Rhyus just sat, staring at the now closed door.

All right, Rhyus told himself after a few long minutes. He threw aside the black-and-white comforter and dragged his legs over the side of the bed.

છાલ્ય

Rhyus made his way up to the main floor, wondering what plans had been set for the day. In the back of his mind, he was grateful for the clothes his hosts had purchased for him.

"Ah, he has risen!" Sultan exclaimed, from a high stool at the kitchen bar. He spun the seat around to face Rhyus who was crossing the last of the basement stairs.

Rhyus looked around the kitchen. "Where's Lenim?" he asked. He had assumed Lenim would be sitting up here waiting, ready to take him around the city.

"Oh, you know. He has important things to take care of," Sultan said, swaying on the stool to the tune playing in his head. Just as before, Sultan wore a low ponytail with pink lenses pushed up on his head where they pinned some of the wilder strands of his wavy hair back from his face.

"Oh." Rhyus wasn't sure what to expect now.

"I suppose that leaves you and me." Sultan had turned back to the bar, but he looked back with a mischievous side-glance from his orange-amber eyes, accompanied by an impish smile.

This left Rhyus just as unsure of what to expect. But the playful look on Sultan's face did draw a smile from him.

"Hungry?" Sultan asked, tossing an object, which Rhyus caught without effort. "Nice catch!" he exclaimed, impressed by Rhyus's immediate reflexes.

"Thanks." Rhyus displayed a crooked grin, but he cringed as soon as he recognized the melon sitting in his hand.

"Not so fond of rabmelons?"

"Well, this was the only thing we had to eat on the entire trip here. So, not particularly."

"Ah." Sultan reached across the bar before spinning back to face Rhyus. "Perhaps bead berries or jin melon?" he asked, holding the assortment of fruits in his open palms.

"Sure." Rhyus approached the bar and traded for the jin melon.

Sultan revealed his charming smile and held up the rabmelon. "You know, I myself am quite fond of rabmelons. They are delicious." He made a face displaying his appreciation, and unexpected to Rhyus, cracked it open with a heavy thump on the counter. He scooped out a large bite with a spoon he had already been using. "Oh, yes," he added, with delight, "delicious, indeed."

"Yeah. Maybe," Rhyus said, but grimaced again as Sultan proceeded with his second bite.

"So," Sultan started, as he finished the rabmelon, tossing the remainder into an open trash can, "would you like to join me in attending a theatrical performance at The Grounds? It's tied to Festus Murus. You may enjoy it."

"Sure," Rhyus said, after putting it to thought, "sounds like a good time."

"Excellent," Sultan said. "Finish that jin melon, and we'll head out. The performance is soon, but we should arrive at The Grounds in plenty of time."

ℜℛ

It was a pleasant show, neither too short nor too long. The players were well prepared, and the production ran smoothly and was quite entertaining.

The show, related to Festus Murus, was a satire of how the wall around Urbs Cereris Arcanae came to be. It displayed the event from the enemies' perspective, the somns from whom the dwellers of Trans Murus had descended.

The show consisted of bright costumes and a minimal setting as well as music. In York's stead was a woman with tight spiraling red hair, leading the musicians.

"Did you like it?" Sultan asked, as they were walking through three neat rows of pink, white, and red blossoming trees surrounding

The Grounds.

"Yes. They put on a very good show," Rhyus said, exiting the low barrier around the grassy square.

"It is always a good show at The Grounds. It is what these somns live for. To perform. To entertain."

"Well, they picked the right profession."

"I certainly agree." Sultan dropped the pink lenses down and shook some of the wild hair back from his face. "Are you hungry?"

It seemed like he had just eaten, but Rhyus realized it had been some time since the jin melon at Lenim's house. "Yeah, actually I am."

"I know just the place. This way." Sultan tipped his head, inviting Rhyus to follow. They carried on, walking side by side as they further discussed the performance.

"Café Kampnel," Sultan said, pointing ahead at a small building that resembled all of the other stores and houses around it. Then again, Rhyus was beginning to identify one place from the next.

Rhyus looked over the café's exterior. *Nothing extraordinary,* he decided. Sultan, on the other hand, was enthralled to be simply standing on the walkway to its entrance.

"I tell you, Rhyus, they make a mean dish here."

-411-

Stepping inside, Sultan led the way up to a little counter. Wooden booths and tables were neatly arranged throughout the large room. There were many aqua and violet pots, containing tall plants with bright colored flowers, placed without blocking the aisles. The café had a very simplistic feel.

A young woman behind the counter stood at once as she spotted them. Short, jet-black hair complimented her sharp appearance, and large, blue hoop earrings matched her wide eyes.

"Yuri Sultan, how are you?" the young woman greeted him with a cheerful smile. Her uniform, a green dress ending just above her knees, with a white apron, clashed with her eyes and earrings, but she looked pleasing nonetheless.

"Miranda," he said, in return, "how's business today?"

"The usual waves."

Apparently Sultan is a regular here, Rhyus thought, as Sultan and the young woman made small talk. *Fitting, I suppose, considering its down-to-the-basics atmosphere and Sultan's free-spirited demeanor.*

"I ordered for both of us, hope you don't mind. I got something you have to try. One of my favorites." Sultan had an expression of great anticipation.

"Oh, sure. No problem," Rhyus said.

Miranda smiled. "I'll bring everything out when it's ready."

"How rude of me. Rhyus, this is Miranda. Miranda, Rhyus. He's a visitor in our parts."

A sheepish note blended into her wide eyes and smile, as she dropped her gaze, commenting, "I have heard about you. Even saw you at the festival, but only from a distance." She looked back up at Rhyus with her royal blue eyes.

"Pleased to make your acquaintance," Rhyus finally said, remembering his manners.

"Yours as well. I hope Sultan is showing you a good time during your stay."

"Definitely." At Rhyus's crooked grin, Sultan gave Miranda a "hah, take that" sort of look.

She laughed, "I wouldn't expect any less of him."

"Why thank you, Miranda. That may just be the nicest thing you've ever said to anyone about me," Sultan teased.

"Not by a long shot. Now you two go take a seat." She smirked, as she shooed them off, turning through a two-way, swinging door leading into the kitchen.

Turning, Sultan led the way to a row of booths along the opposite wall where they took a seat on the violet cushions. Sultan sat where he could view the entire dining room from his position.

As they sat back, relaxing, a sudden smile came over Sultan.

"What?" Rhyus asked.

"Are you really having that good of a time here in Urbs Cereris Arcanae, or were you simply trying to tickle her fancy?" A cheeky attribute dressed Sultan's features.

Rhyus's skin flushed, and he rubbed his neck before folding both hands together on the table. "No. I actually meant it. I've found myself having a very good time. Somewhat to my own surprise, I must admit."

Sultan rolled his brilliant, orange-amber eyes. "Oh, sure." He shook some of the thick, dirty blonde waves from his face and slipped his glasses up, revealing the true vibrancy of his eyes.

"Sultan, can I ask you something?"

"I suppose you *may* ask me something, if you'll just call me Yuri. I think we've reached beyond last names." He offered a good-humored expression.

Rhyus grinned, realizing that Sultan had just concreted their friendship.

"What is it you want to know?"

"What does the city's name mean, Urbs Cereris Arcanae?"

"Ah." Sultan gave a short nod. "It means *the city whose mysteries are secret.*"

"What? What secrets?"

"If I could tell you, they wouldn't be secrets now, would they?"

"I guess not." Rhyus shifted his eyes to the table.

"Now, let me ask *you* something."

"Go for it," Rhyus said, still distracted by what the city's secrets could be.

"You didn't really know you were headed here, to Insula Palam Vita, did you?"

This pulled Rhyus out of his own musings, and he looked up to meet Sultan's gaze. Sultan had just indicated that he considered the two of them friends, but Rhyus wondered whether he might have alternative intentions. Looking into Sultan's liquid eyes, they seemed open and genuine. They were the complete opposite of Lenim's opaque, probing eyes.

"No," Rhyus forced out the word. The decision may not have been wise, but only time would tell.

A few moments passed. "I didn't think so." Sultan's tone remained lighthearted, and his charming smile reappeared.

His returning smile calmed Rhyus's nerves at once. Miranda appeared, taking the last few steps to deliver their food. He hadn't noticed her approaching until she was just steps away. Sultan's question had shaken him.

Sultan displayed a gracious smile, "Thanks."

"Yeah, thanks," Rhyus added.

"No problem. You two enjoy." Miranda smiled kindly and turned away with a small sway in her step as she returned to her seat behind the counter.

"You know," Sultan picked up, "I had the strangest dream last night. I was standing at the edge of the sea, and then, without warning, it hardened into a solid, black surface. I got down on my knees from the sands of the shore, but as I reached out and touched it, it turned to ash and crumbled away until I was left kneeling on a cliff at the edge of the world." Sultan peered with curiosity into Rhyus's emerald eyes. "Strange. Isn't it strange, how real our dreams can seem?"

"Yeah," Rhyus said, contemplating the coincidence of Sultan

bringing up such a topic. "I know what you mean. I myself have been having unusual dreams lately. The world of my dreams seems so real. Sometimes I can't tell which world is which, that one or this. Or, if somehow, they are one and the same. The thing I remember most is lying on a ground of sapphires as they press into my skin…and then there is some sort of stone shelf. I wake up on it, surrounded by waves pounding from every side. No. All except one. There's a stairway that a man comes down. I don't know why, but every time, he knocks me unconscious."

Rhyus looked sightlessly at his plate of food, seeing instead, his dreams playing in fast-forward through his mind. "*So* real."

Sultan watched Rhyus, fixedly absorbing his story. Neither of them paid attention to the wonderful food before them. A new interest flowed through his eyes.

Rhyus's eyes flicked up. "It was only a dream." He shook his head, thinking it foolish and unnecessary to try to make sense of his odd dreams.

"Eat up," Sultan said, still contemplating Rhyus's words. They each picked up a fork and dug in.

"Good lord! This is delicious!" After this initial bite, Rhyus had no difficulty altering to the here and now.

"Isn't it? I thought you might find it satisfactory."

"More than satisfactory. This is the best thing I've ever put in my mouth!" Rhyus declared, taking another huge mouthful.

Sultan smiled.

℘)∞

After finishing their meal, Sultan and Rhyus made their goodbyes and left Café Kampnel, heading in a direction other than Lenim's house. Until evening, they weaved through the city, Sultan pointing out highlights as well as his own, personal favorite places. Once in awhile they stopped to converse with the others, but after a quick farewell, they continued on their tour.

"You seem pretty popular around The Urbs," Rhyus said. Hours had passed since they left Café Kampnel. The suns had set, and numerous colored lanterns cast their warm glow over everything and everyone.

"Well, it's hard not to be recognized in a city this size. It is a decent size, don't get me wrong, but not huge by any means. And Lenim is well recognized, so since I am his main man here in The Urbs…I suppose that brings a good deal of attention." Sultan passed the topic along like it was no big deal.

"Yeah, I guess," Rhyus agreed.

"Where was it you traveled from?"

"Lux Lumetia," Rhyus said, without much thought. They had just exited Pub Ralikoo, Sultan's favorite place to kick back. They had each enjoyed several strong drinks, helping to loosen Rhyus's tongue.

"Ah, the City of Light," Sultan demurred, readjusting his hair into its ponytail. His glasses were back on top of his head.

"Yeah," Rhyus said, in an automatic response.

"And Marion? She's from Lux Lumetia as well?"

"Yeah." Rhyus nodded. They started to make their way back to Lenim's house. "Frankly, I don't know why she even came with me. She doesn't know me. We just met." His voice was a mix of emotions. Confused, annoyed, and even a bit sorry for dragging her along on his crazy voyage. He sighed. *I don't even know who I am.*

Sultan chewed on this. "So, you don't even know one another. You didn't know where you were headed when you left the Crystal City. And now, neither of you know where you are to travel next? But you do plan on moving on, I presume?"

"Basically. What a disaster," he acknowledged, more to himself than to Sultan. He spotted Lenim's house now, just a ways off.

-415-

A mystified expression crept over Sultan's face. His curiosity swayed toward concern as they neared the house. "You'd best be careful, Rhyus. You are feeding speculations. I'm not sure what Lenim has planned for tomorrow, but he's damn well going to want to talk with you."

54: A Trip to Atrum

KyVeerah's eyes opened as he lay in the comfort of the luxurious bedding surrounding him. An instant later, a determined pounding met the bedroom door.

Venn's booming voice accompanied the fist hitting the door, "You up?"

"Yes. I am," KyVeerah said, in an overexaggerated voice, just for Venn. "And a good morning to you too, charming," he muttered, rolling with his back to the door. He pulled the crimson comforter tighter.

"Good. Get up. For real this time."

"Yeah. Right on that," KyVeerah said, offering an obscene gesture, as if Venn could see it.

"Vincent."

"OK, OK! I'm up, I'm up, all right?" He hurled a couple of the crimson and black cased pillows at the door. "I hate mornings," he grumbled, with his face buried in one of the many remaining pillows. He threw the comforter aside, dragging himself from the warm embrace of the bed.

"It's nine-forty. We leave at eleven."

KyVeerah stretched, but he stopped as pain grabbed his side. "Yeah. Sure," he said, standing and flourishing his hand in another obscene gesture that Venn could not see.

"Good," Venn finished. KyVeerah could hear footfalls retreating back down the hall.

Leaning against the black footboard, KyVeerah yawned. *I really, really hate mornings.* Pulling on a pair of lounge pants, he trudged to the bathroom. *At least I didn't have to be ready at first light.*

Before the large mirror over the counter and its double sinks, KyVeerah carefully lifted his arm. The bandages needed changing. *Good lord*, he raised his eyes, aggravated by the nuisance of it all. He peeled the bandages off, tossing them into the trash.

He cringed, examining the larger, stitched up gash. "That ought to leave a scar."

Stripping down, he took a plenty-long shower. As he rung out his hair, a thought hit him. *Atrum Unda. Venn and I are really going to Atrum Unda...together. Who'd have thought?*

After wrapping a towel around his waist, he opened the door, leaning out with his hands on either side of the doorway. "Venn!" he shouted. "Venn!" As expected, he heard movement from the den above. Shortly, Venn came through the door at the end of the hall.

"What?" he barked. "I thought someone was about to strangle you...not that it would be such a horrible thing."

"Come now, you don't really mean that."

Venn raised an eyebrow. "Oh, don't I?"

"I need you to rebandage this," KyVeerah said, changing the subject and raising his arm.

"Blue Ravenna!" Venn turned his head.

"Good Valencia, Venn. It's a mere flesh wound. It's not like my organs are spilling out through it!"

"Vincent!"

"What?"

"Nothing." Venn shook his head. "All right, but if you value ever staying here again, you had best make sure that towel stays where it belongs." KyVeerah grinned at Venn's serious expression.

"Fair enough."

Venn searched the cupboards for materials to take care of the wound. He grimaced as he studied the large gash and the shorter one over his heart. "Could be worse," he eventually stated, trying to convince himself more than KyVeerah.   -417-

"I'm a KyVeerah," he flaunted, "I'll be right as rain before you know."

"Well, for that you're a damn lucky fool," Venn scolded. "And stop fidgeting," he added, as he dressed the wound.

"Can't help it."

"Well, you had better figure out a way. You are lucky that whoever stitched you up took the time to line these tattoos back up."

"Oh, don't you worry. I made sure of that, Venn." KyVeerah was clearly proud of himself. Venn gave him a curious look but didn't ask any further questions. In all honesty, he would rather not know.

"Done," Venn declared.

KyVeerah looked down and then into the mirror. "Excellent. Magnificent job, Venn."

"What did you expect?"

KyVeerah thought this over, and then shrugged.

Venn only shook his head.

"What?"

Venn headed for the door. "Nothing."

"Venn."

"What now?" He stopped in his tracks.

KyVeerah rummaged through a deep drawer, filled with all sorts of odds and ends, finally fishing out a short, stout jar. Pushing the drawer shut with his leg, he tossed the jar to Venn.

"Wet your hair down, or at least dampen it, and work a decent amount of this through it." KyVeerah indicated the black hair running down Venn's back.

Venn gave him a skeptical look.

KyVeerah returned a humorless one. "Trust me, once we get to Atrum, you're going to deeply regret it if you don't. Everyone there uses it to repel the constant rain. If you let your hair turn into a wet rag, you'll stand out like a torch in a tunnel. And we need anonymity!"

Venn tossed the jar back to KyVeerah who returned a confused and offended look that he wasn't taking the advice seriously.

"I'll get to it once you're done in here." Venn turned and walked out of the bathroom, heading to the kitchen for something to eat before they started out on the perilous task before them.

After fumbling through wardrobes in opposite corners of the room, KyVeerah found something to suit him for the destination and task ahead. *I have a feeling it's going to be another long day.*

೮ා೧෪

Just shy of eleven o'clock, Venn found KyVeerah ready to move out. He was sitting in a kitchen chair, leaning back with his boots on the table.

KyVeerah looked at the floor when Venn entered. "You think you ought to clean any of this up before we leave?" He waved an arm toward the sickening melon mess on the far kitchen wall, though making sure not to sound as if he were offering to be of any assistance.

"No."

KyVeerah looked unsure.

"It'll be fine."

"Ready then?"

"Yeah. And get your damn feet off the table. You're not the only one who eats there, you know."

"Then maybe you should clean up the rest of it?" KyVeerah

said, referring to the dried melon pulp and scatter of crystal shards.

"What?" Venn growled.

"Nothing!" KyVeerah threw his feet to the floor, squeezed past Venn in the doorway, and dashed through the double doors and down to The Courtyard. Even from the bottom of the stairway, KyVeerah could make out the deep growl in Venn's throat.

KyVeerah paced the cobblestones, knowing that they could leave once Venn chilled and came down. He studied the great tree rising up through the intended hole in the house and further through the roof. He was watching the double doors when he heard Venn open the set on the second level. He turned away, not wanting to look expectant when Venn appeared.

Venn's tone was flat, asking, "You ready to go?"

"Absolutely." KyVeerah threw his hair back and dropped his shades.

"Would you like the honors?" KyVeerah gestured toward the raised dais near the small, metal fence that surrounded the tree.

"No."

"Crest Falls," KyVeerah said. "That's the portal we will send to." Venn nodded his understanding before reaching up to adjust his rectangular frames.

-419-

KyVeerah moved to the raised dais with the decorative metal rod protruding from the ground just before it. He stepped up onto it and turned to face the forged double doors.

From the point where he now stood, the two white, glimmering statues seemed to look his way. He regarded the two winged women, faces hidden behind their masks. "Guide me well," he said, placing his hands into his jacket pockets.

KyVeerah looked at the ground and then lifted his eyes to the beautiful, stone figures. *Ready or not...Atrum Unda. Crest Falls.*

Once KyVeerah had vanished through the portal, Venn sighed. Taking his turn on the raised stone dais, he pulled the chain from under his shirt, revealing his vessel, the necklace he wore hidden, with a black star sapphire rested proudly as its focal point. Looking at the winged statue on the left, and then to the right, he couldn't believe he had agreed to go back to Atrum Unda after all this time. *Dammit, Vincent...Atrum Unda. Crest Falls.* Then, like KyVeerah, Venn vanished.

55: *From Portal to Passage*

KyVeerah caught Venn's eye as he appeared on the marker of the portal, in this case a large block of black marble with a second smaller square carved into its top. *Hah*, KyVeerah looked away again, a grin spreading over his lips. *I still can't believe I convinced him to come.*

Venn looked up as the rain clouds of Atrum Unda greeted him. He stepped down, sinking into the sapphire granules. Dropping his head, he looked down at the ground trying to consume his boots. He then turned his head, taking in every visible quadrant of his surroundings. An utterly disgusted look unfurled over his every feature. "Yes, it is official."

"What?"

"It's true. I really do hate you."

"Oh, it's not so bad."

Venn stared in disbelief. "You have got to be kidding."

Nearby, a black fountain was placed against a similar, black marble wall. Well, if it were still considered a fountain when water no longer ran through it. But enough rain fell to keep it partially filled. Two statues were placed at opposite edges of the fountain, heads turned to face the very point where Venn stood.

"Well?" Venn pressed.

"What?"

"Let's go find this mythological passageway of yours."

"Oh, right." KyVeerah looked around, and then started northwest. Venn lifted his feet, one exaggerated step after another, following over the sparkling blue ground. Although in the Dark City, the granules glistened.

"These parts look pretty run-down," Venn noted, as they moved through old abandoned buildings.

"Abandoned, yes. Run-down, yes. However, not nearly as bad as some parts where you find city inhabitants living."

"Oh. Perfect," Venn said, a bit dramatically, especially for him. "Hopefully we will run across some of them during our little visit. Maybe grab them some souvenirs from The Tower while we're at it," he continued to pour on the sarcasm.

"Venn…are you feeling OK?"

Venn gave a blank stare.

"All right," KyVeerah muttered, turning back to his trek.

They continued walking until they reached a hill, blanketed entirely in blue. At its summit stood The Tower of Atrum Unda, a looming menace over the city. Heavy mist covered them as they approached.

Venn stopped in his tracks and KyVeerah, recognizing that Venn was no longer moving behind him, stopped as well. He looked back to see what had caused him to halt. Venn was peering up at The Tower through the mist with a hard, unreadable look on his face.

"We…are going to break into…that?" It had been some time since Venn had been to Atrum Unda, and the sight of The Tower staring down threw an immediate veil of angst over him.

KyVeerah glanced up. "Yes. Yes, we are…and we are not going to get caught either."

"Hah!" Venn laughed, causing KyVeerah to jump back a step or two in surprise.

Venn's gone mental.

"Oh, Blue Ravenna. Let's go," Venn said now, passing right on by KyVeerah and starting up the steep hill. "If I die here, I want you to be aware that I am going to haunt you. Forever." There was not a single drop of humor or sarcasm in his words now.

With a side-glance, wondering how serious Venn was about this, KyVeerah walked beside him.

"It's pretty foggy up here."

Shh!" KyVeerah cut him off, with a finger to his lips.

"What now?" Venn said, in a loud whisper.

"Guards," KyVeerah mouthed. "Black Guard."

"Well what now, maestro?" Venn gave a look of accusation.

"Maestro?"

"I thought you were the one on top of things?"

"Just calm down!"

"Calm down?"

"Yes! And for the sake of Valencia, lower your voice!" KyVeerah hissed. "Now, follow me. Just stay close. This fog may work to our advantage."

"So, we walk straight in front of the Black Guard and hope they don't see us because of a little fog?" Venn couldn't believe it. Then again, it was typical KyVeerah. It was no wonder he managed to get himself into so many messes. Venn strangled the empty air in front of him, grumbling "Of all the numbskull..." Nonetheless, after venting, he followed on up the hill.

KyVeerah's voice entered Venn's mind. *"The Sŭsurrus Fountain is far enough away from The Tower that the fog should let us slip right past them. Even after the recent break-in, I doubt there will be more than three or four of them. Besides, they would never expect anyone to try the same thing again."*

"What were you planning if there wasn't fog to cover us?"

"I hadn't gotten that far yet."

Venn shook his head. *"You are definitely going to get us killed."*

"We'll be fine."

"Right."

Continuing with caution, they reached the hilltop. Sure enough, the fog was thicker there.

"Come on. This way. There's no way they could see us through this. And between the sound of the rivers and the water circling The Tower there's no chance."

"I hope you're right. No one better jump out of the fog to tackle our asses...mine anyway."

"Not everything is about you, Venn."

"What?" KyVeerah saying this set Venn aback.

"Yes. That's right." KyVeerah could sense Venn's reaction, despite the fact that he couldn't see him as he followed behind.

"Someday, Vincent."

"Likewise, Venn. Likewise."

Venn gave a low growl.

They moved over the summit, KyVeerah concentrating on the two Black Guardsmen. He'd given far too much credit in thinking there might be three or four soldiers before the entrance gate.

"Watch your step." They had reached the wide stairs at the fountain's base. They sidled up the three steps to the tall ring that formed the lowest level of the fountain. Though the thick fog worked to their benefit, it did pose its own problems.

KyVeerah climbed up. *"Venn, I am going to jump up to the fountain's second level. Give me a second, and then do the same, but be careful. It's slick."*

They made it to the top with both rain and the fountain's spray cascading over them. They looked over the glimmering, black figures. Venn said immediately, *"If we move the marble cape, it reveals this passageway of yours?"*

"How did you figure it out so quickly?"

"For one, someone left it partially revealed, be it this Archives Intruder or one of your old cronies who you claim never use this passage," Venn pointed out. Sure enough, a sliver of the darkness below showed itself through a thin gap where the marble had not been completely moved back into place.

KyVeerah stifled a wince as Venn looked on with a disapproving expression. *"I'm sure it's nothing to worry about,"* KyVeerah said. *"It was probably that Intruder. And he is a problem that I'm certain we won't have to worry about."*

Venn decided to accept this explanation. *"Damn fool. Don't know how they didn't catch him. What kind of somns do they have running this city?"*

KyVeerah shrugged. *"All right, Venn. We have to move this to uncover the rest of the passage. It takes force, but we don't need to be throwing it from the fountain, so be careful."*

Together, they slid the block aside. Each of their tattoos illuminated beneath their clothing as it slowly moved to reveal the passageway's entrance.

Venn's eyes displayed a look of query as he looked down into the narrow entrance. *"You want me to go down that?"* His thoughts had a ring of alarm, as they entered KyVeerah's mind.

"Uh, yeah. What are we waiting for?" KyVeerah edged his legs over the open shaft, dropping onto the ladder, then disappeared down the vertical passage.

Venn stifled his usual grouse, not wanting to attract the Black Guardsmen. Peering down, he saw that KyVeerah had already made it a good way down the ladder.

"C'mon! That fog isn't going to last forever, you know."

Venn sighed and dropped into the narrow shaft. Moving downward, he cringed at the wet, rusted rungs under his hands. Were he any more muscular, the task would have proved impossible. It was touch and go as it was. Shifting awkwardly, Venn managed to squeeze his body on down. *"I hate you."*

"Ah, haven't heard that one in awhile." KyVeerah's thoughts were amused. *"You know, it's not nearly as bad once you reach the bottom. Ah!"* Speaking of the bottom, KyVeerah reached it, tripping over the contorted table at the ladder's base.

"What the hell?" KyVeerah studied the bowed table with the scattered chairs and playing cards.

"What's wrong?"

"Oh, it's nothing."

"No wonder no one uses this passageway," Venn said in disgust, once he reached the bottom. He looked at the blue muck and the items sprawled over the floor. Then he glanced upward, spotting a smashed light fixture with only a few ragged pieces left hanging on the wall. *"Someone sure wasn't having a good day."*

"I would say not." KyVeerah frowned.

"You still think this is a good idea?"

"Do you ever want to find Marion?"

Venn scowled, as moving quickly, they reached the end of the horizontal passage. He observed the second shaft. His face dropped, saying aloud, "No. Hell, no!"

56: A Loss for Words

"*C'mon,*" KyVeerah said, *still speaking through their mental* connection, as he jumped up onto the second ladder and began to climb. Reaching the top, he exerted his energies toward pushing the marble pillar open. He leaned out with caution and looked around, seeing no one. He figured that would be the case.

KyVeerah emerged from the pillar just ahead of Venn. "*Remind me to never do that again.*" Venn passed a glare along with his thoughts. Then, he noted The Tower's interior. "*Whoa.*"

"*Impressive, yes?*"

Venn peered up at the weblike layout of the upper floors, composed of thick glass and glinting black marble. The transparent walkways made it possible to see up for what seemed forever. Every slightest bit of light made its way down to this bottom floor where it reflected with an extraordinary glare.

"*Just don't look at the floor, it'll blind you,*" KyVeerah said, already heading toward the elevators. Not all waited to accept passengers. The southwest elevator was wrapped in warning tape with a sign declaring it temporarily out of service.

"*Interesting,*" Venn said, noticing the twisted metal of the elevator. "*Not just anyone can do that.*"

"*Huh.*" Pressing a silver button, KyVeerah called for an elevator. The northwest elevator chimed, accompanied by an illuminated star.

Leading Venn inside, KyVeerah now pressed the button for floor 80. He caught Venn's questioning side-glance, and said, "*It isn't our final destination, but we will have to switch elevators.*"

"*Why?*"

"*The Tower is tall enough that each elevator only goes a quarter of the way up. We have to switch to the next set of elevators in order to reach the Prisoner's Quarters.*"

Venn continued to give him an uncertain look.

"*Trust me.*"

"*Hah. Trust you,*" Venn jeered. "*Perhaps we should invite Lord Cain out for drinks afterward, too. You know, after we steal one of his prisoners.*"

KyVeerah ignored him. *"If we just act casual while we switch, no one will find us suspicious. They have no reason to. And for the most part, somns here don't thrive on any sort of spoken interaction."*

Venn, looking at the mirrored ceiling, adjusted his glasses and then looked out through one of the elevator's glass walls. Observing the somns walking about, Venn decided KyVeerah might be right for a change. Everyone seemed to keep completely to themselves. He saw only a couple pairs conversing with one another, and neither pair seemed pleased about their encounter.

The elevator came to a sudden stop on floor 80. Another star crystal ignited, the chime sounded, and the metal doors opened.

"Just follow me," KyVeerah said, walking toward the spiral staircase between the ring of elevators. He noticed that the southwest shaft had been blocked off on this level, just as on the bottom floor.

Noticing this as well, Venn said, *"I was right. It's definitely not just anyone who can pull off that kind of damage."*

"You're telling me."

Reaching floor 81, KyVeerah pressed the subsequent button. Venn and he boarded the new elevator, followed by a young woman with light brown hair and very formfitting attire.

KyVeerah waited for her to select a floor before pressing for 130. *"Dammit."* He turned around, keeping the panel blocked from view. She chose a level above where they wanted to exit. Surely she would know that 130 was the Prisoner's Quarters. Maybe she wouldn't pay attention to where they got off.

"She looks young," KyVeerah observed.

"That doesn't mean anything."

"Perhaps she's new and won't suspect anything when we get off at the Prisoner's Quarters." KyVeerah offered Venn a hopeful look.

They stood at opposite corners of the elevator. The young brunette stood in the center, facing the doors and ignoring the two men sharing the confined space with her.

A grin crawled across KyVeerah's face. *"She is attractive."*

"Vincent! Keep focused."

"Oh, I'm fine." KyVeerah turned his grin Venn's way. *"No harm in looking."*

Venn rolled his eyes as the elevator continued to rise. It slowed abruptly as it neared 130. *"Don't look at her or say anything. Not even anything polite."*

Venn threw him a look. *"Yeah. Remember that."*

As the elevator doors slid open, KyVeerah slipped by the woman. She took a mindless step aside, and Venn also made his way out.

KyVeerah searched his memory. *"003H."*

"Is that supposed to mean something to me?"

"That is Fyfe's cell. 003H."

Watchful, Venn took in the numerous cells stretching in every direction. *"Could they ever need this many?"* He started to read the cell's labeling plates.

"Let's hope not."

In short time, Venn figured out how the cells were positioned. *"This way."* They moved with quiet steps to draw as little attention as possible. Stirring noises came from several of the cells. *"This glinting black marble is too visually appealing for prison cells,"* Venn decided.

Having overheard Venn's last thought, KyVeerah was left speechless. Sometimes he really wondered what the hell kind of mental world Venn actually lived in. Shaking it off, he continued forward until Venn came to a halt and pointed to the cell before them.

Stepping up to the door, KyVeerah kept to one side of its horizontal, barred slot. "Fyfe Van Ingen?" he voiced the question aloud. He heard movement. "Fyfe. I know you are in there." A pair of searching eyes appeared, visible through the slot.

"Who...who is it?" the voice from within the cell quavered. In response, KyVeerah moved where the prisoner could see him. "By the mercy of Eve," Van Ingen said, at the sight of him.

Van Ingen was disheveled, and the usual bit of scruff on his face reached well longer than its norm. "Have you come to get me out?" His eyes were lifeless, and the tiny speck of hope in his voice was barely traceable. The short time he had spent here had turned him much for the worse.

"Yes. Yes, we have."

Van Ingen stared with blank eyes. A recent bruise discolored the side of his face. Its colors were bold, even in the shadows of the cell.

"Hold on, Fyfe. We are going to get you out of here." KyVeerah gave him an assuring look. "Venn," he said, as he placed his hand within one of two shallow boxes engraved into the wall beside the cell's door.

Seeing where KyVeerah had placed his hand, Venn comprehended and put his own hand within the second box. KyVeerah jumped as their combined energies connected to create a circuit. Considering his lifestyle, KyVeerah had almost forgotten the extent of Venn's pure, raw power. The cell doors shifted, sliding back a few inches, and then disappeared into the wall.

Motionless, Van Ingen stared at the open space before him. *"I have something for you,"* KyVeerah told the man, who stood dirty and tattered.

KyVeerah unzipped his long jacket, each of the decorative buckles stopping just short of being in the way. He looked at Venn. "He'll stand out like Valencia on a Lux night. Hold this." KyVeerah handed his jacket to Venn.

Under it, yet over his true outfit, KyVeerah had been wearing a thin robe.

"Aren't you full of surprises," Venn said, impressed that KyVeerah had actually planned something ahead of time.

Grinning at Venn, KyVeerah held the robe out so that Van Ingen could step into it. Van Ingen gave a skeptical look before he shifted into the robe. With an uncertain look on his face, KyVeerah turned to Venn.

"Hood up."

KyVeerah nodded, adjusting the hood of the robe. With sympathy, he appraised how horribly the man had been treated. "He needs food and water. And sleep."

"We need to get him out of here. And fast."

KyVeerah took a second to think. "Can you support him, just as much as necessary? We don't want to look suspicious, but I really don't think he'll be able to move too quickly in his condition."

"Yeah, I can do that," Venn said. "What?" he asked, seeing the look on KyVeerah's face.

"I hope he has at least enough strength to make it through the passageway."

Venn wasn't fond of the thought of maneuvering Van Ingen through those narrow, vertical shafts. "We'll make it work."

"Right," KyVeerah said. "Hopefully that little brunette hasn't blabbed about us getting off here."

"If she has, no one's come after us yet. We had better get moving though."

Ding. KyVeerah and Venn exchanged simultaneous looks of horror as the elevator's chime resonated through the air. Van Ingen's body stiffened under Venn's support, muscles rigid with fear.

Venn reverted to their silent communication. *"Shit."*

"Quick. Hide. I'll check things out," KyVeerah said, steering Venn and Van Ingen back into the shadows of the cell.

"You're kidding," Venn growled. He knew coming to The Tower was a bad idea. He hadn't listened to his instincts, and now he was going to pay the price. He was going to die here with his moronic excuse of an accomplice and an already half-dead man. *"Great. My life is in the hands of an idiot."*

KyVeerah frowned, overhearing this.

"What about the cell doors?" Venn asked, ignoring KyVeerah's reaction. *"If they close, we're trapped!"* Venn's body tensed as officious sounding footsteps drew near to their location. KyVeerah flicked his eyes in the direction of the sound.

"They won't. Just stay there! Fyfe mustn't be seen!" With that, KyVeerah tore himself away from Venn and circled the floor as swiftly and silently as possible. Hoping to sneak up on the advancing threat, KyVeerah drew his hidden blade. *"I must reach him before he gets to Fyfe's cell. Please let it be a simple guard surveying one of the less secured cells,"* KyVeerah prayed, in silence.

Moving with stealth, body against the marble of the innermost cells, he caught sight of a Black Guardsman, his back vulnerable. KyVeerah's knuckles whitened on the grip of his weapon. *"I'll silence him before he can even scream."* A deadly glow emanated from behind KyVeerah's shades, a dark look that conveyed his experience and skill with a blade. Readying his attack, he took a deep breath.

That's all it took. KyVeerah's eyes widened as the alert guard attacked, black sword swinging. Instinctively, KyVeerah evaded the blade. Caught in a moment of surprise, he failed to counterattack as the Guardsman landed a blow to the center of his abdomen. Attempting to dodge the brunt of the attack, KyVeerah had twisted the right side of his body away. A scream died fast as the air was driven from him.

KyVeerah stumbled backward, blood seeping from his newly stitched wound. Hot adrenaline coursed through his veins. *"Now, I'm pissed."*

"Vincent!"

"I'm fine! Stay there!"

The Guardsman launched another attack, dark sword aiming for KyVeerah's throat. Leaning back, the thrust slid just inches from his jaw. Without hesitation, KyVeerah buried his pain, as he rolled with unnatural swiftness to place himself behind his attacker.

Before he could react, KyVeerah's blade sliced the man's throat, his body dropping lifelessly to the floor.

"That ought to teach you," KyVeerah said aloud, panting in relief, as he clutched his side. Panic consumed relief as another unknown assailant attacked from behind, choking the air from his lungs. KyVeerah had failed to sense the arrival of two presences entering the cell block, the second's steps as silent and undetectable as KyVeerah's own. If he weren't currently being suffocated, KyVeerah would have been abashed at his sloppiness.

With quick fingers, KyVeerah spun his blade around, but the skilled assailant knocked it from his hand. The blade, clanging against the ground, it spun beyond his reach. Through his peripheral vision, KyVeerah watched his attacker raise a multicurved dagger. Weaponless, KyVeerah's struggle was futile. He couldn't breathe. His vision began to darken.

Suddenly, KyVeerah was hurled forward, as his attacker's weapon flew from his hand. KyVeerah gasped as air rushed to fill his lungs.

Venn had remained hidden, obeying KyVeerah's command after the first scream, but when he had sensed KyVeerah's life energies fading, he had left Van Ingen in the shadows.

KyVeerah's assailant was raising his blade when Venn arrived. Energies flaring to life, his eyes filled with icy rage as he struck, smashing the man's head into a solid, marble wall. Seeing the man bounce back, as vigilant as ever, was *not* what Venn had expected.

KyVeerah fought to stand up while Venn struggled to suffocate the man who had tried to eliminate his companion. The attacker freed himself from the strong hold, plowing a powerful arm into Venn, hurling him across the room. His form became still.

"Venn!"

KyVeerah hastened to his feet, grabbing the multicurved blade that had dropped adjacent to him. KyVeerah prepared to strike but stopped abruptly, sensing the swelling energy within his opponent. An electrical orb of energy balled in the man's hand. KyVeerah edged backward. *"That's not good."*

Venn began to stir. *"Throw it!"*

KyVeerah launched the weapon.

The man growled in pain, yanking the blade from his shoulder. In the momentary distraction, Venn leapt to his feet. Tattoos vibrant with energy, Venn felt the assailant's jaw crumble under his strength. Before he could react, Venn planted his knee upward into the man's abdomen. His head slammed against the floor, and he lay unmoving.

"Y-you saved me," KyVeerah stammered aloud, with delight momentarily triumphing the pain in his eyes.

"Shut up. What the fuck just happened?" Venn snarled, adjusting his glasses.

"We got attacked? By the looks of it, a Black Guard sentry and…" KyVeerah took a moment to inspect the man who nearly killed him. KyVeerah's throat tightened. "Oh, dear Valencia. Look at the insignia on his chest, Venn. That's a…"

"That's a what?" Venn demanded.

"This man is of the Velvet Order. One of Lord Cain's men," KyVeerah informed, horrified. *Shit*, he thought. *This is not good. Most Definitely.*

"Lord Cain. As in one of *his* assassins?"

"Something like that. It makes sense. He would be a somn with enough energy to unlock the cells. At least the less secure ones that require only one powerful somn's energies to be opened. I bet that's why he was here. And *he* was probably just here as an escort." KyVeerah tilted his head to the dead Black Guardsman. "They'll easily dismiss the death of a member of the Black Guard. -431- It happens. But Lord Cain won't ignore *this*. Shit!" KyVeerah's eyes illuminated in panic.

"He's not dead."

Venn and KyVeerah jumped, focusing their attentions to Van Ingen. They had completely forgotten about him during the commotion. Leaning against a wall for support, he added, "He's just unconscious. He will die shortly, but don't worry. Lord Cain won't be hunting you. He'll want to keep this quiet. I doubt he'll even tell his *buddy*, Nyx Crucian."

"It would make him look weak. Especially after The Tower's recent break-in," KyVeerah verbalized his understanding. Van Ingen smiled vaguely, nodding in affirmation.

"You can't know that," Venn argued.

"Believe me. Fyfe *knows*. We can trust his word," KyVeerah countered.

"Well, so much for not getting caught!" Venn fumed, still pissed at the whole situation.

"That doesn't count. I mean, really, what were the chances?" KyVeerah tossed back, having already returned to his usual self. He crossed the room to retrieve his knife, wiping the blood on the shirt of the dead Black Guardsman. *No point in tarnishing my own clothes.* KyVeerah felt justified. Then he glared at Venn, remembering his own blood, now staining one of his favorite shirts. Venn rolled his eyes with a huff. There were indeed disadvantages to having their mental connection open to one another.

KyVeerah turned to Van Ingen. "Ready, Fyfe? We're getting you out of this place." That miniscule fleck of hope flickered to life in Van Ingen's drained eyes. "OK, let's go." KyVeerah turned and headed in the direction of the elevators. Venn begrudgingly followed after, as he helped support the feeble Van Ingen.

KyVeerah sent another mental message, *"We just have to continue to act as normal as possible."*

Venn snorted, but KyVeerah chose to ignore this, continuing, *"The biggest challenge will be keeping Fyfe from seeming unusual, as we make our way back down."* KyVeerah racked his mind, trying to think of any other way out. Nope. The passageway was their only option.

Approaching the elevators, KyVeerah walked forward to press the silver button. He winced, gingerly running fingers over his side, as he hoped no one would be on the elevator. The chime sounded and the northeast elevator's doors opened.

"Thank Valencia," KyVeerah sighed, as he stepped up to the open elevator. It was unoccupied.

57: Business In the Badlands

KyVeerah stepped through the elevator doors. "Oh shit!" He hesitated but then entered. *"Careful Venn, there's a guy in here, just inside the door."* Venn boarded the elevator, guiding Van Ingen who walked just in front of him with the robe on, hood up. They moved to the side of the elevator opposite the young man, who unbeknownst to Venn and KyVeerah was Nyx Crucian's newest recruit, Jett Milan. He looked their way as Venn observed the panel and hit the button for floor 81.

Jett slouched in the corner. He spoke with a quiet monotone, "Sucks doesn't it."

"What did he say?" Venn asked KyVeerah, feeling anything but pleased that the creepy guy had chosen to talk to them.

"Pardon me?" Venn asked, having received nothing but an unknowing look and a shrug from KyVeerah.

"Taking all those leeches to and from their cells, to them frikkin' little *interrogative sessions* or whatever the hell they call them." He made an irritated motion in the air with his hands.

"Leeches?" Venn asked.

"Yeah. You know what I mean. Transporting them damn, blood suckin' slinks to and from their cells." Jett looked Venn in the eye. "Don't worry. You'll pick up on the lingo in no time," he assured, in a dark, detached voice, as he gave Van Ingen the evil eye.

"Hah, brilliant! He thinks we work for them." KyVeerah choked back a laugh.

"Yeah, perfect. Now, are we about off this damn elevator?" Venn did not find this entertaining.

Ding. The chime sounded. Jett peered at the illuminated star from behind his dark hair, and then looked back to Venn. It was evident that something about Venn caught his interest. He waited, allowing everyone to exit before he did so himself.

KyVeerah moved to the center staircase, Venn not far behind with Van Ingen before him. Jett followed just behind, needing to get down to the next floor as well. Venn and KyVeerah hadn't considered that possibility. He watched the trio as they made their way.

"Good luck with that," Jett said, in his detached manner to both Venn and KyVeerah as they had all reached the floor at the bottom of the stairs. He pointed Van Ingen's way.

"Thanks," Venn forced the word.

"I'm sure I'll be seeing you two around." Jett, not coming off quite as creepy when he wasn't slouched in the corner of the elevator, moved down one of the floor's main corridors.

As a new elevator came to receive them, they climbed in. Venn pressed the button for ground level quickly, not wanting anyone else to try boarding. To all of their relief, the metal doors closed.

Once at the bottom, it was a clear shot to the pillar. Venn half carried Van Ingen as he dashed for it, this time leaving KyVeerah as the one tagging behind. "I have an idea," Venn said.

KyVeerah offered a curious look. Venn was quite eager to be getting out and far away from The Tower. He planned to do so without delay. KyVeerah didn't blame him.

"Let me get down into the shaft, and then let Van Ingen stand on my shoulders. He'd be capable of making it down himself, but it will take him far longer in his condition."

KyVeerah gave him an even more curious look.

"Stop that," Venn warned.

"OK, OK. Get." KyVeerah waved an arm.

Venn crawled into the tight space with KyVeerah watching after. "Venn, are you sure—"

"Just do it, Vincent!"

"OK!" KyVeerah turned to Van Ingen and helped him step onto Venn's shoulders. "Just walk the ladder down with your hands." KyVeerah could already tell life was attempting to reenter him.

They made it through the remainder of the passageway, Van Ingen climbing up the second ladder by himself, though very tired and his body aching. Thankful that fog still blanketed the hilltop, they climbed up out of the entrance and helped Van Ingen down the fountain.

Once past the bottom ring, they hurried down the steps and to the base of the sapphire hill.

Van Ingen turned to look where The Tower stood beyond the fog. It was like he had achieved a hundred miles distance by the look on his face. "Thank you." The gratitude he expressed couldn't have been greater.

"Don't mention it," KyVeerah waved it off, but was delighted at having succeeded in freeing him.

His body still aching, Van Ingen nodded, showing his respect and appreciation.

"*Venn,*" KyVeerah said, reentering his mind. "*I need you to take Fyfe and yourself someplace safe.*"

"*And this someplace safe would be where?*"

"Do you have a pen and paper?" KyVeerah asked Venn aloud. Van Ingen was looking about, lost in his thoughts.

"Yeah. I think so." Venn fished through the pockets of his jacket. He retrieved a pen and a folded sheet of paper, handing them over to KyVeerah.

Holding the paper in his right hand, KyVeerah scribbled an address and brief directions. He handed them back to Venn, reentering his mind. "*If nothing else, I'm sure Fyfe will be able to track the address, but I'm sure you'll find it. Oh, one more thing.*" KyVeerah reached into a pocket at his side, unzipping an even smaller pocket within to extract an object from it. He handed over a key, which Venn accepted. "*That'll get you in.*"

"*And where are you off to?*"

"*I have some business that I should tend to as long as we're in the vicinity.*"

Venn locked him in a powerful stare.

"I'm going to have to walk around a bit. Maybe quite a bit," KyVeerah admitted aloud. "Actually, I've a lot to tend to. I probably won't get back until morning. So, don't worry."

This brought an "as if" smile to Venn's lips.

Realization kicked in, eliciting a frown in KyVeerah's own features. "I must be off. Fyfe, I will see you tomorrow." Van Ingen waved him off, and KyVeerah turned on his heels, heading south.

℘℩℘

Clang, clang. KyVeerah pounded the door knocker against the door and its odd surface. *This door used to be quite different*, KyVeerah thought. He was curious as to what happened with the old one. *No one would intentionally choose this makeshift door. Looks like someone made it themselves, and not as an adornment.* He hoped that those he was seeking still lived here. Then the door creaked open with an unpleasant scraping and squeaking. No, this door had not been built or placed well at all.

"Ah, Coraline Fisher," KyVeerah greeted, as he saw a woman with spiraling, black-brown hair and matching dark brown, nearly black eyes.

"Shh!" She threw her index finger up before her lips, peeking out the door to be sure no one else was anywhere within sight. The door made further unpleasant sounds as she forced it further open. "You know we don't use names here," she warned, eyes narrowing, as she pointed a threatening finger.

"Yes." KyVeerah had the compulsion to throw in her first name after the "yes," but he bit his tongue, revealing no more than a charming smile.

"Haven't seen you in a bit," she said, allowing him to step inside. Once he was in, she shut the door as tightly as it would fit in its frame, and then locked it. Good thing the locks and bolts worked.

"Is Donivan...I mean, your husband...home?" Even in KyVeerah's line of business, he was accustomed to speaking to others by name, be it their true name or an alias. Then there was the fact that the Fishers had given him their true names over a bottle of booze and some business at one point in time. Perhaps that was the real problem here, the fact that Coraline and Donivan had broken their own code.

She flashed another warning look. *Eeh, strike two.* "No matter, you and I manage business fine on our own, just the same," KyVeerah tried to distract her from his slip up.

"Yes." She gave him a less harsh, pleased-to-see-you look. Coraline Fisher was three years KyVeerah's junior. Her husband, Donivan Fisher, was twenty-nine, just a year older than him.

"He is aware someone is here. He will be up shortly." Coraline walked to the stove for two mugs of steaming liquid. Her dangling, gold earrings swayed as she moved, and her many golden bracelets jangled with the motion of her arms. As she turned to KyVeerah, her long flowing skirt twirled about her. "Would you care for some hot mallow?" she asked. "It's very fresh. The leaves and herbs we use are grown here in our home."

"No, thank you, I'm fine."

"Are you sure?" she pressed, with an alluring look, dark eyes looking intently and full pouting lips parted ever so slightly.

"Oh, all right," KyVeerah gave in. "One cup would do me well."

Just then, Coraline's husband stepped into the room. "My, my, isn't this a surprise. Haven't seen you in some time," he said, offering KyVeerah a thrilled smile. Donivan was as appealing to the eye as his wife. If they weren't so very good at the business they carried out behind these closed doors, one might suggest they try the streets for a living. They would certainly be much more successful than most.

Donivan Fisher looked like trouble at first glance, as well as every glance thereafter. No one would look away with him around, concerned that he would pick his or her pockets empty. His hair was shaggy, curly black, and a bit messy. He had a black, smartly groomed goatee and a gold hoop earring hanging from his left ear.

Coraline handed them each a cup of hot mallow. Retrieving a mug of her own, she joined the men.

"So, what brings you around these parts?" Donivan asked. An accent lined his smooth words, thicker than his wife's.

"I am in need of some assistance, and I believe you two fit the bill."

Donivan lowered his mug after a cautious sip. He looked up intrigued, deep brown eyes filled to the rim with interest. "How may we assist you?"

"I am in need of a couple of vessels," KyVeerah said. "If my recollection serves me well, you two have a rather adequate collection of them."

Donivan's crafty smile appeared after another drink. "We know you well enough to be sure that your recollections would never serve you poorly."

"We actually just picked up a few new ones." As Coraline said the words "picked up" she smiled, thrilled as if it had been quite an enjoyable task to collect them in adding to their assortment. She turned to her husband. "Would you like me to…?"

"Oh, yes. Would you?" he said, without her needing to finish the thought.

"Certainly." She set her saucer and mug down on the sitting room table before moving across the room and stepping out of view.

"She'll be right back. The doors are secured, yes?" Donivan asked.

"Yes," KyVeerah said, after a swallow, "they are."

"Excellent," Donivan said, in satisfaction. "Please, take a seat." He signaled to the pair of chairs and the couch set around the table. "You're a valuable client. I won't let the mites rob you blind," Donivan assured, showing another cunning grin.

KyVeerah accepted, taking a seat in one of the tattered, fabric chairs that the Fishers had picked up somewhere along the line. Naturally, no piece of furniture around the table matched the others. After his client had taken a seat, Donivan made himself comfortable in the opposite chair. He sat at the edge of the chair instead of sitting back, placing his saucer and mug on the table before him.

Coraline came back into the room, skirt and earrings swinging and her golden bracelets continuing to jangle. KyVeerah set his own mug down on the table as she advanced with a fabric trunk in her arms. He took the trunk from her, placing it on his lap. As he unfastened the latches, Coraline took a seat on the mismatched fabric couch.

Both Fishers watched as KyVeerah opened the trunk, hoping that he would be pleased. They knew that whatever price he was willing to pay, be it money or another offer, it would prove more than sufficient. With KyVeerah, the gain was always well worth the business.

"Well, you do indeed have an impressive hodgepodge," KyVeerah said, after rummaging through the trunk. The Fishers congratulated one another with self-satisfied looks. The arrogant smile and deep scarlet lipstick on Coraline's pouty lips gave her a lascivious appeal. Donivan winked at her thinking KyVeerah wouldn't notice, not that it mattered, just a wrong supposition.

In truth, the trunk contained a remarkable hoard of vessels. More than KyVeerah had ever seen in one place at one time. *I wonder how many of these were stolen?* The question crossed his mind, though knowing would do no good. He could use it to bargain for a lower price, but that would only antagonize his source, and it wasn't as if he couldn't afford full price. Besides, the Fishers were far more in need than he. Nonetheless, KyVeerah assumed that most had undoubtedly been snatched at one point or another. That could be one risky factor when dealing with the Fishers. You couldn't be certain of an item's original owner or which owner the Fishers swiped it from.

All of the vessels were individually wrapped to keep them from tangling or clanging together, as well as to provide a more personal look. If the vessels had just been tossed into the fabric trunk, they would indisputably resemble the stolen items they were. That is exactly what the Fishers had to avoid.

Finally making a decision, KyVeerah closed the trunk. Resecured, he set it on the table among the mugs of hot mallow. Upon it, he placed the two individually packaged vessels he had chosen.

One of the vessels was an anklet. It had a thin, black chain that secured a curved, rectangular plate with a black star sapphire set into its center. The second was a long, silver chain, from which a crystal with silver caps on top and bottom was suspended. A black star sapphire hung within the crystal, like a fossilized creature caught in amber. Thin silver bands over the crystal's surface gave it a slight resemblance to an old hanging lantern.

Coraline formed another pouting smile. "Those are two of our newest additions. I thought they might interest you."

"Excellent," Donivan said, standing from his chair. KyVeerah took this as his signal to stand as well. "What are we accepting as payment today?"

KyVeerah pulled a wad of bills from an inner pocket of his jacket. "Nothing extraordinary today, I'm afraid. But, so far, no living soul has objected to my offering of cash."

"Oh, absolutely." Donivan flashed his cunning smile. "I'm certain it will do us well."

"I hope so. I must go though, I have many things to tend to."

Coraline rose, handing the neatly wrapped items to him, which he placed into a jacket pocket.

"Coraline," Donivan said, looking at the trunk. Leaning forward, she picked it up, and turning to face KyVeerah, smiled. "Come back, anytime." He nodded respectfully, as she made her way back out of the room.

Donivan walked KyVeerah to the door, unlatching the bolts and forcing it open with another horrendous sound. KyVeerah tried to stifle a cringe, but Donivan gave a short laugh. "Yeah, we'll be replacing this thing soon enough. Hey, maybe some of our day's worth can be put to good use here?"

"Glad to be of service."

"Ya take some, ya give some."

"Well, I appreciate your accommodations."

"Come again, anytime."

"Of course." At this, KyVeerah made his way back down the dimly lit Atrum alley.

KyVeerah came to a standstill as he reached a nearby intersection that, to a foreign eye, would look like a million others in this city. He smiled, decicing to add another stop. He was on the move again.

58:An Unforeseen Pairing

"So, just what the hell is a 'perturbation' anyway?"

Helena hadn't intended to start off their conversation in this fashion, but she couldn't help it. She was pissed. It was bad enough that she had never been close to anything resembling a school growing up. But it angered her that some long dead brain-o-crat could make her feel so stupid.

Helena hadn't intended to start off their conversation in this fashion, but she couldn't help it. She was pissed. It was bad enough that she had never been close to anything resembling a school growing up. But it angered her that some long-dead brain-o-crat could make her feel so stupid.

After Albert had taken his leave, she had studied her ass off. All night long. But she felt so unprepared today that she was sure Serlio would see her as no more than just another bratty little schoolgirl. Without even realizing it, she kept reaching into her purse to rub the handle of her knife for comfort.

It was a habit she had tried to break. Some people bit their nails, some popped their knuckles, and some tapped their fingers on the table. Helena stroked her blade.

Serlio wasn't put off in the least. In fact, he smiled. He found her method of coping with stress much less annoying than any of those other options. And, he had reflected, in her line of work, with the type of stresses she faced, it was probably a very useful habit.

She already had the ball rolling. He might as well dive in, so he started. "Perturbation is just a fancy word for disturbance. Breaking down the title of the manuscript is easy. You already know what a Calling is. That's why you're here. An anomaly is just something unusual. Or out of the ordinary. Atmospheric—"

"That I know," she jumped in. "That is like the weather."

He nodded. "So, just like a simple puzzle, put the pieces together."

"OK. A Calling Anomaly would be…hmmm…how a Calling makes something different? And an Atmospheric Perturbation would be…a change in the weather. So, evidently Callings must make the weather do something strange?"

"Close enough. You see, Callings are filled with excess Energy. And Energy is what makes everything go. Everything. To tell you the truth, it isn't just the weather that sees an effect when a Calling is near. Everything and everybody will have some reaction. It just happened that the weather was one of the first things to be noticed.

"But we need to backtrack a little and attack this in an orderly fashion. First we must ask: Where do the Callings get their excess Energy from, anyway? And that goes back to the talk we had yesterday. You do remember the early somns and The Ancients?"

Helena nodded.

"And you recall that they each had different Energies?"

Another nod.

"Good. Then you will remember how the Energies flow side by side using the towers as positive and negative poles. However, the Energies don't always stay in nice straight channels like they are going down the street. Instead, they are more like rivers. They meander back and forth, with currents and eddies.

"They might swing wide, and even double back on themselves. At times they touch. And at times they collide. And when this happens the currents get backed up. And just like water, it tries to find somewhere to go."

"Now, you remember how The Ancients were able to put Energy into a somn?"

Another nod.

"The same thing happens. Except this time it is the Energies that decide who the somn will be." He grinned. "Not really. Most think it is just a matter of coincidence. You know—right time, right place.

"However, there are some who argue quite well, who believe that the Energies have some kind of Cosmic Consciousness and actually choose their host. Either way, some poor sap is walking along minding his own business, when *boom!*

"OK, sometimes it occurs right at birth, but more often it's in adulthood. Being male or female doesn't make much difference. And not all Callings are created equal. Sometimes the Energies just do a little dump, and sometimes it's the mother lode."

"But why are there Callings and Messengers? How do they know how to split it up? And why are they so different?"

Serlio pointed his finger. "That is a great question. It has everything to do with that whole *dichotomy of the universe* thing that we had talked about yesterday. Also, you need to remember that there are two separate sources of the Energies. There are the somns, but also The Ancients. Just because they haven't come back, doesn't mean that their Energies aren't flying around out there.

"Even though they aren't perfectly parallel, equal amounts of the energies just naturally tend to stick together. It basically keeps the universal balance intact.

"Now, just as the two peoples are not the same, neither are their Energies. The Energies of the somns are more brick-and-mortar stuff. It's more involved with strength and brute force. It moves mountains. The Energies of The Ancients is more cerebral and more esoteric. It's more involved with planning and creating. With understanding and control.

"In essence, the two parts make one whole. You have muscles, but without the brain they would just sit, not knowing what to do. On the other hand, the brain might recognize danger, but without the muscles, it couldn't get out of the way."

"Are every Calling and his Messenger always together then? Don't they get sick of each other?"

Serlio actually laughed. "Why, yes my dear. I imagine they surely do!"

He stopped for a moment to gather his thoughts. Taking advantage of the break, he poured them both drinks from the pot. After settling down again, he took an appreciative sip, then began again.

"Remember how we were talking about dipoles? Well as couples go, a Calling and his or her Messenger are about as close to a dipole as you can get. Brutish or sly. Reticent or vocal. Reserved or outgoing. The list goes on and on. Before they meet, someone like you and me would probably like the Messenger. He or she would be quite mature for their age, witty, outgoing, and nice to sit with for hours in deep conversation. On the other hand, your Calling would be pretty lost, bumbling about trying vainly to discover who they are. They would be so full of unused energy that they would be restless and moody." Serlio smiled. "Much like going through adolescence. Only times ten.

"And the Key Calling you keep mentioning? Multiply that by another ten." He scratched his head. "Maybe more. Who knows? There is only to be one. And it is rumored that he will come when times are darkest. I guess that just makes sense because that would be when the cosmic Energies have been the most backed up. The Key Calling receives Energies of both the somns and The Ancients."

Realizing he had shifted track, Serlio picked up where he had left off.

"And to top it off, their rate of development is very different. I guess you can imagine they are trees: The Messenger, who receives his Energies from The Ancients, is very fast growing. He is way ahead of the Calling. But he is like the softwood tree. Fast, but the wood is not as strong. The Calling is like a hardwood tree, slower to develop, but very strong.

"As a matter of fact, since they often have no idea who the other may be—until they finally are united—the cells of the Messenger are affected in some way so that he or she does not age. That helps keep them together, at least physically, until the Calling can catch up—by showing up. Then the Messenger starts aging again.

"There is a small cult of mystics, shall we say, that is housed at each tower. For reasons we don't have time in one session for, they cannot interfere with the natural growth and progression of these beings. However, they can provide a great service to them. And that is by giving each of them permanent markings, or tattoos, that are identical and unique enough to leave no doubt to the pair when they finally do meet.

"The hardest part for them is making absolutely sure that they get the right Callings paired up with the right Messengers. And that is the whole basis for the book you hold in your hand. As I said earlier, every Calling and every Messenger has an effect on everything around them. And each pair has the same unique pattern as to what those effects are. Most of the signs are extremely subtle. Mystics devote their entire life to no other cause. And it is difficult for them."

Helena was crestfallen. "Then how in the world can I ever recognize them? It will be impossible."

Serlio wagged his finger. "No, no, my dear. You see, the basic principles for recognizing a Messenger or Calling are really pretty simple, if you concentrate on the phenomena discussed in your manuscript. If you study and observe, I guarantee you will know when one is near. As I said, the hard part will have already been taken care of by the mystics. Your main job will be to keep your eyes wide open, so you will recognize what you are looking for when you see it."

With that, Serlio clapped his hands much like a teacher dismissing a class. Helena had heard his voice slipping, but was paying so much attention that it hadn't registered.

For a while they sat in silence allowing Helena to absorb what he had said. At length, she was the one who initiated an exit. She stood up. "Thank you so much for everything. And thank you for the manuscript. I promise I will read it until I have every word inked onto my brain." Again she leaned forward to offer a gentle hug. Now it was a real hug. She didn't have to play any more games. She had what she had come for.

When they reached the shop door, just before she stepped through, Serlio gave her a sly half wink, in exact imitation of hers yesterday. "Go on and study, but when you get thirsty don't be a stranger." This time his wink was genuine. Then, with a gentle pat, he had her out the door, much like a mother sending her child off for the day.

Walking down the sidewalk, Helena was at first shocked and filled with embarrassed anger. Why, that old fox had read right through her entire act yesterday. But in a few steps she smiled brightly. Yes, in his Rafter days that old codger had definitely been around the horn and back.

Halfway down the block, she turned to see if he was looking. He was. She smiled a true smile and waved.

He waved back.

59: Flowers for a Friend

Scattered street lamps cast a blue glow over the city via reflections from the sapphire ground. KyVeerah covered several blocks before entering the Corinth Sector and mounting a single wide marble step to knock on a garishly painted silver door.

He heard a single pair of feet moving over the wooden floor. Multiple locks could be heard turning and unlatching. The door opened as far as the chain inside would allow. A young woman peered out through the open crack. "For the love of Adelaide..." she said, in quiet disbelief, closing the door with haste.

KyVeerah continued standing there, looking at the door. He heard the chain slide free, and the door opened as quickly as it had closed.

"Hello, love." KyVeerah rested his hand high on the door frame, grinning ear to ear.

"I can't believe it." Her warm smile widened, as she teased, "I thought you would be as far from this place as your legs could carry you."

"Aren't I just full of surprises."

"Oh, goodness. I'm so sorry, come in," she apologized, in her velvet voice. Pulling the door wider, she waved him to enter. "Give me your jacket."

After hanging it, she closed and locked the door before leading her guest to the sitting room. "Sit down, sit down."

KyVeerah followed her to the couch, sitting with a cringe as sharp pain made itself known. His activities were not helping his wound. She frowned at the fresh bloodstain on his shirt from his earlier altercation in the Prisoner's Quarters.

"Are you OK?" she asked, with true concern.

He attempted to relax as pain gripped his side, trying hard to refrain from baring his teeth. "Oh, yeah," he said, after a breathless moment, waving a hand to dismiss the issue. He patted the couch beside him. "Come. Have a seat, I don't bite. Not normally, anyway."

The young woman shook her head with a smile. She seated herself a few feet to his side.

"How have you been, Tazo?"

"Good, good." She nodded. "And yourself?"

He chewed this over. "You know. Trying not to get into too much trouble. At least nothing I can't get myself out of alive." He bit off his words, knowing that his last remark wouldn't really fly with Tazo.

Her foggy blue eyes filled with alarm. She placed a hand on her leg and leaned toward him. "You are going to get yourself killed!" She couldn't believe he found this kind of talk comical. Almost.

"Oh, I'll be fine," he assured, in an all-too-light manner.

She shook her head again. "You know, it's a good thing you didn't show up later. I have to work the late shift tonight."

"What can I say, I have spectacular timing." He smiled, in arrogance. "Besides, I do have more business to take care of. I just thought you'd be exhilarated that I decided to drop by." A light twinkle showed in his eyes.

KyVeerah leaned forward to a handcrafted crystal vase on the low, black metal table. It was filled with dozens of small blue and violet flowers. Each stretched out on a long, thin stem. Reaching out, he plucked three of them.

"Where have you been?" Tazo asked, watching as he sat back, fiddling with the long stems. She didn't expect a complete answer, but she asked nevertheless.

"Nowhere a decent woman such as yourself should ever be."

"What happened?"

He continued to concentrate on the flowers, shifting them about between his slender, ringed fingers. "What do you mean?"

"You are in pain. And that certainly isn't juice from a rabmelon on your shirt. There's no way of sliding out of this one," she said, trying to present an air of authority.

"I came across an acquaintance I hadn't expected."

"And?" Brow raised, she tapped an insistent finger on her knee.

"And she had a blade. I got cut up a little bit," he said, without going into detail. His voice was level, but she knew that he was understating what had happened. Tazo had enough sensitivity that the painful turmoil that he tried so desperately to keep under wraps was as clear as an open book to her.

Feeling her unconvinced eyes, he paused, securing the flowers' current position with a single hand. He leaned his shoulders back against the upper cushions of the couch. With minor difficulty, he used his other hand to pull his shirt up, revealing many tattoos and the large swath of bandaging covering his right side as well as his chest just over his heart. Fresh blood had seeped through and dried over the lower quarter of the larger dressing. The darkness in his eyes asked whether she was satisfied.

"Adelaide, almighty!" Tazo threw both hands up over her mouth. "That is not a little bit!" she scolded, eyes wide, as she lowered her hands. "Are whatever's under those properly treated at least? Oh lord, please say they are." She gave a deep look of concern, eyeing the newly dried blood. "Those dressings have to be changed!"

KyVeerah pulled his shirt back down. "They will be shortly."

"You promise?" she stressed, with a serious set to her features.

"Yes. It's being well taken care of," he assured, amused by her reaction.

"Well, it damn well better be!" she lectured, still unsure whether she should believe him. In the mean time, he had returned to the flowers. Tazo looked at him with curiosity. Because of the way he was holding them, she could not see what he was doing with them. Finally, he stopped his fiddling.

"Tazo," he said, carefully shifting his position to face her. He put out a hand, palm up.

Her smile was open, and she gently placed her hand onto his, knowing that was what his action requested. "Yes?"

"Has anyone ever told you how radiant you are? I could tell you every day. You brighten this city. If only where you stand, that is more than enough." As Tazo looked at KyVeerah, face flushing, he slid something onto her finger.

Still flushed, she lowered her eyes. KyVeerah had braided the flowers, creating a ring to fit around her finger. The flowers, pale blue, blue-violet, and deep violet sat in a perfect arrangement at the top of her finger.

"You really are something, but you know you are not my type." She smiled kindly. This conversation had occurred before.

"Oh, yes," he said, tilting his head, looking at the other side of the room. "You'd like yourself a dashing, loyal, and all together too well-rounded son of a dagger," KyVeerah teased. He sat silently for quite some time, as a thoughtful expression crossed his face. "I fit the bill for over fifty percent of those things." He gave her a playful look. "Isn't that quite enough?"

They continued talking until nearly two hours had passed. "I must get changed for work," she announced, leaning forward, slapping a hand on his leg and pushing herself up from the couch.

Tazo returned to the sitting room after enough time to shower, do her makeup, and pick out something to wear. KyVeerah had been laying on the couch resting as she readied herself. As she stepped into the room, his jaw dropped.

"Tazo Brooks!"

"What?" She smiled at his perplexed frown.

"Don't you know you are going to a *bar*?"

"Uh, yeah." She looked up out of the corner of her eye. "That *would* be where I work."

"You look far too indecent to go to a bar. Don't you have any idea what kinds of men hang out at bars? Especially in this city."

Tazo's smile widened, and she batted her eyes.

"No." He rotated a finger in the air. "You go put something else on, miss. Men at bars don't deserve to be seeing your pretty little ass and tah-tahs."

Tazo smiled even wider. She rolled her eyes and turned from the room.

"I suppose the makeup can stay," he shouted. "Even though it's covering your beautiful face," he shouted this second part a little louder, as she got further from the room. He closed his eyes, but that didn't keep a new grin from coming to his face.

"Hey!"

KyVeerah's eyes snapped open, looking up to see Tazo standing over him. *Huh. I must've dozed off.*

"Ah," he said, as registration kicked in. "See, doesn't that outfit just feel so much more attractive? Appealing, without giving those naughty boys any visual candy." He flared his eyebrows.

She grabbed a pillow that had fallen to the floor, playfully hitting him with it as he began to laugh. He reacted quickly enough that her blow was partially deflected.

"But really," he said, lowering his arm with caution, "you look absolutely stunning."

"Why, thank you." She gave a small laugh. "I have to head to work, but you stay here and rest. Looks like you need it. You can either stay out here or you can use the bed in the spare room. No one has used it since my cousin moved out."

"Don't I look comfortable here?" He kept a straight face for a second, but then his expression sold him out.

"You are absurd." She hit him with the pillow again before walking toward the side door. "Just use this door when you leave. It'll lock behind you."

He raised an arm with his fingers extended in a farewell gesture. Tazo smiled again, and stepping out, closed it after her. KyVeerah closed his eyes once more, and in less than a minute, he had checked out.

60: Surfacing Uncertainties

Just as had happened the previous morning, or more accurately afternoon, a loud knock sounded at the door of Rhyus's bedroom. This morning, however, it was the persistent knocking that woke him, rather than an all-too-real dream.

Rolling to face the door, Rhyus hoisted himself into a sitting position. The knocking came again.

"Yeah?"

"Morning!" Lenim said, throwing the door open as far as it would go.

Rhyus had expected this today, and unlike the day before, he kept a good portion of his body covered by the comforter to avoid feeling so awkward around his host.

"Ready yourself. We're going for a stroll!" Lenim raised his brows, telling Rhyus he should look forward to such an event. "I'll be upstairs."

Rhyus let out a sigh. "OK." Half willing, he rolled out of bed.

ଛଠ

Rhyus headed upstairs, prepared for what the day might bring. Today Lenim would be in the kitchen waiting. *I wonder if Yuri will be up there too?*

When he reached the top of the stairs, he saw no one. Sweeping the kitchen, still no one. Then he thrust his hand into the air. Turning his head, he looked at the object he had caught without so much as a glance from his peripheral vision.

"Marvelous!"

Rhyus looked where the object had come from. Lenim now stood in a doorway. *He wasn't there a second ago*, Rhyus swore.

"Yuri was so kind as to inform me that you liked the one you had yesterday." Lenim gestured toward the jin melon Rhyus now held in his hand.

"He also informed me that you have remarkably quick reflexes. I see this holds *very* true." Lenim wore a peculiar expression.

As Rhyus looked down at the jin melon, he could feel Lenim's expression weighing heavy on him.

"Go on then. Once you've finished eating we'll head out. Please, have a seat." Lenim extended an open hand toward the kitchen table. Like everything else in the house, the table and chairs must have cost a grand fortune.

℘ℛ

Lenim and Rhyus made their way, weaving through the city, walking without conversation for the first long stretch. *Strange*, Rhyus thought. It normally seemed odd for such silence to be shared between any two somns, yet this was a *peculiarly* comfortable silence.

He noticed that they had kept near the barrier surrounding the city. This time, as Rhyus eyed the white stone, he had no yearning to be back in Lux Lumetia. He had grown fond of The Urbs, and in short time. After all, though it felt like weeks, he had arrived here on Insula Palam Vita only two days ago. Rhyus marveled at how quickly he had acclimated.

"Rhyus," Lenim said.

The words would have seemed out of the blue, but considering the odd silence of their walking, the thought didn't even occur to Rhyus. "Yeah?" he said.

"Do you know of a place by the name of Atrum Unda?"

Returning to silence, Rhyus tried to recall the name. He shook his head. "No."

"Are you certain? The Dark City?"

Rhyus spent another thoughtful moment before shaking his head again. "No," he repeated. "I can't recall."

An expression both confused, yet inquisitive, lined Lenim's features. There was something he couldn't understand.

Rhyus was filled with an urge to ask Lenim why he wished to know, and why he expected him to know such a place, but he resisted. He kept his mouth shut, waiting to see whether a new question would take the place of the first.

"You traveled here from Lux Lumetia." Lenim came to a halt. He didn't dance around the fact that Sultan had relayed this information.

"Yes," Rhyus admitted. There was no point in lying. He already knew the truth.

"And Marion."

"What about Marion?" Rhyus asked, with a little more snap than intended.

"You two don't really even know one another?"

"Well...we met three days before we left Lux Lumetia." The comfort they had shared in their silence had drained entirely. Rhyus now felt the unblinking of Lenim's opaque, midnight eyes, as he probed, reaching for answers.

"Lux Lumetia. Why were you there? How did you get there?" Strangely, Lenim's words were urgent and almost reached a desperate chord as he pressed for answers.

"I don't know," Rhyus admitted, with growing concern. He didn't understand what was going on. He did know that he was not at all fond of Lenim when he fell into these unpleasant moods.

"What do you mean, you don't know?" Lenim's tone was harsh.

"That is exactly what I mean. I don't know. I was unconscious or something. I have no idea how I got there." Lenim was creating an eerie, sickening feeling in the pit of Rhyus's stomach. Something wasn't right.

"Then why Marion?" he demanded. "Why has she come with you? You are telling me that you have absolutely no idea who she is or anything about her?"

"No." Rhyus's answer was blunt. But after the piercing look Lenim sent his way, he added, "Nothing more than the insignificant things one learns about another in such a short time." He shook his head, not knowing what else to say. It was evident that his answers failed to please Lenim, who continued to stare down at him.

But then a change took place. Lenim's eyes retrieved their probes. He shook his head, irritated that he was unable to comprehend something of such immense importance.

"So," Lenim reiterated, "you don't remember anything before finding yourself in Lux Lumetia?"

The harsh quality of Lenim's stare had relaxed, allowing Rhyus to feel a bit more at ease, yet the question was significant. But why?

"No. I don't remember anything before then." Rhyus shook his head. The fact of his unknowing now seemed unnerving. Of course it had crossed his mind a million times, but he figured there was nothing he could do about it. He had hoped it would come back to him in time. However, nothing had yet. A sudden burst of irritable fury shot through him at the tone of this interrogation. He knew Lenim had noted it because a curious change of expression occurred in the second following.

Resigned, Lenim looked away, knowing that Rhyus's every

word held true. He took several steps away in his own frustration, running fingers through his rich, mahogany hair. He finally stood motionless, facing away with fingers interlaced behind his head.

"Come on. I have things to take care of. I'll take you back to the house. Yuri should arrive soon if he isn't there already." Rhyus could see Lenim turning back inward, lost in his own thoughts.

After a good walk, they reached their destination, and Lenim halted. "I will leave you here. As I said, Sultan should be here shortly if he isn't inside already. I will see you this evening."

Rhyus started up the walkway, realizing that Lenim was waiting to make sure that he did so. Once at the door, he turned around to see that Lenim was nowhere in sight.

Entering, Rhyus figured he would head down to his temporary room.

"Hello."

Rhyus jumped, turning his head in the direction of the voice. Caught up in his own thoughts, he had forgotten that Sultan might be there.

"Startle much?" Sultan joked. He sat on a barstool, feet perched on the metal bars.

"Hah, funny."

"Oh. I was going to ask how your walk went. Apparently not so well?"

"Actually, it was a *lot* of fun. Perhaps the best outing I've ever had. An absolute riot."

"Easy on the sarcasm." Sultan gestured to take it down a level, cringing as if it physically pained him.

Rhyus rolled his eyes.

"Oh come on. Was it really so terrible that you can't forget it now to have a good time?"

Rhyus shook his head, sitting next to Sultan. He sported a thick, netted, long-sleeved shirt today, along with a violet bandana around his head. His pink lenses were hooked onto the front of his shirt.

"Bead berries?" Sultan lifted a hand in offering. He had been holding and eating them the whole time.

"No, thanks."

"Oh, come on. Just try one. I insist."

Rhyus laughed at Sultan's persistence. He shook his head again, but this time in a more spirited manner. "Oh, hell. Why not." Tossing them into his mouth, he exclaimed, "Good lord, these are good. I mean *really* good!"

Sultan shrugged. "I told ya. They're mouthwatering."

"Yeah, yeah."

Sultan held a hand out again in temptation, knowing that Rhyus would love more, but that he was too proud to admit Sultan had been right.

A crooked grin slipped out, "Gee, thanks."

Sultan chuckled. "Don't mention it. But really. They are that good."

"All right already! You were 100 percent correct!" Rhyus laughed, surprised how Sultan could always put him in such a good mood.

They sat with a comfortable silence between them. It was more of a shared silence between friends than the isolated silence shared with Lenim.

"So, Lenim tried to pelt me with a jin melon this morning."

Sultan busted out laughing. "Sorry about that. I suppose I should've seen that coming."

"Yeah, thanks for that, Yuri. He told me you had informed him of my good reflexes." Rhyus gave Sultan an accusing, yet lighthearted, look.

"Impeccable."

"What?"

"Impeccable. I told him that you have *impeccable* reflexes." That dazzling smile returned.

"Well, thanks. I guess," Rhyus said, unsure what to say.

"No problem, just an observation. Most impressive, I say."

"Well, lucky for me, or that jin melon would have made it clear through my skull."

Sultan laughed. "Hey, would you like to go back to Café Kampnel for an early afternoon bite? I presume you could use a true meal, no matter how delicious these bead berries may be."

"Yeah. That sounds great."

"What are we waiting for?" Sultan popped the last few berries into his mouth and hopped off the barstool. "Come on."

ഇരു

Opening the door to Café Kampnel, Sultan stepped in after Rhyus. "Miranda, what are you doing here at such an hour?" Sultan asked, with his charming manner. He removed his glasses, hooking them back onto the front of his shirt.

Rhyus recognized the young woman with short-styled black

hair and royal blue eyes. Her dangling crystal earrings matched her green and white dress uniform more than the previous blue hoops, though Rhyus hardly noticed.

"Gwen's son has fallen ill, and I agreed to come in early so that she could go home and tend to him." Miranda stood up, placing a book she had been reading onto a shelf beneath the desk.

"Ah, a logical explanation. It is unusual to see you here anytime before four."

"Yeah, it's that karma bug, you know? I figure if I help Gwen out, something good's bound to come my way." Miranda smiled. Not in a forward way, just an honest smile.

"Certainly," Sultan agreed. "I would assume nothing less."

After Sultan had ordered for both of them, they made their way to the opposite wall, seating themselves exactly as the day before.

"Do you always sit at this booth?" Rhyus asked.

"Mostly. Unless I decide to eat on the go or outdoors. But if that be the case, I know a few ideal locations not too far from here."

Rhyus looked around the dining room. Miranda had returned behind the desk, beginning to read again.

"Have you had any thoughts as to why you ended up here on Palam Vita? In Urbs Cereris Arcanae?" Sultan's liquid eyes were pools of interest.

"Honestly," Rhyus pressed his lips together, "I have no clue."

"What about those dreams of yours? What if they led you here?"

"That's ridiculous." Rhyus shook his head. "How would the boat know my dreams? All I know is that Marion hit the autopilot, and here we are. Who knows if there's a master design to explain why I've ended up here. I am basically some damned guy who can't remember more than the past week of his life, who wasn't happy with where he was and ran away to find himself here with you. Easy enough." Rhyus sighed in irritation, staring out the window.

After a brief silence, Sultan said, "No."

"What do you mean *no*?"

"I don't think that is the case. Whether or not these all-too-real dreams you are experiencing have anything to do with why you are here, I believe there is something more to it. You say 'easy enough,' but I say *too* easy."

"I don't know."

"I am sure these dreams are behind it." Sultan was set on his opinion. Surely something had convinced him. Arms rested on the wooden table, he sat looking at Rhyus. Many beaded bracelets decorated his wrists, and a wide assortment of rings decked his fingers.

Rhyus met his friend's orange-amber gaze. "What makes you so certain? Seems a little outlandish to me."

"Not at all like setting out through The Darkness with no destination, accompanied by a young woman you've known only a couple of days?"

"Yeah, all right, smartass." Rhyus knew Sultan was only poking fun, however he realized how much truth lay behind his jest.

Miranda approached, setting two plates of food before them. "Enjoy," she said, in short, not wanting to interrupt their intense conversation.

"Thanks, Miranda," Sultan said, and Rhyus gave her a desultory nod.

"No problem," she replied, as she had a thousand times before. Miranda turned back across the room to reclaim her post and carry on reading.

In an attempt to clear his mind, Rhyus dove into the plate of food before him. He took bite after bite, discouraging any sort of continued conversation.

"How the hell do you do it?" Rhyus eventually asked.

Sultan gave him a questioning look.

"You know where to find amazing food. If nothing else, that is one thing I do know."

Sultan offered a closed-mouth smile, so as to not reveal the bite he had just taken.

"Knowing good food when you come across it isn't so difficult. You just have to find it," Sultan said, with his typical smile once he had swallowed.

"Yeah, maybe." Rhyus took another bite.

✎ ✐

By the time they left Café Kampnel, it was well into the afternoon. They had sat chatting with one another, and had made conversation with Miranda for a while as well, before leaving the café. Rhyus decided he was definitely fond of Miranda. She was high-spirited and full of joie de vivre. It was no wonder Sultan and she got along so well.

Many quiet hours passed as they wandered walkways that Rhyus hadn't yet explored. They stopped by specialty stores here and there and occasionally took time to make conversation with others. Though unnecessary, Sultan apologized multiple times that nothing exciting or out of the ordinary was scheduled to take place.

Rhyus finally reminded him that he had already attended more planned events than he could have ever expected. Accepting this, Sultan seemed much more content.

Sometime around eight thirty, Sultan led them back to Pub Ralikoo where they joined some of his close acquaintances for a few rounds of drinks. Rhyus enjoyed hanging out with Sultan and the others. According to Sultan, they enjoyed having him around as well and had told him to be sure to bring Rhyus back.

His third day in The Urbs, and Rhyus was beginning to recognize somns and locations. All of the homes and shops that had originally seemed identical to Rhyus now stood apart from one another. After leaving the pub, Rhyus and Sultan continued to wander aimlessly around the warmly lit city.

Smiling to himself, Rhyus thought, *Things are finally starting to look up.*

61: Destined?

Rhyus realized that Sultan and he were heading in the direction of the single entrance to Urbs Cereris Arcanae. "Where are we going?" he asked, with an inkling that they were moving toward something particular, despite the fact that they had been wandering aimlessly for the hours since leaving Pub Ralikoo.

"There's something I think you'd be interested in seeing," Sultan said, but his words contained less enthusiasm than Rhyus had become accustomed to.

"Are we leaving the city?" Rhyus asked, remembering the trek through Trans Murus on the day of his arrival on Insula Palam Vita. It had been light outside then. The thought of Trans Murus in the dark of night was not appealing.

It would be very dark beyond the wall. Ravenna would be the only visible moon, as they traveled through Trans Murus and the thick vegetation beyond. Nothing bad about that, except that its blue-violet tint made it the darkest of the five moons, casting off precious little light.

"Yeah, we are," Sultan answered, not commenting on Rhyus's sigh, though typically he would have picked up on it. "That's not a problem, is it?"

"Oh, no, I was only wondering." Rhyus sensed something strange, even eerie. He looked up to the top of the glittering, stone wall where the glowing orbs hovered, protecting the city and its dwellers, while warning those beyond the barrier from coming near.

Nearing the tall, narrow doors, Rhyus saw the two guards, standing on either side of them. *Why must there be guards protecting the city from within?* Rhyus wondered. *Why would anyone want to leave?*

"Hello," Sultan greeted the guards, less animated than customary. These guards resembled those Rhyus had seen by the doors the day Lenim brought him into The Urbs. Though holding some similarity, their dress and look was quite different than those he had earlier seen. Their masks also differed, but they wore masks nonetheless.

The guards nodded before sidestepping to slowly push the heavy doors open. Just as the previous guards had recognized Lenim, these guards recognized Sultan as his right-hand man.

He followed Sultan out into Trans Murus. Whatever feeling Rhyus had just moments ago taken as eerie was worth a laugh. The feeling enclosing him now was none other than the epitome of eeriness.

"You OK?" Sultan asked, as Rhyus dropped a step behind him instead of taking his side as usual.

Rhyus's pulse raced. He feared Sultan might hear his heart attempting to break free from his chest. It was pitch black after exiting the well-illuminated inner city. Rhyus found it impossible to distinguish any of his surroundings. Black was all he could see in any direction. Looking back, he couldn't even see the entrance now that the guards had closed the doors. The only things visible were the glowing orbs high above the ground, but their light reached outward, not downward.

"Yes," Rhyus choked on the lie. He was not OK. Definitely not. He knew that Sultan didn't need to ask to know that this was so.

As they made their way through Trans Murus, neither Rhyus nor Sultan spoke another word. As his eyes adjusted to the utter darkness, he saw many somns standing and squatting, scattered over the dirt ground. Rhyus nearly screamed, however he only managed a strangled gasp. They did not stare at the pair of trespassers, but that didn't comfort Rhyus in the least.

Sultan made no remark about them. Lowlifes. *That is how Lenim referred to the dwellers of Trans Murus. Yuri probably sees them in no better light*, Rhyus thought. He could feel his hands shaking, and the air quavered within his lungs as they did their best to carry out their only task. Breathing.

The air was still, silent. Beyond Trans Murus, Rhyus could hear the rustling of trees and other vegetation. He even heard some sort of animal cry out every now and then, but whether or not that was in any way reassuring, Rhyus was uncertain.

Trying to ignore the existence of the Trans Murus dwellers, he shivered again. They may as well be corpses, but their presence unsettled him as Sultan and he made their way. He could discern the trees just beyond the edge, and he wished they could only reach it faster. *But over my dead body would I be willing to run through Trans Murus. They may look like the living dead, but who's to say that rushed movement wouldn't spark their awareness?*

Sultan didn't look back. He simply continued to move steadily toward the forest's edge with the knowledge that Rhyus was near behind. Finally, they stepped past the first thin line of trees, and slowly more trees and undergrowth started to close around them.

For a short-lived moment, Rhyus felt a great sense of relief that they had stepped beyond Trans Murus. Then he realized that they couldn't be any safer out in the dark forest at night. He fought the urge to ask Sultan where they were headed.

While they walked, many thoughts formed in Rhyus's mind. *What if he's taking me back to the boat? What if they believe me a threat for some reason? What if they send me out to sea on the boat and then ambush it before I get too far? Wait! Why even bother with the boat? It would be a cinch to just dispose of me here in the forest. Maybe they'll tie me to a tree and just wait for the wild animals to find me.* The thoughts within his mind became increasingly catastrophic as he followed Sultan deeper and deeper.

"This way." Sultan gestured with an arm, as he angled off the path they had been following. It was still exceptionally dark, especially with the trees looming overhead, but Rhyus's eyes had become further adjusted.

Rhyus's pulse finally slowed as his vision further improved, and as he became more accustomed to the woods. They had been walking for some time, and nothing had threatened them. He hoped that remained the case, and refused to let his mind wander into another state of panic.

"We are nearly there," Sultan said.

Something about him still seemed off. Rhyus's eyebrows lowered as he contemplated the fact. He hadn't been his usual lively self since they started for the exit of Urbs Cereris Arcanae. *Maybe it's just the necessity of traveling through Trans Murus and the forest that has him out of character,* Rhyus thought. *Perhaps he will come back around once we reach our destination.*

Sultan came to a halt. "We're here."

"Where exactly is *here*?" Rhyus asked. Looking around, his concerns raised themselves again. There was nothing to see, other than dark forms that he assumed to be plant life. Nothing more than that.

"Give me just one second," Sultan said, though Rhyus wasn't sure he had meant to say the words out loud.

Squatting, Sultan reached down to pick up a small handful of leaves. Through the dark, Rhyus strained his eyes, watching. He held one leaf between the tip of his index finger and thumb while the rest were pressed against his palm by the three remaining fingers.

When Sultan moved a handful of steps further, Rhyus followed.

Rhyus felt the texture of the ground change. They were no longer walking on soft soil, but instead on hard ground.

Sultan took a few steps to the side on this new hard floor. Retrieving something from his pocket, he crouched down again. A tiny flame ignited from something in his hand, and he dipped the small, individual leaf into it until it caught fire. The original flame went out, and Sultan extended his arm.

Rhyus watched Sultan release the fiery leaf, letting it fall to the floor. Just when it seemed it should hit the ground, it landed in a square pool of liquid. Flames erupted into a dance over the liquid's surface. Sultan moved about, repeating the action, igniting pools, until long rows of flame stretched out on either side of them.

Sultan held out his hands. "Light."

Rhyus analyzed their surroundings. It was definitely not what he was expecting.

"What do you think?" Sultan asked, arms crossed before his chest and a curious look on his face.

"Impressive," Rhyus said, as he looked around.

The large, rectangular construction reminded Rhyus of The Courtyard of Umbra Halls. On the other hand, it was extremely different. This place had a mysterious feel to it. Although surrounded by darkness and the woods, it felt very comfortable. Very safe.

This court was built of sandstone. The ground, smooth at one time, was now quite worn. It was evident that a large sandstone wall had once surrounded the entire perimeter, with exception of the open archway entrance, though only portions of it remained.

On sections of the wall that still maintained their original height, arches were discernable. The arches had once topped the entire wall, clear around the court.

"Rhyus," Sultan called, after giving him time to examine the structure. He curled his fingers, beckoning Rhyus to come to him.

"This place," Sultan said, "has been around easily a thousand years." He did not look at Rhyus, but instead at what remained of the court. "Come, look at this."

Rhyus followed Sultan's voice toward the head of the court where two statues stood, larger than ordinary men.

The statue to their left was formed of slick, black stone. Silver flecks within it reflected the light of the liquid pools brilliantly. The statue to their right was made of a shimmering white stone that Rhyus knew was Lux stone. The two figures seemed to be a recent addition, at least in comparison to the original sandstone structure.

Analyzing the two stone figures as they neared, Rhyus saw that they were nearly identical. Both statues were robed with hoods draped over their heads, hiding their faces from view. They had wings that were not raised back behind them, but rather draped forward in a curved manner, cloaking the sides of their bodies.

The only real difference between them, other than the stone from which they were constructed, was the position of their hands. Each held their hands out before them. The dark figure with hands folded one over the other, one palm facing upward and the other downward. The light figure held its hands side by side, palms facing upward, forming a bowl in accepting or giving an offering.

Sultan pointed downward. The two statues stood against the back wall of the court on stone platforms hovering only slightly over a watery surface. A trapezoidal pool was sunk into the ground with its shorter side situated toward Rhyus and Sultan. A low border ran around the basin just above ground, and the water in the pool was dark blue; however, it was unusually transparent.

Through the dark water, Rhyus could easily see its bottom where an intricate design had been carved into the floor. Looking closer, he saw that although the pool was built of the original stone, the carvings at its bottom were in perfect condition.

"Hand carved." Sultan had read his thoughts again. "Built at the same time as the rest of the original structure. Flawless still. After a thousand years. Remarkable isn't it?"

"But how?" Rhyus couldn't believe that the underwater carving could have been part of the original structure.

Sultan's eyes flicked to the side, toward the court entrance. He had not intended Rhyus to notice, but he had. A droll expression crept over Sultan's face. Curious, Rhyus turned his head.

"Lenim?" Rhyus did not mean to say this out loud. Then, in the same moment as she spotted him, Rhyus saw her. Marion.

"What are you playing at?" Rhyus accused, turning back to Sultan whose gaze was averted, looking down into the dark pool. Sultan said nothing. He merely stood unmoving, gazing down at the glassy surface of the still water.

"What's going on," Marion demanded of Lenim, from the entrance. Although she was standing at the opposite end of the lengthy court, Rhyus heard her words perfectly, as clear as if she were just yards from him.

Instead of answering, Lenim stepped beyond the arched entrance, gliding over the sandstone floor. Marion remained beneath the archway until Lenim nearly reached Rhyus and Sultan. Even then, Marion's slow steps halted when she reached half the distance to where the three men now stood.

"Sultan. Rhyus." Lenim came to a standstill, bowing low in greeting. As usual, his straight, rich hair fell forward. "Marion," Lenim said, as his way of telling her to join them. Even though he faced the head of the court, away from Marion, he knew that his voice would carry back to where she stood.

Lenim stared, with his opaque, midnight eyes, up at the statues—first to the white, and then to the black where his eyes lingered until he felt Marion's presence behind him. With a beckoning finger, he brought her closer.

Though hardly willing, Marion took the last steps to Lenim's side. The expression on her face was displeased, and she refused to look at Rhyus. Instead, painted in curiosity, she directed her eyes toward the pool and the high standing figures.

"Why are we here," she demanded, unwilling to accept the silence.

Lenim adjusted his stance, standing as tall as his slender form would allow. "We are here," he began, "because I believe I know where you two are destined to travel."

"Destined," Rhyus scoffed, in a hushed choke.

Lenim's harsh eyes snapped in his direction, the rest of his face still pointed straight ahead. "Yes, destiny. You know, the task to which you have been preordained," he mocked, in a heightened state of irritation. "By the useful assistance of Madam Corvin, Sultan, and indirectly yourselves, I have discerned the true reason you two started this voyage together and the place you are both destined to travel."

"I will *not* be going anywhere with *him*!" Marion spat, with a threatening arm toward Rhyus. Rhyus narrowed his eyes, angry at the tenor of her outburst.

"Well, that may put a damper on things. It will surely slow you down." Lenim raised his eyebrows with a disapproving look in response to her statement and demanding tone.

"What do you mean?" She still demanded answers, though trying her best to dampen her inappropriate tone. She was lucky he allowed her some slack through unwarranted respect and his understanding of her anger toward her former traveling companion, for no matter the cause, no one spoke to Lenim in such a way.

"Well, you see," Lenim began again, "I have ascertained that you are both receiving subliminal messages of a place beyond Palam Vita. A true place, but a place I would not typically recommend to anyone. Particularly two somns who are still as fresh and inexperienced as yourselves."

"Why?" A twisted curiosity grew within Rhyus. "Why wouldn't you send us or anyone else there?"

"Let's see." Lenim lifted his unblinking eyes toward the blackened sky overhead, collecting his thoughts, which had scattered during his attentions to those around him. He brought his eyes back down. "You two have traveled here from Lux Lumetia, the Crystal City, yes? The City of Light?"

"Yeah," Rhyus said. Marion, at Lenim's side, nodded. Her eyes remained fixed on the pool's still surface.

Lenim paused. "Try to imagine a place that is everything other than what you have been accustomed to during your time in Lux Lumetia. Judging by what I know, I don't believe you have had the necessity of dealing with the underbelly of your fair city?"

Neither Rhyus nor Marion replied, but Lenim easily picked up on their silent confessions. "This other city you two have seen. Picture in your minds, darkness and never-ending rain. Most somns you encounter will be a patchwork of deceit and lies. Most are dreadfully dangerous on one level or another. Their entire culture is one of dealing and counter dealing. You can expect to be kissed and stabbed at the same time. There is no live-and-let-live. Power corrupts. And, for them, power is everything.

"I do believe both of your subconscious minds are leading you to the City of Dark Water. But I will not allow it unless you agree to travel there together." Lenim's face was expressionless, as he awaited an answer.

All the while, Sultan remained silent, staring down into the water but avoiding the two stone figures reflecting back up at him. He knew this wasn't his time to speak. This discussion was Lenim's jurisdiction, not his own.

"Right," Marion blurted, after a moment of stretched hesitation. She and Rhyus had both known from the start that they were not meant to remain here on Insula Palam Vita. They just hadn't known their next move. "Fine. All right. I'll go with him." Her words were strained, but if Lenim felt this strongly, it must be the right decision. Right?

Lenim angled his head down to Rhyus, face still expressionless, eyes unblinking.

Rhyus demurred, "Yeah, OK. Let's do this."

"Splendid." Lenim turned his head from Rhyus, remaining unreadable.

"Wait. Aren't we taking the boat?" Marion showed a blended look of concern and confusion.

Lenim gave a single, blunt laugh, throwing his head back. "No. Oh, no." He shook his head in wonder. "I cannot believe you two did such a thing in the first place." That wide grin reappeared over Lenim's slender lips for the first time during this little gathering.

Uncomfortable, Rhyus and Marion passed a short, puzzled look between themselves. They wondered, *If not the boat...then what?*

"You see these statues?" Lenim pointed toward the two robed figures, their wings partially cloaking their forms. "They are part of something greater, not just décor to our sandstone structure. Do you two have any knowledge of portals?"

Rhyus and Marion passed another uncertain look. "No," Rhyus said.

"No." Marion's answer echoed Rhyus's own.

"I had a feeling not." Lenim shifted his eyes from one to the other before turning back to the stone figures. He shook his head again. Considering the overwhelming power of The Darkness, he continued to find the fact that Rhyus and Marion had survived boat travel from Lux Lumetia to Insula Palam Vita incredulous. Their inner strength was much greater than either of them realized.

Sultan lifted his head now toward Lenim. His orange-amber eyes reflected the fiery lights along the ground.

"This court we are standing on happens to contain such a portal. In fact, you are viewing an important piece of it at this precise moment." Rhyus and Marion cast looks Lenim's way. "These statues here before us create two of the three points necessary for all portals to function." Lenim swiveled around. "That patterned piece there," he pointed to a circular design carved long ago into the sandstone, a few steps from where they all stood, "is the third." They all turned to look down at this third point.

"Portals such as this have made quick and easy travel possible. However, they are only known of and used by somns in high authoritative positions or those who have connection to such somns. As for you two...well, you are lucky to have my assistance.

"Don't think that just anyone is going to willingly allow you through a portal. They won't. In fact, you will not speak of this portal or court to others, or of portals in general, after this discussion. This is most critical. Is this clear?" At the hard look from Lenim, Rhyus and Marion nodded.

"Yuri," Lenim said. Their contrasting eyes made brief contact, and Sultan nodded. Without a word, Sultan left the little circle the four of them had formed and headed across the length of the court toward its entrance.

Rhyus, watching after him, was disappointed, yet curious as to where Lenim was sending him. He continued to watch the archway after Sultan vanished, unable to understand what just happened. He just now realized how much he had come to lean on Sultan for emotional support.

Finally, Rhyus turned his attention away from the entrance, but before another moment had passed, he sensed Sultan's return. Rhyus's eyes narrowed as Sultan stepped through the archway, carrying something with him. *Wait*, Rhyus thought, as Sultan made his way back. *Is that my bag? And Marion's?*

"Is that my bag?" Marion asked, in accusation. Turning to Lenim, she expected an answer.

"Yes. I had Sultan and Madam Corvin pack your belongings, as well as some small necessities we thought would do you well, nothing big. I collected your bags and brought them out here earlier while taking care of a bit of business." Lenim stated this as a matter of fact. Nothing said he had to give them an answer, but he didn't see this as a big deal.

"How long have you been planning this?" Marion asked.

"Only since early this morning."

Marion continued to stare at him, unsure how to feel about all of this.

Lenim raised his eyebrows. "Do you want me to send you to your new destination or not?"

"Yes," Marion said, as she dropped her gaze from Lenim's probing eyes.

Lenim turned his unblinking eyes to Rhyus. "You two ready, then?"

Rhyus exhaled a heavy breath. "Yeah." He cast a glance Sultan's way, feeling betrayed. Sultan, realizing this, kept his eyes from meeting Rhyus's own.

Lenim turned back to Marion, and she nodded.

"Marvelous. First, a few key things to inform you of before we send you on your way." Rhyus and Marion looked to him, awaiting their instructions. "First, this will seem an odd sensation, you both being first-time travelers.

"Second, I have to remind you that this is a very dark place and a perilous voyage. I cannot stress this enough. It is just coming on three o'clock in the morning. It is late, I know, but I have chosen this time for a specific reason. At this time of morning, the majority of the Dark City's dwellers will be drunk enough that you should be able to outwit them. Or they will be passed out or otherwise sleeping.

"This point is vital. You absolutely must find somewhere you can hole up, at least temporarily, before the city's inhabitants begin to waken. This time range is the safest for where you are headed. It is mandatory that you make all your decisions together. Make them wisely. If you don't, there will invariably be unpleasant consequences to face. And that is putting it lightly. Do you both understand all of this?" Again, Rhyus and Marion nodded. "Prepare yourselves. This will be some experience for you both."

Lenim looked at Rhyus with his unblinking eyes and shifted in brief toward Sultan. Picking up his feet, Rhyus headed in his direction. As he approached, Sultan made an effort to straighten up, his eyes still reflecting the small, pooling flames.

"You know, I really am sorry for all of this. I wanted to tell you what was being planned." Sultan kept his voice low, but regardless, Rhyus wondered whether Lenim would still overhear his words. "Lenim is a gracious man, but he is our supreme leader. You understand?" His eyes were serious, yet a small tinge of hope showed through them.

"Yes. I understand, Yuri."

"Good." A silent moment passed between them. "Well," Sultan said, in breaking it, "I do believe this is what you are meant to do, but I hope things will bring us together again in times to come. It's been real." Sultan pulled the glasses with their pink lenses from the front of his thick-netted shirt and slid them into place without disturbing the bandana over his ears. He raised an arm, and Rhyus stepped forward. They gave one another an amiable pat on the back.

"Thanks," Rhyus said, stepping back.

"For what?"

"I have to agree. I feel that this is the right thing to do. I must go to the Dark City. But I've truly enjoyed my time here. In the most part, due to you."

Sultan's charming smile showed itself for the first time since they had started for the exit of Urbs Cereris Arcanae. "Oh, come off it."

"Really." Rhyus grinned. "But yeah, I hope we run into each other again somewhere, sometime." They shared a final departing nod, and then Rhyus returned to Lenim and Marion.

"Ready?" Lenim asked, with a stony expression.

"Ready as I'll ever be."

"Marion?" Lenim wanted to be sure she was truly ready to face what was to come.

Marion's lips were a tight line, but she answered, "OK."

Lenim walked over to the circular design carved into the sandstone floor. He waved a hand, beckoning Rhyus and Marion to follow.

"It looks like a dream catcher," Marion said.

"One thing is for sure. This isn't going to keep away the nightmare that is going to become your reality."

Rhyus wondered if Lenim thought Marion would back out at the last second.

"Rhyus, I want you to go first. Marion will be just behind you. Don't let her be there alone, not for as much as a minute."

Rhyus looked up. "I'm ready."

"All right. Marion, won't you step aside, just a couple of steps or so should suffice," Lenim requested. "Yes, that'll do just fine," he said, as Marion took a few steps to the side. Sultan moved forward and put a hand on her shoulder. He could see that she was beginning to look a little uneasy.

"Rhyus. Face in the direction of the statues at the head of the court, and make sure your feet are planted within the circle marker on the ground."

"Right."

Lenim placed a hand into a pocket of his long sweater-jacket, retrieving a pair of shiny, black stones. As Lenim extended his arm, Rhyus reached out his hand to accept one of them. "Rhyus, I will be standing just a short bit before you during your sending. One thing I need you to do is to move off of the new marker once you reach the other end of the portal. If you do not do this, it will not reopen, and I will not be able to send Marion. That is vital."

"Got it."

"Do *not* do so yet," Lenim gave Rhyus another stern look, "but when you are ready to send, all you need to do is hold that stone and think the name Atrum Unda, Ĭnauro Manor. Atrum Unda is the true name of the Dark City, and the Ĭnauro Manor is the portal to which you will send."

Rhyus noticed Marion. He couldn't tell if she was more nervous about him sending and spending that miniscule fraction of time alone, or to be sent herself after him.

"Ready?" Lenim's tone was now very serious.

"Yes."

"Then off you go. We will meet again." Lenim took a couple steps back to avoid interfering with the invisible lines between Rhyus and the stone figures on their platforms over the pool.

Rhyus flashed one last look at Marion and then Sultan beside her, his hand still resting in comfort upon her shoulder. Sultan gave him a reassuring nod. Rhyus turned back to face Lenim and the statues. *Here we go*, Rhyus thought, as he closed his eyes and took in a deep breath. He reopened them. *Atrum Unda. Ĭnauro Manor.*

The very instant in which Rhyus thought its name he saw the darkness in Lenim's midnight eyes disappear. They became translucent with iridescent rings of blue around the irises. The stone in Rhyus's hand began to feel hot as it vibrated rapidly. A high-pitched frequency filled his ears. He realized that it was coming from the stone itself. He glanced down at it for a split second.

Lenim's voice blended with the high buzz, "Just look ahead of you, Rhyus."

Rhyus obeyed, forcing his gaze back up to Lenim's peculiar eyes.

The intense, high-pitched buzz grew louder, as its pitch raised an octave. As the frequency increased, the air became thick and heavy. He felt a constraint wrapping around him, pulling ever tighter.

Then, just as the high-pitched buzz reached the point of intolerable pain, and he was certain that he would be crushed to the core...everything dropped. The sound. The constraint. Gone.

62: Memos with Miniature Wings

The messenger beetle had successfully delivered its urgent message from Callis Morgandy. Now it was Jereth Tavokk's turn to respond with an equally imperative message. He opened the mouth of the tiny, metallic beetle, and its eyes began to glow as it projected a written message of its own, relaying its instructions for further use:

> You may record your message now. Your voice will trigger the beetle, automatically beginning your recording session. To end your recording session, simply press the beetle's mouth closed.

"Callis, my dear friend. I am pleased to inform you that I do have a bit of good news. Then again, I have a bit of *unpleasant* news just the same. First off, I apologize for the late return of our little winged messenger. I have had quite an eventful day. And I must say, the arrival of your message was, well, quite a surprise. But don't get me wrong. It is always good to hear from you, always good to hear your voice, Cal.

"As far as your inquiries go: You are most accurate in your assumption that I have heard about The Archives break-in. And don't give yourself too hard of a time. If the Intruder were in fact Vincent KyVeerah, he would have been able to get past anyone who tried to stop him. He is the craftiest of devils, that one.

"At this current moment in time, I am unable to tell you too much about this Vincent KyVeerah. He is a rather reclusive man. However, I do know that he is very skilled and has an impressive reputation in the underground businesses as it goes.

"Speaking of which, how long does this thing record, I wonder? I see you did finally invest in the memory chip. Told you it would be worth it. [A small chuckle.] Hope you didn't give Mordion too hard of a time. But anyway, back to the point, Cal.

"You will be happy to know that my arrival is scheduled for this very evening, as my business will come to an end with time enough to return. We shall meet at our usual place. Plan on eleven thirty."

That all having been said, Tavokk abruptly snapped the beetle's mouth shut. Once again, the beetle's eyes began to glow, projecting a new message:

Message recording successful. Ready for release.

Satisfied with the new memory chip that was being put to use, Tavokk released the metallic beetle into the air.

"Well, Callis," he spoke, into the empty air, "I suppose I shall see you tomorrow."

63: Facing Propositions

Overall it had been quite a productive day. After her meeting with Serlio, Helena had gone straight home and buried her nose in the manuscript. At first the passages seemed as muddy as when she first opened it. But as she read, she began to see patterns emerging. She found that Serlio had been right. Once she stopped trying to understand every little detail, and stepped back to see the larger picture, it began to make sense.

Seeking respite, Helena headed to her favorite bar, the Wishing Well. Her eyes came to rest on the vibrant blue neon sign. Only second to its neighbor, the Cosmos, the Wishing Well was one of the hottest spots for the nightlife of Atrum Unda.

Helena situated herself on a stool up at the bar's counter. Time passed as Helena fiddled with the glass stem of her current drink, bright pink in color with a floating zestfruit peel ringlet as a final touch. Lost in her thoughts, Helena absentmindedly looked up from her drink and gazed into the large mirror anchored on the bar's wall. *My, my, this is a pleasant turn of events.*

&)(&

Holding the intricately designed key between her thumb and forefinger, Ezra scowled. She didn't know whether to be more pissed at Callis for following her or for stealing her access key. *Callis. The arrogance of that man! It's going to cost him his life one of these days. Hopefully it will be by my hand.* Her light-green eyes filled with a wicked gleam, as she stared at her distorted reflection in the back of the key's smooth surface.

Ezra's scowl deepened. *Who am I kidding? The only way to dispose of Callis Morgandy is for Nyx to do it himself.* Ezra gave a small snort at the thought. *Nyx Crucian? Harm his precious golden boy? He'd never do it. Callis is far too valuable.*

Ezra pondered for a moment. *I suppose it would be a breeze for Armani and Julian to exterminate Callis, but they adore him almost as much as Nyx. It makes me sick.* She cursed under her breath, scolded herself for dwelling on such a pessimistic, absurd notion.

Dismissing the key, she placed it into an outer coat pocket, momentarily burying the vexing thoughts of Callis. She turned her attention back to her current assignment, Helena Meretrix.

From her position at the opposite end of the bar, Ezra had a clear view. Helena sat with her back angled toward Ezra who watched with minor interest as the White Band member finished her cocktail.

Ezra sighed in irritation. *What an incredible waste of time. She hasn't done a damn thing in twenty minutes.* Just as she formed these thoughts, Helena stirred, rising from her seat and moving Ezra's way in heading for the exit.

ဢ෬

From the reflection in the mirror behind the bar, Helena had seen Ezra Stark of the Black Band. More importantly, she had seen Ezra holding her access key to the crown of The Dome. Helena knew a golden opportunity when she saw one, and she wasn't about to pass it up. *Ezra is practically flaunting the thing in my face.* A sly grin spread over Helena's painted lips.

Helena observed as Ezra placed her access key into an outer pocket of her coat, and at that moment, Helena decided it was time to make her move. Pushing out from the bar, she stood and strode in the direction of both Ezra and the bar's doors.

Ezra sat with her head hung low, concealing her drink as her hair formed a curtain around it. With unnatural swiftness, Helena swiped past Ezra, barely touching her in the process. Helena continued on, exiting the Wishing Well.

Out in the refreshingly cool air and light rain, Helena made her way up the spiraling stairs encircling the bar as they led up out of the pit. She paused as she reached the top of the set of wide stairs, coming to the landing on which the Sŭsurrus Fountain and The Tower sat. Triumphant, Helena unclenched her hand. Resting in her palm was a silver key. Ezra Stark's access key.

Once this is all over, I'll have to thank that bitch, Ezra. Helena strolled down from the vast hilltop and off into the night with a single thought running through her mind. *One piece. One more piece is all I need. I must find that rumored Calling.*

ဢ෬

Ezra straightened her posture once she felt that Helena had left the premises. *Strange. I wouldn't have thought Helena dense enough not to recognize a member of the Black Band. I suppose it is quite dim in here, and I made sure to keep my face concealed, but still.*

Ezra stood up, throwing her payment on the bar. A small smile crossed her lips as she headed for the exit. *I shouldn't complain. Her ignorance makes my job that much easier. Foolish Helena. All too soon, her plans will be revealed, followed by her downfall.*

ഇൽ

Hearing a high-pitched whistle, Callis Morgandy made his way, only a towel wrapped around his mid-section, across his flat and into his immaculate kitchen to retrieve the screaming kettle from the stovetop. He then poured the steaming, hot water into a mug with a bag of his favorite ginger mallow. Once brewed, Callis took the mug to the kitchen table to let it cool while he resumed his previous task of dressing for the day. After making himself decent, Callis returned to the dining table to relax and enjoy his drink.

Thrumming his fingertips along the cool surface of the table, he began to plan out his day. *Jereth still hasn't contacted me with information. Not yet, anyway. That doesn't leave me with much for options, though I would like to look into this Helena Meretrix matter. If she's looking for a powerful Calling, then maybe I should be looking for one as well. To be more exact, I need someone who would know where to find such a powerful Calling. If I can do that, I might be able to figure out what it is that she wants this Calling to do.*

Callis frowned as a sense of frustration kicked in. *Where am I going to find anyone like that?* As Callis mused over this, the slanting rain drummed against the windows, becoming increasingly louder until it thrashed against the windows and the side patio door off of the kitchen–dining room area. Suddenly, something crashed against the window, though not hard enough to damage the glass.

Callis snapped from his thoughts to see what had begun to persistently hit against the glass of the patio door. As he approached, he saw the small, flying object ramming repeatedly against the glass, trying to gain access to his home. A silver messenger beetle. The beetle programmed to locate Callis, wherever his location, had sensed him from outside.

Unable to comprehend the glass barrier, the beetle had inadvertently continued colliding with the door until catching its target's attention. Callis opened the patio door, allowing the flying mechanical beetle to enter his home. Once inside, Callis caught the small beetle in his hand.

After retrieving Jereth Tavokk's message and storing the beetle in its proper place, Callis thought, *finally—tonight I'll meet with Jereth and learn of Vincent KyVeerah. But first things first.*

℘ℭ℞

Callis crossed through many sectors of Atrum Unda until he reached The Dome in the Hollow Sector. Not knowing where else to go, he decided that The Dome would be the best place to find a lead on someone who could expand his knowledge on Callings. After making his way up to the Black Band's commons room, Callis came to a halt right outside the frosted doors. He could hear very distinctive voices on the other side of the doors. *Oh, Ravenna. Might as well get this over with.* Not pausing to second-guess his action, Callis entered the commons room. "What the hell?"

Walking into the room, Callis stumbled into a disturbing scene, one he had not expected. Upon one of the lounge's leather couches sat Armani Saint and Julian Gallows with none other than Jett Milan between them. Jett was just as grim as Callis was surprised. With all eyes now on Callis, Armani shouted joyously, "Callis, what a pleasant surprise! Come over and join us!"

Making an unpleasant face, Callis strode across the room to where the other three sat. Armani began, "We were just hanging around with our newfound friend, Jett Milan."

Julian chimed in, "You remember him of course, Cal? Jett Milan of the White Band?"

Callis started to answer, but Armani, rolling his eyes, said, "Jules, you have no place to talk. You had no recollection of our pal, Jett, until just the other day."

"Too true, Armani," Julian laughed, as he roughly slapped Jett on the back in a friendly manner. Friendly, at least for Julian Gallows. Jett leaned forward on the couch, having had the wind knocked out of him. His eyes widened with dark fury. He slowly turned, giving Julian a menacing look. This caused Julian to cackle even louder.

Armani added, jovially, "Careful Jules. Our Jett has a bite to him."

Julian shared a hopeful, yet wicked, grin. "Let him. I could do with a little bit of fun." Julian waited for Jett to take him up on his offer, but the young man simply sighed and slumped against the back of the couch. Julian frowned in disappointment.

Callis, assessing the situation, could read that Jett wasn't as enthused with his new company as Armani and Julian were. His black hair hung over even darker eyes, which remained stone cold. Callis winced.

Armani pulled Callis from his thoughts. "Just don't stand there, Cal. Come and join us." Armani flashed one of his radiant, unnaturally charming smiles. Callis wasn't deceived by Armani's friendly demeanor. His demonic, crimson eyes told a different, more forceful story, revealing what truly lay beyond the façade. Callis sighed and felt about as put off as Jett.

Julian laughed. "Atta boy, Cal. We were beginning to think you didn't like us."

Callis flicked a reproachful look Julian's way. Julian didn't seem fazed by Callis's hostile attitude. As a matter of fact, he took great delight from it. Julian reacted this way because he knew Callis would discern his attitude and become even more aggravated.

Reluctant, Callis headed to a nearby seat. Before situating, he took notice of the assorted rambles on a low table, primarily issues of *The Atrum Chronicles*, mixed amongst other odds and ends.

Callis looked at the mess with disdain. "Really, this is disgusting. Some of this looks over a week old. Have either of you ever heard of—" Callis's voice cut mid-sentence. He grabbed up the newspaper, examining it in an ominous silence.

Armani and Julian exchanged curious glances while Jett merely raised an eyebrow. Turning to Jett, Armani informed, "Don't mind him. Callis does this all the time." Armani placed a slender finger upon his lips. "Yes, actually, it's quite common."

Waving his fingers in front of Jett, Julian added, "Yeah. Cal here is all doom and gloom." Julian, appreciating his own words, cackled bluntly.

Ignoring his not-so-esteemed colleagues, Callis peered at the article of a discarded *Chronicles* issue from the weeks past. *Fyfe Van Ingen. Why didn't I think of it before? This is the guy that's been ranting on about the coming of the Key Calling. Hmm, this describes him as acutely insane.* Callis cast a side-glance at Armani and Julian.

Looking at the duo, he recalled that it was they who were in charge of questioning the prisoner. *Nyx doesn't send the likes of Armani Saint and Julian Gallows to interrogate a crazy man. Unless, of course, that man knows something that he shouldn't. Something Nyx would wish to know.* Callis clutched the paper tighter. *Like the whereabouts of the Key Calling.*

Callis made an instantaneous decision. *I need to meet with the man, Fyfe Van Ingen.* He scowled. *No one is going to give Callis Morgandy the authorization to meet with him, at least not for awhile. Not after the whole Intruder incident. But perhaps if someone else were to retrieve the authorization papers...*

Callis swiveled his gaze to where Jett sat. "Milan, you're coming with me," he said. "Now." Armani, Julian, and Jett all simultaneously looked up at him.

Frowning, Armani protested, "Now, Callis. We found Jett first. You can't just take him."

"Yes, I can. He's not a toy. He's an assassin. I'm going to put him to work, and if you two have any qualms with it, by all means, take it up with Nyx."

Armani and Julian stared at Callis with severe looks. Julian darkly probed, "What sort of work?"

Without hesitation, Callis said, "It's *private*." Julian made to protest, but Armani held up a hand to silence him.

"As you wish, Callis. But you better make sure to return him to us unharmed," Julian said, with a sharp warning from his aqua eyes. Armani agreed, knowing that they couldn't take this up with Nyx, nor would they want to. Armani and Julian knew, very well, that Nyx did *not* approve of them entertaining themselves at the expense of White Band members.

Taking the *Chronicles* issue with him, Callis swept out of the room. Jett jumped to his feet, taking his first, and probably only, chance at escaping Armani and Julian. His dark, unenthused features revealed a single ignited spark of hope. This lasted only a split second before he returned to his usual expression. He followed Callis out of the lounge and into the outer corridor. Once beyond the frosted doors, Callis stopped in his tracks and threw up a hand, signaling for Jett to halt. Jett proceeded to do so and waited.

Callis turned on his heels, holding up the *Chronicles* issue before Jett's face. "You recognize this man?"

Jett, unblinking, replied, "Yes. What—" At that moment, Armani and Julian threw the frosted doors open and strolled out of the commons room. Callis shot both of them a dangerous look.

Armani held his hands up in surrender. He mockingly said, "Just passing through. We're not eavesdropping on your 'private' conversation. We're moving right along, see?" Callis scowled and stared after them until their forms disappeared down another hall.

Returning to Jett, Callis continued, "I need you to obtain Van

Ingen's admittance papers so that I may speak with him."

Raising an eyebrow, Jett's query was toneless, "Why should I do this...for *you*?"

Callis glowered. "Because if you don't, I'll send you straight back to them." Callis jerked his head in the direction, which Armani and Julian had just left. Jett cocked his head to the side, peering around Callis's shoulder. There was no way he was going back to *them*. Jett made an unpleasant expression and returned his gaze to Callis.

Dryly, he answered, "Very well. I'll do it. I'm guessing you don't want anyone else knowing of this?"

Callis nodded. "Yes. Can you manage that?"

"Don't insult me." Jett's eyes hardened. "You'll get Van Ingen's papers." With that, he sauntered off and away from Callis, finished with their conversation.

Callis watched him for a moment. Jett Milan could be trouble in the future. He'd have to keep an eye on him.

ഈറ

Armani and Julian entered Nyx Crucian's office, strolling in without bothering to knock. Nyx kept his back to them, gazing out the dark tinted windows and peering down over the city. His stance remained rigid with hands clasped behind his back and his pale, silver hair trailing down past his shoulders. Armani cleared his throat, assuming that Nyx hadn't heard them enter.

Nyx slowly turned his head, followed by his whole body. He arched an eyebrow in slight surprise. "You're early."

Julian feigned a hurt look. "Ouch. That's really upsetting, sir." Armani took it upon himself to silence Julian by elbowing him, none too kindly, in the side.

"Mind your manners, Julian," Armani warned, slowly enunciating Julian's name. He gave Armani a dirty glare but remained silent all the same. Armani looked expectantly toward Nyx. "You had need of us?"

Nyx calmly paced before the tinted windows. "Yes. I have an assignment for you two." They waited in stillness. Nyx continued, "I need your assistance in acquiring a certain artifact for me."

Armani's exquisite brows furrowed with interest. "An artifact?"

"Yes. It is called the Chrem Larose."

Now serious, Julian questioned, "How are we to obtain this Chrem Larose?"

Nyx strolled over to the long glass table separating him from Armani and Julian. He placed his fingertips upon its cool surface, leaning menacingly over it. His glacial eyes matched his icy voice. "There is a man that goes by the name of Niall Trace. He operates a small underground business dealing in rare antiques. He resides within the Valentine Sector. Collect this for me. Today."

Julian shifted his gaze toward Armani. Armani, maintaining eye contact with Nyx, said, "As you wish, sir. Julian and myself will retrieve this artifact for you, but we will do it upon our own leisure. We will *not* be rushed."

Nyx's eyes seared with arctic fury, taking on an unnatural luminescence. He clutched his hands into tightly bawled fists, his knuckles showing white. Before he could utter a sound, Armani interrupted, "After all, we are already burdened with the task of hunting down The Archives Intruder. We will bring you the Chrem Larose, I assure you. Just at our own pace."

Nyx assessed the situation. Before him stood his two most formidable and deadly assassins, not to mention the most feared demonic duo that Atrum Unda had ever seen. It would not be beneficial to engage them in combat. They were far too valuable.

Nyx adjusted his stance into a less rigid pose. In a clipped voice, he said, "Very well. I will grant your request. I warn you. Do not take too much time. I can be a patient man. But that patience won't last long."

Armani nodded his understanding. "Of course."

Nyx displayed a sinister look. His inferiors needed to keep their place in mind.

"Dismissed."

୫୦୧୨

After leaving The Dome, Callis squandered the hours away. He arrived at the Cosmos around a quarter to eleven in the evening. *Jereth's message said he would arrive around eleven thirty. Being early won't hurt. Who knows, maybe Jereth will arrive early as well.* Callis smiled to himself knowing very well that Jereth Tavokk never arrived early.

Entering the Cosmos, Callis headed to his usual spot in the shadows at the back of the bar. Tazo, having seen Callis enter, approached him. With a genuine smile, she asked, "Can I get you anything, Cal?"

"Just a quell blue, please," Callis ordered himself a nonalcoholic beverage. He knew that there would be plenty of time to drink once Tavokk arrived.

Taken by surprise, Tazo said, "Sure thing. Expecting anyone, Callis?"

Tilting his gaze, Callis lightly replied, "Thank you, Tazo." Dismissed, Tazo left to fetch Callis's quell blue. He thoroughly relaxed for the first time in what felt like ages.

Now I wait.

୨୦୫

Helena had been doing her homework. She had not only been reading, but she had spent endless hours studying the city and its streets about her. She felt this was the first time she had ever seen her own world. She now knew her surroundings intimately. She knew exactly which way the winds blew, which direction smoke trailed from each chimney, the directions different flowers faced. She even knew which way the blades of grass leaned, and how far. These, and thousands of other details, she had cataloged in her mind. Every hour of every day, the awareness of her world grew. From the manuscript, she knew exactly how they might be affected.

-480-

She congratulated herself on a job well done. If anyone with an inkling of extra Energy entered her domain, she would know in a heartbeat. She was ready.

64: A Long Awaited Reunion

With lightning flashing off in the distance and the scent of new rain on the breeze, Jereth Tavokk placed a hand on the handle of the door to the Cosmos. Entering, he spotted his crimson-haired friend.

Passing the bar, he tilted his head forward to catch the eye of Tazo. He winked over his dark shades in greeting and continued on to the booth where Callis sat. Callis, sensing the nearing presence of another, looked up.

An impish smile crawled over Tavokk's lips. "Don't you have anywhere else to hang out? Perhaps you should get some friends."

Callis flashed a crooked grin. "You know, I do have a damn good friend. At least I thought he was until he left me for the last week. The week that may very possibly have been the worst week of my life."

Taking a seat opposite Callis, Tavokk nodded in thought, smile widening. "How horrid. What kind of somn would do such a thing? It's a good thing you have me to make up for such neglect."

Callis laughed, "I'll consider that. So, tell me of your travels."

Time passed as the two men sat, heads together, talking vaguely of Tavokk's most recent business ventures, as well as Callis's unfortunate week, past dealings, and current underground gossip. After a bit, the two removed their elbows from the table and sat back, more casual and relaxed. Tavokk glanced over at the bar where Tazo postponed the making of another round of drinks they had ordered.

"I believe some lovely lady over there is waiting for one of us to summon her," Tavokk said, with a jerk of his head and a sly smirk. Callis, looking where Tavokk had gestured, saw Tazo. He peered at her from behind his hair with his head tilted downward, signaling her over with the flick of his middle and forefinger.

Promptly, Tazo whipped up their drinks and emerged from behind the bar, strolling on over to their table and setting their drinks before them. Smiling, she said, "Here you go, boys. You two looked like you were talking business, so I thought I would give you a minute before bringing you your new round."

"You need not hesitate," Tavokk said, "we never let business interfere with our drinking." Callis tried to hold back a smirk, only a crook of his mouth turning upward. Tazo, noticing, gave him a knowing smile.

Callis caught this, and his face dropped back into its stony cover. He dismissed her. "Thank you, Tazo. We'll let you know if we need anything else." Still smiling, she nodded and took her leave.

Taking a swallow of his drink, Callis registered Tavokk's attire for the first time this evening. Curiously, he asked, "Sporting new wares, I see? Some business trip."

Tavokk glanced down at his current night's attire. A wide smile spreading across his face, he shrugged. "What can I say? A souvenir?" Callis laughed shortly at this. After a moment, Callis regained his composure, all lightheartedness removed. Tavokk had been expecting this. He took another large swallow from his glass.

Unsmiling, Callis got straight to the point. "Jereth. I know you've just returned, and you know I wouldn't bother unless it was of great importance." Tavokk nodded, displaying his comprehension. Callis continued, "I need to know what information you have on the man called Vincent KyVeerah."

Gravely, Tavokk mused, "I must admit that I don't have much information in my possession to give regarding Vincent KyVeerah, but I'll share what I can."

"Any information you do have will be most helpful."

"Very well. I have heard of him through my travels, and I must say, he has quite the reputation on the underground circuit."

"Such as?"

"Well," Tavokk took a brief pause for consideration, "he is *very* good at what he does. Almost as good as me, dare I say," Tavokk added, with a crooked grin, after which his face reverted back to its stern disposition. He continued, "*If* Vincent KyVeerah is the Archives Intruder…you are in quite the bind, my friend. This is not a man easily detected, which is why he is so successful in his work."

Callis began, "I understand, but surely —"

"Callis," Tavokk interrupted, "this man makes his living being undetectable. Vincent KyVeerah will not be found unless he wants to be. And my guess is, since he so recently sought something out from The Tower Archives, he probably won't be seen again for quite some while." Before Callis could respond, Tavokk finished, "I'm sorry, my friend. I know this isn't what you wanted to hear, but that's the only information I can give you on him."

After a moment, Callis spoke, "You have no other information on him? What he looks like? Place of residence? Anything?"

"I'm afraid I can't help you there. Truthfully, Callis, I wouldn't have the slightest idea where to tell you to start looking for him," Tavokk said, with a thoughtful look. Callis retreated into himself. Tavokk, for a change, wasn't able to read what his friend was thinking.

Looking up, Callis's eyes had a foreboding look in them. "I believe you when you say he's good, but he will falter."

"Cal—"

Callis cut him off, voice dark and rigid. "No," he said. "Listen, Jereth. He slipped up. Back at The Tower. If he slipped up once, he will slip up again. And when he does, I'll be waiting for him. Every breath he takes from now until he is eliminated is mine!"

Tavokk's eyes widened with surprise. He had never seen his friend quite like this. This was serious.

"I can see your determination. Tread carefully, my friend," Tavokk warned. He began to stand. With a farewell, he said, "I must be going. It's getting late and I have unfinished business to tend to before the morn. It was good seeing you, Cal. Till we meet again."

Callis joined him in standing. "If you must go, then yes. Till we meet again."

ဆာ

After having left the bar and his friend, Callis Morgandy, just shy of two in the morning, Tavokk had headed to take care of some unfinished business. Some ties had been left loose, given his recent departure, but now that he had returned, he knew that such things had best be taken care of, the sooner the better.

ဆာ

Tavokk's business took longer than presumed, requiring a good handful of hours to deliver promised trinkets and important pieces of documentation to various clients.

After a long time walking, he approached his building. He climbed the grated stairs up to his flat in quick time. It was well nearing seven in the morning, and he was ready to lie down for some shut-eye.

As Tavokk was about to reach into his pocket to retrieve his house key, he had an inkling, sensing that the door was unlocked. A curious look came over his face. Cautious, he raised his hand to the door handle and opened it.

As he took a half step through the door, Tavokk's eyes jolted immediately over to the couch where a man was sitting in the shadows of the morning. The man looked up and met his gaze. Tavokk remained silent, peering into the dark flat as the intruder spoke to him.

"Hello, KyVeerah."

65: A New World...of Calamity

Rhyus snapped his eyes open. He hadn't even realized they were clamped shut. He did notice, however, that the shiny black stone in his hand had become very cold. He stared at it for a short second, and then raised his eyes again, looking around this new place. His emerald eyes narrowed. *Where the hell am I?*

Quickly, he looked back down at his hand. What had a second ago been a stone had, in fractions of a second, turned to a lump of ash. The instant his gaze landed upon it, it crumbled from its once identifiable form. Rhyus looked at it in curiosity. Tilting his hand sideways, the ash fell, and he clapped his hands together to remove as much of the remainder as he could.

Wiping his hands on his denims, he started to further analyze his surroundings. Suddenly, remembering he needed to move off of the third point of the portal, he jumped down from the elevated stone. It had a hexagonal shape, and now that Rhyus was on the floor, it stood as high as his mid-thighs.

Looking at the ground, where a smashed crystal statue lay in a thousand scattered pieces, Rhyus decided that someone must have tried to disguise the portal by making it look like a marble stand for a statue or sculpture to be set upon. In spite of this, the trained eye would have recognized it as a portal with ease.

On the wall before him, Rhyus saw the other two pieces of the portal suspended several yards up. The impressive statues were only partial figures, lifelike and leaning out from the wall where they had been frozen in space. They held their hands out before them in an offering manner, with wings spread out behind them, extending very near to the wall. Each of these men wore a mask over the upper portion of his face.

A disturbance filled the air, and Marion now stood on the pedestal. Her eyes were clamped shut just as Rhyus's had been.

Marion opened her eyes, blinking a few times before looking around. Her eyes found Rhyus, but then she looked at her hand where the stone had crumbled into loose ash. She jerked her hand back, causing the ash to fly from it in a falling cloud, then raised her hand toward her mouth, blowing in an attempt to remove what remained. Wiping her hand against her leg, Marion turned back toward Rhyus, who had come nearer.

Rhyus extended an arm, offering a helping hand. Marion gave him a displeased look but accepted. Grabbing his hand, she jumped down from the pedestal, careful not to land on any big chunks of shattered crystal.

Marion studied the disorder around them. "Where are we?"

"Must be some old abandoned house. By the looks of it though, whoever did live here had a good deal of money on their hands."

"What do we do now?"

"Well, I guess we should get out of this house, for one. It appears to be abandoned, but I get the feeling that there's someone, if not several somns, here. Probably sleeping at this hour, but still. I'd hate to be here when they wake." Rhyus gave Marion a guarded look, and she nodded in agreement.

Crystal-like geshem tiles covered the black marble floor beneath them. Together, Rhyus and Marion moved as quietly as they could, looking for a way out. Beautiful, though dusty and deserted, the home exuded an eerie atmosphere.

As they moved through it, they found every room of the house to be equally impressive, each decorated at high expense. *Why would anyone abandon this place?* Rhyus found the fact peculiar. Reaching the Ĭnauro Manor's entryway, Rhyus and Marion looked up the three stories to the high ceiling. This room had been left completely open, clear to its highest point.

A geshem chandelier still hung suspended from the ceiling. It was large enough that Rhyus was amazed it still remained, regardless of its thick cables and chains.

"Wow," Marion said, in fascination, "it's beautiful." The chandelier was a distinct contrast against the sleek blackness of the surrounding ceiling, walls, and floors. A narrow white rug, stretching over the open space from the entry, also added a contrast to the same geshem tiling that covered every room they had been through. Lights from street lamps outside spilled over the entryway through tall windows, which flanked an ornate set of black double doors.

Cautious, they walked over the lengthy rug toward the front doors. Rhyus noted, without much surprise, that the locks were already unhinged, as he reached for the handle.

"What?" Marion asked.

"Nothing," Rhyus lied, but when Marion gave a hushed gasp,

he knew that she had seen the unhinged locks as well. She cast him an urgent look.

Placing his hand on the door's handle, he wanted to yank it open, but proceeded slowly, lest it make a sound, drawing unwarranted attention. He opened the door just wide enough for them to slip through.

Signaling Marion to go ahead, he changed his mind, deciding it was better for him to take the first step. Who knew what was out there. Searching all about, Rhyus stepped from the house. He dropped his eyes, distracted as his feet sank an inch or more into the sparkling, sapphire granules covering the ground.

Strange, he thought. There wasn't a soul in sight. Or, if so, they were camouflaged, huddled drunkenly up against building walls.

"OK," Rhyus said quietly. At his signal, Marion stepped outside, pulling the door until it closed with only a hushed click.

Just as Rhyus had done, Marion looked curiously down at the granules of the city floor. "That's different," she said. Rhyus nodded in agreement, still keeping a steady eye on their surroundings in case something might decide to pop out of one place or another.

"I don't think I like this place," Rhyus said, in his own hushed voice. Peering about, he saw only an assortment of sleek black marble buildings with no contrast except for the city floor and the silver flecks, which reflected light from the streetlamps. Even the lamps themselves were black.

"Dreary, isn't it?"

"Yeah. And dark." Rhyus gazed at the sky, realizing that none of the five moons could be seen, only a cloud covering. He did spot a large rotating light source as it skipped across the blanketing clouds.

Rhyus looked to the left and then to the right. "Well. What do ya think?" It didn't appear that they could go any direction and find a safe place to stay. He wondered what it was they were supposed to be doing here.

Marion glanced about. "I don't think it really matters."

Rhyus nodded. Marion's words solidified his speculation. "All right then." As he stepped away from the false protection of the Ĭnuaro Manor, a steady falling rain greeted him. On impulse he started to the left, and Marion followed with no idea where they might be headed or where in the city they might be.

Lenim was right, Rhyus thought, as they moved over the dazzling blue ground. The few somns they saw were passed out, having indulged themselves more than they should have. Nevertheless, walking by their unaware bodies sent apprehension through Rhyus and Marion, as they continued toward some unknown destination.

Trying not to let her anxiety show, Marion asked, "Are we going to make a habit of this?"

"What do you mean?"

"Heading out from wherever we are with absolutely no idea where we are going or what to do once we get there?"

"You're right," Rhyus said. "Let's hope not."

"So why *are* we here?" Marion asked, after another moment of silence.

"I really haven't the slightest idea. The only thing I can figure, from what everyone has been telling me, is that I must be meant to do *something* important. But I don't know what."

"Hmm," Marion mulled this over. "Even if that's so, why do I need to be here?" She looked at Rhyus, as they continued forward. They moved through the Dark City for some time, occasionally turning, just to feel like they were getting somewhere. Rhyus made sure to veer away from the black, spiraling tower looming high over the city. Marion had admitted that she too preferred to keep a good distance from it. As if the city weren't shady enough, the dark structure exacerbated its ominous nature.

"Hey!"

Rhyus and Marion jumped at the voice behind them. They had been walking for a couple of hours. Until now, no one had tried to speak to them, nor had anyone they'd passed even looked conscious enough to do so.

Marion grasped Rhyus's left hand. They had come to a complete stop. The voice was shouting at them. They could feel its urgency. Slowly, Rhyus turned to the right, keeping Marion behind him as he faced whoever had called out.

Across the way stood a young woman, staring straight at them. She had nothing with her except a red sequined clutch. Her very scanty dress was also a bright, bold red.

Well, she obviously isn't trying to hide from anything or anyone, Rhyus thought.

Though neither gave any indication that she was fine in doing so, she casually approached them. The dim city lights gave her lightly tanned skin a delicate glow. Her hips swayed with her thin feminine form as she moved.

The dress she wore was very short. In fact, it was a damn good thing it wasn't an inch shorter. As for the top…Rhyus couldn't help but give notice as it draped low, revealing the tops of her large breasts. She was wearing a long gold necklace that laid, with a small ruby pendant, falling to a point between her bosoms, visible just an inch above the dress's red fabric. Marion gripped Rhyus's hand tighter as the stranger neared.

"Are you two lost or in need of a place to stay?" she asked, coming to stand just an arm's length from Rhyus. She was much too close for comfort considering they had just met. And they hadn't even done that yet, technically. Her strawberry blonde hair was styled short, but angled shortest in the back and fell longer until it reached toward her chin at its longest point in the front. Framing her face attractively, its color caused her contrasting green eyes to stand out with a feral light.

After a hesitant moment of observation, Rhyus finally answered, "No."

"Are you sure?" She shifted her head causing her oversized, gold earrings to shift the same. "I do have a place you can stay if you need? Even if just for tonight? It's not far." She put forth the question, making the offer sound very tempting. Rhyus was almost mesmerized by the purring lilt of her voice, but snapped out of it when Marion squeezed his wrist and hand with both of hers.

Rhyus shook his head. "No, thanks. We're fine."

The young woman pressed her painted lips together with a doubtful look. She surveyed the situation, noting how Marion had sidestepped behind Rhyus, squeezing his hand for comfort.

Unknown to Rhyus or Marion, the young woman had been aware of their presence within an hour of their arrival. She had expected that when the time came, she would note some minute signs. But the Energy trail they were throwing off around them was—to her trained senses—like following a tram of explosives. She was almost giddy with the knowledge that this almost had to be the Key Calling. If not, he was mighty damn close. Of all her readings, there was not a single description of a Calling who disrupted the natural Energies with anything close to this magnitude.

She had been following them for some time, and was usually close enough to catch their conversations. She had bided her time to see if they would say more. She finally grew impatient and decided that Rhyus's comment about doing something important was a legit enough reason to intervene.

"My name is Helena," the young woman said, attempting a new

approach.

"Rhyus." He nodded his head in greeting. "This is Marion," he added. He tugged his arm, trying to get Marion to come out from behind him, but she refused. This stranger seemed harmless enough. Unhappy with Rhyus and his positive response toward the stranger, Marion gave him an unkind squeeze, nails digging into his flesh.

He yelped, forcefully yanking his arm out of Marion's grasp with a scowl. Marion, realizing she may have pushed it too far, took a small step out from behind Rhyus, trying to make it up to him.

Helena took the moment to analyze, as she scanned Marion from head to toe. This little brunette was of no interest to her, merely a nuisance. But if she had to put up with the girl to get to this guy, Rhyus, then she would force herself to do so.

"You know," Rhyus said, causing Helena to return her gaze to him with a revived feeling of optimism. She gave him an intrigued gaze, batting her eyelashes, as he looked into her similarly colored eyes. "We actually do need a place to stay," Rhyus said. Both Helena and he noticed Marion's half-stifled sigh of displeasure at this comment.

Helena revealed a sincere smile, but its intentions were nothing near innocence. "You can stay at my place if you'd like? It isn't too terribly far from here." She put the offer in the form of a question, but addressed a "come-on" look to insure his response. Now that she had found him, she sure as hell wasn't going to let him go. The girlfriend might be a problem. But given a little time, she would find a way to dispose of her.

Rhyus took a moment. "Yes. That would be great."

"Rhyus!" Marion shouted, not even bothering to soften her reaction to this strawberry strumpet.

"What?" He turned to face her, irritated. "Marion, we need a place to stay. What's the problem?"

"No," she said, casting a warning look. "We can find somewhere else."

He narrowed his eyes. "I don't know if you've been paying attention, Marion, but this place doesn't seem as friendly as you're suggesting. If you think you can find somewhere more accommodating, go for it." Rhyus's words were straightforward, even harsh. "I'm going with her." He didn't glance at the strange woman, Helena, for confirmation. There was no need.

The whole scene caused a thorough sense of twisted delight to flood Helena. Everything was falling together far easier than she could have planned. The best part of all was that it hadn't required any significant effort or planning on her part. Her twisted smile returned to her face.

Marion stared up at Rhyus with an agonized sense of betrayal. She had actually started to believe he was reverting back to the kind self that she had befriended in Lux Lumetia. But now the pain of his hostility showed on her features. "Fine," she spat, staring into those emerald eyes. He looked blankly back at her.

Marion couldn't believe it. He didn't even care.

Without another word, she turned on her heel and stamped off in the direction that Rhyus and she had just moments ago been walking, together. *Bitch*, Marion thought, grudgingly, toward the tramp with her strawberry blonde hair, big boobs, and slutty attire. As she walked away, alone, her eyes began to well. *Dammit Rhyus*.

&)CR

"You ready to go then?" Helena asked, adding a bit of allure to prevent Rhyus from turning around and stopping Marion. As she took a step nearer, an appealing spicy woodland fragrance flooded his senses.

Rhyus hesitated, but only for a second. "Yeah." He returned his full attention to the copper-toned young woman with the almost nonexistent red dress and similarly painted lips.

"This way." Helena, just a hand's breadth from him now, signaled Rhyus to come along, as she placed a carefully manicured hand on his upper arm. She turned him in the direction opposite of Marion. They walked side by side, taking a quick turn at the very first corner. Helena wanted to block any opportunity for Rhyus to look back and see his former companion.

She led the way, as they weaved between glinting, black marble buildings. The only somns they passed had been out for some time. "Don't worry about them," Helena said. Rhyus wasn't sure he could dismiss them as easily as she did, but the fact that she considered them harmless was reassuring. Though unconscious, the somns kept him on edge. But he would never admit it to Marion. Or Helena.

Together, they made their way over many, many blocks. "I thought you said you lived nearby?" Rhyus was wary. Yet he didn't want to upset the one soul who had offered him lodging in this sketchy metropolis.

His comment didn't offend her. It didn't even cross her mind to take offense at his doubtful inquiry. "Oh, I forgot that I had ventured so far." The lie slid through her teeth more naturally than if she had rehearsed it. She had only said that it was "not far" to convince Rhyus to come with her.

"Don't worry though, it's not much farther now. I promise." Helena offered a smile. Rhyus, blinded by her feminine allure, should have seen the bad intentions displayed right along with it. But he looked right on past them.

As the new acquaintances carried on, a slow feeling of remorse slipped into Rhyus's awareness. He shouldn't have let Marion go off alone. Shame fell over him as he peered around at his surroundings. He lifted a hand, rubbing at the back of his neck, regret eating at him. He came to a halt.

It took a couple of steps for Helena to process this. But once she realized it, she twisted around on her gold, wedge heels. "What's wrong?" she asked puzzled.

"I have to go back."

"What?" Displeasure snapped into her voice, but she immediately covered it up with another plastic smile. "What?" she asked calmly this time. Sprinkling on a hopefully convincing dash of concern.

"I shouldn't have let her go off alone," Rhyus said. "I'm going to go find her."

Helena fought the impulse to scratch his eyes out. Fighting to maintain control of the situation, she looked straight ahead at Rhyus. Her face remained unreadable except for the frustration leaking out through her narrowed eyes.

Rhyus turned his attention from Helena, missing her obvious frustration as a result of his distracted state. He looked back in the direction from which they had come. Turning back to Helena, who managed to regain a look of composure, he waited expectantly for some response.

"Yes," she finally said. "Of course."

Rhyus felt that he should leave her with some sort of final comment, but a loss for words filled him. Angling his head, he glanced back down the walkway behind them.

Drawing Rhyus's attention back to her, Helena started, "Before you leave…" She retrieved a folded piece of paper that resembled a book page, tore the blank top portion from it, and refolded the rest, placing it back into the sequined clutch. Then she retrieved a bottle of liquid eyeliner, finding no other writing tool.

Holding the strip of paper in the palm of her hand, Helena wrote down an address. She folded it, careful to smear the black eyeliner script as little as possible. Holding out her hand with the folded paper, she waited for Rhyus to reach out and accept it, watching with sad eyes as he did so. He lowered his arm back down and put the paper into a pants pocket.

Looking up at Rhyus, she waited for him to meet her gaze. "In case you change your mind," she said. She stepped nearer to him, placing what she hoped came off as a comforting hand on the side of his shoulder. "Good luck finding her," she said, in false compassion. "Rhyus," she gave a concerned turn of her painted lips, concern as fake as the nails on her fingertips, "don't be too surprised if she's too stubborn to accept your apology or your wishes to remain with her."

Rhyus looked into Helena's green eyes before shifting his attention to the glittering, blue granules. He considered her words and slowly nodded his head. He admitted to himself that he wouldn't be shocked if Marion gave that exact response.

Helena lowered her hand but met Rhyus's gaze once more. Maintaining close proximity, she gave him directions for finding the address she had written down. In case he changed his mind and wished to track her down.

"Well, Rye, I hope to be seeing you around." Helena hardly noticed Rhyus flinch at the pet name. She offered a seductive smile, accompanied by a sensuous stroke of the arm before continuing on the course the two of them had been taking. Hips swaying as she walked away.

Rhyus couldn't help but smirk as he watched. He shook his head, and then headed back the opposite direction.

৪৩৫

Coming to a standstill, Rhyus released a sound that resembled something between a sigh and a growl. He had been wandering around for hours and had found absolutely no sign of Marion. "Dammit," he muttered, under his breath. He moved a hand to the back of his neck, clenching his teeth in frustration.

Lowering his arm, Rhyus looked down at his watch. Just shy of seven. If not for the rain, the suns would have already made their appearance. He tilted his head back, exasperated. He thought of how he could be sitting in a warm home, if he had simply continued along with Helena. But no, instead he was out walking pathetically around in the endless rain like someone's damn lost little pet.

Rhyus ran a hand through his hair. It had become thoroughly soaked, not unlike his jacket and every single inch of his clothing. His messenger bag remained at his side with its single strap slung over his shoulder and across his chest. He briefly wondered about its contents. After a minute, he remembered the bag's water repellant quality with a wave of gratefulness. At least he would have dry clothes to change into once he get out of the rain. If he ever did get out of it.

Taking a couple of steps toward the nearest building, Rhyus leaned back against its slick, wet surface. It wasn't like his hair and clothing could become any further saturated. He leaned his head back against the wall, the rain falling over his face.

"Rhyus!"

For a split second, Rhyus thought the voice had been all in his head, but unfortunately he came to know that would require more luck than he had in store. There was no mistaking that voice.

Venn. Rhyus's heart dropped to the pit of his stomach.

Requiring all of his strength of mind, Rhyus slowly turned his head in the direction the voice had come from. Sure enough, there stood Venn, all too close for comfort. In Rhyus's opinion, the sole fact of Venn being present anywhere in this world was too close for comfort. Now he stood a mere ten yards away.

Rhyus turned his head from Venn. He tried to find something else to look at, anything other than Venn.

"Rhyus," Venn said, approaching with urgent steps. Venn looked all about before bringing his focus back to Rhyus, all the while moving forward. "Where is Marion?" he demanded, looking Rhyus hard in the eye.

It took all of Rhyus's self-control not to turn away in apprehension, expecting to be pummeled. Silence clung heavy on the air until Rhyus finally said, "Not with me."

Venn's eyes widened just a fraction. "What do you mean, she's not with you?" he shouted, though stifling it enough to bring it down to a more hushed level. Venn wasn't intending to draw attention to the two of them.

"I *mean* she was with me, and now she's not."

Incredulity burned deeper into Venn. "Then where the hell is she?" He stood very near to Rhyus now, in a threatening stance with a single arm extended, hand pressed flat against the wall.

"I don't know where she is," Rhyus said. He didn't bother to tell Venn why Marion wasn't with him or that he had been trying to track her down for the last two hours. The fewer words he had to speak to Venn, the better. As Venn processed Rhyus's words, his disbelief transformed into solid rage.

Venn growled, and Rhyus had to use all of his control, once again, to not turn away in fear. Cowering before Venn was something Rhyus was not willing to do, even if it took every remaining ounce of control. He couldn't help but think of Venn as some sort of savage beast.

It really wouldn't be all too surprising if he attacked and ripped my limbs from my body. Rhyus fought the image in his mind. He continued to peer at the ground several yards past Venn, instead of looking up at him. The fact only added to Venn's fury.

"You have no idea where she is?" It was difficult for Venn not to reach forward and pick Rhyus up by the neck of his jacket, or solely his neck.

"No," Rhyus said bluntly, braving a short glance up at Venn's menacing, glowing eyes.

"You're coming with me." Venn growled again, grabbing Rhyus by the drenched clothing over his shoulder. He turned and began to half drag Rhyus along with him.

"No!" Rhyus used all of his force to yank himself out of Venn's grasp with one quick motion, which Venn hadn't been prepared for. Rhyus was quite surprised that his jacket hadn't torn apart in the moment as he jumped back a couple of steps, readying himself for a next lunge from Venn.

Venn turned back, eyes narrowed into illuminating slits. He gave Rhyus a heavy glower as an immediate response failed to come to him. A low growl emitted from the back of his throat, and he stared at Rhyus for a long, hard minute.

"You want to be alone?" Venn roared. "Fine!" Without waiting for Rhyus to respond, Venn spun around and stormed off. "No wonder she left you!" he spat back. Rhyus watched, incredulous, as Venn was slowly swallowed by the darkness of the city.

Realizing the rigid tension in his body, Rhyus willed it to loosen. *Of all the somns I could run into, it just had to be Venn. Really. What the hell are the chances?* Rhyus drew a deep breath, continuing to watch the shadows where Venn had vanished. The very chance of meeting Venn here was more unreal to Rhyus than any of the dreams that had been plaguing him.

Rhyus returned to the wall. He leaned his head back against it and closed his eyes as water spilled over his face. *Venn doesn't even care about me. I don't even know why I'm wasting my time out here. Marion is probably more than happy to be rid of my presence. But maybe...*

Reaching into his pocket, Rhyus retrieved the small, folded piece of paper he had been given. *Helena.* He unfolded the strip, peering down at the slightly smudged black letters and numbers forming the address Helena had told him to come to if he changed his mind. He carefully refolded the paper in an attempt to keep from smudging the script any further.

She actually cares about me, Rhyus thought, as resentment washed over him. *Maybe even has feelings for me.* He recalled how she had looked at him and stroked his arm with one of her delicate hands, as he was about to turn and walk away from her, only to search for Marion who probably didn't even want him to find her anyway.

Hey, maybe I have feelings for her too. He opened his eyes and brought his head forward moving his body, with a thrust of determination, away from the wall. He pushed forward, crunching back over the sapphire ground on a trip to find the address where he had been assured he could find a warm welcome. Where he could find Helena.

66: Marking to the Messenger

The oversized door knockers made a clunking sound as they made contact with the wooden door. Like so many other doors Rhyus had passed, this one was painted black. It hadn't taken too long to locate the address with its numbers posted just above the door. *Definitely not the ritziest area*, Rhyus thought, as he waited for someone to answer.

Shortly, he heard someone unhinging a multitude of locks. *Wow, talk about security*, he thought. But then, once again, it struck him that he hadn't landed in the friendliest city.

The door opened a crack, and a soft glow emitted around a woman's face, as she examined her visitor. *Helena?* It took him a second to be certain. She smiled wide and held up a finger indicating for Rhyus to hang on one moment. She closed the door and unfastened the last two chains holding the door to its frame.

Opening the door, wide this time, Helena motioned Rhyus to come in. "I'm so glad you've come," she bubbled. Her smile was true, but if Rhyus hadn't shown up at her door, she had already made plans to go after him later that day. This just made things a whole lot easier on her part. She was not about to let him slip by now that she had found him.

Rhyus entered Helena's home, and she turned to resecure the door. Circling around to look at Rhyus, she threw a hand before her mouth, smiling in amusement. "You are absolutely soaking!" She lowered her hand, all of her features giggling with mirth. She hadn't really had a lot of encounters with outsiders, and seeing someone so improperly dressed for Atrum Unda was something she'd never run into.

"Come, come." She waved him further into her home, to a living room with a welcoming fireplace. Multicolored flames danced wildly within it. He observed his new hostess, as he trailed along. She had changed out of the slinky red dress and into a tiny green nightgown. It had a thin band of black lace, just beneath her breasts, and a wider band lining the bottom. There were slits on either side, and it was about the same length as the dress she'd worn at their earlier encounter. The shade of the nightgown matched her green eyes well, but it matched the color of Rhyus's eyes even more closely.

Rhyus passed Helena, coming to a stand near the stone hearth. He slipped the strap of his messenger bag over his head, setting it down on the floor where a rug covered the hardwood floor. He unzipped his hooded sweatshirt, frowning at how supersaturated his clothing had become. Not that it was any surprise considering the endless hours he had spent wandering about in the rain. The feeling of the soaking wet clothes clinging to his body was very uncomfortable.

"Would you like me to find something you can wear for the time being?" Helena asked, as she watched Rhyus peeling the sweatshirt's sleeves from his arms. She continued to find this all rather humorous. Nevertheless, she recalled her manners and hurried to help him with his sweatshirt, hanging it on one of several hooks beside the fireplace. Steam began to rise from it in a white cloud.

Rhyus shook his head. "No, thanks. I've got something to change into." He motioned toward his bag on the floor.

"Oh," Helena said, "they're OK?"

Rhyus looked up, a grin reaching his lips. "They're dry, if that's what you mean by OK."

Helena flushed at this. "Yeah, sorry." She glanced down to her hands before returning her gaze to Rhyus. "Oh!" She realized he had gripped the bottom edge of his undershirt—raising it an inch or two. A questioning look asked whether she planned to watch him change. After all, she hadn't offered another place for him to do so, and he was not about to stay in these clothes another minute.

Helena turned around, stunned to find that she was blushing. Watching wouldn't have bothered her in the least if he hadn't made it such an awkward situation. Rhyus also turned from his hostess, as he continued to remove his shirt. He looked around. Not wanting to throw the drenched shirt onto anything it may ruin, he was quite unsure what to do with it. Helena had been generous to offer him a place to stay, and he would hate to damage anything.

Helena twisted her head for a peek, just before Rhyus pulled the sleeveless, gray undershirt over his head. *Oh, my*, she thought, enjoying the sight of her houseguest.

Rhyus laid the shirt out over the hearth, unsure what else to do with it. He crouched down by his bag for a pair of dark denims and a black, sleeveless undershirt. He retrieved underclothing from his bag with a shake of his head. It wasn't every day that he changed with a voluptuous woman in the same room, especially in such close proximity. He started to unzip his soaked denims when he was startled by an unexpected yelp.

"Of sins and Ravenna!" Helena exclaimed, throwing a hand over her mouth, green eyes wide in astonishment, as she spotted Rhyus's tattoo.

In response to her dramatic gasp, Rhyus twisted around with a questioning, concerned look. He had forgotten about his unzipped pants. "What?" he asked, in alarm.

"I was right about what a very important somn you are!" She lowered her shaking hand, eyes still wide.

"What do you mean?" he asked, unsure what she was talking about. He ran a hand through his wet hair, as he looked at Helena, puzzled and shirtless.

"A Calling. By all the moons. You are a Calling. I was right!" She was overjoyed.

Rhyus swallowed as her words sank in. He remembered back to Lux Lumetia at the piazza. And he recalled the talk Venn had with him, or more so the conversation Venn had begun to have with him. At the time, he wondered why Venn had decided on such a topic of conversation. But it made sense. Why else would someone as reserved as Venn even broach such a subject with a virtual stranger?

Rhyus bent down to fiddle with his messenger bag, trying to give himself time to think. *Could it really be possible? I am a Calling?* He didn't want Helena to know he was completely ignorant in case she was telling the truth. So he kept his mouth shut.

"It just so happens that I know your Messenger." Helena's eyes were wide with surprise.

"Huh? Who?" Rhyus asked, having only half heard her.

"Jereth Tavokk. Your Messenger." Helena displayed a knowing look, waiting for Rhyus to comprehend. Watching Rhyus now, the realization that Rhyus really had no clue, hit her. She was exultant. Fate truly was on her side. Her expression altered in twisted amusement. But then, recovering immediately with her consummate skills at lying, she looked up with a serious expression. "Oh," she said, in false sympathy. "You had no idea, did you?" She raised two fingers to her lips and looked up into Rhyus's eyes, still acting with her false sense of pity.

A thoughtful look crossed Rhyus features as he mulled over what Helena had said. He turned her words over in his mind. *A*

Calling? The thought was too much. He tried to deny it. *But what if it's true?*

"You must get some sleep," Helena interrupted Rhyus's thoughts. "You look exhausted."

Rhyus lifted his eyes back to his hostess. "What? Sorry." He shifted his eyes, knowing that it was rude of him not to listen to her words, but his mind had been preoccupied.

"Sleep," she said. "We both need to get some sleep. I promise I will explain some things once we have rested."

Rhyus nodded. *It would definitely be nice to get some answers.* He displayed a curious look as Helena walked from the room without giving any bit of explanation. After a short moment, he began to wonder whether he was supposed to follow. Before he had a chance to make up his mind about going after her, she reappeared around the corner.

"The couch all right?" Helena asked, moving nearer to Rhyus.

He watched Helena in her slick, emerald nightgown as she came close, and then turned to bend a bit forward, placing a couple of blankets down onto the couch. "Hmm?" she said, standing back up, facing him with very little space separating them.

Apparently, she doesn't have spatial issues, Rhyus decided, as she stood back up. "Huh? Oh, oh yeah, that's fine." He nodded, not wanting her to feel he was ignoring her.

"You're sure? You can keep the fire going. It gets a little chilly out here." She raised a hand and placed it on his bare upper arm, as she offered her concern. Her hand was very cool. And as it rested just below his shoulder, goose bumps spread over his flesh. Helena smiled at his skin's immediate response to her touch.

She raised her hand further, twirling her fingers through his long, dark bangs, still wet from the rain. It was unusual for anyone in Atrum Unda not to have a good amount of product worked through his or her hair to keep it styled, as well as to repel rainwater. She pushed his bangs slowly back and slid her hand gently down the side of his face, pressing her body even closer.

As Helena reached up with her other arm, sliding both hands now to the back of his neck, Rhyus moved his hands to her hips with the thin, slick fabric beneath them. In that instant, Helena pulled him tightly against her, and standing up on her toes, brought her lips to meet his.

Rhyus squeezed her tighter as their kiss became more intimate. Helena wrapped her arms around Rhyus's torso, hinting for him to drop down to the couch. He did just that. She leaned forward over him, kissing his neck and his ear. Things were becoming quickly more heated as he ran his hands along her thighs.

"See," Helena whispered, into his ear, "aren't you glad you let her go."

Her hushed comment brought Rhyus back to immediate reality — the reality that he, Rhyus, had let his traveling companion, Marion, walk off on her own in this sinister city. The reality that Marion had offered to come along on this little adventure as a friend and to be of assistance to him. Thinking about this all now, Rhyus was filled with remorse. He understood that he had failed, abandoning Marion and her benevolence.

"No." Rhyus's response was hardly louder than Helena's own whisper, but it was terse. He grabbed Helena's thin feminine form and lifted her away. Now, instead of leaning right into him, she found herself sitting further away on the couch, discarded.

The expression on her face was hurt, but inside she was annoyed more than anything, angry that she had been rejected.

"Sorry," Rhyus said, as he rubbed a hand over his eyes. "I'm just exhausted. It's been a really long day. A really long week, at that." He shrugged a weak apology.

"No, I understand," Helena said. She decided to use his explanation to satisfy herself about how he had possibly been able to brush her aside. "We both need rest." Helena gave him a sweet look of understanding, as she pushed herself up from the couch. "My bedroom is just around that corner, second door down the hall, if you need anything. I'll see you after a bit." She spun around, and he watched her walk off, the green nightdress undulating with her hips.

"Yes, goodnight," Rhyus said, before reregistering the fact that it had already began to reach into mid-morning. Once he heard the door to Helena's room close, he laid down. He grabbed the pair of dry underclothing he had removed from his bag before Helena and his little episode. His face flushed in the dark as he reached down to notice that his pants had been unzipped all along. He continued to change out of the rest of his wet clothing, and then unfolded the blankets, tossing them over himself.

Rhyus rested his head on one of the couch pillows and closed his eyes. No matter his exhaustion, Helena's comment had layered on a heavy coat of guilt. As he lay in the silence of the unfamiliar home, in the unfamiliar city, he struggled with his conscience until sleep mercifully reached forth and pulled him under.

℘℘℘

"Morning." Rhyus blinked his eyes open, as Helena set a glass on an end table just beyond the edge of the couch. She placed a second glass by the couch's other arm before turning back to the kitchen.

Rhyus rubbed at his eyes. He reached down and grabbed the black undershirt and dark denims. Throwing off the blankets, he pulled them on before Helena returned with two plates of food in her hands.

"Hungry?"

"Am I," he eagerly said. Grateful, he accepted the plate and pulled the blankets aside to clear a place for Helena.

Rhyus and Helena enjoyed their meal, as they engaged in laid-back conversation. The food Helena prepared for them may not have been on the level of some of the food Sultan had introduced him to, but it was still pretty good. And furthermore, he appreciated her troubles of making him any meal at all.

After eating, Helena offered Rhyus a shower. She had taken one before beginning their meal. Even after hours of walking through the rain, Rhyus found the shower most gratifying. Pleasant, not at all like the feeling brought on by the ominous rain and its accompanying darkness.

When Rhyus made his way back to the living room, he found that Helena had grabbed one of the blankets from the couch and spread it out over the portion of the rug nearest to the fireplace, which she had relit during his absence. Helena had seated herself on the blanket with a mug of steaming liquid. Actually, there were two mugs. She had readied a drink for him as well.

Marvelous timing. He gave her a small grin.

Reaching forward, Helena patted the ground, gesturing Rhyus to take a seat. As he sat, she retrieved pillows from the couch, tossing a couple to her guest, and then situating the others for her own comfort.

Helena watched as Rhyus made himself comfortable. Once situated, he glanced up to find her eyes still on him. "I can't believe you're a Calling," she said, with a smile. "And Jereth Tavokk's Calling, at that," she added, giving a short, giggling laugh.

Rhyus displayed a questioning expression while his mind recircuited, preparing to pick up on the brief conversation Helena and he had started after his arrival early this morning. He glanced back to his hostess, as she took a cautious sip from her mug.

"So, how is it you know that Jereth Tavokk is my Messenger? Or that I'm a Calling at all?" Rhyus gave a skeptical look.

"Oh!" Helena set her mug down, excited to explain. "Your tattoo." She directed a finger. "Messengers and Callings receive identical markings to declare their identities as such and to address their bond. This also gives them certain abilities or powers."

Rhyus's skepticism thickened, but then lifted, replaced by a revived resentment toward Venn as he thought back to their time at the piazza once again. *Venn must've known about this. I bet he avoided telling me anything vital to keep me in the dark!* His eyes narrowed, thoughts causing him to become increasingly infuriated.

"You OK?" Helena asked, along with one of her looks of false concern. In all honesty, she found his reaction more entertaining than anything.

"Yeah," he lied, shrugging her question aside.

"Rhyus," Helena said, her eyes full of proposition.

He flicked his eyes back to her eager gaze. "Yeah?"

"If you are Jereth Tavokk's Calling…that would make you the Key Calling."

Rhyus didn't comprehend.

"The *Key* Calling, Rhyus! The one and only!" Her words were quiet, but her eyes reflected every ounce of her exhilaration. "Do you know what this means, Rhyus?"

His features reverted to their skepticism. "No. I don't."

Oh, by the lunar goddesses, this is the ultimate dream! Helena rolled her eyes in delight behind closed lids. Taking a deep breath, she brought herself back into full control.

"Rhyus." Helena scooted inches closer to emphasize the significance of what she was about to say. "As the Key Calling, it is your destiny to have the powers of The Ancients."

Rhyus laughed. *There's that phrase again. "Your destiny,"* he ridiculed voicelessly.

"The Ancients, Rhyus! Possessing their power means strength and wisdom beyond all others. It will bring you strength by means you could only dream of."

"I don't think that someone with memory loss is meant to have that kind of power. Especially when that someone can't remember more than the past week of his life."

Though Rhyus was unable to see it, Helena was only telling him what she thought would prove to her benefit. It was true, the fact that she now knew Rhyus was a Calling, as well as the whole bit about the tattoo markings that bonded a Calling and his or her Messenger. But Helena had no idea whether Rhyus could be the Key Calling. Nevertheless, considering what Serlio Young had said, there was chance that even a very strong Calling could pull off what she was planning. So, who was to say that Rhyus couldn't be that very Calling she needed?

"Rhyus! Don't you see?" Helena leapt on the fact of his memory loss, using it to her own advantage. "Following this destiny, *your* destiny, will help you regain your memory." Helena looked Rhyus straight in the eye, trying to convince him of her lies.

Rhyus gave only a thoughtful look.

"Oh, Rhyus! I can't believe you have been left so in the dark on all of this," she said, with plastic sympathy. "Rhyus, it is your birthright to control all four of the world's Towers and the power contained within them and channeling between them."

"The Towers," Rhyus said, under his breath.

"Yes, The Towers. They are corroding, and they need their powers to be revitalized by the Key Calling. By *you*, Rhyus." Though much of what Helena was telling Rhyus was full of deception, her words were actually much truer than she was aware.

"A sign," Rhyus muttered.

"Hmm?" Helena asked, having not quite caught his words.

"It's true, isn't it?" He looked at Helena with expectant eyes, wanting her to push him that last bit into believing all she was telling him.

"Yes. Of course."

Rhyus explained the portion of the dream he had just nights ago, the part where the four Towers had risen from the city floor, growing in their power until, one by one, they began to crumble away.

"Yes!" Helena exclaimed, reaching out and putting a hand on top of his. "See, you *do* know! This is what you are meant to do," she reassured, secretly thinking it odd that he had this dream of The Towers. For a moment, she felt a twinge of consternation. It could be possible she was overreaching. She wondered if perhaps he just might be the Key Calling after all.

Maybe this will help me gain the respect I deserve, Rhyus told himself, his thoughts immediately drifting to Venn above all others.

"OK, Rhyus." Helena crossed her legs before her. "I suppose you are ready for me to fill you in on the first mission you will need to carry out in order to begin your path toward your ultimate purpose."

Rhyus looked at her with total concentration, completely absorbed in her web of deceit. He now fully believed both her truths and her deceptions. "What must I do?" He was ready to learn of his first task.

"First, I must tell you that I am part of a secret society that has been looking for the Key Calling." Although this was partly true, the association she worked under had many other aspirations. "The leader of this secret society is a man named Nyx Crucian," Helena boasted, of her superior and his organization, trying to put a good light on him in Rhyus's mind. "I am Nyx's second in command," Helena said, with a proud smile, though this was a lie if she had ever told one.

She went on to explain that Nyx had three bands under his command. The top, containing his most highly valued and skilled assassins, was his Black Band. Following was his Crimson Band, and lowest was his White Band. In truth, Helena was in Nyx's White Band, and not even the most valued of its members. Helena watched Rhyus swallow her lies.

By now, the time had already slipped into early evening. Helena moved on in her own personal plan, explaining to Rhyus, with ever more detail, exactly what his mission was going to require. In actuality, Helena only wanted Rhyus to follow this course in order for her to please Nyx and to significantly raise her status. And from there, she would eventually come to have power over him as well. She didn't care a lick about helping Rhyus for his own sake.

Rhyus and Helena spent the rest of the evening indoors, relaxing with casual time and conversation. She told him that he must be very well rested for the next day. "Our course of action depends on it," she declared.

"Do you feel confident about your mission?" Helena asked. She wanted to make sure he wasn't going to screw up her plan or back out.

"Yes," Rhyus answered, with a self-assured nod.

"Excellent." Helena displayed a bright smile, concealing many thoughts and pleasures. "Rhyus. Tomorrow your life will turn for the best." Her two-faced smile widened.

67: Lost and Found

Staring up at the ceiling, Callis tried to recall the pleasant dream he had been having before the strident blare of his morning alarm dragged him into reality. He could feel it resting on the edge of his mind, but it was no use, he couldn't recollect any piece of it. Although fully awake, he had no desire to leave the comfort of his bed just yet. Instead, he stared at the ceiling, reflecting upon the previous night's events.

It was good to see Jereth last night. But now that I think about it, he didn't provide me with any information of real value. Odd, he is usually packed with information. If Jereth can't even collect the goods on him, this Vincent KyVeerah must be one slick character, indeed. Draping a muscular arm over his head, on the pillow, Callis reflected more deeply into his conversation with Jereth Tavokk.

It seemed as though Jereth knew more than he let on. I suppose he did just get back from whatever the hell he was doing. Knowing Jereth, it was undoubtedly something high-risk. Callis grinned at the thought. *What doesn't involve high risk with Jereth Tavokk? I'm sure his mind was just distracted with other important matters.* He shrugged it off, figuring he'd have another opportunity to question Tavokk before long, when he was less distracted.

Tossing aside the comforter and sheets, Callis climbed out of bed. Stretching, he began to plan out his day. *I might as well head over to The Dome. Perhaps Jett has obtained Van Ingen's papers. He strikes me as one who completes his work accurately and efficiently. Besides, with no new leads on Vincent KyVeerah, this is my next chance for a profitable break.*

ℰℭ

Callis crossed over the city walkways to The Dome. He broached the main entrance, taking the southeast elevator to the level where the White Band resided. As the metal doors parted, Callis spotted him.

"Jett Milan. Perfect timing. Just the somn I needed to see," Callis said.

Jett's eyes showed alarm at Callis Morgandy's unexpected appearance, but they quickly reverted to their usual nonchalant state. Toneless, Jett held the day's issue of *The Atrum Chronicles* up before Callis. "Have you seen this?" Jett's unfeeling gaze rested upon Callis as he read the headline of the front page. It read *Wild Man, Fyfe Van Ingen, on the Run.* Callis leapt from the elevator, approaching Jett with predatory swiftness to snatch the paper from his hands.

"What!" Callis growled, staring in disbelief at what he was seeing. *This can't be true!* His eyes seared with fiery rage.

Jett gripped Callis's forearm with surprising force, dragging him through the frosted glass doors into the White Band's lounge. Releasing his hold, Jett turned his attention on the other two occupants of the room, his comrades, Stella Black and Wylan Norwood. With a commanding stare, Jett ordered them to leave, "Disperse. Now."

The total lack of emotion in Jett's voice was chilling, and more authoritative than one might expect. Both Stella and Wylan looked uneasily between Jett and the Black Band's Callis Morgandy. Registering the tension in the atmosphere, they proceeded to scurry from the room.

Still irate, Callis snapped, "Why would they listen to *you*?" He still clutched the paper, crushed into an indefinable form.

Incredulous, Jett looked at Callis with disdain. "You've got to be kidding." Jett knew with certainty that his superior skills far outmatched those of any other White Band member, despite the fact that he was the most recent addition to the group. Callis scowled at Jett's unsatisfactory answer, but he chose to pursue it no further.

Resuming his detached demeanor once more, Jett returned to the matter at hand. "After we last spoke, I went to The Tower to obtain Van Ingen's papers, however, I was denied any authorization, even with *subtle* threats." A wondering smile appeared on Jett's face as he stared off absently. Callis gruffly cleared his throat, snapping Jett from his daydreaming.

Jett looked back at him, unblinking. "I suspect that Van Ingen made his escape sometime before I reached The Tower. Annoying, isn't it?" Jett displayed his clear lack of interest in the whole matter.

Callis growled, "You think!"

Jett was not at all fazed by the crimson-haired assassin as he turned and stalked out of the room.

After leaving The Dome and making a few insignificant stops, Callis decided to call it a day. It was still early, but he had no tolerance left to deal with anyone. *By Ravenna, I swear, if one more thing fucks up today, I might just mutilate someone into nonexistence.*

Ezra's heeled boots crunched over the blue granules of the city. Her mind processed the events of the past two days as she made her way to The Dome. Following Helena had proved to be fruitless thus far. *Last night was even worse than the day before at that Scribe's Den!*

She had learned nothing of the slightest significance the day she followed Helena to that little shop. And then last night, Ezra had decided to retire as Helena headed toward *another* bar, sure to lead to yet *another* uneventful night. Ezra's lips puckered at the thought of the skimpy, red dress Helena had been wearing. Amazing her breasts didn't fall right out.

In Ezra's mind, the day's only event worthy of note was Callis's suspicious activity, which happened to be the exact reason she was reporting back to The Dome so soon with nothing to tell Nyx of Helena's supposed plan. As she walked, Ezra's consciousness began to trail to thoughts of Callis. She clutched her sharp, manicured nails into a tight fist. A cataclysmic anger started to bubble up in her throat. She could feel herself on the verge of a shrill scream as her fury continued to rise to the surface.

How dare he! The nerve of that impudent bastard! Intruding on my assignment, of all things. Her light green eyes trembled. When Nyx hears of this insolence...

The Dome stood in the near distance, as Ezra came to a halt. A thought caught in her mind, and her breath in her throat, as an unsettling chill ran down her core. Nyx. Her eyes widened even further, but this time masked by absolute horror.

By The Ancients, he was...no, he couldn't be...following me? Could Nyx have sent him to trail me? Ordered him to see if I was sufficiently completing my assignment? An ominous inkling trickled into her bones. Ezra took one hesitant step forward, and then halted again.

Lingering spiteful feelings from two days before, mixed with her new feelings of fear, caused Ezra to become even more anxious. *Callis. Was the stunt you pulled at The Tower a test? As well as following me? Perhaps Nyx sent Callis to evaluate me. To see if I'm on top of my game.* Her brow furrowed. *It does seem likely that Nyx would send his golden boy to spy on me. Does it? Shit. This could just be Callis acting wayward and fucking with me once again. But what if it's not?*

Uncertainty filled Ezra as she tried to make sense of these new revelations. *Nyx will surely wish me to report Callis's erratic behavior and obvious disobedience.* A forbidding force clutched her from the inside. *But if Callis is carrying out direct orders from Nyx...the repercussions of my failure will be severe.* She shrieked in worried frustration. *I just can't be sure which it is!*

She began to take another step forward but turned abruptly on her heels at the last second, stalking in the opposite direction, away from The Dome and out of the Hollow District.

℘ↄႹ

Armani and Julian crossed over into Atrum's Valentine Sector, a dreary place under even drearier skies. As they walked side by side, stepping in unison, Julian asked, "So, tell me why we are hunting down this...uh...what's his name again?"

"Niall. Niall Trace. And we are looking for him because Nyx ordered us to, Jules. I should think that would be obvious," Armani replied, maintaining his sense of calm, the large hoop earring swaying with each step.

"No. What I meant was, why are we locating this Trace guy *today*? Especially after you made a point to tell Nyx that we were taking our time on this one?" Julian asked.

Armani's mouth curved into a charming smile. "Just because we are *retrieving* this artifact, doesn't mean that we're going to hand it over to Nyx immediately." A wicked grin of understanding crawled over Julian's handsome features.

In less time than expected, the duo reached their destination. The building before them was constructed of black rough brick. It was decrepit, much like the other structures filling the Valentine Sector. Armani and Julian entered the disreputable shop and gazed at their surroundings. The interior appeared as run-down as the exterior of the building. A scurvy man in his forties emerged from a back room, a bit dislocated from the shop itself. The man stood behind the main display case of antiquities, as Armani and Julian drew near.

He addressed them, "We're closed, so you'll have to leave."

Armani flashed one of his most elegant smiles. "But it's still quite early in the day."

The shopkeeper barked, "Don't care. Now remove yourselves before I do."

Armani made a clucking noise with his tongue, waving a slender finger in front of the man. He replied, "I do *not* take to rudeness very well, Mr. Trace." Armani knew he had assumed the man's identity correct as Niall's eyes flooded with surprise.

"How do you know of me?" Niall questioned, in suspicion. Armani's demonic eyes were disturbing, shaking the man to his foundation. Julian remained silent, but he resonated just as forbidding an air as Armani.

"Oh, that doesn't really matter. What matters is that you have what we are seeking."

Niall didn't know who sent these dubious men, but he knew it couldn't be good. He could tell these two were trouble. He had to dispose of them. Niall withdrew a long blade from beneath the display case, but before he could put it to use, Armani intervened with an unnatural swiftness and grabbed Niall's wrist from behind. With a quick flick, Armani snapped it, and Niall instantly dropped the blade with a shrieking cry of pain.

Armani kicked the blade to the side, as he said, "I don't believe you will be needing that, Mr. Trace." Julian languidly walked around and picked up the weapon.

Examining it, Julian declared, "Ooh. This is lovely."

Armani addressed him, "Jules, would you be so kind as to restrain our friend, so that I may secure the shop?" Julian slid the blade under his belt.

"With pleasure," Julian answered, taking hold of Niall's uninjured arm and pinning it up behind his back while kicking the man from behind, forcing him to the ground. He clutched Niall's shoulder with his free hand while Armani walked to the front of the store, closing the window shutters and locking the door.

He returned to where Niall knelt, restrained by Julian. Bending his knees, with his hands clasped together, Armani looked Niall in the face. "Much better. Now we don't have to worry about being disturbed. It'd be best if you would cooperate with us. We are busy men, after all." Armani's voice was filled with a disconcerting sweetness accompanied by a warm smile. Niall began to quiver with fear as he tried to stifle his whimpering at the pain in his broken wrist.

Armani's musical voice rang, "Now, Mr. Trace, my associate

and I are looking for a rare artifact. I believe you've heard of it. The Chrem Larose?"

Niall began to sputter nervously, "I-I've never heard of i-it."

All suggestions of friendliness dispersed from Armani. As his gaze darkened with displeasure, Julian's aqua eyes shone with excitement. Still speaking to Niall, Armani looked up at Julian. "Wrong answer."

Julian put pressure on Niall's pinned arm, wrenching it higher behind his back, as he held him down by the shoulder. The force caused the connecting tendons and ligaments to snap like thick, metal cable cords, the unraveling ends splaying apart. Niall released the most disgusting gurgle of a scream, as horrendous as the obliteration of his arm. His arm dangled limp and useless at his side when Julian released it.

Armani shushed the man, "Be still and quiet or we'll be forced to silence your screams. Wouldn't want to disturb the neighbors now, would we?"

Niall started to whimper, "Please...please..."

"Let's try this again, Mr. Trace. It would be oh so wonderful if you would tell us the whereabouts of the Chrem Larose," Armani said, ever so kindly. A bubbling cry escaped Niall, as he writhed in pain.

He managed, "I d-don't know. I s-sold it. T-To a strange man."

Armani's flawless features creased into a probing frown. "Is this the truth?"

Undeniable honesty showed through Niall's eyes, as he pleaded, "Y-yes. I s-swear it's the t-truth."

"How unfortunate," Armani enunciated, with slow spoken words. His voice was deadly, and all beauty from his features turned cruel and unforgiving. Armani recovered from his bent position, standing slowly.

He directed a quiet look at Julian, "Jules."

A wicked grin spread across Julian's face. He withdrew Niall's blade from his belt. In a quick moment, Niall released a short scream, and then nothing more.

₮)⌓

Armani and Julian left the boundaries of the Valentine Sector. "How disappointing," Armani said. "Nyx will not be pleased, to say the least. I suppose it's fortunate that we have some time before we have to present it to him."

Julian added, "I wouldn't worry too much about it. At least we were able to have some fun. I know, let's celebrate with drinks at the Wishing Well." Julian stopped in his tracks, realizing that Armani wasn't at his side.

Turning back, he called, "Armani?"

Armani stood a few yards away, looking toward a figure in the near distance. Julian followed Armani's stare, and his jaw dropped. He couldn't believe what he was seeing.

Armani's voice echoed the look upon Julian's face. "By Eve, is that *Adaveen*?"

68: For Better, For Worse

"Fyfe? Lord, man, you nearly scared the wits out of me!" The man, Fyfe Van Ingen, merely offered a smile in response. "And you know, the name's Tavokk in these parts. You go around this city nowadays calling me KyVeerah, and you may as well throw me in a guillotine yourself."

Van Ingen's smile remained in place, the colorful bruise still dark on the side of his face. His arms rested on the back of the black couch, a drink held in one of his hands. Van Ingen raised the glass in greeting, and then took a sip, reveling in the smooth fire at the back of his throat. "You and this double life of yours, or whatever exactly it is you are doing. Don't you ever worry that it will catch up with you one of these days?" The man's accent was evident as much so as the genuine concern lacing his words.

"Fyfe, my good man, you worry too much. That is your problem. Well, that amongst others. Particularly the one about you going off the deep end, babbling all over the city walkways and having your ass hauled off to The Tower's Prisoner's Quarters." KyVeerah gave him a side-glance. "Yeah. That was a good one."

"Only sayin', maybe you should be more responsible and watch your back. Otherwise, you'll never know what's comin' after you." Van Ingen gave a warning look.

KyVeerah stood, silently looking off into space, as he considered this. Then he looked down at an untidy accumulation of *The Atrum Chronicles*, all of them with tears and bent edges from having been forced under the door in their delivery. On the front page of the paper at the top of the pile, a headline in a bold, large font read *Man Fallon: To be Released Early on Authorized Orders*. KyVeerah didn't think much of it. However, the issue received early this morning, which had fallen to the side of the pile, did catch his attention. This one read *Wild Man, Fyfe Van Ingen, on the Run*.

KyVeerah turned his head back toward Van Ingen who was lugubriously taking another swallow from his glass, before he said, "I still say you worry too much."

"Suit yourself, chum, but I say you'd be better off safe than sorry."

"I suppose we'll worry about that when the time comes then, shall we?"

"Aye."

Looking about the flat from where he stood, a puzzled look came over KyVeerah. His bedroom door was open as was the door to the bathroom. "Where is Venn?"

"Oh, you won't be findin' him here." Van Ingen looked at KyVeerah and made a face holding much more meaning than he was revealing. He tilted the glass again.

"And what is that supposed to mean?"

"What that means, is that Venn is out searching the walkways of Atrum Unda as we speak."

"What?" KyVeerah shouted. "Venn hates this city! By Valencia, why would he be out roaming its walkways?"

Van Ingen looked back up at KyVeerah with one of those "you've got to be kidding me" sort of looks. He left a moment for silence. "Vincent. It's not so hard to figure out."

KyVeerah stared blankly again. Then, his eyes widened. "No."

"Oh, yes." Van Ingen gave him a wink. "Knew you could figure it out on your own."

"What in the hell made him think it was a good idea to go out and wander the city looking for them on his own?" KyVeerah was infuriated by the fact that Venn hadn't stayed put, at least until he could return home. "For the love of Valencia!" KyVeerah threw his head back, exasperated, interlacing his hands behind his neck. He dropped his arms back down, turning to the front door. He heard Van Ingen's quiet voice, just before he reached for the handle.

"KyVeerah," Van Ingen warned.

Exhaling, and feeling quite conflicted, KyVeerah halted with his hand upon the door's handle.

"You need sleep."

"How do you know?" KyVeerah snapped.

Van Ingen said nothing. He only proceeded to take another drink, arms still resting on the back of the couch and his body sunk into its cushions.

"Hey, what are you drinking anyway?" KyVeerah asked. Van Ingen pointed to a bookshelf adjacent to the couch. KyVeerah cringed. "That's what I figured." It was unquestionably the best booze in the house and consequently the priciest. "You do seem to be doing much better this morning?" KyVeerah asked, in further question as the realization occurred to him.

"Aye. A little rest, food, and water will do a man wonders. Not to mention the salubrious drink provided by his host." Van Ingen raised his glass in a toast, though maintaining his elbow's resting position.

KyVeerah pressed his lips together and nodded. "I suppose this holds true."

"And that's a mighty nice jacket you've got yourself there," Van Ingen motioned KyVeerah's way.

KyVeerah shifted his eyes down to the deep blue-violet jacket, and then back up to Van Ingen. "Yes, impressive, isn't it?" he said, proud of the gift from his dear friends, Cyrus and Killian Vanaché. "Well, glad to see you back to your usual self." KyVeerah nodded again. Then, reluctantly following Van Ingen's wise advice, he half-willingly made his way into his bedroom.

Throwing the door shut a little harder than intended, KyVeerah flinched. He shrugged, unzipping the long jacket and tossing it onto the chair in the corner.

The urge to simply collapse onto his bed was tempting, but he fought it, instead proceeding to remove his boots. KyVeerah pushed them aside, and then reaching up, grimaced while he pulled his shirt off over his head, leaving the tattoos covering his back revealed. He gritted his teeth as the motion caused a wave of pain to emanate from his side. Removing his denims, he climbed into bed. It wasn't as opulent as his bed in Umbra Halls, but it still felt good to be back in his Atrum home. No effort required, he fell asleep as soon as his head hit the pillow.

෨ඏ

KyVeerah's eyes snapped open as he heard the door to his home slam against its frame. *Shit, I didn't even lock it!* he recalled, after a second of lying with his eyes open. His body was wide awake in an instant. He never forgot to lock the door. One would have to be a complete idiot not to lock his or her doors living in Atrum Unda. Not that it would necessarily stop someone who really wanted in.

Jumping out of bed, he pulled on the denims from the floor where he had previously dropped them. Yanking the bedroom door open with haste, KyVeerah jumped at the sight of Venn who had apparently been on the way to see whether he had shown up. By the looks of Venn, it would have been an even ruder awakening than had just occurred.

From his peripheral vision, KyVeerah saw Van Ingen sit up

on the couch. He had evidently decided to take a doze as well. A questioning look crossed his face as he processed KyVeerah and Venn standing in the entryway, just before the bedroom door.

"I am going to *kill* him," Venn growled wildly, eyes glowing a glacial blue.

KyVeerah leaned back against the doorframe. "Wait. What? Who?"

"That goddamn boy! Your *Calling*, isn't he?"

"Wait," KyVeerah's eyebrows lowered in hesitation, "you saw him?" He looked back at Venn, his eyes widening.

"Yeah, I saw him," Venn spat.

"Like...just now? While you were out?" KyVeerah demanded.

"Yeah," Venn said brusquely. "And he's lucky I didn't snap his fucking neck." His eyes glowed with more intensity.

"You just left him out there?" KyVeerah shouted, in accusation.

"Yup."

"What the hell were you thinking?" he shouted again.

"You know what," Venn snipped back, angling his head forward. "I *tried* to bring him back, but *he* didn't want to come."

"What do you mean?" KyVeerah threw his hands into the air. "Why didn't you just drag his ass back here?" he asked, in thorough disbelief. "Isn't that what you would normally do?" He had returned to shouting. Both of their eyes now glowed, KyVeerah's releasing a violet illumination.

"Do you have *any* idea what that boy is like?" Venn's gaze hardened. "Oh right," he said curtly. "You wouldn't know. You left him for me to look after as soon as he came your way. Tell me, Vincent. Have you ever even laid eyes upon him?"

"Yes. I have, actually. Thanks for asking," KyVeerah said, offended by the ill-intended accusation. "It just so happens there were some other things that had to be taken care of, which is exactly the reason I left him with you! And now you've gone and scared him off! For a second time!" His voice rose with each word. "And what, did you finally manage to scare Marion off for good too? I don't know how she ever lasted with you so long!"

The brilliance of Venn's eyes dropped a level, and he shifted them to the floor.

"What?" KyVeerah asked. The vibrancy of his own eyes dimmed. He hadn't expected that kind of response. Not in the least.

Venn shook his head, eyes still angled to the floor. "She isn't with him."

"What do you mean?" KyVeerah asked, the two of them having nearly reached a level of civil conversation. Van Ingen continued to listen from the other side of the couch.

Venn sighed in frustration. "Apparently they were together," he paused, before shaking his head again, "but she isn't with him now." Venn clenched his hands. "He has no idea where the hell she is, and neither do I. Alone though...at least I hope to Blue Ravenna she's alone." He released a shaking sigh and moved his hands up to his face.

KyVeerah stared at Venn with amazement. He thoughtfully twisted his lips. "So...what now?" he asked quietly, unsure what to do given the unusual situation. He cast a questioning look Van Ingen's way. Van Ingen returned merely an uncertain face and a shrug.

Venn lowered his hands from his face, balling them into fists again, as they moved down to his sides. He shook his head looking KyVeerah in the eye. "We find her."

KyVeerah had a short-lived urge to ask Venn's suggestion involving Rhyus, but he decided otherwise. *Looks like I may have to deal with him on my own*, he thought, feeling rather irritated toward the boy and this whole situation in general.

ᔕᓃᓉ

After long hours of searching the city for any trace of Marion, Venn and KyVeerah returned to KyVeerah's Atrum Unda home.

Before heading out, just shy of twelve o'clock, Van Ingen had been helpful enough to give a general direction of where he sensed Marion could be found. Even with that bit of help, however, they had been unable to locate her. She could have moved to any place in the location's vicinity by the time they reached it. And every moment thereafter would allow her to move even further from them.

KyVeerah unlocked the door, opening it and stepping into his flat. Venn angrily pushed his way between the door frame and KyVeerah. Feeling responsible for the fact that Marion was still out somewhere in this hellish city, Venn proceeded to the couch. He dropped down, threw his elbows on his knees, and put his head in his hands.

"We'll find her," KyVeerah assured, though his words were an empty shell. He had already said this to Venn numerous times. By the look of despair on Venn's face, he was unconvinced. The hours of aimless searching, and Venn's spiraling emotions, had left him feeling exhausted and empty.

Venn did not acknowledge KyVeerah's comment.

Jerking his head from Venn, KyVeerah noticed Van Ingen who stepped forward to hand him a stiff drink. "No show?" Van Ingen asked, in a quiet voice, though he already knew the answer.

KyVeerah's lips pressed into a thin line, and he shook his head, while staring off at nothing in particular. Van Ingen turned to the couch where Venn had seated himself. He extended his arm with a second glass identical to the one he had given KyVeerah. Initially, Venn showed no response, but after a still moment, he sat up straight and accepted, taking several large swallows.

Van Ingen seated himself on the arm of the couch farthest from where KyVeerah stood. He raised a single leg, resting his foot on the couch cushion with his other foot remaining on the hardwood floor.

"You two ought to stay in for the rest of the night," Van Ingen said. Just as he was expecting, both KyVeerah and Venn looked at him with incredulous eyes.

"Both of you are distraught, and neither of you has a clear plan of attack. If you go out and wander Atrum any further, the city is going to deal you both a hand of trouble rather than handing you what you're looking for." Van Ingen was dead serious.

Venn dropped his eyes, and KyVeerah raised his own up toward the ceiling, as each of them chewed over his words. Finally, KyVeerah sighed. "I suppose you may be right." Although he agreed, he was certainly not pleased with the fact. He closed his eyes a moment, as he drew in a breath.

We need to figure a way to locate Marion. And Rhyus. They've probably already met trouble. We must act quickly. Tomorrow we must find them before it's too late. KyVeerah opened his eyes, instantly reconnecting with Van Ingen's powerful stare.

Van Ingen offered a nod, as he broke into KyVeerah's mind. *"Tomorrow you must find Him."*

69: Revelations

Endless hours of wandering peripatetically through Atrum Unda had taken a toll on Marion's mentality as well as her physical condition. She'd never felt so lost and alone, and the relentless rain didn't help her mood, as she clung to the leather jacket she had dug up from the bottom of her bag.

She knew it wasn't a good idea to leave Rhyus and wander off alone, but there was no way in hell she was going with that dumb whore. Plus, strangely, there was some deep part of her that began to feel more comfortable, the longer she walked over the unfamiliar blue walkways.

Marion was happy to be away from that trick, Helena, but her mind was filled with a sense of longing. *I miss Venn. I miss home. And I wish Rhyus hadn't gone with that sleaze.* Marion scolded herself instantly as she formed the last part of the thought. *Stop feeling sorry for yourself, Marion Sunshine. Besides*, she reminded herself, *I'm probably better off without that jerk anyway.*

Separating from Rhyus, Marion's original thought was that she might be able to locate her old acquaintance, Vincent KyVeerah. It had been two years since she had last seen him, but she felt certain that he still lived in Atrum Unda. Her memories of the short time when she lived with KyVeerah were fuzzy, but anything before that was a blank. She thought that if she walked around a bit, something would eventually trigger a memory or look familiar. But nothing. *I don't recognize a single thing in this city. This place is just way too big. I'm such a fool. As if Vincent is just going to spot me by some random, miraculous chance. What was I—*

Marion yelped in sudden surprise as someone grabbed her by the wrist, twirling her around. Out of instinct, she spun and swung her free arm to fend off the attacker. Marion had lightening quick reflexes, but this man was too fast. As though he had anticipated her reaction, he caught hold of that wrist too. He held her in place, as he said in an awed voice, "My goodness. Would you look at this, Jules? It *really* is Adaveen. My, my, I never thought I'd see Adaveen Cooper again. Did you, Jules?"

Marion stopped squirming for a second to examine the man who was holding her in his grasp. His short hair was a striking bronze and a large, hoop earring dangled from one ear. She peered into dark eyes that displayed dancing strips of red, interwoven through blackened irises. His eyes were horrifying, yet beautiful. He was the most gorgeous man she'd ever seen. Suddenly, remembering herself Marion said, "I'm sorry, but you are mistaken. My name is Marion. Not Ada-whatever."

The man looked at her with curious surprise. "Marion? Oh, dear. Oh, dear. Jules, did you hear what our little Adaveen just said?" Astonishment, as well as true concern, lined his words.

Huh? Jules? Just then, Marion noticed the second man standing next to the one with her in his hold. *Oh my.* This man called Jules was just as attractive as the first, though in a different way. His dark brown hair trailed to his shoulders, appearing almost black in the current lighting. *And his eyes.* They were aqua, the most entrancing eyes she had ever seen. One could easily lose him or herself in them. Marion gulped. These men were very unnerving.

Marion was surprised that she felt more intrigued than frightened by these men. She had been staring and hadn't registered a single word either man had said. She snapped her gaze back to the bronze-haired man and blurted, "I'm sorry, who are you? And, um, you had better let me go." She bristled at his harsh grasp.

Baffled, the bronze-haired man blinked and instantly released the grip, which he hadn't meant to be so harsh. "My apologies. Where in the world are my manners? My name is Armani Saint, and my friend next to me is Julian Gallows." He paused, and then added, "You really don't recognize us? Don't remember us at all?"

"No, of course not."

Armani tilted his head, perplexed, yet controlling his amusement. Julian gawked for a minute, then cackled, "This is too good! She has *no* idea who she is!" Julian tried to contain his glee but failed, bursting into another series of harsh cackles, throwing his head back.

Marion stared at the two oddballs before her. *Uh Huh. Time to ditch these bozos.*

☙☙☙

Later that evening, Marion trailed after her new acquaintances, Armani Saint and Julian Gallows. They moved through a massive structure, The Dome, as they referred to it, which was plainly appropriate. As Armani and Julian led her to where she would be staying, she wondered how things had gotten so out of hand.

So much for ditching them. Marion wasn't really sure how Armani had talked her into coming with Julian and him. He had said something about her face and her eyes. She couldn't even recall all the things he had said. *It all happened so fast. Besides that...for the most part, they seem like rather decent somns.*

Confused by her surroundings, Marion spoke up, "Um, excuse me." Both men stopped in their tracks, turning to look down at her.

Armani flashed his charming, angelic smile. "Yes?"

Marion fidgeted at Armani's alluring gaze directed her way. His dark eyes were overwhelming. Snapping out of it, she asked, "You said there were rooms up here? That seems a little odd, especially for a place like this. Why is that?"

"Oh, well it's really quite simple. This floor of The Dome acts as living quarters for the...er...*executive* members when they wish to crash here. There are only a handful of us currently on staff, so there are plenty of rooms available," Armani explained.

Hmm. Still seems pretty odd, Marion thought.

Assuming that they'd resolved her uncertainty, Armani and Julian continued walking with Marion right behind. They stopped in front of a dark frosted door, identical to every other door of The Dome. Armani removed the room's electronic key from a pocket and unlocked the door, after which he held the door open for Marion to enter.

The room was simplistic, yet modern. The back of the room curved outward, to echo The Dome's structure, with thick, dark tinted glass. The remaining walls were a solid blue-gray color. Close to the room's entrance, another door led to a sumptuous bathroom.

Marion observed her surroundings, setting her bag down by the bed. *It's not much to look at, but at least it's tasteful. And safe.*

"Here, you're going to need this," Armani said, handing her the room's key. Need be, he could always find a way to obtain another. Julian hadn't said much since Armani and he came across Marion. His face held an inquisitive yet peculiar stare that rested constantly on Marion. He seemed to be lost in deep thought.

Tilting his head, Julian muttered something, "How *did* you manage to...me...alive...hmm." Armani shot Julian a deadly look, having caught enough of his words. Julian shifted his stance, realizing he must have spoken aloud.

"How did I what? You were mumbling." Marion stared up at Julian. "You know what they say about mumbling," Marion retorted, but her smile dropped the moment she noticed that it had reminded her of Venn.

Curious, Armani said, "I have no idea. What *do* they say about mumbling?" Before Marion could answer, Julian clapped his hands together in exclamation.

"How about I fetch you some fresh towels for the bathroom? Uh, yes, wonderful," Julian said, sidestepping briskly out of the room. Marion and Armani stared at the doorway, not sure what just happened.

"Is he okay? He seems a bit *off*?"

"Oh, sure. I wouldn't worry about it. You'll see, he'll be back to his usual chipper self tomorrow," Armani assured.

Chipper? Hmm. Julian doesn't seem like the chipper type. Marion frowned at herself. *Who am I to be so judgmental? Appearances can be deceiving, right? I'm sure he's a perfectly acceptable somn.*

Armani gently lifted Marion's bag from the floor, offering, "Here. While we're waiting, I'll help you unpack."

"Oh, OK. Thank you," Marion said, with apprehension. She wasn't sure she wanted this man going through her belongings, but she didn't want to be rude, certainly not after Armani and Julian had been so kind to her. As they began to unpack, Marion took her few toiletries to the bathroom. Once out of sight, she had a moment to herself to reflect. These two were definitely a breed apart, and although she had absolutely no recollection of them, she found herself feeling strangely at ease.

"Hey, Armani?" Marion called.

"Yes?"

Marion stuck her head out from the bathroom. "There are a whole bunch of fresh towels in here."

"How curious," Armani began, as Julian returned, seeming a bit detached.

Armani smiled pleasantly at Julian, asking, "Did you grab the towels, Jules?"

Becoming awkward once more, Julian mumbled, "Oh, yes. Right. Well...they were all out of towels. They, umm, are out to the cleaners...to be cleaned." Julian shifted his eyes uncomfortably. Armani gave him an incredulous look, raising a brow.

Turning defensive, Julian barked something incoherent his way, and after having done so, slumped back against the wall, retreating into himself.

Marion emerged from the bathroom, starting to remove her

jacket. Julian altered his gaze absentmindedly to where she stood. He snapped from his thoughts as he observed the clean tear in the left sleeve of her jacket. "Oh, yeah. Sorry about that." Baffled, Marion looked at Julian and then back to the jacket she was now holding before her. She unintentionally dropped it to the floor.

Pulling up the left sleeve of her shirt, she accused, "That would mean you're the one who did this?" In a long line along her left arm was etched a thin, yet obvious, white scar.

Julian winced with guilt. "Yeah. How about we not mention this to Nyx."

Marion frowned. "Who's Nyx?"

Both Armani and Julian's faces dropped in astonishment. They hadn't expected this. Forgetting her name was one thing, but they didn't think it at all possible for her to have forgotten Nyx Crucian.

Armani began to open his mouth, but Julian interrupted with haste, "No one. Never mind. You must be tired. Armani and I will leave you be so you can get some rest. Let's go, Armani." Julian retreated out of the room.

"But—" Armani said, his eyes on Marion.

Julian gave a forceful bark, as he stepped back into the room, "Let's go!" He proceeded to grab Armani by the arm, dragging him out.

Armani called farewell to Marion, "Goodnight, Adaveen. See you in the morning!"

Marion's brows knitted together as the door closed behind them. *I'm going to have to have a talk with them tomorrow. This Adaveen nonsense has to stop. And what was all that about that Nyx character?* Looking at her arm, everything about this place seemed somehow a tilt beyond the normal. She looked down at the bed, which seemed suddenly inviting. *But right now, sleep.* Marion smiled and dropped onto the bed, eyelids already closed.

ঞ৹ল্ড

Exiting the elevator, Callis headed toward the Black Band's commons room. Having taken the previous day off, he felt obligated to at least see if anything of interest was going on. Reaching the frosted glass doors and throwing them open, he looked upon the last thing he ever expected to see again. *Adaveen.*

Callis staggered over to the lounge's pool table, grabbing its edge for support. He couldn't feel his legs or the rest of his body. Lost for words, Callis stared breathless at the scene before him.

Straight ahead, at the mahogany table, a game of cards was being played. The table's occupants were Armani Saint, Julian Gallows, and Adaveen Cooper.

He had to be imagining this. It couldn't be real. *She can't be real. She's...I thought she was...dead.* As he ran his eyes over her, from her bronzed, chestnut hair to her vibrant, healthy form, Callis realized that his assumptions of the past two years had been dead wrong. *She's alive. She came back.*

Armani and Julian exchanged glances, wondering why Callis was being so odd. Marion stared at him with curious eyes, taking in his muscular build, the tattoos, red hair, and numerous piercings, including a lip ring, an eyebrow piercing, and many more lining his ears. Armani chimed in, "Surely Callis, you remember our little Adaveen?" Marion pivoted her gaze from Callis to Armani.

She snapped, between clenched teeth, "For the last time, my name is *Marion*. Not Adaveen." Marion then returned her gaze to the very attractive crimson-haired man with warm brown eyes. "Who are you?"

As her words sank in, Callis felt as if he had been kicked in the stomach.

Answering for Callis, Armani intervened, "Adaveen, this is Callis Morgandy. Don't you remember him?" Armani asked this latter question, already well aware of the answer.

Marion knew this, but she responded anyway. Giving Armani a dirty look, she said, "No. I'm sorry. I don't believe I've had the pleasure. And it's *Marion*."

Julian watched all of this with amusement written all over his face. Armani indulgently looked at her. "So, tell us, *Marion*, what is your last name then?"

Marion looked down at her hands. She flushed brightly. "I don't want to say."

Armani suggested, "Perhaps Cooper?"

Marion's anger flared. "No!" Julian grinned at this little outburst, and Marion decided she really didn't like Julian's "chipper" side.

Armani pressed on. "Well then, what is it?" All three men looked expectantly at her, waiting for her reply.

"Sunshine," Marion said, her voice barely above a whisper.

Armani leaned closer with a hand cupped around his ear. "Sorry, didn't catch that, my dear. What did you say?"

Blushing, Marion heatedly burst, "Sunshine! I said my name is Marion Sunshine!" With all eyes wide, the room went silent.

Armani and Julian blinked in wonder while this reaction left Callis taken aback. *I've never seen her like this. She's...different.*

Julian cracked into a long series of raucous cackles. "Sunshine? Good lord! That is too priceless!" He pounded the table, tears streaming down his face.

Armani's lips upturned. "Well then, Miss *Sunshine*—"

Marion sprang from her seat, fists clenched tight. "Shut up! Both of you!"

Julian leaned back, nearer to Armani, and half-whispered, "Feisty, isn't she?" as he broke into a whole new string of cackles.

At this, Marion sent him the darkest look she could muster. Julian threw his head back, laughing even louder. Armani's grin spread into a crooked smile. Between fits of laughter, Julian gaily added in Callis's direction, "Pay her no heed, Cal. Seems our gal has gone a bit *crazy*." Julian rotated his finger in circular gesture around his temple.

Feeling the need to scream at the top of her lungs, Marion retorted, "I am not! It's not even like I picked it!"

His musical voice filling the room, Armani laughed, "Didn't you now? Well then, who did pick it?"

Ignoring his question, she mumbled, "I wish Venn was here."

Distracted, Armani queried, "Venn what?" He paused, and then smiled, saying in a smart-aleck manner, "You're mumbling."

Marion bit back an inappropriate remark, and said, "Venn KyVeerah. He's my—"

Callis's eyes widened. He felt like he was going to be sick. *What did she say? Did she just say KyVeerah?*

Armani and Julian looked at her with new curiosity. Armani cut her off, "Hold on. Do you mean *Vincent* KyVeerah?"

Marion corrected him, "No. I mean Venn. His brother." She paused, in thought, then continued, "You know Vincent?"

Armani radiated with excitement. Ignoring her question, he held up a hand. "Wait. So, let me get this straight. Vincent KyVeerah... has a *brother*?"

"Yeah. I've been liv—" Marion started, but she was immediately cut off, yet again, as someone burst into the lounge through the frosted glass doors. Everyone turned their attention to the newcomer. A dark-haired young man with similar, unkind eyes walked into the room.

Callis wondered, *How did he get up here on his own? He doesn't have an access key to this floor.*

"Jett, what a pleasant surprise! I'd like you to meet someone!" Armani exclaimed, glowing with even further delight. He waved his hand toward Marion, saying, "This is Adaveen Cooper, a dear lost friend of ours. Adaveen, darling, this is our newest recruit, and recent friend, Jett Milan."

Marion glowered at Armani before addressing the newcomer politely, "The name's Marion. Nice to meet you, Jett." Jett arched an eyebrow at Marion, perplexed by her. He studied her oddly for another fleeting moment.

"Uh, right. Marion."

Armani suddenly remembered the conversation that had been taking place before Jett stumbled in. Jett looked as if he wanted to say something, but Armani blurted, "One moment, Jett." Holding up his index finger, he turned back to Marion with eagerness. "Now, how do *you* know Vincent KyVeerah if you supposedly lost your memory?" Armani looked at Marion, the red bands of his blackened eyes simmering with exhilaration.

"He's the one who found me...and gave me my name," Marion said, adding the last part in reluctance. She scolded herself, in silence, realizing she had been way too talkative. These somns were strangers. Despite their hospitality, strangers were strangers. Trusting them could not only put her in danger, but also those whom she considered family. For the past two years, Venn and Vincent had been her world. She decided to be careful from here on out.

Out of nowhere, Julian cackled. "Sunshine!" Another cackle. "I get it! I forgot how much I like Vincent KyVeerah."

Comforting, Armani patted Marion's arm while whispering to Julian, "Not now, Jules. Vincent has a brother." Julian rolled his eyes. He had also forgotten how fond Armani was of Vincent KyVeerah.

Cutting in to regain the attention of the others, Jett said, "It seems Helena Meretrix of the White Band has been missing for several days now. She hasn't reported back once. You guys know that?"

Before anyone of the Black Band could answer Jett, Marion interrupted, "Helena? Did you say Helena?"

All eyes in the room returned to Marion. Armani lit up, questioning, "Do you know her too?" Marion nodded. Her mouth turned into a pucker at the thought.

Seeing the instant disgust in Marion's eyes gave Julian one more reason to break into new tears of laughter. He barked, between howls, "Oh... yes... She certainly knows our Helena!"

Venomously, Marion scowled. "Yes. I've met that bitch. She's the one who caused Rhyus and me to separate once we arrived here." Realizing that she hadn't mentioned Rhyus to them, as well as forgetting the resolve she had just made not to reveal any more information, she fumed, "Oh! I forgot to mention, I traveled here with a friend, Rhyus Delmar. He'd still be with me if it wasn't for that scheming whore." Marion's distaste for Helena was only too obvious, a mutual feeling, which everyone in the room could relate to.

Callis was quite amused by Marion's revulsion of Helena. It caused him to slip a light grin. He looked around and noticed that the others shared similar expressions. *By Ravenna, she's changed. But she certainly still fits in here.* His initial shock of seeing her again was replaced in part by fascination at this new Adaveen. *Or Marion, I should say.* Callis straightened his stance, as he looked at her in wonder. As Callis was thinking this, another figure stormed into the room. *Ugh. Royce.*

Jett stepped to the side, avoiding the panicked Royce Elwood. "Listen! The worst has come to my attention. Helena Meretrix is missing! I just overheard Angelina telling Stella that Helena hasn't reported in for days. We need to act before Nyx finds out!" Royce blurted, in rushed alarm. Royce's reaction was only to be expected, since Nyx had assigned him the task of keeping an eye on the White and Crimson Bands' members.

Everyone stared at Royce. Armani was first to return his attention to the others, feeling no need to introduce Royce to Marion or vice versa. A sudden thought hit Armani, and a charming smile spread across his face.

Speaking to Julian, Armani shifted his eyes between Marion and Jett. "Oh, Jules, how perfect! One for me and one for you!" It took only seconds for Julian to realize what Armani meant.

Julian's face lit up as well. "But which one do I get?" Marion's brows furrowed in confusion.

Jett caught on quickly, his face twisting, disturbed by the duo's conversation. He edged toward the door. "All right. I did what I came here for, so I'll be leaving now. Good luck." He addressed this last part to Marion. She didn't stand a chance against Armani and Julian, in his mind. Hell. He had barely escaped them himself. Jett disappeared from the room before Armani and Julian came around to react.

"You guys! Did you not hear me? Helena is *missing*," Royce pressed, distraught. Everyone looked at Royce briefly before turning away again, feeling no reason to bother with a response.

Suddenly, Callis recalled something Marion had said. Armani and she had rejoined in discussion, as he turned his full attention to her. Callis walked forward with purpose, interrupting, "Marion. Does this Venn KyVeerah know you and your friend Rhyus are missing?"

Marion was caught off guard by Callis's assertiveness. She babbled without thinking, "Oh, yes. I wrote him a note before we left. I don't even want to imagine how furious he is with us. He'll probably blame Rhyus. Venn and he don't exactly see eye to eye." Suddenly thinking, she shut her mouth. She chastised herself again for saying more than she should have. But she couldn't help it. Not with this charming man, Callis Morgandy, looking at her so deeply. No one had ever looked at her like that before.

Revelation hit Callis. *Ok. Helena is with this friend of Marion's, Rhyus. This Venn character knows that Marion and Rhyus are missing. It's likely he has spoken with his brother, Vincent KyVeerah, and there is a high probability that Vincent is looking for the two of*

them...If I find Helena, I'll find the man looking for Rhyus...Vincent KyVeerah. The Intruder.

A sudden rush filled Callis. This was the exact break he had been searching for. Without so much as another word to anyone, he turned and stalked out of the room, leaving everyone curious as to what had just taken place within the peculiar mind of Callis Morgandy. A terrifying grin grew over Callis's face as he moved down the corridor.

It's only a matter of time now. You are mine, Vincent KyVeerah.

70: Strangers Amongst the Scenery

Helena walked the Atrum walkways of the latter side of morning. A wicked smile played over her lips. This morning, they had returned to her favorite warm, burgundy shade. Plum Desire. *Today, things are going to turn in my favor.* Helena's smile spread over her features as her thoughts sifted through the pages of her plan.

Rhyus had been asleep when she awoke, and still was after she had finished prepping herself for this glorious day. They had stayed up late the previous night, but not nearly as late as the night before. She left Rhyus a note concerning her whereabouts where he would be certain to find it if he awoke prior to her return.

Helena made her way to Shadow Market, the best place to find the goods to fix the perfect breakfast. She walked with a demanding eye. Transparent tents stood protectively over each stall, their products visible, with the exception of trying to view them through the crowding somns.

After purchasing various breads and fruits, she examined an exotic liquor bottle that caught her eye. It looked appropriate for a celebratory occasion.

"Sir, control yourself!"

A vendor from an adjacent stall caught Helena's attention as he argued with a customer. She watched them carry on from the corner of her eye.

"I am in control!" the customer—an intimidating man— hollered. "Just tell me, has anyone seen an unfamiliar young man? Brown hair, green eyes, roughly six feet and slender."

The vendor gave an exasperated sigh. "No, I'm sorry, sir. I told you, I cannot assist you." It was quite clear to Helena that the vendor was ready to be done with this man.

At that, the irate man with long raven hair gave a disgruntled huff before turning away. "Dammit, Vincent," he cursed.

As he stormed off, Helena turned back to the exclusive liquor bottle. "Shit." Her breath caught. *Rhyus.*

Helena's eyes snapped back to the vendor, then scanned the marketplace, searching again for the raven-haired man. Following the direction he had headed, she finally spotted him making his way through the outermost edges of the Shadow Market crowd.

With caution, she watched him continue off alone. He had gone in the direction of a familiar path, a secluded path, which Helena often took. She followed at a slow pace. *I wonder who he is? Who he works for? This isn't good. How does he know about Rhyus?*

Then, Helena picked up her feet at a run. She realized he was moving toward a secluded area. There were no doors off the particular alley he had taken. And it was a long one. If she could make it around to the other side before he got there, she could catch him off guard.

Reaching the far side of the alley that he had taken, Helena quieted her breathing. Fortunately, she carried her groceries in a single strapped bag. She was sure they wouldn't get in the way. She had not purchased much, and besides, she didn't plan this to be a fair fight. The fact that her prey outmatched her in size didn't faze her in the least. Speed and her remarkable ability with a knife were her edge.

Once her breathing returned to normal, she remained motionless against the marble wall. She became merely a part of the shady scenery. Her black jacket was suitable for the city's weather conditions, hooded, chic, and water-repellant. Beneath it she wore a tiny slate-gray dress, accompanied by black tights and knee-high black boots. To her target, she would be but a shadow on the wall.

She thought about stepping out to meet him face to face. She was in the mood to take someone apart. It would be great fun. However, as she had watched him, alarm bells went off in her mind. For a man his size he moved gracefully. And surprisingly fast. She had enough experience to tell her this was not a man to mess with. She had to do this by stealth.

Her heart quickened its pace when she heard the soft sound of his footsteps over the nearby ground.

It had worked. He walked from the alley, right past her. She nearly laughed.

Slowly, she retrieved her blade from one of her boots. She slinked after the man who continued forward, concern weighing heavily on his preoccupied mind.

Still moving soundlessly over the granules, dazzling in the dim lighting, Helena increased her speed.

The moment she reached him, she abruptly channeled the force of her entire body into her arm. With a swift, forceful motion, her arm wrapped around to his vulnerable side, just as he had raised his hands to the back of his neck in frustration. Her blow struck the front left side of his lower abdomen.

She had made a trained hit, and in the immediate second following, she yanked her arm away, using the man's body as a wall to push off from. It gave her enough distance to avoid his reach. Fortunately for Helena, she had reacted quickly enough. For in the instant after she made contact, he had swung out a powerful arm, reaching for her.

He had sensed Helena, but in his distracted state that realization had come a fraction of a second too late. Despite her quick pull-away, and his slower than normal response, he had still reacted quickly enough to grab her wrist. But his grasp only caught the side, and she was able to escape. She barely managed to slip away, heaving herself away from his muscular form.

Helena knew for a certainty that she had hit the man directly on her mark. As he looked down, shocked at his bloodied hand, he grasped her dagger and pulled it from the fresh wound, tossing it aside.

Scurrying away now with quick steps, Helena continued throwing glances back at the unfamiliar somn. His long, dark hair fell down his back, and the bold, red blood fell down his front. He gave one hard look at her through his rectangular framed glasses before stumbling to the nearby wall, struggling even with that short move. He fell against the slick slab of marble and slid down to the ground. Left alone he lay helpless, with only the cool rain to alleviate his suffering.

His eyes began to glow an unforgiving shade of blue, and Helena knew this was the moment to pick up her feet and run. Had he been any less preoccupied, she would have been ripped apart. *He will have bled to death by time anyone finds him*, Helena assured herself. *But I'd rather not stick around as an easy target. Death could surely drag me down as a part of its windfall.* A trace of concern flashed behind her eyes, and she quickened her pace.

71: From the Search to the Hunt

Come morning, about the time the suns would have been rising, though concealed behind dark clouds, Venn and KyVeerah had gone back out in search of Marion. They left Van Ingen at KyVeerah's flat again, though taking his advice on which direction to head.

They spent many hours searching for Marion, but around noon KyVeerah apologized, telling Venn that he needed to find Rhyus. He wished Venn luck, and they parted ways, their separate searches continuing.

ॐ

KyVeerah altered his direction. As Rhyus's Messenger, he had a strong sense of where to seek him out. Regardless of the fact that there were other somns around, he picked up speed. They wouldn't pay him an ounce of attention anyway. A couple of tall street lanterns started to flicker, and when KyVeerah reached them, they went temporarily dark. He vanished.

Although hyperspacing was a useful way to get nearer to Rhyus, it would still require a great deal of walking. After making his way between various black marble buildings over a distance of many blocks, he could feel Rhyus's presence growing stronger, nearer.

Boots sinking into the false sapphires with every step, KyVeerah came to an abrupt stop. A horrible feeling dropped over him from out of nowhere. Out of habit, he looked around, scanning his surroundings.

Using his mental contact, he checked whether everything was all right on Venn's side of things. His eyes narrowed as he opened the connection to receive only buzzing static. *This is definitely not good.* The low energy response wasn't like Venn had blocked him, but instead signaled that Venn's brain had disconnected. Never had KyVeerah run into this in communicating with Venn. *Something is wrong,* he registered immediately. *Very, very wrong.*

Tuning into his senses to determine Venn's current location, KyVeerah spun on his heels and ran. Lights flickered at his heightened energies. Not just the typical sputtering off in the distance, but each one he passed flickered as he raced down the glittering walkway. The dim lights grew brighter and brighter, but just as they reached the point where it seemed they might burst, the rain parted, accepting KyVeerah once again, and he vanished.

The street fell black.

&ocr;

KyVeerah stepped through the parting curtain of rain to find himself at the Shadow Market in the Devan Sector. Altering the focus of his senses, KyVeerah pushed his way through the crowds, moving in the direction he knew would lead him to Venn.

Reaching an abandoned alley, the feeling grew, a powerful throbbing in his mind. He ran its length, and then far ahead where the alleyway opened, KyVeerah saw a still form lying on the ground. "Venn!" KyVeerah's heart plummeted. He ran faster, approaching Venn's fallen form in a fraction of the time it would have taken any ordinary somn. As he neared, he saw it. Blood. Lots and lots of blood.

The blue granules covering the ground of Atrum Unda took longer to absorb the unfamiliar substance, but soon they would manage the task. The granules here hadn't yet begun to break it down. Registering this, KyVeerah knew that this incident had only recently taken place. *If only I had made it here just fifteen minutes earlier*, he cursed himself.

-533-

KyVeerah took a second to look quickly about. They fell upon the object he was hoping to find, glinting with reflected light. He dashed over, snatching it from the ground. A dagger. Not just any dagger though. This one seemed all too familiar.

Fury thickened in his blood as the fact sank in. Whoever had done this was someone he knew, unless the dagger had been stolen and then used, but KyVeerah's gut told him that was not the case. He couldn't place the weapon to its owner on the spot, but he would remember, and when he did, that somn would pay.

KyVeerah wrapped the blade with a bandana from an inner jacket pocket, securing it under his belt. "Dammit!" KyVeerah swore, under his breath. Zipping his jacket, he crouched next to Venn.

Venn was unconscious, though expected, judging by the large amount of blood that had spilled from his body. KyVeerah leaned forward, his knees diving into the mix of granules and blood. He leaned over him, quickly checking his feeble pulse, which was at least present. Next, he examined the wound.

"Shit!" KyVeerah cursed. The hit had definitely been made by the small dagger he had discovered, and that was exactly what this had been. A hit. This wound would be fatal to any commoner, and it would be to Venn as well if he didn't get attention immediately. "Shit!"

With adrenaline and energies flowing, KyVeerah heaved Venn up. Despite the passing moments and millions of spiraling thoughts, KyVeerah knew exactly where they were. His memory of Atrum's streets was remarkable. He knew he had found himself, once again, near Tazo's place.

Knowing there was no other option, he opted to take Venn to her. Tazo Brooks was one of very few somns he would trust with Venn's life. On top of that, Tazo had training in this field. He was not sure how much, but for sake of the situation at hand, he hoped enough.

I must act fast.

ॐ

KyVeerah finally reached Tazo's place, after what seemed an eternity, despite his unnatural swiftness. His tattoos remained illuminated beneath his clothing as fury and adrenaline roared through his veins. Though Venn was much larger, KyVeerah had managed to carry the unconscious man the necessary distance.

Maintaining his balance, he mounted a single, wide marble step. Raising a fist, he pounded urgently on Tazo's silver painted door. With clenched teeth, at the pain searing his own side, he tried to partially control his force. He managed to only dent the door, a fraction of what he could effortlessly have done. He had considered kicking in the door altogether.

If she doesn't answer, he thought, his teeth still clenching hard. He pounded again.

He could hear as feet scurried across the floor, patience lingering on edge. Locks were unhinged with quick hands, and the door opened with a single chain left holding it to its frame.

A panicked face looked out through the crack. "Jereth?" Worry laced Tazo's features in response to the urgent pounding and the look on his face. "Jereth!" She threw a hand up, clasping it over her mouth. Slamming the door, she unfastened the chain in record time and yanked the door back open with both hands.

"What in the world happened?" A rough edge tinged Tazo's velvety voice. Her foggy blue eyes were filled with a combination of horror and disbelief.

KyVeerah shoved his shades up. "Where?" he demanded, eyes blazing violet and irate, an attribute, which Tazo had never witnessed.

Tazo looked around, a bit flustered. "Jereth, put him in here." With hurried steps, she led him toward the kitchen table. Luckily, she had kept it after her cousin moved out, or they would have had nowhere better to lay the unconscious man than the hardwood floor. KyVeerah placed Venn gently on the table, as Tazo moved a chair to prop up his legs.

"Who is he?" Tazo asked, her voice heavy with worry as she examined the man on her kitchen table.

"My brother."

Tazo's eyes snapped up with a new emotion as she accepted that he was telling her none other than the upright truth. "Your brother..." she said, repeating his words. "I didn't know you had a brother!" Looking back down at the unconscious man, she viewed him in an entirely different light. She pressed a hand over her mouth, shaking her head. Her dear friend, Jereth Tavokk, must have an unimaginable amount of trust to bring her a fading somn as dear as his own brother.

"He needs blood," Tazo observed. She couldn't imagine what her friend must be going through, but the look on his face and his aura were unbearable.

"Can you fix it?" KyVeerah pressed, peering intently into her cloudy eyes, as he lightly clasped his long, slender fingers around her arm.

"I-I might be able to fix the wound, but that doesn't guarantee he will...he needs blood." She altered her statement, repeating the one that had been brushed aside.

"No," he said bluntly.

"No?" she nearly shouted. "What do you mean?" She wished her cousin, Reina, were still here. They had both pursued medicine, but Reina, unlike Tazo, had stuck it out.

"Trust me." He attempted to calm her harsh gaze with a reassuring, yet troubled, look from his own unnatural illuminated eyes. "His body has the capacity to make all the blood he needs, but you must repair the damage before his condition worsens." KyVeerah couldn't mask the trepidation in his gaze. "Can you do it?" His words were desperate. "He is my brother." He emphasized each word, hanging on to every last bit of hope, as it drained from him, drop by drop.

"Yes." A single tear ran down Tazo's face and fell from her chin. Seeing him like this was more than she could bear, and the fact that he had decided to trust her with this crucial task placed a huge pressure on her shoulders. "I am his only chance now, he can't have much time left before too much blood has drained. I don't know how he has lasted this long." She put a quick hand on Venn's pale flesh, looking as though death may be lying just at his side.

Without further thought, all emotion evaporated as her previous training kicked into action. There was nothing now but to repair the damage before her as efficiently and thoroughly as possible. As she hastily prepped the body on her table, KyVeerah kept up a running dialogue.

"His blood will replenish quickly in an attempt to heal him." KyVeerah stared down at his brother's motionless form. "He's not just anyone. If you can reverse the damage in time, the wound itself will heal much faster than typical."

ᔔᙍᘒ

Tazo, with some assistance from KyVeerah, managed to fix the wound as best as possible. Although unable to visualize the deepest aspect of the stab wound, she, thanks to her prior education, still possessed the necessary equipment to probe and approximate the tissues along the entire length of the damage path.

In addition, thanks to a particular secretive and peculiar field of training, Tazo had some other things in her possession that were exceptionally uncommon—things of which very few somns knew the potential power. These rare herbs and other items were one of the factors that succeeded in keeping Venn alive, given the circumstances. Some somns claimed these objects contained magic, but Tazo knew that they were just rare and contained remarkable healing capabilities that just hadn't been researched enough yet. That didn't keep others from bad-talking their use, though. So, in more typical medical settings, these items were not utilized.

Somns generally called someone such as Tazo a *Vellen*, meaning that she was a magic user who was in denial of the facts. There were many variations of Vellens. Up until today, KyVeerah would have never imagined Tazo to be a Vellen, and if not for this critical situation, he may never have known.

After drugging Venn with strong anesthetics, Tazo had concocted a rare paste, and with a long swab, had coated the deeper portion of the wound prior to her repair work. The paste, she told KyVeerah, would help him heal rapidly. She also told him that if Venn naturally healed as quickly as KyVeerah claimed, and if Venn's blood could indeed replenish at such an irregular speed, he would most certainly pull through. Having completed treating the deeper wound, Tazo finished the task of stitching up what remained. She concocted a small bit of ointment with more of her unconventional items and rubbed it on his skin, over and around where the dagger had penetrated the flesh.

Her ministrations finished, Tazo laid out some blankets on her couch. KyVeerah moved Venn over to it while Tazo carried final bandaging supplies out to the living room. While KyVeerah rearranged lamps around the couch to improve the lighting, adjusting it to their needs, Tazo tended to Venn as she kneeled down on a pillow set on the floor.

At last she declared that she was finished. KyVeerah gave Venn a long, thoughtful look, then Tazo and he moved back into the kitchen, seating themselves at the cleared table.

⃓⃔

"A Vellen," KyVeerah said, after a chance to unwind. His brother was going to be all right. He had been staring down at the table's surface during a long, serene silence, but now his eyes shifted to Tazo, seated across the table. Tazo did not voice a response, for she knew his comment had been rhetorical, as he had only been turning the thought over in his mind.

"My, you're even more fascinating than I imagined. And believe me, I've imagined a lot." He offered a roguish grin. Tazo smiled. She was pleased that he was able to return to his typical self in the assurance that his brother would recover.

"Thank you," he said, on a more serious note, reaching out to tenderly take her hand. "He would have died." He said this last part more to himself, realizing again how very close Venn had come to meeting Eve.

Tazo displayed that pleasant smile of hers. "Of course."

"I truly apologize," KyVeerah said, with a genuine look on his face, "but I have another favor to ask of you."

"Yes?"

"Could you possibly look after him while I tend to some essential affairs." He bit his lip, as he was unprepared to revisit the sudden surfacing image of his close friend, Jude Hollis. He had left his friends, Cyrus and Killian Vanaché, to watch over Jude, and now he was asking Tazo to watch over Venn. It seemed everyone he truly cared about was floating behind him in a wake of devastation.

"Of course he can stay here! I would be honored to watch over him," she said, before KyVeerah could feel the need to ask further.

"Thank you, Tazo. Thank you, for everything." KyVeerah's words were steeped in gratitude.

Suddenly KyVeerah's eyes narrowed, and a demonic glow began to spill from the open slits. An infuriating awareness had just fallen into his mind's eye. His blood immediately began to boil, and his fingers ran rigid.

Tazo swallowed, giving her friend an uneasy look, eyes wary.

KyVeerah stood up, sending his chair to tumble backward. "I have to go." Without any further ado, he turned for the door, walking with mechanical, controlled steps. He approached it, unfastening the many locks.

Raising his hand to the door's handle, he paused. Tazo had risen from the table and followed him, though staying several strides behind. "I don't know when, but I promise, I'll be back." He didn't turn around to face Tazo, but she knew his promise would hold true.

With a lift of his head, KyVeerah opened the door. He stepped out onto the single step, pausing to take in a slow, deep breath. He exhaled heavy and heated before stepping down, his feet sinking into the sapphire-blanketed ground.

With unwavering steps, he walked back into the darkness of the day. His violet eyes continued to burn like the blood flowing fast with the rapid beating of his heart. There was only one thing that mattered right now...

I must find Helena.

72: And So It Begins

Anxious, Helena slipped into her home, fastening each of its locks and chains with the hand that wasn't covered in blood. *Who was that man?* she wondered, as she finished securing the door. *Whoever he was, he should surely have passed on by now. But what about the other man he referenced? The one he mentioned must also be looking for Rhyus. Vincent, didn't he say?*

As quietly, yet quickly as she could, Helena made her way into the kitchen. She didn't want to wake Rhyus. Despite her efforts, she heard her guest stir when she passed the living room. He had spent a second night on her couch.

Moving to the sink, she turned on the faucet and placed her bloody hand underneath. Her strike had been quick, but his lightning fast reaction had slowed her retreat.

Thoughts raced through her head as she scrubbed at her hand. *They must be working under someone, but who? What if someone saw me return home with Rhyus? What if those looking for him come here?* The very distinct possibility sent a wave of panic through her.

We need to leave here, she decided. *Shutting off the water, she gripped the edge of the sink. No, he needs to eat first. We must make sure that his energy level is up.* She tried not to let paranoia block any better judgments. She was smarter than that. *That is definitely an important factor to the plan.* However, her nerves remained shaken, as she pulled the items of food from her bag.

"Were you out?"

Jumping, Helena whipped around, prepared for a fight. She hadn't heard Rhyus come into the kitchen.

"Yes." She released her breath, as her muscles relaxed and her arms lowered to her sides.

"Are you all right?"

Helena nodded, though not very convincingly.

Rhyus didn't say a word.

"I'm going to make us something to eat. I'll bring it out to the sitting room when it's ready."

Rhyus took the hint and headed back to the sitting room. Helena sighed heavily, turning back to the counter. For a moment, she closed her eyes, trying to block her worries. Reopening them, she pulled her bag over her head and put it aside. She returned to the food and started to prepare their meal.

She tried to look on the bright side. *If I hadn't gone out for food, I wouldn't even know they were on their way to get him.*

₧₨

Helena and Rhyus finished eating and set their plates on the wooden floor near the fireplace. They found themselves sitting, once again, on a blanket cast on top of the rug.

"Rhyus," Helena said, lowering her eyes. She was unsure how much to tell him. However, in a split second, she opted not to share her encounter or the killing of the raven-haired man. "Our plan is moving forward. You have time to shower and get ready, but then we must move out."

Rhyus looked at her, trying to analyze the current Helena sitting before him. She was different today. Anxious. Very anxious. Either something was wrong with their plan or there were outside concerns causing her to feel ill at ease. He nodded, as he said, "All right."

"Have you memorized your course, for when you've gotten inside?" she asked.

Helena had torn a map from a book, and Rhyus had looked over it more than enough times for his planned route to imprint onto his mind. "Yes," he assured.

"Do you have your key? These keys are the only ones with access to the Energy room."

"Yes," he answered again.

"OK. Well, go shower," Helena said, in a distanced voice. She looked back down at the floor, trying once again to push back the paranoia that any minute somebody would kick down her front door. "I'll clean these up," she added, referring to their dishes.

₧₨

Rhyus slung his bag over his shoulder, the strap lying across his chest. Helena had put some product in his hair, saying that it would help him fit into the Atrum crowd and keep him from feeling like a wet animal. She had been frustrated at the fact that he hadn't any sort of water-repellant jacket, but she found one for him to wear after digging through some pile of mystery clothes lying on the floor in her bedroom closet.

"An Atrum essential," she had said, handing it to him and waiting for him to put it on. The long jacket must've belonged to someone of a thicker, more muscular build, not to mention the fact that its dark, exotic look was different from something Rhyus would normally find himself wearing. It surprised him how appealing he looked in it after catching himself in a mirror.

Helena came around the corner. She gave an amused smile as she took in Rhyus's Atrum Unda transformation, and teased, "You need some shades."

"And why's that?" he asked, returning a playful look.

"Then you would fit in perfectly with all the rest of them smug assholes who think they're hot shit wearing sunshades in the dark." Her smile remained on her lips.

"Oh, here," she said, handing out a broad dagger placed within a sheath. "Just in case," she explained, after taking in the look on Rhyus's face. "Just put it on your belt. It won't look at all conspicuous. All somns carry weapons around Atrum."

Rhyus unbuckled his belt and slid it through the wide strap of the sheath. With this new makeover, as well as his current location and company, he hardly felt like himself. *Then again, I haven't since leaving Lux and entering The Darkness. Well, until I met Yuri.* Rhyus blocked the painful thought before it could fully form.

"Ready?" she asked. Rhyus could easily read from the combination of her voice and body language that Helena was feeling both unnerved, as well as relieved, that they were finally leaving.

Rhyus gave a short nod. "Yeah."

"OK, let's go." Helena moved to the door, unfastening its many securities. She pulled the door open and peered out warily before signaling for Rhyus to step out. Following him out, she paused to relock the door.

The two of them started walking, making their way once again over the sapphire ground. During her instruction, Helena had made sure to tell Rhyus to keep cool and act casual, but in his opinion, she was the one having problems with this piece of her own advice.

Rhyus looked up at the light shining brightly from The Tower's uppermost section where the crystal energy source, the main source of the city, was contained. The Tower's brilliant light beamed outward like that of a lighthouse. "This place gives me the creeps," Rhyus said, in a hushed voice.

"Does it?" Helena asked, in an automatic response. She was

only concerned about her own safety and getting Rhyus to carry out the plan she had laid out for him to accomplish. This was her big chance to gain the favor of Nyx Crucian, and ultimately rise above him. Nothing could go wrong.

Helena led the way, weaving between individual buildings and blocks of connecting ones.

Though Rhyus could easily read Helena's apprehension, he had yet to feel any angst of his own. He simply continued to move alongside her, waiting his moment of triumph to stand before him, waiting to prevail.

"We're getting close," Helena said, after having passed through multiple sectors to finally cross into Hollow.

The black buildings currently surrounding them stood tall. They blocked their further surroundings with the exception of some structure Rhyus couldn't identify and the impressive Tower off in the distance behind them, standing up on the high hill, adding to its already impressive height.

After a few more blocks, Helena came to a halt. Rhyus did the same. "There it is," she said, signaling ahead.

They had come to stand at the edge of the ragged outline of buildings bordering what would be a massive clearing if a single, daunting structure hadn't been built right at its center. The structure turned out to be what Rhyus had defined to himself as the "unidentifiable structure."

Rhyus's jaw dropped. "Holy shit." Helena turned to him, surprised by his response. "That's The Dome," he said, not really meaning to voice the words aloud. The feeling of uneasiness that he had been lacking up until this point finally caught up with him, crawling beneath his skin.

The Dome, reaching 160 stories, was a formidable structure with its circumference at ground level filling a two-dimensional area 40 percent larger than The Tower, though The Tower contained 312 stories plus additional height, when considering the cell containing its energy light source.

"I've been here before," Rhyus said. Helena's head snapped back to him, eyes skeptical.

"What do you mean, you've been here before?" she asked. His comment caused her to become further unsettled.

"No." He shook his head, though his eyes remained focused forward on The Dome. "In those odd dreams, the ones where I saw the four towers. I was here."

"Then it will be that much easier for you to carry out your mission and for you to know that you are supposed to do this." Rhyus didn't bother to explain that he had never been *inside* The Dome in either of his dreams. The mentioning seemed irrelevant, and he had studied the map from that torn page a hundred times over. The map that Helena had drawn and written on to explain his course of action.

"Just remember, don't let anything or anyone stop you. This is what you are meant to do," Helena said, looking him hard in the eye. She turned her upper body toward one side of The Dome, directing, "There. That is the entrance. Remember the map. It's just like the map." She turned back to face him. "You have to go now."

Helena raised a hand to the side of Rhyus's face and planted a kiss. He kissed her back, but she pulled away soon after. She offered him a look granting the best of luck, and then turned and ran off in the opposite direction, the way from which they had come.

Rhyus watched her before moving back around, facing The Dome once again. He took in a deep breath. *Hope this goes as planned.*

73: They had it Coming

His destination predetermined, KyVeerah moved with haste, as his feet carried him, bringing him nearer to The Dome with each and every step. He was aware of the fact that Helena Meretrix worked for a man by the name of Nyx Crucian. The very man who had once offered him the position now filled by his close friend Callis Morgandy, unbeknownst to Callis, of course — at least as far as KyVeerah was aware. After all, he was Vincent KyVeerah, now known in the City of Dark Water as Jereth Tavokk. He had his sources and his ways of knowledge, however, the primary piece of knowledge he needed right now was one he didn't happen to have. Helena's current location.

As KyVeerah had sat at Tazo's kitchen table, a maddening realization had occurred to him. Seemingly out of the blue, a memory surfaced of the last time he had encountered the very somn whose dagger was responsible for nearly killing his brother. The memory that incriminated none other than Helena Meretrix.

He had just left the Cosmos after a meeting with his friend, Callis Morgandy, their last one before he had left for Lux Lumetia. Someone had followed him from the bar as he had taken his leave. That very somn had turned out to be Helena Meretrix, who he had surprised by hiding around the bit of tall vegetation at the bottom of the hill. He had caught her in a secure hold while they had a brief *conversation.* At its end, he had teased her, tricking her into trying to kiss him. Some irrelevant comment had angered her, and as she managed to push herself away from him, she had pulled her dagger. The small white scar on KyVeerah's face was almost indiscernible to others, but he saw it vividly every time he looked in the mirror.

KyVeerah's blood simmered. That dagger had been the very same as the one he found next to Venn.

She must have jumped him, KyVeerah thought irately, *jumped him like the coward she is. She wouldn't take the chance at a fair fight if she could help it. But why would she go through the trouble? There's no way she could have known Venn's connection to me. So it's not like this was to be a personal attack meant to indirectly cause me harm.* The uncertainty of just why the attack had taken place didn't help in calming his ferocity. *I'm going to find her, and when I do, I'm going to shred her into a thousand unrecognizable, bloody pieces.*

೫൦രൂ

KyVeerah quickly closed the distance between The Dome and himself, spiraling its outer perimeter rather than marching straight up to it. There was experience and technique backing his prompt, planned movements.

He went from sprint to standstill, nearly falling over himself at the unexpected halt. Once again, his eyes narrowed, a violet illumination spilling forth. His focus was directed down the dazzling walkway, two long blocks down. Even at that distance, he had known her presence...

Helena. Even in his mind, he hissed her name.

As suddenly as KyVeerah came to a standstill, so did Helena. His powerful presence and ferocity had emanated in her direction, and she had stopped, as if fixed in a spotlight. She jerked her head his way, eyes widening, horrified. Fear enveloped her and she couldn't move. She couldn't run. Panic clenched tighter around her. *He knows I have Rhyus.*

KyVeerah's extended fingers were rigid, but slowly and eerily they curled into fists. He could practically smell Helena's fear permeating through the air. In a split second, Helena pulled herself together. She ran.

In the instant that Helena took off, KyVeerah's illuminated eyes snapped wide open. A wicked shot of adrenaline rushed through him along with his energies, and he picked up his feet in a mad dash, spraying blue granules every which way. His senses were locked onto Helena, and now that he had located her, and with his swiftness and agility, there was no chance of her escaping.

The chase carried on at an incredible pace. Helena's feet took her on a rapid dash, but not fast enough to outrun her pursuer. A fact she was well aware of. It would indeed be a rare somn who could outrun Jereth Tavokk.

Panting, Helena ran as fast as her feet would allow. Heart pulsing far too fast, her fear was so strong it nearly caught in her throat, choking her. She knew the space between them would continue to lessen until he caught up to her, then it would be too late.

A desperate hope hit Helena when she spotted an alley beyond the stretch of buildings along which she now raced. She tried to push herself to even greater speed, and as she reached it, she ducked frantically into its cover.

KyVeerah whipped around the corner of the building in the direction Helena had gone, his unzipped jacket flying behind him, and the sapphires scattering all about in a glimmering wave. He had lost sight of Helena when she made it around to this side of the building, but feeling her very near, he continued to run. He bypassed the narrow alley by just a couple steps, but he came to an immediate halt as he realized…

Too late. Helena had sprung from the alleyway, stabbed him in the side of his lower back, and retrieved her weapon. She retreated back toward the alley, as he let out a heart-wrenching sound, part growl and part the most terrorizing scream of rage Helena had ever heard. He struck out a lightening swift hand, grazing her throat with his long nails, ripping long strips of her flesh as she just barely escaped his throat-crushing grasp. As she slipped through his fingers, he recoiled briefly in pain.

Helena's heart pounded harder than ever, as she ran down the alley, taking advantage of her pursuer's distracted moment of agony. Her eyes began to well at the pain from his claws and the overpowering fear of capture. She choked the tears back. As a professional, she understood that they would keep her from seeing any possible opportunities before her. Opportunities, which would be her only chance of survival.

Helena's breath came in sharp bursts, as her lungs refused her full breaths in her terror. She ran harder, faster. She took a turn, wrapping alongside the next building after exiting the narrow stretch. Reaching halfway along this length of connected buildings, she knew he was on the move again.

Eyes tracing every outline of her surroundings, she spotted another break. But would he expect it a second time? She had no alternative. Normally, with her remarkable speed and coordination, it was a rare somn who stood the whisper of a chance against her. But this was no ordinary somn. Ducking into the new opening, she held her hand to her chest. *One strike*, she told herself. *One strike, and I can take him down.* Her hands quavered.

KyVeerah did not bypass this new break, but he didn't notice it until the last second. The altered pathway was again unexpected, and again, an attacking arm struck out from the shadows with the sole intent of jamming straight through his heart.

A howl of pain escaped his lips as he twisted his torso instantly to the side. The knife missed its intended target but sliced wickedly through his arm. Helena panicked at the fact that, due to the torque from his spin, she had lost the grip on her weapon. She turned to run for it. This time her action came too late, for KyVeerah had slashed out in reflex at the new attack, slicing, clean and deep, across her back. She cried out in pain, as she stumbled forward, though instinctively regaining her balance in her fight for survival.

Quickening her pace again, Helena's body screamed with every breath. Her throat was on fire, as was her back, and she could feel hot, sticky blood streaming from her wounds. She had never imagined she would ever face such an opponent. At last, uncontrollable tears burned her eyes. The tears escaped, falling down her face.

She didn't know where to go, where to run. There wasn't anywhere *to* run. So she continued to run forward. She dashed past the current block of buildings and on past the next freestanding one, fearing that she was back within his line of sight.

Spinning around the next corner, she raced down along its shorter side. Just yards from the end of the wall, something unexpected happened. Helena continued to run those last yards, though slowing, almost giddy in her sense of relief.

"Callis!" she gasped. Her flushed, green eyes widened, and a dense hope flooded them. She opened her mouth again to say more in explanation, but the words failed her.

Callis's face was expressionless, but without needing her to further explain, he put out an inviting arm. She ran up to him, still frightened for her life. "Thank...Ravenna," she panted, leaning, trembling, into his muscular form.

Consolingly, Callis wrapped an arm around her lower back. He raised his other arm and whipped around the unseen knife, burying its well aimed tip forcefully into her upper back, down between her ribs, through the edge of her lung, and straight through her heart. In that moment, she looked at him with confused, disappointed eyes.

She lipped a single word, "Why...?"

Just then, the man who had been pursuing Helena appeared around the other end of the building.

As he felt Helena's body fall limp, supported solely by his arm wrapped around her, Callis's eyes changed from their simmering anger into a thorough state of shock. *Jereth?*

KyVeerah's eyes also widened, followed immediately by a consuming sense of alarm. *Oh, fuck...Callis!*

Although he had noticed, KyVeerah paid hardly any attention to

Helena's lifeless, bleeding body. The two men's eyes met, and in that moment, every drop of color drained from Callis's own. In the twinkling of an eye, his entire world had turned upside down.

Though viewing him from afar, KyVeerah knew that Callis had put two and two together. That he, Jereth Tavokk, was the man he had been searching for…Vincent KyVeerah. KyVeerah could feel the blood drain from his face. He stood perfectly motionless while the two stared one another down, refusing to blink, refusing to alter their intense gaze, locked one on the other.

"No," Callis said, under his breath. His closest friend was the very man he had been hunting, the man he had vowed to send to the grave…*The Archives Intruder…The man who has hidden Adaveen for these past two years…The man who was originally offered my position in Nyx's Black Band…and worst of all, he lied directly to my face during our last meeting at the Cosmos.*

Suddenly, the sky erupted with blinding light as an explosion ripped through the atmosphere. The sight was unlike anything ever witnessed.

The aftershock violently shook the ground beneath their feet. Callis lowered Helena's body urgently to the ground before turning back to where the explosion had occurred, The Tower.

The unimaginable force of the explosion had sounded when the enormous, glass cell capping The Tower, the part containing Atrum Unda's main crystal energy source, had burst, every inch of thick glass shattering from its spherical structure. Glass shards blanketed the entire city, showering down, razor sharp, with the already falling rain. The light of The Tower flickered fiercely, unnaturally.

What the…?

Noting the glass fragments filling the dark sky, Callis raised an arm to shield his eyes. He turned back around to face Jereth…He had vanished. The man had taken full advantage of the moment of disturbance, fleeing off into the labyrinth of glinting, black marble.

Callis clenched his hands into fists, and flexing all of the muscles in his arms vigorously, he slowly raised his fisted hands up toward his face in rage. Saturated in frustration, he leaned his upper body forward before arching it abruptly back, and with a sound straight from the bowels of hell, he released a strident, sickening roar.

74: Catalyst

Ezra moved through the falling rain. Again today, she was making her way to The Dome. Her nerves had gotten to her the previous day, and she had chickened out. Not today though. Today she was going to march straight up to The Dome, and she was going to confront Callis about his impudent actions.

After a good distance of walking, Ezra finally reached the main entrance. She entered and moved promptly to the southeast elevator. Punching in the black button, she watched the numbers in the box above the doors decrease as the elevator descended to receive her.

The doors slid open, and she stepped inside. Ezra reached into her jacket pocket...*Callis Morgandy!* She could hardly contain the scream building up within. Her access key was gone. Again.

Well beyond fury, Ezra stormed out of the elevator and out of The Dome. Reaching hardly more than a block from the great structure, she released her shrill scream. "I am going to kill that son of a bitch!"

ℰℭ

Rhyus started toward The Dome's entrance, Helena having taken off the other way. *I wonder if there is something else that she must do in the meantime?* he thought. *Part of the plan that she must take care of, apart from my own mission?*

As Rhyus drew nearer, he tried hard to pull himself together. The concept of going to The Dome had not shaken his nerves, but now that he was approaching its front doors, he became quite uneasy. It took a lot for him to keep a straight face.

The Dome's ground level was rather bare, containing not much more than support pillars and a spiral staircase at its centermost point. *Thank the goddesses*, Rhyus sighed, seeing there was no one in sight. Helena had told him that he'd have to figure out a way into the underground chamber whether someone was present or not. She had informed him that the chances were high that there would be nobody around on the main floor, but he would just have to cross his fingers in hopes that no one would be entering or leaving.

In the absence of others, Rhyus sprinted toward the floor's central point. Coming to the base of the stairs, he dropped carefully to his knees. He placed his hands down on the floor tile just before the first stair, just as Helena had instructed. An unfamiliar sensation met him, a strange electrical tingling, as the tile accepted his energies.

After a moment, Rhyus pulled his hands back up from the floor. He reached into the space just beneath the stair. The concealed strip of flooring just beyond the tile had lowered, and he gripped his fingers around the tile's edge and began to pull it upward toward himself. His tattoo began to burn as his energies strengthened, and the tile came open.

A ladder lined the wall directly beneath the opening. Sliding down through the hole and onto the ladder, Rhyus forced the heavy tile closed after him. The ladder led to a landing, which he jumped to after walking down a handful of rungs. He then moved quickly down a new staircase.

The floor of the vast underground chamber was three stories below ground level. Many pillars stretched high, holding up the visible portion of the building's structure, the part of which somns were aware. Rhyus took in a quick breath. His foot hit the bottom of the stairs. Once more, he thought back to the map Helena had shown him.

Moving quickly, Rhyus made his way through the large apparatuses, taking the path imprinted on the wall of his mind. *What the hell is all of this stuff for?* he wondered, peering about at the sizeable pieces of machinery. After further winding around the strange objects filling the chamber, and walking over the cleared pathway, Rhyus came to stand before a small, black marble room. It was the only actual room he had even come across.

Using the key, Rhyus entered the room. He entered head-on into a scene that was almost unimaginable. The inner walls of the room were constructed of an unknown material. It had a smooth, silvery shimmer, however, it was very different from Lux Lumetia stone. This stone had a pearly iridescence with glints of color reflecting from it.

The room slanted inward to a circular basin. At the center point of this basin was erected a most unusual crystal formation, emitting a rare luminescence. Surrounding the standing stone appeared to be a shallow pool of water that matched the crystal's aura. At closer inspection, Rhyus realized it wasn't water at all.

Sparks of light? he noticed, peering down into the unusual substance. They radiated from the crystal structure, and then slowly floated down, cascading into a dense, nearly seamless pool around its base.

Without thought, he moved forward, stepping into the shallow substance. The pool of sparks caused his skin to prickle as the currents of energy surged around his body. He reached forward, palm open, and placed his hand upon the crystal's surface. Instantly, images flashed through his mind. He could feel his tattoo burn white with heat, though it elicited no pain. He felt that he was being pulled into a stream of light and energy. Images of both Lux Lumetia and Atrum Unda filled his mind's eye.

Rhyus could feel the life force of the sister cities coursing through him. He sensed the pulsing of both city's Towers and their great crystal energy sources. He could feel the river of energy running continuously through both crystals in an unbroken balance. Rhyus, concentrating on the fire of his tattoo marking, began to pull at the energy from Lux Lumetia. Bending the energies to his will, Rhyus changed the course of the stream so that it filtered solely toward Atrum Unda's crystal. He could sense the energy building up steadily as the energy from Lux Lumetia disintegrated.

It's working...I'm actually going to succeed.

After another passing moment, Rhyus felt his energies retract and finally fade away.

His vision returned to normal as he stepped away from the crystal's basin. Just then, the room began to tremble. The crystal started to emit blinding light. A horrendous sound resonated far above at that exact instant, and Rhyus threw an arm before his face in an attempt to shield his eyes from the intense luminosity.

What the...?

75: Commands and Claims

KyVeerah dashed over walkways, as glass shards rained down over the city of Atrum Unda. He ran hard, lights down the path flickering until he reached them, and vanished.

He stepped back out into the falling rain and glass in a section of Atrum far from Callis's location. *He won't find me now*, he told himself, though his certainty swayed. Callis wouldn't give up easily. KyVeerah walked through the treacherous rainfall, as his thoughts altered to a topic of Callis other than the new-formed barrier in their friendship. Helena.

Why the hell did he kill Helena? She had to have done something to provoke him to such an extreme. After all, they worked for the same man. The thought bothered KyVeerah, since there was no way of discovering the reason for the murder, at least not anytime soon.

He observed those around him with a curious expression. The city's somns had begun to panic in response to The Tower's explosion. Once the glass shards ceased to fall from the sky, he peered up at The Tower's colossal cell. The light that usually shined out from it had erupted in a blinding cataclysm, as the energy surging through it had caused the light to blow.

The Tower now stood dark with the exception of bright bolts of static light whipping occasionally across the sky. The rest of the city fell darker with the lack of its central light source. There were only the dim streetlights and the frightening, crackling energy bolts. Some of them even surged in the direction of the city's floor at the somns scattered all about, trying to comprehend what had happened and what it could possibly mean.

*What in the world could have...*his thoughts caught, realizing his tattoo had begun to glow heatedly, the one Rhyus and he shared in declaration of their relationship as Messenger and Calling. KyVeerah's senses strengthened, and he realized what they were trying to tell him. "Oh, Valencia...Rhyus!" Again, KyVeerah picked up his feet, and he began to run, this time with a specific destination in mind.

KyVeerah hyperspaced again, returning to dangerous territory, for The Dome was not far from Callis's current location. He turned in the direction opposite The Tower and raced through the chaos forming out on the city walkways. As the distance between The Dome and KyVeerah closed to the point where the daunting structure stood, once more, just blocks away, a shadowed being leapt out from an alley before him. The shadowed man grabbed a tight hold on KyVeerah, as he ran smack into him.

Shit! Numerous emotions consumed him, but KyVeerah was more irritated than fearful.

At the same moment as KyVeerah was about to issue forth his energies to blow off his captor, a voice entered him. *"You are being careless, KyVeerah…"*

Fyfe, KyVeerah realized instantly. Were it not for his frenzied fear about Rhyus, and the tremendous forceful surges of energy scattering across Atrum Unda like wildfire throughout the city, KyVeerah would have recognized the shadowed man for Fyfe Van Ingen before he had even stepped out from the alley.

"What!" KyVeerah shrieked, trying to escape Van Ingen's grasp in his headlong rush, but the man was stronger than he had assumed, far stronger. He should have known.

"KyVeerah, wait!" Van Ingen demanded, hollering over the loud, disturbed sounds of the city. He held KyVeerah tighter yet. "You must do something. Immediately. You must go to Lux Lumetia. Go to Lord Abel. I don't care how you manage it. Just do it! Tell him that we will be bringing Rhyus to Lux Lumetia. Then you must return to Umbra Halls. I will take care of Rhyus and get *him* back to Umbra Halls. Now go!"

Van Ingen threw KyVeerah aside, releasing his strong hold just before disappearing into the dark and into the swarm of frenetic somns, in the direction that KyVeerah had been running. Toward The Dome. Toward Rhyus.

KyVeerah growled loudly in frustration. He ran his hands a single time through his hair. Begrudging the intervention, and irritated that he hadn't even been given the option of claiming his own Calling, KyVeerah took off in the direction of a nearby portal.

76: Slow-Motion

The aftershock of the explosion Rhyus heard caused the large underground room to quaver forcefully. He could feel the blood drain from his face.

Rhyus turned around and rushed out of the room and back to the staircase at the center of the underground chamber. He raced up the two stories of stairs leading to the landing and jumped onto the ladder connected to the wall before him. Reaching upward, he pushed forcefully against the marble tile. He could feel the unfamiliar sensation of his tattoo heating on his skin as his energies collected, and the heavy tile pushed upward, swinging open on its hinged side.

Climbing up the remainder of the ladder, Rhyus pulled himself out onto the floor of the ground level. Hurriedly, he swung the floor tile back into place, concealing the underground chamber once more. The place was in chaos. Chances were that nobody would notice him, or give it a second thought if they had, as he appeared.

Before anyone could have a chance to find him there on the floor, Rhyus scurried to his feet. He moved away from The Dome's central point and the spiral staircase. As casually as he could manage in his flustered state, he walked across the glinting floor, moving toward the northwest elevator. Helena had told him to take either the northwest or the southeast elevator, and the northwest one appeared to be the less crowded path.

The lights placed throughout The Dome trembled, their crystal light sources brightening and dimming, all the while making an eerie buzzing noise. Somns started to quickly crowd this level of The Dome, panicked by the flickering lights and the large explosion that had sounded in the distance. Everyone spoke in a simultaneous frenzy, but Rhyus ignored their words, only wanting to reach the elevator without being trampled.

Seeing the elevator open, Rhyus moved faster, covering the remaining distance at a sprint, shoving past others as he went, without the slightest care.

Marion slipped out of the elevator, sliding behind Julian once the elevator doors opened and he proceeded out onto the swarming ground level. Julian moved with quick steps, taking in the scene with a disgusted look.

After the others, Armani stepped elegantly out and moved forward. A young man bumped forcefully into him in a mad dash to get into the elevator that Armani had just exited.

The lava red of Armani's blackened eyes erupted, furious at the young man's intolerable insolence. Armani spun around, about to step back into the elevator to teach the damn fool a lesson when Julian yelled out in barking alarm.

"Armani! She's getting away...*again!*"

An even further demonic look falling over him, Armani twisted back around to face Julian.

Marion had decided that her current company may not be the sort she should be spending her time with and had taken advantage of the chaos and frenzy, seeing it as a clear sign. She opted to slip out of the elevator, behind Julian, and make a run for it.

Julian searched through those surrounding him, picking them up, only to realize that they were not Marion, and then discarding them, throwing them ruthlessly aside.

Armani looked around for their rediscovered Adaveen Cooper, but he had a difficult time focusing, enraged by the many somns constantly bumping and shoving into him. With incredible force, he callously shoved them aside, driving many into the hard ground several yards away. The others, he cast harshly into those still standing, knocking multiples down in a single blow.

Rhyus had shoved past those blocking his way and successfully made it onto the elevator before its doors began to close. Once inside, he waited anxiously for the doors to close, fumbling in his pocket for the intricately faced silver key that Helena had stolen from Ezra. He stuck it into the slot, as Helena had told him to do, and pushed the button for floor 160 repeatedly.

The spherical elevator rose rapidly along the curved shaft on the outermost wall. At first, Rhyus stared impatiently down at the black lower half of the elevator, and then he shifted his gaze back up to the silver doors. After what felt like far too long, the elevator came to an abrupt halt. The doors slid open, and Rhyus leapt out.

With hasty steps, he ran down the main corridor, a straight shot to The Dome's center point where another spiral staircase waited. According to Helena, this one went only from floor 157 to floor 160, reserved for the use of Nyx Crucian's most esteemed employees, who were the only ones granted access keys to reach these levels in the first place.

Rhyus reached the stairs and climbed onto them, however the staircase didn't actually end at 160. It continued up to the ceiling where he cranked two wheels, unlocking a thick, tinted glass panel from its surroundings. He forced the panel open and crawled out onto the roof of The Dome.

Helena had told Rhyus that he needed to go there after he fulfilled his task. She had said that from up there he would be able to see the full effects of what he had accomplished and that this was most important.

Now standing on the roof of the structure, he walked cautiously over the slick glass surface. The tilt of the roof slanted so gradually that only the rain sliding off of it would be able to notice it wasn't entirely flat. Following a particular stream of rainwater, Rhyus reached a circular wall that ran clear around the roof. It was very thick and reached waist high, solid except for large slots at the wall's bottom meant for the rain to exit in continuing down the remainder of The Dome's form.

Rhyus looked up to the sky, nearly solid black, cloudy, and releasing the chilling rain that streamed over his face as it fell down over the entirety of Atrum Unda. A violent shiver shot down his spine. He peered to the city floor. Specks of light were apparent from the dim street lanterns, as if substituting for the stars that could not be seen shining far beyond the thick, black-gray clouds above.

Madness had overtaken Atrum Unda, and Rhyus could see the somns, merely pinpricks now, running about, causing more trouble than the city already had going for itself. The Tower, as Rhyus looked its way, had not done what Helena had said would happen as a result of his mission. Instead of more brightly illuminating the city, The Tower stood black. A dark, structural corpse.

Its immense glass cell had blown out, and the crystal energy source had nearly vanished altogether. Only the slightest sputter of light and energy could be seen from where Rhyus now stood. He jumped, startled, as a fierce crack of light and energy blasted across the sky as an unruly bolt of lightning that not even Mother Nature could control.

He felt sick.

Helena was wrong...This is not what was supposed to happen.

Rhyus dropped down, his knees slamming into the solid surface. But he didn't give a damn as the pain shot up from them. He lowered his head and raised a trembling hand to his face.

What have I done?

He raised his chin desperately, to the pouring rain, as another crack of light and energy thrashed across the sky. Rain falling over his face, he closed his eyes.

What...have I done?

Keep an eye out for

The Exile

The Somnambulist Saga

ഇൗരു

Book Two

A.C. MONTGOMERY

CHARACTERS: Lux Lumetia

THE HINGE

Galton

GALTON'S GANG

Flint

Jory

Hewitt

Tyson

Nolan

Ruby Hale

RIVAL GANG

Beck Scofflin

THE TOWER

Lord Abel

Moore Pamby

UMBRA HALLS

☆ Rhyus Delmar

☆ Venn

☆ Marion Sunshine

NORTH MARKET

Jude Hollis

Cassandra Hollis

Mr. & Mrs. Kolby

Archie

BAR: THE CRIMSON GLASS

Mona

Lucille

STORE: RANDAL VANACHE

Cyrus Vanache

Killian Vanache

☆   Most important characters

★   Vincent KyVeerah makes his original appearance in
Atrum Unda where he resides. His next appearance
comes into play when he visits Lux Lumetia.

CHARACTERS: ATRUM UNDA

THE DOME

Nyx Crucian

BLACK BAND

☆ Callis Morgandy
☆ Armani Saint
☆ Julian Gallows
☆ Ezra Stark
Royce Elwood

CRIMSON BAND

Laughlin Carvel
Rastus Evander

WHITE BAND

☆ Helena Meretrix
Jett Milan
Angelina Pratt
Stella Black
Wylan Norwood

THE TOWER

Lord Cain
Vander Boniface

PRISONERS

Fyfe Van Ingen
Fallon
Haley

MORE UNDERGROUND

☆ Jereth Tavokk
★☆ Vincent KyVeerah
Fado
Mordion
Jimmy
Coraline & Donivan Fisher

BAR: THE COSMOS

Tazo Brooks

CHARACTERS: INSULA PALAM VITA

THE URBS

Lenim Velent
Yuri Sultan
Madam Ellen Corvin
Miranda

:About the Author

Christopher Tierney

A. C. Montgomery received an Associate of Occupational Studies degree in Graphic Design, Illustration, and Computer Graphics in May of 2009, while attending The Creative Center College of Graphic Design, located in Omaha, NE. She has also attended the University of Nebraska at Omaha.

Her artistic capabilities, talent with words, and strong ability to connect with fans will assist in gaining IntraSomnium Publishing recognition, and its novel, "The Rafters: Book I of the Somnambulist Saga," will be a book welcome on any fantasy-lover's shelf

Montgomery lives with her husband in Omaha, Nebraska.